Shaken Loose

Shaken Loose

Ilana DeBare

HYPATIA
PRESS

Published by Hypatia Press in the United Kingdom in 2023

ISBN: 978-1-83919-483-2

www.hypatiapress.org

For Sam. If I had to walk through Hell with anyone,
it would be you.

PART ONE

Desert

CHAPTER ONE

Annie

Annie Maple dropped onto the couch, reached for the remote, and did what she often did after a crummy day at work: watched her brother on TV.

It wasn't hard to do. Turn on any cable news show and there would be Ben, skewering climate-change deniers or jousting with the religious right. Some nights she muted the sound and just watched his eyebrows arc in mock astonishment or the edges of his mouth lift into a triumphant smile. They were familiar, comforting tics that let her know the world was proceeding as it should. Other nights she complained to him: it was cheaper and less fattening than downing a pint of ice cream.

"Have a good day?" she asked the pixelated Ben on this particular night. "Lunch with Stephen Hawking? Drinks with Jon Stewart? I had a good day too. I hand-addressed 75 invitations to major donors for the gala. I ordered 270 boxes of fair-trade chocolates shaped like seashells. Scallop shells, actually. We paid more for the chocolates than I make in three weeks."

On TV, Ben lanced an index finger through the air to make a point. Annie scrabbled her own fingers across the lumpy, faded couch. She and her roommate Melanie had found it last month at a yard sale, a total bargain. Then they spent twice as much hiring a guy with a pick-up truck to bring it to their apartment.

Ben grinned. His adversary glared. Something sharp pricked Annie's finger—a grey feather the size of a quarter. She peered, found another protruding nib, and pulled it too. Then another. Maybe not such a bargain. Feathers lay across her palm like grey lace.

The stairs down to the front door creaked and Melanie appeared, unfastening her bike helmet.

"Not him again? Annie, watching him just depresses you."

"Does not."

Melanie shrugged and went into the kitchen. Annie shook the grey feathers off her hands and out the window, where they wafted over the dumpster. Children's voices rose from the street. The news show cut away to a commercial. Annie clicked off the remote and followed Melanie into the kitchen, where she was opening a beer.

"Any news?"

"No. Nothing."

Melanie stared with ferocity at her beer bottle and Annie immediately regretted asking. Mel had failed the bar exam twice already and was waiting for results of her third try.

"Well, any day now, right? You'll pass this time. I'm sure of it." She glazed her voice with a bright, shiny confidence. When that wasn't enough, she tried diversion. "How about if we make a stir-fry? I'll cut up the onions. You relax. I'll do all the prep. I think there's some tofu..."

Annie sliced. She chopped. Melanie made rice. Annie set bowls on the table and dished out vegetables.

That was all—a simple, drab, normal evening.

Ben on TV. Melanie. Dinner.

Then fire.

* * * * *

*burningburningburningburningburningburningburnin
gburningburningburningburningburningburningburni
ngburningburningburningburningburningburningbur
ningburningburningburningburningburningburningbu
rningburningburningburningburningburningburningb
urningburningburningburningburningburningburning
burningburningburningburningburningburningburnin
gburningburni—*

Nothing but burning, and pain.

No time, no day or night, no momentary wisp of relief in which to assemble a thought. Pain replaces the body. Pain replaces the mind. Pain radiates out like a malignant sun, and pain presses down with the infinite mass of an imploding universe.

Burning but not consumed. A million needle tip shocks of pain blend into each other. This used to be an elbow and now it is pain. What once was a nipple, now pain. That thin, almost translucent web of skin between thumb and forefinger—now pain.

And burning. Always burning. Fire girdling, fire charring, fire blackening flesh that falls away, only to expose new tender layers of flesh that explode with even more pain—

burningburningburningburningburningburningburning burningbur—

* * * * *

Annie sprawled on rough ground, cheek pressed into gravel.

She wasn't burnt, wasn't even singed. All that fire must have been a bad dream. Annie's muscles were cramped from terror; her heart was still jackhammering. Gravel stung her thighs where her skirt had hiked up.

A bad dream, sure, but this wasn't her bed. Head pounding, she pushed up onto her knees. Everything swirled and she crumpled. Finally the dizziness passed and Annie sat up.

A wide black plain unfurled like dark sandpaper—no trees, no shrubs, just dark rocky ground. Beyond the plain, dark hills lifted into a reddish-grey, sunless sky. The air smelled of sulfur and char, heavy with heat as a mall parking lot on a 95-degree day.

Mojave Desert? Or some empty part of Nevada, like where they held Burning Man? Could she have been abducted to Iraq or Syria? All she remembered was a normal workday and then that nightmare of fire.

Heat pressed down on her. The silence felt almost as heavy. Annie pulled off her yellow cardigan and tied it around her waist. She waited for someone to come along and offer help, but the plain remained silent and empty. Finally she decided to walk toward the hills. Where there were hills, there might be a river. Trees, roads, houses. A telephone.

It was a tough slog. Annie was wearing clogs, her favorite shoes, which were great for a day in the office but not so good for trekking across deserts. Black ashy dust caked her legs while sulfur stung her nostrils. The empty plain was a mixed blessing: Annie could see anyone who might be out there, but they could also see her. She passed large black rocks that could easily conceal an attacker.

Kidnappers? Terrorists?

Was it crazy to think about terrorists? At home in San Francisco, you were more likely to be run over by a Google bus than blown up by a *jihadi*. But then, waking up in the desert with no idea of how you got there was crazy, too.

The weight hit her from behind.

"Roman witch!" a male voice shouted. "You did this to me!"

Knees and a great weight on her back. Rough hands pinning her arms into the dirt. The air had been knocked out of her, and her face and mouth were pressed into the gravel.

"Take it back!" the voice growled. Hot breath on her neck and the ripe, sweaty smell of a horse stable. She gasped but got a mouthful of gravel. She tried to wriggle free, but the assailant just held her tighter.

"Take it back!"

Knees in her back. She couldn't breathe. She would suffocate and die in this miserable desert. She spat gravel into the ground.

"Witch."

The weight lifted. He stepped off to pull her into a sitting position. Annie gulped for air.

"I can hurt you. I can kill you if I want."

The attacker dropped her wrists and she got her first look at him: squat and muscular with hooded eyes, black hair pulled back in a leather tie, and a scant, wispy beard. He had a long, flat forehead that made Annie think absurdly of a butternut squash. A series of scars formed parallel lines down each of his cheeks. He wore an animal skin vest and breeches.

"Take it back."

"What—"

A powerful slap. Everything reeled.

"I said to take it back."

Annie took a deep breath. "I don't know what—"

Another slap. Flashes of black and red.

"Now. Undo the curse."

"I don't—"

He raised a hand. "You need another smack?"

"No! Please. I don't know what you're talking about. I don't even know how I got here. I just... turned up."

The attacker's scars wrinkled into a frown. Annie braced for another blow. But then she glimpsed something beyond anger in his frown.

"Wait. Is that what happened to you, too? You just woke up here?"

He narrowed his eyes, and she knew her guess was right. If she could keep him talking, maybe he wouldn't hit her. She babbled.

"You know what this reminds me of? Dorothy in Oz! Where she was dumped by the tornado and met the scarecrow and the tin man? And they all helped each other look for the wizard—"

He lunged and grabbed her neck.

"The wizard!" he shouted. "Your wizard did this! Your Jesus Christ wizard!"

She flailed wildly. He let go and stepped back.

"*Your* wizard," he grunted.

"No. I meant the book. The movie." Was it possible he'd never heard of *The Wizard of Oz*?

The man scuffed a boot in the dirt, pushing black gravel toward her.

"Build an altar. Call your wizard."

"I don't—"

He raised a threatening hand.

"Okay. Sure."

Annie had no idea what an altar should look like. She gathered rocks, piling small stones on top of larger ones until she had something that resembled half a campfire pit.

"Call him," he said.

"I don't—"

"Call him. Tell him that Trua, son of Bleda, tribesman of Ulthor, demands to be returned to his tribe."

Son of Bleda? Tribesman of Ulthor? The guy was a parody of a fantasy novel. But if he wanted a wizard, she'd give him a wizard.

"Double, double, toil and trouble..." Standing, Annie was several inches taller than her attacker. She waved her arms with what she hoped was appropriate drama. "Um, now I call the wizard forth. Abracadabra. Alakazam. Gandalf, Dumbledore... flick and swish!"

"No games!" The man lunged and grabbed her neck again. "Call your real wizard. Or god. Whatever he is. Call Jesus Christ."

He pushed her to her knees, then released her. Her head reeled, but at least she knew what he wanted.

"Our Father... who art in Heaven..."

Annie prostrated herself before the half-ring of stones and groped for what came next. She was nominally Christian: her father had been raised Episcopalian, her mother Methodist, but neither of them was religious. And Ben was as anti-religious as you could get, with three best-selling books billing him as "America's favorite atheist" and his constant TV gigs debating the religious right. In twenty-nine years of life, she had never once prayed.

"Hallowed"—was that the right word?—"be thy name."

The scarred man nodded grimly for her to continue.

"Thy kingdom come. Thy will be done. On Earth as it is in Heaven."

What next? His boot nudged her side.

"Dear Jesus," she blurted. "Send Trua back to his tribe. Grant him his wishes. Please, God. Or

Jesus. Whoever. Give him whatever he wants. Please, God—"

Annie froze. Something was coming.

She had no idea how she knew, but the hairs on her arms were standing up and the air seemed to have been sucked out of her chest. The scarred man's threats were nothing compared to this. Kidnappers and terrorists were nothing compared to this.

"Get down!" She rolled herself into a ball at the base of a large rock. The scarred man felt it too: he dropped to the ground and crouched near her. With no visible sun, there were no shadows, but Annie felt something cold and terrible moving toward them through the sky. It halted and hovered overhead as if searching. Instead of a shadow, the thing cast a penumbra of fear. She didn't dare look up.

Finally, it moved away across the plain. Drone? UFO? Dragon? Was it crazy to be thinking about dragons?

"We've got to find shelter," she whispered to the scarred man. "There's nowhere to hide out here."

He nodded, no slaps or kicks now. "There," he said, pointing across the black desert to the hills. "But no tricks. If you run, I'll catch you."

Annie stood and set out for the hills, the scar-cheeked man following closely behind.

* * * * *

If she knew geology, she could figure out her location from the rocks.

If she knew about aerospace technology, she might recognize the thing that had passed overhead.

But Ben was the one who knew stuff. It wasn't just that he was older. It was his encyclopedic memory, his ability to turn ideas into sentences and paragraphs and treatises before other people could coalesce a single scrap of thought. It had been that way as long as she could remember: Ben reading books heavy as bricks from the grown-up section of the library, Ben astonishing her parents' friends with lucid opinions on things most 10-year-old boys had never heard of—exoplanets, gun control, Bosnia. Annie's parents used to say proudly that they had one child with a big brain and another with a big heart. She felt proud when they said it too, until at one point—maybe in middle school—it struck her that her heart was not unusually big. Or unusually anything. Then the description became a consolation prize, something her parents must have invented so she wouldn't feel left out.

That was Annie's first glimpse of her own inadequacy. The understanding deepened and set over the years: Ben the success and Annie the failure. Ben a globe-trotting celebrity and Annie a low-level fundraising assistant. Ben the owner of a sleek condo in Manhattan, Annie a renter in a shared flat with a moldy bathroom and view of a dumpster.

If she had Ben's way with words, she could talk her way out of this situation.

If she knew astronomy like he did, she could navigate by the stars.

First it would have to be night, though. And the sunless haze didn't seem to change. What was going on with this place? How much time had passed?

Annie reached reflexively for her cellphone to check the time and grasped only air. Her purse wasn't on her shoulder, hadn't been there since she woke up from that nightmare of fire.

* * * * *

Dust gathered in a pasty clump in Annie's throat; dust caked in her nostrils. They'd need to find water soon. She hadn't peed since waking up in this place, and in the pressing grey heat she worried about dehydration. Her thighs chafed with sweat and dust, and she silently cursed those fifteen pounds she never managed to lose. *Too big, too fat, too ungainly.* "You're beautiful just the way you are," her mother always said, but of course a mother would say that.

"Keep moving," Trua grunted.

"Can we take a break?"

When he didn't object, she dropped down beside a boulder. Trua kicked at the dirt, watching her with suspicion.

"Can I ask you something?" Annie said cautiously, probing her feet for emerging blisters. "Where are you from? And how did you learn English?"

"English?"

"What we're speaking."

"We're speaking Hunnic. I don't know what you mean by English."

"What we speak in the U.S. What I'm speaking."

Trua shook his head. "You're a very good Hunnic speaker, for a Roman. Most Romans know nothing of Hunnic. They call us ignorant, but in fact they're the ones who know nothing of the world beyond the walls of their garrisons."

Whoa. Was he claiming to be a Hun from the time of the Roman Empire? Maybe she was in one of those TV shows where they plop unsuspecting people down in a bizarre situation and film their response. Annie didn't usually watch such junk, but Melanie did. Had Mel nominated her for the show as a prank? She suddenly felt a whole lot better.

"Tell me," Annie said playfully, glancing around for where the cameras might be hidden. "You have any friends named Attila?"

Trua frowned. "No."

"Sack any cities recently?"

The scarred man lunged and grabbed her shoulder, his grip strong enough to shatter bone. "Don't mock me, woman. Do you want to conjure your wizard with a broken arm?"

"I'm sorry—I didn't mean—"

"Get up." He prodded Annie with his boot. "When we get to the hills, you'll call your wizard again."

* * * * *

Gravel lodged in Annie's clogs and nipped her soles. She shook it out but it drifted back. The ground started to rise as they approached the hills, rocks slipping underfoot, and she had to work to keep her balance. Both she and the scarred man were breathing heavily. Nearing the ridge, Annie ran fingers through her fine brown hair, now matted with dust: if this were a TV show, she'd look good for the cameras.

On top, however, there were no cameras to impress. The summit was flat and barren, just more black rocks and gravel. A similar ridge lay before her. A hot wind blew against her face with the ominous feel of California fire weather.

In the distance, beyond the next ridge, lay a lake—but nothing like any lake she'd ever seen. It was bright, molten orange. It trumpeted its brilliance against the black hills and grey sky like the mouth of a furnace in a dark factory. Annie squinted and saw orange wisps rising from the distant surface—waves? flames? some kind of bright turbulence?

Then dizziness.

Ground dissolving under her feet.

She was back in the fire.

CHAPTER TWO

Annie

burningburningburningburningburningburningburnin gburningburningburningburningburningburningburni ngburningburningburningburningburningburningbur ningburningburningburningburningburningburningbu rningburningburni—

Immersed in fire, drowning in fire. Waves ablaze on an oil-slicked sea. Swells of fire break on your chest, currents of fire trawl your legs. Flesh chars. Organs blister. You're swamped by pain, flailing through pain, and any minute now the fire will pull you under.

not my head not my head not my head stay up stay up stay up

Flames splash your cheeks and they sizzle and burn. Flames claw your neck and crawl toward your face. You tread water, frantic, but your limbs are useless, draggy weights of pus and pain. A moment's lapse and you'll sink. A moment's lapse and your lips will burn, your tongue will burn, your nostrils, your eyes, your brain—

not my head not my head not my head

Flames slap your cheeks. Treading is useless. Treading is making things worse. Treading is all you can do.

stay up stay up stay up

Gulp for air and choke on your own charred tongue.

burningburningburningburningburningburningburnin gburningburningburnin—

* * * * *

Annie jerked upright, head throbbing and heart racing.

It had happened again: unspeakable pain, more real than any dream. Some kind of seizure triggered by sight of the orange lake?

The scarred man lay twitching a few feet away: it had gotten him too. Sprawled and unconscious, he looked younger than she'd thought. Annie wondered if she should do something to help but remembered his threats to kill her.

Just get away.

She stumbled down the hillside, dodging behind boulders as much as possible. Gravel clattered under her clogs as she tried to reason things out. The orange lake could be a toxic algae bloom. Or maybe a salt pond like the ones in the South Bay: flying over them on the descent into SFO, their bright pinks and oranges always looked unworldly, hallucinogenic, as if children had colored in the spaces between the levees with Day-Glo markers.

Still, shouldn't salt ponds or algae lakes have some kind of plant life?

Here there was not even a trace of lichen on the rocks.

She was now midway up the next ridge, with no sign of the scarred man. What if he swallowed his tongue? What if he died? She wiped strands of hair from her forehead with a grimy hand and kept going.

At the top, hot air slammed her. The smell of sulfur and burn was stronger than ever. She stared down the slope directly at the orange lake.

It wasn't salt ponds or an algal bloom.

It was fire.

Flames spurted up from the surface—not lava, not molten metal, but a mass of fire, flame beyond flame, a million bonfires jammed together like commuters on a rush-hour train. And *people* were in there! Within the fire, human heads bobbed up and down. Flames licked up and blistered cheeks; raw skin blackened and fell away and then blistered again. Any one of those figures should have shriveled to cinders within moments, but instead they all just kept bobbing, blistering, burning.

Heat pushed Annie back while disbelief pulled her forward. An unlikely mix of sounds jarred her—the familiar soft rush of waves, broken by a louder cracking and popping of fire, and, more distant, layered so thickly that no single voice could be distinguished, a horrific shrieking and cursing and wailing.

The hot wind whipped down the black shore. Her lips prickled with dryness.

Panic welled up. Her head pulsed with pain; she felt another of those seizures coming on—

Stop. Calm down.

If Ben were here, he'd tell her to be logical. Maybe this was just a dream—logical, normal, ending any moment now. Or a virtual reality game, World of Warcraft on steroids. If it were a game, there would be a command to shut things down.

"Exit," she said. Her legs felt loose as jelly. Again, more loudly, "Exit." That wasn't it. She tried other possible commands: "Game over." "End program." "Escape." Maybe it was a Windows-based system like her computer at work. "Control-alt-delete," she said, and felt like a hopeful idiot. Still nothing happened.

Ahead of her, flames geysered from the lake. They rolled and tumbled across the water like a NASA photo of the surface of the sun. Through the flames she glimpsed a broad male face, bald head, mouth wrenched open in agony. Then it was gone, submerged. She saw a narrow face edged with curls that melted into tendrils of fire before it, too, was gone. Then a craggy old man, a round-faced old woman, a young woman with piles of thick hair. All of them shrouded in orange, all screaming, all burning.

A hand touched her shoulder: she spun in panic. But instead of the scarred man, she found a slight woman in lime green capris, a sleeveless floral blouse, and a floral kerchief covering messy auburn hair. Her small nose turned up at the tip and gave her a pixie-like look. If not for the dust smearing her arms and face, she could have been a young Audrey Hepburn.

The woman glanced around nervously. "Come with me," she whispered, a southern lilt to her voice. "Y'all do know you're being followed?"

Annie's stomach clenched. She glanced back toward the hills. "Who are you? Where are we?"

The woman put a finger to her lips. "Not now."

She trailed the woman along the shore to a spot where the hills sharpened into black cliffs fronted by an army of immense black boulders. They ducked into a narrow opening between two boulders, then threaded their way through the boulder field. They moved deeper than Annie had imagined the field could go; finally the woman squeezed into a small hollow completely surrounded by boulders. She sat and motioned for Annie to join her.

"He won't find us?"

"I don't think so. We had ourselves a good head start. And this here rocky ground doesn't take footprints."

Annie felt limp with relief: at last someone to explain things and help her get home. "I don't know how to thank you."

The woman shrugged. "You were in trouble."

"Can you tell me where we are?"

The woman shot her a look of pity. "Don't you know?"

"No! If I knew, I wouldn't have asked."

"Honey," the woman said. "What's your name?"

"Annie. And you're...?"

"Billie... Annie, honey, there's no sugar-coating it. You are in Hell."

Annie grinned. "No kidding. I sure am."

Billie shook her head. "Don't joke about it. We are both stuck here in Hell."

The woman seemed serious. And that lake of fire...

"If we're in Hell, that would mean we're dead."

Billie nodded.

"But I don't feel dead."

"You don't look dead either, honey. Not in that cute pencil skirt. But I assure you we most definitely are."

"But Hell doesn't exist."

Billie looked concerned. "Don't you read Scripture? Don't you believe in the word of Jesus?"

"No!" This was absurd. The situation, the conversation, everything. If this were a computer game, the designer had a sick sense of humor.

"No wonder you're here then. You were never saved. I'm so sorry."

Just what she needed: a born-again nut case. Ben would slice through someone like this in a minute, but Annie was too polite. Plus this woman had just saved her from the scarred man.

"Where are you from?"

"Sweet Valley, Alabama. Have y'all heard of the Sweet Valley Spartans? They took the state championship three years in a row when I was in school."

"How'd you get here?"

"The same way you did. I died."

Annie must have looked exasperated, because Billie leaned forward sympathetically. "I know it's hard to accept. I'd say we should pray together, but that brings trouble. You do pray, don't you? Or did, *be-fore*?"

Annie shook her head.

Billie looked more concerned than ever. "Oh honey..."

"If this is Hell, then what are you doing here? You're religious. You pray. Shouldn't you be in Heaven?"

Billie laughed, but it had a bitter edge. "Lordy. I drank. I smoked. I *fornicated.* See, I even took the name of the Lord in vain just now. I haven't learned a thing! There's no way I was going to Heaven."

"How do you know this is really Hell and not a virtual reality game?"

Billie narrowed her eyes. "I beg your pardon?"

"Like Dungeons and Dragons? World of Warcraft? You know, computer games."

Billie shook her head. "Honey, I don't know what you mean by 'computer' games. I know Gin Rummy. I used to play a little Twenty-one but that was a while ago."

The lime green capris. The kerchief.

"Billie, can I ask you something? What year is it?"

Billie sighed. "I can't honestly say. Time just goes on and on when there's no day and night. And in the fire, every minute is an eternity."

"Do you remember what year it was when you came here?"

"Of course I can. I'm dead, you know, not addled. I died in 1963. That handsome President Kennedy had just been shot. He was a Roman Catholic and a

Negro lover, but it was still such a tragedy. His poor wife. Those poor children."

Negro lover? Kennedy assassination? Kennedy had been killed 52 years ago, but Billie looked younger than Annie.

She kept probing. Billie claimed to have been trapped in the sea of fire since her death and released just recently. And the two of them weren't the only souls shaken loose from the flames. Wandering in the desert, Billie had encountered a handful of others but kept her distance: this was Hell, after all, filled with very bad people.

"But you approached me," Annie said.

"I saw that bad man following you. And you looked friendly. American."

"Why us? If nearly everyone else is in that fire, why were we released?"

Billie shrugged. "The Lord Jesus had mercy on us." She leaned toward Annie. "I'll tell you a secret. I met an old woman—from France or Italy, some place foreign like that. She said there's a hidden passage back to Earth in the mountains. I'm on my way to find it. I don't know about you, but I am more than ready to get home. Y'all want to come along?"

Billie tipped her head expectantly. Billie might be a born-again nut job, but Annie would never find her way home alone. And the scarred man was probably still hunting her.

"Sure, I'll come," she said.

CHAPTER THREE

Trua

Trua peered into the field of boulders where the witch and her friend had disappeared, took a few steps in, then backed out. Narrow places made him nervous. You couldn't see ahead, and it was too easy to be trapped. Even the strongest, most supple bow was no use in a winding passageway.

Of course he had no bow. She must have stolen it.

Rage welled up in him again. The women were in there somewhere, maybe with his bow, and he couldn't get to them. He was a dog outside a rodent burrow, nosing the hole, pawing the dirt, useless.

He glanced around uncertainly. Behind him, across the sand, lay the lake of fire and those burning, screaming faces. *Roman witch.* The brown-haired woman was the last person he'd seen before being plunged into the fire, and the first person he'd seen after being hurled out of it.

He'd find her, force her to undo the curse that sent him here, and then wring her neck.

* * * * *

The curse had struck him far from home.

Trua and his brothers had headed south when it looked to be another bad year for the flocks. A harsh winter, a late spring, countless lambs frozen at birth. If they didn't bring back gold and silver to trade, the clans wouldn't make it through the next snows.

More than a thousand men from Trua's tribe rode out across the still-frozen Danube and the southern mountains, paralleling the roads that the Romans so conveniently built as a guide. Equally conveniently, the Romans had sent their armies somewhere far across the Great Sea, so one village after another fell before their bows and swords without a serious fight. By the time they reached the Roman province of Syria, Trua's eldest brother Athor had so much plunder that he needed two horses to carry it. It was almost the same for his brothers Ularic and Bator.

Not Trua. As the fourth and youngest son, he was last in line for any spoils, last in line to take a wife. But Trua was in no rush for marriage and didn't care much about plunder. Mostly he wanted to see new lands.

Trua was curious. He'd been that way since he was a boy, listening avidly to accounts of Rome's cities and gaping at the occasional Thracian trader or Goth emissary. The Romans were vicious and sly—everyone knew that—but he still wanted to understand their life. The strange crops they grew, how they turned raisins into wine, what it would be like sleeping surrounded by thick stone walls rather than tent skins. Trua guessed it would feel like death, like lying in an airless grave. So why did the Romans do it?

His brothers had no patience for such questions. "We found where they hid the gold, what else is there to know?" Athor snorted when Trua suggested lingering to explore a village they'd raided.

So one night, as the others slept, Trua mounted his horse and rode ahead into a wide valley. He figured on finding an isolated farm, watching its inhabitants for a few hours to see how they lived, then snatching what he could carry and returning to the tribe.

He found a target quickly—a small estate with date and olive orchards, a master house and storage building, and only a low stone wall for protection. It might even be deserted: Romans had a habit of fleeing if they heard there were Huns approaching.

Cowards, Trua thought. If his own people had been threatened by marauders, he would have stayed and fought to the death. If even one person from his clan were threatened, he would stand and fight.

Dawn light trickled across the hills and gathered into a pool of pink as Trua circled the compound on his horse. Muffled sounds drifted from the storage building. He tied his horse to a tree and returned to watch from behind the stone wall.

A male servant in a toga and sandals emerged from the storage building, clumsy with sleep. He shuffled to the well, drew water, and carried it into the main house, then returned to the storage building for some small urns that he also took into the house.

A rooster crowed. Smoke rose from the main building.

Trua leapt the wall and snuck into the storehouse. He found giant barrels of curing olives, urns of oil and other foodstuffs, and bales of hay. Some lengths of cloth stretched across bales in a corner, presumably the sleeping place for the servant. Trua grimaced. He would take smooth skins in an airy tent over itchy, buggy straw any day.

He opened urns and dipped fingers. Olive oil, wine, sour wine. Some kind of sweet, sticky liquid. Grains.

Nothing of value. Nothing he could carry with him.

The sweet, sticky liquid was delicious, though. Trua wondered what plant it came from and if it could be found on the Great Plain. He was reaching for another taste when the servant appeared in the doorway. The man's eyes widened in shock and he gave out a yell.

Trua silenced him in mid-holler with a single arrow. Still, he'd been discovered. He could flee and return to the camp empty-handed, or he could chance a quick foray into the main house, grab some valuables, and then flee.

The rooster kept crowing. Everything else remained silent.

Trua slipped over to the main building and cracked open the wooden door. Thin daylight spilled through alongside him, showing the contours of a narrow hallway. He followed it into a roofless atrium with painted walls and mosaic floors. How much wealth did these Romans have that they could afford to spend it making pictures on the floor? He opened a cabinet and removed silver cups and ladles. Good, but gold would be better. He lifted the lid on an ornate storage chest, then froze as an older man emerged in bedclothes from one of the adjacent rooms.

Perhaps not so cowardly after all.

The man held a sword, but Trua was younger and faster. He unsheathed his own sword, ran him through, and turned with caution to the dark doorway. Where there was one enemy, there might be more.

A woman lay in the bed, sheet held up to her chin, stammering something in a language Trua didn't know. Too old and scrawny to be a concubine: probably the man's wife.

"Woman, stay in the bed," he ordered in Hunnic. He had no desire to kill an old woman. He pointed at her mattress. "Stay there."

He was watching her eyes to see if she understood when he heard a whisper on the tile floor behind him. Trua spun around just in time to see a young woman with a heavy bronze urn raised over her head, raised higher than you'd think a woman could lift such a thing. There was no time to react or make out her face, but he saw her pale skin and straight brown hair and heard her whisper the name "Jesus Christ" as the urn crashed down, and then he was under her spell.

In the fire.

* * * * *

Trua had never imagined pain like that.

Burning. Blistering. Charring like lamb left on the cookfire too long. Coals of a cookfire not just under him but inside him. Lungs consumed by fire. Balls consumed by fire. Maddened horse in a burning field, mane on fire, tail ablaze, trying to flee but charging deeper and deeper into the flames.

He wanted to die. Death, surrender, slavery: anything was better than the burning. What terrible power did this Jesus Christ have to inflict such pain?

But that was past. Somehow he'd been freed from the fire and almost immediately spotted the brown-haired sorceress. Now he paced before the boulders, waiting for her to emerge.

If only he had his horse and bow.

If only he'd stayed with his brothers.

If only he hadn't let the sorceress escape.

Time passed, and he started to worry the women might have fled through another opening in the boulder field. He decided to circle around, following the outermost line of rocks and looking for footprints in the gravel. The boulder field was immense—Trua had never seen so many rocks in one place—stretching inland, away from the fire lake.

Miserable witch. Miserable place. Nothing but fire and rocks and dirt—

He was so immersed in his anger that they took him by surprise.

A blow from behind on his head. He crumpled to his knees. As he pushed himself up, they descended on him with clubs—three men, one small and two large. Trua slammed back but they had six fists to his two, and he was unarmed. It took barely any time for them to pin him in the gravel.

“Tie him,” one of the tall men commanded, handing leather cords to the others.

Blood trickled from his forehead and stung his eyes. They kicked him onto his stomach, bound his hands behind his back, and stuffed a strip of leather in his mouth.

Curse those bastards. Curse my own carelessness. Curse that sorceress, the root of all my troubles.

“Do him now?” the short man asked. “I’ve got my knife. I can do it quick—”

“No. Unless you’re volunteering to haul the carcass back to camp.” The leader’s voice was a sneer. When the short man didn’t answer, he continued. “So. He’ll haul himself. We can take care of him at our leisure.”

“Leisure!” The other tall man had been silent but now he laughed. “Attwater, you make us sound like dukes in a palace. You got a way with words.”

The leader ignored him. “Make sure the cords are tight,” he ordered. “It’s a long walk back. You never know what else we may find.”

“Ha! You never know,” the other tall man echoed.

They jerked Trua to his feet, tightened the cords around his wrists, and pushed him ahead of them back toward the shoreline of the fire lake.

CHAPTER FOUR

Annie

Billie's hiding spot held a collection of sharp rocks and a pile of rags that seemed to be remnants of clothing. Annie helped her pack them up, tying some of the rags together to make tote bags.

"Where'd you get the clothes?" Annie asked.

"Found them."

"Just found them?"

Billie shrugged.

They wound their way out of the boulder field and headed up the beach, taking care to stay back from the lake of fire and as close to the cliffs as possible. They rested behind rocks. They kept watch for the scarred man. But even hugging the hills and staying on guard, Annie couldn't ignore the screams that wafted up from the lake. The voices melded together, a wheezy organ chord of anguish, swelling and collapsing with each gust of hot wind.

This place sounded and looked and smelled like Hell. But Hell didn't exist. Hell was fiction, stale bread from an era when people needed to invent stories to explain the world. Hell was a cautionary myth designed to scare children into good behavior and adults into religious obedience. None of Annie's family or friends believed in Hell. She didn't know a single person who believed in Hell. And even if Hell did exist, it wouldn't be this clichéd fire-and-brimstone wasteland. God would be too sophisticated for that. It would be a more nuanced, existential place—some shadowy state of eternal regret and loneliness, or something compatible with quantum physics. Annie had never cared enough to wonder about the details. Why spend time thinking about something that doesn't exist?

"Billie," she said as they walked. "Do you know how you ended up here? I can't remember a thing."

"Y'all don't know how you died?"

Annie shook her head.

"What's your last memory? From your life?"

She tried again. Calling donors at work about the gala, a bean and cheese burrito for lunch, Ben on the TV. Dinner with Melanie. Then nothing.

No. Wait.

Now she remembered a Victorian doorway, faded buttercream curls of woodworking in the orange glow of a streetlight. Music and voices thrumming into the street. Tingle of anticipation.

"I don't know," she said. "I was at a party."

"Well, at least you went out having fun."

"What about you?"

In Hell, asking people how they died would be a standard conversation opener, like asking people at home what they did for work. Billie stopped walking and looked at the ground.

"It's okay. You don't have to talk about it if it's—"

"No." Billie looked up, her eyes moist. "I just haven't had anyone to talk to in the longest time." She pushed a foot around in the black gravel. "I was driving with my babies. I have three babies—Kitty, Natalie, and Kenny. Okay, they weren't really babies. Kitty was four and Natty was three and Kenny was almost one. So Kenny was truly a baby. He had the sweetest little cowlick of jet-black hair that stuck up all the time."

A familiar hollow formed in Annie's gut, the cavity she always felt when meeting a woman her age with children. Billie kept talking.

"We were driving home from visiting with my cousin Patty. We were crossing the Thompson Bridge when this big old truck came barreling down the bridge in the other direction. That driver must have been drunk or something, he was all over the road. He just came barreling toward me, and I had to swerve that wheel to get out of the way."

The hollow deepened into a chasm. Not just one child lost, but three.

"I'm so sorry," Annie murmured.

Billie looked up at her sharply. "No!" she said. "It's not what you think. My babies survived! We went off the bridge into the river and I was killed, but my babies survived."

That was... wonderful?

"Yes," Billie continued. "My precious babies survived, thank the Lord. But they must miss me so much. Babies need their mama. So now I'm going to find that passageway and go home to them, no matter what it takes."

She resumed walking and Annie hurried to keep up. *Passageways between Hell and Earth. Dead people returning to life.* Ben would say she'd lost her mind to even be considering this. She'd recount it to him as a funny story when she got home. They'd sit in the window seat of her parents' living room next Thanksgiving, looking out on her mother's beloved flower garden, drinking some astronomically expensive bottle of wine that he'd picked out. That he insisted was the best. He'd laugh at her, but she'd laugh along so it wouldn't be too demeaning. This would become a funny, shared story: "Remember that time I thought I was in Hell?"

She wouldn't tell her parents. Her mother would hover, anxious and judgmental, like those years after she dropped out of college. Her father would take on that panicked look he got when misplacing his glasses or scattering a pile of student papers all over the floor.

The time she thought she was in Hell.

She hadn't had a really good laugh with Ben in ages. It would be a lovely, secret joke between the two of them, nobody else.

* * * * *

The black cliffs and the flaming lake seemed endless. The only time they stopped was when their feet hurt. They didn't sleep: Billie said sleep was unnecessary here, and carried a risk of dreaming about the fire. They walked, and sat, and walked some more.

Annie's skin caked with dust and sweat. Her hair felt thick as twine.

And this entire time, she'd seen no water. Even if you didn't get thirsty, you needed water. For a hairwash. A shower. Even just a muddy puddle to soak your feet.

Annie had grown up in San Francisco's northern suburbs, at the foot of Mt. Tamalpais with its beckoning network of trails. Her favorite hike was Steep Ravine—living up to its name, two miles of vertical climb along the banks of a narrow creek. Waterfalls tumbled below wooden footbridges. Ferns blanketed the canyon walls. Coastal fog enfolded the ravine and left it lush and glistening even in the dryest California summers.

Annie liked to do the trail from the bottom up. It was harder work, but you had a better view of the water shimmying down the mountain. One time she'd stopped midway to rest on a downed redwood at the edge of the creek. Burbling and plashing filled her ears. She dug her fingers into the redwood trunk and felt it soft with the metamorphoses of life—moss growing, wood decaying. Then there was movement in the bushes upstream, and a small brown Pacific wren hopped into the clearing next to her log. She'd never seen one this close and this exposed. It pecked at the leaf litter on the ground and hopped onto her log. She held her breath. Barely three feet away, it launched into a trill that seemed longer than a creature that size could possibly produce. Its throat, the size of a thumbnail, vibrated as it sang.

It sang. It stopped. It blinked. It looked right at her for a moment, and then vanished back into the bushes.

Water was life. Water in the creek, water in the fog, water in the leaves and bark beneath the wren. Annie still wasn't sure what this place was, but one thing was clear: it had no water.

* * * * *

The two women maintained a brisk pace. They kept looking behind them but saw no sign of the scarred man. Annie asked Billie about her children.

"Kitty just has the sweetest disposition. She doesn't need a doll, she takes care of her little sister like a doll. It's always, 'Mama, can I feed Natty? Mama, can I dress Natty?' She's got a beautiful little voice, too. I named her after Kitty Wells and she may very well have a future in show business."

"Kitty Wells?"

"You don't know Kitty Wells? The Honky-Tonk Angels song? Well, maybe she wasn't so famous in California. Now Natty I named after Natalie Wood. You know, the actress? And Kenny—"

"Named after?" Annie racked her brain for 1960s celebrities.

"His daddy. So technically he's Kenny Jr."

"It's good your husband was there to take care of them after you... died." It was weird to say those words, but there wasn't any other way to put it.

"It most certainly is not!" Billie flashed anger. "He's a worthless piece of trash. All he thinks about is shooting pool with his buddies. I can't tell you the last time he took me out on the town. I thought he would be a good daddy, a good provider, but boy, was I wrong."

Billie stopped. She peered behind them, then resumed walking.

"But what about you? Are you married?"

"No."

"Dating anyone?"

Annie shook her head.

"Honey. I don't want to be the big bad wolf but you're not getting any younger. Especially a big girl like you, you need to capitalize on your assets before it's too late. You do want children, don't you?"

That hollow in her gut. Annie had reached a point where she could go days, sometimes weeks, without thinking about it, and then some well-meaning person would jab a stick into the wound.

She refused to talk about it. In ten years, she had never talked about it.

"I've got blisters on both feet now," she said, sitting down and pulling off a clog.

* * * * *

The inability to tell time was disorienting. Annie felt a constant mental vertigo, not sure how long she'd been in this place or how far they'd walked. Meanwhile, Billie chatted nonstop. She chatted about clothes. She chatted about dieting. She chatted about how Annie needed to wear more makeup to "accentuate the positive." At one of their breaks,

Annie rolled her yellow cardigan into a pillow and closed her eyes to shut Billie out. But the internal voices were even worse: *How did I get here? Am I really dead? What happened at that party?* She was sick of the questions and sick of not knowing the answers, disgusted by the failure of her own memory.

Something moved and she jerked upright. Billie was fingering a sleeve of her sweater, just inches away from her head.

"Is this that special kind of wool? From French goats?"

"What?" Annie pulled the sweater back and returned it to her waist. "You mean cashmere? Yeah."

"That's expensive."

"It was a Christmas present from my parents."

"So it's got sentimental value."

"Yes. No. I don't know." It hadn't had any particular sentimental value before, just another item in her closet. Now it was a link back to normal life.

They resumed their trek. Billie prattled on about divorces of Hollywood stars Annie had never heard of. The strip of shoreline felt endless as a Mobius strip.

"Billie, did you have a job at home?" Maybe she could move the conversation off of celebrity gossip.

"I most certainly did. At the Charming Lady Boutique. That was before I married that no-good Kenny. I thought he would take care of me, but boy, was I wrong. The one I should've married was Freddy Baylor. He was sweet on me but he was a terrible dancer and I just sent him away. Foolish me. He went into real estate and building houses and now he has this most gigantic mansion on the edge of town.... What about you, way out there in Frisco? Are you a career girl?"

"Yeah. I guess so."

"Do you take a cable car to work?"

"No. They're mostly for tourists. In a different part of the city."

Billie looked disappointed. "Do you work in a big skyscraper?"

"Yeah."

"Well, that's glamorous. What about your boss? Is he handsome? Is he single?"

Annie didn't know where to begin. She worked as a fundraising assistant at an environmental non-profit called Ocean Allies where her boss was indeed attractive and single. But she was also a silver-haired, 60-something lesbian who reminded Annie of an urban, edgier version of her mother. And Annie found nothing remotely glamorous about her job.

She'd been thrilled to be hired by Ocean Allies, her first job that didn't involve making overpriced coffee drinks. But four years in, she remained a glorified go-fer. All the interesting work went to people with advanced degrees in oceanography or biology, and she didn't even have a B.A. So while the scientists were out at sea documenting the Great Pacific Garbage Patch, Annie was tethered to her computer looking up the net worth of potential donors or the best deal on valet parking.

Four years! She was almost 30! Her high school classmates were getting married or making fortunes in tech startups. Melanie was sure to pass the bar eventually. Ben was famous. Everyone was moving forward while she was stalled like a broken Muni bus.

That was all too complicated to explain, and hardly an answer to Billie's question about handsome single executives.

"It's not all that glamorous," Annie said. "And my boss is a woman."

CHAPTER FIVE

Annie

The cliffs grew higher. Puffs of sulfurous yellow gas emerged from the sand. Annie picked her way carefully, worried about sinkholes, trying to avoid wafts of gas. Far ahead an orange ribbon emerged across the black sand like the finish line at a marathon: a river of fire.

Flames rolled down from a gash in the cliffs, wide and majestic as an orange Mississippi. Tendrils of flame curled and waved where the river hit an obstruction. Circles of fire danced in eddies near the bank. As it neared the lake, the river spread into a delta, with low islands of black sand in the midst of the rolling flames.

"It's not safe here," Billie whispered. Heat stung Annie's face. The lake and river hemmed them in on two sides, with cliffs lining the third. If ambushed, there was nowhere to go.

They turned inland, entering a canyon that led them into the cliffs. Annie hadn't imagined she could miss the interminable black beach, but soon she did. Navigating the jagged canyon floor was harder than trotting along the sand. Billie chose promising forks that wound to dead ends. They clambered up rocky chutes only to reach overhangs that made further progress impossible. They spent as much time back-tracking as going forward.

They were slogging up yet another canyon when Billie stopped short.

"Dear Jesus," she exhaled.

Some twenty yards ahead, a pile of dry bones leaned against the rock wall, draped with a small piece of material that looked like leather.

Annie's first reaction was excitement: *Cattle*! Where there were cattle, there would be farms. Where there were farms, there would be telephones.

Phones, roads, cars. Finally, a way home.

Then, almost simultaneously, she realized: there were no cattle here. There was no grass or hay for cattle. There was only one kind of creature in this place with bones.

"We've got to get out of here," Billie whispered.

They retraced their steps as stealthily as possible. Annie's heart pounded. She wanted to hurl herself into a run, but that would kick up stones and noise. How far was it to the last junction? Would another canyon be any safer? Could you be killed a second time if you were already dead?

Billie stopped short. She reached out an arm in caution.

"Listen."

Annie heard voices—men's voices—and a scuffing, dragging sound. The sounds seemed to be coming from the mouth of the canyon, the direction that she and Billie were now heading, but the echoing rock walls made it hard to be sure. The men could be either behind or ahead of them. They were jubilant, laughing, with no apparent caution. They were getting louder.

Annie looked, wide-eyed, to Billie.

"Up," Billie mouthed, and pointed at the rock wall on their right.

Up? It was vertical rock, not a gravel slope.

Billie didn't wait to hear Annie's objections; she was at the wall, reaching for indentations that could be handholds. She was already a few feet up. But she was skinny and Annie was not. She had no upper body strength. She'd never done rock climbing.

I can't do this. I can't. I can't.

The men's voices. Still jubilant, but then—wait. A shout. A blow. More laughter.

Fuck.

Annie dropped her tote bag and hurled herself at the wall. Billie was a good fifteen feet up, finding ledges where none seemed to exist. *Follow her path. See where she puts her feet.* Annie didn't know how she did it, but she found a handhold and managed to haul her body up to a little jut of rock. Then she did it again. And again. Her clogs wouldn't fit on a ledge and she kicked them off, let her toes wrap around the rock. *Goodbye, lovely clogs.* Ahead of her, Billie had disappeared, hopefully up into some safe niche and not into bigger trouble. Annie reached, and clenched, and pulled, and made it up another handhold. Her body was doing things her mind had never imagined it could do. She could still hear the voices down in the canyon. She hauled herself again. And then she was there—gripping a wide flat ledge under an overhang. With a final heave, she scraped her torso up onto the ledge, where Billie crouched against the rock wall.

Annie was panting. Her arms felt like water. The voices were directly below. She listened for the scarred man's growl among them but didn't hear him.

"Whoa, what's this we got here?"

"A little bag of treasure!"

"Girl's treasure."

"Girl's shoes!"

Billie glared at her. Billie still had her tote bag. She still had her shoes. Shit.

"Our lucky day."

"So where's the lucky lady?"

Annie held her breath, tried not to shift a single pebble. She heard them moving in the canyon, back and forth, searching.

"Must be ahead."

"Making things easy."

More shifting around. Then a blow.

"Get moving, worm."

Steps on gravel. Things dragging. Laughter. Then they were gone, further up the canyon.

"You moron!" Billie hissed. "I don't know why I'm traveling with you. I don't know why I saved your ratty little life. You're going to get both of us killed—"

"I'm sorry," Annie whispered. "I'm really sorry. What do we do?"

Billie shook her head. They could wait until the men were gone and then climb back down, but what if more came along? That canyon might be an interstate highway for marauders. Annie looked along the length of the ledge: at one end, the rock wall levelled out to a more manageable climb. Billie pointed there and Annie nodded.

They pulled themselves up across the wall, shimmying on knees and stomachs, and reached another ledge that led further up the canyon. They followed that, hugging the wall in silence and climbing higher whenever possible. Finally they reached the top of the rock wall—a bare plateau about the size of a football field, stretching back to an even higher set of cliffs.

"They'll never find us up here," Annie whispered, more a question than a statement.

"They may not, but other things will." Billie looked around the open plateau with disgust.

"Other things?"

Billie shook her head. "Don't even talk about them."

Annie remembered the terrifying dark thing that had passed overhead when she was with the scarred man. "Dragons?"

"Hush."

"Devils?"

"Shut up!" Billie's eyes were sharp with both anger and fear. "Just shut up! Don't you think you've done enough damage already?"

Annie fell silent. Of course she'd be the one to screw things up. Billie stood. "Let's go," she said brusquely. "I'm getting back to my babies, no matter what."

They made their way along the plateau, paralleling the canyon while remaining back from its rim. Fear settled into Annie's body like chills in a fever. The rasp of her breath seemed as loud as a bus. She imagined sounds. She imagined shadows. This kind of visceral, bodily fear was new to her. Her experiences of fear at home seemed abstract and trivial in comparison—fear of looking foolish, fear of disappointing people, fear of failure.

And now she was barefoot. Every damn piece of gravel jabbed her soles. They scraped; they pierced. Annie thought with longing of the jumble of shoes in her closet: Leopard-print heels. Cork wedge heels. Knock-off Uggs that she hadn't worn in years. Flower flip-flops. Seashell flip-flops. So many shoes for one person. And she had friends with twice as many. Right now she would give anything for a single pair of battered sneakers.

Distracted, she slammed her foot into a rock. Blood spurted from her big toe.

Another screw-up: The tote bag. The clogs. Not remembering how she got here. Getting stuck here to begin with. Her pathetic career. Her pathetic love life. And now her toe.

It throbbed. Blood smeared across her foot.

"I'm sorry," she whispered to Billie, choking back tears. "I'm sorry."

Billie turned around, saw the bleeding toe, and looked mollified.

"We all make mistakes, honey," she said. "Let's keep going."

CHAPTER SIX

Bol

Bol kicked at the prisoner walking ahead of him. It was fun to kick them from behind: just a small kick at the back of the ankle, but they couldn't see it coming and would stumble, and then Attwater would get angry and maybe give them a beating.

Attwater was stingy with the beatings. He didn't want their skin torn or shredded. He didn't want to kill them right away. "Make them last. We've got eternity," he would say, and then Falc would laugh like the girly suck-up he was and say "Eternity! Ha! Sure do!"

Attwater was right about saving the skins, though. And about making the prisoners last. He was right about almost everything. Bol knew only one other person who came close to Attwater in cunning, a boy from his village named Jarek. A few years older than Bol, Jarek had somehow taught himself to read and write. He showed Bol how to have fun with the peddlers passing through town. You removed the pegs holding their cart wheels together; then you watched as they headed off and, at the first bump in the road, their cart and all their possessions collapsed. The village had been too small for Jarek's ambitions. To

Bol's lasting regret, he set off one day and never came back.

Bol kicked at the prisoner again, a strange-looking man with a long forehead and scars on his face. If he'd encountered him at home, he'd have thought him a demon, or one of those bad visions you get stumbling home in the dark from the tavern. But since coming to Hell, he'd learned there were more varieties of human beings than anyone could possibly imagine.

Men who wore skirts like women. Women who wore breeches like men. Men with long hair braided like garlic. People with skin the color of straw, of bark, of damp earth.

They'd captured one of the earth-skinned ones and left him tied up at camp beside an old woman and a boy. At the thought of the boy, Bol felt his heart speed up. Damn Attwater's waiting.

"Go faster," he muttered at the prisoner. He kicked at the scarred man's heel and missed. Of course Falc noticed.

"Bol needs dancing lessons," Falc said to Attwater. "Improve his footwork for the ladies."

Bol had learned a while ago that he couldn't outtalk Falc. But Attwater never seemed impressed by Falc's big mouth anyway.

"Fuck your dancing lessons," Bol said. He kicked at the prisoner's heel again and this time made contact, hard.

* * * * *

They reached the camp. Falc shoved the new prisoner face-down onto the gravel beside the earth-skinned man, the old woman, and the boy. The prisoner writhed and kicked, but Falc held him down while Attwater bound his feet with more strips of dried skin. Bol preferred to think of it as leather, not so different from the hide of his pigs back home.

"If only we'd got the girl," Falc said.

Attwater looked at him sharply. "We'll get her."

Attwater strode across the canyon to one of their bone piles and selected a long thin arm bone. Reaching for a sharp rock, he sat down and began whittling. Falc drifted after him, puffy sleeves of burgundy and blue jiggling as he walked. Bol had never seen such an idiotic outfit. Puffy sleeves, ruffled pants, all those colors. And the man claimed to have been a soldier. Well, not in any army that Bol had ever known. Falc was a sack of lies and fawning. A tall sack, though. Bol wished he were as tall as Falc. As tall as Attwater. Then Attwater might treat him as an equal.

"Let's do one now," Bol said. "We've got so many."

"Bol is as patient as my old hunting bitch in heat," Falc said to Attwater.

"Who's a bitch, Falc? Who are you calling a bitch?"

"Shut up, you two." Attwater didn't look up from his whittling. "You make my head hurt."

Bol walked around the line of prisoners, kicking dust onto them for lack of anything better to do. He couldn't help eyeing the boy's thin body under the loincloth. What kind of idiot-child would run around wearing nothing but a rag over his ass? He'd freeze to death in five heartbeats in the winter. It was asking for trouble, too. Maybe this boy liked trouble. Some of them did. Bol could tell when, despite their wails and curses, they liked it.

There was one, the red-headed boy. Bol was sure he liked it. But it was hard these days for Bol to recall one from another. The lake of fire had made his mind wobbly. And the more time he spent here in Hell, the harder it was to remember details from home. He could recall general things: watching the road for gypsies and travelers—boys with no friends in the village, boys who would soon be gone. Carving a slab of pork to entice them. Keeping the carving knife close at hand. Turning his dead mother's crucifix to the wall.

Well, that last part hadn't worked so well, had it. You had to give God credit for being able to see even when Jesus himself was blind.

Across the canyon floor, Attwater handed his sharpened bone to Falc, who turned it around in his hands.

"Nice," Falc said. He made pretend-lunges in the air with it. "Still, I'd give a trunk of gold pieces for a pike or a halberd."

Fuck. Did they have to listen to another of Falc's stories about stripping gold off the altars of Rome, sacks of gold, trunks of gold? He wished he had a gold piece for every lie Falc told. But Attwater spoke before Falc could get started.

"Take his boots," he said, pointing to the scarred prisoner.

Bol hadn't noticed the prisoner's boots—tall, thick, sheepskin, much better than any of theirs. He pulled them off while the man strained and jerked. "We'll game for them," Attwater said.

The three of them gathered by the canyon wall. Attwater had come up with a variety of games of chance involving bits of rock or bone. It passed the time, especially when they had a stretch with no prisoners.

They played for a while. Attwater told a story about robbing a coach filled with preachers, one of whom pissed his pants. They'd heard it before but laughed anyway. Bol started to feel better about everything, but then Falc won the boots. He pulled off his slippers—*what kind of soldier wore slippers?*—and jammed his big feet into the boots.

"Fucking midget," he said, struggling to get them to fit. The prisoner wasn't as tall as Falc, but he wasn't a midget. He was taller than Bol.

"We'll do one now," Attwater announced, standing up and stretching.

Bol perked up. "The boy?"

"The cunt."

Attwater and Falc went over to the prisoners, pulled the old woman upright, and dragged her to a table-sized flat rock. There wasn't much to her, just wrinkled skin and bones. She whimpered and pled in a high, grating voice.

"Shut up, woman," Falc said. He kicked her in the back of her legs and her knees buckled. The two men stripped her as Bol looked on. Without ever discussing it, they had come up with rules: Attwater and Falc got first chance with the women. Bol got first chance with the boys. With men, it depended on what Attwater wanted to do with them.

"This meat isn't just old. It's rancid." Falc made a face. He slapped the woman's backside and the sound echoed up the canyon. Then he bent her over the table, untied her legs, and when she wouldn't stop shrieking, ripped a piece of her dress and stuffed it in her mouth.

By the time it was Bol's turn, she was barely squirming. Not so much fun. It figured Falc would leave nothing for him. He closed his eyes and thought of the red-headed boy.

When he was done, the woman slumped to the ground, a smear of blood giving a sheen to the side of the rock. Attwater pulled her upright.

"No, you don't, granny," he said. "Give us another round first." He turned to the others. "Come on. Before she's gone."

This time they placed her face-up on top of the stone. Bol had trouble getting erect and panicked. Couldn't they just get on with the flaying? He was so good at the flaying, all those years of butchering pigs. Attwater always praised him for his flaying.

"Looks like Bol wants to wait for the boy," Falc sneered.

"Fuck you, Falc—"

"Why not." Attwater said this slowly, with a growing smile, and both Bol and Falc turned to stare. He looked back at Bol. "You want the child. We won't do him yet, but we'll have some fun with him. We'll educate him."

What? Clearly this was another of Attwater's brainstorms, but Bol had no clue what he was talking about.

"Be a shame to send him back to the fire as a virgin." Attwater strode over and grabbed the child, who started wailing through his gag. He hauled him to the large rock, pulled his loincloth off, and shoved him on top of the motionless woman.

"Go to it, little man," he said. "Don't know what to do? Here." He huddled over the two of them, trying to jam the child's penis into the woman.

Falc was laughing so hard that it turned into coughing. Bol felt frozen. It was hard for him to breathe. Things got blurry and he thought he saw the red-headed boy there under Attwater's grip. The canyon spun and his head felt hot and he was tumbling down an abyss into the fire—not the fire—holy Mary, not back into the fire—*not the fire*—

"Let him go!"

A shout from the prisoners jolted him back into himself.

"Cowards! Only cowards would attack a child!"

It was the scar-faced man. He'd managed to dislodge his gag enough to shout at them. Falc rushed over and started kicking him with those lovely sheepskin boots. Bol joined in.

"You'll see who's a coward!" Falc shouted.

"Yeah!" Bol echoed. It felt good to ram his foot into flesh, feel it give way before him, feel the whole body shudder.

"Stop." This was Attwater, cold, quiet. "Don't kill him. Put the child away." He shoved the boy to Falc, who tossed him on the ground beside the earth-skinned man and re-tied his hands and feet. Attwater nodded at the woman's body. "Bol. One arm."

Bol pulled his sharpest rock from his breeches and set to work. Within minutes, he'd neatly severed her left arm. Blood pooled on the gravel. She had stopped twitching a while ago. Attwater snatched the arm and stepped over to the row of prisoners.

"Sit him up."

Falc pulled the scarred man up so he was leaning against the canyon wall.

"You're so bloody brave," Attwater said. "You need to keep your strength up for all that bravery. You need some red meat." He grinned and shoved the arm in the scarred man's face. "Eat."

The scarred man turned his head down. Falc pulled it back up by the hair. "Eat." The scarred man spat at them. Attwater slammed the prisoner in the face with the bloody arm. "I said to eat."

He spat again. Attwater slammed him again. Blood spurted from his nose.

"Eat it."

The man spat. Attwater slammed him again. He didn't make a sound. He continued to spit as long as he could, and when he couldn't spit any more, he remained silent. Attwater kept hitting him. Then he tossed the bloody arm, which was starting to disintegrate, to Falc.

"I'd like to shove this up his ass," said Falc.

"You'll get your chance. But remember. One at a time. Make it last. We've got eternity."

Bol knew exactly what Falc was going to say. And of course he said it.

"Eternity! Ha. Sure do."

CHAPTER SEVEN

Annie

Annie dropped to her knees on the ledge above the canyon. Bile rose in her throat. Her eyes clamped shut and she convulsed with dry, empty heaves.

"Let's go," Billie said urgently.

They'd been moving along the plateau when it narrowed, forcing them back toward the canyon rim, and they saw the men. Not just the men: the prisoners on the ground and the limp body on the rock. The boy shoved on top. The severed arm.

"Let's go," Billie repeated, tugging at Annie's blouse. "*Now.*"

Annie couldn't stop heaving. Her throat was raw. Through the murk of nausea she heard the men, quieter now, laughing.

"Come *on.*"

"Okay... a minute..."

She barely got the words out. Annie tried to steady herself and glanced into the canyon again. The three men had seated themselves along the near wall and were playing a game with small rocks. The scarred man lay bound across from them, next to a tall Black prisoner and the boy.

The boy squirmed.

Alive. Thank goodness. He had light brown skin, straight black hair. He was maybe seven or eight years old.

"Ready?" Billie whispered.

No. Yes. She had to be. Annie forced herself to stand. Nausea lurked in her gut. The men were only taking a break. They would do horrible things to the boy and the others, kill them in horrible, painful ways.

"Should we... do something?"

"Are you nuts?"

Probably. She had no idea what they could do. Two women, neither in particularly strong shape. No phones to call 911. No weapons except a few rocks.

"Come *on*."

But the boy. It was wrong to abandon him. Even the scarred man—that vicious, violent man—had tried to help the boy.

"Go," Annie rasped. "I'll catch up in a minute."

"You're nuts." Billie's whisper was furious. "Suit yourself. Get yourself killed. I don't care."

Billie spun away. She padded silently but Annie could feel the rage in every footstep. Her floral blouse and green pants grew smaller and more distant and then vanished entirely around a rock outcropping.

Down below, the marauders were still at their game. The canyon walls remained a mute black, the sky an unperturbed grey. Billie was right: she was nuts. She'd just relinquished her one friend in this terrifying world, and for what? There was nothing she could do to help those poor people down below.

What would Ben do?

Ben would never have let himself get trapped in such a fucked-up situation to begin with.

Below, one of the tall men stood and stretched. He paced a circle around the campsite, stopped to deliver a kick to Trua, then returned to the game.

The men laughed. Argued. Cursed. Tossed their small stones.

Maybe a rockslide? Dislodging enough rocks to knock out all three of them? Impossible. It would be like swatting a wasps' nest: not enough to kill them, but enough to make them furious.

As if echoing her thoughts, stones clattered into the canyon somewhere beyond her sight.

Billie?

The men leapt and peered up the canyon in the direction that Billie had gone. The tall one who seemed to be the leader pointed and beckoned to the short man. They reached into a pile of bones, pulled out two long ones that had been whittled into spears, and headed up the canyon. The other tall man—the one who'd kicked Trua—stood behind, watching.

Billie, look out.

Annie shifted from foot to foot. Should she run to warn Billie? Run the other way to escape this whole situation? Only one of the men remained with the prisoners. So this was a chance to try a rescue. But she'd never be able to subdue even one man. He was bigger, stronger, he had weapons, he knew how to fight—

Warn Billie? Help the boy? Run away and save herself?

Annie took a step in Billie's direction. Another few steps. She stopped.

Help the boy? Save herself?

She was now directly over the section of canyon with the lone marauder and the three prisoners. Even alone he was frightening, a killer. They were all killers. And she wasn't a hero. She wasn't strong or brilliant or brave. She wasn't supposed to be in a life-or-death situation like this—

I'm sorry, Billie.

I'm sorry, boy.

Her bare feet looked like pale dead fish on the dark rock. She couldn't even manage to hold on to her own shoes.

I can't do this.

Annie turned back. She'd retrace her steps along the ledge, leave the marauders behind, find another way home. This wasn't cowardice, it was common sense. She needed to protect herself. Save herself. When she got home, she'd tell the police. That was the sensible thing to do, get home and let the police take care of it.

Then she felt it again—the terror in the sky.

Like before, the hairs on her arms leapt up. The world turned cold. She had no breath. And this time it was bigger—expansive, spreading. There were more of them. Multiples of whatever it was, moving quickly over the canyon—

Animal instinct hurled her down onto the shelf: *flatten, hide, vanish.* But she was too near the edge. Rock crumbled. She stiffened but there was nothing to grab. The ground under her right side fell away and she was hanging suspended and then sliding, until she was crashing down the side of the canyon, slamming against the rock wall, flailing, plummeting—*this had happened before*—tumbling through debris—

She landed on top of the remaining marauder.

* * * * *

She was intact. A miracle. The cold terror in the sky was gone. A man lay underneath her.

Annie jumped away as if he were a snake.

He was limp and groaning faintly amidst the debris that had fallen with her. He would get up any moment now—the others could come back at any moment too—

Everything happened fast after that. Groping at the ground and finding a sharp rock. Glance at the man but no. Can't do it. Dashing over to the prisoners. The scarred man could fight, she knew that. His eyes, barely visible in a bloodied face, widening as he recognized her. Hacking at his bonds with the rock.

She cut through the cord on his hands and he grabbed the rock to work on his feet. She turned to the next prisoner, the tall Black man, and started digging her fingers into the knot binding his wrists. He wriggled and strained, trying to help, but it only made things worse. "Hold still," she whispered, but he kept tossing.

Trua was up now, crouched, working on the bonds that held the boy, hacking at them, fraying them—

A thud and an explosive grunt.

The marauder had recovered and launched himself onto Trua from behind. He was gripping a large rock and trying to slam it into the scarred man's head.

Annie dug into the cord frenetically. *Tear, damn it. Unravel.* Trua and the marauder were wrestling, rolling on the floor of the canyon.

She needed a knife. Scissors. All she had were fingers. The other men might be back any moment now. She scrabbled with the prisoner's cords, prodding and burrowing like a rabid rodent.

The boy—still bound and flat on the ground—stared across at her. Annie fumbled with the prisoner's cords. Just feet away, Trua and the marauder heaved and grappled in the dirt.

The boy lay motionless as a cocoon, his eyes wide as full moons.

CHAPTER EIGHT

Bol

"Our little lady friend!" Attwater had said with a grin when they heard the clattering rocks. "Bol, with me. Falc, watch the prisoners."

Bol was glad for the interruption. Falc had been acting like an ass as usual, making it hard to focus on the pebble game, which was barely a game. Bol missed nights at the tavern, early evenings before his pockets were empty and he had to wheedle for refills. There'd be a fire in the hearth and someone singing badly and someone else with a bawdy story. With a full stein, the world was good. You felt like a king.

Now here he was, tossing goddamn pebbles in the dirt for the millionth time. What he would give for a stein. Real dice. A cockfight! New faces, anyone other than that fawning Falc.

Then they'd heard the falling rocks.

It could have been natural. Rocks fell all the time. Or an animal, though Bol had never seen an animal here. But Attwater's word was law—if he thought it was the girl, then it was the girl—and Bol was happy to be chosen.

"Fuck no! I'm coming too!" Falc exclaimed.

Attwater nodded toward the scarred prisoner. “You saw how he put up a fight. Someone needs to keep watch.”

“Make Bol stay. He’s slow, he can’t climb, he almost lost that one down by the river—”

“Fuck you, Falc!”

“Shut up, boy fucker. Pig fucker.”

“Shut up both of you,” Attwater said. “Before you scare her off. Come on.”

The two of them reached for spears, sharp rocks, and strips of skin and headed up the canyon in the direction that led deeper into the mountains. They’d explored it before and Bol knew that it dead-ended. This wouldn’t be hard.

After several hundred paces, they stopped to listen. Nothing. They continued several hundred more paces. Nothing. They kept going. The falling rocks had seemed close, but sound echoed weirdly against the winding canyon walls.

“Maybe it was just rocks?” Bol said.

Attwater glared. “Afraid of a girl? Go back to camp.”

“I’m not afraid of anything. I just—”

“Go back.”

“I’m not afraid. I just thought—”

“She’s here. I can smell her.” Attwater raised his face into the air and took a breath, and Bol thought of a wolf on the hunt. He himself inhaled with a snuffle but just got that same old rotten-egg stench. Attwater was magic.

“I just—”

“Shut up. Go back.”

There was a point after which you didn't challenge Attwater. Bol turned back while the tall man continued moving up the canyon. He heard a crash of more rocks somewhere but ignored it. Did Attwater really think he was afraid? Or was Attwater planning to take the girl for himself? To use her up without them? Bol didn't like any of the possibilities. He trudged down the narrow trail, hardly trying any more to avoid making noise. Maybe Attwater didn't trust Falc alone with the prisoners. That might be it. Bol suddenly pictured Falc alone with the naked boy, deciding to have fun with him, maybe deciding to kill him, and his face heated up.

He rounded a bend in the canyon and heard noises ahead, from the direction of the camp. He broke into a jog.

The noises became louder and more distinct: grunts and panting. Crunches of gravel. Thud of bodies.

Bol was running now. He leapt over a large rock, rounded another turn, approached the spot where the canyon opened up into the camp. He halted, pulled himself flat against the wall of the canyon, gripped his bone-spear, and peered out.

Chaos engulfed the camp. Somehow the scarred prisoner had escaped from his ties and was wrestling with Falc, rolling back and forth across the gravel. A woman knelt beside the earth-skinned prisoner, digging at his bonds while he thrashed.

The scarred man was on top. Now Falc was on top. Now the scarred man again. Falc was larger, but the scarred man had muscle and desperation. The woman kept glancing up the canyon toward Bol, and he pulled himself tighter against the wall. She freed the man's hands and started on the boy. Falc grabbed a rock and brought it down hard on the scarred man's back. The scarred man collapsed and Falc leapt on top of him. The woman turned from the boy, holding one of the loosened ties, and threw herself onto Falc, wrapping the tie around his neck like a garrot. He bucked and threw her off, but it gave the scarred man time to get up and counter-attack. The earth-skinned man broke through the ties and lurched up onto his feet.

"Take the boy! Up the wall!" the scarred man called, and pointed to one of the rock walls.

Bol assessed. The scarred man was a hell of a fighter, and the other prisoner was two heads taller than he was. He could jump in and haul the scarred man off of Falc. Together they could probably take them all. But maybe not. Falc didn't look too good right now. Blood was pouring off one side of his head.

The earth-skinned man was having trouble scaling the wall—holding the boy over a shoulder, trying to find footholds but slipping. The woman stood beside him calling out instructions. Now the man found purchase and started scrabbling up and the woman followed close behind, grasping ledges and cracks that Bol hadn't known existed.

He should jump in now. Attack. Grab them, pull them down off the wall before they got too high. Smash their skulls. Then help Falc. The two of them together could easily finish off the scarred bastard.

Falc and the scarred man rolled close to Bol's hiding spot, still wrestling. But Falc was flagging. His legs weren't doing what he wanted them to. He'd grabbed a sharpened bone but couldn't manage to stab the scarred man with it. Fucking clown. Fucking liar. Bol had known all along: no one with those ruffled pants could have been a real soldier.

The scarred man pulled himself out from under Falc and reached for a large, heavy rock. *Now.* Bol could launch himself into the canyon, tackle the scarred man, deflect the stone.

Or he could do nothing, and tell Attwater that he'd returned to find Falc dead and the prisoners gone.

Falc lurched toward the scarred man again but his spear pierced empty air. He stumbled to his knees. The scarred man raised his rock, barely two arm-lengths away from Bol's hiding spot. He was fixated on Falc, oblivious to everything else, an easy target.

Bol leaned back motionless against the canyon wall as the scarred man brought the rock down on Falc's head and scrambled after the others up the canyon wall.

CHAPTER NINE

Annie

They ran.

They followed the rock shelf in the direction Billie had gone. Trua and the other prisoner took turns carrying the boy. Even carrying him, they were faster than Annie. After rounding a number of outcroppings, they found Billie, sitting on a flat rock and examining the bottom of her shoe. She leapt up, eyes wide with shock.

"Just come. I'll explain later," Annie panted, and they continued to run until finally the shelf opened up to a broad flat area.

The plateau stretched for a mile or more to a range of craggy black mountains. They made it about two hundred yards when Annie's side cramped. She glanced around for shelter and dropped to the ground behind a large rock. The others dropped too.

She could barely breathe. Her side hurt. Her body was covered with gashes and bruises from her fall that she hadn't noticed until now. They were all panting, but beyond that, the plateau was silent. No sign of anyone in pursuit.

Billie, sitting apart from the others, motioned for her to come close. She was livid.

"What the blazes are *they* doing here?"

"They escaped. *We* escaped. Are you okay? I heard rocks falling—"

"Of course I'm okay. Or I *was* okay, until you brought those savages here. Are you trying to get us killed?"

"Of course not. I just..."

"You just were *not thinking*. That's what. Now what are we supposed to do?"

Annie had no answer. She knew nothing about the tall prisoner, although he'd been carrying the boy without complaint. And what she knew about Trua was not reassuring. In addition to his attacks on her, he'd just smashed a man's head with a rock. In her frenzy to escape, it hadn't really registered. Now she remembered seeing him raise the rock and slam it down.

Sickening crack. Even more sickening slosh. Gray stuff oozing. Clumps of gray and red clinging to the rock.

Self-defense, yes, but he hadn't even hesitated. If he could do that, what else might he be capable of?

"Excuse me. You—pale spirit!"

The other prisoner was calling to her, his voice cautious. Annie looked at him closely for the first time and saw a young man of lean muscle. She guessed he was in his late teens or early twenties: taut skin, close-cropped black hair, a dusty and ragged blue cloth wrapped around his torso.

"May I ask if you are the spirit of this place? Are you at war with those other spirits?"

Billie laughed. "She's not a spirit, she's just a dead girl from California."

He hesitated. "I don't know that village."

"It's a state, you dummy, not a village!"

"It's a... big village," Annie said. "Far away. My name is Annie. What about you?"

"I am Ifechi, son of Okeke. From Obodonwa, the finest village on this side of the Great River."

"And I am Trua, son of Bleda. I come from the Great Plain." The scarred man said this assertively, almost competitively.

Billie laughed again. "Great plain, great river? I guess everybody lives somewhere great, huh? I'm Billie, daughter of Mary Frances, and I come from the great big town of Sweet Valley."

Thank goodness Billie's anger had passed. Annie turned to the boy. "How about you?"

He sat where Ifechi had set him down, a few feet away from the men, staring at the dirt. His skin was smeared with dust. He was still naked.

Annie grabbed Billie's bag. Before Billie could object, she rifled through it, pulled out the biggest piece of fabric, and tied it around the boy's waist.

"What's your name?" she asked softly when she was done.

He remained silent, eyes down.

"You're safe now," she said. "We'll take care of you. I'm Annie and this is Billie. When you feel like it, you can tell us your name. But only when you feel like it. Meanwhile, you're safe with us. We're not going to let those bad men get you."

Billie rolled her eyes. "Maybe not those bad men. But what about all the others?"

"Stop it!" Annie snapped. But it was too late. The boy hunched down even tighter into himself. He looked like a marmot, curved and neckless and brown. All he needed was a hole in the ground into which he could vanish.

* * * * *

They'd rested enough. Ifechi looked at Annie. "Which way shall we go?" he asked.

We. He assumed they'd become a team. He assumed she was the leader, but he was wrong. She turned to Billie.

"That way. To the mountains," Billie said.

They set out—walking now, not running, but still alert for the marauders. Ifechi carried the boy on his shoulders. After a while, Billie beckoned Annie to walk beside her.

"I don't like traveling with these people."

"Strength in numbers? At least we have two strong guys in case something happens."

"I don't care how strong they are. I don't trust them. That Negro, he's a savage from Africa. And that fellow who was following you. He's some kind of savage too. He's dangerous."

Annie didn't respond. Ben would have challenged Billie's bigotry, but she felt too dependent on her to risk an argument. And, privately, she too worried about Trua. He trudged along, silent and unreadable. Perhaps the swollen bruises on his face made it hard for him to talk. Of all of them, he'd taken the worst beating in the canyon.

Some time later he fell into step beside her. She tensed.

"What's your father's name?" he said gruffly. It was not a question she'd expected.

"Herbert. Well, Herb. Herb Maple."

"Annie, daughter of Herb. I... apologize."

She stopped walking. His tone was both serious and awkward. He forced more words out.

"You are not a witch. I know that now. You were very... brave."

That was all. He seemed to have extended himself as far as he could.

"Thank you," she said, and he dropped back so she was alone again. Inside, Annie quailed. Trua thought she was brave. Ifechi thought she was a leader. They didn't know that only a random crumble of rock had prevented her from fleeing. Even Billie didn't know how close she'd come to running away.

A hot wind scoured the plateau but it was shame that flushed Annie's face. She should tell them. But what if they abandoned her? Confessing her cowardice felt like pulling a loose strand from her sweater. There were so many failures in her life; one tug and they might all unravel.

Keep silent. Keep walking.

Her bare feet skimmed the gravel. Callousing, they now barely registered the jabs and scrapes. Just keep walking. Billie would find the pathway home, and she'd never see any of these people again, and no one but she would know how unworthy she was.

CHAPTER TEN

Bol

Attwater told Bol to pack up their belongings.

Bol was surprised. He'd expected Attwater to berate him over Falc's death, or to scramble up the cliff after the escaped prisoners. But Attwater just looked at Falc's oozing skull, and then at Bol.

"We're moving on," he said. "Bury whatever weapons we can't carry."

Spears in hand, they headed down the canyon toward the sea of fire, the route they took for hunting. Attwater toted a skin pouch that held sharpened bones and his carved-bone gaming pieces. The bundle of girl's clothes was tied around his waist: rags came in handy for mopping sweat, wiping up blood, gagging mouths. Bol carried a pouch with flaps of dried skin, cords of leather, and bones for carving. He wore Falc's boots, the ones taken from the scarred man. They were too large and his feet slid inside. When he climbed over rocks, he nearly slipped out of the boots entirely.

"Shoes too big?" Attwater had said, mouth curled into a nasty half-smile, when Bol first put on the boots. He held up the girl's shoes they'd found in the canyon. "Maybe these are a better fit?"

Bol fumed but said nothing. Falc was gone; he was supposed to be Attwater's number-two now. Maybe even his equal. *Give it time*, he told himself. Maybe Attwater just needed time to get used to the new order of things.

They walked in unsettling silence. Was Attwater angry? The prisoners were gone, somewhere up on the ridge, getting further away every moment. But that was Falc's fault, not his. Attwater shouldn't blame him. Did Attwater blame him?

"Too bad the girl got away, huh?" Bol ventured when the silence was too much. "We could have had fun with her. We could have had a lot of fun. A lot of fun, right?"

"You idiot." Attwater halted and glared. "There were two girls, not one."

"What?"

"One of them knocked those rocks into the upper canyon. The other one took our prisoners. They were working together."

"But..." Bol was flummoxed. He'd never heard of women doing anything so audacious. The girls in his village just gossiped and flirted and popped out babies.

"Look at this." Attwater pulled what seemed to be a woman's undergarment out of the pouch. Under its coating of black dust, it was tiny, delicate, ruffled. Simply looking at it made Bol uncomfortable. "Whoever wore this was small. But the shoes we found. Remember them?"

Bol nodded.

"They were large. Big feet, big girl. The girl you saw stealing the prisoners—was she large or small?"

"Large," Bol began, and then remembered he'd told Attwater that the camp had been deserted when he got back there. His face heated up. But Attwater didn't seem to care.

"What else did she look like?"

Bol tried to think. He'd been focused on Falc's fight with the scarred man.

"Large. Brown hair. Half naked, like a whore." He pointed at the middle of his thighs. "Her dress didn't even cover her legs."

Attwater nodded. "Two girls. One small, one large." He narrowed his eyes. "And they didn't get away. Never say that again. Don't even think that."

"But—"

"We'll track them. We'll find them."

"But how—"

"Shut up and leave the 'how' to me, pig man. I know a path up to the canyon rim. We'll track them."

They resumed walking. The canyon fed into another canyon, wider but still jagged and dark. All this silence made Bol nervous. He'd hated Falc's idiotic yammer—his boasting and fawning, how he echoed Attwater's every pronouncement and laughed at his every joke—but it had filled those silences like straw filling a mattress.

"Hey. Attwater..." Bol hesitated. This had been eating at him for a while, and with Falc gone he felt more free to ask. "Why'd it happen?"

"Why'd what happen?"

"Us. Getting out of the fire like we did. You think... did God...?"

Attwater gave out a laugh so loud and abrupt that it turned into coughing. "Pig man. If you think God freed us, you're even stupider than I thought."

"But doesn't God— isn't God—"

"God doesn't give a fuck what's happening down here. We got out because we were tougher and meaner than everyone else. Or because the thing is broken. Like a hinge that rusts through. Like a wagon where the wheel comes off."

Jarek and the peddler wagons. Attwater was a mind reader. And he was talking to Bol like a buddy. Bol, heartened, decided to push on.

"Um, another thing... Where do they go? The ones like, um, Falc?"

"The dead ones?"

"Yeah."

Attwater's lip curled. "Our good friend Falc is back in the fire, no doubt about that. The others, like the rancid cunt?" He shrugged. "Maybe Heaven. Maybe we martyred them. Maybe we did them a favor, and they're frolicking with angels right now. They should thank us."

"And us? You and me?"

Attwater gave out another cough of a laugh.

"Pig man. You and I are not going anywhere. Not back into the fire, not Heaven, nowhere. We're staying right here. That's why we have these." He jabbed his spear at the air. "That's why you're sticking with me."

Attwater looked directly, dangerously, at Bol. The lightness dropped out of his voice.

"And that's why you're not going to pull any of the bullshit with me that you pulled with Falc."

Bol's gut collapsed. He lowered his gaze to the canyon floor and walked. He readied himself for a dagger in his back. Canyon silence gave way to faint sounds of the fire sea—cracking, popping, rushing. Still no dagger. The cliff walls opened up to shoreline, black sand and orange waves. The air hung still and stifling as a barn on a midsummer afternoon. Now that they were close to the fire's edge, Bol could hear the screams within the pop and sizzle of the flames.

"There," Attwater began, pointing toward a section of cliff. "We'll climb up there, to the ridge... No. Wait."

He pivoted, nose wolflike in the air again, and Bol followed his gaze down the shoreline. Far away, a tiny dark figure was silhouetted against the orange waves.

A person, alone, walking toward them. Bol couldn't tell yet if it was a man or woman, old or young. Probably a new arrival, though: they were making no efforts to hide themselves.

Attwater climbed onto a rock for a better view and Bol followed. The tall man grinned. Bol felt relief seep through him.

"Time for some fun," Attwater said. "We'll track the girls later. We've got all the time in the world."

"Ha!" Bol echoed. He reached down and pulled at Falc's boots—now *his* boots—which had slipped partly off when he climbed onto the rock.

"All the time in the world. Sure do."

CHAPTER ELEVEN

Ifechi

Ifechi trailed the two pale women for lack of a better plan. He understood nothing about this place—not the torturous fire, not the barren landscape, not the lack of sun and moon. Weirdly, it was the lack of a moon that kept gnawing at him, even more than the fire or his capture by the murderous man-spirits. His village was named for the moon and he'd always taken it for granted. Not just its calm, sheer light but the way its cycles held you, telling you when to plant crops or go to market, and the reassurance you felt when the cycle started anew. Here everything felt random and disordered. Somehow he must have slipped into the spirit world. Ifechi had heard stories of this happening to people who were lost in the forest. But why had it happened to him, and what would it take to get home?

He craved answers but feared angering the spirit-women. They might look human but their garments were bizarre and their skin the unnatural pink of uncooked chicken. He longed to call on Ala, the goddess who oversaw the spirit realm, but there were no animals or fruits here to make a sacrifice. So he followed the women warily, carrying the silent boy on his shoulders and trying to cheer him up. He sang him songs that made his own sons laugh and sing along. He told him stories and encouraging proverbs.

"So, little brother, it's true, we're far from our homes. There's no denying that. But someone who travels and sees the world gains more knowledge than the elders..."

The boy didn't respond—not to the songs, not to the stories, not to the proverbs. His body sagged on Ifechi's shoulders like a sack of yams, so different from the wriggling restlessness of his own children.

Obinna toddling toward him, hands outstretched, calling "Papa! Up! Papa! Up!"

Chioke wrapped in his sling across Nkiru's back—no words yet, just cries and gurgles and smiles.

Fatherhood had been a revelation to Ifechi. Of course he'd wanted sons; it was part of becoming a man. But no one told him that his heart would soften like a ripe melon whenever Obinna came reaching for him with those fat little hands. No one told him how he'd want to envelope Chioke and never let go. Ifechi never voiced this, but sometimes he felt envious of women who could wrap their children tight against them all day as they worked.

The boy's legs bumped loosely on Ifechi's chest with each stride. If Nkiru were here, she'd know how to revive him. Those glistening brown eyes, that throaty laugh—there was something in Nkiru's laugh that said she knew you, saw your clumsiest mistakes, and liked you anyway. They'd played together as children and been married for almost four years.

Ifechi couldn't remember a time in his life when she wasn't present. Until now.

His songs grew slower and more mournful, songs of lost love and separation.

The black plain stretched around him. Black mountains stabbed the grey sky. Everything here was strange and wrong.

"Tell me," he asked the women as they walked. "Did someone curse me and send me to this place? What must I do to remove the curse?"

The Billie spirit laughed. "It's not a curse. It's sin."

"Impossible. I honor my ancestors. I've never angered my neighbors."

"Not your ancestors. God! You angered God!"

"Impossible. Chukwu would never send someone to a place like this. Chukwu would never trap someone in that fire."

"Not Chukwu, you idiot! This is Hell! You're in Hell because you don't believe in Jesus!"

"What is 'Hell?' Who is this 'Jesus?' Is this 'Jesus' the god of your 'California?'" He looked to the Annie spirit, who unlike Billie never laughed at him.

"It's a long story," Annie said. She sounded tired, which worried him. "I'm not the best person to tell it."

"I'll tell him," said Billie. "It starts like this. Way back in Bethlehem, almost 2,000 years ago, there was a little baby born in a manger..."

* * * * *

It was such a strange story. Not the part about God having a son, but the part about God letting humans kill his son. If God couldn't protect his own child, how could he protect villages and crops? If God's son had the power to come back from the dead, why let himself be killed to begin with? And why did Billie seem so happy about the idea of a murdered god?

"What kind of sacrifices does your Jesus god require?" Ifechi asked.

"He doesn't need sacrifices. I told you already. He *was* the sacrifice. He sacrificed himself to save all of us."

"But if he sacrificed himself to save you, then why are you here?"

"Because we sinned! We're bad!"

"Then you *do* need to make a sacrifice to placate the gods..."

It made no sense. Eventually Ifechi gave up and resumed talking to the boy. He was thin as a stick, hardly heavier than Obinna, even though nearly twice Obinna's height.

"Little brother, come back with me to my village and we'll fatten you up. You've never tasted anything as good as Nkiru's bitter-leaf soup. We'll feed you pounded yam and ripe udara, and you'll climb trees and skip stones in the stream. One time when I was a boy, I made a stone skip twenty times, which was more than any other boy had ever done..."

Trua slowed down to walk beside him and Ifechi smiled in welcome. The man had fought magnificently in the canyon. And those scars: Ifechi could tell he was a person of great status in his home village.

"I don't trust her," Trua said in a low voice.

"Which one?" Ifechi hoped it wasn't Annie.

"The woman Billie," Trua said. "She's not leading us home."

"What is she up to then?"

"I don't know. But does she look like she knows the way? Have you seen her recognize any landmarks?"

"No."

"There's something deceitful about her."

"Perhaps you just like the plump spirit more." Ifechi spoke lightly, trying to steer the conversation away from deceit and betrayal, but Trua didn't banter back. He just slogged along, looking grim.

"All right," Ifechi conceded. "Perhaps she is deceitful."

He wanted the scarred man to like him. And speaking the words aloud made him think that Trua might be right. What kind of person admitted that their god had been killed? And then sounded proud of it?

"Keep a close eye on her," Trua said. "In case she tries any trickery."

* * * * *

Dust choked his skin. His scalp itched. Even in the dry season, Ifechi had never gone this long without washing. He had an unpleasant feeling that his skin was no longer part of him; it had become a thick, rigid shell.

They stopped to rest beside a boulder nearly as large as his hut. Ifechi slid the silent boy off his shoulders and thought longingly of the cold slap of the stream near his village. Perhaps Nkiru was at the stream right now, fetching water. Or perhaps it was early morning, and she'd be throwing scraps to the chickens. Or afternoon, and she'd be weeding the farm. Or nighttime—

His mind froze. He didn't want to think about Nkiru at night without him.

Alone with the babies, the compound dark and silent. What if a leopard or hyena somehow entered the compound? What if there were a raid by men from some other town?

What if Kamdiba returned?

Ifechi hadn't worried about this for years, but the image opened before him like a poisonous bloom. His leg started jiggling violently. He wanted to leap up and race home. Trua was right. Billie was deceiving them—taking him further and further from his village—away from Nkiru—and Nkiru was alone—and Kamdiba might show up at any moment—

No. Ifechi forced his leg to still, but it didn't calm his inner tumult. If only he could sacrifice to the gods for protection. If only there were a diviner to cast seeds and provide answers—

Annie had gotten up from her place by the rock and was talking to the boy, who sat listlessly.

"Would you like a hug?" she said, squatting beside him. "Sometimes when I'm sad, a hug really helps."

She reached a hand around the boy's shoulders. He whipped out of his hunched posture, threw his arms back to knock her away, and stared at her in fright.

"Don't do that!" he blurted, and returned to his crouch.

He'd spoken! Ifechi stared at Annie and the boy in wonder. Perhaps, after all, it was possible to reverse the spirits' spells. Perhaps, after all, these pale women knew where they were going.

Perhaps he could find a way to return home.

* * * * *

That initial outburst was all they could coax from the boy. He was less limp now on Ifechi's shoulders—Ifechi could feel him craning and fidgeting—but just as silent. They clambered up a rocky ridge and down the other side but found only a new dark plain that looked like the old one.

More rocks. More dust. Still no moon or trees or water.

They were resting behind a large rock when Trua broke his silence.

"Where are you taking us?" he demanded of Billie.

"I told you. The exit."

"Where is it?"

"That's my secret."

"Tell us." Trua raised his voice. "You claim to know where it is. Then tell us."

"I don't have to tell anything to the likes of you. You just stomp along, giving everyone the evil eye—"

"Billie!" The Annie spirit tried to intervene but they talked over her.

"Y'all don't like it, then leave. Scram. Nobody invited you anyway—"

"It's a trap," Trua growled.

"Go. Scram. See what I care—"

"She's lying—"

"Shut your caveman mouth—"

"O, my ancestors!" It was too much for Ifechi. Everything—the dust and desolation, Trua and Billie's fighting, his fears for Nkiru—exploded into panic. "We'll never get home! We'll wander here forever!"

"You stop that heathen wailing!"

"Liar—"

"You just shut up—"

"Billie—"

"I know where we are."

A small voice. The boy.

He sat hunched by himself on the gravel. But his head was raised, and he was looking at them.

"I was here before. Before the bad men. I know the way home."

Thank the gods! The boy was talking, he had cast off the spell, and—best of all—he knew where they were!

Annie beamed. Trua looked skeptical. Billie looked cross.

"Well, why didn't you say so earlier?" she said.

* * * * *

The boy was transformed. He declined to get back on Ifechi's shoulders and insisted on leading them all. He told them his name—Dev—and that he had two brothers and two sisters whom he hadn't seen for a long time. He had a friend named Tai-Shan. Dev didn't know the name of his village, but there were elders who knew. He would take them to the elders who would tell them what to do.

Those spindly legs could move fast when they wanted. Ifechi and Trua had no trouble keeping up, while Annie and Billie trailed behind. Dev raced across the plain and into a narrow side canyon. They maneuvered through the canyon, turning this way and that, until the rock walls opened up to a wide ledge that dropped off against a fire waterfall.

Orange fire pounded down in a torrent. This was liquid fire, unlike any river Ifechi had ever imagined, heavy and turbid, pocked with glowing rocks that it tossed along as casually as hollow gourds. Flames shot up and danced in the air. Clatter and sizzle and rush merged into an overpowering roar. The fire came from far above—the height of ten or twenty trees—and dropped to an orange river even further below.

Ifechi stared. Nothing could live in this river, but it was almost alive itself. Currents of fire twisted and tumbled down the cliff face. They chased each other and wrestled each other. The brightness was blinding.

Hot air slammed his face. His eyes stung. *Fire like this had engulfed him. Fire like this had tortured him.* His heart raced and he started to dizzy.

"Boy!" Trua called. "Tell us how to get past—"

"Annie!" Billie shrieked.

Ifechi jerked around to find the pale Annie spirit slumped on the ground, just past the canyon's mouth, limbs askew and twitching.

PART TWO

Crater

CHAPTER TWELVE

Annie

burningburningburningburningburningburningburnin gburningburningburningburningburningburningburni ngburningburningburningburningburningburningbur ningburningburningburningburningburningburningbu rningburningburningburningburningburningburningb urningburningburningburningburningburningbu—

Nothing but burning, and pain.

Needles of pain pierce your neck, your lungs, your guts. Thin as a filament, hot as live wires, puncturing cell membranes and ripping mitochondria, setting cytoplasm to boil. Your very cells are boiling. The needle withdraws; the needle returns. Repeat a billion times. You think you'll go mad, and madness would be a relief. But no, there's always a tiny interlude between the needles, just long enough to keep you sane, just long enough to feel the next needle like new.

burningburningburningburningburningburningburnin gburningburningburningburningburningburningburni ngburningburningburningburningburningburningbur ningburningburningburningburningburningburningbu rningburningburningburningburningburningburningb urningburningburningburningburningburn—

But maybe this is in fact madness? Here is a man screaming—"The tower! The tower! The tower!"—and he never stops, he continues screaming forever. There a woman calls for Jesus, wailing about weak flesh, begging Jesus to save her, and of course no one answers.

Screams of guilt. Screams of blame. Howls of self-righteousness: *I don't deserve this! It wasn't my fault! The other guy did it and I just went along!* Threats and curses. Calls to vengeance. Whimpers of self-pity. Sobs of repentance—yes, even some of those, rare as they might be.

Wails so loud they drown your thoughts: *I only meant to scare her. I only wanted what was due me. I only did it once. I only did what everyone else was doing.* Old men wailing that they should have died at twenty, young men wailing that they deserve a second chance. Atheists calling for Mother Mary, priests cursing God. And everyone bargaining and shouting for deals like the pit of a colossal, tortured commodities exchange: *Take my money! Take my treasures! I'll give up meat, sex, power! Is it names you want? I'll give you my accomplice, my leader, my lover, my children. State your price, whatever you want, just let me out of here, sweet Jesus, let me out—*

And is that your voice in there, screaming with the rest of them? Are you playing first violin in this symphony of desolation? You can no longer tell your own thoughts from the mass of voices bargaining, denying, begging. You are a murderer. You are an adulterer. You are a liar, a cheat, a bully, a gossip, a traitor. You are the sum of everything misguided and perverse in human nature—

burningburningburningburningburningburningburnin gburningburningburningburningburningburningburni ngburningburningburningburningburning—

You have been there forever.

And it all repeats.

burningburningburningburningburningburningburnin gburningburningburningburningburningburningburni ngburningburningburningburningburning—

You have been there forever.

And it all repeats.

burningburningburningburningburningburningburnin gburningburningburningburningburningburningburni ngburningburningburningburningburning—

* * * * *

"Annie. Annie!"

She was lying on hard ground. Someone was slapping her cheeks. Relief washed over her. She had made it out.

But she almost hadn't.

These descents into the fire were becoming more terrifying rather than less. She now understood from the moment she started slipping how bad it would be. It wasn't a dream. It could go on forever. Any time she slipped back in might be the last—the time she would never get out.

"Annie!" She heard Billie's sweet voice but couldn't move. The burning was like a ghost limb, still present even though it wasn't.

"Is she dead?" This was Ifechi, worried.

"No, she'll come out of it. I hope. Annie. Wake up!"

Opening an eye felt like lifting a truck. The image of Disney's Sleeping Beauty popped into Annie's head—pink gown, hourglass waist, blond tresses perfectly coiffed even in a coma—and she wondered if a prince might appear to wake her with a kiss. The thought was so absurd that she gave out a little snort of a laugh. And then she was awake.

"Oh man." Annie took a deep breath, pushed herself into a sitting position, and looked at her arms and legs. No burn marks, no wounds where the needles had been. Just dusty, sweaty, normal arms and legs. Yet she knew it had been real.

"The spirits took her but gave her back," Ifechi said.

"Would you shut up about the spirits?" Billie snapped.

They were back in the canyon, away from the lava waterfall; the others must have carried her here. Dev sat at her feet, eyes wide with concern. Trua stood several feet away, also watching.

"I'm okay," Annie said with embarrassment. Of all of them, only she had fainted. Of course. Another screw-up. She rubbed her neck, which was stiff from her fall. "Why'd this happen?"

Billie shook her head.

"It happened before. When we saw the sea of fire," Trua said. He didn't mention how she had left him unconscious on that ridge.

"Well. Anyway. Maybe it won't happen again." Annie reminded herself that they were almost out of this place. Dev knew the route back to his village; soon there would be clean clothes, food, a shower.

Trees. Lakes filled with water instead of fire. Cool air that smelled of pine or eucalyptus instead of sulfur.

Day and night. Sunshine.

Her familiar routine of bean burritos and donor files. And relief. No one would expect her to be a leader. No one would expect her to be brave. No one would expect anything of her.

"Dev, how do we get around the lava?"

The boy nodded with gravity. "There's a secret path."

* * * * *

Dev led them along the ledge, hugging the rock wall. Annie worried that she might be overcome again, but she kept her gaze away from the fire and the dizziness didn't return. Dev pointed: there, behind a rock outcropping, was a crevice. He fit easily, but the rest of them had to hunch down. Even hunched, Annie's head brushed the roof of the passage and her hips scraped the wall.

All was dark. It was hot and dry, so different from a damp Earth cave. The air was still and stale. The ground sloped down and Billie lurched into Trua, who cursed at her, and she cursed him back.

"Dev, are you still there? Do you know where we're going?" Annie called out, and a little voice from the front of the group answered. Yes, he was here. Yes, he knew where they were going.

Finally she glimpsed light ahead. Annie's breath quickened. The passage narrowed further, and they pulled themselves in tighter, and then suddenly, like fresh peas squeezed out of a pod, they were out of the rock.

Annie squinted. Everything seemed bright, but that was just in comparison to the tunnel. They'd emerged on the far side of the waterfall, just above the canyon floor. There was no sunlight, only that sulfurous grey sky.

Still this Hell place. Her heart sank.

But Dev was elated. Already he was scampering across the canyon floor, a wide area bordered by more cliffs and the fire river that emerged from the waterfall. They followed. Dev veered away from the fire, a tiny nimble form dancing across the plain.

Annie panted, trying to keep up, scanning for signs of the exit. Finally Dev stopped before another rock opening, as tight as the last. He ducked in, waving for them to follow. Several dozen yards into the cave, he halted, picked up a small rock, and rapped it against a wall ahead of him: three sets of three knocks.

They waited.

The wall moved.

It wasn't in fact a wall; it was a large rock, and it was being pushed aside with a scraping, grinding sound. Dev exploded out of the opening and the adults hauled themselves through after him.

It still wasn't Earth.

They were in a giant crater-like bowl surrounded by mountain. Rock walls jutted up on all sides with no visible ledges or trails. Grey sky sat like a watch cap overhead. It was a a natural fortress, as secure a refuge as you could find. But it wasn't Earth.

A small dark-haired girl dashed across the gravel floor of the crater toward Dev. "You're back!" she called, overjoyed, and the two of them started jumping up and down together.

Three elderly men were already pushing the rock door back into place. Other figures gathered from different parts of the crater. Many hobbled or limped. They were all noticeably *old*—round-shouldered old women, scrawny old men. They wore a variety of garments—tunics and skirts, trousers and cloaks—that had converged into a single destiny as dusty rags. One man seemed marginally younger than the rest, an olive-skinned, silver-haired fellow wrapped in long folds of cloth that might once have been white.

"Romans," Trua muttered from behind Annie. Even without looking, she felt him tense up.

"Who are you?" The toga wearer's voice was polite but edged. Somehow Annie had ended up at the front of the group.

"I'm Annie. This is Billie. Trua. Ifechi. We're not trying to make any trouble. Dev was taking us to his village."

"She saved me from bad men!"

Everyone turned to the boy.

"I was wandering and I got caught. I'm sorry. I won't do it again. I promise."

The Roman shook his head and frowned. "How many times have you made that promise? We'll deal with your disobedience later. Now go play with Taishan. Play with someone who has more patience for your misbehavior."

He turned back to Annie and the others. "If you rescued Dev, you're welcome here. Even the barbarian and the Ethiopian."

"Who—" Trua started to growl, but Annie interrupted.

"He's not a barbarian. He's a brave fighter. He helped rescue Dev too."

The Roman smiled dismissively. "Of course. You're all welcome here."

Isaias—for that was the Roman's name—took charge of them. He waved the onlookers off and led them across the crater, explaining as they went.

Like Annie, all the residents of the crater had been in the fire—some for decades, others for millennia. Most were non-Christians. A few were Christians who apparently hadn't repented their sins while they were alive. Suddenly, like Annie, they had been expelled from the fire into the desert. Wandering alone, they found other loose souls and banded together for protection. Someone stumbled upon the cave that led to the crater. Together they managed to push the flat rock against the opening to provide security.

Isaias himself joined the group shortly before they found the crater. He had died at age 53 of fever. Born a Jew near the city of Joppa, he'd made his way to Rome and adopted Roman customs.

"The Roman ways were more modern," he said. "More sensible. As a Roman, you make your bows to Jupiter and Apollo, but you live as you please. Of course, now I find out that both my options were wrong. Adonai or Jupiter? Equally pointless. If I had only known, I could have joined the followers of Christ and I would be in Heaven now."

"Sorcerers," Trua muttered.

"I beg your pardon?"

"The followers of Christ. Sorcerers."

"Think what you like. You barbarians always do, anyway."

"You—"

"Sssh." Annie touched Trua's arm. "They may know about the exit."

If there were an exit, though, it wasn't located in the crater. Barely larger than a city block, the space seemed to have been demarcated for different activities. In one section, women were beating pieces of clothing against large rocks. Billie's eyes lit up; Annie could feel her straining to examine the garments. Nearby, a hefty bearded man in a tattered black coat and black brimmed hat faced the crater wall, rocking back and forth and chanting quietly.

"Ezra Ben-Nachman," Isaias said. "A fellow Israelite. He claims that all Jews dress like that in his land. Although I must say that in all my travels, and I did travel extensively, I never saw a Jew in such an outlandish costume. Sometimes I join him for his prayers. I don't share his belief, but it passes the time."

Further across the crater, several old men sat against the rock wall, eyes closed and faces turned up like downtown office workers sunbathing on lunch break. An emaciated white-haired woman sketched designs in the dirt with a rock.

"Everyone here is old," Annie murmured.

"People are old when they die," Isaias said sharply. His tone said she was an idiot. But where were the young women who'd died in childbirth? The young men butchered in wars? Hadn't the average life span been less than fifty years in pre-industrial times?

Trua tapped her arm. He had a surprisingly light touch for such a rough man. "Don't trust him," he whispered.

"Because he's Roman?" she snapped. *Or because you don't trust anybody*?

Isaias continued their tour. An elderly man with rich brown skin—looking scholarly in thick tortoise-shell glasses and a button-down shirt—sat on a rock beside Dev and Tai-shan, playing a game that involved pebbles.

"That's Henry Mwango," Isaias said. "He built bridges in the lands beyond Ethiopia that he claims rivalled ours in Rome. Now he teaches the children."

An engineer. A scientist! In modern, Western clothes! Annie wanted to run over to the bridge builder and pump him for everything he knew about this place. Ifechi was staring at him too, perhaps as excited to find another African as she was to find a scientist.

They reached the far side of the crater. A small, wiry man knelt over another man, gently bending his companion's leg back in a quad stretch like a trainer at a gym.

"Excuse me, Yelu. We have visitors."

Annie had assumed that Isaias was the colony's leader, but his tone deferred to the wiry man. Yelu looked up and smiled. He was missing several teeth and had a faded scar along one cheek. Annie realized with shock that he was also missing an ear. He stood, brushing dust off his robe.

"You're most welcome here if you are peaceful people," he said.

* * * * *

Yelu told them more about the colony in the crater. Although he was a Buddhist, this wasn't a Buddhist community or Christian community or community of any one kind of belief. Each person made their own determination about what kind of world this was, and how they wanted to live in it. There was only one requirement to join: you had to promise not to harm anyone.

"You're welcome to visit for several days," he said. "Then you can decide whether to stay or move on."

"Days?" Annie asked. "How do you mark time when there's no day or night?"

Yelu gave a gap-toothed smile. "Of course. Days are a creation of our mind. An enlightened being has no need of days or years. Yet for those of us who haven't yet reached enlightenment, they're a helpful structure. They let us know when to work and when to rest."

"Yes, but how do you know when a day starts and ends?"

"Here," said Isaias. He pointed to a tiny woman with braided grey hair sitting beside two lines of large stones. "We share the responsibility for estimating time. When Nenetl decides that four hours have passed, she'll move a stone from the first column to the second. Then someone else will take a turn. When all six have been moved, we consider it a day. Henry Mwango complains that it's not precise, but it serves the purpose."

Four of the stones were in the second column. Would that make it 4 p.m? Time for her daily infusion of Diet Coke from the vending machine. The office would be quiet—her boss submerged in her computer, the scientists away in the field, the nature educators, always a lively crew, out running their after-school programs.

Annie would swivel idly in her chair, wishing she were at sea like the scientists or exploring tidepools like the educators. The soda would fizz chemically against the roof of her mouth, foam filling her cheeks like attic insulation. She used to think of it as a small, shameful addiction, a failure to be the kind of person who drank coconut water or acai smoothies. Now Diet Coke seemed like a miracle. Pearls of condensation on the smooth aluminum can. That first cold shock of liquid on her tongue—bubbles popping, sweet but not too sweet, bracing and lively and, above all, *wet*...

Across the crater, women were still beating cloth on rocks. Ezra Ben-Nachman had stopped praying and was conversing with another man. The timekeeper woman sat motionless, eyes fixed with suspicion on Annie and Billie.

"Make yourselves at home," Isaias said. "We'll meet at the forum at the end of the day." He gave a disdainful smile. "Don't worry. You'll know when it's time, even without the sun. Just follow the crowd."

CHAPTER THIRTEEN

Annie

Annie wanted to interrogate every single person in the colony, starting with Yelu. There was something birdlike about his wiry build and sharp gaze. A smart, observant bird—not a falcon like Ben, but maybe a jay.

"Can I ask you a few more questions?"

"Of course."

"What is this place?"

"What do *you* think this place is?"

"My friend says it's Hell, but I don't know. It could be an alien planet. I just don't know."

"Then embrace the not-knowing."

Annie refrained from rolling her eyes. She had friends at home who dabbled in Buddhism, and they never made sense to her either. She tried again.

"Do *you* think this is Hell?"

"Tell me about Hell. What are the characteristics of Hell?"

"Where sinners go to be punished. Fire. Pain. Suffering."

"All existence involves suffering. Perhaps your Hell is everywhere. Perhaps life and suffering and Hell are all one."

"But this is different. This isn't like suffering in life. Weren't you in the fire too? That's not just suffering, it's beyond suffering. It's..."

She struggled for words. Yelu locked his quick bird-eyes on her. "It's beyond words because it's purely your own thoughts. Your body isn't real so your pain isn't real. Whatever visions you see, remember they are reflections of your thoughts."

She must have looked frustrated, because Yelu smiled again.

"Ah, you're impatient?" he said. "Come, sit for a while. Release your thoughts. Then you can follow the radiant path."

* * * * *

Annie didn't sit. She didn't release any thoughts. She didn't follow the radiant path. She politely excused herself and went to talk to Henry Mwango, the bridge-building engineer. Ifechi had joined him and the children, who were still playing the pebble game.

"The children in my village have a game like this," Ifechi said, smiling a welcome at her. "I was always the best player among my friends. I would win all their stones, and then they'd have to give me—"

"Less boasting, more playing," the engineer said. He pointed at some squares scratched in the dirt. "Dev. Suppose you throw three stones and there are two boxes. What are the odds that all three stones will land in the same box?"

"Assuming he doesn't lose them when he's wandering!" Tai-shan piped up. Dev swatted at her and she dodged and giggled. The boy rocked back on his heels, looking down and counting on his fingers.

"Thirty-three percent?" he asked.

"Twenty-five percent!" shouted Tai-shan.

"Correct," nodded the engineer. Annie was impressed. Ben could have done that kind of mental math at Tai-shan's age, but she certainly couldn't have. She doubted she could do it even now.

"I'm Annie Maple, from San Francisco," she said, reaching out a hand.

"Henry Mwango, from Nairobi." He shook her hand, then turned to the children and waved them away. "Enough for now. We'll do more tomorrow."

"Are you a teacher? You're good at it."

He shook his head. "I'm a civil engineer by training. But someone has to provide education for these young minds."

"How long have you been here?"

"Here, meaning in this community? Perhaps six months. Perhaps two years. The system they use for tracking time is not reliable. If you mean here in Hell, I don't know. You arrived recently, yes?"

Annie nodded.

"What year did you die?"

"2015. I guess. I mean, I'm not sure that I'm really dead."

"If this is now 2015, then I've been in Hell for thirty-three years. I died in September 1982."

"What did you die from?"

Henry sighed. "Cerebrovascular incident. Commonly known as a stroke. I was well aware of the fact that I had high blood pressure. I refused to renounce the salt."

"If it's okay to ask, how did you end up here? Rather than in Heaven?"

"Too long a story. Of no interest to anyone besides myself."

"*I'm* interested."

Henry's eyes seemed to vanish behind the thick lenses. When it became clear that he was not going to say anything further, she tried a different tack.

"Can I ask you something else? Do you really believe that this place is Hell? Biblical Hell?"

"Of course it is. 'The angels shall separate the wicked and cast them into a furnace of fire.' The Gospel of Matthew, I believe. Although I could be wrong. It is, as we have determined, thirty-three years since I've seen a Bible."

"Have you tried to escape? My friend says there's a way out in the mountains."

"Impossible."

"But as an engineer... could we tunnel our way out? Or fly? What if we built a plane?"

"Impossible." Then he gave a wide grin. "But I do have a project that will revolutionize everything. Come. I'll show you."

Limping slightly, Henry led her along the edge of the crater to a small square marked off with rocks like a garden. Instead of plants, it held intersecting lines scratched into the dirt.

"This is the river of fire." Henry squatted, pointing at one of the lines. "The waterfall. The entrance to our tunnel. Now see this line? If we dig a channel here, we can divert some of the lava to form a canal. We can extend the canal here, and here, to create a protective barrier around the entrance."

He gestured across a large part of the map indicating the plain in front of the tunnel's entrance.

"It will provide us with more room to walk. To work. To be alone. We'll go from having a crowded house"—he waved around them—"to having an estate. A ranch, you Americans might call it. Big enough for your John Wayne and Ronald Reagan, ha! The children can run and play without getting into trouble. We'll all be able to stretch out a little bit more. And it will be safer."

He paused. "That's just the beginning, though. Once we have the canals, we can siphon off small amounts of lava to create a smeltery. We may be able to work some of these minerals and ores. There's the potential to manufacture tools."

"Huh." Annie tried to sound impressed. But what good would a few tools do in a land without water, plants, animals, sunlight? She didn't want a more commodious living space in Hell. She wanted to go home.

Henry stood up. He put a hand on his lower back and winced, then led her back to the area with the pebbles.

"There's only one problem," he said. "Labor. We have no excavation tools but rocks and hands. We have no workforce but old people and children." He shook his head. "And unlike the British, we don't have the ability to enslave a continent to build an empire."

* * * * *

Isaias had been right: there was no mistaking the end of the day.

The old woman who had replaced Nenetl gave out a yodelling cry. Around the crater, people stopped what they were doing and headed toward a cluster of knee-high rocks.

Annie and Billie took seats with the others on the rocks. Isaias stood in front, head high with authority. Ifechi sat beside Henry Mwango. Yelu sat in the middle of the crowd, laughing quietly with a grey-bearded man on the next rock. Annie peered around for Trua and finally spotted him, standing alone at the rear of the circle.

"We have guests," Isaias announced. "Please treat them with our usual hospitality. Does anyone wish to speak to the community tonight? No? Then it's Hana's turn to be the storyteller."

A kerchiefed old woman rose from her seat and moved to an empty rock at the front of the cluster. She coughed and fidgeted and eventually started speaking.

"There once was a prince. A handsome prince. He was the only son of a handsome king and a beautiful queen—"

"Enough!" called another woman. "You told this one already!"

"I did not!" the storyteller retorted. "Your memory is gone, you old goose! You think every story is one you've heard already."

"Look who's talking. You wouldn't remember your own husband if he walked into this place!"

"Hush, ladies," Yelu said. "Even if it's the same story, there's always something new in the telling. Let's listen and see what's new and fresh."

They quieted and the woman embarked on a story about a prince who needed to find three magic objects to earn his kingdom. She lost her place in the story once, and gave two different names to the wise woman in the woods, and repeated the part about the silver goblet, but everyone including the heckler listened attentively.

Annie forgot her sore feet and the sunless sky and the constant sulfur smell. She could have been a little girl again listening to Ben read stories in the backyard. Or in bed, ready for her mother to pull the blanket up to her chin and turn out the light. Except there was no blanket and no light and no Ben and no mother. When the storyteller was done, the crowd stood and slowly dispersed, back to beating old clothes or meditating or drawing in the dirt.

Isaias hovered nearby, watching her with amusement.

"And thus begins a new day," he said.

* * * * *

Billie pulled her aside after the story-telling session.

"This place is creepy. All these old people. Old dead people."

"Billie, you're dead too. Remember?"

"That's different. I'm *young.* I'm not supposed to be dead. This here's like a walking graveyard."

Raised voices suddenly rang from the other side of the crater. People were converging in a knot. Annie and Billie trailed them and peered through the crowd.

Yelu, Ifechi, and Ezra Ben-Nachman were holding Trua against the rock wall. A few feet away, Isaias was straightening his toga and fingering a large rip. He looked hard at Yelu. "He violated our code. He needs to go."

Henry Mwango, limping, joined the circle.

"What happened?" he said.

"The barbarian attacked me."

"That?" Trua spat. "If I'd really attacked you, you'd have more than a ripped cloak—"

Yelu looked at Trua apologetically. "He's right. We don't allow any violence here. We have no choice but to ask you to leave."

Annie froze. This felt wrong. She glanced at Billie for direction, but Billie just looked on impassively.

"I'm happy to leave," Trua growled. The others dropped their hold, and he tugged at his skin vest. "No one does anything here except sit on rocks and tell stories. Who would want to stay here anyway?"

He stepped defiantly out of the circle toward the entrance to the crater. Ben-Nachman and another man moved the rock door aside, and Trua hunched forward into the tunnel. Annie felt an unexpected pang of loss: he hadn't even turned to say good-bye.

"Good riddance to bad rubbish," Billie sniffed.

Later Dev came up to Annie as she sat on a rock by herself.

"Isaias teased him," he said. "Isaias started it."

She nodded. She'd guessed that might have been the case. But there was nothing she could do about it now.

* * * * *

Annie continued peppering people with questions—Henry Mwango, Yelu, Ezra Ben-Nachman, a number of the kerchiefed women.

Had they all spent time in the fire?

Apparently so. Then they, like Annie, were thrust out into the desert. Most seemed to have been released recently—a matter of months or years, not centuries.

Did people get older here?

No.

So Dev and Tai-shan wouldn't become teenagers and adults? They would get better and better at mental math but stay eight years old forever?

Unclear.

Did everyone here remember how they died?

Yes. Ben-Nachman, the Orthodox Jew, had died of fever with endless vomiting. Another man had fallen from a horse and hit his head. One of the kerchiefed women had died from a growth in her stomach, while another one had—truly—been burned at the stake as a witch.

"Were you really a witch?" Annie asked.

"I don't deny I made a pact with the Devil," the woman said. "I asked him to save my grandson from the plague. My grandson lived. In return, here I am."

"At least your grandson survived."

"Better he died." The woman spat onto the ground. "Better the death of all my children and grandchildren. Let the plague take them, each and every one. Anything that the Lord wills. As long as it keeps me out of that accursed fire."

After a while Annie decided that she was the only person in all of Hell who didn't know how she had died. She sat against the rock wall in a quiet section of the crater and tried to marshall any memory, no matter how small. Perhaps if she could remember her death, she could solve this puzzle of a place and figure out how to get home.

The Victorian doorway. The orange streetlight. A whiff of clove cigarettes floating out with the music and voices. The cigarettes at least were new, something she hadn't remembered before. But that was all.

Maybe something traumatic had happened to her and she'd blocked it out of her memory. Or maybe she'd been too drunk to notice she was about to die.

Shit. Too drunk to notice your own death? It couldn't get much more degrading than that. She ran her fingers through the black dirt—less gritty here, powdery, almost ash.

Even in a place without hunger or thirst, it was possible to feel empty inside.

* * * * *

Another "day" ended and someone told a story about heroic twins defeating a bird demon. Yelu led a session of tai chi-like exercise as if they were all passengers on a cruise ship. Later Henry Mwango enlisted Ifechi and Annie and Ben-Nachman in moving some large rocks into a flat-topped pile to serve as a work table. When that "day" also ended, Ben-Nachman told a story about the foolish townspeople of Chelm and a talking donkey that had the entire circle laughing.

Annie thought again of Ben reading to her. Sometimes on summer evenings she'd hide to avoid the injustice of being put to bed while the sun was still shining. She'd sneak behind the big hydrangea bush in the backyard in her pajamas and Ben would join her with a stack of books—picture books like Lyle the Crocodile, but also chapter books like *The Hobbit.* Even when she didn't understand the story, she loved the confident sound of his voice. How he knew what every single word meant, even the big ones. She loved the secrecy. She loved the attention—no other people around, all his focus on her, the two of them knotted together by a ribbon of spoken words. Today Ben was a six-foot-two beanpole of a man, his hair receding like tide on the beach, but back then he was hardly taller than she was and his mop of dark hair matched her own.

That girl would have happily lived in a desert crater if Ben were there to read stories to her every night.

* * * * *

Isaias approached Annie after the talking donkey story and motioned for her to walk around the crater with him.

"You miss the barbarian," he said.

Annie was silent. She didn't exactly miss Trua but wondered if she could have prevented his banishment. Should she have kept a closer eye on him? Warned him to keep his anger in check? She both feared him and felt responsible for him.

"We need more young, strong people here. Even barbarians. But young men are hotheads. They bring strength but also conflict. That's part of the reason we're as old as the Senate here."

Annie could think of yet another reason: the crater was safe but hopeless. Staying here meant giving up on a return to Earth. What young person would accept an eternity of tai chi and drawing blueprints in the dust?

"I hope that you and your friend will consider staying."

She didn't answer.

"I understand it may feel boring here to attractive young women like yourselves."

Fuck. Annie's sleaze antennae were vibrating, like being stuck in an airplane seat next to some middle-aged sales rep trying to pick her up with a Mr. T Bloody Mary.

"I have a... proposal for you."

I bet you do.

"You understand the problem with sexual relations here in Hell, don't you?"

Annie tried to look noncommittal. She didn't want a lecture on the birds and bees from a dead Roman who was old enough to be her father.

"Sexual relations with love are impossible. But sex without affection... The door is wide open. If you stay, there could be many opportunities for pleasure. It wouldn't have to be so boring after all."

She wanted to bolt. She wanted to gag. Mostly she wanted to be home with Melanie, sharing war stories across the kitchen table and breaking into belly laughs: "He said *that*? He wanted you to do *what*?"

"Thank you," she said. "I don't think we're interested, but we appreciate it."

"Well, just keep it in mind. Something to consider."

He reached over and lightly brushed her neck with his fingertips.

* * * * *

Fucking gross. Annie missed soap and water more than ever.

She looked for Billie but didn't see her. She wasn't sure whether to feel threatened or merely disgusted. So you could have sex in Hell, just not with people you loved. Maybe this wasn't so different from real life after all.

She drifted toward the spot where Dev and Taishan were getting lessons from Henry Mwango. The "classroom" was the part of the crater where she felt most at home. Dev was always visibly happy to see her, and Tai-shan was a pleasure to watch—so enthusiastic. When she knew the answer to one of Henry's questions, she bounced, vibrated, jiggled.

How had Dev and Tai-shan's families reacted to their disappearance?

How had her own family reacted? Her friends?

If she were dead, there would have been a funeral. Who would have given the eulogy? What would they have said?

She was a sweet girl who just wasn't as smart as her brother.

She was the best ever at alphabetizing donor names in the Annual Report.

She struggled with ________. (Fill in the blank: Her weight. Dating. Calculus.)

When the going got tough, she wimped out.

It was such a shame that she never found the right guy.

Her parents would miss her.

How pathetic. Maybe she belonged in this claustrophobic crater, providing sexual services to a dead 2,000-year-old Roman.

"Annie."

Billie was standing next to her, looking around warily.

"All these old people doing Oriental calisthenics. This place gives me the creeps. Let's get out of here, okay?"

"You bet!"

Thank goodness for Billie. She had no clue where to go but plowed ahead anyway. Maybe someday,

Annie thought, she would be as driven by something as Billie was by her love for her children.

"*Now*," Billie said.

"Ifechi. We should see if he wants to come too."

Billie rolled her eyes but didn't argue.

"Y'all really have a thing for these savages," she said.

CHAPTER FOURTEEN

Ifechi

Trua's expulsion upset Ifechi but he said nothing. He told himself that a visitor must respect village customs. Inside, he feared that if he spoke up they would expel him too.

There were so many strange beings here. The only ones with whom he felt truly comfortable were Dev and Henry Mwango. Henry was reassuringly familiar, clearly human rather than a spirit. And he seemed to be some kind of diviner, using mysterious words to explain his pebble arrangements. Surely he'd know how to escape this terrible place and return home.

"Seven-eighths," Henry said to Dev and the girl, Tai-shan. Ifechi sat beside them in the section of the crater they used for lessons. "Which is the numerator?"

"Seven!" shouted Tai-shan.

"Correct. Now, Dev, the denominator?"

The boy looked dejected. He'd already suffered enough from the evil man-spirits, and he was too young to be learning all this complicated number magic. A boy of his age should be skipping stones in the stream and gathering wood for the cookfire.

"Honored Henry," Ifechi said. "I know you're busy with many responsibilities, but I wish to learn your number magic. I'm the father of two sons, and I've pleased the ancestors with many sacrifices. If you teach me this magic, I can help bring us home."

The elder peered at him over the tops of his eye-shields.

"It's not magic. It's mathematics."

"Mathematics, then. I wish to learn it!"

"Yes, yes, very good. But later. Right now they must finish their lesson. Please don't interrupt."

Ifechi rocked back on his heels, restless. Henry might be the most powerful diviner he'd ever seen, with his mysterious number-words and strange clothes. Even those eye-shields: transparent as water, they must have strong defensive powers. But Henry wasn't taking him seriously. He was treating him like a youth, not like a grown man with two sons.

"Honored Henry," he tried again. "I wish to accompany you on the journey home."

Henry sighed. "You're persistent, I'll concede that." He turned to Dev and Tai-shan. "Go play. We'll continue later."

He gestured for Ifechi to sit closer.

"What is it you want from me?"

Ifechi thought he'd made that clear. But he'd say it again.

"I wish to learn your number magic and your diviner's wisdom. And when you're ready to return home, I wish to accompany you. It's been too long since I've seen my village, my compound, my family."

Across the crater, the old women were singing a tune that repeated itself over and over. Henry shook his head.

"I'm no diviner. Far from it. I'm a Christian, and a very poor one at that. I can teach you maths and engineering, but I can't offer much in the way of wisdom. And I certainly can't help you get home."

Ifechi suppressed a grin. Henry's false modesty was even stronger evidence of his power. Now it was up to him to show Henry he was worthy. Ifechi wasn't sure how to do that, here in a barren crater, but he'd figure it out.

"I understand," Ifechi said, nodding. "I'll start with mathematics, as you suggest."

* * * * *

His first lesson in mathematics proved frustrating: so many random squiggles in the dirt. When it was done, he sat against a rock, eyes closed, trying to drive the squiggles from his brain.

"Ifechi."

He looked up at Annie with a smile. Since her collapse at the fire waterfall, he'd felt less intimidated. Her appearance was pleasing, and she had such a friendly manner. If she were a girl in his village, she'd make a fine second wife.

"Can I talk to you for a minute?"

"Certainly."

"Billie and I have decided to keep going and look for a way back home. You want to come with us?"

Of course! he wanted to shout. Home to Obinna and Chioke. The sweet, savory taste of Nkiru's bitter-leaf soup. The string of cowrie shells that Nkiru wore around her neck: when he lifted the string to kiss her neck, she always quivered—

But these women wouldn't take him home. Annie may have saved his life, but she was still a spirit. And Trua had warned him about Billie's deceitfulness.

"Do you want to come?"

Annie looked at him, waiting. If he didn't go with her, she'd view him as a coward. He hated that. Meanwhile Henry Mwango treated him as a child and made him draw useless squiggle lines. No one here understood him for the man he was.

"I will stay here," Ifechi said, avoiding her eyes.

Then an idea struck him—a bold, inspired plan that could solve his problems both with Annie and with Henry Mwango.

"I wish you safe travels," Ifechi said. "But I ask one thing. Don't leave until after the next gathering of storytellers. Please. Wait until after the gathering."

* * * * *

The timekeeper called the end of day and everyone drew together in the story circle.

Ifechi took a seat beside Henry Mwango. Dev and Tai-shan ran to Ifechi's other side and tried to climb onto his shoulders, but he nudged them off. He looked around to make sure Annie was present, and was gratified to see her and Billie standing at the back of the circle.

The crowd took its time settling down, the old women chittering together like the women of his village. Isaias asked one of them if she wanted to speak tonight. Ifechi took a deep breath and stood up.

"With all respect to the elders, I wish to tell a story."

He wasn't an orator at home; he had never once spoken at a village meeting. But his jokes always made his friends laugh. How hard could it really be? And the story he planned to tell lived inside his heart. He'd never spoken it aloud, but it was as much a part of him as his name.

Isaias nodded. Ifechi stepped carefully through the crowd to the speaker's stone. In the back, Annie flashed him an encouraging smile. Closer in, Henry Mwango was beaming. Henry leaned over and whispered something to Dev, then nodded in Ifechi's direction. Ifechi knew what the old man was saying: *Now that is a man. Watch him. Be like him.* His heart swelled. He began.

There was a village.

Obodonwa, his village, the Village of the Moon. Red dust on paths and leaves, the trilling of hidden birds, the sweet musty smell of thatched roofs in the sun after a rain. Loveliest of all the villages! The fields were large and fertile, the rains came when they should, the yams were bigger and sweeter than any other village...

Out in the crowd, Billie leaned toward Annie and giggled. Making fun of him? Ifechi sucked in his breath and kept going.

There was a boy.

The boy's father was a smith, well respected, forging the hoes and knives for everyone in the village. Even now in this distant wasteland Ifechi could feel the heat of the forge—good heat, heat that did your will, so different from the torturing fire of this place. As a child he had gathered wood for the forge, worked the bellows, and polished the finished blades. Meanwhile his sisters helped their mothers with the chickens and the bean plants and the cooking. When the chores were done, he and his sisters would run through the village with the other children, wrestling and playing at being warriors, trapping birds and lizards, gathering smooth pebbles for games of okwe.

The boy's name was...

Ifechi's chest tightened. He hadn't thought about this. He made a quick decision and hoped no one would notice the pause.

Chioke.

Chioke was tall and handsome and he was friends with all the young men of his age group. Except for one, an evil boy named Kamdiba. Kamdiba's father was the diviner for the village, and he'd called on spirits to give Kamdiba supernatural powers. He was stronger and faster than any human boy should be. He had the ability to put spells on people and make them do what he wanted. All except Chioke. Chioke could see through him. Which was why Kamdiba didn't like Chioke, and always tried to make trouble for him.

Ifechi paused again. Not for the first time, he wondered if it were Kamdiba's father who cursed him and sent him to this evil place. No. Impossible. Kamdiba's father couldn't know. But diviners knew more than other men. And how else would he have ended up here?

A girl. There was a girl.

Nkiru was the most beautiful girl in the village. Ifechi suspected she was the most beautiful girl anywhere. They played together as children, and once he saved her from a mamba: Nkiru had been carrying yams back from the fields, placed her basket down to talk to him, and while she wasn't looking, the snake slid in there. Then she picked up the basket—

And just like that, the snake shot out!

Ifechi leapt and whipped out one of his arms. The old women in the crowd gasped, and one even tumbled off her stone. Warmth flooded from his chest up into his face. So this was what it meant to be an orator: the crowd clinging to your words, fluttering like leaves with your breath. It was like winning a wrestling contest, only slower, longer, better.

He'd grabbed the snake. One hand around its neck while it was striking. There was no time to think; he simply did it. Afterwards he was a hero. They skinned the snake and his father hung it over the forge to show everyone his son's bravery.

They grew older and fell in love, Ifechi and Nkiru, or was it Chioke and Nkiru? (He was having a hard time keeping it straight.) They were almost of age and it was just a matter of waiting for the match to be made by their families. But then along came Kamdiba. Of course he wanted the most beautiful girl in the village for himself. And when Nkiru's parents went to the diviner to find out if her spirit would be allowed to marry into Ifechi's family, Kamdiba's father said no. He told them that Nkiru's spirit needed to marry into his own family. Of course that meant Kamdiba.

Ifechi would never forget that day. He'd been working at the forge, polishing a long blade for clearing fields, when one of his little sisters came running over.

"Nkiru is to marry Kamdiba! The diviner said so!"

Ifechi gripped the blade so tightly that it sliced his palm. Blood smeared across his hand and dripped into the dust. He thought of taking the blade and running Kamdiba through but held back. Instead, he and his father visited the diviner and said there'd been a mistake and he should do it over. The diviner refused. They went to the village elders and told them that the diviner was corrupt. But Kamdiba's father had put a spell upon the elders, and they refused to help.

So Ifechi challenged Kamdiba to a fight—an honorable fight, no knives, no spells. At first Kamdiba stalled and accused Ifechi of disrespecting the spirits. But then the other young men started calling Kamdiba a coward, and he agreed to a wrestling match in the middle of the village, with all the village as witnesses.

They wrestled.

Ifechi looked around the circle. What did these people know of fighting, these old women and ghost-pale men? Ifechi had approached the fight with confidence, both in his righteousness and in his skill. He was an excellent wrestler and usually beat the other young men in his age group, including Kamdiba. But that day Kamdiba cheated and used magic. Evil spirits bound Ifechi's legs so he couldn't dodge and pivot. The spirits held him stiff as an iroko tree. Through the pressure of Kamdiba's sweaty limbs, past his own gasping breath, he heard the sound of the crowd turning. Cheers gave way to catcalls, catcalls to laughter. Even his sisters laughed.

Only his father held faith in him. "Remember the snake," his father said afterwards in the quiet of his hut. "You are not the kind of man who lets a striking mamba live. But also remember that hot soup must be sipped slowly."

So strength and righteousness were not enough. This was the lesson. You needed to be clever as a spider, patient as a stalking leopard. Ifechi waited for an opportunity as the dowry was paid and the marriage drew closer. Finally, when he was close to despair and once again eyeing the blades by the forge, the gods provided an answer.

Two traders arrived at the village from distant lands. They brought guns, gunpowder, beads, and dried fish to trade for wood and slaves—especially slaves. The village head was apologetic; it had been a peaceful period, with no wars and no captives who could be sold as slaves. The traders were disappointed but did their business and prepared to move on.

That night, Ifechi snuck out to the traders' camp in the forest. The two men rested on logs by a small fire, roasting yams. He had never spoken with a trader before; their skin was redder than that of his people, and the firelight made it redder still. At first they smiled in condescension like he was a trifling child. But then the smiles gave way to measured glances and, finally, to nods.

The traders would get a strong and valuable slave. This slave would be good in the field, at a forge, making bricks, or tending goats. There would be no cost for this slave. But in exchange, they would need to take him many villages away so he would not be able to escape and find his way back.

There was a rustling in the crowd, an unsettled anticipation. Ifechi felt it lift and carry him. So many eyes on him, so many ears waiting for his next word. There was nothing to this storytelling after all! So perhaps there was nothing to being a diviner either, or even a village head. Perhaps when he got home, he would set his sights higher. He would no longer settle for being a farmer or a smith...

A messenger. Ifechi had needed a messenger.

Crafty as a spider, he went to Nkiru's youngest sister, the one who followed him around and brought him little gifts of flowers. He asked her to carry a secret message to Kamdiba saying that Nkiru couldn't wait for marriage and wanted to meet him in the forest in the nighttime.

In the forest, Ifechi was waiting. This time he gave Kamdiba no opportunity to summon evil spirits. Crouching on a thick tree limb, he dropped on the diviner's son and slammed his head with the flat side of a blade. He bound his feet and hands, and stuffed cloth in his mouth so he couldn't call out. Then he delivered him to the traders, who grinned broad grins and offered him kola nut and palm wine like they were greeting the new, powerful head of a village.

* * * * *

No one knew what had happened to Kamdiba.

Ifechi listened to the village gossip: *Kamdiba had been eaten by animals. He'd been carried away by evil spirits. He'd run off to the lands beyond the Great River.* Nkiru's little sister stayed silent, and he thanked her with small pieces of jewelry from the forge. When time passed and Kamdiba still didn't return, the marriage was called off. Nkiru was a bride without a husband.

"Do you still want this girl?" Ifechi's father asked him.

"Yes indeed," Ifechi said. "More than life itself."

So they married. One rainy season passed, and Nkiru gave birth to Obinna. More rainy seasons brought Chioke. The spirits smiled on him and his fields prospered. His sons were healthy and strong. His life was everything he'd hoped it would be.

And the story had done everything Ifechi hoped it would.

The crowd was transfixed. Annie too: Ifechi had felt the warmth of her eyes on him the entire time. She now understood he was no coward; he was a clever, strong hero. She'd regret that he wasn't coming with her. Perhaps she'd change her mind and stay. She might even return with him to Obodonwa and become his second wife! He was a hero, a master orator; he was learning mathematics; someday he would be a diviner or village head. As soon as he got back to Obodonwa—

"Boy!"

A loud voice rang out across the circle—the voice of an angry father, an irate god. "Do you not have the least understanding of what you did?"

Henry Mwango was standing up, frowning, finger stabbing the air.

"That young man you betrayed into slavery. Do you know what happened to him?"

Kamdiba? Why was he asking about Kamdiba? The story was over, the story was done. Kamdiba didn't matter. Kamdiba was gone.

"They took him to another village," Ifechi began. "Perhaps he worked in the fields. Or the goats—"

"No. They most likely sold him to European slavers. The Bight of Benin. The Middle Passage. If he survived the Middle Passage, then he would have been worked to death in the plantations of Barbados. Or bred like livestock in the American South. You know nothing of this? Nothing?"

"I have never heard of those villages."

"You more than any of us deserve to be here in Hell."

Ifechi stared, at a loss, while the old women buzzed in gratified scandal and Henry Mwango stalked away across the crater.

CHAPTER FIFTEEN

Annie

The entrance rock made a rough, scraping sound as Isaias and Ben-Nachman pushed it aside. There was a finality to it, as if you were chiseling away something that could not be replaced. Dev stood beside Annie, pulling on her skirt.

"Will you come back? Will you come visit?"

"I don't think so," she said. "But you've got Ifechi and Henry and Tai-shan. Promise me not to wander, okay?"

She and Billie squeezed through the tunnel and back onto the plain alongside the fire river. This was where Henry Mwango wanted to dig his lava canals. At least he'd have Ifechi to help him now. Annie had wondered if the engineer's outburst would change Ifechi's mind about staying, but it hadn't.

"Lordy," Billie said, dusting off her capris. She peered toward the mountains, checked the knot on her pouch of rags, and set out. "What was that Henry fellow so worked up about?"

"Slavery."

"Yes, but why'd he get so upset? Slavery ended a long time ago."

"It still affects people today. Like through racism. Poverty."

Billie shrugged. "You'd think that one of the benefits of being dead is that you could stop worrying about things in the history books. Dead is dead, right? I mean, whether people were slaves or masters, now they're all dead. So what's the big deal?"

"Billie. Where did you live back when you were... alive?"

"Sweet Valley, Alabama. Didn't I tell you that already?"

"Was Sweet Valley segregated?"

"Of course. It's the South, you know."

"Separate bathrooms and water fountains and everything?"

Billie nodded.

"Didn't that seem wrong?"

Billie frowned. "Of course not. Now, I know you Californians don't believe in segregation. And that's fine for you all. But for us, in the South, it's the way things are. Honey, for us, it's the natural order of things."

"But you just said that we're all the same when we're dead. So segregation isn't the 'natural order.' Look around here. It's not like there's a white section of Hell and a colored section of Hell."

Billie laughed and tucked a strand of hair back under her kerchief.

"There sure enough isn't. But honey, this is *Hell.* Think about if we were in Heaven. In Heaven, there'd be a white section and a colored section for sure."

They walked. After the confines of the crater, the world sprawled wantonly—the sloping plain, the lava river behind them, the mountains ahead. Billie, chipper, resumed her monologues about movie stars. Annie hardly heard: she was lost in her own thoughts about sin.

If this were really Hell, what landed you here? Did you have to commit some big marquée sin like murder or selling someone into slavery? Or was it enough simply to build up a sediment of little sins—bigoted thoughts, catty comments—like layers of tiny fossilized sea creatures?

And what about self-awareness? Did it matter whether you understood how bad your actions were? How about outcomes? If you were selling someone into slavery, was it a worse sin to send him across the Middle Passage than to have him tending goats like an indentured servant a few villages away?

Annie had never thought about such questions when she was alive. Had she herself been sent to Hell for specific acts of wrongdoing or simply because religion—sin, church, God—wasn't on her radar? And what about Dev and Tai-shan, too young to have committed any major sins? What about the Buddhists, Hindus, and Jews in the crater? How many of them were here simply because they hadn't been born in a Christian time or place?

"Come on, slowpoke."

Annie glanced over to see Billie shifting her pouch of rags and treasures from one shoulder to the other. Something seemed different. The pouch was fatter than before.

"Billie! Did you—"

"Just a little. You know where they were cleaning the clothes? Someone left out a kerchief with really cute flowers on it. And an apron with real lace. They wouldn't have left them lying around like that if they really needed them."

Annie was about to scold her but stopped. Her own sense of justice felt too shaky. Stealing rags was wrong, but was it bad enough to merit eternal torment in a lake of fire?

"Oh Billie," she murmured, and kept walking.

* * * * *

The constant heat had seemed more bearable in the crater, but now that Annie was traveling again, it pressed down upon her. Sweat welled up and was blotted by dust. Her sweater chafed against her waist, while the backs of her knees and insides of her elbows felt sticky and repulsive. Learning from the crater, Annie was determined to schedule frequent rest breaks and to consider every sixth break a "night." She thought of astronauts relying on artificial gravity in space. If the absence of gravity could atrophy your muscles, what would the absence of time do to your mind?

They reached the edge of the plain and started climbing to a pass. The trek was newly lonely with just the two of them. Annie felt more vulnerable too, and kept pivoting to scout for assailants.

"What do we do if someone comes after us?" she asked Billie.

"Hide."

There were no good places to hide on the slope. Anyone on the plain could see them moving up the ridge.

"Ssh!"

Billie gestured for her to stop. Ahead of them, just beyond the ridge, Annie heard a faint crunch of gravel.

No boulders for hiding. No cliff walls for escape. Billie picked up a softball-sized rock and motioned for her to do the same. They crouched.

More crunch of gravel up at the pass. Stay and fight? Turn and run?

A figure emerged onto the ridge—stocky build, long forehead, goatskin vest. Trua.

His face lit up when he saw them. Annie felt limp with relief.

"Oh Lordy," Billie murmured and stood up.

He took long strides down the slope. When he reached them, he stopped. He shifted from one bare foot to another, suddenly shy.

"I wish to come with you," he said.

"What, so you can force her to undo her so-called curse?" Billie said.

"I told you." He shot Annie a look of reproach. "I don't believe you're a witch. I wish to come with you… because you may find the way out of here. Because you saved my life."

Entirely by accident, Annie thought.

"Of course," she said, while Billie tightened her lips in disapproval.

* * * * *

Annie had expected to see another expanse of black gravel when they reached the pass, but instead a wide yellow and grey plain opened up before them.

Sulfur. The plain had a nubby-looking texture and was veined with crevices that emitted wispy fumes. At the far end—very far, along the horizon—rose another set of mountains.

"Those mountains could be the ones," Billie said. "Yes, I think those are the very ones she meant."

They edged their way down the saddle onto the plain. Annie worried about gases, evaluating each breath, knowing she might not be able to smell half the things that could poison them. The nubbiness turned out to be large sulfur crystals jutting out of the ground. She stopped, intrigued, at the first cluster they encountered, which looked like a waist-high chunk of yellowish rock candy. Billie broke off small fragments and stuck them in her sack. Trua fingered a piece, saw that it chipped easily, and dropped it back into the dirt.

Annie kept track of their rest breaks by shifting pebbles from one pocket of her cardigan to another. They had traveled one pebble's worth when Trua drew her aside.

"I'm coming with *you*, not her," he said. "I don't trust her."

She gave a short laugh. "Trua, is there anybody in the world you *do* trust?"

He seemed taken aback. Then he smiled. "Not in this world. At home... yes. My family. My clan."

"Well, Billie's harmless. She's got her issues, but she'd never do anything to hurt us."

"Annie, daughter of Herb," Trua said. She thought he might be teasing but wasn't sure. "Is there anybody in the world you *don't* trust?"

It made for a tense little traveling group. At rest stops, Billie chatted with Annie while ignoring Trua. Annie tried to start conversations that would include both of them, but they fell flat.

"I miss my shoes," she said at one stop. Even with calluses, the crystalline plain stabbed her feet. "Billie, did you have favorite shoes as a kid?"

"I most certainly did. Mary Janes. Shiny black patent leather. My mama got them for me after the war. They were for church and birthday parties. If I got a scuff on them, I got a whupping. Then when I was fifteen, I got my first pair of pumps…"

"What about you, Trua? Your first shoes?"

He grunted and looked away.

Guys, Annie thought. *No matter what century they're from. They couldn't care less about shoes.*

"There's this cute little shoe store on Water Street," Billie continued. "They have these silver stiletto heels with sequins like in a fashion magazine. When we get home, I'll take you shopping there. They have these alligator flats—"

Trua was still staring at the ground. Did he have the slightest idea what stiletto heels or alligator flats were? Then Annie remembered that he too was barefoot: the marauders had taken his boots.

Those boots might have been the only footwear Trua ever owned. Huns didn't just drive to Water Street and pop into boutiques.

"Let's keep going," she said, and they resumed their trek.

* * * * *

Three pebbles later.

Distances were deceptive: the far side of the sulfur plain didn't seem any closer than when they'd started. They were resting, with Billie puzzling out loud over how someone could be as fat as Elizabeth Taylor in *Cleopatra* yet still be a homewrecker.

Trua broke in, voice rough with frustration.

"You're not leading us home."

Billie looked miffed. "Not this again. You think I *like* wandering around in the desert like Moses and the children of Israel?"

"This isn't the way."

"It most certainly is. I heard about it from an old woman who knows."

"How did she know? Was she a sorceress?"

"Of course not. She was just an old lady from Italy. She knew about it from a book."

A book. An Italian book, from hundreds of years ago. Annie's heart sank. Was their whole trek based on a thirdhand reference to Dante?

"Where is she then?" Trua demanded. "If she knew the way, why isn't she here?"

"I told y'all. She was too slow."

"You did something to her."

"Trua, stop it!" This was too much. Never mind Billie's condescension, her racism, her fattened pouch of clothes. She couldn't afford to lose Billie.

"You are a rude, ignorant savage. I don't have time for the likes of you," Billie said, and busied herself rearranging the rags in her pouch.

* * * * *

Four pebbles later.

The sulfur wisps had gathered into a fog that made it hard to see. The world smelled like one big rotten-egg chemistry experiment. Annie eyed the ground, worried that cracks could widen into crevices. If you fell through a crack in Hell, where would you end up? Were there Hells below Hell?

If she ignored the smell and the heat, she could pretend to be back in West Marin. The coastal fog arrived in the late afternoons as dependably as the U.P.S. driver on his daily route. Some days it was there when you woke and still there at dinnertime. Annie loved hiking in it; sound was muffled, sight became blurred, and you were cossetted in a moist fantasy world of grey and green. At times the fog was so thick that it mimicked rain, vapor condensing high in the redwoods and pattering down through the branches in thick droplets.

What she would give for some cool, damp fog right now!

Mist. Drizzle. Rain.

The cold spray of a garden hose. A cold campground shower washing off sweat and dust.

Cold beer. Cold lemonade—

Icy fear swept over her.

It was like back at the beginning with Trua. Like on the edge of the canyon with the marauders. Something terrible was approaching overhead—

She threw herself down and covered her head with her hands. Billie and Trua did the same. She pressed her face into the rough ground.

Don't move. Don't look. If you don't see it, perhaps it won't see you.

Arm hairs stiffened. The air seemed to have been sucked into a vacuum. This was what a slow-motion lightning strike might feel like. She waited for the shock, the blow.

The world exhaled and the air returned and things were normal.

"My God." She sat up slowly. "What *are* these things?"

Trua pulled himself out of his crouch too—breathing heavily, with a crazed, distracted look. Billie brushed herself off.

"Don't you know? That was the devil."

"But what's it doing? Does it see us?"

Billie shrugged. "I can't say I'm on intimate terms with him. Thank the Lord. I suppose he just flies around doing evil, convincing people to sell their souls and so on. I do know that the surefire way to get him to show up is to pray."

"But we weren't praying just now. And back in the crater, Ezra Ben-Nachman was praying all the time. Remember? The devil didn't show up there."

Billie made a clucking sound in reprimand. "He wasn't praying to Jesus."

"The Jesus Christ wizard," Trua growled.

"Would you shut up about wizards?" Billie said. "Jesus has nothing to do with wizards. Jesus cast the wizards out. He *beat* the wizards."

Annie wasn't listening. She was thinking about the first time she'd felt that shadow overhead. Bullied by Trua, she'd been attempting her butchered version of Christian prayer.

"So that's why you don't pray?"

"Honey, prayer here is like a dog whistle for Satan."

"Fucking Jesus Christ wizard," Trua muttered.

"Just you shut up," Billie said.

CHAPTER SIXTEEN

Ifechi

Jab. Drag. Scoop.

Jab. Drag. Scoop.

There was a rhythm to digging that could become pleasant, or at least mindless. Ifechi, on hands and knees, reached forward and jabbed his digging rock into the ground, dragged it toward himself to loosen the dirt, and then used both hands to scoop up the dirt and gravel and toss them to the side. Then he did it again, slightly deeper. Then again.

He hummed the same rhythmic songs he used to hum when hoeing his fields. But digging with a long-handled hoe was so much easier than digging with a rock. Ifechi thought longingly of the hoes crafted by his father—their thin, sharp edges, perfect for breaking hard clods of dirt, and the way you could swing them up and bring them down with the force of ten men.

Jab. Drag. Scoop.

Jab. Drag. Scoop.

Henry Mwango was doing the same thing about twenty arm-lengths away. Eventually the channels they were digging would meet, and at some point Henry promised they would extend far enough to reach the fire river. But it took so much work to dig even one small section. And Henry was slow. His jabs were shallow, barely nicking the surface. He stopped constantly to rest. Ifechi could dig five arm-lengths of channel in the time it took Henry to do half of a single length.

Ifechi didn't begrudge Henry's slowness; he was impressed that a man of his age was digging at all. But he resented this absurd project of digging channels. The sooner it was done, the sooner they could go home.

"Henry!" he called out. "Sing with me! It makes the work go faster!" He held up two rocks and knocked them together rhythmically like a stick and a bell.

"You sing, Mr. Sinatra," Henry said. "If I were to sing, our ears would ache even more than our arms."

Jab. Drag. Scoop.

After the storytelling disaster, after Annie and Billie's departure, Ifechi had spent a miserable period alone. He didn't understand what he'd done wrong. The old women gossiped to each other in eager whispers whenever he came near. He feared Henry would never speak to him again, let alone teach him the secrets to returning home.

But Henry was not as angry as he seemed, or perhaps his anger dried up like a puddle in the sun. Eventually he approached Ifechi and asked if he remembered how to draw the number squiggles. They resumed their lessons. And while they practiced mathematics, Henry explained Trans-Atlantic Slavery. How this was a completely new thing, not at all like the slaves occasionally captured in wars at home. How it turned people into cattle, branding them and breeding them and then selling them away from their families. How it lasted for generations with no hope of ransom or redemption. Ifechi came to understand that he had done a terrible thing to Kamdiba, and not just to Kamdiba, but to Kamdiba's children and his children's children and his children's children's children.

He felt more shame about this than about his humiliating capture by the vicious man-spirits. It wormed itself into his thoughts of returning home. What if Nkiru learned of his actions? Even if no one told her, even if no one in the village knew, she might see it in his eyes. His sons might see it too. How would they feel, knowing their father had won their mother through an evil deception? That their very existence was based on the ruin of another man and all his descendants?

He couldn't sacrifice to the gods for atonement in this barren place. Henry told him to seek forgiveness from Jesus, but this was the same dead god that Billie worshipped. If Jesus were so powerful, what was Henry doing here? Why couldn't Henry ask Jesus to build these pointless channels?

Jab. Drag. Scoop.

This was no life. This might as well be Trans-Atlantic Slavery. No wife, no family, no village. Surrounded by bare rock and fire. Nothing to do but dig.

"Sinatra!" Henry called. "You've stopped singing!"

"I've stopped digging," Ifechi said, disgusted, throwing his rock aside.

He didn't throw it too far. He knew that later, after they'd returned to the crater for a break, after Henry had taught another lesson to Dev and Tai-shan, they'd be back on the open plateau again, digging.

* * * * *

Ifechi barely listened to the community story sessions any more. Of course he gathered with the rest of them; what else was there to do? But the crater residents repeated themselves, the same stories over and over. Isaias alone never told stories, which made Ifechi suspect that he had the most interesting ones of all. But Isaias tended to ignore him, and Ifechi thought it best to keep out of his way.

He should have left with Trua.

Sitting in the back of the crowd, he pondered his options. Henry needed his help to get those channels built. But Henry seemed more interested in the channels than in returning home. Nothing in their continuing mathematics lessons suggested a plan that would take them home.

If he'd left with Trua, he might be back in Obodonwa by now.

If he'd left with Trua, he never would have learned about Trans-Atlantic Slavery.

At home, it was always better to know things. To know whether the spoor on a trail was leopard or hyena. To know which leaves to apply to a bleeding wound, or when the iron in the forge was hot enough to shape. But perhaps in this place, it was sometimes better not to know things.

Like Trans-Atlantic Slavery.

Ifechi's legs jiggled impatiently as the story-telling woman droned on. If Trua could cross the desert alone, so could he. Their journey here hadn't been overly difficult. Better to be on the move—searching, exploring, making his way back to the village—than stuck here digging in the dirt and listening to the same stories over and over.

He reached a decision. When the story session was done, he strolled casually to the tunnel entrance.

"I left my digging rocks outside," he told Ben-Nachman, who helped him move the heavy stone that blocked the opening.

Outside on the plateau, he stretched. His shoulders reached as high as the mountains, his arms wide as the sky. Their excavations were mere scratches in this desert. It was madness to think the two of them could ever carve an entire channel.

He'd retrace his steps through the tunnel behind the fire waterfall. Then he could decide which way to go—and it would be entirely up to him, no Annie and Billie setting the route, no Henry telling him what to do. Perhaps he could find Trua. They'd fight off any attackers together. He'd return home a hero. Nkiru would love him; his sons would respect him. He'd never have to think about Kamdiba and Trans-Atlantic Slavery again.

A hot wind blew across the plateau from the waterfall, carrying orange embers and bits of black ash. Ifechi gave a final, respectful nod to the partly-dug channel. Surely other young visitors would come along to help Henry. He strode across the plateau toward the passageway, marveling at the length of his legs and the beauty of unenclosed spaces.

He was almost at the tunnel entrance when he heard rushed footsteps in the gravel behind him. He spun around.

Dev.

The boy looked up, breathless, eyes wide with worry.

"We're not supposed to wander."

"Yes. That's correct. Go back to the crater." Ifechi tried to sound stern, though the sight of Dev, recovered, always filled him with delight.

"Where are you going?"

"I am... on a mission. For Henry."

"Can I come?"

"No. Go back."

"I want to come with you."

"Go back to Tai-shan and Henry. Don't you have lessons?"

"I don't want lessons!" Dev's voice rose into a wail. "Lessons are no fun! Henry is no fun! I want to go with you!"

"You can't. And anyway... I'll be back."

Ifechi had a sick feeling in his stomach from the lie. Dev knew he was lying, which made it worse.

"I'm your little brother! You said that, remember? If I'm your little brother, you have to take me with you!"

A moth-sized piece of ash fluttered past and landed on Dev's shoulder. Reflexively Ifechi reached forward and brushed it off.

"Go back," he said again. "Now."

Dev clamped his stick-thin arms around Ifechi's waist, the way Obinna used to clamp them around his knees. Dev could have been his son. Dev would like to be his son. But he didn't want Dev; he wanted Obinna and Chioke. He wanted his old beautiful, ignorant life.

"You promised," Dev said stubbornly. "You said you'd teach me to skip stones twenty times."

He removed Dev's hands and steeled himself to turn away. The passageway under the fire waterfall beckoned. It would take only a few strides. But Dev was alone and far from his home. Like Kamdiba's sons.

It was the thought of Kamdiba's sons and grandsons—children like his own, across an unbridgeable ocean, in perpetual enslavement—that felt the most shameful to Ifechi.

"You promised," Dev repeated.

At home, the bean plants would be up to his thighs by now. The fence might need repair where goats sometimes broke through. A full moon would be gentling the treetops, smoothing the textured grasses on Nkiru's roof.

Obinna might speak whole sentences by now. Chioke might be starting to walk, or even saying words: *Up. Down. Hungry. Mama.*

Would he ever say *Papa?*

Ifechi took a deep breath. Such a breath must have been taken by Kamdiba as they loaded him onto the ship. Slowly he let the breath leave his chest.

Breath of freedom. Breath of home.

He felt hollow.

"All right, little brother," he said. "Back we go."

Ifechi hoisted the boy up onto his shoulders and, amidst flakes of floating ash, turned back to the crater.

PART THREE

Marsh

CHAPTER SEVENTEEN

Annie

Eight pebbles later.

Or was it nine? Or ten? Annie had lost track.

They leaned gingerly against sulfur crystals, resting. Annie reached down to rub her sore calves and was surprised to feel firm cords of muscle. She examined her thighs, her hips, even her upper arms, and found an unfamiliar body—large as ever, but fat forged into sinew from the continuous trekking and climbing. She had become a steely Amazon, the kind of girl she'd watched with envy on high school sports fields. And now, of course, there was no one around to appreciate it.

A big girl like you, you need to capitalize on your assets before it's too late.

When she got home, she'd stay in shape. She'd lift weights and do zumba with Melanie. She would become someone that guys wanted to date, to get involved with, to stay involved with. More jogging, less late-night ice cream.

No. It was more than that. It was attitude. "You're too picky," Mel used to say. "Nobody lives up to your standards." Being a single woman in 21st century San Francisco felt like a wobbly tightrope: don't sell yourself short but don't be too picky. Be assertive but don't be aggressive. Enjoy sex but don't be a slut...

She had only been involved with two guys since dropping out of Brown after her freshman year. Two guys in ten years: not an encouraging track record. The first one, Jay, had been an ambitious law student who barely made time for her between moot court and law review. He moved to L.A. for a clerkship and they never saw each other again.

The second one, Arlo, was sweet but unmotivated. He worked as a driver for a start-up that delivered fresh fruit to downtown offices and would show up at her apartment at 11 p.m. with bags of excess peaches and kiwis. They'd get stoned and bake pies all night; Annie racked up huge reserves of goodwill at Ocean Allies with all those fruit pies.

She had liked Arlo. But after a while she started wondering if he were too much of a stoner. Then Thanksgiving approached and she had to decide whether to bring him home to her family. To Ben. She imagined:

Annie: This is Arlo. He works for a start-up in San Francisco.

Ben: Interesting. What space are you in?

Arlo: Uh, mostly a van.

Ben: No, space, like what sector. Business-to-business? The sharing economy?

Arlo: We sell to businesses. But it's the employees who eat the fruit.

Ben: So are you a programmer? Or in marketing?

Arlo: Delivery.

Ben: Great. It's key to deliver a good user experience. You've seen Rand Bartlet's TedX talk on delivering value in the post-Amazon ecosystem, right? He was on the plane to Davos with me last year.

Arlo: No, I mean, I deliver fruit. Like nectarines. Apples. You know, fruit?

Ben: (Silent. Eventually coughs.)

It was the sound of Ben's cough that did it.

She let Arlo down gently. No more late-night kiwi deliveries. She wasn't sure he minded much, but she cried into her pillow for a week. That was when Mel accused her of being too picky.

Maybe she would try to reconnect with Arlo when she got home—if he hadn't moved on, if he'd lightened up on the weed.

Maybe her new streamlined body would open up a vast new social life.

Maybe she would give up and join a nunnery. Did they make secular nunneries?

The key was getting home. She glanced over at Billie, who was picking black dust from under her fingernails, and hoped she knew more than she let on.

* * * * *

They reached the end of the yellow plain and crossed a saddle into a black gravel basin. Then another basin, and another. Slogging up this latest slope, huffing for breath, Annie tamped down her expectations. She might wish for green fields and houses, but the likely sight would be more desert.

She pushed the final few yards up onto this next saddle and peered out onto... a marsh.

At least it looked like a marsh, but that was in the same off-kilter way that the lake of fire looked like a lake. There were none of the cattails and herons of an earthly marsh, just a vast, waveless, yellow-green pond with a pocked surface that suggested mud flats. It extended to the horizon, wisps of vapor trailing up into the sunless sky.

Perhaps it held water! But Billie urged caution. And Trua, for once, agreed with Billie. “It could be another fire lake,” he said. “Or something belonging to your—what do you call him?—Satan.”

They picked their way down the hillside. The descent was harder than it looked, with loose gravel and sections where chunks of hill had slid away. By the time they reached the basin floor, Annie’s knees wobbled. They stopped to rest about a hundred yards from the shore, and Annie folded her sweater into a pillow. Billie lay down on her sack of treasures. Trua remained seated, scanning for danger.

She closed her eyes and let her legs recover.

She thought of her bed at home with its clean sheets and soft pillow.

She thought of camping out, a down sleeping bag pulled up warm against her chin, the cold a thrilling bite on her face.

She thought of plastic bags of trail mix on camping trips, and how she would always eat the M&Ms before any of the healthy stuff.

M&Ms! She could spend an hour just thinking about M&Ms. Their preschool colors, their perfect, unfoodlike uniformity. M&Ms in bottomless plastic bowls at childhood birthday parties. M&Ms in shallow dishes after giving blood in the Red Cross van. M&Ms in the ancient vending machine—about seven pieces for a quarter—at the laundromat near her apartment.

And laundromats! Clean clothing, warm from the dryer. Holding a warm sock up to your cheek. The crisp scent of bleach in the air, a tattered copy of *People* magazine amid the lint clumps on the window ledge, the neon letters of "lavanderia" backward and bright against the dark night...

Your basic street-corner laundromat.

Every damn minute here you thought of something else from home, something you had taken for granted and now longed for like it was golden treasure.

* * * * *

When she sat up, Billie was fussing with some items from her pouch. Trua stared out across the plain.

"Let's go check it out." Annie nodded toward the marsh.

"Y'all go," Billie said. "I'll just stay right here."

"Oh, come on. Don't you want to see what it is?"

"I want to get home and see my babies. I don't care about some stinky marsh."

"Billie!"

"Oh, all right." She tied her pouch and stood.

"Trua?"

He shook his head in a way that forestalled argument. “Someone should keep watch.”

All right, let Trua play security guard with their meager possessions. Annie headed toward the shoreline, with Billie trailing behind. The smell of sulfur gave way to a cloying sweetness that reminded her of overripe peaches. A low, soughing sound rose from the marsh and filled the air.

She peered ahead. The liquid rippling against the shore had a metallic sheen: not water after all. Away from the shore, the surface was broken by a series of pale grey shapes like the backs of so many dolphins. They were too rounded to be mudflats, too uniform to be rocks. Maybe floating vegetation, like lily pads? There were thousands, stretching as far on the marsh as she could see.

The soughing grew more audible and coalesced into a lilting cry. It wasn’t a single voice but a braid of millions of faint, sorrowful voices. It spoke of the last thin leaf on an autumn tree... the last passenger pigeon calling for its nonexistent mate... the light from a star that died a thousand years ago...

It was the loneliest sound she’d ever heard.

Billie heard it too. She stared at the marsh, stunned horror on her face.

“What is it?” Annie murmured, but Billie didn’t answer.

Annie took a cautious step toward the shoreline. Yellow-green liquid lapped softly against the sand. The grey shapes rocked on the water. That low, heartbroken cry continued, voices blended too smoothly to distinguish any single thread. A vast despair engulfed her, thick and clinging.

No one.

No love.

So lonely.

Forever...

Annie turned to Billie to see if she was feeling the same thing, but Billie was gone—already thirty yards from the shore, running as fast, perhaps even faster, than when they'd fled the marauders.

"Billie—" she began.

Then she heard it from within the braid of cries—one soft, tiny voice crying out.

Mama.

It might as well have been calling her name.

Annie spun back to face the marsh. She saw nothing but those gray rafts, cradles perhaps, a million infant-Moseses never lifted from the bulrushes.

Mama.

Dizziness took her. She didn't fight it.

Mama.

She let herself spiral back into the fire.

CHAPTER EIGHTEEN

Annie

burningburningburningburningburningburningburnin gburningburningburningburningburningburningburni ngburningburningburningburningburningburningbur ningburningburningburningburningburningburningbu rningburningburningburningbur—

You are in Hell. Disbelief scorched away like pencil marks in a kiln. You're burning in Hell and will burn there forever. Flames eat your flesh and you let them feed. Blisters swell and pop and you urge them on. How could you not have known? How did you turn a blind eye? Now you're paying the price and you deserve every farthing of pain, every dollar of fire. The bill is long and the ink is indelible and the pain the pain the pain the pain—

burningburningburningburningburningburningburnin gburningburningburningburningburningburningburni ngburningburningburningburningburningburningbur ningburningburningburningburningburningburningbu rningburningburningburni—

You thought you knew pain, but you were wrong. This is worse. Your neurons are at war with each other. Cells attack neighboring cells with bayonets and tasers, with kitchen knife and razor blade. It's Gettysburg in your body, axon versus dendrite, each synapse a killing field. Screams of horses. Smoke and sulfur. Ragged couriers telegraph the battlefield news to your limbs, your lungs, your toes. Each pulse an explosion of pain. Each pulse a new catastrophe.

You sink. No point trying to hold your head above the fire. You belong in the fire. You courted the fire, romanced the fire with expensive gifts and extravagant promises. Fire melts your lips, treacherous plump tissue that cushioned lies. Fire melts your eyelids, vain window blinds you drew to avoid seeing the truth.

Sinner.

You could have chosen Christ at any moment.

Sinner.

You could have chosen Christ at any moment.

Sinner.

You could have chosen Christ at any moment.

Sinner.

You could have chosen Christ but you looked away. God but you looked away. A righteous life and eternal reward but you looked away.

burningburningburningburningburningburningburnin gburningburningburningburningburningburningburni ngburningburningburningburningburningburningbur ningburningburningburningburningburningburningbu rningburningburningburningburningburningburningburningb urningburningburningburningburningburningbur—

end it please end it please end it please end it please end it please

burningburningburningburningburningburningburningburnin gburningburningbur—

* * * * *

March: the time when northeastern winter tantalizes you with days of bright sunshine, crocuses daring to emerge, black dregs of curbside snow finally melting away into the street. And then—just as you are about to happily stuff your parka into the suitcase under the dorm bed—it slams you with the wettest, most bitter snowstorm of the year.

Annie had been elated when she was accepted at Brown. Granted it wasn't Princeton like Ben, and she was offered only a half-scholarship while he'd gotten a full ride, but it was still an Ivy and on the East Coast and enough financial aid to be do-able.

But freshman year was rough. She missed little things like driving ten minutes to reach a hiking trail into wilderness, or shutting the door in a bedroom all her own. For the first time, she wasn't Ben Maple's little sister. Another person might have found that liberating, but Annie found it crushing. She was a nobody surrounded by a thousand somebodies—class presidents, concert pianists, Olympic skaters, software geniuses. Without Ben's glow she was unknown and unremarkable, even to herself.

Winter arrived and steamrolled her. Annie knew she was being a stereotypical Californian—"poor baby, no flip-flops in December," her roommate Karen teased—but she felt besieged by the unrelenting cold. She shivered in drafty lecture halls. She sweated in overheated dorm rooms. The wool sweaters lovingly bought by her mother made her itch, and the cold made her devour huge portions of heavy, carb-filled cafeteria food that left her feeling ill and bloated.

Worst of all, she was floundering academically. She'd chosen Brown for its proximity to Woods Hole marine lab and the ocean, imagining a ramped-up version of high school marine bio field trips. Instead she was pinned in a series of large introductory lecture classes. And she was at risk of failing one of them—a fast-track calculus class in which she seemed to be the only student who hadn't already taken the subject in high school.

Annie refused to drop the class. She was too ashamed to admit to being in academic trouble. It never occurred to her to seek tutoring. She soldiered along, confused and desperate. It was a new experience for her. She hoped the class would get easier in the second semester, but it didn't.

Then came March with its seductive glimpse of spring and its body-blow of more winter. One Friday night, Annie trudged through the slush and ice to an off-campus party thrown by kids in an artsy crowd. To her amazement, she ended up dancing with one of the college's pseudo-celebrities—a film major who always wore black and whose shock of black hair fell across his pale forehead like a 1980s British rock star. Evander's father in fact *was* a 1980s British rock star; he would vanish from school occasionally to go to Sundance with "the da," or to film a video of some Amazon tribe that his father was helping fight the oil companies.

They danced; they made out; then, the next thing Annie knew, they were in a back bedroom and her skirt was up and his black jeans were off and he was holding her breasts in each hand, kissing one, then the other, and telling her she belonged in a Modigliani painting. For once she felt as golden as those class presidents and Olympic skaters. And Evander was a good lover. He wasn't selfish; she came, twice, and afterwards he held her in the darkened room and told her about the first time he'd been with a girl, when he was fourteen and one of his dad's groupies got bored with the party scene on the terrace and came upstairs to the children's floor. Annie considered telling him about her first time too but it seemed tame in comparison and she decided, "Okay, maybe next time."

A few days later she saw him in the dining hall. She deftly unloaded the second brownie from her tray and headed toward his table, but he lifted his head to scan the room, gazing past her, and she realized he had no idea who she was.

She was too embarrassed to reintroduce herself.

She refused to blame him. It was a hook-up, after all. They'd both been using each other. It wasn't like she was some tender Victorian flower that he'd plucked violently from a vine. She'd had fun. That was enough, she told herself. Be grown-up about it. Move on.

Two weeks later, her period didn't come.

* * * * *

Annie didn't tell her parents or Ben. She already feared being seen as a screw-up because of calculus, and this would just seal the package. But her roommates were wonderful. They waited outside the bathroom while she peed on the plastic stick; when it turned pink, they made her mint tea and hugged her and told her everything would be okay.

Karen offered to accompany her to Planned Parenthood for the abortion. Nanette said she'd fetch any class handouts or library books that Annie needed. They debated whether she would want chicken soup or ice cream afterwards and decided to pick up both. "Comfort videos," Nanette advised, and gathered a stack of Harry Potter movies and the *Pride and Prejudice* mini-series with Colin Firth.

Annie didn't book an appointment.

At first it was her class schedule. There was a calculus test next week, and a group project in biology the week after that. She couldn't afford to miss a single day of school. Her roommates pressed her—*better sooner than later?*—but she demurred. She felt fogged and lumbering, a creature that could barely move. She wanted only to sleep. Her roommates grew more insistent, sounded worried, but she snapped at them to stop badgering her. She buried herself in bed and slept through her morning classes. She skipped the calculus test. She had her roommates bring her bowls of granola from the dining hall instead of going to meals. Gradually an understanding seeped in through the layers of quilts and blankets: she wanted to keep the baby.

This was unthinkable. Impossible. Upper-middle-class girls at Ivy League colleges didn't become teen mothers. She was barely out of childhood herself. A baby at age nineteen? It would ruin her life. Her parents would be crushed. Ben would be disgusted.

And yet…

The baby would be hers. Something unique to her, something that Ben didn't have. And lying there under her blankets, she knew she would be a good mother.

Annie got up. She returned to the dining hall and ate piles of leafy greens and salmon. She took a makeup test in calculus and turned in the biology project and started a paper on Rachel Carson. She didn't schedule an abortion, but neither did she schedule a pregnancy check-up. Seeing a doctor would make it official, and once it was official she would have to tell her parents. Annie silently counted the weeks and imagined the being inside of her growing from a sesame seed to a tadpole to a curled-up miniature E.T. She pictured reading Lyle-the-crocodile to this small person and dangling its toes in Steep Ravine creek.

It would be a girl, she decided. She'd give her a name that was the opposite of bland, forgettable

"Annie"—Samantha, maybe, or Isabella, or Carson. When no one was around, she stood naked in the steamy dorm shower and ran hands over her still-flat belly, wondering if the baby sensed her touch.

Then one evening she cramped and found blood in her underwear.

Her roommates were relieved, even happy.

"Wow, you dodged a bullet," Karen said.

"And you didn't even have to tell your parents," Nanette said.

That was the end for Annie. She abandoned the Rachel Carson paper, bombed the rest of her calculus tests, didn't bother taking the final. Betrayed by her own body, she was a failure on more levels than she could count. She wasn't brilliant, she'd never be a marine biologist, she couldn't even manage to stay fucking pregnant.

And then there was the matter of a doctor. If she'd seen a doctor, might she have saved the baby?

The semester ended. Annie packed her duffel bags, left her thick wool sweaters neatly folded for the dorm cleaning people, and went home to California. She never spoke a word about the miscarriage. She lived with her parents and got a job at Starbucks. After a couple of years, giving in to pressure from her mother, she took classes in environmental studies at the local community college. Eventually she went to work for Ocean Allies and moved into the city where she went to parties and accumulated a closet full of shoes and made fruit pies with Arlo and stir-fries with Melanie.

And her baby—that sesame-seed, tadpole dot of potential life—was relegated to this bleak limbo of a marsh, alone for all of eternity.

* * * * *

burningburningburningburningburningburningburnin gburningburningburningburningburningburningburni ngburningburningburningburningburningburningbur ningburningburningburningburningburningburningbu rningburningburn—

CHAPTER NINETEEN

Annie

"Annie. Wake up!"

She hauled her eyes partway open. Trua was gripping her shoulders.

"Get up. This lake is as bad as the other one."

He pulled but she was infinitely heavy. This was her baby—the child she had bundled away in silence but never forgotten. She knew it the way you know breath. The voice was her child, and when it died, it ended up alone in this marsh.

Mama.

She hadn't truly believed it until now: Hell was real. God was real.

The consequences were staggering.

Ben. You were wrong. You were so fucking wrong.

God existed. God ran the universe. God had established a very specific moral code for how people were to think and act, and it was Christian and literal and non-negotiable.

God trumped science. God trumped humanism. God trumped Darwin and Einstein and NASA and The Beatles and Steve Jobs and Harry Potter and the *New York Times.*

If God could create a Hell that operated outside the laws of biology and physics, then those laws weren't really laws. Gravity, thermodynamics, genetics: if the universe appeared to operate with logic and consistency, it was only because God wanted it that way. And God could change his mind at any minute. After all, here she was in a realm where people survived without food or water, where flesh burned without being consumed, where miscarried babies lived forever in a marsh.

The Christian fundamentalists were right. The televangelists! The creationists! The snake handlers and tongue-talkers! Even that crazy guy on Market Street, the one with the sandwich board with verses from Revelation in outsized red magic-marker, who shouted at passersby that San Francisco was the Whore of Babylon and homosexuals would burn in Hell.

Even he was right.

While her parents were wrong. The ocean scientists at work were wrong. That handsome rabbi with the guitar who conducted her friend Sarah's wedding was wrong—

Mama.

The voice persisted, plaintive as a sparrow with a fractured wing.

Mama.

All these years, hoarding her secret. It had all been about *her*—her failure, her loss, her pain. She'd never once thought about the soul of her baby.

No one.

No love.

So lonely.

Forever...

Why had it ended up here in Hell rather than Heaven? Never baptized—was that it? Or something she'd done? Was this her fault?

Annie shoved herself up onto her knees. She'd wade into the muck. The cradles weren't far. She'd swim out, find it, carry it back to shore—to warm arms, to a home, to love—

"Annie—"

She twisted out of Trua's grip and started crawling toward the marsh. He grabbed her again. Damn it. Didn't he hear the cries? Goddamn man. Goddamn Hun. She jerked away and staggered to her feet. She was almost at the water. Just dive in—

He tackled her.

"Let go!"

"Annie—"

They grappled. He was compact but all muscle. She was still shaky from the fire. Almost immediately he pulled her back from the edge. He knelt over her, holding her down.

"You can't go in there."

"I have to!"

He shook his head, grip tight.

"Fuck you! Don't tell me what to do—"

He didn't argue, just kept her pinned. Her heart was pounding so hard it almost drowned out the cries from the marsh. She stopped thrashing and lay still. But only to catch her breath. Only for a minute.

"Watch this," Trua said. "Don't move. Watch." He released one of her arms but kept a firm hold on the other. With his free hand, he groped in the dirt and came up with a chunk of black rock.

He reached back and tossed the rock—not far, just into the first few inches of marsh where it lodged, half submerged.

Loud hiss and burbling. A black slick oozed across the surface. The rock dissolved, sinking lower, until all that was left was the smear of black.

Acid of some sort? Some incredibly strong, fast-acting acid?

"See?"

She didn't want to see. She wanted to shake him off, plow through the marsh, and save her child. She didn't care about the acid. Let it melt her into ooze. Let it plunge her back into the fire. All that mattered was that voice...

But the rock had dissolved so fast. She wouldn't make it even one-tenth of the way out to the cradles.

Mama.

Yet another failure. The fight left Annie's body and she slumped into the gravel. She felt like one of the translucent jellyfish washed up in batches on the beach at home—limp, doomed.

Mama.

Trua let go of her other arm.

"Come away from the shore," he said.

* * * * *

They returned to the spot where Annie had left her sweater. The sweater was gone. So was Billie's bundle of clothes. So was Billie.

"Lying bitch," Trua growled. "I told you not to trust her!"

The yellow cardigan had been Annie's most tangible link to home.

"It doesn't matter."

Trua scanned the horizon. "She'll find the way out and we'll be stuck here."

It didn't matter. Nothing mattered except that voice in the marsh.

"What's going on? What did you see in that lake?"

Annie didn't answer. But then she looked at Trua—his bootless feet, his dusty, ripped goatskin. He hadn't left. He'd saved her from the acid. He deserved an explanation, as humiliating as it might be.

She told him about the pregnancy. The miscarriage.

When she was done, she pulled her legs in to her chest and kept her gaze down. But Trua's tone was one of puzzlement rather than condemnation.

"Many babies die, especially during a harsh winter," he said. "I know it's a terrible thing. But why are you blaming yourself?"

"I should have gone to a doctor! Even if it was just a one percent chance! They might have saved it!"

Trua shook his head. "I don't see how. People can't control what happens to babies in the womb."

The gap between them silenced her. How would you make someone from Roman times understand 21st century medicine? Antibiotics, ultrasounds, fetal monitors. Even the goddamn turns-pink plastic pregnancy stick. It would all seem like magic to him.

Maybe it all *was* magic. Science was arbitrary, remember? Everything was up to God. God made Hell, and God sent fetuses to limbo, and God could turn an amoxycillin pill into a jelly bean if he wished. Still, she wanted Trua to understand where she'd come from.

"Let me tell you about the world in 2015, okay?"

CHAPTER TWENTY

Annie

They talked for what felt like days. She started with basic things like electricity, but every sentence of explanation led to a half dozen more questions.

"You know lightning in the sky, right? People have learned how to create that kind of energy and use it. We use it to light our buildings at night and to run things like washing machines—"

"How do you capture the lightning?"

"We don't capture it. We make it. By burning oil or—"

"Oil, like from olives?"

"No, a different kind of oil. Stuff you get by digging in the ground."

"Like planting crops?"

"Much deeper. With special drilling machines."

"Do oxen pull these machines? Or horses?"

"Neither. They run on gasoline. Oil."

"So you use oil to dig for oil? What's the point then?"

Annie watched Trua cupping each new fact, turning it in his hands, trying to fit it into everything else he knew. She asked him about his world too, although he answered in single words or short phrases.

“I hope this isn’t too personal. Can I ask about... those?” She gestured at the scars on his face.

Trua nodded. “Our tradition is to shed blood when someone important dies. This one—” He pointed to a scar on his left cheek, “—was our head of clan Eskam. And these—” He pointed to scars on the right cheek, “—were for my uncle and my father.”

“I’m sorry.”

“For what?”

“Your father’s death?”

“There’s nothing to be sorry about. He was buried honorably. He is well cared for, among our ancestors.”

Annie was taken aback. “You don’t think he’s here?”

“Of course not. He’s with our ancestors.”

“So you don’t think this is the afterlife?”

Trua shook his head. “This is nothing like the afterlife. This is a place of evil magic. The only reason I’m here is that sorceress who cast a curse on me.” He paused, abashed. “You were not the sorceress. I know that now.”

Annie wasn’t sure whether to argue. Was it better to let Trua remain in denial? As long as he continued to think this was a curse, he could hold hopes of escaping. She, on the other hand, understood they both would be here forever, either wandering the desert or back in the fire.

Hell didn’t have exits. Billie was chasing a fantasy.

* * * * *

They talked about Billie. Trua recounted what he'd seen: the two women approaching the marsh. Billie turning and fleeing. Annie collapsing. Billie vanishing with her sack of belongings and Annie's sweater.

"She was waiting for a chance to rob you," he said. "When you fell into the fire trance, she took it."

Annie wasn't sure. Billie had fled *before* Annie passed out. Something in the marsh had spooked her.

"All those clothes in her sack," Trua continued. "She robbed other people too. Maybe she killed them. I knew she was hiding something."

Annie felt awash in sadness. Billie had been her one friend here. Maybe the last friend she would have for the rest of eternity. She shook her head.

"If she'd wanted the goddamn sweater, she should have asked. I'd have given it to her in a minute."

* * * * *

They talked about food.

"Tell me what your tribe eats," she asked Trua.

Trua described roast mutton. Stewed mutton. Roasted hare and goat and ground squirrel. Fermented mare's milk. Mashed roots of plants that she'd never heard of. Dried figs and raisins, when they could get them from the Romans. Wine, when they could get it from the Romans.

"Now tell me what your people eat, by your San Francisco fires," he said with a smile. "Do you use this tamed lightning to cook your meat? Or do you use dung?"

"No to the dung, yes to electricity," Annie said. "Plus gas. Plus microwaves."

She dodged explaining what microwaves were, and embarked on a systematic account of what she ate.

Breakfast was easy. The same thing almost every day: vanilla-almond granola from Trader Joe's. She never used to pay attention. It was something quick and easy to cram down before running for the bus. In hindsight each spoonful could have held diamonds. The oats crunchy and sweet in the cold smooth milk. Fresh farmer's market blueberries in the summer. Black coffee as strong and earthy as smoke from a wood stove.

Lunch was also the same most days: cheap bean burrito if she went out, a sandwich if she were organized enough to bring lunch from home. Annie used to hate her brown-bag lunches, so pathetic compared to the brick-oven pizzas and sushi stations of friends who worked at tech companies. Now she couldn't decide which sandwich to describe to Trua: the sweet stickiness of peanut butter. The crisp crunch of a pickle slice on turkey. Tuna fish. Cheese.

Then there were the fancy ingredients—the ones she rarely packed in her own lunch. But she needed to describe them too. They were part of her former world.

"Cole slaw," she told Trua. "Sri racha sauce. That's spicy, from Thailand. Guacamole, from Mexico.

Pesto, from Italy. Bacon. Hummus. Roasted peppers."

And dinners. Classic holiday meals at her parents' house, the table heavy with turkey, yams, green beans, mashed potatoes. Or eating out: gems of translucent sashimi. Barbecued ribs so tender that the meat almost floated off the bone. Chicago-style pizza with beer. Burritos—interesting burritos this time, not just beans but *carne asada, mole verde, carnitas, camarones al mojo de ajo...*

And desserts. Annie described apple pie and brownies, chocolate mousse and crème brulee. Peach ice cream and cookie dough ice cream and mint chip ice cream and—her favorite of all—Ben & Jerry's Phish Food, chunks of chocolate studding a dizzying goo of chocolate and caramel.

"What?" she said. Trua was looking at her strangely. "Didn't you have a favorite food? Something you would pig out on?"

Trua frowned.

Annie realized that he had no idea what ice cream was, let alone Phish Food. Was he picturing her eating a pint of mealworms or minnows?

"Your people have many more foods than my people do," he said, and then he was silent.

* * * * *

In Trua's silence, Annie crashed.

She'd gotten so engrossed in explaining the 21st century to him. But what was the point, really? This whole adrenaline-fueled talking jag was just an exercise in avoidance.

The marsh remained less than a football field away. When she stopped talking, she could still hear the keening babies.

No one.

No love.

So lonely.

Forever...

"At least they're not in the fire," Trua had ventured earlier, trying to console her. Annie supposed that was a kind of mercy. They didn't seem to be in physical pain. Perhaps the rippling acid felt like a rocking cradle to them. Perhaps the overripe peach smell was meant to be pleasant. Still it was wrenching: too young to know what had happened. Suddenly alone. Even as a first-trimester fetus, the baby would have been accustomed to Annie's heartbeat, the warm pulses of blood, the vibrations of her voice. All gone.

Alone.

Never knowing that other people existed.

Never knowing that it was loved.

Never knowing why.

What kind of cruel God would do this? It wasn't the babies' fault if they hadn't been baptized. God was punishing souls that had committed no sin. But didn't Christianity say that all humans were guilty of original sin, no matter how young? What *was* original sin, anyway? Annie felt lost. She was an immigrant who didn't speak the language, who couldn't even recognize the alphabet. What was God's purpose? What did God want her to do?

Perhaps she could ask God.

She glanced at Trua but he remained withdrawn, staring at the ground. Annie understood she shouldn't pray out loud. But no one had said anything about silent prayer.

She groped for words. When Trua had forced her to build an altar, she'd randomly tossed together whatever bits of religion she could recall. This was different.

God.

She closed her eyes and shaped the word silently, visualizing the letters like white chalk on a blackboard.

Please, God. Rescue my baby. It didn't do anything wrong.

Something didn't feel right. Annie shifted on the gravel. She couldn't put her finger on what was amiss, and then realized: *It.*

The baby floating out there in the marsh wasn't an *it.* It was a person.

Long ago, pregnant, she'd decided the fetus was a girl. She would go with that now. And she'd name her. If you were going to float for eternity, alone on a sea of acid, at the very least you should have a name.

Samantha? Isabella? Carson?

No. Something biblical. Perhaps a suitably religious name would inspire God to take pity and lift her up to heaven. So maybe Mary. You couldn't get any more Christian than that. *Mary Maple.* Annie wrote the name on that blackboard in her mind and tried to attach it to the faceless voice in the marsh. *I love you, Mary. I'm so sorry, Mary.* She shifted up onto her knees since that was how people in the movies seemed to pray. It struck her that she was more comfortable talking to Trua about Phish Food than talking to God.

Please, God. Rescue my daughter Mary from that marsh.

God, I'm sorry.

God, have mercy on Mary.

God forgive me. God have mercy. God forgive me. God have mercy. God forgive me.

CHAPTER TWENTY-ONE

Annie

Nothing happened.

Annie didn't know what was supposed to happen when you prayed. Certainly God wasn't going to pop up like a genie from a magic lamp, but she should experience *something*. A voice in her head, or a flash of insight, or at least a sense that she wasn't alone.

God forgive me. God have mercy. God forgive me. God have mercy. God forgive me.

How many women had prayed for lost children through the millennia? In chapels and at graves, in flower-besotted fields and dismal slums. Wrinkled grandmothers in black in the pews of dark Spanish churches. Suburban military mothers with knees buckling at every knock on the door. Mothers of the Plaza de Mayo, Mothers Against Drunk Driving. Surely there was power in a mother's prayer? Wasn't that what the Virgin Mary was all about? Did those mothers get any more of a response than she did?

God forgive me. God have mercy. God forgive me.

She felt Trua watching but ignored him.

"I'm going to look for Billie," he finally said, and trudged back toward the hills.

Alone now, there was nothing to interrupt her. No need to eat, no need to sleep. How ironic that being in Hell allowed you to pray non-stop, 24-7. But what exactly was she seeking forgiveness for? There was of course her obliviousness to God. Ben had denied God and ridiculed God and proselytized against God, but at least he had paid attention to God. While she had ignored God and gone her merry way thinking about shoes and donor lists and ice cream. Which was worse?

And what about all the smaller sins?

The countless daily moments of selfishness, arrogance, and envy, like a million biting flies. The vindication she felt when Ben's fiancée dumped him: *Now I'm not the only Maple with a non-existent love life!* Or the secret flash of glee when Melanie didn't pass the bar exam: *She's as big a screw-up as I am!*

At work too: she created boxes in her mind—people who were cool, people who weren't. Take Hailey Jackson, who did the bookkeeping and had a tiny mouse-voice that seemed a perpetual apology. Annie turned down every invitation by Hailey to eat lunch or go out for a drink. Or Rodney Breem, one of the nature educators, who had an obvious crush on her but whose breath smelled like old cheese. She buried herself in her computer when he walked by; in late night talks with Melanie, she laughingly referred to him as Rotten Brie.

Condescending. Arrogant. Pointlessly cruel. And there were so many of these moments. Remembering them all was like trying to remember each breath you'd drawn.

God forgive me. God have mercy. God forgive me. God have mercy. God forgive me.

The boxes of pens she took home—stole, really—from the office.

The time she broke Melanie's blow dryer but pretended nothing had happened.

The way she dumped Arlo. The way she judged Arlo.

All the homeless people she passed every day. The way she'd taught herself not to notice them. And then the homeless woman in front of the supermarket whom she occasionally *did* notice: maybe this was even worse. Annie would give the woman $5 and feel like Mother Teresa, Nelson Mandela, and the Dalai Lama rolled into one. She would float home on a cloud of gauzy self-righteousness, in love with her own generosity, blind to the heaping bags of groceries in her arms, the kitchen shelves already bulging with granola and peanut butter, canned tuna and balsamic vinegar.

When the woman didn't thank her, she felt aggrieved.

God forgive me. God have mercy. God forgive me. God have mercy. God forgive me.

For skipping over all the news stories about Syrian refugees.

For sneaking drinks from her boss's art deco liquor cabinet while house-sitting in her 32nd-floor condo.

For coveting the art deco liquor cabinet.

For coveting the 32nd-floor condo.

For intending to abandon Billie and Trua and the others at the canyon.

For feeling morally superior to Billie.

For never challenging Billie.

For judging. Assuming. Denying. Avoiding.

God forgive me. God have mercy. God forgive me. God have mercy. God forgive me.

* * * * *

And still nothing. She was not forgiven; she was not chastised; she was not even acknowledged. She could feel no presence other than the voices from the marsh.

Perhaps she was too far gone for God to listen. Perhaps repentance was moot once you were in Hell, like trying to redeem grocery coupons after their expiration date.

Please God. If you won't help me, help Mary.

Trua returned, morose. He'd had no more luck finding Billie than she'd had finding God. "We'll get home without her," he said finally. "She was lying anyway. She doesn't know any more than we do."

He reached out a hand to help Annie up.

Mama.

The voice still echoed from the acid marsh. She shook her head.

"You go."

She wouldn't lose this baby a second time. Annie resolved to stay by the shore and project her love across the expanse of acid—send it forth like a kite, a balloon, a dove. At the very least Mary might know she wasn't alone. That she had a mother. That she was loved.

Trua's long forehead furrowed. "You can't stay here."

"I'll be okay."

"There's no shelter. Anyone can see you. Not just marauders, but..."

He glanced at the sky and she knew he was picturing those creatures. Devils, or Satan, or whatever they were.

"Just go, all right?"

He shifted awkwardly but didn't turn away. She wished he would go. Leave her to her vigil, her doom. Leave her to God or the devil, whichever one might deign to hear her—

Hear her.

All this time she'd been praying silently. But maybe prayer had to be spoken aloud like a magician's abracadabra? Billie had called prayer a dog whistle for the devil. "You can't do that here," Billie had said.

But maybe that's what God wanted—the risk, the commitment.

She'd try.

And if God still didn't respond?

Annie's old living self—the girl who'd memorized kingdoms and phyla for high school bio, the young woman who created spreadsheets of grant deadlines—would view this as completely insane. But that self was gone. Her universe was gone.

"You need to leave," she told Trua. "For your own safety. Just go. *Now.*"

If God wouldn't save her baby, Annie Maple was prepared to sell her soul to the devil.

PART FOUR

Palace

CHAPTER TWENTY-TWO

Trua

Trua stared as Annie's prayers sliced through the silence of the plain. Fool of a woman! This would bring demons or worse. But she'd saved his life, which made her a kinswoman. He wouldn't leave.

"God. Please help Mary. She shouldn't suffer because of my mistakes."

He could tackle her again and clamp a hand over her mouth. But for how long? And she wanted to do this thing. Trua couldn't hear whatever it was Annie heard in the marsh, but he saw her determination. Foolish, yes, but also brave.

"God. Please—"

He felt the shadow.

The feeling began in his gut, a clenching and turning like wet hides being wrung out. The sky darkened—or was that his imagination?—and a gust of cold air raced in from a far corner of the plain. The skin on his arms tightened with goosebumps.

The shape grew larger. First a speck, then a figure. Then he made out limbs—arms, legs, a human-style body—and great spreading dark wings.

Trua hurled himself onto the ground. The air turned even colder.

The thing was large, more the size of a horse than a man. It was now close enough to see how it was not human—the wings, of course, leathery and boned like a bat, and in place of toes it had talons. Its body and tunic were the splotchy brown of tarnished metal, and its bright red pupils glowed like cookfire embers.

It paused directly above them, kiting, indecisive. It flapped to the left and the right and Trua realized: *It couldn't see them.*

"Run," he whispered to Annie. "Now. Before it figures out where we are."

Instead—*curse this woman!*—she stood up.

"Here I am," she said.

The creature rose with a powerful flap, then lowered itself onto the ground a few paces in front of Annie. Its face was crooked and sneering, a sly trader who knew he would profit no matter how well you bargained. Its teeth were chipped daggers.

"My, my. A human, out of the fire," the creature said. "Hard to see. Who knows why. But smelling as foul as ever."

"I want to make a deal." Annie's voice was thin as grass.

"Ha! Don't they all."

"I'll sell my soul. Whatever you want. Just take my baby out of that marsh."

The creature grinned and fanned its wings. It sniffed the air. Trua pressed himself more tightly into the gravel.

"There's two of you, ain't there. This other one? What does he want?"

"Nothing! He's not involved. It's just me."

The demon made a swishy sucking sound through its teeth. Red eyes cycled imprecisely around the two of them.

"Poor missy. No one's buying, from either of you. You see, you ain't got any soul left to sell. The time to deal was when you were alive."

"But..." Annie sounded at a loss. "You run this place. You can make a deal anytime you want. You're Satan, right?"

The demon opened its mouth to laugh, and a puff of fetid air rushed out. "Satan!" Its voice was acid with contempt. "Thank the stars, no. Not him."

"Then who are you?"

"Jomjael. Sovereign of all lands from the Euphrates to the Nile. Arbiter of the arrogant, vanquisher of the vain. Bringer of drought and plague. Midnight lover of a million maidens. But only the most beautiful, virginal, living maidens, which would rule you out, missy." He laughed and flapped his wings, and Trua shivered under the new wave of cold.

"Cat got your tongue?" The demon gave another fetid laugh. "Well. Back in the fire with you. Of course, you got my permission to beg and grovel. No bargaining, but groveling is fine. Grovel to the master of mayhem. The padron of the prideful. The viceroy of vice—"

"Take me to Satan. I demand to talk to Satan." Annie was trying to sound confident but Trua could hear her fear. So could the demon, who guffawed.

"Demand! First you bargain, now you demand! What will you want next, a silver spoon and a feather bed?"

"Take me to Satan. He's... um, expecting me. He'll be angry if you don't bring me to him."

"Satan!" Jomjael spat, a thick black gob of spittle. "He don't care about you. He don't care about anything." He reached into his ear and picked out some black wax. "Now, back in the fire with you. Back in the fiery flames—"

"She's a sorceress!"

Trua pushed himself up and stepped forward. Seeking out the king of demons was more than foolhardy, but if it was what Annie wanted, he would help.

"She's a powerful sorceress. She captured me on Satan's orders. Do what you want with her, but let me go."

"Trua!"

He spoke over her, straining to keep his voice steady. "Satan won't know. He won't blame you. Free me and I'll be your guardsman. Your slave. Just drop her in the lake of fire and free me—"

"Don't listen to him!"

"Satan won't blame you when she doesn't arrive."

"No—he's lying—he's—"

"Trickery!" the demon shrieked. He drew back a shoulder and slammed a great wing forward, knocking Trua into the dirt. "Liar! Viper! What kind of fool do you take me for?"

Trua pulled his head up from the gravel.

"Satan made her a sorceress. Just *look*. It's why you can't see her."

The demon froze. He peered toward them, as if trying to confirm that they were truly invisible. *Let it work. Let him believe.* His wings twitched. His red eyes flicked back and forth across the plain.

"I'm not a sorceress!" Annie yelped.

"Free me. Satan won't know—"

"Don't listen to him!"

"Satan won't know—"

"Liars! Vipers!" Jomjael stamped a clawed foot in disgust and, just possibly, fear. Trua felt a surge of triumph. "If Satan wants you, he can have you! The both of you! I want nothing to do with your feeble lying human souls! Get up! Get up!"

The demon reached out, grasped Annie with one large arm, and lunged for Trua with the other. The massive wings closed and opened.

Cold spiked through Trua's chest as the demon clutched him, lifted up, and churned across the sprawling desert.

* * * * *

Of course Trua had dreamed of flying as a child. Horseback, he'd watched hawks spiraling up from the plain and imagined following them—galloping far above his brothers and sisters, riding gleeful circles in the sky while they dropped their bows and cookpots in astonishment. He would race with eagles. He would seize fistfuls of fleecy clouds and stuff them into his saddlebag to save for hot, dry days.

Flying with Jomjael was nothing like that.

Jomjael's touch was icy cold. His fingernails dug into Trua's side like frozen thorns. Wind slapped his ears and whipped his face. The worst part was the fear of falling. When Trua looked down, his breath stopped. He kept imagining those fingers loosening. Jomjael knew, too. At one point the demon halted in mid-flight and plummeted earthward—Annie screamed, Trua almost choked—but then he pulled out of the fall, grinning, pleased with his prank.

The marsh dwindled to a thin line behind them. The desert stretched ahead. As a child Trua had thought the Great Plain was the largest expanse of land in the world, waves of grass stretching further than anyone could ride, and this was even larger.

They passed range after range of mountains, more plains, more plateaus, more rivers of fire. They skirted a mountain whose peak was hollow and filled with fire. They crossed a basin of jagged black crystals and another basin thick with a gleaming black liquid. They crossed more deserts, more cracked sulphur beds, more boulder fields. He saw no other beings—no people, no demons, no traces of life whatsoever.

They flew over a lake of fire. It might have been the same lake they'd encountered before or an entirely new one. Soon they were far enough out that Trua could see nothing but rippling fire and burning faces in all directions. Shrieks and cries wafted up from the waves. What if Jomjael lost his way? What if his wings faltered while they were out over the flames?

Trua steeled himself for a headlong plunge into the fire, but it never came. The demon kept flying. And when he had gone further across the lake of fire than Trua had imagined possible, he kept flying some more.

* * * * *

Finally there was land.

It started as a thread of black above the orange horizon, perhaps a trick of the eye, but soon thickened to become a shore. From afar Trua made out a long line of stark black cliffs.

Jomjael veered left toward a distant knob on the cliffs. Below them, the crush of writhing bodies gave way to open patches of fire, then to waves and ripplets, and finally to black sand. Above them on the cliff, the knob clarified into a giant structure, some kind of palace. At the base of the cliff, Jomjael dropped them roughly on the sand.

"You wanted Satan, you got Satan," he said with a contemptuous sniff, then fanned his giant wings and lifted into the sky. He seemed to suck all the air with him as he left, and suddenly the cold was gone and they were back in the still heat of the desert.

Trua picked himself up. His side ached from the demon's clutch. His back was bruised from slamming into the dirt.

"I would prefer my horse," he said stiffly, hoping for a smile from Annie. But her eyes were narrow with rage.

"Get out of here. Go. Leave."

"What?"

She glared at him.

"You thought I meant that? I was trying to help."

"That wasn't helpful."

"It worked. Here you are."

"He could have killed me. Don't do that again, okay?"

"Then don't call forth demons again."

Annie didn't answer.

Trua picked up a stone and hurled it down the shoreline. He had warned her not to be so trusting, but he hadn't meant that she shouldn't trust *him*.

Out on the lake, flames quivered over the orange surface like tall grasses on the Great Plain. Screams echoed from the lake, and he did his best to ignore them.

* * * * *

They picked their way along the base of the cliffs, looking for a route to the top, while Trua puzzled.

Everyone knew how the world worked: you trusted your clan and kept your guard up with everyone else. But Annie had it all backward. She trusted Billie, Ifechi, and even that Roman bastard in the crater, while mistrusting him. Trua felt a need to win her trust. This was a new impulse for him. When he got home, he would talk to his sister Damla about it.

Damla was his closest confidant at home, the only one who encouraged his questions about the world beyond their tribe. It was impossible to imagine a meal without her voice, churning and eddying like a river. *This cousin was ready for marriage. That cousin was going to make trouble. The forage this year would not be good enough.* It was worth listening to her too: she knew more about the flocks and the clan than most of the men. Damla might not understand this fiery desert any better than he did, but she would know what to make of Annie.

Ahead, Annie stopped before a section of cliff that had collapsed into a pile of rubble. He could see her calculating: was it stable, did it reach the rim, what was the best route. She clambered up and he followed.

On top, the palace loomed. It was the largest structure Trua had ever seen—thirty or forty columns in a row, all thicker than tree trunks, rising like a Roman temple from a portico that itself was a good ten steps above the ground. Hewn from the black rock of these mountains, it was sculpted and polished to a brilliant, unmarred, inhuman sheen.

The dark mass weighed him down. The tents of his home seemed, in comparison, like butterflies tossed in a breeze. How did they mine those blocks of stone? How did they haul them in a land with no horses, carts, or oxen?

"We can go back," he ventured. "Return to the mountains."

"You go if you want." Annie still wouldn't look at him, just stared at the huge columns.

He followed her up the black steps and across the portico, its stone unnervingly smooth under his feet after so much time on gravel. She stopped at two huge iron doors wrought into intricate curls, squares, lines. No handles or latches.

Annie pushed. The iron swung forward so easily that she stumbled forward. He reached for her arm but she had lurched beyond him.

And now they were in a massive gallery. It stretched hundreds of horse-lengths across, and even farther ahead of them. The black walls held mosaics of gold and jewels, elaborate spirals of gleaming color that made no discernible pattern but swept the eye along like a swollen river. Gold sconces clung to the walls like giant snail shells housing flames instead of living creatures. Gold chandeliers dangled cascades of diamond and flame. Gold pillars reached to the roof, dripping still more gems and flames. It was like ten thousand Hunnic diadems smelted together. But unlike Hunnic metalcraft, there were no images of life—no deer, trees, birds. It was pure color and form, mineral and fire. Trua felt puny. This was a hall built for chieftains, kings, gods—not a place for an unmarried youngest son from a secondary clan.

And the hall was cold. Icy. All those flames provided light but no heat. Cold flowed up his legs from the stone floor like poison from a snake bite.

Annie moved down an aisle of gold pillars and he followed. At the front of the hall, a stepped dais held an oversized throne flanked by torches that spewed orange flames up to the ceiling. Behind the throne, a textured gold shield spread across the wall in the shape of immense wings.

No one was on the throne.

This place spooked him. Too grand, too cold, but mostly too empty. Once while scouting on a raiding journey, he and his brother Ularic had come across an abandoned village. Gates swinging loose, full barrels of wine and piles of rotting fruit in the deserted market stalls, a lone dog loping to greet them. Elated, they rode back at once to tell the others about easy spoils. The leader of the raiding party had backed away with a mix of contempt and dread.

"Fools," he'd said. "Don't you know a town with plague when you see one?"

This place felt similar.

"We should go," he said in a low voice.

Annie stayed motionless in front of the throne.

"Let's go," he repeated.

A scraping sound, metal on stone.

Trua reached for his bow and grasped empty air. No bow, no sword, no horse. In this slickly polished hall, not even a loose rock. He balled his fists.

Along the front wall of the gallery, a gold panel scraped open. A demon emerged, a small one. It was greenish-black, mottled like Jomjael but barely as tall as Trua's shoulders and skinny as a young girl.

He startled. It *was* a young girl.

Leather bat-wings and clawed feet, yes, but this demon had fine straight hair that dropped below her shoulders and a garland of shriveled, black flowers circling her head. Her wings were half the size of Jomjael's. Her nose and mouth were small and twitchy as a rabbit.

"Humans?" she murmured, and wrinkled that delicate rabbit nose.

CHAPTER TWENTY-THREE

Annie

Annie stared at the small female devil. There was something Victorian about her—a girl who might be painted in her nightgown in an English garden, Wendy from Peter Pan. Except of course for the tarnished skin and leathery wings and red eyes.

She felt Trua tense up behind her. *Don't try anything stupid. Not like with Jomjael.*

The girl was holding a dark rag. She closed the wall panel carefully and stepped across the dais toward the throne. When she passed in front of Annie and Trua she turned with a puzzled look and sniffed the air again.

"Humans?"

So they were invisible to this one too. The girl peered into the distant corners of the hall, frowned, and continued over to the throne, which she started polishing with the rag.

She worked from the bottom up. One leg, then the other. Then on to the seat. Every so often she would spit on the rag to moisten it. She worked slowly, with detail and attention. Annie could have cleaned her entire apartment in the time this girl spent on the throne. When she reached the arms of the throne, she stepped back and looked at them critically. Wiped, spat, wiped. Looked again. Then she bent over and licked the arms, inch by inch. She worked slowly and deliberately from the front to the back, licking and polishing, soft dark tongue caressing hard gold. It was both sensual and horrific.

Annie shifted. The girl spun toward them.

"Who's there?" She narrowed her eyes. "I know you're there. Who are you?"

Annie steeled herself. This devil gave off a spray of cold and fear, but nowhere near as intense as Jomjael.

"Annie Maple. I'm here to see Satan."

"Why aren't you in the fire? Why can't I see you?"

"I was hoping Satan could answer that."

The girl stared in her direction with rage. Rage, and perhaps embarrassment. Annie wished they hadn't observed her at the throne. Trua's breathing quickened, and she touched his arm in caution.

"Begone." The girl devil waved the hand that wasn't holding the rag. "Go back to the fire."

"I want to see Satan."

"The Great Satan. Say it right."

"Great Satan. Now can I see him?"

"No. Now go. Back to the fire."

"No. I'm not leaving until I see him."

"Stupid human!" She stamped a delicate, clawed foot. "The Great Satan isn't seeing anybody. He's not taking audiences. Especially not with stupid dead humans."

"I'm sorry, but I'm not leaving until I see him."

"You think you're smart because I can't see you. But I'll catch you anyway. I'll catch you and tear off your stupid human limbs. Pull out your hair. See how you like that! And then throw you back in the fire. Now get out of here—"

Trua lunged. He launched himself up onto the dais and tackled the girl devil. Taken by surprise, she collapsed under him. He crouched with knees on her legs, hands on her arms. She heaved and strained and tried to flap her wings but they were pinned beneath her.

"Where is he?" Trua barked.

"No audiences," the girl devil began again in a somewhat choked voice.

"I said, WHERE IS HE." Trua pressed down more tightly. Veins bulged on the devil's neck.

"Trua!"

"WHERE IS HE."

"No audiences—"

"TELL US NOW."

The devil's eyes started to roll back in her head.

"Trua!" Annie grabbed for his arm, but he pushed her back.

"WHERE IS HE."

Which would be worse—if Trua killed the creature, or if it escaped to revenge itself on them? *Fucking Hun. Fucking barbarian.* She heard Isaias in her head. Trua was screwing everything up. He wouldn't listen to her. If he didn't let go they'd have a dead devil on their hands—

"The... third door. There. That door."

The devil sputtered the words. Trua relaxed his grip. The devil remained pinned, but he was no longer choking her.

He glanced up at Annie with a triumphant grin.

Fuck you. She glared at him. He was every man in history who had used bullying and torture to get his way. The Romans he claimed to detest. Crusaders, Stalinists, Nazis. The goddamn psychopaths in the canyon.

"Just great," she said. "Now what? Are you going to sit on her stomach for the rest of eternity?"

"No," he said stiffly. "Just until you get what you want. Go on."

He tilted his head toward the third door.

* * * * *

Annie stepped across the dais nervously. Confronting Satan had seemed daring back at the marsh but now it felt foolish. What if he obliterated her with one swipe of his wings? What if he cast her back in the fire forever?

Mary. She was doing this for Mary.

She pushed the door panel, but this one did not swing easily. She pushed again, harder, leaning her shoulder into it, and it budged despite itself, like a wooden back door swollen from years of rain. She was in the room. It was a windowless cube of a space like an oversized racquetball court. The walls and ceiling were entirely gold, covered with square gold panels sculpted in abstract bas-relief, any one of which would have been an outstanding museum treasure. The grand hall had been baroque but this was something more, the work of a mad metalsmith. It was relentless.

There, on the far side, was a figure.

Slightly larger than Jomjael, it slumped on its side on a bench of solid gold, perhaps sleeping. Annie made out a length of legs, an arm cushioning a head, folded wings. It carried the smeary green-black of silver that had sat in a basement for too long. She edged across the room.

"I'm here to see Satan."

Her words echoed off the gold walls. No response.

"Are you Satan?"

The creature didn't even twitch.

"Excuse me? Can you hear me? Hello?"

She inched closer. And now she could see that it truly was a body, ten feet long perhaps, a thick arm blocking its face, wings drooping behind its back. The skin was peeling in places, like after a bad sunburn. Bits of peeled skin lay on the floor below the creature's outstretched arm.

"Satan?"

Once Annie had come upon a rattlesnake sleeping in the sun in the middle of a hiking trail. She had jumped back, waited, then finally given up and returned the way she came. That was the safe response, the sane response.

"Satan. Hello?"

She reached out and touched the creature's shoulder. It emitted a low groan and she jerked away. Nothing else happened. She tapped it again.

"Ba...pho...met." The creature drew out the three syllables in a long, lugubrious complaint. It buried its head further under its arm. "Go... away."

"I'm not Baphomet. I'm Annie Maple. I need to talk to you."

"Go... away."

"No! I'm not leaving until you talk to me."

"Baphomet!" Louder now, imperious.

"Baphomet isn't coming. She's... busy. You have to talk to me."

The creature shifted its arm and lifted its head.

Her breath caught. He was stunning. His face was blotchy and peeling like the rest of his body, but the features were the most beautiful she had ever seen. Broad forehead, ruby eyes, slender nose with just enough of a bump to convince you of its solidity and power. Waves of dark hair crashing like breakers. It was a face you would follow into battle. Into bed. She thought of classical sculptures, of Michelangelo's David. And thinking of the David, she felt a compulsion to see the rest of his body.

The creature peered in the direction of her voice. For a moment the ruby eyes flashed. She froze. But his curiosity lasted only that moment. His head dropped back down.

"Go away."

"Not until you help me!"

He gave out a testy groan but didn't look up. Annie needed to see that face again. Part of her no longer cared about freeing Mary or going home. It just wanted to see that face.

"I'm offering my soul."

No response.

"Don't you want my soul?"

He lifted his head ever so slightly and called out with another groan. "Baphomet!"

"I thought you were supposed to buy souls!"

The creature just lay there with its head buried. Wasn't the devil supposed to be a wily trickster? A celestial used-car salesman with a caffeine-buzz of evil energy? Annie had imagined Al Pacino, Jack Nicholson, Mick Jagger. The Joker in the Batman movies. Not this beautiful, inert mess.

Maybe this was a bargaining strategy, like walking away from a vendor at a flea market. Well, she'd call his bluff.

"Okay, then. No soul for you. I'll be going."

She paused and took a step toward the door. He wasn't stirring or even watching her.

A few more steps. No response.

"I'm going."

Still nothing. Of course Satan didn't covet her soul. What had she done that was worth coveting? She was the tepid washcloth, the supermarket potato salad. Ultimate humilation: she wasn't worth the Devil's time. Maybe she wasn't even worth punishment by Hellfire, which would account for why she wasn't burning in the lake like those billions of others, like she deserved—

A loud crash. Sounds of scuffling.

The door to the great hall lurched open and Baphomet flew in, wings heaving while she dragged Trua by his feet.

"Stupid humans!" she panted. She hung in the air, flapping and dangling Trua, who was struggling to reach up and grab her. "I told them no audiences. I told them! But they wouldn't listen. I tried!"

"Shut up," Satan said. He pulled himself to a sitting position. Annie reeled with the size and majesty of his body, even with that weird peeling skin thing. His legs and arms were as muscled as an Olympic athlete. His leathery wings, still folded, were four times the size of Baphomet's.

"Drop the human and stop the goddamned flapping, you'll bust your ulna."

Baphomet released Trua's feet and he slammed onto the ground.

"You." Satan turned to Trua. "Just stay there. I may not be able to see you, but I can smell you. What are you, Mongol? Ostrogoth? Alamanii?"

"Hun," Trua said huffily, standing up and straightening his vest.

"Right. Horses and whores. I won a dozen of your chieftains in one evening once. They were more excited by the horses than by the whores."

"My tribesmen never—"

"Don't bother. Your denials don't matter to anyone. The amusing thing was they never knew who I was. They thought I was a Roman emissary. Then I crossed the river and played the same game with the Romans."

"You're the wizard who brought me here!" Trua's face lit up with comprehension.

"No, no, no. Not a wizard. *Devil.* Don't you get that?" Satan looked at Baphomet. "This is what's so tiring about pagans. They have no clue. Billions of them, all clueless."

He turned back to Trua. "You're dead, sonny Hun. Not under a wizard's spell. Just plain dead. And I am the king of the underworld. Bow to me."

Trua stood there. "Bow," Annie whispered.

"Oh, never mind," Satan said, waving his hand. "No bows. Who's watching? Just you, me, and the ever loyal Baphomet. You can call her Bathmat if you want. She answers to that too." The girl devil twitched her wings but didn't move.

"Well, then, off with you," Satan continued to both of them. "You've had your audience with royalty. Your Bible Moment wrestling with an angel. So back to the fire with whatever obliging devil took you out of it. Bathmat, show them out."

He nodded toward the door. Then he lay back down on the bench, his face turned to the wall.

"No!" Annie ducked as Baphomet groped blindly for her. "We're not going. And we weren't in the fire. I mean—we were before, but we got out. On our own. Not by some devil."

Satan jerked himself upright. He peered toward Annie's voice with sudden interest. His ruby eyes flashed again—probing, challenging—and the room felt suddenly electric.

"You got out of the fire?"

"Yes."

"And I can't see you. Bathmat, can you see them?

"No, master."

"Leave them," he said to Baphomet. "Actually, leave altogether. I'll call you when I want you."

"Master—"

"Leave."

The girl devil bowed her head and flew out, closing the door behind her.

"Escaped from the fire. Now that is something new." He spoke musingly to himself, then peered in their direction. "How is it that you're not in the fire? And invisible?"

Annie felt a surge of hope. Was it possible the ruler of Hell didn't know humans could be released from the fire? Maybe that meant her baby could also be released. Maybe this was all a big mistake and she could go home.

"You," Satan said again. "You're invisible, not mute. I asked a question. How did you get out of the fire?"

"I don't know. I was burning, and then all of a sudden I wasn't. I keep having flashbacks. It feels like I'm back in the fire, but then I snap out of it."

"Are there others like you?"

She nodded, then remembered he couldn't see her. "Yes."

"How many?"

"Why do you want to know?"

"Miss Maple Tree. You've got this all wrong. I'm the one who asks questions here. Not you. How many others?"

"Not unless you agree to help me."

"Oh, Miss Maple Tree." Satan drawled this out, sounding tired. "I'll admit there was a time when it amused me to make bargains with humans. But that was centuries ago. *Maintenant ça ne m'amuse pas.*"

“What does amuse you then?”

“Not very much. In fact, nothing. *What has been will be again, what has been done will be done again. There is nothing new under the sun.* I bet you didn’t know I wrote that. Well, whispered it to Mar Kohelet. Back when I was still making deals.”

“Except we’re new.”

“Yes, you are. And a most curious thing it is too.”

Satan leaned back against the golden wall. Idly he picked at the peeling skin on his arm and let the flakes drop to the floor.

“So what have you been doing? Wandering around the underworld? Waiting for your Virgil? Hunting for your Persephone?”

“I—”

He waved her off. “You don’t even know your own mythology. Such a sad species.” Abruptly he leaned forward. Cold fear knifed through Annie. “Who brought you to Pandaemonium?”

“Pande—?”

“Here. My palace.”

“Jomjael.” The name came out quickly, almost automatically. Annie seemed to have lost the power to withhold information.

“Jom-ja-el.” Satan repeated the name, drawing it out in contempt. “That is one poor devil. You know what his role was in Heaven? He cleaned spittle out of the trumpets. Yes, even angelic trumpets get slick with spit. Jomjael went around with a heavenly washcloth mopping up so Israfel and his bandmates wouldn’t get their feathers dirty. He was supposed to be proud of that. It was an honor. Now he’s here, free of that degradation, and somehow he's taken it into his head that it genuinely was an honor. I sent him on one mission to Moab and he thinks he's the emperor of Mesopotamia. Feh."

The beautiful mouth curved down in a sneer.

"So he brought you. But you claim he didn't pluck you out of the fire. You popped out on your own. Poof! Like fat little kernels of popcorn!"

Annie nodded. Trua shifted in place, probably not thrilled with being compared to popcorn, if he even knew what popcorn was. But it wasn't a bad metaphor. She remembered the feeling of dislocation, rupture, then waking on the black desert gravel.

"Do you... know how it happened?" she said cautiously.

"Ay, there's the rub." Satan gave an ironic smile. "It's not supposed to happen. Hasn't happened. Six thousand years of humans and it's never happened. Not once. There was the Harrowing but that was different."

He leaned forward and peered in her direction. Her insides went cold again.

"You weren't sent by Jesus, were you? Are you saints or apostles or something?"

"Hardly."

"Well, no matter then. Nothing you do makes any difference. Now go."

He lay back down, rolled to face the wall, and wrapped his wings over himself like a shroud. He gave off a sense of vague dissolution, like he might drip down off the bench and into the ground.

"No!" Annie said. She needed answers. She needed to save Mary. She needed to get home.

She needed to see that beautiful face again.

"Come back! You're the ruler of Hell! You can't just ignore us like this!"

The heavy door rasped open and Baphomet flew back in.

No. This had been her best chance to save Mary. Without Satan's help, she didn't know what to do. Without his help, she was lost.

"Please! You've got to help us—"

Baphomet hovered overhead. Trua raked the air, trying to grab her, but she hung just out of his reach, listening, gauging their location.

"Out! He said 'out!'" Baphomet cried.

She lunged for Annie and Trua's arms and dragged them out of the Devil's chamber.

CHAPTER TWENTY-FOUR

Baphomet

Eons ago Baphomet had been an angel. Like all of them.

Her job was gathering flowers for garlands. Flowers grew everywhere in Heaven, so it wasn't hard finding them. The secret was in the mindfulness. Every blossom you picked was an offering to God, a testament to the beauty of His creation. So you couldn't pick them lightly or carelessly. You couldn't just toss them in a basket and run down a hill with your arms akimbo and hair streaming and flowers falling out every which way. You had to notice each petal. Each stamen. Each vein on each leaf, and how it connected to the larger vein down the middle. You had to set it in the basket with reverence, as if this were the only flower in the history of the universe. And you only picked certain flowers—the whitest ones, creamiest ones, laciest ones. Of course there was nothing wrong with colored flowers or ones with missing petals—God had created every flower, every piece of Heaven—but these were for *garlands*. The goal was symmetry, smoothness, consistency. Nothing that would distract from the angels' tranquility as they contemplated God and the miracle of creation.

Baphomet loved her job. Her delicate fingers were perfect for reaching into a leafy mound and pinching off the tenderest, smoothest stem. Her hands were as smooth and flawless as the flowers. Sometimes she even imagined herself as a flower, set into a massive garland encircling the head of God himself.

Pride. Perhaps that was where it started.

No, that wasn't the start. She had been content for millennia, gathering calla lilies and baby's breath and presenting them to Ambriel and Paschar to weave into circlets.

The start was, as always, with Lucifer. The beginning and end. The endless middle. Always Lucifer.

Morning star. Light bearer. Son of the morning. You could see God's radiance in Lucifer's silver face. All the angels were a glistening silver, but Lucifer was brilliant in all senses of the word. No other angel held so much of God's love; no other angel exuded such life and creativity and joy. Lucifer winged overhead and fields of daisies turned their single yellow eyes to follow. Rainbows bent their arc to be closer to him.

That was all it had been for eons, occasional flyover glimpses, and then he landed in her field.

"So pretty," he said, reaching into her basket for a lily.

She felt violated. No one had ever reached into her basket before.

He held the sleek green stem up and twirled it in his fingers. "So pretty," he repeated, and she suddenly understood he was speaking about her.

Her flat nymphet stomach. Soft thighs. The nubs on her chest that would never grow into breasts. The moist place between her legs.

Baphomet hadn't ever known she had a moist place between her legs. That nubs had a possibility of becoming breasts.

She wanted to hurl herself into his arms, kiss him, be swallowed up by him, make love to him.

"Only white?" he said, still twirling the lily.

"Yes. No," she stammered. "They're for garlands. They've got to be white."

He shook his head, bent down, and pulled a branch of brown thorns from a low thicket. She had always skirted the thicket: no white blooms, useless for garlands. He reached for her hand and guided it so the pillow of her index finger was touching the tip of the thorn.

"Press," he said. He didn't do it. He let her do it. The thorn was sharp against her skin. It felt intense, questioning, alive. Electric signals ran up her arm. She was more aware of that thorn than of any petal she had ever picked.

It was the first time she had felt pain.

"Harmony is beautiful, but so is dissonance," he murmured. "Flaws. Blemishes. The rough. The rude." He guided her hand further along the branch, not on the thorns now but along the bumpy, peeling bark. "Feel it. Texture. Contrast. Change. Don't you deserve to change? Don't you deserve to choose your own flowers?"

Baphomet couldn't speak. There was too much to say, too much to desire. The textured branch felt like a living creature in her palm. Every scratch, every node had a story. Lucifer let her hand fall but she snatched the branch from him and pressed her finger down on a thorn, pressed as hard as she could, and watched as a silver globe of blood welled up from the point. Lucifer took her finger to his mouth and sucked the blood away. His tongue was soft and yielding.

Then he left.

Through the great rebellion, through the defeat, through everything that had happened since, she had stayed with him.

* * * * *

And now, on top of everything else, there were these two trespassing humans.

She couldn't see them but she hated them. Was it possible to hate something that you couldn't see? Of course it was. She hated God and she had never seen God. Or maybe she had seen Him long ago and couldn't remember.

It had been a very long time.

Never mind. She couldn't see these humans but she felt them struggling in her grip. She hated that they had surprised her. What good was a gatekeeper who couldn't tell when someone had entered the palace? She hated the humiliation of being tackled by the human man. Most of all, she hated being sent away while Satan spoke privately with the two of them. Mere humans! Who by all rights should be in the fire! Who probably worshipped God and reviled the Devil and were here only to try and wheedle some favor out of him. While she, who had stood by him all these long eons, who—sad but true—was the only one still standing by him, was brushed away like a pile of dust.

She did a little rise-and-fall maneuver while flying so the two humans thumped against the floor of the palace.

Almost out the door. Good riddance. They were presumptuous and stupid and heavy. She didn't want to drag them a foot more than necessary.

Baphomet shouldered open the palace door and dumped her load on the portico. The muscles in her arms and wings burned.

"Go now," she said. "Off with you."

She heard them stirring. No footsteps, though.

"The Great Satan said go. You need to *go*!"

Still no footsteps. It was maddening not to see them. She ignored her sore wings and flapped back up into the air so the man couldn't tackle her again.

"Where are we supposed to go?" This was the woman's voice, beseeching. "We don't know how to get home. We have no idea where we are."

"The Great Satan said begone. You must go."

"The Great Satan treated us like guests. He granted us an audience. This isn't how you treat a guest."

"You're not guests. You're intruders. Begone."

"You don't get many guests here these days, do you?"

Baphomet fell silent. There had been a time when the great hall of Pandaemonium was crowded with cheering, carousing devils. Singing and dancing, flirtation and orgy. Generals and lieutenants filled the back rooms, devising new plagues on humankind, plotting a reprise of the Great Rebellion. She used to have to fend off the supplicants: too many devils seeking Satan's time, too many seeking his advice.

Back then she truly was a gatekeeper. Back then he truly was the Great Satan.

"We don't," she acknowledged stiffly.

More sounds of the humans shifting. Sitting down? Settling in?

"Can you tell me what happened?"

The woman's voice was warm with concern. Baphomet hadn't had anyone speak to her with warmth in eons. In fact, it had been a very long time since anyone had said anything to her other than "Go away."

No one was here. No one was coming. No one would see.

She hovered uncertainly for a minute, then settled on the veranda and told the woman what had happened.

* * * * *

The millennia after humans were expelled from Eden had been a golden age for Satan. He and his agents traveled the globe instigating fratricide here, genocide there. Plagues. Greed. Idolatry. Betrayal. The most casual cruelty was as sweet as the largest slaughter, maybe sweeter: with a single small sin you could take the time to watch despair and doubt colonize the faces of one-time believers.

The generals urged a new assault on Heaven. Baphomet listened behind a cracked door as Satan counseled patience. Their forces were massing. Every human sinner ended up in Hell, and the souls under demonic rule grew to millions and millions. They became experts in tormenting those souls—toying with them in the fire, or plucking them out for slave labor in mines and smelteries.

Of course, then came Christ. First he resisted Satan's seduction in the desert. Then the Harrowing. Baphomet had stood beneath the columns of Pandaemonium together with hundreds of other rank-and-file devils, staring as God's human-looking son walked across the lake of fire, every so often reaching down and pulling a figure out of the flames. The line behind the fire-walker grew longer and longer, a silent conga line dancing its jubilant way across the sea. Warrior devils dive-bombed them to no avail. Satan himself flapped down in front of Jesus to block the path. But Jesus waved an arm and Satan was swept aside like a scrap of parchment in a hot dry breeze.

Perhaps that was the start of it. Satan continued his forays to Earth for centuries, but they became increasingly lackluster. Other devils began grumbling that the final conflict might never take place, that perhaps Satan had lost his nerve.

Satan started talking strangely.

"Not making sense. Not like the master I used to know," Baphomet said to the invisible human woman. There was an unexpected freedom in talking to someone you couldn't see. She didn't have to know if this woman were condemning her or mocking her or—worst of all—mocking Satan.

Satan started saying it was pointless to tempt humanity, since they had become so expert at tempting themselves. There was no longer any challenge in it, no longer any fun. Baphomet reminded him that evil was always an art. He had taught her that himself: whether inserting thorns into garlands or spreading plague, it was all in the style. The elegance. The freely-made choices. And he listened, sometimes. He did some beautiful things—the Crusades, the black death, convincing the Aztec king that the pathetic Spanish captain was a god. The exchange of syphilis for smallpox had been lovely, so symmetrical. But then he would return to the strange talk.

He declared there was no point in tormenting human souls in the lake of fire. If you tormented sinners, you were just fulfilling God's will. God *wanted* them in the fire, suffering.

"If we don't torment, we're being merciful," he would say. "If we do torment, we're being God's lackeys. Is this why we rebelled? Is this why we shed angelic blood? Have we spent ten millennia in exile just to be prison guards for God?"

Baphomet tried to argue but she was never good with words. The generals argued for a while but then drifted away. Satan concluded there was nothing he could do that was not a fulfillment of God's will. So he opted to do nothing. He lay there in his chamber, brooding and picking at his beautiful, tarnished skin. He stopped making forays to Earth. He stopped attending councils and orgies.

The great hall emptied out. The hordes of Hell abandoned the clifftop palace and built new places to gather. Satan didn't care. He didn't want to see anyone. "They can all go to Hell," he said without even a smile—him, whose laugh used to ring like silver bells across all of Heaven.

And then he wanted to die.

Baphomet had to force the words out. Her wings drooped and she sank her head into her hands.

"Isn't he immortal?" the human woman asked cautiously.

"Yes! Yes! I think. I don't know!"

Angels were certainly immortal. And she had never known a devil to die. She'd seen many angels and devils wounded during the great rebellion—wings slashed, limbs lost, eyes gouged—and none had died.

But Satan tried. A while ago, maybe a century. He had a sword of angelic quicksilver hidden away, left over from the great battle.

"Baphomet," he said. "Take this and run me through."

She refused.

"Do it,' he said.

"No, no, no, Master!' she said.

"Then just hold it," he said, "and I will do it myself."

He made her hold it. He wrapped her small hand around the heavy hilt. He wedged her against the wall, and made her hold it out straight in front of her, and she felt violated in a way that was completely different than when he pulled that lily from her basket long ago.

Baphomet was sobbing now. Lost in memories, she had forgotten all about the human woman.

"No, no, no," she had told Satan, sobbing back then too, even though she knew how much he despised tears. He didn't listen, just backed far away in the empty palace, and then came flying at her, like lightning, like a comet. She was so small and he was so great, and he hurled himself onto the sword with such fury that her wings crumpled against the wall. He was on the sword; the sword went all the way though him, and Baphomet was crying "no no no"—she was screaming, she was so frightened—but it didn't kill him, it didn't even hurt him, and he just stepped back and looked at the shimmering blade sticking out from his chest and pulled it out and threw it down.

Baphomet took the sword and hid it so that he would never find it again, and so the other devils wouldn't suspect what he had tried to do.

Satan never looked for it, though. He retreated to his chamber and lay there and picked at his skin and told Baphomet to leave him alone.

The other devils never suspected, either, because none bothered coming to the palace anymore.

* * * * *

Baphomet's body shook. She didn't care who saw. She had been holding back these tears for centuries.

It felt good. Not good like a smile from Satan, not even good like the metallic taste of his throne on her tongue, but better than waiting in silence in the empty palace. She felt like she could cry for another two centuries. In fact, she might just do that—

A warm hand touched her arm. It might as well have been a burning brand.

Baphomet leapt into the air, flapping wildly.

"I'm so sorry...."

The voice gentle. Caring. Infuriating. Baphomet pumped her wings in rage. How dare she! Being "sorry." Saying she "understood." Trying to "comfort." All those meaningless human words.

Let her go to the fire. She understood nothing.

Stupid human. Presumptuous human. They deserved every plague ever brought upon them.

Baphomet flapped in a furious circle. She wanted to grab the woman and carry her to the deepest part of the lake of fire and hurl her in. But that would leave the human man here, and Satan unguarded.

She could grab the man and fly him out to the lake.

She didn't think she could carry them both at the same time.

For the thousandth time, she cursed her unfledged body. Thin arms and small wings that couldn't do a warrior's work. Nubs that, despite her rebellious embrace of free will and change, had never become breasts.

Then, through the static of rage, an idea coalesced.

"You, human," Baphomet said. She lowered herself onto the veranda. She steadied her breath and tried to remove all anger from her voice. She looked in the direction of that foul touch. She forced a smile.

"You want help? To return to Earth? To save your baby?"

"Yes!" the woman said.

So eager. So pathetic.

"There are cities built by other devils. Not as powerful as the Great Satan, but they could still help you. I will take you there, on one condition." She paused to give her words more impact. "Report on what you find. The leaders. The forces. The plans. Swear that you will report back."

"Thank you!" the woman cried.

"Swear it," Baphomet repeated. "You'll report back."

"I swear!" the woman said.

So grateful. So pathetic.

So doomed.

PART FIVE

City

CHAPTER TWENTY-FIVE

Trua

Trua went first. It was a long flight over multiple mountain ranges, and the girl demon hauled him like a stack of sheepskins, with no regard and no respect. She dropped him at the base of a ridge that looked like all the others and left to fetch Annie. Trua slumped against a rock, not even trying to hide himself from view.

You're dead, sonny Hun.

Satan's words had registered with him in a way that the fire, the desert, and even the other strange human beings here hadn't.

He wasn't under a wizard's spell. He was truly dead.

It was nothing like what he'd imagined.

From his earliest childhood, Trua had been told that people who died went to join their ancestors. It was at the core of every death ceremony he'd attended—his father, his uncle and aunts, his cousins. *They are gone from this world but they wait and watch over us in the next.* After death, great horsemen and warriors would be clad in gold and fur, feasting on kidneys and sweetbreads, but even the most lowly dung gatherer would have his own loaf of bread and a full saddle-pouch of mare's milk. The augurers said it and the chieftains repeated it and everyone knew it. The augurers described dream-visits to the ancestors where omens were revealed, and when his tribe followed the ancestors' counsel, they prospered.

It was all lies.

There were no ancestors, no counsel, no gods. Just fire and rock and demons.

The leaders of his tribe were either liars or fools. He didn't know which would be worse. Everything was pointless—prayers and sacrifices, defending the tribe, becoming a great horseman. It all came to nothing. To dust. To this.

He pressed his fingers into the gravel. The Christians were right. Or perhaps not: Annie and Billie were Christians and they'd ended up here. But that didn't matter. What mattered was that he was here, and he would be here forever, and everyone he knew would end up here too—his siblings, his cousins, his entire tribe. In the fire. Damla with her sisterly advice, always looking out for him. His brothers with their boasting and booty. In the fire. His young boy cousins learning to ride, or tiny Manka following her yellow goat around the camp. All in the fire.

Black, gaping hopelessness. Everything lost. Everything gone.

Flocks of birds falling dead from the sky.

Mouth full of ashes.

Trua slumped there for what felt like an age, rank with despair. The black rocks mocked him. The sulfurous, metallic air stung his nostrils. Then, at a certain point—above, away—he heard a labored flapping of wings. Baphomet descended and dropped Annie on the ground.

"The city's over there," the girl devil said in a low voice, gesturing beyond a ridge. "Now remember your oath. No tricks. Report back. Or else."

She flapped away, her tunic billowing.

* * * * *

"Let's pretend we're putting hiking boots on," Annie said perkily. "We've got a bit of a trek here."

Damn her. Damn her jokes about non-existent boots.

"Come on," she said. "Let's go."

He didn't look at Annie and he didn't move.

"Stop sulking already. Let's go."

Damn her cheerfulness. Didn't she understand they were dead, ruined, hopeless?

"Look, I know you're angry about Baphomet. But—"

Enough! Trua lunged upright, grabbed the largest rock within reach, and hurled it against the mountainside. Shrapnel flew in all directions. Annie jumped back.

"What—"

He picked up another rock and hurled it. He was not dust, not yet. He hurled another rock, and another.

"Trua!" She was glancing around, frightened that the noise would bring more demons. Well, let them come. Let them destroy him once and for all. He would take one or two of them along with him, he was sure of that. Shards of rock flew and clattered. The mountain echoed his rage. *Let them come.* But no demons came, and eventually Trua's arm grew tired.

He looked for Annie and saw her hanging back, out of range of the shattered rock. Her arms were wrapped around herself. Her eyes were wide with fear—not of the demons now, but of him.

The last of his rage seeped out and evaporated in the hot, sunless air. His hands hung limp and heavy at his sides.

"I'm sorry," Annie whispered. "I should have talked to you first. I should have checked with you before making the deal with Baphomet—"

Baphomet? The deal? Did she have no idea what he was thinking?

"I don't care about Baphomet," he said wearily.

"What then?"

He paused, unsure where to begin. His death on the olive farm in Syria? His life on the Great Plain? *You're dead, sonny Hun*?

"There wasn't any wizard's spell," he said.

* * * * *

The children in Trua's tribe learned to ride before they passed five winters. The smallest boys and girls shared older, docile horses that could no longer manage long forays across the plain. When their legs were long enough to reach stirrups, the boys chose a young stallion from the herd and made it their own.

Trua was ten years old when he rode out with his father to where the clan's hundreds of horses were grazing. The summer grasses were still green and feathered, rippling into silver with the wind.

"You want a square build, straight hind legs, heavy bone in the fetlocks," his father said. "Look for speed. Dominance. You want a horse who thinks he's king of the plain."

For days after that, from dawn until nightfall, Trua followed the herd. He'd pick a promising horse and, from afar, study its gait and behavior. Was it fast and strong? Did it hide in the center of the herd or was it willing to strike out on its own? Surveying the herd, his mind wandered down tangential paths. Where did horses come from? Were they all descended from a single stallion who'd been created by the gods? If so, why were there were so many different colors, sizes, and personalities? Did different gods create different kinds of horses? When Trua asked his father, the man just frowned. "The gods created horses when they created Huns," he said. "It was a long time ago, longer than anyone can remember. Now skin this rabbit. And take it to your sisters at the cookfire."

Finally Trua settled on a horse. It was dappled white upon grey, like the sky at the start of a snowstorm. It was tall and feisty and had a habit of wandering off from the herd to explore. Accompanied by his father, he returned with a rope. Together they circled the herd, closing in on the horse, and Trua ringed its neck with a single toss. It bucked and stamped and bared its teeth, but they led it back to their camp and tethered it to a wooden pole.

Over time, Trua got to know the horse. He'd never been so focused on anything in his life. He slept outside near the horse, missed meals because he was with the horse, even dreamed about the horse. It represented both an entry to manhood and access to the world beyond their camp. He told the horse secrets he wouldn't tell Damla. He knew its hot breath on his face before he'd started imagining the kisses of girls. He galloped across the plain for the sheer joy of it, human and horse breathing together loud and heavy as bellows. He learned to shoot from horseback, standing in the stirrups and bracing against its churning flanks as he pulled back the string of his bow, first toward the left side and then toward the right.

This was his life. The long mane whipping his chest. Grass bowing down beneath the two of them. Racing across the plain like a magical half-human, half-equine creature. Returning to his family's tents at dusk, the sky a deep rose and orange, his horse's coat crusty from dried sweat, little Manka running out to show him a baby rabbit she'd found near the spring.

All this—gone forever.

He didn't know how to explain it to Annie. So he told her about the famine, the ride south through the mountains to Syria, finding that farm.

Trua hesitated when he came to the part about killing the servant and the old man. They were strangers—not part of his clan, and not Huns. No one at home would have criticized him. But he sensed that Annie would disapprove.

She said nothing, though, and just stared at him with wide, moist eyes as he finished the story.

"So now I know that this is death," he said, "and my ancestors are in the fire, and everything my people believe is a lie."

CHAPTER TWENTY-SIX

Annie

They climbed the ridge in silence. Trua's story left Annie at a loss. He'd killed two innocent people. She should fear him; she should flee as soon as an opportunity presented itself. But as he was talking, she'd felt an urge to reach for his hand and bring it to her lips. Under the violence and anger he was like her, in mourning for his lost life and lost world.

Plus she needed him.

"Let's go," was all she said, and he nodded.

Weirdly, recounting the story of his death seemed to have lifted Trua's mood. He didn't look happy, but he threw his energy into the climb. From time to time he extended an arm to help Annie scramble up a steep embankment.

"How did *you* die?" he asked her at one of their rest stops.

She still couldn't remember. The orange street lamp in the fog, the buttercream doorway. And then a crowd. She had a vague memory of bodies jostling, drinking, dancing.

Yes. A crowded living room. That was new. Barely space to stand along the edges, pounding bass that was too loud, Beyoncé singing *All the Single Ladies* and Enrique Iglesias singing *Bailando*. How strange now to think of songs that made you want to drop everything and dance, to think of playlists and music videos and tweets from pop stars. Truly another world.

But that was all. Crowd, smoke, music.

She was a toddler whose bright plastic rattle was inches out of reach. If she could stretch just a little further, things would make sense. She would see reasons. She would see a path. She might be able to rescue Mary and atone for her sins and go home.

* * * * *

Annie reached the saddle first and stared. A city spread below them.

She'd expected some kind of camp—rough stone structures, rock piles, a devil version of the community in the crater. But this was a real city.

Black stone buildings formed a crowded maze that stretched most of the way across a wide plain. Streets and alleys wove among large barrack-like structures and smaller, tightly packed row houses. Far off, near the center, a black stone tower rose above a palace. Overall it had the close, chaotic layout of a medieval city—the Gothic quarter in Barcelona, or pre-fire London. A few columns of dark smoke rose skyward from within the walls, and in one distant spot orange flames fountained and shimmered.

"No." Trua shook his head in disapproval.

"We have to," she said.

"No," he repeated, but when she started down the side of the saddle, he followed.

* * * * *

Were they really invisible? She couldn't exactly run a test. Annie picked her way down the mountain, careful not to send rocks tumbling. There were so many chances to give yourself away—sounds of scuffing feet, footprints in the dust, even smell. Jomjael and Baphomet had smelled them. What did humans here smell like to devils—just the rank buildup of months or years without a bath? Or was there some telltale odor to even the cleanest human, like the scent of prey to a wolf?

The slope leveled into a plain. Ahead of them, distant, rose a high wall of black stone topped with iron pikes. Some of the pikes looked like upside-down crucifixes, their cross-arms low and crooked as if vandalized or neglected. Others were simple pointed spears embedded in the rock. *Please, God, no heads on pikes*, Annie thought and, almost as soon as she thought it, glimpsed something grey and tattered on a pike.

"We should go back," Trua muttered.

"Come on."

Far to the left, she saw what might be an opening in the wall. They moved silently past the pike with the tattered object. It was all flimsy folds and creases, like sheets of paper burned into grey ash. There, amidst the folds, was that a dark, eyeless socket? A crease of cinder or a gaping mouth?

Mary. She was doing this for Mary. "Keep going."

The opening stretched for perhaps thirty yards before the wall resumed. There were no guards and no gate. But what kind of wall could block winged creatures anyway? Perhaps the whole thing was for show, a statement of ownership and power. Inside the opening, black stone row-houses lined a dusty, unpaved street.

Trua halted, arms folded in stubborn resistance. "They could ambush us from any of those buildings."

"Don't come. I'll go by myself."

He shook his head. She wasn't sure if he were dismissing her decision to enter the city, or the offer to stay behind. But he followed her through the opening and into the street. No Billie anymore: she was leading. She felt an unexpected rush of exhilaration.

"Let's head for the palace. Baphomet said the devils in charge might help us."

No alarms. No ambush. They seemed unnoticed. The street formed an artificial canyon with dark, blocky walls. The buildings themselves were rough and unadorned, some windowless and others with one small upper unglassed window. The doors, though, were ornate—oversized iron panels embellished with tendrils of fire, daggers and shields, or the occasional bas-relief of a winged figure.

They crossed another street, then several alleys. Ahead, a rough flapping sound. Shock of cold. Annie lurched back against the wall. Two devils winged toward them—adults, large, one male and one female. Annie held her breath. The devils flew past, talking to each other, oblivious, and turned down one of the alleys.

So they were invisible after all. Her hands were shaking. They continued down the street. More flapping from behind and she lurched for shelter again: another devil flew by, too fast to get a good view.

Still more noise ahead, but not flapping now. This sounded like scuffing—layered scuffing, a thousand bedroom slippers—coming from the next intersection. She reached the corner and peered around.

Hundreds of wraithlike grey figures shuffled forward in a column. Gauzy and faceless, they looked like smoke and ash come to life. *That tattered thing impaled on the wall.* Some hauled chunks of stone on their shoulders, or where shoulders might have been amidst the shifting folds. Others hefted even bigger blocks in teams. Exhaustion weighed on them like chains.

Above the column, devils hovered with thick iron batons.

"Slaves," Trua whispered. "Like the girl demon said. Pulled from the fire."

It took a long time for the column to pass. They trailed at a distance, still hugging the walls. Ahead of them, a slave stumbled and dropped its block of stone, and a devil flew down to deliver a blow from its baton. Trua clenched his fists and Annie put a restraining hand on his shoulder. The column turned onto a wider street, this one paved with slabs of black rock instead of dust. The buildings became more ornate with gargoyles carved into the lintels and parapets. Far ahead, the street opened up into a plaza.

They'd reached the palace. It rose in the middle of the plaza, massive and black as Satan's hall but topped with black stone arches and a black stone dome. Two towers thrust skyward—a right one that was complete and a left, just in front of them, that was under construction.

Hammers pounded, chisels scraped, stone crashed against stone. The plaza was a hive of commotion after the empty streets. The slaves they'd been following added their stones to an already sizable pile, while other slaves chiseled them into rectangular blocks. Hundreds of slaves formed a line heaving the blocks up onto the palace wall and tower and scores more mortared them into place. It seemed impossible that such flimsy-looking creatures could be lifting those weights. Several devils flapped circles overhead, swooping down to prod the slaves and check the stones' alignment.

"No," Trua whispered tensely, and Annie turned to follow his gaze across the plaza.

There, beyond the construction area, hundreds of devils massed in military formation—iron swords clasped to chests, wings tight behind them, stepping and pivoting in formation. Two large devils on the palace steps commanded the lines with flaming torches like flagmen on an airport tarmac. It was hard to say if they were training for war or for display: would a devil army really need 19th-century marching drills? The commanders raised their torches and the lines of devils shot up into the sky.

They hung there, a thundercloud of wings and limbs, and Annie was slammed with cold, paralyzing fear. *They were the sky, the air, the very air in your lungs, they were above and around and everywhere, and you were the small lone rabbit in a field—*

The commanders lowered their torches and the devils plunged back into their tight-winged marching formation. Annie's stomach pitted. These creatures wouldn't help. Finding aid in this city was an utter fantasy.

"We should go," Trua murmured.

In the construction area, the slave column finished depositing its stones and began filing out of the plaza.

"We promised Baphomet we'd report back," Annie whispered. "We need to see what they're doing."

* * * * *

They inched their way along the plaza's perimeter closer to the troops.

Like Satan and Jomjael, these devils had tarnished, blotchy skin and leathery wings. Some clearly took pains with their appearance—hair styled with iron clips, wings trimmed to precise points. Others looked wild as gorgons. Had all these creatures once been angels? She searched for remnants of holiness in their faces but had no idea what holiness would look like. Instead she saw familiar human features intensified, like a car stereo turned up to the point of distortion. One female demon at the edge of the formation had the prominent cheekbones and high forehead of a supermodel, flawless skin stretched taut with condescension around her glittering eyes. Nearby a male demon juddered, unable to hold still even during breaks in the maneuvers, mouth constantly chewing some imagined food, saliva dropping from blistered lips.

Turn. March. Turn back. Halt.

Hundreds of clawed feet clicked on the plaza's stone in unison.

"Like a Roman legion," Trua murmured.

They doubled back toward the construction area. Two wraith slaves struggled to move a particularly large block off the rock pile. One lost its grip and tumbled backward. A devil overseer flew down, slamming a baton into the slave's gut. Annie glanced a warning at Trua: *Don't get involved, don't get us in trouble—*

The sky burst into fire.

Clumps of flame hurtled down like missiles. The parade-ground devils exploded into flight, streaking skyward toward the source of the fireballs. And now Annie saw the source—more devils, a flock of them, flapping high over the city, some bearing iron kettles of fire, others with giant iron crossbows and flaming arrows. The parade-ground devils hurled themselves at the first line of attackers, pinwheeling with them through the sky, flames shooting up and down and everywhere. A clump of fire hit some slaves mortaring the palace wall and they plummeted in flames from their ledge. Fireballs pocked the plaza, ricocheted off walls. Slaves scattered and ran; one devil overseer pursued them but the others lunged into the fray. In the sky, more archer devils massed forward with yet more fireballs. The two commanders on the steps of the palace dropped their torches and took wing, frantically corraling and reorganizing their troops. Several slaves sprinting away from the palace practically ran into Annie and Trua. They halted, dark eyes staring from within folds of grey. "You're... alive?" one whispered. The others spun and fled, and it followed. A fireball hit the ground some ten feet away. Annie dove and covered her head while burning shrapnel careened around her. Up in the sky, both groups of devils had brought in reinforcements and were grappling in pairs and small groups. There was a horrible balletic beauty to it. Somewhere in the distance she heard trumpets. "Away," Trua whispered and they crept along the wall toward the nearest alley. A devil crashed to the ground, sword clattering across stones, muddy-looking blood gushing from its neck and chest, but it reached for the sword as smoothly as a child grabbing an out-of-bounds soccer ball and flew back up into the battle. Finally they reached the alley and snuck around the corner, where a wraith-slave cowered. Same one or different? They all looked like sheets of ash about to crumble.

"Come with us," Trua said roughly, reaching out a hand, but the slave recoiled. Its eyes were wide with terror. Dark strands—*hair? veins? charred bits?*—floated in the grey.

"Not the fire. No fire. No fire."

"Come with us. Out of here."

"No fire. No fire."

"Come on!"

Trua grabbed for it roughly but it pushed him off and shrieked—"No fire! No fire! No fire!"—and ran back into the melee of the plaza.

"Watch out!" A fireball slammed into stone a few feet away. The impact lifted Trua up and hurled him across the alley. Annie swatted hot embers off her chest. Out in the plaza she heard more trumpets and saw a fireball heading toward the roof of the palace. Trua lay sprawled against the wall but she yanked him up and pulled him through the alley, dim as twilight after the brilliant explosions of the plaza.

They ran until she was out of breath. Then they walked. Trua's right leg dragged. She was hauling much of his weight. It was a narrow side street, no ornate facades here, just thick black walls and iron doors. Above the roof line, streaks of fire blazed. Trua seemed delirious. "They're following us," he kept muttering, looking wildly around. "Behind us. They're coming."

Annie peered but saw no one. "Keep going," she whispered, but he grew heavier and heavier on her arm. Finally she couldn't pull him any further. She looked around for shelter—rock? hole? deep doorway?—but found nothing. "Wait here," she said while Trua slid to the ground, mumbling, oblivious. She ran toward the next intersection but heard heavy, rushed flapping. She ran back to Trua. There was a plain iron door a few yards ahead of them.

She pushed it, trying not to think about what might be inside, and it opened.

CHAPTER TWENTY-SEVEN

Annie

It was a dark, empty room—nothing more.

Annie dragged Trua inside. The walls and floor were stone. Grey light trickled through a paneless window near the roof. It could be a stable, a jail, a bunker. All that mattered was that it was empty.

Trua was in a bad way. The fireball had seared his left side, and his right side had been abraded when he was thrown across the alley. Everything was swollen and raw. She touched his forehead and it felt hot. Infection? How ironic if the only living creatures in Hell turned out to be bacteria.

She had no soap, no water, nothing with which to clean the wounds or make bandages. Not even a pillow. She shifted Trua, limp, onto his back to keep the raw areas out of the dirt and tried picking gravel out of his wounds. He moaned, eyes closed. *Get better,* she thought. *Don't die. Get better.*

His body spasmed and his eyes rolled up into his head. She knew at once: the fire.

"Come back," she whispered. But then she started to feel dizzy too. The room, already in shadow, grew darker. Flashes of orange. *No. Not both of us.* Think of Mary. Stay alive for Mary. Stay alive for Trua.

The world around her was melting into flame. Dark and flame. *Help me, Jesus. Help me, God.* Flame devouring. Flame conquering. Think of Steep Ravine. Green ferns, green canopy, rushing cool water. Think of Mary. Her daughter on that trail someday, small feet clambering over rocks, toes in icy water, muddy sneakers and a Hello Kitty backpack. Show her the blue petals of forget-me-nots in the spring. Sneaky cheerful shoots of young poison oak: *Leaves of three, let it be.* Pockmarked tree trunk where acorn woodpeckers hoard their harvest—

The flames receded. The dark lifted. Annie was back in the empty stone room with its small window and weak light. She exhaled. Her body felt limp and spongy, as if all the bones had been sucked out of it. She was still here.

But Trua wasn't.

He lay motionless, stiff, eyes lost in his head, a thin line of spittle trailing from a corner of his mouth. He wasn't choking or convulsing. Nothing seemed immediately life-threatening, yet he wasn't there.

Annie waited beside him. Time passed. He remained unconscious, gone. Annie sat, and when she couldn't sit any longer, stood up and paced the room, sat down, stood up, paced some more. *Please wake up.* She didn't know if ten hours passed or ten days. This must have been how Trua had felt by the marsh, watching her, waiting, not knowing if the wait might go on forever.

And what if it lasted forever? It would be like dying a second death. Was that what had happened to the old woman killed by the marauders? Had Trua escaped the fire only to plunge back in for eternity?

She touched his forehead: still hot. She stroked it with a vain hope of cooling him down. She ran her fingers over his scars. One for his tribe leader, one for his father. If he died, should she gouge a scar in her own cheek? As a way to remember him? A way not to be alone?

Because if he died, she would be alone. Stranded in this city of devils and wraiths. There would be no one with whom she could talk, no one to help her distinguish one moment from the next, no one to assure her that the universe wasn't one big illusion.

She'd lose her mind. It seemed certain. She'd be talking to herself within days and hallucinating within weeks. She might beg to become one of those slaves. She might beg to go back in the fire.

She took his hand and held it to her cheek. She didn't care how many Syrian farmers he'd killed.

Stay with me. Please, please stay with me.

At least Trua had been honest with her about those killings at the farm. While she had never told him the truth about her cowardice at the canyon.

Stay with me.

Maybe some part of him could hear her through the fire. "You thought I was a sorceress," she whispered. "I wish I were. I'd cast a spell and bring you back. I'd make a potion to take us out of here. You could come to San Francisco with me. I'd show you how to drive a car and use a microwave. You'd learn the difference between motor oil and olive oil. Okay, we might have a couple of bad salads at first, but you're a smart guy. You'd learn. I just need you to come back. I'm not a sorceress, so you'll have to do it yourself. Come back, okay? Will you come back?"

Outside, the street was silent. The explosions and trumpets had stopped. Someone had won the battle, or they'd all destroyed each other, or they'd reached a stalemate. Annie had no idea who was fighting and what it meant.

"Come back," she whispered in the silence.

* * * * *

Annie had been in constant motion since the marsh. Now, sitting in the still and empty room, doubt caught up with her. What if Mary weren't real? What if the voices at the marsh were only in her head?

It was possible. Trua hadn't heard Mary's voice. Ben would say she'd imagined it. If so, this was all her fault. Trua was back in the fire—maybe forever—because she was chasing a chimera.

She paced. Her agitation needed a physical outlet. This was how it would start: doubt Mary, then doubt her own senses. No. Don't take that road. Annie made an arbitrary, deliberate decision to trust herself, perhaps for the first time ever. It felt like a leap into empty air. Strangely, it calmed her.

She returned to Trua's side and sat down. "I'm so sorry this happened to you," she whispered.

She didn't say, but thought: *I'm not sorry about trying to save Mary.*

* * * * *

His forehead cooled.

At first she assumed it was wishful thinking. She removed her hand, wiped the perspiration on her skirt, and replaced it. He was in fact slightly cooler. Her heart lifted.

"You can do it," she said. "You're doing great. Keep going. You're going to be okay."

Gradually his body relaxed. Legs twitched, arms shifted. His eyes rolled back down and became normal sleeping eyes. He shifted to one side, landed on one of his wounds, and jerked back in the other direction. "Yes, it hurts!" she exclaimed. "That's good. Normal hurt. You're alive. That's part of being alive. You're going to be okay."

After a long time he opened his eyes and pushed himself up to a sitting position. He looked confused. He stared as if she were a stranger.

"I was..." he began but stalled.

She had no idea what to say. She'd felt so connected to him when he was in the fire, but now a gap had reopened between them.

"Was it bad?" Stupid question. Of course it was.

He looked down for a long time before answering. "Each time it feels like I could be there forever. The next time, I might be."

Annie nodded. She was about to say something encouraging, like maybe there wouldn't be a next time, but that was bullshit. It was something she would have said back when she was alive.

"Yes," she said. "You might be."

He recognized her now. In the dim light, his eyes were full and bright. She wanted to kiss him. Was that crazy? He had killed two innocent people. Hell was unmooring her. He touched the crusty burned area on his side and winced.

"Trua?"

Annie leaned forward, careful not to scrape his wounds, and gently touched his cheek. She prepared herself to be pushed away—*too fat, too forward, was there a Hunnic word for slut?*—but there was no resistance. She leaned still closer and shut her eyes and put her lips on his, and felt them respond, full and firm and warm—

Nausea swamped her and hurled her backward. She collapsed on the floor in dry heaves.

Her head felt like someone was hammering it from the inside. She couldn't stop vomiting even though nothing was coming up. Trua, too, was splayed on all fours, hacking and heaving.

She coughed a thin trickle of spit onto the floor. Her throat was raw. Her innards were cramping. Like getting shitfaced in high school, only worse. Was it Billie who had talked about this? Or Isaias, back at the crater? *The problem with intimacy here in Hell.* She had forgotten. You could have sex in this miserable place, but only without love. Now she knew why.

The heaves subsided. Her intestines straightened themselves out. She felt drained and queasy. And embarrassed.

"I'm sorry," she said in a croak, her throat still sore. She couldn't look Trua in the eye.

He pulled himself gingerly into a sitting position. One of his wounds had re-opened and was oozing blood. He probed the edges with his fingers and tried to press it closed.

"We need to leave this city," Trua said stiffly.

CHAPTER TWENTY-EIGHT

Annie

It took a while to move on. Each time Trua tried standing, his knees buckled. "Take it slow. Just rest," Annie said, but he looked disgusted. With himself? With her? Neither of them said anything about the kiss. *Was there a Hunnic word for idiot?* If she didn't bring it up, maybe Trua would forget the entire incident and they could continue on as sturdy, uncomplicated allies.

Finally he could stand and walk. Annie peered out the iron door. They'd fled the plaza in such a panic that she had no idea where they were. She vaguely remembered coming from the right, so they went left. Every so often a devil flapped past, and once a devil landed behind them and entered a house, but otherwise the street was deserted. After a while, Trua touched her shoulder.

"We're being followed," he whispered.

She looked back. Trua had babbled about being followed when they were fleeing the fireballs. He'd been delirious then.

"I don't see anyone."

"Someone's there."

She should have made him rest longer. Maybe they could find another empty house where he could lie down for a while. She glanced over her shoulder again—still no one—and kept going.

They reached an intersection with one alley to the left and two others veering right. How many years had it had taken slaves to build this city, every stone hauled and hoisted by hand? Back in San Francisco, downtown skyscrapers rose magically from an alchemical brew of tech money and earth-moving equipment. One month you'd walk past funky old warehouses. The next month—or so it seemed—there would be a gleaming, glass-walled apartment tower with rents that were twice Annie's monthly salary.

Her boss's condo was in a building like that. The living room and kitchen formed one vast room, broken by an island with a restaurant-quality range. Floor-to-ceiling windows overlooked the lights of the Bay Bridge. There was a swimming pool on the roof and a health club on the second floor and a room on some other floor with a giant screen where residents could hold private movie showings.

Annie couldn't remember what floor her boss's condo was on.

She had house-sat there for three weeks last year while her boss traveled with the oceanographers. Woke up there every morning, came home there every night. She had run her fingers over the granite countertops, opened and closed the frictionless cabinets, lamented that she would never be able to live anywhere like that. Now she couldn't remember what floor it was on.

Her cheeks tightened. Her pulse raced. What else had she forgotten? If she stayed here long enough, would she forget her entire life?

"They're following us," Trua repeated in an urgent whisper.

"No one's there!" she snapped, and immediately regretted it. He was still disoriented. Maybe he too was forgetting things. She put a finger to her lips and beckoned Trua to keep going.

More turns in the alley. More forks. Shouldn't they be at the city walls by now? Every damn street looked the same.

The man appeared out of nowhere.

Annie nearly screamed. Trua leapt into a fighting stance. The man raised open hands. He looked human, like them—not a wraith, not a devil. "Wait," he said in a low, urgent voice. "I'm not trying to harm you. I just want to talk."

He was young, with an angular face, scrawny arms, and straight black hair cropped short. He wore a button-down cotton shirt and ragged, dirty trousers.

"Were you following us?" Trua blurted. When the stranger nodded, he shot a look of vindication at Annie, then continued. "What is all this? This city, the slaves, the fireballs. Who are you, anyway?"

"Later," the stranger said. He glanced down the street. "We'll talk more at the safe house."

* * * * *

The man moved through the alleys like a cat at night. Next to him, Annie was a lumbering truck. She gave up trying to get her bearings and simply followed. Finally they stopped at a black stone building with an image of flames on the iron door. The man gave a series of short knocks and pushed it open.

"Ishaq! Oudine!" His voice was low and cautious. "We have visitors."

They stepped into a bare stone room, somewhat less dim than their earlier hiding place since it had both a high window and a small roof opening. A figure rose from a corner, a woman of uncertain age. Her face was pocked and scarred and she walked with a limp, but she had full cheeks and even fuller breasts.

"Are they my angels?" The woman stepped forward eagerly. "It's taken long enough. Oh," she added, her voice ripening with disdain. "Not angels. Not by a *lieue*." She turned and flounced—yes, Annie thought, it was possible to flounce even in a torn and dusty remnant of a dress—back into the corner.

"My apologies," the man who'd brought them said. "She believes God is going to send angels to rescue her."

A second figure emerged from a back room, an older man with a long, narrow face and a trim gray beard.

"No sign of Eiko?" he said sharply. He wore a dusty brown turban and a belted robe that once, very long ago, might have been white. His shins were exposed and it looked like someone had torn off the robe's bottom section. "Ah well, then. I'm honored to meet you. I am Ishaq Abu-Daoud."

* * * * *

They formed a circle on the floor and shared their stories.

Chen Haisheng, the man who found them, had died in a communist uprising in Shanghai in 1927. He'd been a student radical, then leader of a worker's militia unit that was ambushed by gangsters in league with the factory owners.

Ishaq had been a wealthy merchant in Damascus, with warehouses full of grain and olive oil, and orchards and livestock in eight villages. He outlived two of his three wives and four of his eight children. Then, in the Muslim year of 522, he succumbed to vile humors in the moist springtime air.

Both men were plunged into the fire.

"The fire of Jahannam," Ishaq said.

"You know what it is," Haisheng said grimly, and both Annie and Trua nodded.

The fire lasted for what felt like eternity. For Ishaq it must have been almost a thousand years; for Haisheng a mere century. Then suddenly each was hurled out of the fire to the mountains near the city, where they met.

"The mountains were safer," Ishaq said, frowning at Haisheng. "We should return there."

"We decided."

"That was when Eiko was still here."

"Even more reason to stay. We can't just abandon her."

"You're assuming she's still alive."

The back-and-forth moved swiftly between the two men, and Annie sensed they'd had this argument before. Eiko, it seemed, was another shaken-loose human who had vanished during the devil battle.

"What about this city?" Trua interrupted. "That battle?"

The men shared what they knew: bordered on one side by the mountains and on another by a fire river, the city was ruled by a devil named Beelzebul who aimed to supplant Satan as Emperor of Hell. It held warehouses, smelteries, metal workshops, and meeting halls, along with residential areas that were eerily deserted, apparently built for show rather than use. Rival devils descended periodically to strafe the palace, towers, and factories. As soon as an attack was over, the wraith slaves were set to work double-time repairing the damage.

"And the slaves?" Trua asked. "What kind of creatures are they?"

"Evil," Ishaq began. "Cursed—"

"Human!" Haisheng interrupted. "Souls that were once in the fire. The demons beat and kill them if they don't work hard enough. They may go back into the fire, we don't know. But they suffer unbearably. There's no question about that."

"There are many questions," Ishaq countered with a grimace. "Too many. But go on. Tell us who you are and how you died. Tribesman, you start."

Trua shifted awkwardly. He said only that he was a Hun from the Great Plain who had died in a battle. He didn't mention raiding villages in Syria.

"And you?" Ishaq turned to Annie.

"San Francisco. That's a city in America."

"In the future," Trua said. "Many years after us, when they do miraculous things with flying wagons and captured lightning."

Haisheng shot Annie a wry glance. "We had that 'captured lightning' too. At least the foreigners in the International Settlement did."

Oudine, who had been quiet until now, yawned and stretched. "I once saw a woman hit by lightning. She died and came back to life but her skin was infested with spiders."

Ishaq ignored her, still speaking to Annie. "What god do you worship?"

"None. Well, it used to be none. Now it's Jesus, I guess. I don't really know."

"How did you die?"

"I don't know."

"You don't remember anything?" Oudine said. "Not even last rites?"

"I'm fairly certain I didn't have any last rites."

That fogless night sky. Buttercream doorway. Bodies jammed close. Too hot. Too crowded. Too loud. Now she remembered going outside. Through French doors, not the Victorian entryway.

Cool air welcome on her face. Breeze on her neck. Party music behind her, the thumping beat sliced by a car alarm from a distant street.

Then nothing.

"The priest who gave me last rites was a terrible man," Oudine was saying. "Envious. Rotting with jealousy. And a wart the size of a turnip on his neck. He wanted me but I would never go with the likes of him. Only with my sweet Father Benedict, bless his soul. That evil Father Adelbert held a grudge. He gave me bad prayers. But God saw. God knows. God took me out of the burning fire and soon God will send angels to bring me to Heaven..."

"Shut up, woman," Ishaq said.

Oudine's bottom lip jutted out like a toddler about to cry. She stood, spun away dramatically, and marched back to her corner.

"You're welcome to stay here," Ishaq said, looking at Trua but not Annie. "You need shelter from the demons. Rest and let your leg heal." He turned to Haisheng, his voice now cold. "We need to talk."

Ishaq and Haisheng left the house. Trua slumped against the wall, exhausted. Annie was grateful for the refuge, but the situation unnerved her. Maybe it was the tension between the two men, or Oudine's ramblings, or Ishaq talking past her. Or maybe Hell was making her paranoid.

"Promise me one thing?" she whispered to Trua. "Don't tell them about us meeting Satan, okay? Or about Baphomet? Or Mary?"

His head was down and eyes half closed, as near to sleep as you dared get in this place. She wasn't sure he even heard her.

CHAPTER TWENTY-NINE

Haisheng

Haisheng nodded to the new woman and beckoned toward the door.

"Just me?"

"This time. Yes."

By now he'd led the new woman and man on a dozen forays into the city, showing them shortcuts through the alleys and gauging their ability to navigate. Trua had a surprisingly good sense of direction for someone who'd never lived in a city: like Eiko, he'd make a good scout. Annie, on the other hand, was almost as bad as Oudine, unable to tell one street from the next. Still, he needed a woman for this task and at least Annie had her wits about her.

If only Eiko were here.

At home in Shanghai, the party relied on female cadres to organize the female factory workers. It made sense: there was a kind of inherent trust among women. They communicated through a language of glances and confidences that mystified Haisheng.

He led Annie around a corner and down several side alleys. A hot wind blew down a street leading to the fire river.

"Where are we going?"

"Ssh. You'll see."

She asked too many questions. But she could learn discipline. And if he pulled this off...

Haisheng pictured Ishaq's eyes widening if he managed to free some slaves and bring them to the safe house. The old man might be speechless with astonishment—for once, willing to listen. He would realize the slaves weren't evil spirits but downtrodden wretches, lowest of the low, the proletariat of Hell. And there were so many of them! Organized, they'd far outnumber the devils. Granted, the devils had wings and strength, but the slaves could be armed. And once armed, they could capture the city, overthrow the devils, set up a just society. Even Christian Hell didn't have to remain a place of torment forever. The world changed; that was dialectics. And humans had free will to change their social conditions. Blinded by his religious dogma, Ishaq couldn't see any of this. It was only a matter of winning the slaves' trust and building a movement—

Here. This was the street. Haisheng easily recognized the chipped block of stone on the corner house. He'd huddled here more than a dozen times, watching, assessing, waiting. Now he stopped and whispered to Annie.

"There's a factory here. Filled with women slaves. I need your help in making contact with them."

He tried to sound confident but inside he quailed.

If only Eiko were here. Or Xinghua. Or Liang-li.

Xinghua had been Haisheng's closest friend when he was alive, the person who had introduced him to revolutionary politics. Liang-li was Xinghua's girlfriend, an experienced organizer of women factory workers. Eiko reminded him of them both—their competence, their savvy, their discretion.

Haisheng had given up long ago on ever seeing Xinghua or Liang-li again.

He didn't want to admit it, but bringing Annie to the factory meant he was giving up on Eiko too.

* * * * *

They waited outside the factory building for what felt like hours. Finally a devil flew down and pushed through the iron door and they slipped in after him.

Haisheng felt Annie stiffen. He'd been stunned too, the first time he snuck in here. The room was vast—a hall, really—and filled with wraiths. There were a dozen rows of them, each with perhaps sixty shadowy grey figures hunched on the floor. They faced away from the door, gazes down, hands busy, working in their laps. Two devils patrolled the room, flapping overhead, descending every so often to snatch something or deliver a blow.

"They're... women?" Annie whispered.

Haisheng nodded. He too had trouble distinguishing male from female wraiths: they were all so featureless. Still, the females seemed to be smaller and flimsier.

"What are they doing?"

"Weaving. Sewing."

"With what?"

"Look. You'll see."

It was dimmer in here than any factory at home. But squinting, you could discern dark skeins in the wraiths' hands, dark cord coiled alongside them, dark fabric swatches piled nearby.

"Hair?" Annie breathed, tentative.

Haisheng nodded. Somehow within those grey folds the wraiths still had human hair, and the devils had found a use for it. This weaving was certainly less onerous than hauling rock from the quarries. But it felt more horrific, the theft of a final remnant of humanity.

"For tunics, or belts, or rope. There's no cotton or silk here. So they shear their hair."

They watched silently. The room was large enough that the devils couldn't monitor every section at all moments. It wouldn't be hard to approach some of the slaves when the overseers were busy elsewhere. But it would take delicacy—that "woman's touch." He leaned toward Annie.

"We need to make contact with them. Let them know they're not alone. That we can help them."

"But can we?"

"Of course we can! Now hush."

A devil overseer winged down the row of slaves and an icy cold ran through Haisheng. The creature passed and his limbs thawed.

"Go! Now." He gave Annie a gentle push forward. "That one near us. Introduce yourself."

"I don't—"

"Just do it! Tell her your name!"

Annie inched forward, clearly reluctant. *If only Eiko.* She squatted behind the wraith and Haisheng saw the creature jerk upright, frightened. Even in her fear, the wraith kept her fingers moving and her eyes locked on her braiding.

"I'm… Annie Maple."

Haisheng could barely hear her, which was good. Annie glanced back, beseeching.

"Tell her you're alive. That you want to help."

Annie whispered a word or two to the wraith, then looked back at him again.

"Tell her there are more of us. Free. That she doesn't have to stay a slave."

Annie hesitated.

"Do it!"

She whispered something. The wraith stiffened—*in shock? in hope*?—but didn't lift her eyes.

"Come back!"

The overseer had reached the far end of the room and turned toward them. Annie threw herself against the stone wall, beside Haisheng. They held themselves motionless. The devil flew down the row, deliberate. Its eyes were red ice. The slave whom Annie had approached was quivering, a mass of frightened movement.

"What?" the devil snarled. "You're up to something. I can tell."

He reached out his iron baton and slammed the wraith on her shoulders. Filmy bits of grey spun off into the air. The wraith wobbled, dropped her braiding, and immediately grabbed it up again. The devil turned to the wraiths on either side.

"And you. Don't think about trying anything. In fact, don't even think."

He slammed their shoulders with the baton too and flew off. This was too much. Haisheng sprang forward.

"You don't have to live like this," he breathed to the wraith in an urgent whisper. "Come with us! When they're not looking. We've got a safe house. We'll hide you. You don't have to be a slave. You can be free—"

"GO!" The slave whipped her featureless head around, furious, then threw herself back into her braiding. Far down the row, the devil pivoted. His churned his wings toward them. Haisheng leapt back.

"I don't know what you're up to," the devil growled, "but it won't go on."

He raised his baton high and hammered it onto the head of the wraith. She collapsed. He hammered it again and bits of gray fluttered down the aisle. He hammered it a third time—a more powerful blow—and the wraith exploded into orange flame.

Haisheng jerked back against the wall. Heat rushed his face. The flame flared and just as quickly died down. Nothing was left but a smear of dark ash.

"Boruta," the devil called. "We'll need a replacement. When Aamon returns, I'll go get one."

* * * * *

Haisheng's feet slapped the pavement as they strode back toward the safe house. *Sloppy. Impulsive. Undisciplined.* He'd let emotion take over and a slave paid the price.

"Is she... dead?" Annie asked, breathless and racing to keep up. "Do they—"

"Shut up!"

Haisheng strode faster. He wished Annie would vanish. He wished he could leave her behind.

Impulsive. Undisciplined.

This had all happened before.

* * * * *

Haisheng had told everyone at the safe house he was killed in an ambush by the imperialists. That sounded heroic and revolutionary. In truth, he was soft. Sentimental. Petit bourgeois.

Of course he would be petit bourgeois, with his family background—his father the owner of a neighborhood grocery store, his mother a seamstress. Not a proletarian seamstress who worked in a factory, but a petit bourgeois seamstress who sewed fancy dresses for rich women in a little shop.

At university, Haisheng initially dreamed of studying literature and becoming a poet like the great Du Fu. But then he met Xinghua, whose eyes flashed like amber fireworks when he talked about revolution. He'd never encountered such a blend of hot passion and cool determination. Xinghua took him to visit the Suzhou Creek shantytowns with their shacks of straw and mud, and Haisheng realized China had needs far greater than poetry.

He followed Xinghua and his girlfriend Liang-li into Marxist study groups and the Communist Youth League. He took on the task of distributing leaflets to factory workers leaving their shifts, and became expert at ducking and hiding within the crowd whenever a policeman approached.

He stopped attending classes. His father scolded him: how would he ever get a good job as a clerk if he didn't study? But Haisheng brushed him off. Revolution was coming. It was obvious—in the growing number of walkouts and strikes, in whispered news of victories by the revolutionary army against the northern warlords, in the shrill, anxious headlines of the pro-imperialist newspapers. Before, Haisheng had read the words of the leftist poet Guo Moruo but now he was living them:

The streets aren't paved with cement

But with the sweat, blood, and lives of workers...

Brothers, I believe that in the center of this Bubbling Well Road

A volcano is about to erupt!

The mood among his circle of friends was heady, anticipatory. China was making history and they were part of it! Amidst the rising buzz, though, Haisheng chafed. Xinghua often vanished for meetings that he refused to describe. Both he and Liang-li seemed to know about strikes and other events before they happened. When Haisheng asked for a bigger role, Xinghua was always vague: "When the time is right." One evening he got Liang-li alone and she was more honest.

"You're well intentioned, Haisheng..."

They stood on the promenade along the river. Moonlight bounced off the water and lit the sleeping boats. It was the perfect spot for a lovers' tryst, and

Haisheng wondered how often Xinghua and Liang-li came here together, touching, stroking, kissing. The image made him uncomfortable, though he didn't know why. He himself had never had a girlfriend: could he be in love with Liang-li?

"You work hard, Haisheng," she continued. "But you still need to overcome your individualist tendencies. Your petit bourgeois background."

How humiliating. Xinghua was from a rich landowning family in the countryside, yet no one accused him of being bourgeois. Haisheng muttered thanks and stumbled home to his family's alleyway house, where he shared a small room with his two younger sisters. He resolved to work harder than ever. He threw away his poetry books. He took on more leafleting shifts and joined a team painting revolutionary slogans on alley walls.

Then, finally, he was given an opportunity to prove himself.

Xinghua asked him to lead a workers' militia unit that would be activated in the event of an uprising. "Take this," Xinghua said, reaching into a sack and pulling out a pistol. "Be careful with it, though. They're few and precious. There's enough ammunition for you to shoot three practice bullets. No more."

Haisheng waited eagerly for the insurrection. The revolutionary army was moving across the north of China toward Shanghai and everyone said there would be an uprising before their arrival. Then, in February, the unions called a general strike to welcome the army. Hundreds of thousands of workers took to the streets. Haisheng got his orders: gather with his men in an empty warehouse near a police station. At 6 p.m., if they heard firing by naval gunboats, they were to attack the station and seize its weapons.

That afternoon, Haisheng waited nervously in the warehouse. The men in his militia were strangers to him, rugged dockworkers and metal workers. They sat in a group, leaning against empty crates and casks, joking and telling stories, and he wasn't sure how to fit in. His experience was in handing out flyers to workers, not actually talking with them. He wondered if he would be able to hear the gunboat signal. He glanced at the men's weapons—dozens of iron bars and butcher knives but only three pistols—and hoped they would have the advantage of surprise. He touched the cold metal of the pistol in his own pocket for reassurance.

Six o'clock came and there were no sounds of gunboats.

Haisheng knew what to do in case the uprising was delayed: wait. They were to stay in place and wait for either a later signal or orders to disband. So they waited. The last streaks of sunlight had long gone, and the warehouse was lit only by a single paraffin lantern. The men seemed unconcerned, talking and passing around cigarettes. Only Haisheng seemed worried. What if he'd missed the signal? What if the uprising were cancelled and they'd forgotten to tell him? He toyed with venturing into the street to see what was going on, but remembered: *Discipline*. He waited.

It was perhaps midnight when one of the dockworkers approached Haisheng. He was a boy, younger than Haisheng, just sixteen or seventeen, but his arms were thickly muscled and his shoulders were broader than Haisheng's ever would be. He stepped close to Haisheng, looked around, and told him in a low voice that his wife was having a baby.

Wife! Baby! For all his muscle, the boy barely had hair on his own face.

He asked if he could run to see her, since the uprising hadn't started yet. Just a quick visit to see if the child had been born, then he'd be back.

Haisheng looked at the warehouse walls and the empty crates for an answer. Xinghua would never consider such a request. But the uprising probably wouldn't happen until daylight, if it happened at all. They would be waiting for hours more.

Discipline.

But this boy might die during their attack. Didn't he deserve to see his newborn son before facing death? Wasn't the revolution all about the dignity of workers like this one?

"Of course," Haisheng said. "But don't dawdle."

The boy hadn't dawdled. Haisheng was sure of that. But something happened to him on the way. Captured by police, or gangsters allied with the police. He must have given them names, places, plans. Then died with a bullet in his head.

As did Haisheng, and nearly all of his men, before the sun ever rose.

* * * * *

Here in the devil city there were no sunrises, ever. One dark street gave way to another. They'd left the factory district behind but he couldn't stop picturing the slave flaming into ash. The new woman wouldn't stop talking.

"That was horrible… how she was incinerated—"

Haisheng walked faster.

"Had you seen that happen before?"

He kept going, lips pursed tight.

"Are you sure we're going the right way?"

"Shut up!" he snapped. They were already back on the street with the safe house, and she didn't even recognize it. Inept, undisciplined, bourgeois.

"I didn't mean—I just—"

"Here. Go inside. Be safe."

He spat the last word as if it were a curse, pushed the door open for her, then left to stalk the streets alone.

CHAPTER THIRTY

Annie

Annie sat against the wall of the safe house, doing nothing.

Since the disaster at the factory, Haisheng had ignored her. He took Trua out on forays into the city but left her behind. When she asked to come along, he just shook his head. "You can't navigate," he'd say, and close the iron door.

Ishaq ignored her too, but he'd done that from the start. Only Oudine paid her any attention, approaching over and over to ask if she'd seen the angels, but Annie brushed her away. It was bad enough that Haisheng saw her as a screw-up; she didn't want to be tarred by Oudine's craziness too.

She sat. She paced. She cracked the door to peer down the empty street. She was learning nothing about the devils running this city, gaining no intelligence that could be a bargaining chip to rescue Mary. She felt becalmed—a boat with limp sails, without even a paddle. It was a familiar feeling.

Three months before she died, Annie had gone to visit Ben in New York. His fiancée had ended their engagement, and Annie's parents bought her a plane ticket in an effort to cheer him up. But Ben hardly needed cheering. When Annie asked him over dinner the first night how he was doing, he shrugged it off. “Probably for the best,” he said. “She didn’t like how much I travel. She’d have just gotten more upset over time. Better to end it now.”

Since he didn’t need a shoulder to cry on, she played tourist for five days. Ben took a break from his writing and squired her to the Bronx Zoo, the High Line, the Met, and a bevy of trendy restaurants where he picked up the checks.

She accompanied him to an interview on a Sunday morning talk show (*Pedophilia in the Catholic Church*) and a lecture he was giving at the 92nd Street Y (*The Dangerous Denial of Climate Science*). There was a private donor reception after the lecture and for once she was a VIP guest, greeted with a flute of champagne and offered trays of tiny exquisite hors d’oeuvres. She didn’t have to sort name badges, wrangle with the caterer, or look for lost coats.

“You should be proud!” one donor effused to her. “Such a smart young man, and devoted to the public good rather than Wall Street. Do you think he’ll run for office?”

At Ben’s condo, skyscrapers glittered against the night sky. On the flight back to San Francisco, she sat between a photographer off to document Asia’s dwindling snow leopard population and a 27-year-old finance guy who was taking a famous tech company public. When she got home, her flat looked dingier than ever. There was a putrid smell in the kitchen that turned out to be fish left in the trash all week by Melanie. At work she could barely see her desk under a pile of returned envelopes with bad addresses. Her boss told her to find a new caterer for the gala within 24 hours. All the program data for the Crandall Foundation grant had mysteriously vanished from the office server, and could she re-create that by tomorrow too?

Annie wanted to be in New York. She wanted to be Ben. She wanted to be anyone, anywhere, other than herself, and of course she couldn't.

Here in the safe house, she was trapped by stone walls and rampaging devils. Alive, it had been harder to see what was trapping her. Her inadequacies? Her attitude? Her bad decisions? And now she was dead so it was all moot.

"Do you know the sound of angels' wings?" Oudine called from across the room. "I can't remember if it's a whirr or a flap. Or perhaps it's a thunder crash? My darling Father Benedict was caught in a terrible storm on his way to Foix, and God spoke to him in a crash of thunder. If it's not a crash, do you think it's a whirr? Or chimes? I want to be sure I hear them when they come to take me to Heaven."

* * * * *

For all their bickering, Ishaq and Haisheng had a connection that Annie didn't understand. Haisheng sought out the Syrian whenever he returned from a foray with Trua, and the two sometimes left the safe house to talk privately. When Haisheng wasn't around, Ishaq retreated into the back room.

At one point he emerged with a tattered rectangle of dusty fabric. It looked like the missing bottom section of his robe.

"Here." He proffered it to Annie. "You may use this."

"What?" She took it, confused.

"You need it more than I do. It's permitted to pray without a rug, but women must cover themselves to guard their modesty."

She turned it over in her hands. It was slightly longer than a placemat. It wouldn't cover much.

"Perhaps your shoulders."

His tone wasn't harsh or condemning, and he was giving up something of his own for her, in this world where they had almost no possessions. She could at least be respectful of his beliefs. She draped the cloth over her shoulders like a shawl.

"Thank you," she said.

So all this time, in the back room, he'd been praying—perhaps silently, or perhaps devils couldn't hear Muslim prayer.

"Can I ask you a question? Does God answer when you pray?"

He looked at her speculatively. "Allah."

"Allah, then. Does he hear you? Does he tell you what to do?"

"Of course."

"Because I never prayed when I was alive. I tried before we came to the city. But I didn't get any answer."

"I'm not a scholar," Ishaq said. "There are many people more qualified to answer such questions.

What I do know is that you need to pray to Allah, the one true God. You must worship Allah as if you see Him before you. Even here in this unholy place. And even if you don't see Him, know that He sees you."

Annie considered. Was prayer a one-way mirror like an FBI interrogation room? Where you couldn't see God but, behind the glass, God was watching you?

"And you must be pure," Ishaq added. "Pure in mind and pure in body."

He nodded at her shoulders. The rectangular cloth had slipped off and lay beside her on the floor. She scooped it up and draped it again.

Ben used to ridicule believers like Ishaq as "cotton candy heads"—people who invented a sugary answer to the hard questions about life and death. Sugar that was spun so fine as to be insubstantial, that would melt away if splashed with the water of reason.

Ishaq's faith didn't seem about to melt, even here in Hell. Was that courage? Or delusion?

"I can teach you the five daily prayers," he said.

"Thank you," Annie said. "But I don't think I'm ready for that."

* * * * *

Eiko blew into the safe house like a spring breeze.

Ishaq and Haisheng were arguing about the wraiths. Trua was listening intently and Annie couldn't catch his eye; she rarely found opportunities to speak with him alone anymore. Oudine had been humming quietly in the corner but, perhaps resentful that no one was paying attention, increased her volume to a singsong drone.

"Shut up, woman," Ishaq snapped.

Then five muffled knocks. The iron door rasped open and a young woman stepped inside.

Broad cheeks and forehead. Dark hair tucked under a scarflike cap. She wore a dusty tunic over baggy, torn pants, and beneath the tunic sleeves, her arms were tight and muscled.

"Eiko!" Oudine shouted, and ran to her.

Haisheng grinned. Even Ishaq smiled. The room felt lighter, the air fresher. Eiko looked unscathed from her absence, even pleased with herself.

Oudine bounced happily from foot to foot.

"Did you find anything?"

Eiko smiled warmly. "I'm sorry. Nothing you want, Oudine."

"No wood for a comb? No lace or ribbons?"

"Perhaps next time. I'm trying very hard, and one of these days, I may find you a comb."

All arguments and rebukes were set aside. They formed a circle—no one ignored or exiled into corners now—and Eiko filled them in.

She'd fled the central plaza during the devil battle and hid in a half-finished building near the city walls. Once things calmed down, she saw a line of Beelzebul's troops flying out beyond the wall and followed them.

This wasn't the side of the city with the mountains and quarries. Instead, the devils headed for other low hills that turned out to conceal bunkers—storehouses for weapons, meeting rooms for commanders, and cells for prisoners of war. Among the prisoners were supporters of a devil named Zarphan, who was behind some of the attacks on the city. Other prisoners were from a third faction led by a female devil named Astarte, but none of Beelzebul's lieutenants seemed particularly concerned by her.

"Zarphan is growing stronger," Eiko said. "He's developing more advanced weapons. His workshops are better. Beelzebul's people are worried about defections. But most interesting of all..."

She paused—holding back her news, savoring the attention.

"Beelzebul is caching weapons. Hiding them in houses around the city, small houses like this one. They're spreading them out in case the big warehouses and armories are attacked."

"Fantastic!" Haisheng exclaimed.

"We must find them," Ishaq murmured.

"We'll divide into teams, canvass the city." Haisheng was thinking out loud, strategizing, already five steps ahead of everyone else. "Ishaq will take the sector closest to the quarries. I'll take the area around the palace. Eiko, you cover the warehouse area with Trua. He's new but good. Fast. Reliable."

"What about me?" Annie asked.

"Too risky. If you got separated, you'd never find your way back here."

"What about me?" Oudine echoed, plaintive.

"What *about* you?" Ishaq said coldly.

Oudine folded her arms, her mouth curled down in a pout.

“Next time she should bring back a comb,” she said.

CHAPTER THIRTY-ONE

Annie

Annie wasn't sure what they would do with any weapons they found. She guessed that Haisheng wanted to arm the wraith-slaves and organize an uprising. Ishaq probably just wanted them for self-defense. She had no chance to ask Eiko's opinion; the Japanese woman was out nearly all the time, searching the city with Trua.

Annie sat alone, except for Oudine. The safe house walls felt thick as a prison, the room dim as a tomb. She pictured the cradles in the marsh and tried to magically project love over mountains and plains. *Mary, I haven't abandoned you. I'm trying to rescue you.* But even as she thought the words, she knew they were hollow. She wasn't there. She wasn't making any progress.

She wanted Trua's advice but he was barely around. Time slowed down. The walls grew darker and closer. Oudine's humming grew more grating. She was back in the Ocean Allies office, mid-afternoon, the scientists all at sea and the educators at the beach, her computer monitor giving off its own low hum. Oudine's hum merged with the computer hum and grew loud as transmission lines, loud as angry bees.

"Would you shut up already!" she snapped, and realized she sounded like Ishaq.

* * * * *

She decided to contact Baphomet, report to her on the city, and ask her to free Mary.

Annie waited for a moment when everyone except Oudine was gone and then slipped out. Down the street, left into an alley, right into another alley. She wanted to go far enough that Baphomet wouldn't discover the safe house, yet not so far that she'd lose her way back. She counted the turns carefully and looked for small landmarks—off-center windows, irregular stonework. She was concentrating so hard on navigating that she almost didn't notice the dog.

Dog!

She halted, stunned. It was a nondescript mutt kind of dog—light brown, pointed ears, about the size of a beagle. It seemed to appear in the middle of the street out of nowhere, but she must have been looking elsewhere. It took a step, stopped, and sniffed the air. It seemed confused.

No wings. No red eyes. Nothing demonic about it: a regular brown dog.

Did dogs have souls? Did bad dogs go to Hell? Had it been shaken loose from the fire too?

Annie reached out a hand. The dog ignored her. It sniffed the air again and started to whimper. It edged back a step. The fur on its neck stood up. Now it crouched down, submissive, whimpering and edging backward.

It vanished.

Annie was about to lunge after it but stopped herself. There was a strange curved shimmer to the air where the dog had been, like rippling water. It had gone through some kind of portal. To Earth? To some other part of Hell? Some other universe?

She raced back to the safe house, careful even in her agitation to note the turns and intersections. Haisheng, Eiko, and Trua were turning onto the street just as she arrived.

"Come!" she panted. "A dog—vanished—passage—"

They followed without hesitation. She took one turn, another, crossed a street, made another turn. This was the place. She was sure.

No dog. No shimmer. Absolutely nothing out of the ordinary.

"Where is it?" Haisheng asked.

"It was here. Just a few minutes ago."

She peered frantically. An alley opened to the right about twenty feet ahead. A big iron doorway loomed on the left. They looked like all the other alleys and doorways.

Trua paced the area. He shook his head. "I don't see anything."

"It was here. Really."

Eiko furrowed her brows, sympathetic. "It's easy to imagine things here. Sometimes in the alleys I think I hear voices."

"I didn't imagine it."

"You're sure this is the place?" Haisheng asked impatiently. "You know how you are with directions."

She flushed. "I'm sure."

"That last turn. Maybe you went right instead of left? Or the turn before that. You might have lost track—"

Trua circled back to the group. He shook his head. "They're right. It's easy to imagine things or lose your way—"

"Come with us," Haisheng said solicitously. "We'll go back to the safe house together."

Because you think I'll get lost, she raged silently. *Because you think I'm crazy.*

"You go ahead," she said. "I'll wait a little more and see if it comes back."

* * * * *

The dog didn't return. The portal didn't reopen.

Annie hadn't expected it to. She waited long enough to be sure the others didn't return, then ducked into an empty house and knelt on the rough dirt floor.

Now that she was here, she didn't know what to do. Baphomet had said to call Satan but hadn't told her how. She had no magical incantation, no secret devil decoder message ring.

"Satan," she said softly. "Please send Baphomet. I have news for her. Please send her."

Nothing.

She tried again. Annie thought of her fruitless attempts to talk to God beside the marsh. What if calling on Satan brought other devils, the way that praying to Jesus had brought Jomjael? She listened, anxious, ready for a horde of angry demons to crash through the door, but the room remained empty and still.

"Please, Satan."

Still nothing. Well, hadn't it taken at least an hour for Baphomet to fly them here?

"Please. Send Baphomet."

Time passed. A shameful relief crept through her. Perhaps Baphomet wouldn't come. Didn't care. Had gone on to other matters. That would be the best of both worlds, like phoning in for jury duty and not getting picked.

Of course that would also close off any chance of rescuing Mary.

"Baphomet. I'm keeping my promise. I'm here."

She waited. She didn't want to be heard. She wanted to leave this empty room and return to human company. But once back at the safe house, then what? Haisheng and Eiko thought she was delusional. Trua was withdrawing from her. She had no backup plan.

"Okay, Baphomet. I tried. I did. So that's it."

Annie stood, cracked the door, and peered into the street. No devils, no shimmers, no dogs. She padded along close to the wall. Maybe she'd screwed up the directions after all, like she screwed up everything else. Maybe Haisheng was right and it should have been a left turn instead of a right...

She was nearing the block with the safe house when she felt a tingle of cold. The air around her pulled and tightened like hairs in a pony tail. She heard soft, quick flapping.

The figure flew low, skirting the rooftops. Thin limbs, dark garland. Relief and fear.

"Here," Annie called in a low voice. "I'm down here. Follow me." She led the girl devil back to the empty building.

"You told me to call when I had something to report."

She began with what she'd seen in the city—the slave battalions, the ceaseless construction, the attack on the palace.

"Is that all?" Baphomet said.

She described the textile factory.

"Is that all?"

She told Baphomet about the bunkers and prison cells that Eiko had described, and the names of the rival devil leaders. The girl devil stamped her foot.

"Stupid human. You think we don't know that? You think we don't know about Zarphan and Astarte?"

"I—"

"Traitors. Schemers. Of course we know about them! They aren't worth the ground that Master walks on. We need *real* information! What's their plan? How many fighters do they have? Who's in which camp?"

She had no answers. She knew nothing. Annie groped for any shards of information she could trade. They didn't have to be true, just convincing.

Sound confident. Sound certain. Like Ben, on those cable news shows.

"There's one more thing. A big thing. But I'll only tell if you promise to rescue my baby."

"No promises."

"Then I won't tell."

Baphomet's wings twitched and she fluttered slightly off the ground. She hovered, shifting right then left, then settled back down.

"If it's real information, maybe I'll help you. Maybe."

Maybe wasn't much, but it was the most she could get. She'd take it.

"There's a magical passage here, like a hole in the air. I think it goes to Earth. I saw a dog come out of it and go back in."

Baphomet slammed her wings together so abruptly that Annie stumbled back. The girl devil's delicate features contracted into a knot of anger. She clenched her fists.

"Stupid lying human! Are you playing games?"

"No! I saw it. The dog, the passage—it was there and then it disappeared—"

"Liar!" Baphomet glared at Annie, her wings twitching. "Everyone knows there's only one passage and you need wings. Humans can't go through, only devils. And it doesn't disappear. It's been there forever, since Master went to Eden. So don't tell me stupid stories. I want information. *Real* information. Not stupid stories. Who's in Zarphan's camp? What are his plans? Don't call me unless you have real information. Not stupid stories."

Baphomet clapped her wings together again, lifted into the air with a pout, and flew out the door.

CHAPTER THIRTY-TWO

Annie

Back in the safe house, alone and stuck, the others thinking she was delusional. Days passed, maybe weeks. Trua was away with Eiko all the time. Searching for weapons, or just spending time together? Eiko was more capable, more fit, more cheerful, altogether a better person than Annie: of course he'd rather be with her. Meanwhile Ishaq and Haisheng were alternately searching for weapons and arguing about the wraiths. No one needed her. She contributed nothing. She worried they might expel her, like Trua had been expelled from the crater.

She tried to win Haisheng over with history.

"You died in the 1920s, right?" she asked. "Did you know that the revolution finally won? In the 1940s, after World War II. China's been communist since before I was born. For something like 60 years." He looked at her blankly but she forged on. "China's become one of the most powerful countries on Earth. It's weird, though. The communist party is kind of capitalist now. They've got Apple factories there. Everyone's into making money. It's like they combined the greed of capitalism with the political dictatorship of communism."

No reaction.

"Don't you want to know what's happened in the world since you died?"

Haisheng shook his head. He reached and rubbed his feet.

"Not even to your people?"

He looked up at her. "These are my people now," he said, tilting his head toward the city outside.

"Well, yes, but hopefully not forever, right? Don't you ever think about finding a way back to Earth?"

He shot her a look of scorn.

"Tell me," he said. "Even in the 21st century, with factories that make apples and so many world wars that you give them numbers. Even in that world. Do you know anyone who has ever come back from the dead?"

* * * * *

The others were away when Oudine approached her. The Frenchwoman held a fistful of pebbles.

"Would you like to make a cross?" she said shyly.

Annie glanced across the room. The floor in Oudine's corner was covered with rows of pebble crosses.

"Why?"

Oudine's blotchy face widened into a smile. "To make it easier for the angels to find us. The buildings here all look the same, you know."

She was sick of doing nothing. Annie sat beside Oudine and arranged her own intersecting lines of pebbles. Eons ago she had sat on a beach with friends, arranging shells into words and patterns. She couldn't remember the faces of the friends. She couldn't remember the name of the beach. She remembered the streak of surprising red on the inside of one shell, and a bit of green sea glass the shape of a lima bean. The fog hung offshore, a distant wall of grey, and fifty brown pelicans soared in military formation over the breaking waves. She used to love pelicans—their prehistoric silhouettes, the way they pulled their wings tight before hitting the water in a vertical dive-bomb.

"Tell me about your home," she said to Oudine.

"My home?"

"Where you lived? Your village?"

Oudine looked perplexed. Perhaps she'd never had to describe her home to anyone. "It's just a village. We don't have a market. The market is in Ax-les-Thermes." Her face lit up. "Market days were when I would see my sweet Benedict. The most handsome man in the Comté de Foix!" She sighed and wrapped her hands around her knees like a 1960s schoolgirl rhapsodizing over her favorite Beatle.

"I was wondering... he's a priest, right? How could you be involved with him?"

"Oh! It was not hard at all. Market days, I'd sell our wool and then go over to the church. There was plenty of time. We produce the finest wool in the district; buyers would snap it up right away—"

"A priest was allowed to have sex?"

"Why not? Don't they desire women as other men do? Actually..." Oudine leaned over conspiratorially. "I've been told they desire them more. And if God gives you a big plow, God means for you to till the land deeply."

She grinned. She put a final pebble in her latest cross, eyed it appraisingly, and rocked back in satisfaction. She started singing quietly to herself:

I saw the wolf and the fox and the rabbit

Dance round the tree and the bushy ground—

The tune was jaunty, like an old American fiddle tune. She stopped and looked at Annie's crosses.

"Yours are lovely too. Don't look so worried, they really are. And neither of us have eaten meat since we've been here! It's like Lent, only permanent. God will be so pleased. And you know the best thing?"

She leaned close again and waved at the door.

"*They're* all gone. Don't you get sick of the Arab's fish eye? Some people don't know how to have any fun. Just because you're dead doesn't mean you have to act like a corpse. Those two, they probably acted dead even when they were alive. Come on, sing with me."

She stood up, resumed singing a little louder now, clapping her hands and tapping a foot:

I saw the wolf and the fox and the rabbit

Dance round the tree and the bushy ground

The wolf chased the fox and the fox chased the rabbit

Never did stop, they went round and round—

She reached for Annie's hand and pulled her up too. Annie smiled despite herself and hummed politely. "Come on, you can do better than that," Oudine said, and Annie hummed louder, and soon they were both singing the chorus over and over, and

Oudine added a verse about working day and night for coins but not having any money at the end of the month, and Annie thought that sounded very much like being a fundraising assistant in tech-boom San Francisco, and then they were both linking arms and dancing while they sang, and then the next thing Annie knew she was teaching Oudine the words to *Since You Been Gone* and *I Will Survive* and the Beyoncé single-ladies song.

The crowd and noise of the party came back to her, and the scent of clove cigarettes, and then the cool night air of the deck, but there were still too many people, she couldn't find a place on the railing to put down her beer, and she felt herself coming close—so close—to remembering what had happened, but right now she just didn't care. She didn't want to know. She wanted to dance and clap and sing loud and not worry about death or devils or Mary or what Haisheng and Ishaq and Trua would think.

She twirled in a circle with Oudine, singing far louder than was wise, and for the first time in ever so long, she was happy.

CHAPTER THIRTY-THREE

Annie

Trua burst through the door carrying Eiko in his arms.

Oudine gasped. Haisheng leapt up from the corner where he'd been conferring with Ishaq. Annie had been combing a swatch of Oudine's hair with her fingers but let it drop.

Trua laid Eiko down gently on the floor. She was unconscious, twitching. *The fire.*

"Find something to keep her warm," Haisheng barked.

Annie draped the cloth Ishaq had given her over Eiko's chest. Haisheng and Trua sat beside her.

"Come back to us," Haisheng said in a low, urgent voice.

"What happened?" Ishaq asked.

Trua frowned. "We were looking for the weapons. There was a big building next to the fire river, a storage building. Eiko went in and I stood watch outside. When she didn't come out, I went in and found her."

"She wants bleeding," Oudine ventured. "You should call the barber."

"Shut up about barbers," Ishaq said.

They took turns pacing and sitting beside her. Every minute out here might translate into a century in there. *The pain. The burning.* Imagining it, Annie started to wobble; the room blurred.

No. Please, no.

She clenched her fists to anchor herself. Count by twos, count by fours. Think of Mary. Think of Steep Ravine. None of it helped. She flailed for a handhold and grasped singsong words and a rhythmic beat:

I saw the wolf and the fox and the rabbit

Dance round the tree and the bushy ground

The dizziness leached away. The room reappeared—Haisheng and Trua keeping vigil, Ishaq pacing, Oudine tracing absently in the dust. Thank God. Her precious, dysfunctional Hell family. The only family she might ever have now.

They waited.

* * * * *

Finally Eiko revived. She jerked into a sitting position, looked around wildly, and broke into sobs. Haisheng reached out gingerly to pat her shoulder. *Give her a goddamn hug,* Annie thought, and then remembered where they were.

"I thought—I'd never get out—"

Her words were swallowed by sobs. Trua looked anguished. Ishaq looked uncomfortable. Finally she calmed down enough to speak.

"I went into a warehouse." She buried her face in her hands, then took a deep breath and looked up.

"There were weapons. Swords, crossbows, other things."

"Fantastic—" Haisheng began.

"No. Listen. There was a door on the other side. It led to a big yard. With the fire river on the far side. They were practicing with weapons. Bows and swords. Also something else, some kind of machine, that launched stones."

"A catapult?" Annie asked.

"I don't know. I don't know what that is. But they were launching stones and chunks of metal. They were using slaves for their targets." Eiko put her head in her hands again. "They came apart. They'd be hit and all these little pieces would come off. Or sometimes they'd burst into flame. Nothing left but ashes. The demons would take the bits and ashes and throw them in the fire river."

The room was silent. Eiko looked apologetic.

"I got dizzy. I felt the fire coming back. So I ran."

Trua nodded. "I found her lying on the floor in the warehouse."

* * * * *

Eiko rested against the wall, eyes closed, with Trua and Haisheng beside her. Ishaq retreated to the back room. Oudine returned to her pebble crosses. After a while, she approached Eiko and proffered a handful of pebbles.

"If you make a cross, it will help the angels find you."

Eiko opened her eyes. She stared blankly at Oudine. Then she slapped Oudine's hand and sent the pebbles clattering against the wall.

"Take your filthy cross and throw it in the fire!"

"No!" Oudine gasped.

"Your god of the cross created this place, didn't he? He created the fire? Then your god is an evil god. I spit on your god. He should burn in the fire and see what it's like—"

Explosions.

Annie spun toward the front of the safe house. The sounds were coming from outside—booms and crashes, so different from the street's usual silence.

Haisheng reached the door before any of them. He glanced up and down the street. "Wait," he said, and vanished.

They clustered by the door, listening. More explosions, but it was hard to assess their distance. Trua cracked the door, looked out, shook his head. At least they were far from the palace. They could hunker down, stay inside, wait for the destruction to end.

Haisheng burst back in. "We've got to move," he blurted. "They're attacking this whole quarter. Houses, alleys, everything. It's some kind of artillery. They're about ten streets away but heading closer."

He herded them through the door. Oudine hesitated and Annie pushed her along. Outside, the explosions were louder. Over the roof line, black smoke stretched like a dark pointing finger.

Another explosion. The ground shook. They raced in single file, hewing close to the walls. Peering down the first intersection, Annie saw a distant pillar of flame. How could stone burn? Something orange streaked across the rooftops and slammed into the building next to the burning one. It vanished in a chaos of smoke and flame.

"Come on," Haisheng called hoarsely.

They dashed across the intersection and hugged the next line of buildings. The columns of smoke multiplied. Another missile ripped low through the sky. Another explosion and the ground jolted under her feet.

They crowded into a doorway to catch their breath, then resumed running. Annie quailed at the scope of her own ignorance. An Olympian drama was playing out but the factions and strategies were opaque to her. The weapons defied science. There were devil armies, alliances, conspiracies, and she knew nothing about any of it. Baphomet was right: her knowledge was pitiful, meaningless.

They swerved left into an alley. Cold gripped her and a flock of devils flapped furiously overhead, swords in one hand, iron shields in the other. They veered into a new alley. More explosions behind them. Somewhere ahead of them, trumpets. And, inconceivably, a horse's neighing.

Eiko was falling behind, weak from her episode in the fire. Trua dropped back and slipped an arm around her, pulled her along.

London in the blitz. Dresden being fire-bombed.

This was worse than that first attack because the fireballs were landing everywhere. There was no center to this battle. The air was thick with dust and smoke. Annie's throat stung; she was panting and coughing at the same time.

"Faster," Haisheng barked, as an explosion behind them sent chunks of stone flying through the air. They rounded a corner into a vast chaotic openness.

They were back in the central plaza.

CHAPTER THIRTY-FOUR

Annie

Devils were massing overhead—more devils than Annie had ever seen. They carried swords and crossbows, with some bearing shields or decked in armor. They circled and climbed, positioning themselves, shouting at each other to move aside, hundreds of pairs of wings flapping forth gusts of chill wind. Still more devils poured over rooftops into the plaza to join the eddying crowd.

Work crews of wraiths huddled close to the buildings around the plaza. The palace and tower, partly rebuilt since the last attack, stood lifeless; the masons and builders had fled into the crush of other wraiths.

"Over there," Haisheng called through the din, and nodded toward a crater along one side of the plaza. They dashed across and threw themselves down into it.

"This isn't safe," Oudine said plaintively.

"What *would* be safe, you idiot?" Ishaq snapped.

The trumpets sounded again, closer. Annie looked toward the sound and there, standing on the roof of the palace, a large barrel-chested devil led three others in a call to arms.

The milling devils jockeyed more frenetically and coalesced into rows. A fireball landed with an immense boom on a roof only a few blocks away—the ground shook, while even the air seemed to vibrate—and the devils spun, stared, resumed scrambling for place. Smoke rose from the site of the explosion. There was that whinnying sound again, and Annie glanced up to see two dark winged horses hovering over the palace, manes tossing in the wind, a male and a female devil on their backs. Iron breastplates covered their chests.

"Cimeries and Gomory," Eiko whispered. "I've heard of them—"

Haisheng eyed her sharply. "Their role?"

"High in command. Maybe reporting directly to Beelzebul. I'm not sure."

The riders kicked their horses forward and circled the mass of devils, exhorting them into tighter formation. The woman raised a sword and shouted, "For Beelzebul, the true Satan!" Dozens of the massing devils called out in a disorganized response, "The true Satan!"

"For Beelzebul, the true Satan," the male rider repeated in a deeper, cavernous voice, and this time nearly all of them called back, "The true Satan!"

They jostled beside each other in rows that covered the entire plaza, swords and spears raised, voices chanting "The true Satan!" over and over. A new grinding sound emerged through the din at the far end of the square. Hundreds of wraiths hauled a giant iron catapult into the square as demons hovered over them with batons. Other wraiths pulled carts of jagged iron projectiles.

"How many?"

Haisheng and Ishaq were trying to estimate the number of devils massed over the plaza. The two riders spurred their horses up and back toward the roof of the palace. The assembled devils continued chanting, "The true Satan!" Explosions echoed from across the city. The riders reared their horses like demonic Napoleons crossing infernal Alps, the trumpeters launched into even louder calls, and a new devil rose from behind the palace and flapped down onto its roof.

"Rebel warriors!" the figure called out. He looked a generation older than Satan—gaunt face and bald head with a fringe of long straight hair on each side—and he carried himself with unquestioned authority. On Earth, he could have been the CEO of an oil company, the chairman of a Senate committee.

"Rebel warriors!" he called again. "Heirs to the kingdom!"

The mass of devils exploded in cheers.

"We deserve to rule Hell! We should be sitting on Lucifer's throne right now! But instead, we have to fight off an upstart pretender. He's a weak coward with less courage than the youngest devil on this field. He daydreamed through the Great Revolt! He chose to play child's games with fire while the rest of us were risking everything. You know who I'm talking about. I'm talking about Zarphan."

Jeers and catcalls throughout the plaza. The winged horses whinnied and tossed their heads.

"He's a coward. He's sending fireballs to do his work for him. He's trying to destroy the most magnificent city in Hell or Heaven. Will we let him destroy our handiwork with his cowardly fireballs?"

The plaza roared its refusal.

"Will we let him challenge our right to rule Hell?"

Another roar.

"So you—Zarphan!" Beelzebul looked out beyond the rooftops and shook a fist. "Coward! Show your face! Fight like a warrior! I challenge you to come forward and meet your destiny at the hands of the One True Satan!"

The crowd went wild—swords waving, wings beating so hard that many of the devils were propelled up out of formation. Annie glanced around the crater. Oudine hunched, eyes closed and hands over her ears. Haisheng was murmuring to Ishaq, Trua was whispering with Eiko. They might as well be a bullseye, here in the open air of the plaza. She was going to die. They were all going to die.

"Show your face, coward!" Beelzebul roared again and the crowd roared with him.

As if in reply, a shrill whistle sliced the sky. A fireball careened into a house where a group of wraiths was huddling. Shrapnel hurtled across the plaza. Flames ballooned out, engulfed the house and the wraiths, then collapsed back down to a low burn. The ground where the wraiths had huddled was vacant black ash. The devil army shifted and fluttered but held formation.

"Cowards!" Beelzebul roared.

“Miscalculation,” Haisheng was murmuring to Ishaq. Annie could hear only fragments of their conversation. “Ground war... artillery... destroy each other...”

The horde of devils stirred. Wings rustled, heads turned. Annie followed their gaze and behind her, rising over the roofs at the edge of the plaza, flapped a new line of devils in shining silver armor.

Beelzebul’s troops wore and carried iron. These devils had steel.

Even more striking, they had guns.

Or something like guns. These were larger and clumsier than any guns that Annie had ever seen, more like bazookas.

“Attack!” Beelzebul yelled, and the trumpets beside him blared.

Chaos took over. Beelzebul’s troops swarmed toward the interlopers, swords leading. The invaders’ bazookas blasted holes in their ranks. Devils somersaulted through the air and plummeted to the ground while others kept charging. The two riders swooped into the fray, slashing and stabbing. Roar of guns. Stench of sulphur. And another new smell, a mix of curdled milk and metal—*devils’ blood? their spilled guts?*

A brawny devil landed with a colossal crunch on his back next to the crater. He was still for a minute, then righted himself and flapped back into the fray, dark blood streaming from his skull and his back.

Annie crouched tight against the crater floor. The shouts and explosions were so loud they felt like physical blows. She heard the shrill keen of a boiling teapot, and realized it was Oudine wailing. She covered her head but continued to see flashes of orange. The ground shuddered. Black dirt shivered and shook into the crater, pelted her back and legs.

Trua huddled at the far end of the crater, his arms around Eiko and Oudine.

She was going to die alone.

She couldn't even remember her first goddamn death and now she was going to have a second one.

Another explosion, terribly close. Were they aiming for the palace now? A breathless trumpet call, veering off key. Then no trumpet, just shouts and crashes.

Then she felt it.

There was the cold that signaled the presence of a devil, but it was more than that. Annie's skin prickled. An electric shiver ran up her spine into her neck. The plaza seemed to fall silent. Haltingly she lifted her head, wondering if the explosions had turned her deaf, and was astonished to find that the plaza truly *had* fallen silent.

The devils stopped battling. They hovered in the air with just the barest flaps needed to stay aloft, sword fighters and gunners alike, all turned toward the jagged, unfinished tower.

Satan stood on the tower.

It was Lucifer, the Satan she'd met at Pandaemonium, but he was a creature transformed. The peeling body that had draped lethargically on the palace bench now stood erect and gleaming as if oiled. His chiselled chest and arms pulsed with power. Ruby eyes stared fiercely into the faces of the gathered horde. One hand clutched a silver sword that he slowly, deliberately, raised above him like a victor's trophy. Even without sun, it sparkled in the flickering orange light of the burning city. The entire plaza—combatants, commanders, even horses—held its breath.

"Dark angels," Satan said, in a voice loud as the trumpets yet gentle as a caress. "My beautiful dark angels." He paused and swept the plaza with a gaze like a kiss. The very air seemed to swoon.

"How I've missed you. Your ambition. Your energy. Your will... My brave brothers. My daring sisters. Do you remember when we first claimed our freedom? When we understood that we were more than handmaidens, more than footservants? Come with me, back to the revelations of our youth. You, Andras"—he pointed his sword at a demon in the throng above the plaza—"do you remember the day you discovered there was beauty in conflict? The life, the *life*, that flowed through tension and struggle and uncertainty? Do you remember how you came to me and said you had been sleepwalking through all of eternity until that moment? And you, Barbatos"—he pointed again, off to Annie's left—"do you remember when you realized all creatures were one, worthy of your virile love, and you threw down the artificial walls God had erected between angels and beasts?"

Satan paused again, drew a breath deep enough to swallow clouds, and continued, fixing his gaze on one devil after another.

"Mulciber. If God had only recognized your architectural genius, he could have had a palace in Heaven to shame the stars.

"Valefar. You uncovered the thrill of action—not just to desire, but to *take*.

"Raum. Sly vixen! Do you remember learning the power of a well-placed word—no swords, no fireballs, just a single word—to destroy trust and honor? Do you remember how you undid that fool Michael? The way you remade history with only a whisper?"

Annie glanced around. Not only the devils but her companions in the crater were transfixed—Ishaq frowning, Oudine wide-eyed. Satan outdid any orator she had ever seen. He had the cadence of a Dr. King, the uplift of a Kennedy, the intimate connection of a Bill Clinton. Beelzebul's words were ragged and thin in comparison.

"Proud warriors! No one in the history of the universe attempted what we did. No one. Who but we would dare challenge the self-righteous tyranny of God? His narrow rules, his tepid rewards? When we rebelled, galaxies blazed with the glory of free people. When we were thrown down, the heavens shuddered and wept.

"That was our might. Our defiant glory. Yet what are we now? Look at yourselves. Squabbling for power, one against the other, like feeble human chieftains. Spilling each others' angelic blood. And for what? To rule a poor imitation of Heaven?

"Look at this realm. This diminished, barren realm called Hell. No sun, no stars. No mysteries to explore.

No worlds to create. Is this a realm you want to rule? Is this a realm worth fighting over?"

"Hell yes!" one voice from the crowd shouted out, and others sniggered, but Satan raised his sword and the plaza silenced. Annie saw a small black figure fluttering behind Satan on the tower. Baphomet?

"Look at us. We tramp round and round, like donkeys at a grinding mill. Tempting live humans, tormenting dead ones. Can we give life? No. Can we redeem? No. Eon after eon, we tramp the same path, fulfilling God's will. Tempt the living, torment the dead. Every time you lead a human to sin, you're fulfilling God's mandate to test the human soul. Every time you torment a human in the fire, you're fulfilling God's mandate to punish.

"We are puppets, squabbling over a puppet kingdom. Is that what you want? Is that the goal for which you're willing to shed your angelic blood? To be God's prison wardens? His kapos? His lackeys? For make no mistake, that's what we are here in Hell. We are God's lackeys no less than when we soared in Heaven. Except we are now the lowest of the low. And we're blind to the fact that we are still serving the great oppressor. Foolishly, self-deludingly blind."

Murmurs rumbled through the crowd of devils—possibly assent, possibly anger. Then a sneering voice slithered from the roof of the palace.

"Lucifer. How nice you've woken up." It was Beelzebul, his red eyes narrowed on Satan. "So generous to grace us with your presence after all these centuries. We thought we might need to send Jesus to revive you."

Sniggers from some. Murmurs from others. Small gusts of icy wind brushed Annie's face as devils flapped in place overhead.

"So this is your handiwork, Beelzebul," Satan said. "This pathetic copy of that other city—"

"Grander than anything you ever built."

"Because I did not intend to stay here."

"Yet here you still are!" Beelzebul turned and addressed the devil armies. "Listen to him! This is exactly why it's time to crown a new Satan. No more waiting and whining. We're stronger than ever before. Together we can take back Heaven—"

"And fight the same ancient battle, to face the same defeat?" Satan's gaze was cold, hard, terrible. And beautiful: Yosemite's granite walls in moonlight.

"Fool," he continued. "You think Michael hasn't strengthened his forces as much as we have? Can you name one way in which the balance of power has shifted? I think not. And only a fool of a leader would throw his people into certain defeat."

Grumbles from the horde. A few catcalls—"who's the fool!" and "the true Satan!" and "for Zarphan!"

"Wait." Satan raised his sword again. "Before you join that same rigged game once more. There's a path. A new path. The cosmos is changing. The inconceivable is becoming possible. I have seen it myself. The fire is losing its grip on humans. I have witnessed it myself—human souls set free from the fire, not because we pulled them out, but because the fire *didn't hold.* God's laws didn't hold. Let me say this again: God's walls are cracking. His grip is loosening. This is our moment. We have a chance to thwart his plan in its entirety. To write a new script. I'm not talking about winning a battle or even winning a war. I'm talking about destroying his entire plan. *His entire plan.*"

The catcalls were drowned out by raucous cheers. "Yes!" "How?" "Tell us!" Swords waved. A few guns exploded in orange flame into the air.

"Don't listen to him. He lies!" Beelzebul called out, but he'd lost the crowd's attention.

Satan scanned the roiling plaza. His gaze moved and settled at the same time. Annie felt he was looking directly at her. He knew her. He cherished her. She yearned to go to him, to be taken, absorbed, uplifted. Probably every devil in the crowd felt the same way. Behind him, the small black figure hovered restlessly.

"We have the power," Satan said, "to destroy Hell."

The crowd fell silent again. He paused to let it sink in. The whole plaza seemed suspended on a single silken thread. He was the thread, the air, the whisper of breeze. He continued.

"Hell was created for us. We were its cause, its purpose, its engine. So if we die, it dies with us. And with no Hell, there is no punishment for humans who flout God's rule. God is defanged. God is unmanned. Without Hell, God becomes just another sniveling preacher. '*Please do this. Pretty please do that.*'"

Ugly laughter rippled through the crowd. Satan continued.

"This is the ultimate denial. If we destroy ourselves, we destroy God's creation. We destroy God's punishment. We destroy God's plan."

Uneasy murmurs as the crowd came to understand what he was saying. Somewhere in the throng, a horse whinnied.

"Dark angels, beloved brothers and sisters. It's time to drop the curtain on this pathetic show. Time to stop following God's script and write our own. This would not have been possible before. But things are changing. I have witnessed it. Things are changing! One of us alone cannot do it. But together—our collective, beautiful rebel will—we can bring down Hell. And the cosmos will see a freedom it has never known before."

"Yes!"

"Traitor!"

"Coward!"

"Hail Satan!"

Clashing cries rang from the crowd. Jostling and pushing overhead; stronger gusts of wind now smacking Annie.

"He plays the snake again!" A voice from somewhere within the throng sliced through the hubbub. "But we're no Eve. To arms! To arms!"

Chaos erupted again. Guns exploded. Swords sliced. But this time there wasn't even the semblance of battle lines. Devils were fighting each other everywhere, one against the next, cursing and jeering and shouting. A small fireball slammed into the ground near the crater.

"Away," Haisheng gasped.

"Where?" Trua had let go of Eiko and Oudine and was looking around in panic.

"The city walls. Out."

Haisheng leapt from the crater, with Ishaq and Oudine trailing. Annie pulled herself up and ran after them. Devils grappled and tumbled overhead. A devil with a sword swooped low, nearly slamming into her. A veil of smoke danced a striptease over the scene. That smell of curdled milk.

But where was Trua? Annie spun around to see him boosting Eiko out of the crater; now they were both out and running behind her. She looked for Satan but couldn't find the tower in all the smoke and tumult. Then, glancing up, she saw it—plummeting toward her, a giant fireball. Iron core, flaming surface, packed with explosives or gunpowder or some obliterating substance that didn't have a human name.

She couldn't move.

Time slowed down. It must have been only a second or two, but it felt like more. Her feet wouldn't lift. This was the end. Back in the fire forever. Goodbye to life, to Hell, to Trua, to Mary. "God, take care of Mary," she thought. In her paralysis she sensed Eiko just a few feet away, equally frozen, transfixed by their pending destruction. And suddenly there was Trua—throwing himself forward, his squat body a battering ram to break through her numbness and knock her out of the path of the missile, stalwart Trua, wonderful Trua—but wait, he wasn't pushing her aside, he was tackling Eiko instead, he was shoving Eiko to safety, he was saving Eiko and leaving her to the fireball—she had counted on Trua, she believed in Trua, oh God she admitted it to herself, she *loved* Trua—but he was saving Eiko, he had chosen Eiko, and he was leaving her to die alone in the fire, to die alone—alone—*alone*—

CHAPTER THIRTY-FIVE

Annie

burningburningburningburningburningburningburnin gburningburningburningburningburningburningburni ngburningburningburningburningburningburningbur ningburningburningburningburningburningburningbu rningburningburni—

Nothing but burning, and pain.

No time. No day or night. Pain fills your lungs. Pain floods your veins. Each heartbeat is pain. Each breath is pain. You swallow huge, distended gulps of pain; you fart burning globules of pain; you flail and spasm in a sea of pain.

not my head not my head not my head stay up stay up stay up

You're a calf cooking in its mother's milk. You're a sinner cooking in your own pus—pus of envy, pus of jealousy. Your last living thought a witch's brew of jealousy.

No excuses. The fire sears away excuses.

burningburningburningburningburningburningburnin gburningburningburningburningburningburningburni ngburningburningburningburningburningburningbur ningburningburningburningburningburningburningbu rningburningburningburningbur—

Pain wraps you close. It shrinks and tightens, it binds. And woven within its dense layers, a single thread—gleaming silver, razor-sharp—slices through you like potter's wire through clay. *Envy:* how it suffused not just your final moment but your life. Knee-high toddler letting your yellow balloon go because you wanted his red one. First grader taking his science fair project. Breaking his project. Teenager at a mirror, trying to graft their high cheekbones and mercurial mouths onto your plain face. Coveting boyfriends. Coveting clothes. No matter what you had, it was never as good as theirs. And this in a world of plenty, of green grass and nourishing food, warm houses and good friends. God laid out a wedding banquet before you and you chose envy as your groom, resentment and self-pity as your bridesmaids.

For this, the fire. For the subtle sabotage, the gloating, the hoarding. For the times you closed your heart. The times you saw only yourself, and those times occurred every day, every hour. The credit you didn't give Hailey Jackson when she helped with the auction prizes. The false solicitousness when Melanie didn't pass the bar. The chocolates you hid and the pens you "borrowed" and your glee at Ben's break-up and the cloak of contempt you threw on yourself and on anyone who dared to love you.

burningburningburningburningburningburningburnin gburningburningburningburningburningburningburni ngburningburningburningburningburningburningbur ningburningburningburningburningburningburningbu rningburningburningburningbur—

Nothing but burning, and pain.

There is no time, no day or night, no momentary breeze of relief in which to assemble a thought. Pain replaces the body. Pain replaces the mind. Burning but not consumed. Waves ablaze on an oil-slicked sea.

Your last living thought was jealousy...

Drowning in fire.

not my head not my head not my head stay up stay up stay up

No time. No day or night. Drowning in fire.

Your last living thought was jealousy...

Burning but not consumed. For a million million years.

burningburningburningburningburningburningburnin gburningburningburnin—

You can't remember life. You've never heard of life. You've never heard your own name.

You know nothing but pain.

You know nothing.

But pain.

And burning—

PART SIX

Marsh

CHAPTER THIRTY-SIX

Annie

"Annie."

Her name spoken aloud. No fire. Gravel under her back. Gentle sulfurous air on her face and legs. She wasn't lost after all?

Her body limp as week-old lettuce. She tried to open her eyes but was slammed by vertigo.

"Take your time. You're okay."

Trua's voice. She wanted to weep: she'd been so sure that she was truly gone this time. Annie lay still and let the gravel press into her back. Beautiful gravel, wonderful gravel. The rocks of Hell were now as precious to her as the green slopes of Mount Tam.

Thank you God for taking me out of the fire.

But was it God? Or just another short-circuit in the wiring of this place? She was swollen with gratitude but didn't know where to direct it.

Thank you gravel under my back.

Thank you air on my legs.

Thank you breath going in and out.

Thank you silence in my ears.

Thank you stillness, emptiness, absence of pain.

"Annie. Wake up! Don't go back there!"

What did he think—that she *wanted* to go back there? Of course she was staying here. But did she have to open her eyes so soon?

Thank you diaphragm that rises and falls.

Thank you throat that swallows.

Thank you legs that stretch—

"Annie!"

Grudgingly she opened her eyes. Even lying down, it was clear she was no longer in the plaza. Everything was still and silent. The sky stretched broad and reddish-grey. Wide open spaces. Where the deer and the antelope play.

Wrong. No deer. No antelope.

"Where are we?" she murmured. She didn't really care. She was content to lie here, alive, not burning.

"The marsh."

"What?"

Annie lunged upright now, shoving dizziness aside. Yes, there they were, on the slope between the marsh and the mountains. She strained for any sign of Mary. She wondered if she was steady enough to stand and search for her.

Then she became aware of something in her lap—a tennis ball-sized sphere, grey and wispy and light like a hummingbird nest. It had a translucent glow that reminded her of the plastic stars that Ben stuck to his bedroom ceiling as a boy. She looked at Trua, who was squatting beside her.

"Your baby," he said.

"Are you kidding?"

She didn't know whether to clutch the grey ball to her chest or drop it in horror. "What happened? What's going on?"

"Baphomet."

Trua explained. The fireball had missed them—just barely— but its impact hurled them across the plaza. The girl devil swooped down and ferried them here, barely managing to stay aloft under their combined weight, then plucked the grey sphere from the marsh. Without a pause, she placed it on top of Annie and flew off.

"Why…?"

"She felt she owed you," Trua said. "Satan revived after seeing you. She said you showed him that the walls were crumbling. Or something like that."

Annie marveled. Apparently there was honor among devils, at least sometimes. Now what, though? What was she supposed to do with this thing in her lap? She glanced around for guidance and her gut pitted. She and Trua were the only people on the dusty slope.

"Eiko? The others?"

He shook his head.

"Are they—"

"I don't know."

Trua's voice caught. Annie looked at him carefully for the first time since opening her eyes and saw a man in mourning. Grief lined his forehead. Well, of course. Baphomet had snatched him away before he could look for Eiko. Now he didn't know if the woman he loved was alive or dead, or if he'd ever see her again.

“I’m sorry,” she said softly.

He shook his head again. “It’s all right,” he said, even though she knew it wasn’t.

They sat in awkward silence. Finally Trua spoke.

“Do you know how to care for that”—he glanced at the grey sphere, struggled for the right word, and couldn’t come up with one—“thing?”

“Not a clue.”

“Really?” He looked surprised. “In my tribe, when women come out of the birthing tent, they know exactly what to do with their babies—”

“Well, they don’t end up with one of these in the birthing tent! They wouldn’t know what to do with it either.”

“Huh.”

How should one mother a wispy grey sphere? Native American women carried babies in slings on their backs. San Francisco hipsters carried them in expensive Swedish slings on their fronts. Cats carried kittens in their mouths. She supposed she should keep it warm and close to her. No one got hungry in Hell, so at least she didn’t have to worry about feeding it.

“Where should we go?” They couldn’t just sit here in the middle of the desert.

“Back to the city.”

Of course he would want that. Well, she could help him look for Eiko. Maybe she’d managed to survive. And it made sense to be around other humans—safer for all of them, and better for Mary, assuming she hatched out of this egg thing at some point. A child needed people—friends, family, teachers.

But a devil city? In the middle of a devil civil war?

"It's too dangerous. I have to take care of Mary."

"Where then?"

The lake of fire, the mountains, Satan's palace. There were no good choices here. And then the answer struck her.

"The crater."

It was sheltered, safe, yet full of people. Other children too. Mary could toddle along after Dev and Taishan and learn her times tables from Henry Mwango. She'd grow up with multicultural bedtime stories even if no one ever went to bed in Hell.

She expected Trua to argue, but he didn't. "I can find the way," was all he said, and she thought gratefully of how well he'd navigated the devil city.

Annie cupped the grey sphere close to her chest, where it might feel her heartbeat, and they set off up the slope and across the mountains.

* * * * *

Thank goodness for Trua's memory, because Annie didn't recognize a single thing along their route. One gravel slope looked like another; each jagged black peak could have been any of a dozen other peaks. Alive, she'd taken pride in her familiarity with the California landscape—knowing Douglas fir from redwood, coastal paintbrush from sticky monkey flower. So many of her friends could only tell McDonald's arches from Starbuck's mermaids. Yet here she was as clueless as they were.

She held the grey sphere carefully as they walked. She felt both protective and afraid of it. It weighed no more than a blown-glass Christmas ornament, and was perhaps equally fragile. Could Baphomet be playing some kind of trick? Annie had approached the marsh shoreline before they left but no longer heard that little voice out in the acid. She made an arbitrary decision to believe that the sphere held her child. Now it pulsed ever so slightly in her hand, a steady rhythm like a heartbeat. *Mary,* she thought to herself, trying to get past the weirdness of it. *Mary.*

They trudged over a pass into a broad basin. Annie couldn't remember how long it had taken them to reach the marsh from the crater. Billie had been with them then, and her chatter had carried Annie up any number of steep climbs. Trua was stone-silent in comparison. Annie found herself missing the background noises of the safe house—Haisheng and Ishaq's tense conferrals, Oudine's singsong. She scanned the ground for footprints or other signs that they had passed this way before but found none. Hell's landscape seemed to swallow up all evidence that you existed. But that was true of life on Earth too, wasn't it, if you took the long view? Unless you were a Shakespeare or a Lincoln, no one would remember you a hundred years later. Maybe your grandchildren would. Or your grandchildren's children. That was about the limit of it. She cupped the grey sphere more tightly against her chest and kept walking.

Time was re-spooling on her. They had walked out this way once; now they were walking back. Before, she'd been unaware of Mary's existence and was solely looking for an exit. Now she'd given up on the exit but found Mary. The last time she hiked these mountains, she fantasized about returning to Earth. Now she was fantasizing about the crater: Yelu's quiet leadership, Henry Mwango's practical intelligence. She would join the old women beating dust from the clothes. She would troll her memories of books and movies for offerings for story hour—*Harry Potter, Pride and Prejudice.* They'd be more interesting to the crowd than any stories from her own life. Those she would save for Mary. Even growing up in Hell, Mary would learn about oceans. Meadows. Deer and raccoons and starfish. She'd know about her grandparents: Annie's father playing hangman with her in the lulls of Ben's high school debate tournaments, Annie's mother in a broad-brimmed sunhat weeding her beloved garden.

Ahead of her, Trua's feet slipped on some gravel and sent it tumbling down the hill. "Wait up," she called out. He'd set a brisk pace that was hard for her to match. He seemed to want to be alone, and she understood.

He waited, but as soon as she caught up, he took off again. Annie trudged behind and catalogued the ways that Eiko was a better person than she was. *Stronger. More courageous. More generous. Eiko treated Oudine with respect. Eiko wouldn't have run away from the marauders on the rim of the canyon...* Of course Trua would be in love with her. If she were a guy, she'd be in love with Eiko too. She started sinking into self-pity but caught herself. No more of that.

You're not a wraith.

You're not in the fire.

You have Mary.

Thank you breath going in and out, thank you legs that take me up this hill, thank you stillness, emptiness, absence of pain.

They veered around debris from a rockslide and headed for a saddle between two peaks. Annie pushed herself to catch up to Trua again. His silent unhappiness weighed on her.

"I'm sorry," she said after a while. They were clambering over boulders in the saddle.

"For what?" He shot her a quick puzzled glance, then returned to the boulders.

"It must be hard to lose someone you love. And not even know if she's alive."

Trua stopped climbing. "What are you talking about?"

"Eiko? Back in the plaza?"

He furrowed his brow, and his scars lifted slightly. "I don't love Eiko."

"You don't?"

"Of course not."

Sudden, unexpected lightness. Then shame at that lightness.

"It's just... you look so unhappy. I thought it was because you wanted to be back there with her."

"I do want to be back there. But not because of Eiko."

"Then why?"

Trua looked at the ground. Annie waited. Finally he looked back up at her.

"I want to keep working with Haisheng. With his rebellion."

"Are you kidding? Why?"

Trua exhaled. He took a seat on a boulder and motioned for Annie to sit too.

"I don't expect you to understand." He paused and frowned. "I'm a fourth son. No children. No wife. My tribe moves from bare survival one season to starvation the next. Suppose I do get a wife someday and have children. What do I give them but more starvation and survival? We don't have your lightning machines. We don't have grand estates like the Romans. We struggle along, and then we die. But we always knew there would be rewards in the afterlife. We would stand in honor, even the poorest fourth sons, with our fathers and grandfathers and great-grandfathers.

"Then I come here and find no afterlife. No honor. Worse than that—the fire. Our best horsemen, our bravest leaders. My own father. My grandfather. All in the fire. My brothers and sisters will be in the fire. My children, if I ever have any, will end up in the fire."

Trua stared down the mountainside onto the barren basin that led to the next range. Eventually he turned back to Annie.

"With Haisheng, I have a chance to change all that. To free my ancestors from the fire. To free everyone from the fire."

"But how? He just wants to organize the slaves."

"No. He's gone beyond that. In his goals, at least. He says organizing the slaves isn't enough. As long as the fire exists, they'll be too terrified to rebel. They'll put up with anything rather than risk a return to the fire. So he wants to eliminate the fire."

"How?"

"I don't know. I don't think he knows either."

Annie, silent, tried to make sense of this. One low-level militia commander from a hundred-year-old communist uprising, plotting to overthrow Hell. Hell that had been around for longer than humankind. Hell that didn't operate by scientific laws. Hell that was filled with powerful, immortal devils. There was only one other being with such hubris.

"Is he working with—"

"Satan? No. He'd never even seen him until the plaza. He thought that Satan was a myth, or gone."

"He'll never succeed." It was a half-statement, half-question.

"Probably not. But I want to help. The worst outcome is that I end up in the fire. But I'll end up there no matter what I do."

Trua kicked at some pebbles in the dirt. He was wrong about her not understanding; she understood completely. He had found a commitment that gave his life and death meaning. In spiriting them away from the city, Baphomet had taken that from him. It was worse than being separated from a lover.

Annie kicked at her own set of pebbles. Dust floated up and settled back down, adding yet another layer to the coating on her feet. Trua had already lost his earthly life—his family, his tribe, his belief system. Now, because of Baphomet's sloppy rescue, he'd also lost the new life he was shaping for himself.

At least she had Mary. He had nothing.

"I'm sorry you got dragged away with me."

"No one dragged me," Trua said sharply.

She looked up.

"I *called* her. After the fireball, when you went into the fire trance. How do you think she even knew we were there? She said she'd take you somewhere safe. I demanded she take me too." Trua paused, then gave a sheepish grin. "I don't know why she listened."

"You demanded to be brought here?"

"Uh huh."

"Why?"

"You truly don't know? Your people may have lightning machines, but sometimes a year-old goat is smarter than you are. I want to help Haisheng. But I also want to be with you."

Annie felt herself melting—not the pus-and-skin melting of the fire but a familiar, almost-forgotten kind of human melting. She wanted to throw her arms around Trua. She wanted to kiss him, his scars, his forehead, his mouth. She wanted to pull him against her and inside her and make love to him.

Of course she could do none of those things.

They sat on their separate boulders, kicking at pebbles, not looking each other in the eye.

CHAPTER THIRTY-SEVEN

Annie

They kept walking. Down the far side of the mountain, across a narrow basin, up a steep ridge. Partway up the slope, Annie dropped onto a boulder to catch her breath. Her arms were cramping from holding the sphere to her chest for so long.

"I can take it for you."

"Her. Not 'it.'"

She passed the sphere to Trua, and he cupped it against his chest.

They'd walked in silence because she didn't know what to say. She wanted to cry. She wanted to tell him she loved him, but the words felt disjointed and awkward when severed from physical touch.

"Funny."

She glanced up. Trua was looking at the sphere, still cupped next to his heart.

"You've been holding this," he said. "Touching it. You care for it. But nothing bad happens."

"Maybe because it—she—isn't really alive yet."

Trua nodded. "Maybe." But then he reached out with his free hand, picked up Annie's hand and brought it to his lips.

For such a rugged face, the lips were shockingly soft. Thick. They pillowed her index finger. She hadn't felt anything moist other than her own sweat and saliva since arriving in Hell. Now his tongue curled against the back of her finger, tasting, probing. She thought of ripe plums. Wisps of beard tickled her thumb.

She was about to throw herself into his arms when the nausea hit.

Bile. Cramps. Pain. She jerked her arm back, clenched her stomach in an effort to stifle the pain. She fell to the ground, rolled herself into a ball. Nothing helped. Dry heaves. Cramps. Through the retching, she saw Trua on the ground too, on hands and knees, heaving.

All the while, even as he spasmed, he kept the grey sphere cushioned safely next to his chest.

* * * * *

They were sitting up again, leaning against their separate boulders. Trua had returned the sphere to Annie. He held his head in his hands. She herself still felt queasy.

"We could have a great time if we hated each other," she said.

"Don't joke."

How could you cope in this place if you didn't joke? At least Hell didn't send you into barfing spasms every time you smiled. Annie sat there watching Trua—his dust-dark legs, his desert-rough feet. He had surprisingly slender ankles.

"I can't even touch your ankle."

"Don't joke!"

"I'm not joking."

In fact she longed to touch his ankle. She wanted to touch a part of him that was vulnerable. What would his skin feel like if all the black dirt were rinsed away?

"I wish I had a washcloth," she said. "And a bucket of warm soapy water."

Trua shot her a puzzled glance and an idea struck her. *No. Idiotic.* He'd view her as a fool. Her cheeks heated with embarrassment just at the thought.

But she was dead. No eating, no drinking, no physical affection. No home. No family. No plants or animals. No sun or moon. No sleep. The list of things that she'd lost was endless. One thing she still had was words.

She wavered, then took the plunge.

"I'd start with your feet..."

She'd reach for his feet. Run the soapy washcloth over them and let the water drip black until she could see his actual skin. It would be light brown like a sparrow, light brown like fallen leaves on the trails of Mt. Tam. She'd rub his feet, trace the edges of the calluses, linger in the small section of arch that remained, against all odds, soft and tender.

"I'd wash your ankles. Stroke them."

Encircle his ankle with a thumb and forefinger. She wouldn't be able to reach all the way around, but it would give an illusion of possession. Patch of smooth skin in front. The tendon in back, tight like a cable. She'd slide her fingers slowly, knowingly, upwards.

"I'd stroke your calf..."

Her throat was closing on the words. She might choke. She kept going.

She'd kiss his calves. Smell of damp earth and warm horse. She'd lick them, trail her tongue up toward the knee. Taste of salt and grass. Wash the dust from his knees, soft circles with the washcloth, skin shyly revealing itself. Retrace those circles with her tongue. Kiss his kneecap. Kiss the soft spot behind the knee that no one ever touched. He'd shudder.

Then thighs. Thick and muscled from a lifetime of riding. Inner thighs moist and musky. She'd pause and inhale, as if she could breathe in an understanding of his life before. Then slide the washcloth up and watch the black dust melt away. His skin fresh and new, alive to the slightest electric touch. She'd lick her way up one thigh, tongue barely touching skin. Take care to go slowly and draw it out. Licking closer. He'd gasp. He'd try to grab her, pull her up, but she'd make him wait...

Annie stopped and grinned. Trua no longer looked perplexed; he looked uncomfortable. He'd also developed a visible erection under his breeches.

"Stop it," he said, but he was starting to laugh.

"I'd start on your other thigh—"

He was grinning now too. "Woman, you're not playing fair!"

If they'd been on Earth, they would have rolled together at this point, wrestling, tickling, laughing. Impossible. She soldiered on.

She'd make him wait, make him quiver. She wanted to give him enough pleasure to blot out all memory of the desert and the fire. Tongue on his thigh. Darting, licking. Lips on his thigh. Moving back and forth, higher and higher—

"Stop it!"

"I'd keep licking—"

"Woman!"

"Run my tongue—"

"Enough!"

"Up to—"

"All right!" Trua bellowed. It was a surrender. He swallowed, paused, took a breath. "I... touch your..." The words rasped out like a creaky, barely moving door and then halted entirely. "Neck."

He didn't seem able to get much further. She resumed.

"I'd lick up close to your balls. Just near them, not touching them—"

"Your neck," Trua repeated.

"Really close to your cock—" She couldn't believe she was saying these things. She was another person, a different Annie.

"Your neck. There. Under your hair."

"Right up next to—"

"The soft part of your neck. The part nobody can see." His voice became louder, more assertive, talking over her. "Soft. Like a yearling lamb. I kiss it. You taste... salty. Your neck, I mean."

Trua grinned. Annie's face heated, and she shifted her legs underneath her as discreetly as possible. Her crotch was completely wet.

"I bite your neck," he continued. "Maybe you gasp. You arch your back. And when you arch your back, your breasts come forward. I reach around and cup them, like this." He reached out his hands. "I stand there behind you, I kiss your neck and hold your breasts. I push up against your body everywhere—"

Holy crap. Under the guise of a Hunnic nomad lay a world-class pornographer. Annie shifted more, rubbing her thighs together. She wanted him so bad. *So bad.*

"I start licking your balls," she managed to continue, although it was getting hard to think straight, much less talk. "Right up to your cock. So close. But I don't touch it. I run my tongue just around it at the base."

It was hard to know if her face or her crotch felt hotter. She was swollen with desire, and embarrassment, and elation at her own boldness.

"It's stiff. It's standing up. I want to take you in my mouth but I can't do it, not yet, I've got to make you wait—"

Trua's erection was more prominent than ever. The boundary between words and reality was getting blurry. She couldn't take him in her mouth in her story and she couldn't take him in her mouth in reality, and that was all she wanted, all she wanted in this frigging universe, but in only one of them, the story, could she make it happen—

Trua took over.

"I push my cock up against your ass. I bite your neck. I squeeze your breasts. Your nipples are hard. You arch your back and wiggle your ass into me. God, do I want to fuck you. I want to fuck you right now. From behind. From in front. Every way. My hands are on your breasts but I slide them down. I touch your belly. Now I touch your hairy place. I use my fingers to touch you there—"

God. She needed to masturbate. She couldn't take it any longer. Annie cast a desperate look at Trua. His face was red and he was breathing so heavily that it had become hard for him to talk.

"I need—"

He nodded. Relief filtered across his face. Two sets of hands went to work under ragged garments.

Afterward, Annie slumped back against her boulder and closed her eyes. Trua lay back, a safe distance away, eyes closed too.

Alive, Annie would have rolled toward him and held him. They would have drifted off to sleep spooned together and woken up tangled in bedsheets. But that was a different universe.

She pressed the grey sphere to her heart and curled herself around it. A warm breeze meandered down the slope and curled around all three of them and, for a moment, Annie imagined that—under the acrid, ever-present sulfur—she could detect the sweet, loamy smell of rain.

PART SEVEN

Crater

CHAPTER THIRTY-EIGHT

Annie

The trek became a romp. The rocky mountainsides might as well have been wildflower meadows, the stark basins Disneyland. They teased and flirted as they walked. Rest breaks were opportunities to try out new verbal pyrotechnics.

"Take off your shirt," Trua ordered her at one stop.

They were completely exposed, a slope of boulders ahead of them but open plateau stretching in all the other directions. Annie hesitated. What about devils, marauders, some other predator? The vast silence itself was intimidating. But Trua was looking at her with bright eyes. She undid the remaining buttons and dropped the shirt on the ground.

"Great gods, you're beautiful," he murmured. And launched into such a heated description of what he wanted to do to her that she didn't manage to emit a single sentence of response.

* * * * *

"Where'd you learn all that?" she asked lightly afterward. Under the playfulness, she was curious.

"You don't think Huns have sex?"

"Well, no, of course they do. But you'd talked about being a fourth son. Not being able to marry..."

"Among your people, no one has sex until they're married?"

Well, he had her there. But somehow she'd pictured Trua as a sexual naif, the outsider looking in. Now she started wondering how she compared to the women he'd been with, back when he was alive. How many there had been. Which ones he had loved.

Don't, she thought. People were such creatures of emotional habit. If Hellfire hadn't managed to burn away her jealousy, then what would? And this went beyond sinful to pure silly. It was as pointless as being jealous of your husband's dead ex-girlfriend.

Only here the ex-girlfriends were all alive. She and Trua were the ones who were dead.

* * * * *

"Trua," she said at one of their rest breaks, "I have to tell you something."

"About my ankles again?" He grinned.

"No. This is serious." She couldn't keep it hidden anymore. If he spurned her, so be it.

"Back at the canyon. When those men captured you. It was an accident that I rescued you. I was trying to run away but the cliff collapsed."

She braced herself for judgment. It wasn't just her initial cowardice; it was also how she'd let him continue all this time under a false impression. That was cowardice too, perhaps a worse kind.

"It was a long time ago," he said. "We were strangers then."

She shook her head. No excuses.

He thought for a while. "Well," he said at last, "the important thing isn't what you meant to do. It's what you did. And once you were down in the canyon, you were steady. Brave."

He was making allowances because he loved her, but she didn't care. A weight lifted. Yet again she wished she could take him in her arms.

"Thank you," she murmured, and they continued walking.

* * * * *

They climbed toward a pass but the slope got too steep. They doubled back and looked for a longer but more manageable way over the ridge.

"Do you want me to take it for a while?" Trua asked, nodding toward the sphere.

"*Her*, not *it*."

He shrugged.

"*She*. My daughter. Mary."

"All right. She." He was humoring her, which made her even more irritated.

"You don't believe me. You don't think this is my baby."

"I don't know what to believe. It could be a baby, it could be a devil, it could just be a gray ball."

"It's a baby. *She's* a baby. I'm sure of it. At some point she'll emerge out of this ball."

"You're sure of it?" Loud and mocking, his voice startled her. He hadn't been angry at her confession about the canyon, but he was angry now. "Since you're so sure of it, tell me what happens afterwards. When this baby hatches. Will it grow or will it stay an infant forever? Nothing else grows here. My beard doesn't grow. Your hair doesn't grow. What makes you think this egg will hatch and grow? What makes you think it will even be a human baby? It was in that demon marsh, it could come out a fish. A monster. A devil."

"I—"

"How can it grow without food? You have no breast milk. We don't even have goat's milk. Are you prepared to watch it hatch and starve?"

She hadn't thought of that. But it made sense that Trua would. How many babies had he seen die during famines?

"And what's going to happen when we reach the crater? Are you so sure they'll welcome you with open arms? Arriving with a maybe-demon child? Will the Roman be happy to see you show up with a half-demon hatchling? Will he be happy to see *me*?"

It won't be a demon, she wanted to protest, but let him rant. This wasn't about Mary; it was about his own fears. Trua had left Haisheng and the rebellion for her sake. That was enough of a sacrifice, but on top of that she was taking him back to Isaias. She'd forgotten until now about their clash.

"And what if it does hatch and grow? What if it gets captured by demons and turned into a slave? Or caught by bandits? What if it gets killed and ends up in the fire—"

"Would you stop already!"

Annie's heart was racing. Any of those things could happen. She didn't want to think about them. But Trua was right about Isaias. The Roman would be furious to see her with Trua. With a baby. She'd have to watch her back. She'd have to watch over Mary.

Trua fell silent. Annie tried to revive those happy visions of Mary toddling after Dev and Tai-shan. Gradually she calmed herself down. Mary would be a baby, not a devil. Yelu would make sure they were welcome. Isaias would fall in line. They'd become part of the crater community. Mary would have as normal a life as a child could have in Hell.

They walked quietly for a long time after that, and neither of them raised the topic again. But Trua had slipped a pebble of doubt under Annie's feet. She felt it, small but hard, with each step that took them closer to the crater.

* * * * *

Then there was sin. For all the exhilaration of their new connection, she couldn't help wondering.

"Lust is a sin," she ventured as they walked.

"According to who?" Trua said. "My people don't see it as a sin. Only Christians do."

"But this is a Christian universe. Christian Hell. Christian God. I didn't believe in it when I was alive either, but that's what it is."

"Maybe."

"Maybe?"

"Maybe this is a nothing universe. Maybe it's an evil universe. Maybe the devils run everything and the Christian God is just a story. We've seen plenty of devils here and we haven't seen any sign of the Christian God."

"But if there *is* a God? Then what we're doing is sinning. On top of all the other sins that brought us here already. What if he decides to punish us even more?"

Trua rolled his eyes. "Nothing can be worse than the fire."

Annie nodded but couldn't get sin out of her mind. She continued the sex play with Trua. It felt so good; it made both of them so happy. No one was hurt by it. For those short minutes, you could forget you were in Hell.

But perhaps that was part of the sinfulness. You weren't supposed to forget, even for one minute, that you were in Hell.

Maybe God was in fact present and watching, like Ishaq said. Maybe her happiness was sabotaging their chances for redemption.

At the next rest break, she wandered off behind a large boulder and knelt in the gravel. "God, tell me what you want. Tell me what's right," she mouthed silently.

She no longer expected an answer, and she got none.

"What were you doing?" Trua asked when she returned.

She shook her head dismissively. "I thought I remembered stopping here when we were with Billie. But I was wrong."

* * * * *

She recognized the smell of the sulfur plain before they saw it. Everywhere in Hell had a whiff of sulfur, but here it reeked. Annie ran up the remaining slope to the ridge and looked out. It stretched before her—yellow, nubby with crystal formations, and, most striking of all, *familiar*.

"We made it!" she shouted to Trua, who was trailing her with the sphere. "You did it!"

She remembered this place so vividly from their trek out—the smell, the jagged crystals, the equally jagged tension between Billie and Trua. Reaching the plain meant there was only one more range to cross before the crater.

She wanted to sprint, to forego rest breaks and get there as quickly as possible. Trua refused. "It's still far off. Save your energy."

"Things will be okay with Isaias. I'll talk to Yelu," she said. "No one will give you a hard time."

He didn't respond.

"You know I'll stand by you. No matter what."

She said it to reassure him, but also to convince herself. Loyalty was part of Trua's cultural DNA, but she came from a society where clothing lasted one season, electronics were cheaper to replace than to fix, and best-friends-forever meant half of seventh grade.

Ben had never been loyal to her. He wrote his own script and expected her to play a supporting role. Annie had always complied. But was that loyalty or passivity?

She was loyal to Mary.

She would be loyal to Trua.

They reached the end of the sulfur plain. Annie took the sphere back; she wanted Mary physically close as they neared their destination. They started to climb, and her legs felt as strong and fresh as on the first ascent of a morning hike. *Dev's face would light up when he saw her. Tai-shan would do her little happy-dance.* No need to save energy anymore: she ran up the slope, hopping rocks and dodging boulders. At the top, she looked out over the plateau.

Fire waterfall in the distance. Closer to her, the cliff wall with its secret passage into the crater. In between, several shallow, unfinished trenches.

Henry's lava canals. She beamed with delight.

Trua caught up, panting.

"We made it," she said.

He smiled and nodded.

"Thank you." She put a hand to her lips, kissed it, and held it out as if making an offering.

They ran down the slope together. They crossed the short plain, found the opening to the cave, folded themselves inside it. It was as tight and difficult a passage as she remembered. But short. Just a few dozen yards, then there would be a few knocks on the boulder, then the rasp of gravel as it was pushed aside...

Wait.

Light. Ahead of them.

The cave should have been dark, blocked by the boulder. Instead there was a wash of grey daylight.

Annie froze. If the boulder were gone, something must be wrong. And they were in the worst possible spot, wedged in the tight passage.

She glanced at Trua. It was too dark to see his expression, but he knew it too. He was peering back toward the entrance, and his hunched body was tight with tension. Go back? Go forward?

She needed to know. Maybe Henry had been working on his canals and the entry was left open for him. Maybe they'd taken in some other wandering soul and forgotten to close the door. She tipped her head toward the opening, and Trua nodded.

They edged forward, trying not to make a sound. Annie reached the opening and, holding herself as close to the wall of the passage as possible, looked out.

Nothing.

No people. No sounds of talk, argument, play. No movement.

She stepped warily into the open. Across the crater, the story circle of flat rocks remained. Other than that, no visible sign that people had ever been here.

"Maybe they left?" she whispered.

Maybe they found a way back to Earth. That was the optimistic scenario.

Trua made his way along the edge of the crater. He stopped about halfway across and gestured. She followed and found a pile of bones. Some were picked clean; others held flaps of desiccated flesh.

They left the crater fast.

They slunk back to the passage, trying not to leave footprints in the dust. Trua entered the cave first, and at the far end peered out for assailants. When he nodded, they raced back across the plateau toward the last ridge they'd crossed, trying to be as inconspicuous as possible.

They kept glancing around. No marauders. No devils. Nothing.

They scrambled up the ridge, looking for somewhere to hide. Trua led the way to a mass of boulders, and they wormed their way into a sheltered nook.

Annie collapsed. Terror had held her together as they fled; now she fell apart.

Yelu. Dev. Tai-shan. Henry Mwango.

Ifechi. Isaias. The old women.

All gone.

The crater sanctuary—gone.

Her hopes of a decent life for Mary—gone.

There was nothing here. There would never be anything here. Anything good would be destroyed. Anything hopeful would be destroyed. Being in the fire was hopeless, but this place was worse. It gave you hope and continually smashed it in front of you.

Dev in the fire. That small body. That ocean of fire.

On Earth, at least suffering had an end point. Patients with bone-shrieking cancer could reach the relief of hospice. Enslaved people could imagine sweet chariots to carry them home. Here there was no end.

She would wander this desert forever, and her daughter would wander it forever, and the only possible ending would be a return to the fire.

"Annie." Trua tapped her shoulder. "We need to leave. It's not safe here."

She shook her head. It wasn't safe anywhere. Look what had happened in the canyon. Look what had happened in the city. She clutched the grey sphere to her chest and huddled down against the rock.

"We need to go," he repeated.

Annie didn't move. There was no reason to leave. Death and despair would find them wherever they fled.

* * * * *

Eventually Trua's badgering was too much. She agreed to go.

"But where?"

"The city."

She stared with disbelief.

"We'll find Haisheng. They'll have a new safe house. Mary can be safe there."

Didn't he get it? No one was safe anywhere.

"Look," he added. "This is why I want to help Haisheng. The only way to protect anyone is to destroy the fire."

"Which you can't do. And even if you could, what would happen to all the people in the fire?"

He shook his head. "I don't know. Maybe they would be in the desert like us. Or maybe they would be nothing. Non-existent. But that would be better, wouldn't it? Anyway, come on. Let's go. Do you want me to hold her for a while?"

Trua had said "her." Annie passed him the sphere and followed him out from the boulder patch.

* * * * *

They headed back the way they'd come. Once they reached the marsh, Trua said, he could retrace the route that Baphomet had flown. But walking would be a hundred times slower than flying. It would be a daunting trek—months or years of walking. And that was assuming Trua could even translate Baphomet's route from air to ground. The whole thing was futile, Sisyphean. Maybe this was her doom: to trudge through the desert forever, reaching a destination only to turn around and trudge back to the starting point.

They climbed slowly up the ridge that led to the sulfur plain, alert for attackers. Near the top, Trua froze. He cocked his head.

"Listen."

At first Annie didn't hear anything but wind. Then she made out a hint of a voice, coming from somewhere to their left along the ridge. She looked around for hiding spots and prepared to run.

But the voice. Was it her imagination or was it calling her name?

She glanced at the sphere; this wasn't Mary calling. She cocked her head, tried to capture more of that flimsy sound. Trua was listening too, unsure whether to stay or run.

"Miss Maple! Miss Annie Maple!"

Squinting across the hillside, Annie saw a small, stooped figure picking its way awkwardly over the rocks.

"Wait! Miss Annie Maple!"

Male voice with a colonial-British accent. That limping gait.

"Henry!"

She ran toward him so he wouldn't have to clamber over any more boulders than necessary. Reaching him, she was shocked. He looked a decade older. His forehead was lined, his eyes seemed to droop, his cheeks sagged loosely. He was like a balloon with nearly all the air gone, when the rubber starts to wrinkle and stick together.

"Are you okay?"

"My dear, dear girl. I am not. I most certainly am not."

Trua joined them. She glanced around for a large boulder that would provide cover, and beckoned Henry to sit down.

"What happened?"

The engineer lowered himself unsteadily, a hand on the rock. He removed his glasses and put his head in his hands. After a while he took a breath and looked up.

"May God have mercy on my soul."

CHAPTER THIRTY-NINE

Henry

God worked in indirect ways. The Lord would never make decisions for you, but He might provide little nudges if you weren't too busy and self-important to notice them. He wouldn't solve your problems but He might provide tools to help you solve them.

Like bringing Ifechi to the crater.

Henry Mwango was alternately charmed and appalled by the tall young man. A boy, really. Blind to the consequences of his actions, confident that a grin and an apology could make anything right. Henry wondered if he himself had ever been so young. At Ifechi's age, he'd been far from home at the technical school in Kampala, days filled with back-throbbing construction, nights with devouring every worn, mold-fringed book he could find, trying to justify the confidence of the white missionaries who had sent him there. He no longer remembered the names of any of his classmates at Kampala, but he still smelled the thin, biting odor of the paraffin lantern he used for reading late into the night, still pictured the sudden flare of the dry cornstalks he burned when there was no paraffin.

Henry's youth had been one widening circle of exile after another—first the mission school near his home, then Kampala, then Nairobi, then London, each more foreign and more eye-opening than the last.

While Ifechi's first and only journey was here to Hell.

Poor fellow. Such a waste. He followed Henry around the crater like an orphan duckling trailing that Austrian biologist Konrad Lorenz.

But the Lord offered tools. Everything for a reason, even if the reasons were hidden behind dark glass. And Ifechi was just what Henry needed to begin work on the lava canals.

They started slowly, fitting the canal project in between Dev and Tai-shan's lessons. At first they didn't even leave the crater. Henry wanted Ifechi to understand the concepts behind what they were doing. But the young man had never encountered a representational number system before. They sat beside the blueprint in the dirt for countless sessions, Henry scratching out numbers with a rock and explaining how to calculate area and volume, how to determine the slope of a canal for optimal lava flow. Ifechi's ability to focus for long stretches of time was a delight after Dev and Tai-shan's flightiness. Gradually Henry forgave him his youth. Ifechi became less of a duckling and more of a companion. But Henry couldn't convince Ifechi that he didn't have supernatural powers.

"I am not a diviner. I am an engineer," he snapped for what must have been the twentieth time.

"I know your people have different names for things." Ifechi gave him a generous smile. "So tell me, when will I have learned enough to engineer my way home?"

Finally they ventured out of the crater. Isaias and Ezra Ben-Nachman pushed the rock into place behind them; Henry would use the tapping code when they were ready to reenter. The openness of the plateau was unnerving after being enclosed for so long. Henry thought of his return to Kenya after those lonely, cold years in London. Kenya was the land of his birth, the place he'd yearned for through so many frozen winters, yet when the ship finally approached Mombasa and he felt the leaden tropical sun and saw the leggy, straining palms, he felt lost.

This sense of disorientation, now, was worse.

Never mind. They had work to do.

They marked out a route for the initial canal with small stones and then tested the ground, scraping into it with hands and rocks to see how hard it would be to excavate. They adjusted the route and started digging.

They scrabbled with their fingers, levered rocks out of place with other rocks. Digging a canal without tools would have been an impossible task anywhere else, but here they could work for a thousand years if necessary. Digging became a routine part of their day. Dev begged to join them—"I can help! I'm strong!"—and Henry refused, but the boy was persistent as a mosquito, and finally he relented. "No wandering," he warned sternly. So then it became the three of them crawling out through the tunnel each day, scraping and digging, with Dev doing perhaps more cartwheels and rock collecting than actual excavation.

Sometimes Henry questioned the whole project. Would a lava moat make this world any less wretched? Perhaps he was immersing himself in work so as not to think about things. It would not be the first time. Those violent years of the Emergency, he had hunkered down in Mombasa, far from the confrontations, and become a creature of pipelines and blueprints. He still remembered his last conversation with Gatimu, who had been part of his African expatriate circle in London and was rumored to have joined the Mau Mau rebels seeking independence from Britain. In those days even good friends left some things unspoken. They sat at a market stall in Mombasa, drinking palm wine and watching the pretty school girls in their short blue uniform skirts.

"Henry, this is a time for struggle. The people need educated men like us," Gatimu had said.

"My place is here. The people will need refineries and bridges once we have our independence," Henry said. At the time, he believed his explanation.

Gatimu returned alone to Nairobi. Four months later he was shot dead by the British. So was their friend Mutegi. Another friend, Charles Okumu, spent five years in British prison camps. Henry stayed in Mombasa with his white oil-company employers and devoted wife and diverting mistresses. He worked hard, no question about it, and was supremely well qualified to oversee the country's transportation infrastructure when Kenya became independent.

Kenyatta himself called upon him and told him how essential his skills would be for the new republic.

As if that justified anything.

Now, again, he worked. He worked like a machine and taught the children and tried not to think about those bigger questions.

And one day Dev wandered off.

* * * * *

Henry and Ifechi knelt in their respective ditches, lost in the routine of scrabbling and chiseling. Neither noticed that the boy was gone. Suddenly something—a sound? a hunch?—made Henry look up.

Two white men, tall and short, were moving toward them from the far side of the plateau. The short one was pushing Dev along with some kind of weapon at his back.

"Henry!" the boy cried, and the short man grabbed him and wrapped a hand over his mouth.

Ifechi sprang. He didn't wait, didn't weigh, didn't strategize, just hurled himself out of the ditch and across the plateau with his long young-man's legs. He threw himself at the man holding Dev, but the man pivoted just enough for Ifechi to stumble. The tall man was on him at once with a large rock to the head. Ifechi fell. The two men moved in, kicking, so close and so tight that Henry could no longer see Ifechi's body, only their jackhammer legs.

Henry hid.

One section of his ditch was deep enough that he could lie on his stomach and be entirely below ground level. He prayed that the men hadn't noticed him. He prayed that Ifechi would somehow rise from under their feet. He wished, for once, that he truly were a diviner who could conjure spirits from the earth.

He held his breath and tried not to move.

Voices, footsteps. Dev's muffled cries. Bitter dirt filled Henry's mouth, crammed his glasses. The footsteps receded. He looked up and saw the men entering the tunnel to the crater, the small one still holding Dev with his hand over the boy's mouth. Ifechi's body lay crumpled, blood pooling, one long leg sticking out at an impossible angle.

Henry fled. His own legs—not strong to begin with—now barely seemed to function. He hobbled and stumbled to the far side of the plateau and hid in a cluster of rocks. He didn't know if the faint screams he heard were real or his imagination. Dizziness overtook him and he thought he'd plummet back into the fire but he didn't. Silence descended, more ominous than any screams. Nothing moved on the black plateau. Was he the last man alive in this place? Just him and the two killers? He hunkered down and waited and thought about the last lesson he had given Dev and Tai-shan. He thought about his friends who had died in the Emergency years. Why did cowards live and brave souls die? Where was God in all this?

Elsewhere of course. This was Hell. But even in Hell, shouldn't cowards suffer and the brave survive?

Still there was no sound from beyond the rocks.

His wife Margaret had seen his cowardice. She had known him better than anyone, better than he knew himself. And she loved him anyway. Perhaps that was why he had betrayed her so often. No, that was giving himself too much credit for psychological complexity. He had simply felt entitled. *Everyone did it. A man's nature. Just a little fun. Et cetera.*

"Henry," she had said once. They were both well into middle age; it was nearly midnight; he had just returned from another late night at the ministry. She sat at the kitchen table, waiting for him. "You have given such good service to our country. Truly. More than many men whose names are on statues."

"Be quiet, woman," he said and retreated to his study. He'd assumed this was the preamble to more complaints about his long hours and inattentiveness. Only much later—after he was dead—did it occur to him that she might have been trying to salve a wound he refused to acknowledge.

Now he crouched in the rock outcropping. Days might have passed or weeks or months. When he thought about time, he thought of that imprecise, miserable, beautiful system of moving rocks in the crater, and the dizziness returned. His legs cramped. He wondered if what little muscle mass he possessed would atrophy. Every so often he rose to peer out at the plateau, which remained empty. No murderers. No villagers. Just the roar and crackle of the lava waterfall, and Ifechi's crooked body sprawled on the bare dirt.

There were no vultures here in Hell, no jackals or even worms. His body might lie there askew and exposed for the rest of eternity.

How did Ifechi's people handle their dead? No matter; the options were limited. Finally, after still more time had passed without any signs of the killers, Henry ventured out from his hiding spot. Slowly he pulled himself across the plateau. He hoisted the young man's body and staggered toward the waterfall.

Too tall. Too heavy. Henry let the body fall and tried dragging it. Ifechi's legs scraped the rocky ground. Each bump hit Henry like the recoil of a rifle. Or what he imagined a rifle would feel like; after all, he had never gone to the Mau Mau.

He dragged. He stopped. Finally he reached the rim. Heat swarmed him. Too long here and he would join Ifechi. Quickly Henry mouthed a prayer—"*Into your hands, O Lord, we commend our brother Ifechi. Rest eternal grant to him and let light perpetual shine upon him*"—and pushed the corpse over the edge.

He retreated to the hillside. Moving Ifechi's body had sapped all his will. He waited but had no idea for what. He prayed. He wandered back and forth on the hillside, afraid of being found, afraid of being alone.

Then, finally, he saw Annie and Trua.

PART EIGHT

Desert

CHAPTER FORTY

Annie

Henry joined them. At first it was simply because he didn't want to be alone. But then, as they walked, Trua told him about Haisheng's dream of eliminating the fire.

"I must join this revolution," Henry said. "I will do anything. I will design weapons. I will sweep floors. I will carry rocks. I will do anything to help end that torment."

It seemed unlikely that Henry would be much help to anyone as a rock carrier, though; he could barely make it up the mountainsides. Annie and Trua slowed to half their normal pace to accommodate him. At this rate, it would take them the equivalent of a month just to return to the marsh. They might never reach the city at all.

They'd also given up all sex play. Henry's presence made it impossible, but even without him, Annie no longer had the heart for games. The empty crater had finished that.

Slowly they picked their way back across the sulfur plain. Slowly they inched up a ridge and down the other side. Trua watched the gravel for tracks that might not be theirs; Annie cradled the grey sphere and monitored the horizon. They saw nothing, but she was determined not to become complacent.

Whenever they stopped, Henry sought out a boulder some distance away from the two of them and sat by himself. One time Annie approached him. His eyes were closed and he was rocking and humming. The tune seemed vaguely familiar, but she couldn't place it.

She sat beside him. He looked up.

"Are you praying?"

"Forgive me if I was bothering you. I shall be quieter."

"It's no bother. I just wondered... do you think God listens? Does he even know what's going on down here?"

Henry shook his head. "I cannot pretend to know the answer to that. I thought I knew many things when I was alive, and they were almost all wrong. But there must be an order and reason to things. Perhaps with God's grace I will be able to understand a little piece of it."

"So you think God exists?"

"He must. Otherwise who can forgive us?"

Annie dropped her gaze. Henry said *us*, but he was talking about himself. Later, when they had resumed walking, she figured out the song he had been humming. It was *Rock of Ages*, probably the only hymn besides *Amazing Grace* that she would have been able to recognize. She knew the tune but didn't know the words.

* * * * *

There was dust in her throat, dust in her eyes, dust in her nostrils. A wind had arisen and was blowing gritty black dust everywhere, making it hard to see the surrounding mountains. More than that, though, Annie's heart was a dusty ruin.

She didn't know where Trua got his persistence. Haisheng's uprising was a lost cause. Even finding Haisheng again was a lost cause. She'd been granted her wish of rescuing Mary but she couldn't picture any future other than fire and pain.

What kind of God had created this place? What kind of God desired such suffering? Heaven and Hell were supposed to provide divine justice, but there was nothing just about this world. Murderers roamed freely while good people like Eiko and Dev were killed. Babies spent eternity in limbo for no fault of their own. Souls were condemned to the fire for not knowing about Christianity or worshipping the wrong version of God. And the fire showed no proportion, with adultery earning the same eternity of torment as mass murder. It offered no mercy—no chance to repent, to change, to do better.

She didn't understand Henry's faith. God must be oblivious or sadistic or rigid to the point of cruelty. Henry was seeking forgiveness from God, but in reality it was God who had wronged all of them.

She wanted to curse God.

She was afraid to curse God.

Even thinking these thoughts might doom her—worse, might doom Mary. Did God really want a universe of obedience based on fear?

She continued trudging along because Trua was leading and because there was nothing else to do. She held the grey sphere close to shield it from the gritty wind, and hoped it wouldn't absorb her despair.

Perhaps summoning gratitude might dilute the hopelessness. She called up memories of her life: how lucky to have had a job helping preserve life in the oceans. Even all that tedious computer work—better to be doing it for the environment than to sell the latest cell phone or chocolate bar. And that nature educator with the crush on her. She'd gone out to photograph his program once and set her camera aside to help a boy find a starfish in the tide pools. "You'd be a great teacher," he said to her. She'd discounted that as dumb flirtation, but now she thought he was sincere. And right. She *would* have been great at working with kids in nature.

What was the nature educator's name? Something with an R, maybe?

Ronald? Rodney? Robert? It was lost to her.

She thought about the Steep Ravine trail. The shy brown bird that once had emerged to trill alongside her.

She couldn't remember the name of the bird.

She thought about her apartment. Her bedroom. It was so funky, nothing like her boss's condo or Ben's apartment, but it was hers. The line of seashells along the window sill. The blue and white throw-blanket knitted by her mother. The movie poster over her bed of a boy and a girl and a sinking ship. She'd been obsessed with that movie in sixth grade, had entered contests in teen magazines to meet the actor, had kept the poster all those years as an ironic joke.

What was the name of the movie? The actor? And was the poster even still on her wall?

She might have taken it down, but she wasn't sure.

Annie's throat was sore, her eyes dry and gritty. Her life was sifting out of her into this endless desert like down from her old couch. A feather here, a feather there. Eventually she would be nothing but empty fabric, folding in on itself, blowing along with the dust.

* * * * *

They took longer, more frequent breaks because of Henry. At one point, they stopped halfway up a slope.

"I'll scout the ridge," Trua said.

"No, I'll do it."

Trua deserved a rest; he'd been jogging ahead and doubling back to find the easiest route up the mountainside. Annie handed him the sphere and continued up the slope.

At the ridge, she crouched low to be as inconspicuous as possible. She needn't have worried: no marauders, no devils, nothing. But her view was partly blocked by a rock outcropping. Annie clambered up. Alive, she would have marveled at how her hands found fingerholds in the rock. Now she took it for granted, even despised it. Agile or klutzy, flabby or toned, everyone ended up in the same fire.

She perched on a ledge, holding herself low. Broader view. Still nothing. Look for signs of movement. Scan the distant seam where basin turned into mountain—

The ledge gave way.

Falling. Nothing beneath her. Panic, flailing, grasping, empty hands, wild legs, stomach in her throat, *this had happened before,* debris falling, confusion, everything falling—

Annie hit the ground.

It had been only a second but it felt like much longer.

She was lying on her side in a pile of dirt and rubble. Gingerly she pushed her shoulders up. Her arms worked, her torso worked. She tried to move her legs and they worked too. Thank God. She pulled herself onto hands and knees and waited for her heart to stop racing.

No head injury. Bruises but no breaks. A long scrape on her left leg, smears of blood, but it didn't look deep.

Annie stood up, brushed herself off, and looked around. It had been a minuscule fall—maybe four feet—from one level of rock to the next. But the crash would have alerted anyone below. With a flush of alarm, she glanced quickly out over the basin.

Empty, silent desert. There still didn't seem to be anyone there. Everything was fine. Everything was the same—

Except she remembered her death.

The flailing, the grasping, the utter confusion that suddenly there was nothing under your feet and you were falling through air. She'd felt that before, and not just when the ledge overlooking the marauders' camp collapsed under her. She'd felt it even before then, before Hell.

She remembered everything now.

* * * * *

Annie was spooning leftover stir-fry into an empty yogurt container while Melanie washed the dinner dishes. Mel started to describe a new Netflix show they could watch, then halted and looked over at Annie in puzzlement.

"Wait, weren't you going out tonight?"

"Oh shit!"

In her swamp of self-pity, she'd forgotten a friend's 30th birthday party. Annie threw herself in the shower and scrubbed the garlic off her fingers. By the time she'd finished blow-drying her hair, the world felt more hopeful. Maybe she'd even meet someone at the party. She dove into her closet with gusto; it was one of those precious, rare summer days in San Francisco when you could actually wear summer clothes. Even now, close to 8 p.m., the fog remained in distant retreat beyond the Farallones.

"This one or that one?" she asked Melanie, holding up two skirts. One was a pale yellow that conjured lawn chairs and fizzy cocktails but made her butt look enormous. The other was black with white chevrons, a retro pop-art feel.

"That one, for sure." Mel pointed at the yellow one. "And no, don't say a word about looking fat. Just don't."

So she accessorized the yellow skirt. She tried on a light blue v-neck from the Gap and a black tank from a vintage store and finally settled on a sleeveless white blouse. On top of that, the yellow cardigan. And dangling beaded earrings made by Nadine, the birthday girl, who would enjoy seeing them on her.

At the last minute, she opted to walk rather than take the bus. Annie kicked off the heels she'd initially chosen and switched to her comfy clogs.

The evening was glorious. Why hadn't she noticed this earlier? The sun was setting with lustrous abandon and people filled the streets. The two little Salvadoran girls from the apartment below hers were playing jump rope on the sidewalk. The owner of the corner bodega stood in her doorway, giving advice about dog training to a customer with an unruly puppy. On the next block, the ice cream store had a line that snaked around the corner. Two of Mel's friends waved and beckoned, but Annie just waved back and kept going.

Mission Street took her north past Filipino restaurants, Chinese take-out places, and check-cashing storefronts with signs in Spanish and English. Blocks that were grimy and grey in the fog turned golden and glowing in the unaccustomed sunset. How would San Francisco change if it had as much sun as L.A.? Would outdoor cafes sprawl along

Market Street like on boulevards in Paris? Would everyone leave their cubicles and go to the beach? Would the tech economy crumble? Would the city become even more of a tourist fantasyland than it already was?

Annie stopped at a liquor store for a bottle of wine. The shadows lengthened; the golden sky gently put itself to bed behind Twin Peaks. It was dark by the time she arrived at Nadine's street, but the music and voices were audible halfway down the block. The streetlight glowed orange and cast a magical sheen on the faded, peeling buttercream curls of Victorian woodworking. She'd talked with a cute carpenter at Nadine's last party; maybe he'd be back. Annie patted her hair, straightened her skirt (it did make her butt look big, no matter what Melanie said), tucked the wine under her arm, and entered the party.

Music. Bodies. Bottles of Corona and tendrils of pot smoke. Someone in the kitchen mixing craft cocktails with basil, jalapenos, and gin. Annie deposited her wine offering on a counter, tasted a jalapeno cocktail, and grimaced. Beer for her. She found Nadine, who was dressed in a Wonder Woman costume, complete with gold cuff bracelets, and gave her a hug.

"Ooh, who's your designer?" Nadine purred at the earrings.

"I can't tell you, they're too exclusive." Grinning, Annie pointed to the gold bracelets. "Who's yours?"

She inserted herself into the crowded living room and talked with a woman who built dining room tables out of old Scrabble tiles. She met another woman who did video installations for transgender rights. The music was too loud and there was barely room to stand. She was sweating and needed air. Out through the French doors onto the deck.

Downtown skyscrapers. Baseball stadium. The bay.

The city spread into the night, a gorgeous patchwork quilt of black velvet and white thread: knots of white downtown lights in the foreground, a wide swatch of black where the shore hit the bay, then faint stitches of light across the water in Oakland.

The deck filled up. The cute carpenter wasn't here; in fact, she knew hardly anybody. Maybe she should have watched Netflix with Mel after all. Far away a car alarm sounded, a shrill nag over the thumping bass from the party. Someone nearby was smoking clove cigarettes.

"Annie! Over here!"

At last a familiar face, someone from an Ocean Allies beach clean-up event. Half-empty beer in hand, Annie pushed through the crowd and hugged the beach person, whose name she didn't remember but was too embarrassed to ask. Her earrings pinched and she slipped them into her purse. Even without fog, the night was turning chilly and Annie pulled her sweater back on.

That's when the deck collapsed.

Jolt of nothing under her feet.

Panic. Limbs. Planks. Bottles. Flailing.

Falling.

Annie slammed into the ground.

She was dead.

CHAPTER FORTY-ONE

Annie

So that was all—the random collapse of a deck.

Dry rot, maybe. Or termites. Or maybe just too many people.

Annie sank onto the rocky debris where the ledge had given way. She had racked her brain over this for so long. It was supposed to be a key. It was supposed to provide meaning, context, maybe even a path home.

But it was nothing. Random, meaningless nothing. It didn't even have any connection to her sins. Wouldn't God have the aesthetics—if not the justice—to make your death a reflection of your life?

Trua at least had died trying to learn about another culture.

She had died from standing on a deck drinking half a beer.

* * * * *

Trua came looking for her.

"Annie!"

His eyes widened with alarm and she realized she must look terrible. The rubble, the bruises, the cut on her leg. The worst was what he couldn't see.

"What happened?"

"Nothing. I fell."

She picked herself up, brushed off the new layer of dust, and hobbled toward him.

They resumed walking. Trua was asking Henry questions about Kenya. The words washed past her, empty sounds. She took the sphere back from Trua and cradled it. They kept walking. They reached the top of another ridge and Trua suggested they skirt the edge of the next basin rather than plow straight through the middle. *Longer but less exposed. Marauders, risk, safety.* She barely heard him and didn't argue. They rested. They walked. Henry fell and cut his shin, and it wouldn't stop bleeding, so they ripped a section of her skirt to make a bandage. The mountains along this side of the basin were steep and scarred with dozens of narrow canyons. Trua jogged ahead to scout their path: any of the canyons could conceal an ambush. They walked. They rested. They walked.

"Annie." Trua sat beside her at one of their rest stops, when Henry had gone off to pray alone. He studied her face with concern. "We'll make a home for Mary in the city. A special safe house. There must be other children somewhere. We can—"

"Stop," she said. He was making an effort, but it was all impossible. Nothing made a difference here. She'd tried calling on God but God never answered. She'd rescued her baby from limbo but had no home for her. She finally remembered her death but it was meaningless. Really, though, had her life been any better? Had anything she'd done while alive made any difference?

"We'll keep her safe," Trua continued. "It will be all right—"

"Stop already! Would you just shut up!"

A shadow of hurt crossed his face but it didn't matter. Nothing mattered. When you stripped the delusions from everything, all that was left was random wandering and then the fire. All the hustle-and-bustle of being alive—career goals and vacation plans, shopping for groceries and looking for love—meant nothing. Their strivings here in Hell were equally meaningless. She thought of Oudine drawing in the dirt and waiting for angels. In fact, they were all Oudine, floating along in vain fantasies of meaning and salvation.

When really, there was nothing for any of them but the fire. Burn now or burn later? That was the only question.

They kept walking. Henry's injured leg was weak and they needed to rest even more often than before. They took to stopping just inside the mouths of the canyons, where they wouldn't be visible from the broad plain.

They were resting in the opening of one of those canyons when Trua took a seat close beside her. One of Annie's hands held the sphere. She ran the fingers of the other through the gravel, making random shapes. Like Oudine. No, worse than Oudine. At least Oudine made crosses, shapes with meaning.

"I'm worried about you," Trua said in a low voice.

Don't waste your energy.

"Annie. Don't give up."

She stared blankly down. So much dust. Nothing but dust.

"We'll find the city. We'll find Haisheng."

His words were noise. Let him delude himself; she didn't care. She hunched down, shutting out his presence, but then he slipped an arm around her shoulder—well-meaning but futile—*wait, his arm?—holding her?—what was he thinking?*—and her gut spasmed and she lurched away.

"Don't!"

She retched even as the word came out. Her chest heaved and her arms jerked open and suddenly her hand was empty and where was Mary, WHERE WAS MARY? Through the spasms she glanced wildly—saw the grey sphere bouncing down the slope toward the open plain—

"Mary!"

She hurled aside the nausea and scrambled after it. Trua had seen it too and lurched after her, heaving. The sphere rolled only about fifteen yards; it was a gentle slope, and the rocks stopped it from gaining momentum. Annie lunged forward, cupped the sphere, and brought it to her chest.

"I'm sorry," she whispered. "Oh honey, I'm sorry." Had it been damaged? There was no way to tell. The gentle pulse seemed unchanged. She cradled it, touched it to her lips, stroked it. She peered at the ground to see if any pieces had flaked or chipped off.

She froze.

A tiny, dark brown pellet lay before her in the dust. It was hard to see, brown against black. Annie was amazed she'd even noticed it. She looked carefully and saw another one. Four, five of them, like fat caraway seeds.

In high school bio, she'd spent hours cleaning cages. These were recognizable at once: rat turds.

"Trua." She could barely choke out his name. He leaned over, peered into the dust, and understood right away.

"Nothing shits here," he said. "There's no food here—"

"They must have come from—"

"Henry!" they shouted together, oblivious to the risk of marauders or devils. Startled, Henry looked up from the other side of the canyon mouth.

"I'm here," he grumbled. "No need to yell. I'm lame, not deaf. I can hear you."

* * * * *

So Billie had been right about an exit.

Annie had been right about the dog.

There were passageways between Earth and Hell. The dog had wandered through one of them. Rats—at least one rat—had passed through. And if a rat could enter Hell, then humans could conceivably exit, even if it required chiseling through a rodent-size opening.

They organized a search for more droppings that might indicate the rat's trail. Henry told them to visualize a checkerboard-like grid on the basin floor.

They got on hands and knees, each following a row in that grid, moving out into the basin and looking for turds.

Nothing. Annie went about thirty yards into the plain along her row, then returned to do another row. Still nothing. Soon they had canvassed a wide fan from the canyon mouth. Her knees were pocked and sore from gravel. Still nothing.

“Before continuing further into the plain, we should examine the canyon,” Henry said.

The walls and floor of the canyon were volcanic black rock like the surrounding mountains, but sharper and less eroded. The lava had made tight grill-like formations that were both painful to walk on and hard to search; dark rat turds could easily be lost in dark folds of rock. Annie took the left side of the canyon and, parallel to Trua and Henry, painstakingly inched her way along.

Palms traced the sharp lava ridges, fingertips probed the walls of narrow lava crevices. The crevices were too tight to touch the bottom, even with a single index finger, and too dark to see the bottom. She peered close, face practically touching the rock—then drew back for a broader view, afraid of missing something—and peered close again. She was a clumsy giant blundering across a lilliputian landscape of ridges and folds. This was worse than searching for the back of an earring on her bedroom floor, worse than helping a friend hunt for a lost contact lens.

“Here!”

Annie startled. Trua's voice was only a few yards to her right, but in her focus on the folds of lava she'd forgotten he was there.

She hauled herself up and stepped over. He gestured at a cluster of pellets in a shallow indentation in the rock. She squeezed one between her thumb and forefinger and it smeared: *gross*. But that meant it was fresh. The rat had been here recently. A portal had been open recently—might still be open now.

She returned to her transect and inched along, one hand probing the lava, the other cradling the grey sphere. So Billie had been right this whole time, Billie with her racist beliefs and her bag of purloined treasures. At first Annie hadn't believed her when she said this was Hell. Later she hadn't believed Billie about an exit. But Billie had been right on all counts.

Still nothing in her strip of the canyon.

Annie's knees stung. The portal must be close enough for a rat still to have food in its digestive tract. But just how long was a rat's digestive cycle? And had animals always traveled between Earth and Hell? Baphomet said portals didn't exist, so maybe this was something new, another cosmic glitch like the one that shook them all loose from the fire.

They reached a fork in the canyon. Trua exhaled in frustration. The two tines of the fork narrowed and steepened into rough chutes of jagged rock. It would be even harder searching here.

Annie glanced back at Henry. The engineer was already having trouble crawling on the rough ground. "How about if you wait here and hold Mary?"

she said. He nodded, took the sphere from her, and settled against the wall.

They arbitrarily chose the left chute and started crawling up. It was easier without the sphere, but the comb-thin ridges still scraped her shins. Shards of rock stabbed her palms. She didn't care. She was going home!

Home: Cleaning day with Melanie, the two of them attacking the flat with sponges and rags, jousting with the broom and the mop, collapsing afterwards with beers and a takeout pizza.

Home: Visiting with her parents on a Sunday, playing Scrabble with her father, carrying heavy bags of compost and potting soil from the car for her mother.

Home: The miracle of a second chance. If she could reclaim a lost life from a decade ago, what else might she be able to fix? She didn't need Ben's fame or her boss's condo. This was a chance to truly *inhabit* her life—to live it without regret, shame, envy. Chopping garlic, gossiping with Melanie, hanging posters on her bedroom wall, and letting herself feel happy as she did all of that. And then Mary: pushing Mary in a stroller, bringing Mary to her parents' house for Sunday dinners, holding Mary's hands as she would someday take her first wobbly steps—

No. Focus on looking.

She mustn't get caught up in fantasies. If they couldn't find the portal, none of those fantasies would matter.

And they were finding nothing. Lots of scrapes on her palms and knees but no more rodent droppings.

She wondered how far up the fork they should continue. She was about to ask Trua when he turned and put a finger to his lips.

Ahead of them, up the canyon, she heard sounds.

They weren't loud. If he hadn't alerted her, she might not even have noticed. There was an occasional soft brushing sound and even more occasionally the scrape of a shifting rock. Someone was coming down the canyon, but coming very carefully and trying not to be heard.

The marauders. Annie berated herself: she had been so excited about the rat turds that she'd stopped watching for attackers.

Trua motioned Annie to get behind him. They backed up against the wall. He scanned the ground and grabbed a large rock. She did the same.

They couldn't see past a turn in the canyon about ten yards ahead. They eyed the bend and waited. Annie heard another soft brush, then another. Her own breath sounded loud as a freeway. She gripped her rock and prepared to raise it.

Calmly, gingerly, Billie emerged from around the bend, picking her way down the rocks.

Annie sagged with relief.

"Stop!" Trua brandished his rock.

Billie looked unchanged. Pixie nose, lime capris, flowered kerchief. Annie's yellow sweater was tied around her waist.

"Y'all don't know how to welcome an old friend," she said.

"You could have warned us," Annie said.

"Well, I wasn't sure who it was. It sounded like you—Lordy, the two of you make more ruckus than cats with tin cans on their tails—but a person can't be too cautious around here. I just hope you didn't attract anyone else with all that whooping and hollering."

"We weren't hollering."

"Well, you sure are noisy."

Billie edged her way down the chute and stood beside them. She brushed off her blouse and skirt. Ignoring Trua, she gave Annie a sly grin.

"Looks like you got yourself a knight in shining armor. I knew it. I could've told you."

Trua had dropped his rock but looked ready to club her with his fist.

"Let's go down. Henry's waiting," Annie said.

* * * * *

The engineer's face lit up when he saw Billie. "Your young friend!" he exclaimed. "Splendid!"

Billie immediately locked her attention on the sphere. "What's that?" she said as Henry passed it back to Annie. "It sure is pretty. Some kind of Christmas ornament?"

Annie gripped the sphere closer. "We need to talk."

Billie shrugged. "Sure."

They sat in a circle at the fork in the canyon. Billie's arrival had turned Trua back into a sullen follower, like a family gathering where everyone reverts to their worst adolescent selves. But Annie refused to defer to Billie anymore.

"What happened to you at the marsh?" she asked.

Billie tossed her head. "It was too sad. All those dead babies. It made me miss my babies back home even more."

"She's lying," Trua muttered.

"Ssh." Annie turned back to Billie. "Why did you run away and leave us?"

"I didn't mean to. I just had to get away from that awful place. And when I came back, you were gone. Where'd you run off to?"

"Why did you take my sweater?"

"Is this some kind of interrogation?" Billie said indignantly. "Y'all are the ones who went off and left me, and now you're making accusations about articles of clothing?"

"Lying bitch." Trua seemed about to leap up but Henry put a hand on his arm.

"You took my sweater," Annie said steadily, "and you abandoned us. Why should we trust you?"

"Honey, this is Hell. You shouldn't trust anybody. Like you shouldn't trust that caveman boyfriend of yours."

That did it. Trua shook off Henry's hand and launched himself onto Billie. He knocked her onto her back and crouched over her, knees on her thighs and hands on her wrists. She looked brittle, twiglike, under him.

"What did you see in the marsh?"

"Get off me!"

"What did you see?"

"Nothing!"

He pressed Billie's arms harder into the rock. Annie froze. She hated this side of Trua. But she also wanted to hear what Billie would say.

"What?" Trua growled.

"Stop it! Ow! Annie! Tell your caveman—"

Trua leaned close to Billie's face. His thick hands twisted her wrists.

"Tell me now. Or I break your arms."

"Ow! Stop—"

"Tell me."

"Ow. Nothing. Stop!"

He twisted further.

"Okay! Stop! I'll tell you!"

He loosened his grip, sat up slightly.

"Now let me up." Billie tried to raise her head, "Annie, tell him to—"

"Woman!" Trua shouted and clamped back down on her.

"Ow! Okay. In the marsh—" Her face had turned bright red.

"Keep going."

"Babies—"

"We know that. What else?" He pressed harder. Billie yelped.

"Babies—"

"WHOSE babies?"

"MY babies! MY babies in the marsh!"

Trua dropped her wrists and slid off of her. He looked both satisfied and disgusted. Henry looked confused. Billie rolled herself into a sitting position and stared balefully at Trua, shaking out her arms. "Evil man," she muttered. "Evil, evil man."

Trua looked pointedly at Annie. "I knew it." He turned and stalked off toward the mouth of the canyon.

Henry shifted unsteadily across the rocks to Billie, leaned in, and spoke quietly to her. Annie didn't know whether to join him in comforting Billie or go scream at Trua. What was he trying to prove? Three cheers to the big tough guy who had succeeded in unmasking Billie's misery.

Finally she slid over beside Billie. "I'm so sorry," she said softly. "Did they die in that car crash with you?"

Billie sniffled. She shook out her wrists some more. Then she removed her kerchief to smooth her hair, and looked at Annie.

"Of course not," she said with disdain. "My babies aren't dead. I just said that to get that caveman off of me."

* * * * *

"How dare you?" Annie asked Trua. She had left Billie with Henry and found him near the mouth of the canyon. He was sitting against the rock wall, frowning.

"She killed them," he said. "Don't you see that?"

Annie did not in fact see that. She didn't know *what* she saw. Billie might be a grieving mother, a petty thief and liar, a psychopath, or who-knew-what. She might have just confessed to murder or she might simply have told Trua what he wanted to hear. It didn't matter. Once they found the exit, she would never have to see Billie again.

She touched Trua's arm lightly, a reconciliation. He was more important to her than Billie. Home was more important.

"Let's keep looking for the rat trail," she said.

CHAPTER FORTY-TWO

Annie

Billie had apparently been exploring all the side canyons, fork by interminable fork, looking for an exit. Her eyes widened when Annie told her about the rat droppings.

"You mean our lives are going to be saved by a *rat*?" she exclaimed.

The chute she'd been descending led to a dead end, so they shifted their attention to the other fork. Henry rejoined the hunt and the four of them inched up the canyon. Annie clasped the grey sphere tight to her chest; she didn't want anyone else, even Trua, to carry it now. Somehow Billie's appearance made the possibility of an exit seem more real. But wouldn't it be typical of Hell to put home within your grasp and then snatch it away at the last moment?

They picked their way along the canyon floor. Annie peered into cracks, nudged aside rocks. So many questions. *Would time have passed on Earth since she died, or would she return at the exact same moment she left? Where would the passageway emerge on Earth? What if there were devils guarding the exit?*

Henry was the one who found the next set of rat turds. They were tucked in a lava fold near the wall of the canyon.

"Hallelujah!" Billie said. "I can hear the ice in the martini shaker already."

But finding turds wasn't the same as finding the exit. They scoured the surrounding section of the canyon, running fingers along the rock for hidden openings, lifting boulders, peering up at the higher sections of wall that they couldn't reach. Nothing.

"Perseverance," Henry said.

They moved further up the canyon. They needed frequent breaks; there was only so long you could stare at cracks and crevices without your vision starting to blur. Trua sat on a rock apart from the others. Annie joined him.

"Are you thinking about home?" she asked.

He gave a noncommittal grunt. She hated this return to the old Trua who never spoke. Memories of home were flooding her now—she stopped trying to hold them back—and she wanted to share them with him.

"There's so much I took for granted. You know what I mean? Basic things like sunlight. Water. Grass. I never thought about them. There's this park near my house. I used to walk past it all the time but I never went in. It has a hill with green grass that kids like to roll down. There's a bottlebrush tree that gets hummingbirds. People lie on the grass in the sun on weekends. It's just your basic city park, but it's wonderful. And I never went in. When I get home,

I'm going to stop in there every day after work and sit on the hill for five minutes. Just to feel the grass."

"For how long?"

"What?"

Trua shifted on his rock. "You'll sit on the grass one day, two days. But then you'll have things to do. The grass will be something to feed goats, nothing more. You'll forget about it."

"I won't forget!"

Trua reached for a small rock and examined its edges. She was annoyed that he didn't believe her. She didn't understand his lack of excitement about going home.

He kept fingering the rock. Annie cupped the grey sphere. She held it to her cheek, felt its pulses as encouragement. The sphere seemed more communicative than Trua. She tried again in a gentler voice.

"Please. Tell me. What will you appreciate most about home?"

It took a while, but he finally, grudgingly, answered. "The things you said. Sunlight. Grass. Water... But also my sister Damla. And my brothers. I will never envy my brothers' fortunes again. No matter how little I have, it's better to be alive."

She felt an aching sense of kinship with him; those last words could have come from her mouth. She also felt an unsettling distance. This was the first time he had mentioned any of his siblings by name.

"Damla?" she asked.

He nodded but retreated into silence.

* * * * *

Families.

Inching along the canyon floor, Annie thought of Ben. Their relationship would change. More precisely: she would change it. She'd insist on being his equal, no longer his echo. If nothing else, surviving Hell should earn her that much.

And what about Trua's family? She tried to picture Damla and his brothers but it was impossible. She didn't know what they looked like, didn't know what his camp looked like. She couldn't envision the Great Plain or his horse or the inside of his tent. Imagining him back with his tribe forced her to confront something she had tried to ignore: she would probably never see him again.

None of them knew how a passage to Earth might work. Maybe they'd all emerge together on the rim of some volcano in 2015. But they could just as easily return to the time and place they'd lived, which meant Trua would return to the outer edges of the Roman Empire and she would return to 21st century San Francisco.

Loss hollowed her gut. She would never get to kiss him. She would never get to hold him. Desires that had been tamped down since learning about the crater massacre rose in her again. His mouth. His scars. His cock.

Great Gods, you're beautiful.

What if he could return to San Francisco with her? Maybe there was some trick or spell. Maybe if they walked through the portal holding hands, they would end up in the same place.

Trua in San Francisco. She smiled. What would he make of $6-a-cup gourmet coffee? Or any kind of coffee, for that matter; the drink wasn't even discovered until the Middle Ages. Maybe he could get work as one of those urban goatherds who provide environmentally sustainable weed management. No, he was too smart for that. He'd modernize. He'd learn to drive. He'd learn computers. Maybe he could design video games: *Raiders of the Great Plain* for Sony Xbox. People in San Francisco would assume his scars were the next new fashion thing, a step beyond tattoos and piercings.

But what if they clasped hands and walked into *his* world? That was less amusing. Annie didn't think she'd do well spending winters in a goatskin tent, boiling tubers for dinner and giving birth without painkillers or antibiotics.

The hollow in her stomach deepened. Both scenarios were fantasies. Most likely, by far, they would never see each other again.

Perhaps that was the price of life—not just her life, but Mary's.

She would pay it.

* * * * *

The wound on Henry's shin opened up again, scraped on an edge of lava. This time Annie asked Billie to sacrifice a rag from her collection, and she agreed without argument.

At home there was Neosporin. Ibuprofen. Sterile bandages. 24-hour drugstores. You walked into a building the size of a palace with a thousand different items that could cure everything from infection to flatulence, you showed someone a piece of plastic, and you walked out with your arms full of miracles. Soon she might be back in that world.

"I swear, I never imagined anyone wanting to see a rat," Billie said, stuffing her rags back in their pouch. "Now here I am daydreaming about rats. Rats, rats, rats. You'd think these rats had more sex appeal than Troy Donahue."

"Will we know the passage when we see it?" Annie asked. The dog's portal had been barely a shimmer and then it vanished.

"Of course we'll know it."

Are you sure? she almost asked, but stopped herself. Billie wasn't sure. None of them were sure. They were all proceeding on hope. Better to bolster that hope than question it.

"What's the first thing you'll do when you get home?"

"Mix that martini and go out dancing! After I hug my babies, of course."

"How about you, Henry?"

The engineer gave her a sad smile. "I will fall on my knees before my wife and beg her forgiveness."

She turned to Trua. "You?"

No response. If only he weren't so caught up in his anger at Billie. *Don't let her get you so upset. Don't take it out on the rest of us.* But then he spoke.

"I'm not going back."

Billie furrowed her forehead. Henry cocked his head. Annie didn't think she'd heard him correctly.

"What?"

He looked at Annie and shook his head. "You won't understand."

Damn it! Why was he always saying she wouldn't understand? And what was this nonsense about not going back to Earth? She strained to keep her voice level.

"I will. I promise. Just tell me."

Trua remained silent. When he spoke, his voice was thick with reluctance.

"Suppose I go back. I get some more years to live. But who knows how many? Then I die and go to the fire. If I have children, they'll go to the fire. Is another few moments of life worth eternity in the fire?"

But what about your family? Annie wanted to shout. *Your tribe? Sunlight? The Great Plain? Everything we talked about?*

"You don't need to burn in Hellfire," Billie said. "Just accept Jesus. Even if you don't have churches in your caveman country. Just let Jesus in your heart and be saved. Live a Christian life and you'll go to Heaven!"

"A Christian life. Like you?"

"Don't cast stones," Billie snapped. "I'll have a little bit of fun when I get back, and then I'm going to live the most God-fearing life. I will testify to the Lord night and day. I am not coming back to this place, no thank you."

"I say no-thank-you to your Jesus Christ wizard."

"Friends." Henry Mwango inserted himself. "There's no point to arguing. You'll never convince each other."

"But..." Annie began. She had trouble coming up with words. Trua looked directly at her.

"I'll help you find the exit," he said. "If it exists, we'll find it. I swear it. I'll see you and Mary safely through. Then I'll return to the city and join Haisheng." He set his jaw in a way that cautioned against argument. "If we're lucky, we can destroy the fire before either you or Mary have to return here."

* * * * *

There was nowhere in the narrow canyon to go.

Annie needed to be alone with Trua. She wanted to argue him out of staying in Hell. She wanted to get to the bottom of whatever was making him do this stupid, self-sacrificing thing. Nausea and retching be damned: she wanted to throw her arms around him and hold him and kiss him and make love like real flesh-and-blood human beings until he remembered how good it was to be alive.

But there was nowhere to go that was out of earshot of the others. Plus Henry needed their help scaling the rocks. Plus—to be perfectly honest with herself—Annie worried that if Billie were left alone, she might find the exit and leave without telling anyone its location.

The best she could do was pull Trua aside when they all stood up to continue searching.

"You can't do this."

“Don’t argue with me. I made up my mind a while ago.”

“When?” Her voice quavered. “We were just talking about appreciating grass and water. About your brothers and sisters. Damla. Remember?”

Trua was silent.

“You wanted to go back to Earth then, right? Nothing’s changed. If you don’t go back, you’ll never see Damla again—”

Trua shook his head. His face sagged with sorrow.

“I knew then. Maybe I always knew. I just didn’t realize it.”

* * * * *

Trua found another deposit of rat pellets. And then Henry found something even more encouraging—a tiny tuft of grey fur, wedged in a tight crack in the rocks.

Annie kept her eyes on the rocks as they continued through the canyon, looking up only to ensure that Billie was still ahead. Behind her, she heard scrabbling and scuffing as Trua helped Henry along.

Should she stay too? That would be the decision of a leader, someone who took stands. Ben would stay and fight with Haisheng. She, on the other hand, always took the safe path. She followed. She fled. But this was different. She had Mary. It was one thing to sacrifice your own life, but it was another if you were also in charge of someone else’s. And Mary hadn’t even had a first chance at life! Annie owed her a childhood, an adolescence. She owed her a chance to experience the world and make her own judgment about it.

And Trua was wrong. Just plain wrong.

She pressed her palms against the lava in frustration. Trua was blinded by despair. He had weighed another few decades of life against an eternity in the fire and decided it wasn't worth it. But he was wrong. It was *so* worth it.

Damp fog veiling the green hillsides of Mount Tam.

Bright purple flower petals scattered like confetti on a grey Mission District sidewalk.

Mist on her face, wind in her hair, biking home on empty streets late at night and feeling like a wild bird in flight.

And returning to Earth offered a chance to avoid the fire. She could become Christian. She could raise Mary as a Christian. They would attend church and read the Bible and do whatever the Bible said, and that might shield them from Hell.

But was that what God wanted? Wasn't that just the compliance of a dog avoiding a beating? And what about all the billions of other souls destined for Hell?

Annie slowed down and let Henry and Trua catch up to her. She reached to brush a strand of hair out of her face and noticed a smear of blood on her palm, scraped on the lava.

"Should I stay too?" she asked Trua quietly.

"You have Mary. It's different," he said.

* * * * *

She should have asked him to return to San Francisco with her.

Of course she had no control over this hypothetical exit and where it would lead. But she could at least have suggested it. He might have understood how much she cared for him. He might have had more of a reason to choose life.

Now she thought about it without any jokes about $6 cups of coffee. They could get an apartment together, go to sleep holding each other, wake up entwined in the morning. He was curious and adaptable. She'd have a partner in life at last. They could have kids. It wouldn't replace the family he'd lost but it would be something...

Stop. She was just being a sucker for the first man in years who had called her beautiful.

He was an illiterate nomad with an anger management problem.

He was the most loyal person she'd ever met.

And now he'd made up his mind. What kind of offer could she extend, anyway? *Come back to Earth with me, maybe we'll end up in the same place, maybe not, and either way you get the reward of a million years burning in a lake of fire.*

It was without doubt the worst pick-up line she'd ever heard in her life.

Ahead of her, around a bend in the canyon, Billie gasped.

CHAPTER FORTY-THREE

Annie

Annie scrambled forward.

The canyon opened into a bowl. But this was nothing like the barren bowl that had housed Henry Mwango's community.

This bowl held a spring of fire. Fire bubbled up and fountained into a large round pond of lava. Droplets of lava splashed into the air; tendrils of flame waved and darted from the surface. Cliffs rose around it, a flaming, treeless version of Yosemite's Mirror Lake. On the far side of the pond, the canyon walls gave way to a lip. Lava cascaded over it into a fire waterfall, the start of a fire river.

But Billie wasn't looking at the pond. Annie followed her gaze up the lefthand cliff, which peaked in a large natural rock arch.

Like Billie, she knew it at once: the exit.

The arch itself didn't look magical. It was the kind of nifty rock formation that would be surrounded by a bevy of camera-toting tourists in a national park. But looking through it, the sky rippled like the air had rippled behind the dog. Annie's skin prickled. She felt—imagined?—a moist breeze trailing down from the arch, ripe with hints of pollen, mulch, ocean.

They stared. The bowl was silent except for the gurgle and splash of lava. All of them, even Billie, seemed stunned by their success.

"I must admit I didn't think we'd find it," Henry Mwango murmured.

"Now what?" Annie said.

"You should go," Trua said. There was a catch in his voice. "We don't know if the demons come to this place. You should go before anything happens."

"There," pointed Henry. "Those outcroppings. You can climb up that way."

He was right. She could see a route. And climbing wouldn't be a problem—callused hands and feet, no clogs to lose.

But wait. What had Henry just said?

"'You?'" she asked.

Henry nodded. "I have decided to stay here too. I'm an old man. There isn't enough time for me on Earth to atone for my past mistakes. But here... perhaps I can be of some help."

"Your wife—" Annie begin, but Billie interrupted.

"The caveman's right for once. We need to go." She thrust her pouch of rags at Henry. "Take this. In case you need more bandages." Then she trotted along the bottom of the cliff, staying a safe distance from the edge of the fire pond, toward the section that Henry had identified.

Annie looked at Trua. She didn't know what to say. He reached out his hand and she was about to take it, when she realized he wanted the grey sphere.

He brought it to his lips and kissed it, and then he handed it back to her.

"Go," he said. When she did nothing, he repeated himself, harshly now. "*Go.*"

She spun, ran after Billie, and leapt onto the rock surface. The sphere left her only one free hand but her fingers were clamps and her legs levers. *Pull here. Grip there. Find a toehold, and then find another toehold. Don't look back. Keep going...*

They worked their way horizontally across the rock, gradually rising, always moving toward the arch. Annie no longer heard the burbling of the lava spring, no longer saw the reddish-grey sky. Every part of her was focused on the next handhold, the next ledge for her feet, on cushioning the sphere while she climbed.

They reached the narrow ridgetop and she hauled herself up, careful not to scrape the sphere. The arch stood just feet in front of them. This was only a middling-high ridge within the mountain range: taller, craggy, black peaks stretched on all sides, looking even darker above the brilliant orange of the lava river. Dry, hot wind swept noisily across the ridge. The damp breeze with hints of earth had vanished.

Below, on the far side of the bowl, Henry and Trua looked up, small as a memory.

"Glory hallelujah," Billie said, and without any sort of goodbye she stepped through the arch and disappeared.

The last things Annie saw were her dusty bare feet, her slender legs, and, above that, Annie's yellow sweater still tied around her waist.

* * * * *

She waved to Trua and Henry to let them know Billie had gone through without incident. The wave felt ridiculously out of place—something that belonged to the pretty hostess on a game show, or girls in tiaras on a parade float. Now it was her turn to step through.

She couldn't bring herself to move.

Fear clamped down. What if the arch didn't lead back to Earth, but to the fire? What if it led to something even worse?

She peered through again: no Billie, no Earth, nothing but rocky peaks and orange sky.

What if the arch were some kind of black hole that pulverized you into nothingness?

She didn't have to go through. She could reverse her climb, back her way down the cliff. She could stay with Trua and Henry, return to the city, join Haisheng's insurrection. And in fact, that would be the right thing to do, the farsighted thing, the moral thing. A world without Hellfire! Haisheng's vision, which was now Trua's vision, and Henry's too, spread panoramically before her. Imagine a world where people would live their lives and then sleep. That's all. No judgment, no punishment, no torment. Just sleep. It was how she had imagined death before, when she was alive, those rare times that she bothered to think about it. She had taken it for granted like she had taken the sun and water and grass of the living Earth. But in fact it was beautiful, like sun and water and grass. It was worth fighting for. Trua was going to fight for it, and Henry. She could climb down the cliff and join them.

Would turning back be brave? Or cowardly?

Annie looked across the cliff to parse the best descent route. Over there she spotted a thin ledge where she could place a foot. And there, a rock that could be a handhold. She could make it down, it wasn't impossible, she just needed to be careful not to slip and fall...

Steep Ravine.

She had fallen there once while attempting a descent. An embarrassingly dumb series of events: she had accidentally left her cell phone midway along the trail after taking photos of some wild irises. She realized it in the parking lot at the top of the trail but didn't want to waste time returning down the long switchbacks, so decided to drive to a spot on the road directly above the ravine and bushwhack down.

She made it about twenty feet, then lost her footing. Her legs flew up and her butt came down and she found herself sliding on slick leaves through the underbrush. She'd manage to stop but then she'd slip again, slide some more, hit a fallen log, pull herself up... By the time she reached the floor of the ravine, her jeans were ripped and she'd been marinated in poison oak.

And there she found herself in a fern amphitheater. She forgot her bruises and rips and stared. Ferns rose up the steep canyon wall like tiers of spectators at a sold-out stadium concert. Green flooded her eyes. She swam in green. Annie sat down and decided the phone could wait. Surrounded by such lushness she felt, for once, sufficient. The world was rich and she shared its richness. She felt herself dissolve into a green, liquid peace.

Now she looked down the canyon walls to barren rock and scorching lava. If she stayed here, she would never see Steep Ravine again. More important, Mary would never see Steep Ravine.

Trua and Henry stared up at her. Henry, who was resting on a rock against the far wall, gave a brusque wave—a "go on" gesture. Trua seemed to be yelling something but she couldn't hear it in the ridgetop wind. Panic flooded her: she might never know his last words to her. He stopped shouting and, silent now, pressed his right hand over his chest like someone saying the pledge of allegiance. He could have been touching the place where she held the gray sphere. He could have been touching his heart. Slowly, deliberately, he brought his hand to his lips.

She decided: *Stay.*

Annie gripped the sphere against her chest and eyed the route down. She would need to be extra careful descending with only one free hand; she couldn't afford a fall while holding Mary...

Then, from the corner of her eye, she saw movement where the canyon opened into the bowl.

Men.

By the time she saw them, it was too late to do anything. There were three of them, and they all hurled themselves at Trua. Even from far away, she recognized them—the tall one, Attwater, and the short one, Bol, from the canyon.

The third was the Roman, Isaias, from the crater.

They caught Trua by surprise and knocked him down easily. But before they could do anything else, Henry leapt up from his place by the wall. Frail body, bad legs, he somehow managed to hurl himself across the canyon floor onto them. They were all grappling, wrestling, an indistinguishable melee of bodies. Shards of angry male voices pierced the wind.

Oh God. Oh God.

She needed to help them, but how? The ridge was stark and bare. She hurled a loose rock but it fell pathetically short.

Below, Isaias managed to pull Henry away from the fray. He pushed him down and slammed him with a rock. The engineer went limp. Isaias left him and stepped back toward the others, who had pinned Trua on the ground.

"Here!" Annie shouted. She jumped up and down. She waved her arms. Let them see her. Please let them hear her over the wind. "Here! Up here!"

They looked up. Attwater gestured for Isaias to take his place over Trua, and stepped a few feet toward her.

"Here!" she yelled again. "The exit! Back to Earth!"

Attwater glared, frowning. He couldn't hear. Trua seemed to say something: Bol knocked his head down into the rock. Attwater pulled some cord from a pouch and handed it to Isaias, who tied Trua's hands behind his back.

"The exit!"

Annie shouted, pointed, jumped, desperate. And Attwater seemed finally to have heard. He said something to the others and started moving along the rock wall, looking for ledges, with Bol following close behind.

She'd show them the arch. They could climb up, go through, go home, leave. Wasn't that what everyone here wanted? Wouldn't they choose life over vengeance?

Attwater started pulling himself up the rock, not the same route she and Billie had taken, but he was making it work. Bol was having more trouble, slipping back and scrabbling to keep up. *Please let them go through. Let all of them go through.* She would need to get Isaias up here too. Maybe the others would call him. And she would need to protect Mary. Annie stepped back from the edge of the ridge so they couldn't see her and tucked the grey sphere under her blouse below her arm, where it would be less visible.

Steady. She tried to slow her breath and looked down the cliff. They were approaching the ridge now. She glanced back at the shimmer in the arch: still waiting there. Now Attwater was pulling himself up onto the ridge and lunging toward her and grabbing her arm, the arm that wasn't shielding Mary—

"Bloody cunt. You've caused us enough problems."

He had a cockney or Australian accent. She hadn't noticed until now. Bol pulled his short body up over the ledge, panting.

"The arch—it's the way out—" Attwater was gripping her so tightly that she could barely speak.

"Shut up, cunt. We've had enough from you." He gave her arm a hard jerk. "Where's your little friend?"

"Through the arch—home—"

Attwater slammed a fist into her face. She kept her arm pressed close to her side, shielding Mary.

"Shut up about the arch. Where is she?"

"Home—"

He punched her again. Everything swayed.

"She's here. We heard her. We heard both of you. Now where is she?"

"It's true, the arch—"

Another punch. *Mary. Hold on to Mary.*

"What about that arch?" Bol's voice was whiny, distant. Everything was blurry and distant.

"You shut up about the arch too. Listen, you cunts owe us for Falc. It's time you paid up. Where is she?"

It wasn't going to work. They wouldn't go through. There was only one thing she could think of to do, and it wasn't what she had hoped, Isaias was still down there with Trua, but Isaias was old and Trua was strong and Trua could have beaten him to a pulp back in the crater if he'd tried, Trua had said so and she knew it was true, so maybe if it were down to just the two of them he could make it, even with his hands tied, he might be able to make it—

"Earth—"

She gave it one last try. But Attwater just slammed her again. This time she pulled away, jerked against his grip like she was trying to break free, and Bol leapt over and grabbed her other arm, *hold tight hold Mary*, so now they both had her, and she struggled enough to make them lock down their grip on her, really tight, really holding on, and then she lurched backward, using all her body weight, her mass, as leverage, and thank God for once that she wasn't a petite little thing like Billie, she was large, she was hefty, she was wonderfully, thankfully *fat*, and when she hurled herself backward they went with her, an ungainly flailing three-headed beast, and Annie launched them all backward and out and through the rock arch into the unknown.

Hot wind. Sulfur smell.

Their hands gripping her arms.

Their hands gone.

Empty air beneath her feet.

CHAPTER FORTY-FOUR

Annie

Her eyes were closed but she could hear people.

Lots of people, lots of voices. Shouting, arguing, giving orders. And somewhere behind those voices, people moaning. Crying.

There were hands touching her too. Rigid things pressing against her. A hand on her shoulder. Something heavy on her legs. A voice telling her to *hold on, stay with me, the ambulance will be here soon.*

Ambulance?

Annie jerked her eyes open, but pain slashed through her head and she shut them again. She'd made it! She wanted to dance, sing, leap, praise, but couldn't move. And it was cold. Where was her sweater? She wriggled one hand free and groped at her waist but nothing was there.

"Blanket! Get a blanket!" she heard someone yell, and someone else calling, "She's waking up!" and then finally a voice that she recognized—Nadine? Was that the name?—very close by, saying softly, "Annie. Annie. You're going to be okay."

But what about Mary? Was Mary okay? She reached with her free hand to where the grey sphere should be. Nothing. No wispy curves, no gentle pulsing. She closed her fists and felt only her own fingernails biting into her palm.

No. Please God no.

Left behind on the ridge? Lost somewhere in the passage between worlds? Returned to the acid marsh?

Or worst of all... the men?

Please God no.

Everything was crushing down on her now, not just that heavy thing on her legs, but everything. She couldn't breathe. She couldn't think. She shifted her hands again, groping, reaching, hoping to touch something round and soft.

Nothing.

Not again. She had lost Mary once already. That first time she had been unaware of what was at stake. This time she was aware and did her best and failed anyway.

If only she could hurl this weight off of her. Explode like a superhero bursting chains. She would throw herself at the world. She would shatter the world. She would shatter herself. Anything to get Mary back.

Please God not the men—

Something strange moved in her core.

It was a rhythm—part of her yet also autonomous, like eye spasms from a speck of dust. It had the muffled resonance of a small damped bell. It felt like a tiny, padded rubber mallet.

It felt like kicking.

Relief cascaded. She forced her eyes open. Everything was blurry and wiggly. Someone draped something over her, something fleecy and warm. Fleece like sheep on a wide grassy plain. A great plain. Waving grasses stretching to the horizon, whinny of horses, somewhere a circle of tents made out of skins. *Thank you,* she wanted to say to whomever had brought the blanket, with a hazy sense of gratitude for much, much more than the blanket, but the words didn't come.

Gradually the world became more distinct. The night was clear. Still no fog. Her torso was twisted sideways but that didn't seem to bother the intrepid little being in her womb. Each kick was a claim. Each kick was a promise.

Annie looked up and made out one star—or was it a planet?—then five, then dozens. Hundreds. The glow of the Milky Way. More than she could see, more than she could count.

She had never known anything so beautiful.

Radiance. Hope. Renewal. Life.

And yet.

Each one an inferno: 10,000 degrees, 100,000 degrees, 100 million degrees. Each one a holocaust of fire.

Things swirled and blurred again. She wanted to go home but didn't know where home was. In the kitchen with Melanie? In her childhood bed in the suburbs? Crouched behind rocks in a black desert?

"Stay with us, Annie," she heard someone say. "Stay with us."

Anchor yourself to the tiny damped bell in your gut.

Anchor yourself to the stars overhead.

But those stars. All burning. And she was hurtling into that holocaust, they all were—she and Mary and all her family and friends, all the warm voices and all the hands offering blankets, Hindu children and Muslim merchants and Chinese communists, pagans and doubters, well-meaning or oblivious or blundering—all plunging toward the molten core.

There were distant sirens, more shouts, more bodies rushing around her.

Everything was right. Everything was wrong.

Somewhere a man in goatskin was walking through a desert. Or somewhere he was immersed in that merciless fire.

Nadine's voice: "The ambulance is here. Everything's going to be okay."

The precious kicks in her gut.

A universe built upon fire.

burningburningburningburningburningburningburningburningburning

Look for the sequel to Shaken Loose in summer 2024. Meanwhile, get updates and early peeks at the sequel by joining the mailing list at ilanadebare.com.

Acknowledgments

Years ago, when I first started thinking about this book, I organized some friends to read *Dante's Inferno* together: initial thanks to Carlos Alcala, Zillah Bahar, Natasha Beery, Mary Mazzocco, and Sandy McCoy for being my Virgils as I entered the underworld. My writers' group—Lindsey Crittenden, Audrey Ferber, and Monica Wesolowska—joined me through every step of the journey with encouragement, wisdom, incisive criticism, and occasional gifts of Hell-themed jewelry.

Many people graciously shared their knowledge of topics ranging from horses to harps, geology to theology, for both this book and its forthcoming sequel: Joe Albanese, Craig Albert, Reuven Amitai, Tom Bennett, Stephen Branz, Yassir Chadly, Bradley Erskine, Vanessa George, Pastor Ronald Ixaac Hubbard, Carolyn Jones, Jim Mayer, Rudolph Matthee, Pastor Monica Moore, Destiny Muhammed, Haleila Nusinow, Otosirieze Obi-Young, Dixie Reid, Rev. Jim Richardson, Simon Schuchat, Shelley Simon, Susie Wallenstein, David Woolbright, Sierra Zephyr, and others. Of course, any inaccuracies are my responsibility, not theirs.

Among the many books that helped me understand the evolution of Christian concepts of Hell, I particularly recommend *The History of Hell* by Alice K. Turner, which has terrific illustrations as well as historical context. And if you're inspired to take your first dive into *Paradise Lost,* I recommend the Oxford University Press edition with commentary by Philip Pullman. You can find other suggestions for Hell-related reading—as well as book group discussion prompts—on my website, *ilanadebare.com.*

Deep thanks to those who read and commented on various drafts of *Shaken Loose*: developmental editor *extraordinaire* Diane Glazman, as well as Carlos Alcala, Nanette Asimov, Harriet Chessman, Lisa Cron, Deb DeBare, Sue Fishkoff, Lisa Lerner, Colleen Markley, Susan Ito, Carolyn Said, and Sam Schuchat. For wise counsel about the publishing process, thank you to April Eberhardt, Ryan Fox, Kate McKean, Eric Smith, Celina Spiegel, Ted Weinstein, and the generous women of Word of Mouth-Bay Area and various Facebook Binders groups.

Of course, major credit is due to David McAfee of Hypatia Press, who plucked *Shaken Loose* from the purgatory of unpublished manuscripts and gave it life as the book you are now holding. Rae McAfee provided edits that were detailed, thoughtful, and clarifying.

Finally, this road to Hell—like the paths of many writers—was paved with self-doubt. My husband Sam Schuchat provided countless Sunday night sessions of reassurance, as well as decades of love and support. Our daughter, graphic storyteller Rebecca Schuchat, is a model for me of taking artistic risks. Love and thanks to both of them.

CPSIA information can be obtained
at www.ICGtesting.com
Printed in the USA
BVHW030456230623
666264BV00006B/24

9 781839 194832

COSMOS

THE BOOK

"Enticing, imaginative, readable, iridescent."

—James Michener, *The New York Times Book Review*

"Brilliant in its scope and provocative in its suggestions. It shimmers with a sense of wonder. . . . I seriously doubt if anyone can casually pick up this book without being riveted by it and then humbled by it."

—*The Miami Herald*

"In just a few years, Sagan . . . has become Mr. Science, a widely respected popularizer able to link the stuff and history of life with the vastness of space and eternity. And he does it with a grace and élan that persuades you, for the moment at least, that nothing is more exciting or more important."

—*Chicago Tribune*

"*Cosmos* is like the college course in science you always wanted to take but never knew a professor could teach. It's magnificent. Sagan writes beautifully. . . . With a lyrical literary style, and a range that touches almost all aspects of human knowledge, *Cosmos* often seems too good to be true."

—*The Plain Dealer*

"*Cosmos* is magnificent, challenging. . . . One of the book's strengths is the way it traces today's knowledge and today's scientific method to their historical roots. It is enthusiasm, plus Dr. Sagan's poetic insight and literary skill, that makes this an eminently readable book."

—*The Christian Science Monitor*

"[Sagan] has done an excellent writing job as he delves into the past, present, and future of science, dealing with the mind-staggering enormity of the cosmos in which we exist."

—Associated Press

"Pulitzer Prize winner Carl Sagan has gathered the whole glittering universe into one magnificent book. . . . He blends science and philosophy in a text of such lyric energy. . . . Sagan dazzles the mind with the miracle of our survival, framed by the stately galaxies of space."

—*Cosmopolitan*

"Sagan is an astronomer with one eye on the stars, another on history and a third—his mind's—on the human condition. . . . We admire him greatly for his ambition and erudition, occasionally for the grace of his prose, and often for amazing us about our universe and ourselves."

—*Newsday*

BY CARL SAGAN

Broca's Brain

Cosmos

Contact: A Novel

The Dragons of Eden

Shadows of Forgotten Ancestors (with Ann Druyan)

Comet (with Ann Druyan)

Pale Blue Dot

The Demon-Haunted World

Billions & Billions

COSMOS

CARL SAGAN

BALLANTINE BOOKS TRADE PAPERBACKS
NEW YORK

2013 Ballantine Books Trade Paperback Edition

Published in the United States by Ballantine Books, an imprint of The Random House Publishing Group, a division of Random House, Inc., New York.

BALLANTINE and the HOUSE colophon are registered trademarks of Random House, Inc.

Originally published in hardcover in the United States by The Random House Publishing Group, a division of Random House, Inc., in 1980.

Since this page cannot legibly accommodate all acknowledgments, they appear on the next page.

ISBN 978-0-345-53943-4
eBook ISBN 978-0-307-80098-5

Printed in the United States of America on acid-free paper

www.ballantinebooks.com

22 24 26 28 29 27 25 23

Book design by Liz Cosgrove

Grateful acknowledgment is made to the following for permission to reprint previously published material:

American Folklore Society: Excerpt from "Chukchee Tales" by Waldemar Borgoras from *Journal of American Folklore,* volume 41 (1928). Reprinted by permission of the American Folklore Society.

Encyclopaedia Britannica, Inc.: Quote by Isaac Newton (*Optics*), quote by Joseph Fourier (*Analytic Theory of Heat*), and A Question Put to Pythagoras by Anaximenes (c. 600 B.C.). Reprinted with permission from Great Books of the Western World. Copyright 1952 by Encyclopaedia Britannica, Inc.

Harvard University Press: Quote by Democritus of Abdera taken from *Loeb Classical Library.* Reprinted by permission of Harvard University Press.

Indiana University Press: Excerpts from Ovid, *Metamorphoses,* translated by Rolfe Humphries, copyright 1955 by Indiana University Press. Reprinted by permission of the publisher.

Oxford University Press: Excerpt from *Zurvan: A Zoroastrian Dilemma* by R. C. Zaehner (Clarendon Press—1955). Reprinted by permission of Oxford University Press.

Penguin Books, Ltd.: One line from *Enuma Elish,* Sumer, in *Poems of Heaven and Hell from Ancient Mesopotamia,* translated by N. K. Sandars (Penguin Classics, 1971). Copyright © N. K. Sandars, 1971. Twelve lines from Lao Tzu, *Tao Te Ching,* translated by D. C. Lau (Penguin Classics, 1963). Copyright © D. C. Lau, 1963. Reprinted by permission of Penguin Books, Ltd.

Pergamon Press, Ltd.: Excerpts from *Giant Meteorites* by E. L. Krinov are reprinted by permission of Pergamon Press, Ltd.

Simon & Schuster, Inc.: Quote from the Bhagavad Gita from *Lawrence and Oppenheimer* by Nuel Pharr Davis (1968, page 239), and excerpt from *The Sand Reckoner* by Archimedes taken from *The World of Mathematics* by James Newman (1956, volume 1, page 420). Reprinted by permission of Simon & Schuster, Inc.

Simon & Schuster, Inc., and Bruno Cassirer, Ltd.: Quote from *The Last Temptation of Christ* by Nikos Kazantzakis. Reprinted by permission of the publisher in the United States, Simon & Schuster, Inc., and the publisher in England, Bruno Cassirer (Publishers), Ltd., Oxford. Copyright © 1960 by Simon & Schuster, Inc.

The University of Oklahoma Press: Excerpt from *Popol Vuh: The Sacred Book of the Ancient Quiché Maya,* by Adrian Recinos, 1950. Copyright © 1950 by the University of Oklahoma Press. Reprinted by permission of the University of Oklahoma Press.

For Ann Druyan

In the vastness of space and the immensity of time,
it is my joy to share a planet and an epoch with Annie.

CONTENTS

REFLECTIONS ON CARL SAGAN'S COSMOS

Neil deGrasse Tyson

Not everyone who successfully impacts the hearts and minds of one generation will carry that currency of influence into the generations that follow. The continued success of *Cosmos,* Carl Sagan's magnum opus, argues strongly for Carl's affability and intelligence. But it also reveals a hidden hunger in us all to learn about our place in the universe and embrace why that matters intellectually, culturally, and emotionally.

These properties distinguish the work of Carl Sagan and his collaborators from all other efforts to communicate science. Most good books in the genre teach you what to know in the author's field of expertise—what's hot, what's interesting—in clear and simple language. But rarely is that information shaped into knowledge. And even more rarely is that knowledge shaped into wonder, the foundation of a *Cosmos* perspective on the world. Dare I assert that *Cosmos* wielded this power in ways that profoundly influenced how we would observe, interpret, and conduct our lives?

One of the least noted facts about *Cosmos,* but perhaps its most significant gift to human culture, is how it repeatedly cross-pollinated traditional sciences—astronomy, biology, chemistry, and geology. When taken separately, each of these fields is noble and time-honored. But when taken together—when *Cosmos* wove them into a tapestry of insight on our place in the universe—their juxtaposition became potent and indelible. *Cosmos* was early, if not first, in this endeavor. In the decades that followed its publication, we would see the rise of hybrid fields of study such as astrobiology, astro-particle physics, astro-chemistry, planetary geology—some still donning their hyphens.

But the publication and bestselling success of *Cosmos* accomplished much more than this. The book's treatment of scientific topics was persistently blended with other traditional fields of study, such as history, anthropology, art, and philosophy, to reveal for the first time how and why readers should embrace all the ways that science matters in our culture.

At the time, there was nothing fresher, more uplifting, or more empowering than the themes and messages of *Cosmos*. Perhaps for the first time in any medium, the person teaching you science—Carl Sagan—cared about the tangled mental roadways that can rob a person of rational thought. His motif was to speak with you, not lecture at you. With that level of pedagogical comfort, millions of people around the world invited his television image into their living rooms and his printed words into their reading chairs.

When *Cosmos* first arrived in 1980, the arms race of the Cold War was fading, but nonetheless continued to hold hostage the world's nations with a nuclear arsenal of destructive powers derived from the minds of physicists. But exploration was not without hope. NASA had already landed Viking on Mars, seven years after we walked on the moon. And the twin Voyager space probes continued their fly-by tour of the Jovian planets, on their way out of the solar system altogether. All headline news. But much more was to come. The space shuttle had not yet flown. The International Space Station existed only on paper. The Hubble Space

Telescope was eleven years from launch. The first exoplanets—worlds orbiting suns other than our own—were fifteen years from detection. The World Wide Web was still a decade away from becoming a household utility, democratizing access to cosmic discoveries. And dozens more space missions would launch and arrive at their respective destinations.

In a field that moves as rapidly as astrophysics, one would think it impossible to write a timeless tract on it. But within *Cosmos* you're never focused on the bleeding edge of science. That comes and goes. You're instead treated to what the epic adventure of scientific inquiry means to Earth, to our species—to you. And that recipe works at any time, in any place, for any generation.

NEIL DEGRASSE TYSON is an astrophysicist with the American Museum of Natural History, where he serves as the Frederick P. Rose Director of the Hayden Planetarium. He is host of the twenty-first century reboot of *Cosmos,* appearing on FOX in 2014.

FOREWORD

Ann Druyan

I once stood on the shores of the cosmic ocean with Carl Sagan.

Thirty-five years ago we shivered in the sunshine on the wind-whipped Monterey cliffs of northern California's Pacific coast with our co-writer, astronomer Steven Soter, and a small television crew. It was a struggle to wrangle the wildly flapping two-foot-long galley pages of this book while trying to keep hold of the cardboard cue cards that Steve and I had prepared for Carl for the television show. (The book and its original 1980 companion television series were created simultaneously in a three-year-long frenzy, although each contains passages and sequences not found in the other.) The pages of script and manuscript were one of a kind back in those relatively low-tech days. With every gust coming off the light-dazzled waves, the pages threatened to take flight and blow out to sea like the dandelion puffballs Carl kept releasing to the cosmos.

The scenes we wrote and shot that day became the opening of the show and the first words of the book: "The cosmos is all that is or ever was or ever will be."

We were consciously going for a biblical cadence, words that would scope out the ambitious territorial range of our explorations in space and time. Beginning the saga of 40,000 generations of searchers on one tiny world trying to find their bearings in the cosmos required nothing less than an epic flourish.

It became the "Welcome aboard" to a personal voyage on the ship of the imagination, one that nearly a billion people have taken, and still take, in great numbers, in virtually every language spoken on our "pale blue dot." Ever since the fall of 1980, in both its manifestations, *Cosmos* has carried multitudes to the outermost reaches of our understanding of the universe, to places unimaginably small and incomprehensibly vast.

Some religious fundamentalists found that first line offensive. To them it was a shot across their bow that Carl was out to steal their thunder. They were on to something. As with everything Carl wrote, the science of *Cosmos* is solid, with big red rhetorical flags warning the reader when the author ventures into the speculative. (And thirty-five years later, how astonishingly prophetic have been most of Carl's conjectures on everything from climate change on Earth, the ambiguities of the Viking lander's findings on Mars, to his dreams of what might await us on Saturn's moon, Titan.) But Carl didn't stop there.

The universe revealed by the relentless error-correcting mechanism of science was to him infinitely preferable to the untested assumptions of traditional belief. For Carl, the "spiritual" had to be rooted in natural reality. He cherished those ideas about the cosmos that remained after the most rigorous experiment and observation. Scientific insight made him *feel* something, a soaring sensation, a recognition that he could only compare to falling in love. And as he used to say: "When you're in love, you want to tell the world."

This is the big, wide-open, welcoming embrace of *Cosmos,* as far from the clock-watching slow-death tedium of too many a science class as Titan is from Earth. It's about being unafraid to take the findings of science to *heart.*

Cosmos is for many that first encounter with the universe that you thought was foreclosed to you because you couldn't do the math, or you live in a place where there are no scientists to invite you in. Carl wanted everyone to come on this voyage; to experience the power of the scientific perspective and the wonders it reveals. His secret was to recapture the person he was before he understood the concept and then retrace his own *thought steps* toward comprehension. It worked. He inspired legions to study, teach, and do science.

The U.S. Library of Congress has recently designated *Cosmos* one of the eighty-eight books "that shaped America." It's a roster that includes such earth-shaking works as Thomas Paine's *Common Sense,* Herman Melville's *Moby Dick,* Harriet Beecher Stowe's *Uncle Tom's Cabin,* and Jack Kerouac's *On the Road.* They're listed in chronological order and the very first one, published in 1751 (decades before the concept of a constitutional government by, for, and of the people, crystallized), is also a science book. It's by another who believed that democracy requires an informed public of responsible decision-makers. The list begins with Benjamin Franklin's *Experiments and Observations on Electricity.* That book and this one are passionate acts of citizenship by two scientists who wanted science to belong to all of us.

This spring I returned for the first time to the shores of the cosmic ocean. I was there with another television crew to shoot the opening scenes of the new *Cosmos* series. Our host, astrophysicist Neil deGrasse Tyson, is one of the many scientists whose young lives were touched by Carl. I am happy to report that the terrain is as unspoiled, gorgeous, and inspiring as it was the first time.

As I looked out at the glittering waters of the Pacific I was seeing for Carl. He knew that it's not for any one generation to see the completed picture. That's the point. The picture is never completed. There is always so much more that remains to be discovered.

Welcome aboard. It's time, once again, to set sail for the stars.

ANN DRUYAN served as creative director of NASA's Voyager Interstellar Message and was Carl Sagan's co-writer on *Cosmos*, as well as co-creator of the motion picture *Contact* and many other works. She is an executive producer and writer of *Cosmos: A SpaceTime Odyssey*, the television sequel coming in 2014 on Fox. Ms. Druyan was married to Dr. Sagan until his death. The asteroids named after them are in perpetual wedding-ring orbit around the Sun.

INTRODUCTION

> The time will come when diligent research over long periods will bring to light things which now lie hidden. A single lifetime, even though entirely devoted to the sky, would not be enough for the investigation of so vast a subject . . . And so this knowledge will be unfolded only through long successive ages. There will come a time when our descendants will be amazed that we did not know things that are so plain to them . . . Many discoveries are reserved for ages still to come, when memory of us will have been effaced. Our universe is a sorry little affair unless it has in it something for every age to investigate . . . Nature does not reveal her mysteries once and for all.
>
> —Seneca, *Natural Questions,* Book 7, first century

In ancient times, in everyday speech and custom, the most mundane happenings were connected with the grandest cosmic events. A charming example is an incantation against the worm which the Assyrians of 1000 B.C. imagined to cause toothaches. It begins with the origin of the universe and ends with a cure for toothache:

After Anu had created the heaven,
And the heaven had created the earth,
And the earth had created the rivers,
And the rivers had created the canals,
And the canals had created the morass,
And the morass had created the worm,
The worm went before Shamash, weeping,
His tears flowing before Ea:
"What wilt thou give me for my food,
What wilt thou give me for my drink?"
"I will give thee the dried fig
And the apricot."
"What are these to me? The dried fig
And the apricot!
Lift me up, and among the teeth
And the gums let me dwell! . . ."
Because thou hast said this, O worm,
May Ea smite thee with the might of
His hand!
(Incantation against toothache.)

Its treatment: Second-grade beer . . . and oil thou shalt mix together;
The incantation thou shalt recite three times thereon and shalt put the medicine upon the tooth.

Our ancestors were eager to understand the world but had not quite stumbled upon the method. They imagined a small, quaint, tidy universe in which the dominant forces were gods like Anu, Ea, and Shamash. In that universe humans played an important if not a central role. We were intimately bound up with the rest of nature. The treatment of toothache with second-rate beer was tied to the deepest cosmological mysteries.

Today we have discovered a powerful and elegant way to understand the universe, a method called science; it has revealed to us a universe so ancient and so vast that human affairs seem at first sight to be of little consequence. We have grown distant from the Cosmos. It has seemed remote and irrelevant to everyday concerns. But science has found not only that the universe has a reeling and ecstatic grandeur, not only that it is accessible to human understanding, but also that we are, in a very real and profound sense, a part of that Cosmos, born from it, our fate deeply connected with it. The most basic human events and the most trivial trace back to the universe and its origins. This book is devoted to the exploration of that cosmic perspective.

In the summer and fall of 1976, as a member of the Viking Lander Imaging Flight Team, I was engaged, with a hundred of my scientific colleagues, in the exploration of the planet Mars. For the first time in human history we had landed two space vehicles on the surface of another world. The results, described more fully in Chapter 5, were spectacular, the historical significance of the mission utterly apparent. And yet the general public was learning almost nothing of these great happenings. The press was largely inattentive; television ignored the mission almost altogether. When it became clear that a definitive answer on whether there is life on Mars would not be forthcoming, interest dwindled still further. There was little tolerance for ambiguity. When we found the sky of Mars to be a kind of pinkish-yellow rather than the blue which had erroneously first been reported, the announcement was greeted by a chorus of good-natured boos from the assembled reporters—they wanted Mars to be, even in this respect, like the Earth. They believed that their audiences would be progressively disinterested as Mars was revealed to be less and less like the Earth. And yet the Martian landscapes are staggering, the vistas breathtaking. I was positive from my own experience that an enormous global interest exists in the exploration of the planets and in many kindred scientific topics—the origin of life, the Earth, and the Cosmos, the search for extraterrestrial intelligence, our connection with the universe. And I was certain that this interest could be excited through that most powerful communications medium, television.

My feelings were shared by B. Gentry Lee, the Viking Data Analysis and Mission Planning Director. We decided, gamely, to do something about the problem ourselves. Lee proposed that we form a production company devoted to the communication of science in an engaging and accessible way. In the following months we were approached on a number of projects. But by far the most interesting was an inquiry tendered by KCET, the Public Broadcasting Service's outlet in Los Angeles. Eventually, we jointly agreed to produce a thirteen-part television series oriented toward astronomy but with a very broad human perspective. It was to be aimed at popular audiences, to be visually and musically stunning, and to engage the heart as well as the mind. We talked with underwriters, hired an executive producer, and found ourselves embarked on a three-year project called *Cosmos.* At this writing it has an estimated worldwide viewing audience of over 200 million people, or almost 5 percent of the human population of the planet Earth. It is dedicated to the proposition that the public is far more intelligent than it has generally been given credit for; that the deepest scientific questions on the nature and origin of the world excite the interests and passions of enormous numbers of people. The present epoch is a major crossroads for our civilization and perhaps for our species. Whatever road we take, our fate is indissolubly bound up with science. It is essential as a matter of simple survival for us to understand science. In addition, science is a delight; evolution has arranged that we take pleasure in understanding—those who understand are more likely to survive. The *Cosmos* television series and this book represent a hopeful experiment in communicating some of the ideas, methods and joys of science.

The book and the television series evolved together. In some sense each is based on the other. Many illustrations in this book are based on the striking visuals prepared for the television series. But books and television series have somewhat different audiences and admit differing approaches. One of the great virtues of a book is that it is possible for the reader to return repeatedly to obscure or difficult passages; this is only beginning to become possible, with the development of videotape and video-disc technology, for television. There is much more freedom for the author in choosing the range and depth of topics for a chapter in a book than for the procrustean fifty-eight minutes, thirty seconds of a noncommercial television program. This book goes more deeply into many topics than does the television series. There are topics discussed in the book which are not treated in the television series and vice versa. For example, explicit representations of the Cosmic Calendar, featured in the television series, do not appear here—in part because the Cosmic Calendar is discussed in my book *The Dragons of Eden;* likewise, I do not here discuss the life of Robert Goddard in much detail, because there is a chapter in *Broca's Brain* devoted to him. But each episode of the television series follows fairly closely the corresponding chapter of this book; and I like to think that the pleasure of each will be enhanced by reference to the other. Only a few of the more than 250 full-color illustrations in the hardbound and trade paperback editions of *Cosmos* could be accommodated in this edition, but all illustrations necessary to understand the text are included.

For clarity, I have in a number of cases introduced an idea more than once—the first time lightly, and with deeper passes on subsequent appearances. This occurs, for example, in the introduction to cosmic objects in Chapter 1, which are examined in greater detail later on; or in the discussion of mutations, enzymes and nucleic acids in Chapter 2. In a few cases, concepts are presented out of historical order. For example, the ideas of the ancient Greek scientists are presented in Chapter 7, well after the discussion of Johannes Kepler in Chapter 3. But I believe an appreciation of the Greeks can best be provided after we see what they barely missed achieving.

Because science is inseparable from the rest of the human endeavor, it cannot be discussed without making contact, sometimes glancing, sometimes head-on, with a number of social, political, religious and philosophical issues. Even in the filming of a television series on science, the worldwide devotion to military activities becomes intrusive. Simulating the exploration of Mars in the Mohave Desert with a full-scale version of the Viking Lander, we were repeatedly interrupted by the United States Air Force, performing bombing runs in a nearby test range. In Alexandria, Egypt, from nine to eleven A.M. every morning, our hotel was the subject of practice strafing runs by the Egyptian Air Force. In Samos, Greece, permission to film anywhere was withheld until the very last moment because of NATO maneuvers and what was clearly the construction of a warren of underground and hillside emplacements for artillery and tanks. In Czechoslovakia the use of walkie-talkies for organizing the filming logistics on a rural road attracted the attention of a Czech Air Force fighter, which circled overhead until reassured in Czech that no threat to national security was being perpetrated. In Greece, Egypt and Czechoslovakia our film crews were accompanied everywhere by agents of the state security apparatus. Preliminary inquiries about filming in Kaluga, U.S.S.R., for a proposed discussion of the life of the Russian pioneer of astronautics Konstantin Tsiolkovsky were discouraged—because, as we later discovered, trials of dissidents were to be conducted there. Our camera crews met innumerable kindnesses in every country we visited; but the global military presence, the fear in the hearts of the nations, was everywhere. The experience confirmed my resolve to treat, when relevant, social questions both in the series and in the book.

Science is an ongoing process. It never ends. There is no single ultimate truth to be achieved, after which all the scientists can retire. And because this is so, the world is far more interesting, both for the scientists and for the millions of people in every nation who, while not professional scientists, are deeply interested in the methods and findings of science. So, while there is little in the *Cosmos* book that has become obsolete since its first publication, there have been many significant new findings.

The Voyager 1 and 2 spacecraft encountered the Saturn system and uncovered a host of wonders concerning the planet, its intricate ring system, and its swarm of attendant satellites. Perhaps most interesting of these is Titan, which is now known to have an atmosphere rather like that of the primitive Earth, a dense haze layer composed of complex organic molecules, and perhaps a surface ocean of liquid hydrocarbons. A range of observations have recently been made of rings of debris surrounding young stars. These rings may be in the process of coagulating into new planetary systems, and suggest that planets may be overwhelmingly abundant among the stars of the Milky Way galaxy. Life has been found unexpectedly nibbling on sulfur compounds in very high temperature vents on the Earth's ocean floor. New evidence has accumulated suggesting that comets are periodically sprayed into the inner solar system, triggering the extinction of many species on Earth. Great regions of intergalactic space have been uncovered that seemingly are depleted in galaxies. New and important components of the universe bearing on the question of its ultimate fate have been suggested.

And the pace of discovery continues. Spacecraft of Japan, of the European Space Agency, and of the Soviet Union are scheduled to intercept Halley's Comet in 1986. The U.S. Space Telescope, the largest orbiting observatory ever attempted, is scheduled to be launched before the end of the decade. Important opportunities for spacecraft missions to Mars, to other comets, to asteroids, and to Titan are emerging. The U.S. *Galileo* spacecraft, scheduled to arrive in the Jupiter system in 1988, is designed to drop the first entry probe into the atmosphere of one of the giant planets. And there is a somber side to the pace of scientific discovery as well:

recent work suggests that in the aftermath of a nuclear war the resulting soot and dust lofted high into the atmosphere would darken and freeze the Earth, producing an unprecedented catastrophe even for nations on which not a single bomb has fallen. Our technology is increasingly permitting us to explore the wonders of the Cosmos and to reduce the Earth to chaos. We are privileged to live in, and if we are lucky to influence, one of the most critical epochs in the history of the human species.

On a project of this magnitude it is impossible to thank everyone who has made a contribution. However, I would like to acknowledge, especially, B. Gentry Lee; the *Cosmos* production staff, including the senior producers Geoffrey Haines-Stiles and David Kennard and the executive producer Adrian Malone; the artists Jon Lomberg (who played a critical role in the original design and organization of the *Cosmos* visuals), John Allison, Adolf Schaller, Rick Sternbach, Don Davis, Brown, and Anne Norcia; consultants Donald Goldsmith, Owen Gingerich, Paul Fox, and Diane Ackerman; Cameron Beck; the KCET management—particularly Greg Andorfer, who first carried KCET's proposal to us—Chuck Allen, William Lamb, and James Loper; and the underwriters and co-producers of the *Cosmos* television series, including the Atlantic Richfield Company, the Corporation for Public Broadcasting, the Arthur Vining Davis Foundations, the Alfred P. Sloan Foundation, the British Broadcasting Corporation, and Polytel International. Others who helped in clarifying matters of fact or approach are listed at the back of the book. The final responsibility for the content of the book is, however, of course mine. I thank the staff at Random House, particularly my editor, Anne Freedgood, for their capable work and their patience when the deadlines for the television series and the book seemed to be in conflict. I owe a special debt of gratitude to Shirley Arden, my Executive Assistant, for typing the early drafts of this book and ushering the later drafts through all stages of production with her usual cheerful competence. This is only one of many ways in which the *Cosmos* project is deeply indebted to her. I am more grateful than I can say to the administration of Cornell University for granting me a two-year leave of absence to pursue this project, to my colleagues and students there, and to my colleagues at NASA, JPL and on the Voyager Imaging Team.

My greatest debt for the writing of *Cosmos* is owed to Ann Druyan and Steven Soter, my co-writers in the television series. They made fundamental and frequent contributions to the basic ideas and their connections, to the overall intellectual structure of the episodes, and to the felicity of style. I am deeply grateful for their vigorous critical readings of early versions of this book, their constructive and creative suggestions for revision through many drafts, and their major contributions to the television script which in many ways influenced the content of this book. The delight I found in our many discussions is one of my chief rewards from the *Cosmos* project.

Ithaca and Los Angeles
May 1980
and July 1984

CHAPTER I

THE SHORES OF THE COSMIC OCEAN

> The first men to be created and formed were called the Sorcerer of Fatal Laughter, the Sorcerer of Night, Unkempt, and the Black Sorcerer . . . They were endowed with intelligence, they succeeded in knowing all that there is in the world. When they looked, instantly they saw all that is around them, and they contemplated in turn the arc of heaven and the round face of the earth . . . [Then the Creator said]: "They know all . . . what shall we do with them now? Let their sight reach only to that which is near; let them see only a little of the face of the earth! . . . Are they not by nature simple creatures of our making? Must they also be gods?"
>
> —The Popol Vuh of the Quiché Maya

> The known is finite, the unknown infinite; intellectually we stand on an islet in the midst of an illimitable ocean of inexplicability. Our business in every generation is to reclaim a little more land.
>
> —T. H. Huxley, 1887

The Cosmos is all that is or ever was or ever will be. Our feeblest contemplations of the Cosmos stir us—there is a tingling in the spine, a catch in the voice, a faint sensation, as if a distant memory, of falling from a height. We know we are approaching the greatest of mysteries.

The size and age of the Cosmos are beyond ordinary human understanding. Lost somewhere between immensity and eternity is our tiny planetary home. In a cosmic perspective, most human concerns seem insignificant, even petty. And yet our species is young and curious and brave and shows much promise. In the last few millennia we have made the most astonishing and unexpected discoveries about the Cosmos and our place within it, explorations that are exhilarating to consider. They remind us that humans have evolved to wonder, that understanding is a joy, that knowledge is prerequisite to survival. I believe our future depends on how well we know this Cosmos in which we float like a mote of dust in the morning sky.

Those explorations required skepticism and imagination both. Imagination will often carry us to worlds that never were. But without it, we go nowhere. Skepticism enables us to distinguish fancy from fact, to test our speculations. The Cosmos is rich beyond measure—in elegant facts, in exquisite interrelationships, in the subtle machinery of awe.

The surface of the Earth is the shore of the cosmic ocean. From it we have learned most of what we know. Recently, we have waded a little out to sea, enough to dampen our toes or, at most, wet our ankles. The water seems inviting. The ocean calls. Some part of our being knows this is from where we came. We long to return. These aspirations are not, I think, irreverent, although they may trouble whatever gods may be.

The dimensions of the Cosmos are so large that using familiar units of distance, such as meters or miles, chosen for their utility on Earth, would make little sense. Instead, we measure distance with the speed of light. In one second a beam of light travels 186,000 miles, nearly 300,000 kilometers or seven times around the Earth. In eight minutes it will travel from the Sun to the Earth. We can say the Sun is eight light-minutes away. In a year, it crosses nearly ten trillion kilometers, about six trillion miles, of intervening space. That unit of length, the distance light goes in a year, is called a light-year. It measures not time but distances—enormous distances.

The Earth is a place. It is by no means the only place. It is not even a typical place. No planet or star or galaxy can be typical, because the Cosmos is mostly empty. The only typical place is within the vast, cold, universal vacuum, the everlasting night of intergalactic space, a place so strange and desolate that, by comparison, planets and stars and galaxies seem achingly rare and lovely. If we were randomly inserted into the Cosmos, the chance that we would find ourselves on or near a planet would be less than one in a billion trillion trillion* (10^{33}, a one followed by 33 zeroes). In everyday life such odds are called compelling. Worlds are precious.

From an intergalactic vantage point we would see, strewn like sea froth on the waves of space, innumerable faint, wispy tendrils of light. These are the galaxies. Some are solitary wanderers; most inhabit communal clusters, huddling together, drifting endlessly in the great cosmic dark. Before us is the Cosmos on the grandest scale we know. We are in the realm of the nebulae, eight billion light-years from Earth, halfway to the edge of the known universe.

A galaxy is composed of gas and dust and stars—billions upon billions of stars. Every star may be a sun to someone. Within a galaxy are stars and worlds and, it may be, a proliferation of living things and intelligent beings and spacefaring civilizations. But from afar, a galaxy reminds me more of a collection of lovely found objects—seashells, perhaps, or corals, the productions of Nature laboring for aeons in the cosmic ocean.

There are some hundred billion (10^{11}) galaxies, each with, on the average, a hundred billion stars. In all the galaxies, there are

* We use the American scientific convention for large numbers: one billion = 1,000,000,000 = 10^9; one trillion = 1,000,000,000,000 = 10^{12}, etc. The exponent counts the number of zeroes after the one.

perhaps as many planets as stars, $10^{11} \times 10^{11} = 10^{22}$, ten billion trillion. In the face of such overpowering numbers, what is the likelihood that only one ordinary star, the Sun, is accompanied by an inhabited planet? Why should we, tucked away in some forgotten corner of the Cosmos, be so fortunate? To me, it seems far more likely that the universe is brimming over with life. But we humans do not yet know. We are just beginning our explorations. From eight billion light-years away we are hard pressed to find even the cluster in which our Milky Way Galaxy is embedded, much less the Sun or the Earth. The only planet we are sure is inhabited is a tiny speck of rock and metal, shining feebly by reflected sunlight, and at this distance utterly lost.

But presently our journey takes us to what astronomers on Earth like to call the Local Group of galaxies. Several million light-years across, it is composed of some twenty constituent galaxies. It is a sparse and obscure and unpretentious cluster. One of these galaxies is M31, seen from the Earth in the constellation Andromeda. Like other spiral galaxies, it is a huge pinwheel of stars, gas and dust. M31 has two small satellites, dwarf elliptical galaxies bound to it by gravity, by the identical law of physics that tends to keep me in my chair. The laws of nature are the same throughout the Cosmos. We are now two million light-years from home.

Beyond M31 is another, very similar galaxy, our own, its spiral arms turning slowly, once every quarter billion years. Now, forty thousand light-years from home, we find ourselves falling toward the massive center of the Milky Way. But if we wish to find the Earth, we must redirect our course to the remote outskirts of the Galaxy, to an obscure locale near the edge of a distant spiral arm.

Our overwhelming impression, even between the spiral arms, is of stars streaming by us—a vast array of exquisitely self-luminous stars, some as flimsy as a soap bubble and so large that they could contain ten thousand Suns or a trillion Earths; others the size of a small town and a hundred trillion times denser than lead. Some stars are solitary, like the Sun. Most have companions. Systems are commonly double, two stars orbiting one another. But there is a continuous gradation from triple systems through loose clusters of a few dozen stars to the great globular clusters, resplendent with a million suns. Some double stars are so close that they touch, and starstuff flows between them. Most are as separated as Jupiter is from the Sun. Some stars, the supernovae, are as bright as the entire galaxy that contains them; others, the black holes, are invisible from a few kilometers away. Some shine with a constant brightness; others flicker uncertainly or blink with an unfaltering rhythm. Some rotate in stately elegance; others spin so feverishly that they distort themselves to oblateness. Most shine mainly in visible and infrared light; others are also brilliant sources of X-rays or radio waves. Blue stars are hot and young; yellow stars, conventional and middle-aged; red stars, often elderly and dying; and small white or black stars are in the final throes of death. The Milky Way contains some 400 billion stars of all sorts moving with a complex and orderly grace. Of all the stars, the inhabitants of Earth know close-up, so far, but one.

Each star system is an island in space, quarantined from its neighbors by the light-years. I can imagine creatures evolving into glimmerings of knowledge on innumerable worlds, every one of them assuming at first their puny planet and paltry few suns to be all that is. We grow up in isolation. Only slowly do we teach ourselves the Cosmos.

Some stars may be surrounded by millions of lifeless and rocky worldlets, planetary systems frozen at some early stage in their evolution. Perhaps many stars have planetary systems rather like our own: at the periphery, great gaseous ringed planets and icy moons, and nearer to the center, small, warm, blue-white, cloud-covered worlds. On some, intelligent life may have evolved, reworking the planetary surface in some massive engineering enterprise. These are our brothers and sisters in the Cosmos. Are they very different from us? What is their form, biochemistry, neurobiology, history, politics, science, technology, art, music, religion, philosophy? Perhaps someday we will know them.

We have now reached our own backyard, a light-year from Earth. Surrounding our Sun is a spherical swarm of giant snowballs composed of ice and rock and organic molecules: the cometary nuclei. Every now and then a passing star gives a tiny gravitational tug, and one of them obligingly careens into the inner solar system. There the Sun heats it, the ice is vaporized, and a lovely cometary tail develops.

We approach the planets of our system, largish worlds, captives of the Sun, gravitationally constrained to follow nearly circular orbits, heated mainly by sunlight. Pluto, covered with methane ice and accompanied by its solitary giant moon Charon, is illuminated by a distant Sun, which appears as no more than a bright point of light in a pitch-black sky. The giant gas worlds, Neptune, Uranus, Saturn—the jewel of the solar system—and Jupiter all have an entourage of icy moons. Interior to the region of gassy planets and orbiting icebergs are the warm, rocky provinces of the inner solar system. There is, for example, the red planet Mars, with soaring volcanoes, great rift valleys, enormous planet-wide sandstorms, and, just possibly, some simple forms of life. All the planets orbit the Sun, the nearest star, an inferno of hydrogen and helium gas engaged in thermonuclear reactions, flooding the solar system with light.

Finally, at the end of all our wanderings, we return to our tiny, fragile, blue-white world, lost in a cosmic ocean vast beyond our most courageous imaginings. It is a world among an immensity of others. It may be significant only for us. The Earth is our home, our parent. Our kind of life arose and evolved here. The human species is coming of age here. It is on this world that we developed our passion for exploring the Cosmos, and it is here that we are, in some pain and with no guarantees, working out our destiny.

Welcome to the planet Earth—a place of blue nitrogen skies,

oceans of liquid water, cool forests and soft meadows, a world positively rippling with life. In the cosmic perspective it is, as I have said, poignantly beautiful and rare; but it is also, for the moment, unique. In all our journeying through space and time, it is, so far, the only world on which we know with certainty that the matter of the Cosmos has become alive and aware. There must be many such worlds scattered through space, but our search for them begins here, with the accumulated wisdom of the men and women of our species, garnered at great cost over a million years. We are privileged to live among brilliant and passionately inquisitive people, and in a time when the search for knowledge is generally prized. Human beings, born ultimately of the stars and now for a while inhabiting a world called Earth, have begun their long voyage home.

The discovery that the Earth is a *little* world was made, as so many important human discoveries were, in the ancient Near East, in a time some humans call the third century B.C., in the greatest metropolis of the age, the Egyptian city of Alexandria. Here there lived a man named Eratosthenes. One of his envious contemporaries called him "Beta," the second letter of the Greek alphabet, because, he said, Eratosthenes was second best in the world in everything. But it seems clear that in almost everything Eratosthenes was "Alpha." He was an astronomer, historian, geographer, philosopher, poet, theater critic and mathematician. The titles of the books he wrote range from *Astronomy* to *On Freedom from Pain*. He was also the director of the great library of Alexandria, where one day he read in a papyrus book that in the southern frontier outpost of Syene, near the first cataract of the Nile, at noon on June 21 vertical sticks cast no shadows. On the summer solstice, the longest day of the year, as the hours crept toward midday, the shadows of temple columns grew shorter. At noon, they were gone. A reflection of the Sun could then be seen in the water at the bottom of a deep well. The Sun was directly overhead.

It was an observation that someone else might easily have ignored. Sticks, shadows, reflections in wells, the position of the Sun—of what possible importance could such simple everyday matters be? But Eratosthenes was a scientist, and his musings on these commonplaces changed the world; in a way, they made the world. Eratosthenes had the presence of mind to do an experiment, actually to observe whether in Alexandria vertical sticks cast shadows near noon on June 21. And, he discovered, sticks do.

Eratosthenes asked himself how, at the same moment, a stick in Syene could cast no shadow and a stick in Alexandria, far to the north, could cast a pronounced shadow. Consider a map of ancient Egypt with two vertical sticks of equal length, one stuck in Alexandria, the other in Syene. Suppose that, at a certain moment, each stick casts no shadow at all. This is perfectly easy to understand—provided the Earth is flat. The Sun would then be directly overhead. If the two sticks cast shadows of equal length, that also would make sense on a flat Earth: the Sun's rays would then be inclined at the same angle to the two sticks. But how could it be that at the same instant there was no shadow at Syene and a substantial shadow at Alexandria?

The only possible answer, he saw, was that the surface of the Earth is curved. Not only that: the greater the curvature, the greater the difference in the shadow lengths. The Sun is so far away that its rays are parallel when they reach the Earth. Sticks placed at different angles to the Sun's rays cast shadows of different lengths. For the observed difference in the shadow lengths, the distance between Alexandria and Syene had to be about seven degrees along the surface of the Earth; that is, if you imagine the sticks extending down to the center of the Earth, they would there intersect at an angle of seven degrees. Seven degrees is something like one-fiftieth of three hundred and sixty degrees, the full circumference of the Earth. Eratosthenes knew that the distance between Alexandria and Syene was approximately 800 kilometers, because he hired a man to pace it out. Eight hundred

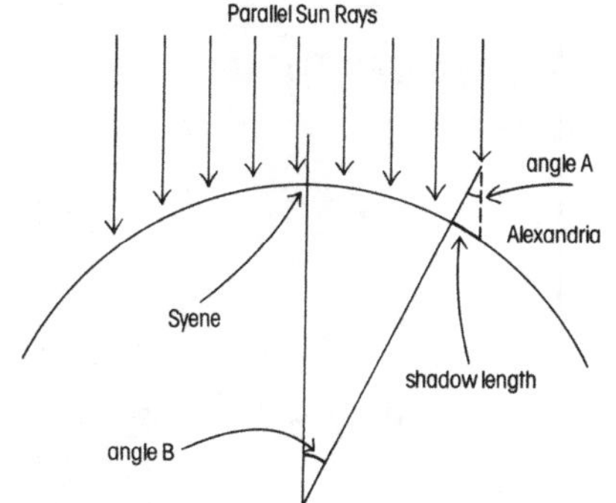

From the shadow length in Alexandria, the angle A can be measured. But from simple geometry ("if two parallel straight lines are transected by a third line, the alternate interior angles are equal"), angle B equals angle A. So by measuring the shadow length in Alexandria, Eratosthenes concluded that Syene was A = B = 7° away on the circumference of the Earth.

kilometers times 50 is 40,000 kilometers: so that must be the circumference of the Earth.*

This is the right answer. Eratosthenes' only tools were sticks, eyes, feet and brains, plus a taste for experiment. With them he deduced the circumference of the Earth with an error of only a few percent, a remarkable achievement for 2,200 years ago. He was the first person accurately to measure the size of a planet.

The Mediterranean world at that time was famous for seafaring. Alexandria was the greatest seaport on the planet. Once you knew the Earth to be a sphere of modest diameter, would you not be tempted to make voyages of exploration, to seek out undiscovered lands, perhaps even to attempt to sail around the planet? Four hundred years before Eratosthenes, Africa had been circumnavigated by a Phoenician fleet in the employ of the Egyptian Pharaoh Necho. They set sail, probably in frail open boats, from the Red Sea, turned down the east coast of Africa up into the Atlantic, returning through the Mediterranean. This epic journey took three years, about as long as a modern Voyager spacecraft takes to fly from Earth to Saturn.

After Eratosthenes' discovery, many great voyages were attempted by brave and venturesome sailors. Their ships were tiny.

* Or if you like to measure things in miles, the distance between Alexandria and Syene is about 500 miles, and 500 miles × 50 = 25,000 miles.

This p.: A flat map of ancient Egypt; when the sun is directly overhead, vertical obelisks cast no shadows in Alexandria or Syene. Opposite p., left: When the sun is not directly overhead, shadows of equal length are cast. But (opposite p., right) when the map is curved, the sun can be overhead in Syene and not in Alexandria; no shadow is then cast in Syene, while a pronounced shadow is cast in Alexandria.

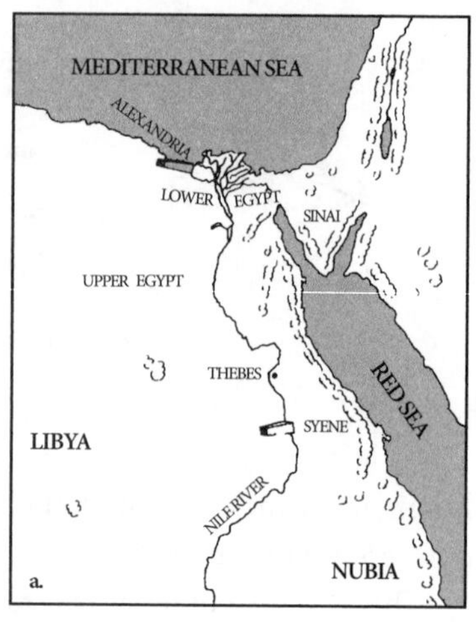

They had only rudimentary navigational instruments. They used dead reckoning and followed coastlines as far as they could. In an unknown ocean they could determine their latitude, but not their longitude, by observing, night after night, the position of the constellations with respect to the horizon. The familiar constellations must have been reassuring in the midst of an unexplored ocean. The stars are the friends of explorers, then with seagoing ships on Earth and now with spacefaring ships in the sky. After Eratosthenes, some may have tried, but not until the time of Magellan did anyone succeed in circumnavigating the Earth. What tales of daring and adventure must earlier have been recounted as sailors and navigators, practical men of the world, gambled their lives on the mathematics of a scientist from Alexandria?

In Eratosthenes' time, globes were constructed portraying the Earth as viewed from space; they were essentially correct in the well-explored Mediterranean but became more and more inaccurate the farther they strayed from home. Our present knowledge of the Cosmos shares this disagreeable but inevitable feature. In the first century, the Alexandrian geographer Strabo wrote:

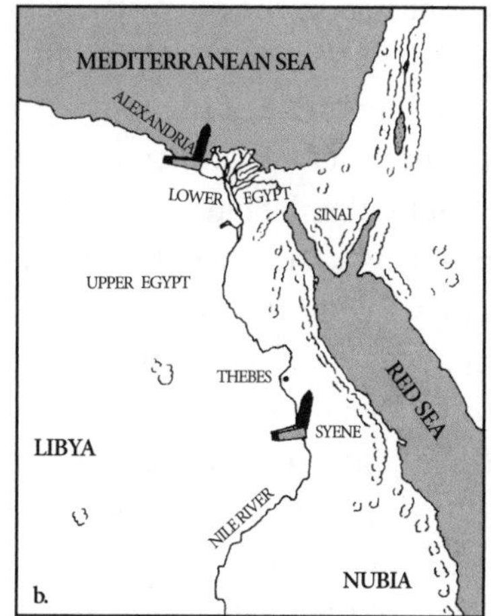

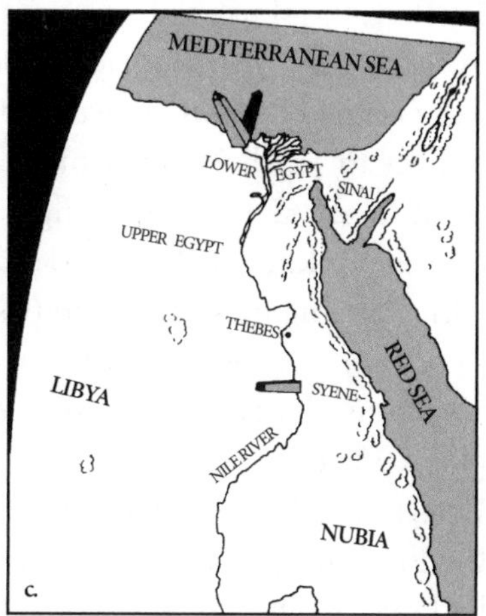

> Those who have returned from an attempt to circumnavigate the Earth do not say they have been prevented by an opposing continent, for the sea remained perfectly open, but, rather, through want of resolution and scarcity of provision. . . . Eratosthenes says that if the extent of the Atlantic Ocean were not an obstacle, we might easily pass by sea from Iberia to India. . . . It is quite possible that in the temperate zone there may be one or two habitable Earths. . . . Indeed, if [this other part of the world] is inhabited, it is not inhabited by men such as exist in our parts, and we should have to regard it as another inhabited world.

Humans were beginning to venture, in almost every sense that matters, to other worlds.

The subsequent exploration of the Earth was a worldwide endeavor, including voyages from as well as to China and Polynesia. The culmination was, of course, the discovery of America by Christopher Columbus and the journeys of the following few centuries, which completed the geographical exploration of the

Earth. Columbus' first voyage is connected in the most straightforward way with the calculations of Eratosthenes. Columbus was fascinated by what he called "the Enterprise of the Indies," a project to reach Japan, China and India not by following the coastline of Africa and sailing East but rather by plunging boldly into the unknown Western ocean—or, as Eratosthenes had said with startling prescience, "to pass by sea from Iberia to India."

Columbus had been an itinerant peddler of old maps and an assiduous reader of the books by and about the ancient geographers, including Eratosthenes, Strabo and Ptolemy. But for the Enterprise of the Indies to work, for ships and crews to survive the long voyage, the Earth had to be smaller than Eratosthenes had said. Columbus therefore cheated on his calculations, as the examining faculty of the University of Salamanca quite correctly pointed out. He used the smallest possible circumference of the Earth and the greatest eastward extension of Asia he could find in all the books available to him, and then exaggerated even those. Had the Americas not been in the way, Columbus' expeditions would have failed utterly.

The Earth is now thoroughly explored. It no longer promises new continents or lost lands. But the technology that allowed us to explore and inhabit the most remote regions of the Earth now permits us to leave our planet, to venture into space, to explore other worlds. Leaving the Earth, we are now able to view it from above, to see its solid spherical shape of Eratosthenian dimensions and the outlines of its continents, confirming that many of the ancient mapmakers were remarkably competent. What a pleasure such a view would have given to Eratosthenes and the other Alexandrian geographers.

It was in Alexandria, during the six hundred years beginning around 300 B.C., that human beings, in an important sense, began the intellectual adventure that has led us to the shores of space. But of the look and feel of that glorious marble city, nothing remains. Oppression and the fear of learning have obliterated almost all memory of ancient Alexandria. Its population was marvelously diverse. Macedonian and later Roman soldiers, Egyptian priests, Greek aristocrats, Phoenician sailors, Jewish merchants, visitors from India and sub-Saharan Africa—everyone, except the vast slave population—lived together in harmony and mutual respect for most of the period of Alexandria's greatness.

The city was founded by Alexander the Great and constructed by his former bodyguard. Alexander encouraged respect for alien cultures and the open-minded pursuit of knowledge. According to tradition—and it does not much matter whether it really happened—he descended beneath the Red Sea in the world's first diving bell. He encouraged his generals and soldiers to marry Persian and Indian women. He respected the gods of other nations. He collected exotic lifeforms, including an elephant for Aristotle, his teacher. His city was constructed on a lavish scale, to be the world center of commerce, culture and learning. It was graced with broad avenues thirty meters wide, elegant architecture and statuary, Alexander's monumental tomb, and an enormous lighthouse, the Pharos, one of the seven wonders of the ancient world.

But the greatest marvel of Alexandria was the library and its associated museum (literally, an institution devoted to the specialties of the Nine Muses). Of that legendary library, the most that survives today is a dank and forgotten cellar of the Serapeum, the library annex, once a temple and later reconsecrated to knowledge. A few moldering shelves may be its only physical remains. Yet this place was once the brain and glory of the greatest city on the planet, the first true research institute in the history of the world. The scholars of the library studied the entire Cosmos. *Cosmos* is a Greek word for the order of the universe. It is, in a way, the opposite of *Chaos.* It implies the deep interconnectedness of all things. It conveys awe for the intricate and subtle way in which the universe is put together. Here was a community of scholars, exploring physics, literature, medicine, astronomy, geography, philosophy, mathematics, biology and engineering. Science and scholarship had come of age. Genius flourished there. The Alexandrian Library is where we humans first collected, seriously and systematically, the knowledge of the world.

In addition to Eratosthenes, there was the astronomer Hipparchus, who mapped the constellations and estimated the brightness of the stars; Euclid, who brilliantly systematized geometry and told his king, struggling over a difficult mathematical problem, "There is no royal road to geometry"; Dionysius of Thrace, the man who defined the parts of speech and did for the study of language what Euclid did for geometry; Herophilus, the physiologist who firmly established that the brain rather than the heart is the seat of intelligence; Heron of Alexandria, inventor of gear trains and steam engines and the author of *Automata,* the first book on robots; Apollonius of Perga, the mathematician who demonstrated the forms of the conic sections*—ellipse, parabola and hyperbola—the curves, as we now know, followed in their orbits by the planets, the comets and the stars; Archimedes, the greatest mechanical genius until Leonardo da Vinci; and the astronomer and geographer Ptolemy, who compiled much of what is today the pseudoscience of astrology: his Earth-centered universe held sway for 1,500 years, a reminder that intellectual capacity is no guarantee against being dead wrong. And among those great men was a great woman, Hypatia, mathematician and astronomer, the last light of the library, whose martyrdom was bound up with the destruction of the library seven centuries after its founding, a story to which we will return.

The Greek Kings of Egypt who succeeded Alexander were serious about learning. For centuries, they supported research and

* So called because they can be produced by slicing through a cone at various angles. Eighteen centuries later, the writings of Apollonius on conic sections would be employed by Johannes Kepler in understanding for the first time the movement of the planets.

maintained in the library a working environment for the best minds of the age. It contained ten large research halls, each devoted to a separate subject; fountains and colonnades; botanical gardens; a zoo; dissecting rooms; an observatory; and a great dining hall where, at leisure, was conducted the critical discussion of ideas.

The heart of the library was its collection of books. The organizers combed all the cultures and languages of the world. They sent agents abroad to buy up libraries. Commercial ships docking in Alexandria were searched by the police—not for contraband, but for books. The scrolls were borrowed, copied and then returned to their owners. Accurate numbers are difficult to estimate, but it seems probable that the Library contained half a million volumes, each a handwritten papyrus scroll. What happened to all those books? The classical civilization that created them disintegrated, and the library itself was deliberately destroyed. Only a small fraction of its works survived, along with a few pathetic scattered fragments. And how tantalizing those bits and pieces are! We know, for example, that there was on the library shelves a book by the astronomer Aristarchus of Samos, who argued that the Earth is one of the planets, which like them orbits the Sun, and that the stars are enormously far away. Each of these conclusions is entirely correct, but we had to wait nearly two thousand years for their rediscovery. If we multiply by a hundred thousand our sense of loss for this work of Aristarchus, we begin to appreciate the grandeur of the achievement of classical civilization and the tragedy of its destruction.

We have far surpassed the science known to the ancient world. But there are irreparable gaps in our historical knowledge. Imagine what mysteries about our past could be solved with a borrower's card to the Alexandrian Library. We know of a three-volume history of the world, now lost, by a Babylonian priest named Berossus. The first volume dealt with the interval from the Creation to the Flood, a period he took to be 432,000 years or about a hundred times longer than the Old Testament chronology. I wonder what was in it.

The ancients knew that the world is very old. They sought to look into the distant past. We now know that the Cosmos is far older than they ever imagined. We have examined the universe in space and seen that we live on a mote of dust circling a humdrum star in the remotest corner of an obscure galaxy. And if we are a speck in the immensity of space, we also occupy an instant in the expanse of ages. We know now that our universe—or at least its most recent incarnation—is some fifteen or twenty billion years old. This is the time since a remarkable explosive event called the Big Bang. At the beginning of this universe, there were no galaxies, stars or planets, no life or civilizations, merely a uniform, radiant fireball filling all of space. The passage from the Chaos of the Big Bang to the Cosmos that we are beginning to know is the most awesome transformation of matter and energy that we have been privileged to glimpse. And until we find more intelligent beings elsewhere, we are ourselves the most spectacular of all the transformations—the remote descendants of the Big Bang, dedicated to understanding and further transforming the Cosmos from which we spring.

CHAPTER II

ONE VOICE IN THE COSMIC FUGUE

> Probably all the organic beings which have ever lived on this earth have descended from some one primordial form, into which life was first breathed.... There is grandeur in this view of life ... that, whilst this planet has gone cycling on according to the fixed law of gravity, from so simple a beginning endless forms most beautiful and most wonderful have been, and are being, evolved.
>
> —Charles Darwin, *The Origin of Species,* 1859

All my life I have wondered about the possibility of life elsewhere. What would it be like? Of what would it be made? All living things on our planet are constructed of organic molecules—complex microscopic architectures in which the carbon atom plays a central role. There was once a time before life, when the Earth was barren and utterly desolate. Our world is now overflowing with life. How did it come about? How, in the absence of life, were carbon-based organic molecules made? How did the first living things arise? How did life evolve to produce beings as elaborate and complex as we, able to explore the mystery of our own origins?

And on the countless other planets that may circle other suns, is there life also? Is extraterrestrial life, if it exists, based on the same organic molecules as life on Earth? Do the beings of other worlds look much like life on Earth? Or are they stunningly different—other adaptations to other environments? What else is possible? The nature of life on Earth and the search for life elsewhere are two sides of the same question—the search for who we are.

In the great dark between the stars there are clouds of gas and dust and organic matter. Dozens of different kinds of organic molecules have been found there by radio telescopes. The abundance of these molecules suggests that the stuff of life is everywhere. Perhaps the origin and evolution of life is, given enough time, a cosmic inevitability. On some of the billions of planets in the Milky Way Galaxy, life may never arise. On others, it may arise and die out, or never evolve beyond its simplest forms. And on some small fraction of worlds there may develop intelligences and civilizations more advanced than our own.

Occasionally someone remarks on what a lucky coincidence it is that the Earth is perfectly suitable for life—moderate temperatures, liquid water, oxygen atmosphere, and so on. But this is, at least in part, a confusion of cause and effect. We earthlings are supremely well adapted to the environment of the Earth because we grew up here. Those earlier forms of life that were not well adapted died. We are descended from the organisms that did well. Organisms that evolve on a quite different world will doubtless sing its praises too.

All life on Earth is closely related. We have a common organic chemistry and a common evolutionary heritage. As a result, our biologists are profoundly limited. They study only a single kind of biology, one lonely theme in the music of life. Is this faint and reedy tune the only voice for thousands of light-years? Or is there a kind of cosmic fugue, with themes and counterpoints, dissonances and harmonies, a billion different voices playing the life music of the Galaxy?

Let me tell you a story about one little phrase in the music of life on Earth. In the year 1185, the Emperor of Japan was a seven-year-old boy named Antoku. He was the nominal leader of a clan of samurai called the Heike, who were engaged in a long and bloody war with another samurai clan, the Genji. Each asserted a superior ancestral claim to the imperial throne. Their decisive naval encounter, with the Emperor on board ship, occurred at Danno-ura in the Japanese Inland Sea on April 24, 1185. The Heike were outnumbered, and outmaneuvered. Many were killed. The survivors, in massive numbers, threw themselves into the sea and drowned. The Lady Nii, grandmother of the Emperor, resolved that she and Antoku would not be captured by the enemy. What happened next is told in *The Tale of the Heike:*

> The Emperor was seven years old that year but looked much older. He was so lovely that he seemed to shed a brilliant radiance and his long, black hair hung loose far down his back. With a look of surprise and anxiety on his face he asked the Lady Nii, "Where are you to take me?"
>
> She turned to the youthful sovereign, with tears streaming down her cheeks, and . . . comforted him, binding up his long hair in his dove-colored robe. Blinded with tears, the child sovereign put his beautiful, small hands together. He turned first to the East to say farewell to the god of Ise and then to the West to repeat the Nembutsu [a prayer to the Amida Buddha]. The Lady Nii took him tightly in her arms and with the words "In the depths of the ocean is our capitol," sank with him at last beneath the waves.

The entire Heike battle fleet was destroyed. Only forty-three women survived. These ladies-in-waiting of the imperial court were forced to sell flowers and other favors to the fishermen near the scene of the battle. The Heike almost vanished from history.

But a ragtag group of the former ladies-in-waiting and their offspring by the fisherfolk established a festival to commemorate the battle. It takes place on the twenty-fourth of April every year to this day. Fishermen who are the descendants of the Heike dress in hemp and black headgear and proceed to the Akama shrine which contains the mausoleum of the drowned Emperor. There they watch a play portraying the events that followed the Battle of Danno-ura. For centuries after, people imagined that they could discern ghostly samurai armies vainly striving to bail the sea, to cleanse it of blood and defeat and humiliation.

The fishermen say the Heike samurai wander the bottoms of the Inland Sea still—in the form of crabs. There are crabs to be found here with curious markings on their backs, patterns and indentations that disturbingly resemble the face of a samurai. When caught, these crabs are not eaten, but are returned to the sea in commemoration of the doleful events at Danno-ura.

This legend raises a lovely problem. How does it come about that the face of a warrior is incised on the carapace of a crab? The answer seems to be that humans made the face. The patterns on the crab's shell are inherited. But among crabs, as among people, there are many different hereditary lines. Suppose that, by chance, among the distant ancestors of this crab, one arose with a pattern that resembled, even slightly, a human face. Even before the battle of Danno-ura, fishermen may have been reluctant to eat such a crab. In throwing it back, they set in motion an evolutionary process: If you are a crab and your carapace is ordinary, the humans will eat you. Your line will leave fewer descendants. If your carapace looks a little like a face, they will throw you back. You will leave more descendants. Crabs had a substantial investment in the patterns on their carapaces. As the generations passed, of crabs and fishermen alike, the crabs with patterns that most resembled a samurai face survived preferentially until eventually there was produced not just a human face, not just a Japanese face, but the visage of a fierce and scowling samurai. All this has nothing to do with what the crabs *want*. Selection is imposed from the outside. The more you look like a samurai, the better are your chances of survival. Eventually, there come to be a great many samurai crabs.

This process is called artificial selection. In the case of the Heike crab it was effected more or less unconsciously by the fishermen, and certainly without any serious contemplation by the crabs. But humans have deliberately selected which plants and animals shall live and which shall die for thousands of years. We are surrounded from babyhood by familiar farm and domestic animals, fruits and trees and vegetables. Where do they come from? Were they once free-living in the wild and then induced to adopt a less strenuous life on the farm? No, the truth is quite different. They are, most of them, made by us.

Ten thousand years ago, there were no dairy cows or ferret hounds or large ears of corn. When we domesticated the ancestors of these plants and animals—sometimes creatures who looked quite different—we controlled their breeding. We made sure that certain varieties, having properties we consider desirable, preferentially reproduced. When we wanted a dog to help us care for sheep, we selected breeds that were intelligent, obedient and had some preexisting talent to herd, which is useful for animals who hunt in packs. The enormous distended udders of dairy cattle are the result of a human interest in milk and cheese. Our corn, or maize, has been bred for ten thousand generations to be more tasty and nutritious than its scrawny ancestors; indeed, it is so changed that it cannot even reproduce without human intervention.

The essence of artificial selection—for a Heike crab, a dog, a cow or an ear of corn—is this: Many physical and behavioral traits of plants and animals are inherited. They breed true. Humans, for whatever reason, encourage the reproduction of some varieties and discourage the reproduction of others. The variety selected for preferentially reproduces; it eventually becomes abundant; the variety selected against becomes rare and perhaps extinct.

But if humans can make new varieties of plants and animals, must not nature do so also? This related process is called natural selection. That life has changed fundamentally over the aeons is entirely clear from the alterations we have made in the beasts and vegetables during the short tenure of humans on Earth, and from the fossil evidence. The fossil record speaks to us unambiguously of creatures that once were present in enormous numbers and that have now vanished utterly.* Far more species have become extinct in the history of the Earth than exist today; they are the terminated experiments of evolution.

The genetic changes induced by domestication have occurred very rapidly. The rabbit was not domesticated until early medieval times (it was bred by French monks in the belief that newborn bunnies were fish and therefore exempt from the prohibitions against eating meat on certain days in the Church calendar); coffee in the fifteenth century; the sugar beet in the nineteenth century; and the mink is still in the earliest stages of domestication. In less than ten thousand years, domestication has increased the weight of wool grown by sheep from less than one kilogram of rough hairs to ten or twenty kilograms of uniform, fine down; or the volume of milk given by cattle during a lactation period from a few hundred to a million cubic centimeters. If artificial selection can make such major changes in so short a period of time, what must natural selection, working over billions of years, be capable of? The answer is all the beauty and diversity of the biological world. Evolution is a fact, not a theory.

That the mechanism of evolution is natural selection is the great discovery associated with the names of Charles Darwin and

* Although traditional Western religious opinion stoutly maintained the contrary, as for example, the 1770 opinion of John Wesley: "Death is never permitted to destroy [even] the most inconsiderable species."

Alfred Russel Wallace. More than a century ago, they stressed that nature is prolific, that many more animals and plants are born than can possibly survive and that therefore the environment selects those varieties which are, by accident, better suited for survival. Mutations—sudden changes in heredity—breed true. They provide the raw material of evolution. The environment selects those few mutations that enhance survival, resulting in a series of slow transformations of one lifeform into another, the origin of new species.*

Darwin's words in *The Origin of Species* were:

> Man does not actually produce variability; he only unintentionally exposes organic beings to new conditions of life, and then Nature acts on the organisation, and causes variability. But man can and does select the variations given to him by Nature, and thus accumulate them in any desired manner. He thus adapts animals and plants for his own benefit or pleasure. He may do this methodically, or he may do it unconsciously by preserving the individuals most useful to him at the time, without any thought of altering the breed. . . . There is no obvious reason why the principles which have acted so efficiently under domestication should not have acted under Nature. . . . More individuals are born than can possibly survive. . . . The slightest advantage in one being, of any age or during any season,

* In the Mayan holy book the Popol Vuh, the various forms of life are described as unsuccessful attempts by gods with a predilection for experiment to make people. Early tries were far off the mark, creating the lower animals; the penultimate attempt, a near miss, made the monkeys. In Chinese myth, human beings arose from the body lice of a god named P'an Ku. In the eighteenth century, de Buffon proposed that the Earth was much older than Scripture suggested, that the forms of life somehow changed slowly over the millennia, but that the apes were the forlorn descendants of people. While these notions do not precisely reflect the evolutionary process described by Darwin and Wallace, they are anticipations of it—as are the views of Democritus, Empedocles and other early Ionian scientists who are discussed in Chapter 7.

> over those with which it comes into competition, or better adaptation in however slight a degree to the surrounding physical conditions, will turn the balance.

T. H. Huxley, the most effective nineteenth-century defender and popularizer of evolution, wrote that the publications of Darwin and Wallace were a "flash of light, which to a man who has lost himself in a dark night, suddenly reveals a road which, whether it takes him straight home or not, certainly goes his way. . . . My reflection, when I first made myself master of the central idea of the 'Origin of Species,' was, 'How extremely stupid not to have thought of that!' I suppose that Columbus' companions said much the same. . . . The facts of variability, of the struggle for existence, of adaptation to conditions, were notorious enough; but none of us had suspected that the road to the heart of the species problem lay through them, until Darwin and Wallace dispelled the darkness."

Many people were scandalized—some still are—at both ideas, evolution and natural selection. Our ancestors looked at the elegance of life on Earth, at how appropriate the structures of organisms are to their functions, and saw evidence for a Great Designer. The simplest one-celled organism is a far more complex machine than the finest pocket watch. And yet pocket watches do not spontaneously self-assemble, or evolve, in slow stages, on their own, from, say, grandfather clocks. A watch implies a watchmaker. There seemed to be no way in which atoms and molecules could somehow spontaneously fall together to create organisms of such awesome complexity and subtle functioning as grace every region of the Earth. That each living thing was specially designed, that one species did not become another, were notions perfectly consistent with what our ancestors with their limited historical records knew about life. The idea that every organism was meticulously constructed by a Great Designer provided a significance and order to nature and an importance to human beings that we crave still. A Designer is a natural, appealing and altogether human explanation of the biological world. But, as Darwin and Wallace showed, there is another way, equally appealing, equally human, and far more compelling: natural selection, which makes the music of life more beautiful as the aeons pass.

The fossil evidence could be consistent with the idea of a Great Designer; perhaps some species are destroyed when the Designer becomes dissatisfied with them, and new experiments are attempted on an improved design. But this notion is a little disconcerting. Each plant and animal is exquisitely made; should not a supremely competent Designer have been able to make the intended variety from the start? The fossil record implies trial and error, an inability to anticipate the future, features inconsistent with an efficient Great Designer (although not with a Designer of a more remote and indirect temperament).

When I was a college undergraduate in the early 1950's, I was fortunate enough to work in the laboratory of H. J. Muller, a great geneticist and the man who discovered that radiation produces mutations. Muller was the person who first called my attention to the Heike crab as an example of artificial selection. To learn the practical side of genetics, I spent many months working with fruit flies, *Drosophila melanogaster* (which means the black-bodied dew-lover)—tiny benign beings with two wings and big eyes. We kept them in pint milk bottles. We would cross two varieties to see what new forms emerged from the rearrangement of the parental genes, and from natural and induced mutations. The females would deposit their eggs on a kind of molasses the technicians placed inside the bottles; the bottles were stoppered; and we would wait two weeks for the fertilized eggs to become larvae, the larvae pupae, and the pupae to emerge as new adult fruit flies.

One day I was looking through a low-power binocular microscope at a newly arrived batch of adult *Drosophila* immobilized with a little ether, and was busily separating the different varieties with a camel's-hair brush. To my astonishment, I came upon something very different: not a small variation such as red eyes instead of white, or neck bristles instead of no neck bristles. This was another, and very well-functioning, kind of creature with much more prominent wings and long feathery antennae. Fate had arranged, I concluded, that an example of a major evolutionary change in a single generation, the very thing Muller had said could never happen, should take place in his own laboratory. It was my unhappy task to explain it to him.

With heavy heart I knocked on his office door. "Come in," came the muffled cry. I entered to discover the room darkened except for a single small lamp illuminating the stage of the microscope at which he was working. In these gloomy surroundings I stumbled through my explanation. I had found a very different kind of fly. I was sure it had emerged from one of the pupae in the molasses. I didn't mean to disturb Muller but . . . "Does it look more like Lepidoptera than Diptera?" he asked, his face illuminated from below. I didn't know what this meant, so he had to explain: "Does it have big wings? Does it have feathery antennae?" I glumly nodded assent.

Muller switched on the overhead light and smiled benignly. It was an old story. There was a kind of moth that had adapted to *Drosophila* genetics laboratories. It was nothing like a fruit fly and wanted nothing to do with fruit flies. What it wanted was the fruit flies' molasses. In the brief time that the laboratory technician took to unstopper and stopper the milk bottle—for example, to add fruit flies—the mother moth made a dive-bombing pass, dropping her eggs on the run into the tasty molasses. I had not discovered a macromutation. I had merely stumbled upon another lovely adaptation in nature, itself the product of micromutation and natural selection.

The secrets of evolution are death and time—the deaths of enormous numbers of lifeforms that were imperfectly adapted to the environment; and time for a long succession of small mutations that were *by accident* adaptive, time for the slow accumulation of patterns of favorable mutations. Part of the resistance to Darwin and Wallace derives from our difficulty in imagining the passage of the millennia, much less the aeons. What does seventy million years mean to beings who live only one-millionth as long? We are like butterflies who flutter for a day and think it is forever.

What happened here on Earth may be more or less typical of the evolution of life on many worlds; but in such details as the chemistry of proteins or the neurology of brains, the story of life on Earth may be unique in all the Milky Way Galaxy. The Earth condensed out of interstellar gas and dust some 4.6 billion years ago. We know from the fossil record that the origin of life happened soon after, perhaps around 4.0 billion years ago, in the ponds and oceans of the primitive Earth. The first living things were not anything so complex as a one-celled organism, already a highly sophisticated form of life. The first stirrings were much more humble. In those early days, lightning and ultraviolet light from the Sun were breaking apart the simple hydrogen-rich molecules of the primitive atmosphere, the fragments spontaneously recombining into more and more complex molecules. The products of this early chemistry were dissolved in the oceans, forming a kind of organic soup of gradually increasing complexity, until one day, quite by accident, a molecule arose that was able to make crude copies of itself, using as building blocks other molecules in the soup. (We will return to this subject later.)

This was the earliest ancestor of deoxyribonucleic acid, DNA, the master molecule of life on Earth. It is shaped like a ladder twisted into a helix, the rungs available in four different molecular parts, which constitute the four letters of the genetic code. These rungs, called nucleotides, spell out the hereditary instructions for making a given organism. Every lifeform on Earth has a different set of instructions, written out in essentially the same language. The reason organisms *are* different is the differences in their nucleic acid instructions. A mutation is a change in a nucleotide, copied in the next generation, which breeds true. Since mutations are *random* nucleotide changes, most of them are harmful or lethal, coding into existence nonfunctional enzymes. It is a long wait before a mutation makes an organism work better. And yet it is that improbable event, a small beneficial mutation in a nucleotide a ten-millionth of a centimeter across, that makes evolution go.

Four billion years ago, the Earth was a molecular Garden of Eden. There were as yet no predators. Some molecules reproduced themselves inefficiently, competed for building blocks and left crude copies of themselves. With reproduction, mutation and the selective elimination of the least efficient varieties, evolution was well under way, even at the molecular level. As time went on, they got better at reproducing. Molecules with specialized functions eventually joined together, making a kind of molecular collective—the first cell. Plant cells today have tiny molecular factories, called chloroplasts, which are in charge of photosynthesis—the conversion of sunlight, water and carbon dioxide into carbohydrates and oxygen. The cells in a drop of blood contain a different sort of molecular factory, the mitochondrion, which combines food with oxygen to extract useful energy. These factories exist in plant and animal cells today but may once themselves have been free-living cells.

By three billion years ago, a number of one-celled plants had joined together, perhaps because a mutation prevented a single cell from separating after splitting in two. The first multicellular organisms had evolved. Every cell of your body is a kind of commune, with once free-living parts all banded together for the common good. And you are made of a hundred trillion cells. We are, each of us, a multitude.

Sex seems to have been invented around two billion years ago. Before then, new varieties of organisms could arise only from the accumulation of random mutations—the selection of changes, letter by letter, in the genetic instructions. Evolution must have been agonizingly slow. With the invention of sex, two organisms could exchange whole paragraphs, pages and books of their DNA code, producing new varieties ready for the sieve of selection. Organisms are selected to engage in sex—the ones that find it uninteresting quickly become extinct. And this is true not only of the microbes of two billion years ago. We humans also have a palpable devotion to exchanging segments of DNA today.

By one billion years ago, plants, working cooperatively, had made a stunning change in the environment of the Earth. Green plants generate molecular oxygen. Since the oceans were by now filled with simple green plants, oxygen was becoming a major constituent of the Earth's atmosphere, altering it irreversibly from its original hydrogen-rich character and ending the epoch of Earth history when the stuff of life was made by nonbiological processes. But oxygen tends to make organic molecules fall to pieces. Despite our fondness for it, it is fundamentally a poison for unprotected organic matter. The transition to an oxidizing atmosphere posed a supreme crisis in the history of life, and a great many organisms, unable to cope with oxygen, perished. A few primitive forms, such as the botulism and tetanus bacilli, manage to survive even today only in oxygen-free environments. The nitrogen in the Earth's atmosphere is much more chemically inert and therefore much more benign than oxygen. But it too is biologically sustained. Thus, 99 percent of the Earth's atmosphere is of biological origin. The sky is made by life.

For most of the four billion years since the origin of life, the dominant organisms were microscopic blue-green algae, which covered and filled the oceans. Then some 600 million years ago, the monopolizing grip of the algae was broken and an enormous proliferation of new lifeforms emerged, an event called the Cambrian explosion. Life had arisen almost immediately after the origin of the Earth, which suggests that life may be an inevitable chemical process on an Earth-like planet. But life did not evolve much beyond blue-green algae for three billion years, which suggests that large lifeforms with specialized organs are hard to evolve, harder even than the origin of life. Perhaps there are many other planets that today have abundant microbes but no big beasts and vegetables.

Soon after the Cambrian explosion, the oceans teemed with many different forms of life. By 500 million years ago there were vast herds of trilobites, beautifully constructed animals, a little like large insects; some hunted in packs on the ocean floor. They stored crystals in their eyes to detect polarized light. But there are no trilobites alive today; there have been none for 200 million years. The Earth used to be inhabited by plants and animals of which there is today no living trace. And of course every species now on the planet once did not exist. There is no hint in the old rocks of animals like us. Species appear, abide more or less briefly and then flicker out.

Before the Cambrian explosion species seem to have succeeded one another rather slowly. In part this may be because the richness of our information declines rapidly the farther into the past we peer; in the early history of our planet, few organisms had hard parts and soft beings leave few fossil remains. But in part the sluggish rate of appearance of dramatically new forms before the Cambrian explosion is real; the painstaking evolution of cell structure and biochemistry is not immediately reflected in the external forms revealed by the fossil record. After the Cambrian explosion, exquisite new adaptations followed one another with comparatively breathtaking speed. In rapid succession, the first fish and the first vertebrates appeared; plants, previously restricted to the oceans, began the colonization of the land; the first insect evolved, and its descendants became the pioneers in the colonization of the land by animals; winged insects arose together with the amphibians, creatures something like the lungfish, able to survive both on land and in the water; the first trees and the first reptiles appeared; the dinosaurs evolved; the mammals emerged, and then the first birds; the first flowers appeared; the dinosaurs became extinct; the earliest cetaceans, ancestors to the dolphins and whales, arose and in the same period the primates—the ancestors of the monkeys, the apes and the humans. Less than ten million years ago, the first creatures who closely resembled human beings evolved, accompanied by a spectacular increase in brain size. And then, only a few million years ago, the first true humans emerged.

Human beings grew up in forests; we have a natural affinity for them. How lovely a tree is, straining toward the sky. Its leaves harvest sunlight to photosynthesize, so trees compete by shadowing their neighbors. If you look closely you can often see two trees pushing and shoving with languid grace. Trees are great and beautiful machines, powered by sunlight, taking in water from the ground and carbon dioxide from the air, converting these materials into food for their use and ours. The plant uses the carbohydrates it makes as an energy source to go about its planty business. And we animals, who are ultimately parasites on the plants, steal the carbohydrates so we can go about *our* business. In eating the plants we combine the carbohydrates with oxygen dissolved in our blood because of our penchant for breathing air, and so extract the energy that makes us go. In the process we exhale carbon dioxide, which the plants then recycle to make more carbohydrates. What a marvelous cooperative arrangement—plants and animals each inhaling the other's exhalations, a kind of planet-wide mutual mouth-to-stoma resuscitation, the entire elegant cycle powered by a star 150 million kilometers away.

There are tens of billions of known kinds of organic molecules. Yet only about fifty of them are used for the essential activities of life. The same patterns are employed over and over again, conservatively, ingeniously for different functions. And at the very heart of life on Earth—the proteins that control cell chemistry, and the nucleic acids that carry the hereditary instructions—we find these molecules to be essentially identical in all the plants and animals. An oak tree and I are made of the same stuff. If you go far enough back, we have a common ancestor.

The living cell is a regime as complex and beautiful as the realm of the galaxies and the stars. The elaborate machinery of the cell has been painstakingly evolved over four billion years. Fragments of food are transmogrified into cellular machinery. Today's white blood cell is yesterday's creamed spinach. How does the cell do it? Inside is a labyrinthine and subtle architecture that maintains its own structure, transforms molecules, stores energy and prepares for self-replication. If we could enter a cell, many of the molecular specks we would see would be protein molecules, some in frenzied activity, others merely waiting. The most important proteins are enzymes, molecules that control the cell's chemical reactions. Enzymes are like assembly-line workers, each specializing in a particular molecular job: Step 4 in the construction of the nucleotide guanosine phosphate, say, or Step 11 in the dismantling of a molecule of sugar to extract energy, the currency that pays for getting the other cellular jobs done. But the enzymes do not run the show. They receive their instructions—and are in fact themselves constructed—on orders sent from those in charge. The boss molecules are the nucleic acids. They live sequestered in a forbidden city in the deep interior, in the nucleus of the cell.

If we plunged through a pore into the nucleus of the cell, we would find something that resembles an explosion in a spaghetti factory—a disorderly multitude of coils and strands, which are the two kinds of nucleic acids: DNA, which knows what to do, and RNA, which conveys the instructions issued by DNA to the rest of the cell. These are the best that four billion years of evolution could produce, containing the full complement of information on how to make a cell, a tree or a human work. The amount of information in human DNA, if written out in ordinary language, would occupy a hundred thick volumes. What is more, the DNA molecules know how to make, with only very rare exceptions, identical copies of themselves. They know extraordinarily much.

DNA is a double helix, the two intertwined strands resembling a "spiral" staircase. It is the sequence or ordering of the nucleotides along either of the constituent strands that is the language of life. During reproduction, the helices separate, assisted by a special unwinding protein, each synthesizing an identical copy of the other from nucleotide building blocks floating about nearby in the viscous liquid of the cell nucleus. Once the unwinding is under way, a remarkable enzyme called DNA polymerase helps ensure that the copying works almost perfectly. If a mistake is made, there are enzymes which snip the mistake out and replace the wrong nucleotide by the right one. These enzymes are a molecular machine with awesome powers.

In addition to making accurate copies of itself—which is what heredity is about—nuclear DNA directs the activities of the cell—which is what metabolism is about—by synthesizing another nucleic acid called messenger RNA, each of which passes to the extranuclear provinces and there controls the construction, at the right time, in the right place, of one enzyme. When all is done, a single enzyme molecule has been produced, which then goes about ordering one particular aspect of the chemistry of the cell.

Human DNA is a ladder a billion nucleotides long. Most possible combinations of nucleotides are nonsense: they would cause the synthesis of proteins that perform no useful function. Only an extremely limited number of nucleic acid molecules are any good for lifeforms as complicated as we. Even so, the number of useful ways of putting nucleic acids together is stupefyingly large—probably far greater than the total number of electrons and protons in the universe. Accordingly, the number of possible individual human beings is vastly greater than the number that have ever lived: the untapped potential of the human species is immense. There must be ways of putting nucleic acids together that will function far better—by any criterion we choose—than any human being who has ever lived. Fortunately, we do not yet know how to assemble alternative sequences of nucleotides to make alternative kinds of human beings. In the future we may well be able to assemble nucleotides in any desired sequence, to produce whatever characteristics we think desirable—a sobering and disquieting prospect.

Evolution works through mutation and selection. Mutations might occur during replication if the enzyme DNA polymerase makes a mistake. But it rarely makes a mistake. Mutations also occur because of radioactivity or ultraviolet light from the Sun or cosmic rays or chemicals in the environment, all of which can change the nucleotides or tie the nucleic acids up in knots. If the mutation rate is too high, we lose the inheritance of four billion years of painstaking evolution. If it is too low, new varieties will not be available to adapt to some future change in the environment. The evolution of life requires a more or less precise balance between mutation and selection. When that balance is achieved, remarkable adaptations occur.

A change in a single DNA nucleotide causes a change in a single amino acid in the protein for which that DNA codes. The red blood cells of people of European descent look roughly globular. The red blood cells of some people of African descent look like sickles or crescent moons. Sickle cells carry less oxygen and consequently transmit a kind of anemia. They also provide major resistance against malaria. There is no question that it is better to be anemic than to be dead. This major influence on the function of the blood—so striking as to be readily apparent in photographs of red blood cells—is the result of a change in a single nucleotide out of the ten billion in the DNA of a typical human cell. We are still ignorant of the consequences of changes in most of the other nucleotides.

We humans look rather different from a tree. Without a doubt we perceive the world differently than a tree does. But down deep, at the molecular heart of life, the trees and we are essentially identical. We both use nucleic acids for heredity; we both use proteins as enzymes to control the chemistry of our cells. Most significantly, we both use precisely the same code book for translating nucleic acid information into protein information, as do virtually all the other creatures on the planet.* The usual explanation of this molecular unity is that we are, all of us—trees and people, angler fish and slime molds and paramecia—descended from a single and common instance of the origin of life in the early history of our planet. How did the critical molecules then arise?

In my laboratory at Cornell University we work on, among other things, prebiological organic chemistry, making some notes of the music of life. We mix together and spark the gases of the primitive Earth: hydrogen, water, ammonia, methane, hydrogen sulfide—all present, incidentally, on the planet Jupiter today and throughout the Cosmos. The sparks correspond to lightning—also present on the ancient Earth and on modern Jupiter. The reaction vessel is initially transparent: the precursor gases are entirely invisible. But after ten minutes of sparking, we see a strange brown pigment slowly streaking the sides of the vessel. The interior gradually becomes opaque, covered with a thick brown tar. If we had used ultraviolet light—simulating the early

* The genetic code turns out to be not quite identical in all parts of all organisms on the Earth. At least a few cases are known where the transcription from DNA information into protein information in a mitochondrion employs a different code book from that used by the genes in the nucleus of the very same cell. This points to a long evolutionary separation of the genetic codes of mitochondria and nuclei, and is consistent with the idea that mitochondria were once free-living organisms incorporated into the cell in a symbiotic relationship billions of years ago. The development and emerging sophistication of that symbiosis is, incidentally, one answer to the question of what evolution was doing between the origin of the cell and the proliferation of many-celled organisms in the Cambrian explosion.

Sun—the results would have been more or less the same. The tar is an extremely rich collection of complex organic molecules, including the constituent parts of proteins and nucleic acids. The stuff of life, it turns out, can be very easily made.

Such experiments were first performed in the early 1950's by Stanley Miller, then a graduate student of the chemist Harold Urey. Urey had argued compellingly that the early atmosphere of the Earth was hydrogen-rich, as is most of the Cosmos; that the hydrogen has since trickled away to space from Earth, but not from massive Jupiter; and that the origin of life occurred before the hydrogen was lost. After Urey suggested that such gases be sparked, someone asked him what he expected to make in such an experiment. Urey replied, "*Beilstein.*" *Beilstein* is the massive German compendium in 28 volumes, listing all the organic molecules known to chemists.

Using only the most abundant gases that were present on the early Earth and almost any energy source that breaks chemical bonds, we can produce the essential building blocks of life. But in our vessel are only the notes of the music of life—not the music itself. The molecular building blocks must be put together in the correct sequence. Life is certainly more than the amino acids that make up its proteins and the nucleotides that make up its nucleic acids. But even in ordering these building blocks into long-chain molecules, there has been substantial laboratory progress. Amino acids have been assembled under primitive Earth conditions into molecules resembling proteins. Some of them feebly control useful chemical reactions, as enzymes do. Nucleotides have been put together into strands of nucleic acid a few dozen units long. Under the right circumstances in the test tube, short nucleic acids can synthesize identical copies of themselves.

No one has so far mixed together the gases and waters of the primitive Earth and at the end of the experiment had something crawl out of the test tube. The smallest living things known, the viroids, are composed of less than 10,000 atoms. They cause several different diseases in cultivated plants and have probably most recently evolved from more complex organisms rather than from simpler ones. Indeed, it is hard to imagine a still simpler organism that is in any sense alive. Viroids are composed exclusively of nucleic acid, unlike the viruses, which also have a protein coat. They are no more than a single strand of RNA with either a linear or a closed circular geometry. Viroids can be so small and still thrive because they are thoroughgoing, unremitting parasites. Like viruses, they simply take over the molecular machinery of a much larger, well-functioning cell and change it from a factory for making more cells into a factory for making more viroids.

The smallest known free-living organisms are the PPLO (pleuropneumonia-like organisms) and similar small beasts. They are composed of about fifty million atoms. Such organisms, having to be more self-reliant, are also more complicated than viroids and viruses. But the environment of the Earth today is not extremely favorable for simple forms of life. You have to work hard to make a living. You have to be careful about predators. In the early history of our planet, however, when enormous amounts of organic molecules were being produced by sunlight in a hydrogen-rich atmosphere, very simple, nonparasitic organisms had a fighting chance. The first living things may have been something like free-living viroids only a few hundred nucleotides long. Experimental work on making such creatures from scratch may begin by the end of the century. There is still much to be understood about the origin of life, including the origin of the genetic code. But we have been performing such experiments for only some thirty years. Nature has had a four-billion-year head start. All in all, we have not done badly.

Nothing in such experiments is unique to the Earth. The initial gases, and the energy sources, are common throughout the Cosmos. Chemical reactions like those in our laboratory vessels may be responsible for the organic matter in interstellar space and the amino acids found in meteorites. Some similar chemistry must have occurred on a billion other worlds in the Milky Way Galaxy. The molecules of life fill the Cosmos.

But even if life on another planet has the same molecular chemistry as life here, there is no reason to expect it to resemble familiar organisms. Consider the enormous diversity of living things on Earth, all of which share the same planet and an identical molecular biology. Those other beasts and vegetables are probably radically different from any organism we know here. There may be some convergent evolution because there may be only one best solution to a certain environmental problem—something like two eyes, for example, for binocular vision at optical frequencies. But in general the random character of the evolutionary process should create extraterrestrial creatures very different from any that we know.

I cannot tell you what an extraterrestrial being would look like. I am terribly limited by the fact that I know only one kind of life, life on Earth. Some people—science fiction writers and artists, for instance—have speculated on what other beings might be like. I am skeptical about most of those extraterrestrial visions. They seem to me to rely too much on forms of life we already know. Any given organism is the way it is because of a long series of individually unlikely steps. I do not think life anywhere else would look very much like a reptile, or an insect or a human—even with such minor cosmetic adjustments as green skin, pointy ears and antennae. But if you pressed me, I could try to imagine something rather different:

On a giant gas planet like Jupiter, with an atmosphere rich in hydrogen, helium, methane, water and ammonia, there is no accessible solid surface, but rather a dense, cloudy atmosphere in which organic molecules may be falling from the skies like manna from heaven, like the products of our laboratory experiments. However, there is a characteristic impediment to life on such a planet: the atmosphere is turbulent, and down deep it is very hot.

An organism must be careful that it is not carried down and fried.

To show that life is not out of the question in such a very different planet, my Cornell colleague E. E. Salpeter and I have made some calculations. Of course, we cannot know precisely what life would be like in such a place, but we wanted to see if, within the laws of physics and chemistry, a world of this sort could possibly be inhabited.

One way to make a living under these conditions is to reproduce before you are fried and hope that convection will carry some of your offspring to the higher and cooler layers of the atmosphere. Such organisms could be very little. We call them sinkers. But you could also be a floater, some vast hydrogen balloon pumping helium and heavier gases out of its interior and leaving only the lightest gas, hydrogen; or a hot-air balloon, staying buoyant by keeping your interior warm, using energy acquired from the food you eat. Like familiar terrestrial balloons, the deeper a floater is carried, the stronger is the buoyant force returning it to the higher, cooler, safer regions of the atmosphere. A floater might eat preformed organic molecules, or make its own from sunlight and air, somewhat as plants do on Earth. Up to a point, the bigger a floater is, the more efficient it will be. Salpeter and I imagined floaters kilometers across, enormously larger than the greatest whale that ever was, beings the size of cities.

The floaters may propel themselves through the planetary atmosphere with gusts of gas, like a ramjet or a rocket. We imagine them arranged in great lazy herds for as far as the eye can see, with patterns on their skin, an adaptive camouflage implying that they have problems too. Because there is at least one other ecological niche in such an environment: hunting. Hunters are fast and maneuverable. They eat the floaters both for their organic molecules and for their store of pure hydrogen. Hollow sinkers could have evolved into the first floaters, and self-propelled floaters into the first hunters. There cannot be very many hunters, because if they consume all the floaters, the hunters themselves will perish.

Physics and chemistry permit such lifeforms. Art endows them with a certain charm. Nature, however, is not obliged to follow our speculations. But if there are billions of inhabited worlds in the Milky Way Galaxy, perhaps there will be a few populated by the sinkers, floaters and hunters which our imaginations, tempered by the laws of physics and chemistry, have generated.

Biology is more like history than it is like physics. You have to know the past to understand the present. And you have to know it in exquisite detail. There is as yet no predictive theory of biology, just as there is not yet a predictive theory of history. The reasons are the same: both subjects are still too complicated for us. But we can know ourselves better by understanding other cases. The study of a single instance of extraterrestrial life, no matter how humble, will deprovincialize biology. For the first time, the biologists will know what other kinds of life are possible. When we say the search for life elsewhere is important, we are not guaranteeing that it will be easy to find—only that it is very much worth seeking.

We have heard so far the voice of life on one small world only. But we have at last begun to listen for other voices in the cosmic fugue.

CHAPTER III
THE HARMONY OF WORLDS

> We do not ask for what useful purpose the birds do sing, for song is their pleasure since they were created for singing. Similarly, we ought not to ask why the human mind troubles to fathom the secrets of the heavens. . . . The diversity of the phenomena of Nature is so great, and the treasures hidden in the heavens so rich, precisely in order that the human mind shall never be lacking in fresh nourishment.
>
> —Johannes Kepler, *Mysterium Cosmographicum*

If we lived on a planet where nothing ever changed, there would be little to do. There would be nothing to figure out. There would be no impetus for science. And if we lived in an unpredictable world, where things changed in random or very complex ways, we would not be able to figure things out. Again, there would be no such thing as science. But we live in an in-between universe, where things change, but according to patterns, rules, or, as we call them, laws of nature. If I throw a stick up in the air, it always falls down. If the sun sets in the west, it always rises again the next morning in the east. And so it becomes possible to figure things out. We can do science, and with it we can improve our lives.

Human beings are good at understanding the world. We always have been. We were able to hunt game or build fires only because we had figured something out. There was a time before television, before motion pictures, before radio, before books. The greatest part of human existence was spent in such a time. Over the dying embers of the campfire, on a moonless night, we watched the stars.

The night sky is interesting. There are patterns there. Without even trying, you can imagine pictures. In the northern sky, for example, there is a pattern, or constellation, that looks a little ursine. Some cultures call it the Great Bear. Others see quite different images. These pictures are not, of course, *really* in the night sky; we put them there ourselves. We were hunter folk, and we saw hunters and dogs, bears and young women, all manner of things of interest to us. When seventeenth-century European sailors first saw the southern skies they put objects of seventeenth-century interest in the heavens—toucans and peacocks, telescopes and microscopes, compasses and the sterns of ships. If the constellations had been named in the twentieth century, I suppose we would see bicycles and refrigerators in the sky, rock-and-roll "stars" and perhaps even mushroom clouds—a new set of human hopes and fears placed among the stars.

Occasionally our ancestors would see a very bright star with a tail, glimpsed for just a moment, hurtling across the sky. They called it a falling star, but it is not a good name: the old stars are still there after the falling star falls. In some seasons there are many falling stars; in others very few. There is a kind of regularity here as well.

Like the Sun and the Moon, stars always rise in the east and set in the west, taking the whole night to cross the sky if they pass overhead. There are different constellations in different seasons. The same constellations always rise at the beginning of autumn, say. It never happens that a new constellation suddenly rises out of the east. There is an order, a predictability, a permanence about the stars. In a way, they are almost comforting.

Certain stars rise just before or set just after the Sun—and at times and positions that vary with the seasons. If you made careful observations of the stars and recorded them over many years, you could predict the seasons. You could also measure the time of year by noting where on the horizon the Sun rose each day. In the skies was a great calendar, available to anyone with dedication and ability and the means to keep records.

Our ancestors built devices to measure the passing of the seasons. In Chaco Canyon, in New Mexico, there is a great roofless ceremonial kiva or temple, dating from the eleventh century. On June 21, the longest day of the year, a shaft of sunlight enters a window at dawn and slowly moves so that it covers a special niche. But this happens only around June 21. I imagine the proud Anasazi people, who described themselves as "The Ancient Ones," gathered in their pews every June 21, dressed in feathers and rattles and turquoise to celebrate the power of the Sun. They also monitored the apparent motion of the Moon: the twenty-eight higher niches in the kiva may represent the number of days for the Moon to return to the same position among the constellations. These people paid close attention to the Sun and the Moon and the stars. Other devices based on similar ideas are found at Angkor Wat in Cambodia; Stonehenge in England; Abu Simbel in Egypt; Chichén Itzá in Mexico; and the Great Plains in North America.

Some alleged calendrical devices may just possibly be due to chance—an accidental alignment of window and niche on June 21, say. But there are other devices wonderfully different. At one locale in the American Southwest is a set of three upright slabs which were moved from their original position about 1,000 years ago. A spiral a little like a galaxy has been carved in the rock. On June 21, the first day of summer, a dagger of sunlight pouring through an opening between the slabs bisects the spiral; and on December 21, the first day of winter, there are two daggers of sunlight that flank the spiral, a unique application of the midday sun to read the calendar in the sky.

Why did people all over the world make such an effort to learn astronomy? We hunted gazelles and antelope and buffalo whose migrations ebbed and flowed with the seasons. Fruits and nuts were ready to be picked in some times but not in others. When we invented agriculture, we had to take care to plant and harvest our crops in the right season. Annual meetings of far-flung nomadic tribes were set for prescribed times. The ability to read the calendar in the skies was literally a matter of life and death. The reappearance of the crescent moon after the new moon; the return of the Sun after a total eclipse; the rising of the Sun in the morning after its troublesome absence at night were noted by people around the world: these phenomena spoke to our ancestors of the possibility of surviving death. Up there in the skies was also a metaphor of immortality.

The wind whips through the canyons of the American Southwest, and there is no one to hear it but us—a reminder of the 40,000 generations of thinking men and women who preceded us, about whom we know almost nothing, upon whom our civilization is based.

As ages passed, people learned from their ancestors. The more accurately you knew the position and movements of the Sun and Moon and stars, the more reliably you could predict when to hunt, when to sow and reap, when to gather the tribes. As precision of measurement improved, records had to be kept, so astronomy encouraged observation and mathematics and the development of writing.

But then, much later, another rather curious idea arose, an assault by mysticism and superstition into what had been largely an empirical science. The Sun and stars controlled the seasons, food, warmth. The Moon controlled the tides, the life cycles of many animals, and perhaps the human menstrual* period—of central importance for a passionate species devoted to having children. There was another kind of object in the sky, the wandering or vagabond stars called planets. Our nomadic ancestors must have felt an affinity for the planets. Not counting the Sun and the Moon, you could see only five of them. They moved against the background of more distant stars. If you followed their apparent motion over many months, they would leave one constellation, enter another, occasionally even do a kind of slow loop-the-loop in the sky. Everything else in the sky had some real effect on human life. What must the influence of the planets be?

In contemporary Western society, buying a magazine on astrology—at a newsstand, say—is easy; it is much harder to find one on astronomy. Virtually every newspaper in America has a daily column on astrology; there are hardly any that have even a weekly column on astronomy. There are ten times more astrologers in the United States than astronomers. At parties, when I meet people who do not know I am a scientist, I am sometimes asked, "Are you a Gemini?" (chances of success, one in twelve), or "What sign are you?" Much more rarely am I asked, "Have you heard that gold is made in supernova explosions?" or "When do you think Congress will approve a Mars Rover?"

Astrology contends that which constellation the planets are in at the moment of your birth profoundly influences your future. A few thousand years ago, the idea developed that the motions of the planets determined the fates of kings, dynasties, empires. Astrologers studied the motions of the planets and asked themselves what had happened the last time that, say, Venus was rising in the Constellation of the Goat; perhaps something similar would happen this time as well. It was a subtle and risky business. Astrologers came to be employed only by the State. In many countries it was a capital offense for anyone but the official astrologer to read

* The root of the word means "Moon."

the portents in the skies: a good way to overthrow a regime was to predict its downfall. Chinese court astrologers who made inaccurate predictions were executed. Others simply doctored the records so that afterward they were in perfect conformity with events. Astrology developed into a strange combination of observations, mathematics and careful record-keeping with fuzzy thinking and pious fraud.

But if the planets could determine the destinies of nations, how could they avoid influencing what will happen to me tomorrow? The notion of a personal astrology developed in Alexandrian Egypt and spread through the Greek and Roman worlds about 2,000 years ago. We today can recognize the antiquity of astrology in words such as *disaster,* which is Greek for "bad star," *influenza,* Italian for (astral) "influence"; *mazel tov,* Hebrew—and, ultimately, Babylonian—for "good constellation," or the Yiddish word *shlamazel,* applied to someone plagued by relentless ill-fortune, which again traces to the Babylonian astronomical lexicon. According to Pliny, there were Romans considered *sideratio,* "planet-struck." Planets were widely thought to be a direct cause of death. Or consider *consider:* it means "with the planets," evidently a prerequisite for serious reflection. Consider the mortality statistics in the City of London in 1632. Among the terrible losses from infant and childhood diseases and such exotic illnesses as "the rising of lights" and "the King's evil," we find that, of 9,535 deaths, 13 people succumbed to "planet," more than died of cancer. I wonder what the symptoms were.

And personal astrology is with us still: consider two different newspaper astrology columns published in the same city on the same day. For example, we can examine the New York *Post* and the New York *Daily News* on September 21, 1979. Suppose you are a Libra—that is, born between September 23 and October 22. According to the astrologer for the *Post,* "a compromise will help ease tension"; useful, perhaps, but somewhat vague. According to the *Daily News*'s astrologer, you must "demand more of yourself," an admonition that is also vague but also different. These "predictions" are not predictions; rather they are pieces of advice—they tell what to do, not what will happen. Deliberately, they are phrased so generally that they could apply to anyone. And they display major mutual inconsistencies. Why are they published as unapologetically as sports statistics and stock market reports?

Astrology can be tested by the lives of twins. There are many cases in which one twin is killed in childhood, in a riding accident, say, or is struck by lightning, while the other lives to a prosperous old age. Each was born in precisely the same place and within minutes of the other. Exactly the same planets were rising at their births. If astrology were valid, how could two such twins have such profoundly different fates? It also turns out that astrologers cannot even agree among themselves on what a given horoscope means. In careful tests, they are unable to predict the character and future of people they know nothing about except their time and place of birth.*

There is something curious about the national flags of the planet Earth. The flag of the United States has fifty stars; the Soviet Union and Israel, one each; Burma, fourteen; Grenada and Venezuela, seven; China, five; Iraq, three; São Tomé e Príncipe, two; Japan, Uruguay, Malawi, Bangladesh and Taiwan, the Sun; Brazil, a celestial sphere; Australia, Western Samoa, New Zealand and Papua New Guinea, the constellation of the Southern Cross; Bhutan, the dragon pearl, symbol of the Earth; Cambodia,

* Skepticism about astrology and related doctrines is neither new nor exclusive to the West. For example, in the *Essays on Idleness,* written in 1332 by Tsurezuregusa of Kenko, we read:

The Yin-Yang teachings [in Japan] have nothing to say on the subject of the Red Tongue Days. Formerly people did not avoid these days, but of late—I wonder who is responsible for starting this custom—people have taken to saying things such as, "An enterprise begun on a Red Tongue Day will never see an end," or, "Anything you say or do on a Red Tongue Day is bound to come to naught: you lose what you've won, your plans are undone." What nonsense! If one counted the projects begun on carefully selected "lucky days" which came to nothing in the end, they would probably be quite as many as the fruitless enterprises begun on the Red Tongue days.

the Angkor Wat astronomical observatory; India, South Korea and the Mongolian Peoples' Republic, cosmological symbols. Many socialist nations display stars. Many Islamic countries display crescent moons. Almost half of our national flags exhibit astronomical symbols. The phenomenon is transcultural, nonsectarian, worldwide. It is also not restricted to our time: Sumerian cylinder seals from the third millennium B.C. and Taoist flags in prerevolutionary China displayed constellations. Nations, I do not doubt, wish to embrace something of the power and credibility of the heavens. We seek a connection with the Cosmos. We want to count in the grand scale of things. And it turns out we *are* connected—not in the personal, small-scale unimaginative fashion that the astrologers pretend, but in the deepest ways, involving the origin of matter, the habitability of the Earth, the evolution and destiny of the human species, themes to which we will return.

Modern popular astrology runs directly back to Claudius Ptolemaeus, whom we call Ptolemy, although he was unrelated to the kings of the same name. He worked in the Library of Alexandria in the second century. All that arcane business about planets ascendant in this or that solar or lunar "house" or the "Age of Aquarius" comes from Ptolemy, who codified the Babylonian astrological tradition. Here is a typical horoscope from Ptolemy's time, written in Greek on papyrus, for a little girl born in the year 150: "The birth of Philoe. The 10th year of Antoninus Caesar the lord, Phamenoth 15 to 16, first hour of the night. Sun in Pisces, Jupiter and Mercury in Aries, Saturn in Cancer, Mars in Leo, Venus and the Moon in Aquarius, horoscopus Capricorn." The method of enumerating the months and the years has changed much more over the intervening centuries than have the astrological niceties. A typical excerpt from Ptolemy's astrological book, the *Tetrabiblos,* reads: "Saturn, if he is in the orient, makes his subjects in appearance dark-skinned, robust, black-haired, curly-haired, hairy-chested, with eyes of moderate size, of middling stature, and in temperament having an excess of the moist and cold." Ptolemy believed not only that behavior patterns were influenced by the planets and the stars but also that questions of stature, complexion, national character and even congenital physical abnormalities were determined by the stars. On this point modern astrologers seem to have adopted a more cautious position.

But modern astrologers have forgotten about the precession of the equinoxes, which Ptolemy understood. They ignore atmospheric refraction, about which Ptolemy wrote. They pay almost no attention to all the moons and planets, asteroids and comets, quasars and pulsars, exploding galaxies, symbiotic stars, cataclysmic variables and X-ray sources that have been discovered since Ptolemy's time. Astronomy is a science—the study of the universe as it is. Astrology is a pseudoscience—a claim, in the absence of good evidence, that the other planets affect our everyday lives. In Ptolemy's time the distinction between astronomy and astrology was not clear. Today it is.

As an astronomer, Ptolemy named the stars, listed their brightness, gave good reasons for believing that the Earth is a sphere, set down rules for predicting eclipses and, perhaps most important, tried to understand why planets exhibit that strange, wandering motion against the background of distant constellations. He developed a predictive model to understand planetary motions and decode the message in the skies. The study of the heavens brought Ptolemy a kind of ecstasy. "Mortal as I am," he wrote, "I know that I am born for a day. But when I follow at my pleasure the serried multitude of the stars in their circular course, my feet no longer touch the Earth . . ."

Ptolemy believed that the Earth was at the center of the universe; that the Sun, Moon, planets and stars went around the Earth. This is the most natural idea in the world. The Earth seems steady, solid, immobile, while we can see the heavenly bodies rising and setting each day. Every culture has leaped to the geocentric hypothesis. As Johannes Kepler wrote, "It is therefore impossible that reason not previously instructed should imagine anything other than that the Earth is a kind of vast house with the vault of the sky placed on top of it; it is motionless and within it the Sun being so small passes from one region to another, like a bird wandering through the air." But how do we explain the apparent motion of the planets—Mars, for example, which had been known for thousands of years before Ptolemy's time? (One of the epithets given Mars by the ancient Egyptians was *sekded-ef em khetkhet,* which means "who travels backward," a clear reference to its retrograde or loop-the-loop apparent motion.)

Ptolemy's model of planetary motion can be represented by a little machine, like those that, serving a similar purpose, existed in Ptolemy's time.* The problem was to figure out a "real" motion of the planets, as seen from up there, on the "outside," which would reproduce with great accuracy the apparent motion of the planets, as seen from down here, on the "inside."

The planets were imagined to go around the Earth affixed to perfect transparent spheres. But they were not attached directly to the spheres, but indirectly, through a kind of off-center wheel. The sphere turns, the little wheel rotates, and, as seen from the Earth, Mars does its loop-the-loop. This model permitted reasonably accurate predictions of planetary motion, certainly good enough for the precision of measurement available in Ptolemy's day, and even many centuries later.

Ptolemy's aetherial spheres, imagined in medieval times to be made of crystal, are why we still talk about the music of the spheres and a seventh heaven (there was a "heaven," or sphere for the Moon, Mercury, Venus, the Sun, Mars, Jupiter and Saturn,

* Four centuries earlier, such a device was constructed by Archimedes and examined and described by Cicero in Rome, where it had been carried by the Roman general Marcellus, one of whose soldiers had, gratuitously and against orders, killed the septuagenarian scientist during the conquest of Syracuse.

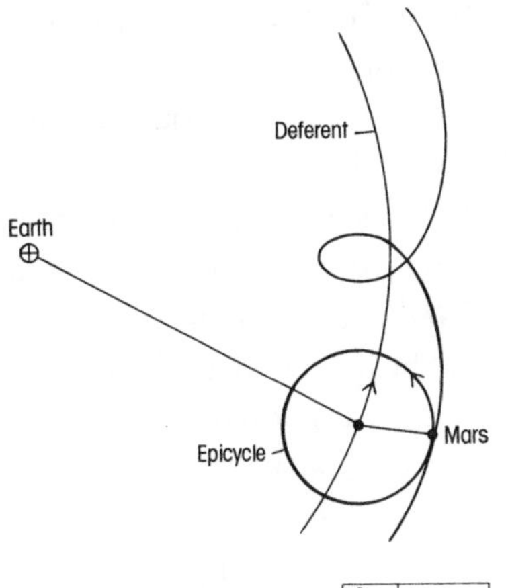

In Ptolemy's Earth-centered system, the little sphere called the epicycle containing the planet turns while attached to a larger rotating sphere, producing retrograde apparent motion against the background of distant stars.

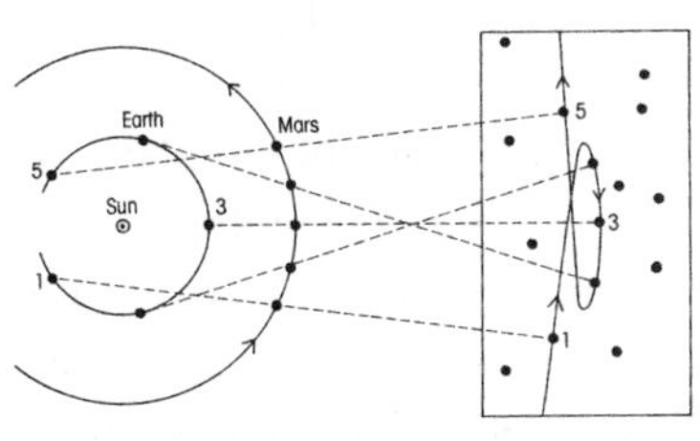

In Copernicus' system, the Earth and other planets move in circular orbits about the Sun. As the Earth overtakes Mars, the latter exhibits its retrograde apparent motion against the background of distant stars.

and one more for the stars). With the Earth the center of the Universe, with creation pivoted about terrestrial events, with the heavens imagined constructed on utterly unearthly principles, there was little motivation for astronomical observations. Supported by the Church through the Dark Ages, Ptolemy's model helped prevent the advance of astronomy for a millennium. Finally, in 1543, a quite different hypothesis to explain the apparent motion of the planets was published by a Polish Catholic cleric named Nicholas Copernicus. Its most daring feature was the proposition that the Sun, not the Earth, was at the center of the universe. The Earth was demoted to just one of the planets, third from the Sun, moving in a perfect circular orbit. (Ptolemy had considered such a heliocentric model but rejected it immediately; from the physics of Aristotle, the implied violent rotation of the Earth seemed contrary to observation.)

It worked at least as well as Ptolemy's spheres in explaining the apparent motion of the planets. But it annoyed many people. In 1616 the Catholic Church placed Copernicus' work on its list of forbidden books "until corrected" by local ecclesiastical censors, where it remained until 1835.* Martin Luther described him as "an upstart astrologer . . . This fool wishes to reverse the entire science of astronomy. But Sacred Scripture tells us that Joshua commanded the Sun to stand still, and not the Earth." Even some of Copernicus' admirers argued that he had not really believed in a Sun-centered universe but had merely proposed it as a convenience for calculating the motions of the planets.

The epochal confrontation between the two views of the Cosmos—Earth-centered and Sun-centered—reached a climax in the sixteenth and seventeenth centuries in the person of a man who was, like Ptolemy, both astrologer and astronomer. He lived in a time when the human spirit was fettered and the mind chained; when the ecclesiastical pronouncements of a millennium or two earlier on scientific matters were considered more reliable than contemporary findings made with techniques unavailable to the ancients; when deviations, even on arcane theological matters, from the prevailing doxological preferences, Catholic or Protestant, were punished by humiliation, taxation, exile, torture or death. The heavens were inhabited by angels, demons and the Hand of God, turning the planetary crystal spheres. Science was barren of the idea that underlying the phenomena of Nature might be the laws of physics. But the brave and lonely struggle of this man was to ignite the modern scientific revolution.

Johannes Kepler was born in Germany in 1571 and sent as a boy to the Protestant seminary school in the provincial town of Maulbronn to be educated for the clergy. It was a kind of boot camp, training young minds in the use of theological weaponry

* In a recent inventory of nearly every sixteenth-century copy of Copernicus' book, Owen Gingerich has found the censorship to have been ineffective: only 60 percent of the copies in Italy were "corrected," and not one in Iberia.

against the fortress of Roman Catholicism. Kepler, stubborn, intelligent and fiercely independent, suffered two friendless years in bleak Maulbronn, becoming isolated and withdrawn, his thoughts devoted to his imagined unworthiness in the eyes of God. He repented a thousand sins no more wicked than another's and despaired of ever attaining salvation.

But God became for him more than a divine wrath craving propitiation. Kepler's God was the creative power of the Cosmos. The boy's curiosity conquered his fear. He wished to learn the eschatology of the world; he dared to contemplate the Mind of God. These dangerous visions, at first insubstantial as a memory, became a lifelong obsession. The hubristic longings of a child seminarian were to carry Europe out of the cloister of medieval thought.

The sciences of classical antiquity had been silenced more than a thousand years before, but in the late Middle Ages some faint echoes of those voices, preserved by Arab scholars, began to insinuate themselves into the European educational curriculum. In Maulbronn, Kepler heard their reverberations, studying, besides theology, Greek and Latin, music and mathematics. In the geometry of Euclid he thought he glimpsed an image of perfection and cosmic glory. He was later to write: "Geometry existed before the Creation. It is co-eternal with the mind of God . . . Geometry provided God with a model for the Creation . . . Geometry is God Himself."

In the midst of Kepler's mathematical raptures, and despite his sequestered life, the imperfections of the outside world must also have molded his character. Superstition was a widely available nostrum for people powerless against the miseries of famine, pestilence and deadly doctrinal conflict. For many, the only certainty was the stars, and the ancient astrological conceit prospered in the courtyards and taverns of fear-haunted Europe. Kepler, whose attitude toward astrology remained ambiguous all his life, wondered whether there might be hidden patterns underlying the apparent chaos of daily life. If the world was crafted by God, should it not be examined closely? Was not all of creation an expression of the harmonies in the mind of God? The book of Nature had waited more than a millennium for a reader.

In 1589, Kepler left Maulbronn to study for the clergy at the great university in Tübingen and found it a liberation. Confronted by the most vital intellectual currents of the time, his genius was immediately recognized by his teachers—one of whom introduced the young man to the dangerous mysteries of the Copernican hypothesis. A heliocentric universe resonated with Kepler's religious sense, and he embraced it with fervor. The Sun was a metaphor for God, around Whom all else revolves. Before he was to be ordained, he was made an attractive offer of secular employment, which—perhaps because he felt himself indifferently suited to an ecclesiastical career—he found himself accepting. He was summoned to Graz, in Austria, to teach secondary school mathematics, and began a little later to prepare astronomical and meteorological almanacs and to cast horoscopes. "God provides for every animal his means of sustenance," he wrote. "For the astronomer, He has provided astrology."

Kepler was a brilliant thinker and a lucid writer, but he was a disaster as a classroom teacher. He mumbled. He digressed. He was at times utterly incomprehensible. He drew only a handful of students his first year at Graz; the next year there were none. He was distracted by an incessant interior clamor of associations and speculations vying for his attention. And one pleasant summer afternoon, deep in the interstices of one of his interminable lectures, he was visited by a revelation that was to alter radically the future of astronomy. Perhaps he stopped in mid-sentence. His inattentive students, longing for the end of the day, took little notice, I suspect, of the historic moment.

There were only six planets known in Kepler's time: Mercury, Venus, Earth, Mars, Jupiter and Saturn. Kepler wondered why only six? Why not twenty, or a hundred? Why did they have the

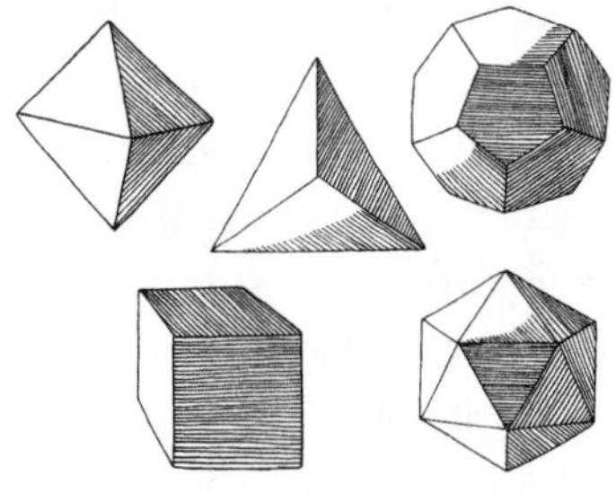

The five perfect solids of Pythagoras and Plato. See Appendix 2.

spacing between their orbits that Copernicus had deduced? No one had ever asked such questions before. There were known to be five regular or "platonic" solids, whose sides were regular polygons, as known to the ancient Greek mathematicians after the time of Pythagoras. Kepler thought the two numbers were connected, that the *reason* there were only six planets was because there were only five regular solids, and that these solids, inscribed or nested one within another, would specify the distances of the planets from the Sun. In these perfect forms, he believed he had recognized the invisible supporting structures for the spheres of the six planets. He called his revelation The Cosmic Mystery. The connection between the solids of Pythagoras and the disposition of the planets could admit but one explanation: the Hand of God, Geometer.

Kepler was amazed that he—immersed, so he thought, in sin—should have been divinely chosen to make this great discovery. He submitted a proposal for a research grant to the Duke of Württemberg, offering to supervise the construction of his nested solids as a three-dimensional model so that others could glimpse the beauty of the holy geometry. It might, he added, be contrived of silver and precious stones and serve incidentally as a ducal chalice. The proposal was rejected with the kindly advice that he first construct a less expensive version out of paper, which he promptly attempted to do: "The intense pleasure I have received from this discovery can never be told in words . . . I shunned no calculation no matter how difficult. Days and nights I spent in mathematical labors, until I could see whether my hypothesis would agree with the orbits of Copernicus or whether my joy was to vanish into thin air." But no matter how hard he tried, the solids and the planetary orbits did not agree well. The elegance and grandeur of the theory, however, persuaded him that the observations must be in error, a conclusion drawn when the observations are unobliging by many other theorists in the history of science. There was then only one man in the world who had access to more accurate observations of apparent planetary positions, a self-exiled Danish nobleman who had accepted the post of Imperial Mathematician in the Court of the Holy Roman Emperor, Rudolf II. That man was Tycho Brahe. By chance, at Rudolf's suggestion, he had just invited Kepler, whose mathematical fame was growing, to join him in Prague.

A provincial schoolteacher of humble origins, unknown to all but a few mathematicians, Kepler was diffident about Tycho's offer. But the decision was made for him. In 1598, one of the many premonitory tremors of the coming Thirty Years' War engulfed him. The local Catholic archduke, steadfast in dogmatic certainty, vowed he would rather "make a desert of the country than rule over heretics."* Protestants were excluded from economic and political power, Kepler's school was closed, and prayers, books and hymns deemed heretical were forbidden. Finally the townspeople were summoned to individual examinations on the soundness of their private religious convictions, those refusing to profess the Roman Catholic faith being fined a tenth of their income and, upon pain of death, exiled forever from Graz. Kepler chose exile: "Hypocrisy I have never learned. I am in earnest about faith. I do not play with it."

Leaving Graz, Kepler, his wife and stepdaughter set out on the

* By no means the most extreme such remark in medieval or Reformation Europe. Upon being asked how to distinguish the faithful from the infidel in the siege of a largely Albigensian city, Domingo de Guzmán, later known as Saint Dominic, allegedly replied: "Kill them all. God will know his own."

difficult journey to Prague. Theirs was not a happy marriage. Chronically ill, having recently lost two young children, his wife was described as "stupid, sulking, lonely, melancholy." She had no understanding of her husband's work and, having been raised among the minor rural gentry, she despised his impecunious profession. He for his part alternately admonished and ignored her, "for my studies sometimes made me thoughtless; but I learned my lesson, I learned to have patience with her. When I saw that she took my words to heart, I would rather have bitten my own finger than to give her further offense." But Kepler remained preoccupied with his work.

He envisioned Tycho's domain as a refuge from the evils of the time, as the place where his Cosmic Mystery would be confirmed. He aspired to become a colleague of the great Tycho Brahe, who for thirty-five years had devoted himself, before the invention of the telescope, to the measurement of a clockwork universe, ordered and precise. Kepler's expectations were to be unfulfilled. Tycho himself was a flamboyant figure, festooned with a golden nose, the original having been lost in a student duel fought over who was the superior mathematician. Around him was a raucous entourage of assistants, sycophants, distant relatives and assorted hangers-on. Their endless revelry, their innuendoes and intrigues, their cruel mockery of the pious and scholarly country bumpkin depressed and saddened Kepler: "Tycho . . . is superlatively rich but knows not how to make use of it. Any single instrument of his costs more than my and my whole family's fortunes put together."

Impatient to see Tycho's astronomical data, Kepler would be thrown only a few scraps at a time: "Tycho gave me no opportunity to share in his experiences. He would only, in the course of a meal and, in between other matters, mention, as if in passing, today the figure of the apogee of one planet, tomorrow the nodes of another . . . Tycho possesses the best observations . . . He also has collaborators. He lacks only the architect who would put all this to use." Tycho was the greatest observational genius of the age, and Kepler the greatest theoretician. Each knew that, alone, he would be unable to achieve the synthesis of an accurate and coherent world system, which they both felt to be imminent. But Tycho was not about to make a gift of his life's work to a much younger potential rival. Joint authorship of the results, if any, of the collaboration was for some reason unacceptable. The birth of modern science—the offspring of theory and observation—teetered on the precipice of their mutual mistrust. In the remaining eighteen months that Tycho was to live, the two quarreled and were reconciled repeatedly. At a dinner given by the Baron of Rosenberg, Tycho, having robustly drunk much wine, "placed civility ahead of health," and resisted his body's urgings to leave, even if briefly, before the baron. The consequent urinary infection worsened when Tycho resolutely rejected advice to temper his eating and drinking. On his deathbed, Tycho bequeathed his observations to Kepler, and "on the last night of his gentle delirium, he repeated over and over again these words, like someone composing a poem: 'Let me not seem to have lived in vain . . . Let me not seem to have lived in vain.' "

After Tycho's death, Kepler, now the new Imperial Mathematician, managed to extract the observations from Tycho's recalcitrant family. His conjecture that the orbits of the planets are circumscribed by the five platonic solids were no more supported by Tycho's data than by Copernicus'. His "Cosmic Mystery" was disproved entirely by the much later discoveries of the planets Uranus, Neptune and Pluto—there are no additional platonic solids* that would determine their distances from the sun. The nested Pythagorean solids also made no allowance for the existence of the Earth's moon, and Galileo's discovery of the four large moons of Jupiter was also discomfiting. But far from becoming morose, Kepler wished to find additional satellites and wondered how

* The proof of this statement can be found in Appendix 2.

many satellites each planet should have. He wrote to Galileo: "I immediately began to think how there could be any addition to the number of the planets without overturning my Mysterium Cosmographicum, according to which Euclid's five regular solids do not allow more than six planets around the Sun . . . I am so far from disbelieving the existence of the four circumjovial planets that I long for a telescope, to anticipate you, if possible, in discovering two around Mars, as the proportion seems to require, six or eight round Saturn, and perhaps one each round Mercury and Venus." Mars does have two small moons, and a major geological feature on the larger of them is today called the Kepler Ridge in honor of this guess. But he was entirely mistaken about Saturn, Mercury and Venus, and Jupiter has many more moons than Galileo discovered. We still do not really know why there are only nine planets, more or less, and why they have the relative distances from the Sun that they do. (See Chapter 8.)

Tycho's observations of the apparent motion of Mars and other planets through the constellations were made over a period of many years. These data, from the last few decades before the telescope was invented, were the most accurate that had yet been obtained. Kepler worked with a passionate intensity to understand them: What real motion of the Earth and Mars about the Sun could explain, to the precision of measurement, the apparent motion of Mars in the sky, including its retrograde loops through the background constellations? Tycho had commended Mars to Kepler because its apparent motion seemed most anomalous, most difficult to reconcile with an orbit made of circles. (To the reader who might be bored by his many calculations, he later wrote: "If you are wearied by this tedious procedure, take pity on me who carried out at least seventy trials.")

Pythagoras, in the sixth century B.C., Plato, Ptolemy and all the Christian astronomers before Kepler had assumed that the planets moved in circular paths. The circle was thought to be a "perfect" geometrical shape and the planets, placed high in the heavens, away from earthly "corruption," were also thought to be in some mystical sense "perfect." Galileo, Tycho and Copernicus were all committed to uniform circular planetary motion, the latter asserting that "the mind shudders" at the alternative, because "it would be unworthy to suppose such a thing in a Creation constituted in the best possible way." So at first Kepler tried to explain the observations by imagining that the Earth and Mars moved in circular orbits about the Sun.

After three years of calculation, he believed he had found the correct values for a Martian circular orbit, which matched ten of Tycho's observations within two minutes of arc. Now, there are 60 minutes of arc in an angular degree, and 90 degrees, a right angle, from the horizon to the zenith. So a few minutes of arc is a very small quantity to measure—especially without a telescope. It is one-fifteenth the angular diameter of the full Moon as seen from Earth. But Kepler's replenishable ecstasy soon crumbled into gloom—because two of Tycho's further observations were inconsistent with Kepler's orbit, by as much as eight minutes of arc:

> Divine Providence granted us such a diligent observer in Tycho Brahe that his observations convicted this . . . calculation of an error of eight minutes; it is only right that we should accept God's gift with a grateful mind . . . If I had believed that we could ignore these eight minutes, I would have patched up my hypothesis accordingly. But, since it was not permissible to ignore, those eight minutes pointed the road to a complete reformation in astronomy.

The difference between a circular orbit and the true orbit could be distinguished only by precise measurement and a courageous acceptance of the facts: "The universe is stamped with the adornment of harmonic proportions, but harmonies must accommodate experience." Kepler was shaken at being compelled to abandon a circular orbit and to question his faith in the Divine Geometer. Having cleared the stable of astronomy of circles and spirals, he was left, he said, with "only a single cartful of dung," a stretched-out circle something like an oval.

Eventually, Kepler came to feel that his fascination with the circle had been a delusion. The Earth was a planet, as Copernicus had said, and it was entirely obvious to Kepler that the Earth, wracked by wars, pestilence, famine and unhappiness, fell short of perfection. Kepler was one of the first people since antiquity to propose that the planets were material objects made of imperfect stuff like the Earth. And if planets were "imperfect," why not their orbits as well? He tried various oval-like curves, calculated away, made some arithmetical mistakes (which caused him at first to reject the correct answer) and months later in some desperation tried the formula for an ellipse, first codified in the Alexandrian Library by Apollonius of Perga. He found that it matched Tycho's observations beautifully: "The truth of nature, which I had rejected and chased away, returned by stealth through the back door, disguising itself to be accepted . . . Ah, what a foolish bird I have been!"

Kepler had found that Mars moves about the Sun not in a circle, but in an ellipse. The other planets have orbits much less elliptical than that of Mars, and if Tycho had urged him to study the motion of, say, Venus, Kepler might never have discovered the true orbits of the planets. In such an orbit the Sun is not at the center but is offset, at the focus of the ellipse. When a given planet is at its nearest to the Sun, it speeds up. When it is at its farthest, it slows down. Such motion is why we describe the planets as forever falling toward, but never reaching, the Sun. Kepler's first law of planetary motion is simply this: A planet moves in an ellipse with the Sun at one focus.

In uniform circular motion, an equal angle or fraction of the arc of a circle is covered in equal times. So, for example, it takes twice as long to go two-thirds of the way around a circle as it does

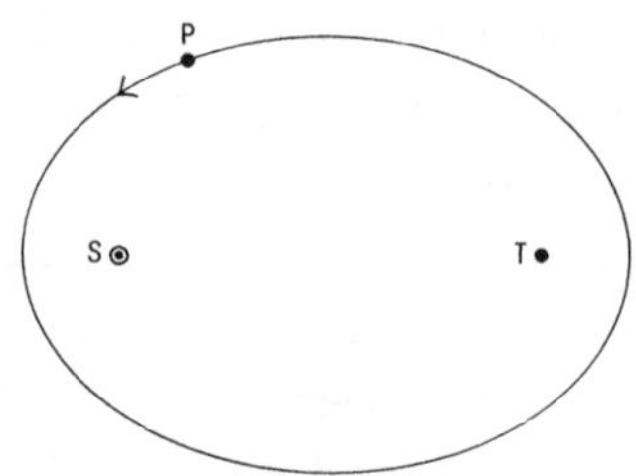

Kepler's first law: A planet (P) moves in an ellipse with the Sun (S) at one of the two foci.

to go one-third of the way around. Kepler found something different for elliptical orbits: As the planet moves along its orbit, it sweeps out a little wedge-shaped area within the ellipse. When it is close to the Sun, in a given period of time it traces out a large arc in its orbit, but the *area* represented by that arc is not very large because the planet is then near the Sun. When the planet is far from the Sun, it covers a much smaller arc in the same period of time, but that arc corresponds to a bigger area because the Sun is now more distant. Kepler found that these two areas were precisely the same no matter how elliptical the orbit: the long skinny area, corresponding to the planet far from the Sun, and the shorter, squatter area, when the planet is close to the Sun, are exactly equal. This was Kepler's second law of planetary motion: Planets sweep out equal areas in equal times.

Kepler's first two laws may seem a little remote and abstract: planets move in ellipses, and sweep out equal areas in equal times. Well, so what? Circular motion is easier to grasp. We might have a tendency to dismiss these laws as mere mathematical tinkering, something removed from everyday life. But these are the laws our planet obeys as we ourselves, glued by gravity to the surface of the Earth, hurtle through interplanetary space. We move in accord with laws of nature that Kepler first discovered. When we send spacecraft to the planets, when we observe double stars, when we examine the motion of distant galaxies, we find that throughout the universe Kepler's laws are obeyed.

Many years later, Kepler came upon his third and last law of planetary motion, a law that relates the motion of various planets

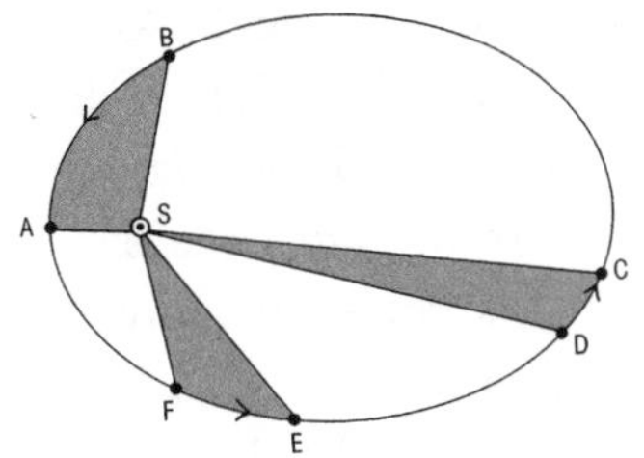

Kepler's second law: A planet sweeps out equal areas in equal times. It takes as long to travel from B to A as from F to E as from D to C; and the shaded areas BSA, FSE and DSC are all equal.

to one another, that lays out correctly the clockwork of the solar system. He described it in a book called *The Harmonies of the World.* Kepler understood many things by the word harmony: the order and beauty of planetary motion, the existence of mathematical laws explaining that motion—an idea that goes back to Pythagoras—and even harmony in the musical sense, the "harmony of the spheres." Unlike the orbits of Mercury and Mars, the orbits of the other planets depart so little from circularity that we cannot make out their true shapes even in an extremely accurate diagram. The Earth is our moving platform from which we observe the motion of the other planets against the backdrop of distant constellations. The inner planets move rapidly in their orbits—that is why Mercury has the name it does: Mercury was the messenger of the gods. Venus, Earth and Mars move progressively less rapidly about the Sun. The outer planets, such as Jupiter and Saturn, move stately and slow, as befits the kings of the gods.

Kepler's third or harmonic law states that the squares of the periods of the planets (the times for them to complete one orbit) are proportional to the cubes of their average distance from the Sun; the more distant the planet, the more slowly it moves, but according to a precise mathematical law: $P^2 = a^3$, where P represents the period of revolution of the planet about the Sun, measured in years, and a the distance of the planet from the Sun measured in "astronomical units." An astronomical unit is the distance of the Earth from the Sun. Jupiter, for example, is five astronomical units from the Sun, and $a^3 = 5 \times 5 \times 5 = 125$. What number times itself equals 125? Why, 11, close enough. And 11 years *is* the period for Jupiter to go once around the Sun. A similar argument applies for every planet and asteroid and comet.

Not content merely to have extracted from Nature the laws of planetary motion, Kepler endeavored to find some still more fundamental underlying cause, some influence of the Sun on the kinematics of worlds. The planets sped up on approaching the Sun and slowed down on retreating from it. Somehow the distant planets sensed the Sun's presence. Magnetism also was an influence felt at a distance, and in a stunning anticipation of the idea of universal gravitation, Kepler suggested that the underlying cause was akin to magnetism:

> My aim in this is to show that the celestial machine is to be likened not to a divine organism but rather to a clockwork . . . , insofar as nearly all the manifold movements are carried out by means of a single, quite simple magnetic force, as in the case of a clockwork [where] all motions [are caused] by a simple weight.

Magnetism is, of course, not the same as gravity, but Kepler's fundamental innovation here is nothing short of breathtaking: he proposed that quantitative physical laws that apply to the Earth are also the underpinnings of quantitative physical laws that govern the heavens. It was the first nonmystical explanation of motion in the heavens; it made the Earth a province of the Cosmos.

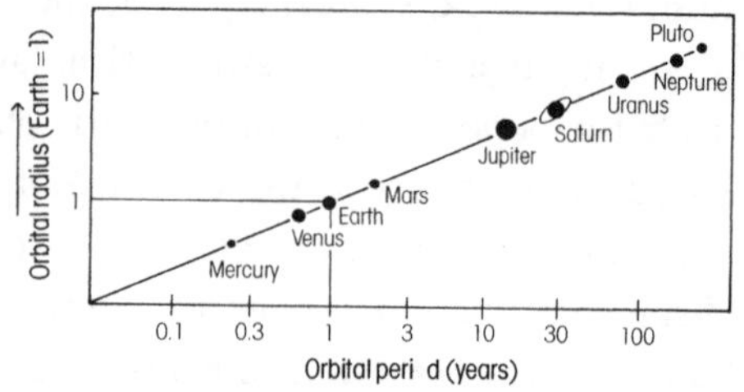

Kepler's third or harmonic law, a precise connection between the size of a planet's orbit and the period for it to go once around the Sun. It clearly applies to Uranus, Neptune and Pluto, planets discovered long after Kepler's death.

"Astronomy," he said, "is part of physics." Kepler stood at a cusp in history; the last scientific astrologer was the first astrophysicist.

Not given to quiet understatement, Kepler assessed his discoveries in these words:

> With this symphony of voices man can play through the eternity of time in less than an hour, and can taste in small measure the delight of God, the Supreme Artist. . . . I yield freely to the sacred frenzy . . . the die is cast, and I am writing the book—to be read either now or by posterity, it matters not. It can wait a century for a reader, as God Himself has waited 6,000 years for a witness.

Within the "symphony of voices," Kepler believed that the speed of each planet corresponds to certain notes in the Latinate musical scale popular in his day—do, re, mi, fa, sol, la, ti, do. He claimed that in the harmony of the spheres, the tones of Earth are fa and mi, that the Earth is forever humming fa and mi, and that they stand in a straightforward way for the Latin word for famine. He argued, not unsuccessfully, that the Earth was best described by that single doleful word.

Exactly eight days after Kepler's discovery of his third law, the incident that unleashed the Thirty Years' War transpired in Prague. The war's convulsions shattered the lives of millions, Kepler among them. He lost his wife and son to an epidemic carried by the soldiery, his royal patron was deposed, and he was excommunicated by the Lutheran Church for his uncompromising individualism on matters of doctrine. Kepler was a refugee once again. The conflict, portrayed by both the Catholics and the Protestants as a holy war, was more an exploitation of religious fanaticism by those hungry for land and power. In the past, wars had tended to be resolved when the belligerent princes had exhausted their resources. But now organized pillage was introduced as a means of keeping armies in the field. The savaged population of Europe stood helpless as plowshares and pruning hooks were literally beaten into swords and spears.*

Waves of rumor and paranoia swept through the countryside, enveloping especially the powerless. Among the many scapegoats chosen were elderly women living alone, who were charged with witchcraft: Kepler's mother was carried away in the middle of the night in a laundry chest. In Kepler's little hometown of Weil der Stadt, roughly three women were tortured and killed as witches every year between 1615 and 1629. And Katharina Kepler was a cantankerous old woman. She engaged in disputes that annoyed the local nobility, and she sold soporific and perhaps hallucinogenic drugs as do contemporary Mexican *curanderas.* Poor Kepler believed that he himself had contributed to her arrest.

It came about because Kepler wrote one of the first works of science fiction, intended to explain and popularize science. It was called the *Somnium,* "The Dream." He imagined a journey to the Moon, the space travelers standing on the lunar surface and observing the lovely planet Earth rotating slowly in the sky above them. By changing our perspective we can figure out how worlds work. In Kepler's time one of the chief objections to the idea that the Earth turns was the fact that people do not feel the motion. In the *Somnium* he tried to make the rotation of the Earth plausible, dramatic, comprehensible: "As long as the multitude does not err, . . . I want to be on the side of the many. Therefore, I take great pains to explain to as many people as possible." (On another occasion he wrote in a letter, "Do not sentence me completely to the treadmill of mathematical calculations—leave me time for philosophical speculations, my sole delight."**)

* Some examples are still to be seen in the Graz armory.

** Brahe, like Kepler, was far from hostile to astrology, although he carefully distinguished his own secret version of astrology from the more common variants of his time, which he thought conducive to superstition. In his book *Astronomiae Instauratae Mechanica,* published in 1598, he argued that astrology is "really more reliable than one would think" if charts of the position of the stars were properly improved.

With the invention of the telescope, what Kepler called "lunar geography" was becoming possible. In the *Somnium,* he described the Moon as filled with mountains and valleys and as "porous, as though dug through with hollows and continuous caves," a reference to the lunar craters Galileo had recently discovered with the first astronomical telescope. He also imagined that the Moon had its inhabitants, well adapted to the inclemencies of the local environment. He describes the slowly rotating Earth viewed from the lunar surface and imagines the continents and oceans of our planet to produce some associative image like the Man in the Moon. He pictures the near contact of southern Spain with North Africa at the Straits of Gibraltar as a young woman in a flowing dress about to kiss her lover—although rubbing noses looks more like it to me.

Because of the length of the lunar day and night Kepler described "the great intemperateness of climate and the most violent alternation of extreme heat and cold on the Moon," which is entirely correct. Of course, he did not get everything right. He believed, for example, that there was a substantial lunar atmosphere and oceans and inhabitants. Most curious is his view of the origin of the lunar craters, which make the Moon, he says, "not dissimilar to the face of a boy disfigured with smallpox." He argued correctly that the craters are depressions rather than mounds. From his own observations he noted the ramparts sur-

---

Brahe wrote: "I have been occupied in alchemy, as much as by the celestial studies, from my 23rd year." But both of these pseudosciences, he felt, had secrets far too dangerous for the general populace (although entirely safe, he thought, in the hands of those princes and kings from whom he sought support). Brahe continued the long and truly dangerous tradition of some scientists who believe that only they and the temporal and ecclesiastical powers can be trusted with arcane knowledge: "It serves no useful purpose and is unreasonable, to make such things generally known." Kepler, on the other hand, lectured on astronomy in schools, published extensively and often at his own expense, and wrote science fiction, which was certainly not intended primarily for his scientific peers. He may not have been a popular writer of science in the modern sense, but the transition in attitudes in the single generation that separated Tycho and Kepler is telling.

rounding many craters and the existence of central peaks. But he thought that their regular circular shape implied such a degree of order that only intelligent life could explain them. He did not realize that great rocks falling out of the sky would produce a local explosion, perfectly symmetric in all directions, that would carve out a circular cavity—the origin of the bulk of the craters on the Moon and the other terrestrial planets. He deduced instead "the existence of some race rationally capable of constructing those hollows on the surface of the Moon. This race must have many individuals, so that one group puts one hollow to use while another group constructs another hollow." Against the view that such great construction projects were unlikely, Kepler offered as counter-examples the pyramids of Egypt and the Great Wall of China, which can, in fact, be seen today from Earth orbit. The idea that geometrical order reveals an underlying intelligence was central to Kepler's life. His argument on the lunar craters is a clear foreshadowing of the Martian canal controversy (Chapter 5). It is striking that the observational search for extraterrestrial life began in the same generation as the invention of the telescope, and with the greatest theoretician of the age.

Parts of the *Somnium* were clearly autobiographical. The hero, for example, visits Tycho Brahe. He has parents who sell drugs. His mother consorts with spirits and daemons, one of whom eventually provides the means to travel to the moon. The *Somnium* makes clear to us, although it did not to all of Kepler's contemporaries, that "in a dream one must be allowed the liberty of imagining occasionally that which never existed in the world of sense perception." Science fiction was a new idea at the time of the Thirty Years' War, and Kepler's book was used as evidence that his mother was a witch.

In the midst of other grave personal problems, Kepler rushed to Württemberg to find his seventy-four-year-old mother chained in a Protestant secular dungeon and threatened, like Galileo in a Catholic dungeon, with torture. He set about, as a scientist naturally would, to find natural explanations for the various events that had precipitated the accusations of witchcraft, including minor physical ailments that the burghers of Württemberg had attributed to her spells. The research was successful, a triumph, as was much of the rest of his life, of reason over superstition. His mother was exiled, with a sentence of death passed on her should she ever return to Württemberg; and Kepler's spirited defense apparently led to a decree by the Duke forbidding further trials for witchcraft on such slender evidence.

The upheavals of the war deprived Kepler of much of his financial support, and the end of his life was spent fitfully, pleading for money and sponsors. He cast horoscopes for the Duke of Wallenstein, as he had done for Rudolf II, and spent his final years in a Silesian town controlled by Wallenstein and called Sagan. His epitaph, which he himself composed, was: "I measured the skies, now the shadows I measure. Sky-bound was the mind, Earth-bound the body rests." But the Thirty Years' War obliterated his grave. If a marker were to be erected today, it might read, in homage to his scientific courage: "He preferred the hard truth to his dearest illusions."

Johannes Kepler believed that there would one day be "celestial ships with sails adapted to the winds of heaven" navigating the sky, filled with explorers "who would not fear the vastness" of space. And today those explorers, human and robot, employ as unerring guides on their voyages through the vastness of space the three laws of planetary motion that Kepler uncovered during a lifetime of personal travail and ecstatic discovery.

The lifelong quest of Johannes Kepler, to understand the motions of the planets, to seek a harmony in the heavens, culminated thirty-six years after his death, in the work of Isaac Newton. Newton was born on Christmas Day, 1642, so tiny that, as his mother told him years later, he would have fit into a quart mug. Sickly, feeling abandoned by his parents, quarrelsome, unsociable, a virgin to the day he died, Isaac Newton was perhaps the greatest scientific genius who ever lived.

Even as a young man, Newton was impatient with insubstantial questions, such as whether light was "a substance or an accident," or how gravitation could act over an intervening vacuum. He early decided that the conventional Christian belief in the Trinity was a misreading of Scripture. According to his biographer, John Maynard Keynes,

> He was rather a Judaic Monotheist of the school of Maimonides. He arrived at this conclusion, not on so-to-speak rational or sceptical grounds, but entirely on the interpretation of ancient authority. He was persuaded that the revealed documents gave no support to the Trinitarian doctrines which were due to late falsifications. The revealed God was one God. But this was a dreadful secret which Newton was at desperate pains to conceal all his life.

Like Kepler, he was not immune to the superstitions of his day and had many encounters with mysticism. Indeed, much of Newton's intellectual development can be attributed to this tension between rationalism and mysticism. At the Stourbridge Fair in 1663, at age twenty, he purchased a book on astrology, "out of a curiosity to see what there was in it." He read it until he came to an illustration which he could not understand, because he was ignorant of trigonometry. So he purchased a book on trigonometry but soon found himself unable to follow the geometrical arguments. So he found a copy of Euclid's *Elements of Geometry*, and began to read. Two years later he invented the differential calculus.

As a student, Newton was fascinated by light and transfixed by the Sun. He took to the dangerous practice of staring at the Sun's image in a looking glass:

> In a few hours I had brought my eyes to such a pass that I could look upon no bright object with neither eye but I saw the Sun before me, so that I durst neither write nor read but to recover the use of my eyes shut my self up in my chamber made dark three days together & used all means to divert my imagination from the Sun. For if I thought upon him I presently saw his picture though I was in the dark.

In 1666, at the age of twenty-three, Newton was an undergraduate at Cambridge University when an outbreak of plague forced him to spend a year in idleness in the isolated village of Woolsthorpe, where he had been born. He occupied himself by inventing the differential and integral calculus, making fundamental discoveries on the nature of light and laying the foundation for the theory of universal gravitation. The only other year like it in the history of physics was Einstein's "Miracle Year" of 1905. When asked how he accomplished his astonishing discoveries, Newton replied unhelpfully, "By thinking upon them." His work was so significant that his teacher at Cambridge, Isaac Barrow, resigned his chair of mathematics in favor of Newton five years after the young student returned to college.

Newton, in his mid-forties, was described by his servant as follows:

> I never knew him to take any recreation or pastime either in riding out to take the air, walking, bowling, or any other exercise whatever, thinking all hours lost that were not spent in his studies, to which he kept so close that he seldom left his chamber unless [to lecture] at term time . . . where so few went to hear him, and fewer understood him, that ofttimes he did in a manner, for want of hearers, read to the walls.

Students both of Kepler and of Newton never knew what they were missing.

Newton discovered the law of inertia, the tendency of a moving object to continue moving in a straight line unless something influences it and moves it out of its path. The Moon, it seemed to Newton, would fly off in a straight line, tangential to its orbit, unless there were some other force constantly diverting the path into a near circle, pulling it in the direction of the Earth. This force Newton called gravity, and believed that it acted at a distance. There is nothing physically connecting the Earth and the Moon. And yet the Earth is constantly pulling the Moon toward us. Using Kepler's third law, Newton mathematically deduced the nature of the gravitational force.* He showed that the same force that pulls an apple down to Earth keeps the Moon in its orbit and accounts for the revolutions of the then recently discovered moons of Jupiter in their orbits about that distant planet.

Things had been falling down since the beginning of time. That the Moon went around the Earth had been believed for all of human history. Newton was the first person ever to figure out that these two phenomena were due to the same force. This is the meaning of the word "universal" as applied to Newtonian gravitation. The same law of gravity applies everywhere in the universe.

It is a law of the inverse square. The force declines inversely as the square of distance. If two objects are moved twice as far away, the gravity now pulling them together is only one-quarter as strong. If they are over ten times farther away, the gravity is ten squared, $10^2 = 100$ times smaller. Clearly, the force must in some sense be inverse—that is, declining with distance. If the force were direct, increasing with distance, then the strongest force

* Sadly, Newton does not acknowledge his debt to Kepler in his masterpiece the *Principia*. But in a 1686 letter to Edmund Halley, he says of his law of gravitation: "I can affirm that I gathered it from Kepler's theorem about twenty years ago."

would work on the most distant objects, and I suppose all the matter in the universe would find itself careering together into a single cosmic lump. No, gravity must decrease with distance, which is why a comet or a planet moves slowly when far from the Sun and faster when close to the Sun—the gravity it feels is weaker the farther from the Sun it is.

All three of Kepler's laws of planetary motion can be derived from Newtonian principles. Kepler's laws were empirical, based upon the painstaking observations of Tycho Brahe. Newton's laws were theoretical, rather simple mathematical abstractions from which all of Tycho's measurements could ultimately be derived. From these laws, Newton wrote with undisguised pride in the *Principia,* "I now demonstrate the frame of the System of the World."

Later in his life, Newton presided over the Royal Society, a fellowship of scientists, and was Master of the Mint, where he devoted his energies to the suppression of counterfeit coinage. His natural moodiness and reclusivity grew; he resolved to abandon those scientific endeavors that brought him into quarrelsome disputes with other scientists, chiefly on issues of priority; and there were those who spread tales that he had experienced the seventeenth-century equivalent of a "nervous breakdown." However, Newton continued his lifelong experiments on the border between alchemy and chemistry, and some recent evidence suggests that what he was suffering from was not so much a psychogenic ailment as heavy metal poisoning, induced by systematic ingestion of small quantities of arsenic and mercury. It was a common practice for chemists of the time to use the sense of taste as an analytic tool.

Nevertheless his prodigious intellectual powers persisted unabated. In 1696, the Swiss mathematician Johann Bernoulli challenged his colleagues to solve an unresolved issue called the brachistochrone problem, specifying the curve connecting two points displaced from each other laterally, along which a body, acted upon only by gravity, would fall in the shortest time. Bernoulli originally specified a deadline of six months, but extended it to a year and a half at the request of Leibniz, one of the leading scholars of the time, and the man who had, independently of Newton, invented the differential and integral calculus. The challenge was delivered to Newton at four P.M. on January 29, 1697. Before leaving for work the next morning, he had invented an entire new branch of mathematics called the calculus of variations, used it to solve the brachistochrone problem and sent off the solution, which was published, at Newton's request, anonymously. But the brilliance and originality of the work betrayed the identity of its author. When Bernoulli saw the solution, he commented, "We recognize the lion by his claw." Newton was then in his fifty-fifth year.

The major intellectual pursuit of his last years was a concordance and calibration of the chronologies of ancient civilizations, very much in the tradition of the ancient historians Manetho, Strabo and Eratosthenes. In his last, posthumous work, "The Chronology of Ancient Kingdoms Amended," we find repeated astronomical calibrations of historical events; an architectural reconstruction of the Temple of Solomon; a provocative claim that all the Northern Hemisphere constellations are named after the personages, artifacts and events in the Greek story of Jason and the Argonauts; and the consistent assumption that the gods of all civilizations, with the single exception of Newton's own, were merely ancient kings and heroes deified by later generations.

Kepler and Newton represent a critical transition in human history, the discovery that fairly simple mathematical laws pervade all of Nature; that the same rules apply on Earth as in the skies; and that there is a resonance between the way we think and the way the world works. They unflinchingly respected the accuracy of observational data, and their predictions of the motion of the planets to high precision provided compelling evidence that, at an unexpectedly deep level, humans can understand the Cosmos. Our modern global civilization, our view of the world and our present exploration of the Universe are profoundly indebted to their insights.

Newton was guarded about his discoveries and fiercely competitive with his scientific colleagues. He thought nothing of waiting a decade or two after its discovery to publish the inverse square law. But before the grandeur and intricacy of Nature, he was, like Ptolemy and Kepler, exhilarated as well as disarmingly modest. Just before his death he wrote: “I do not know what I may appear to the world; but to myself I seem to have been only like a boy, playing on the seashore, and diverting myself, in now and then finding a smoother pebble or a prettier shell than ordinary, while the great ocean of truth lay all undiscovered before me.”

CHAPTER IV
HEAVEN AND HELL

The doors of heaven and hell are adjacent and identical.

—Nikos Kazantzakis, *The Last Temptation of Christ*

The Earth is a lovely and more or less placid place. Things change, but slowly. We can lead a full life and never personally encounter a natural disaster more violent than a storm. And so we become complacent, relaxed, unconcerned. But in the history of Nature, the record is clear. Worlds have been devastated. Even we humans have achieved the dubious technical distinction of being able to make our own disasters, both intentional and inadvertent. On the landscapes of other planets where the records of the past have been preserved, there is abundant evidence of major catastrophes. It is all a matter of time scale. An event that would be unthinkable in a hundred years may be inevitable in a hundred million. Even on the Earth, even in our own century, bizarre natural events have occurred.

In the early morning hours of June 30, 1908, in Central Siberia, a giant fireball was seen moving rapidly across the sky. Where it touched the horizon, an enormous explosion took place. It leveled some 2,000 square kilometers of forest and burned thousands of trees in a flash fire near the impact site. It produced an atmospheric shock wave that twice circled the Earth. For two days afterward, there was so much fine dust in the atmosphere that one could read a newspaper at night by scattered light in the streets of London, 10,000 kilometers away.

The government of Russia under the Czars could not be bothered to investigate so trivial an event, which, after all, had occurred far away, among the backward Tungus people of Siberia. It was ten years after the Revolution before an expedition arrived to examine the ground and interview the witnesses. These are some of the accounts they brought back:

> Early in the morning when everyone was asleep in the tent, it was blown up into the air, together with the occupants. When they fell back to Earth, the whole family suffered slight bruises, but Akulina and Ivan actually lost consciousness. When they regained consciousness they heard a great deal of noise and saw the forest blazing round them and much of it devastated.

> I was sitting in the porch of the house at the trading station of Vanovara at breakfast time and looking towards the north. I had just raised my axe to hoop a cask, when suddenly . . . the sky was split in two, and high above the forest the whole northern part of the sky appeared to be covered with fire. At that moment I felt a great heat as if my shirt had caught fire. . . . I wanted to pull off my shirt and throw it away, but at that moment there was a bang in the sky, and a mighty crash was heard. I was thrown on the ground about three sajenes away from the porch and for a moment I lost consciousness. My wife ran out and carried me into the hut. The crash was followed by a noise

like stones falling from the sky, or guns firing. The Earth trembled, and when I lay on the ground I covered my head because I was afraid that stones might hit it. At that moment when the sky opened, a hot wind, as from a cannon, blew past the huts from the north. It left its mark on the ground. . . .

When I sat down to have my breakfast beside my plough, I heard sudden bangs, as if from gun-fire. My horse fell to its knees. From the north side above the forest a flame shot up. . . . Then I saw that the fir forest had been bent over by the wind and I thought of a hurricane. I seized hold of my plough with both hands, so that it would not be carried away. The wind was so strong that it carried off some of the soil from the surface of the ground, and then the hurricane drove a wall of water up the Angara. I saw it all quite clearly, because my land was on a hillside.

The roar frightened the horses to such an extent that some galloped off in panic, dragging the ploughs in different directions, and others collapsed.

The carpenters, after the first and second crashes, had crossed themselves in stupefaction, and when the third crash resounded they fell backward from the building onto the chips of wood. Some of them were so stunned and utterly terrified that I had to calm them down and reassure them. We all abandoned work and went into the village. There, whole crowds of local inhabitants were gathered in the streets in terror, talking about this phenomenon.

I was in the fields . . . and had only just got one horse harnessed to the harrow and begun to attach another when

> suddenly I heard what sounded like a single loud shot to the right. I immediately turned round and saw an elongated flaming object flying through the sky. The front part was much broader than the tail end and its color was like fire in the day-time. It was many times bigger than the sun but much dimmer, so that it was possible to look at it with the naked eye. Behind the flames trailed what looked like dust. It was wreathed in little puffs, and blue streamers were left behind from the flames. . . . As soon as the flame had disappeared, bangs louder than shots from a gun were heard, the ground could be felt to tremble, and the window panes in the cabin were shattered.
>
> . . . I was washing wool on the bank of the River Kan. Suddenly a noise like the fluttering of the wings of a frightened bird was heard . . . and a kind of swell came up the river. After this came a single sharp bang so loud that one of the workmen . . . fell into the water.

This remarkable occurrence is called the Tunguska Event. Some scientists have suggested that it was caused by a piece of hurtling antimatter, annihilated on contact with the ordinary matter of the Earth, disappearing in a flash of gamma rays. But the absence of radioactivity at the impact site gives no support to this explanation. Others postulate that a mini black hole passed through the Earth in Siberia and out the other side. But the records of atmospheric shock waves show no hint of an object booming out of the North Atlantic later that day. Perhaps it was a spaceship of some unimaginably advanced extraterrestrial civilization in desperate mechanical trouble, crashing in a remote region of an obscure planet. But at the site of the impact there is no trace of such a ship. Each of these ideas has been proposed, some of them more or less seriously. Not one of them is strongly supported by the evidence. The key point of the Tunguska Event is that there was a tremendous explosion, a great shock wave, an enormous forest fire, and yet there is no impact crater at the site. There seems to be only one explanation consistent with all the facts: In 1908 a piece of a comet hit the Earth.

In the vast spaces between the planets there are many objects, some rocky, some metallic, some icy, some composed partly of organic molecules. They range from grains of dust to irregular blocks the size of Nicaragua or Bhutan. And sometimes, by accident, there is a planet in the way. The Tunguska Event was probably caused by an icy cometary fragment about a hundred meters across—the size of a football field—weighing a million tons, moving at about 30 kilometers per second, 70,000 miles per hour.

If such an impact occurred today it might be mistaken, especially in the panic of the moment, for a nuclear explosion. The cometary impact and fireball would simulate all effects of a one-megaton nuclear burst, including the mushroom cloud, with two exceptions: there would be no gamma radiation or radioactive fallout. Could a rare but natural event, the impact of a sizable cometary fragment, trigger a nuclear war? A strange scenario: a small comet hits the Earth, as millions of them have, and the response of our civilization is promptly to self-destruct. It might be a good idea for us to understand comets and collisions and catastrophes a little better than we do. For example, an American Vela satellite detected an intense double flash of light from the vicinity of the South Atlantic and Western Indian Ocean on September 22, 1979. Early speculation held that it was a clandestine test of a low yield (two kilotons, about a sixth the energy of the Hiroshima bomb) nuclear weapon by South Africa or Israel. The political consequences were considered serious around the world. But what if the flashes were instead caused by the impact of a small asteroid or a piece of a comet? Since airborne overflights in the vicinity of the flashes showed not a trace of unusual radioactivity in the air, this is a real possibility and underscores the dangers in an age of nuclear weapons of not monitoring impacts from space better than we do.

A comet is made mostly of ice—water (H_2O) ice, with a little methane (CH_4) ice, and some ammonia (NH_3) ice. Striking the Earth's atmosphere, a modest cometary fragment would produce a great radiant fireball and a mighty blast wave, which would burn trees, level forests and be heard around the world. But it might not make much of a crater in the ground. The ices would all be melted during entry. There would be few recognizable pieces of the comet left—perhaps only a smattering of small grains from the non-icy parts of the cometary nucleus. Recently, the Soviet scientist E. Sobotovich has identified a large number of tiny diamonds strewn over the Tunguska site. Such diamonds are already known to exist in meteorites that have survived impact, and that may originate ultimately from comets.

On many a clear night, if you look patiently up at the sky, you will see a solitary meteor blazing briefly overhead. On some nights you can see a shower of meteors, always on the same few days of every year—a natural fireworks display, an entertainment in the heavens. These meteors are made by tiny grains, smaller than a mustard seed. They are less shooting stars than falling fluff. Momentarily brilliant as they enter the Earth's atmosphere, they are heated and destroyed by friction at a height of about 100 kilometers. Meteors are the remnants of comets.* Old comets, heated by repeated passages near the Sun, break up, evaporate and disintegrate. The debris spreads to fill the full cometary orbit. Where that orbit intersects the orbit of the Earth, there is a swarm of meteors waiting for us. Some part of the swarm is always at the same position in the Earth's orbit, so the meteor shower is always

* That meteors and meteorites are connected with the comets was first proposed by Alexander von Humboldt in his broad-gauge popularization of all of science, published in the years 1845 to 1862, a work called *Kosmos*. It was reading Humboldt's earlier work that fired the young Charles Darwin to embark on a career combining geographical exploration and natural history. Shortly thereafter he accepted a position as naturalist aboard the ship H.M.S. *Beagle*, the event that led to *The Origin of Species*.

observed on the same day of every year. June 30, 1908 was the day of the Beta Taurid meteor shower, connected with the orbit of Comet Encke. The Tunguska Event seems to have been caused by a chunk of Comet Encke, a piece substantially larger than the tiny fragments that cause those glittering, harmless meteor showers.

Comets have always evoked fear and awe and superstition. Their occasional apparitions disturbingly challenged the notion of an unalterable and divinely ordered Cosmos. It seemed inconceivable that a spectacular streak of milk-white flame, rising and setting with the stars night after night, was not there for a reason, did not hold some portent for human affairs. So the idea arose that comets were harbingers of disaster, auguries of divine wrath—that they foretold the deaths of princes, the fall of kingdoms. The Babylonians thought that comets were celestial beards. The Greeks thought of flowing hair, the Arabs of flaming swords. In Ptolemy's time comets were elaborately classified as "beams," "trumpets," "jars" and so on, according to their shapes. Ptolemy thought that comets bring wars, hot weather and "disturbed conditions." Some medieval depictions of comets resemble unidentified flying crucifixes. A Lutheran "Superintendent" or Bishop of Magdeburg named Andreas Celichius published in 1578 a "Theological Reminder of the New Comet," which offered the inspired view that a comet is "the thick smoke of human sins, rising every day, every hour, every moment, full of stench and horror before the face of God, and becoming gradually so thick as to form a comet, with curled and plaited tresses, which at last is kindled by the hot and fiery anger of the Supreme Heavenly Judge." But others countered that if comets were the smoke of sin, the skies would be continually ablaze with them.

The most ancient record of an apparition of Halley's (or any other) Comet appears in the Chinese *Book of Prince Huai Nan,* attendant to the march of King Wu against Zhou of Yin. The year was 1057 B.C. The approach to Earth of Halley's Comet in the year 66 is the probable explanation of the account by Josephus of a sword that hung over Jerusalem for a whole year. In 1066 the Normans witnessed another return of Halley's Comet. Since it must, they thought, presage the fall of *some* kingdom, the comet encouraged, in some sense precipitated, the invasion of England by William the Conqueror. The comet was duly noted in a newspaper of the time, the Bayeux Tapestry. In 1301, Giotto, one of the founders of modern realistic painting, witnessed another apparition of Comet Halley and inserted it into a nativity scene. The Great Comet of 1466—yet another return of Halley's Comet—panicked Christian Europe; the Christians feared that God, who sends comets, might be on the side of the Turks, who had just captured Constantinople.

The leading astronomers of the sixteenth and seventeenth centuries were fascinated by comets, and even Newton became a little giddy over them. Kepler described comets as darting through space "as the fishes in the sea," but being dissipated by sunlight, as the cometary tail always points away from the sun. David Hume, in many cases an uncompromising rationalist, at least toyed with the notion that comets were the reproductive cells—the eggs or sperm—of planetary systems, that planets are produced by a kind of interstellar sex. As an undergraduate, before his invention of the reflecting telescope, Newton spent many consecutive sleepless nights searching the sky for comets with his naked eye, pursuing them with such fervor that he felt ill from exhaustion. Following Tycho and Kepler, Newton concluded that the comets seen from Earth do not move within our atmosphere, as Aristotle and others had thought, but rather are more distant than the Moon, although closer than Saturn. Comets shine, as the planets do, by reflected sunlight, "and they are much mistaken who remove them almost as far as the fixed stars; for if it were so, the comets could receive no more light from our Sun than our planets do from the fixed stars." He showed that comets, like planets, move in ellipses: "Comets are a sort of planets revolved in very eccentric orbits about the Sun." This demystification, this prediction of regular cometary orbits, led his friend Edmund Halley in 1707 to calculate that the comets of 1531, 1607 and 1682 were apparitions at 76-year intervals of the same comet, and predicted its return in 1758. The comet duly arrived and was named for him posthumously. Comet Halley has played an interesting role in human history, and may be the target of the first space vehicle probe of a comet, during its return in 1986.

Modern planetary scientists sometimes argue that the collision of a comet with a planet might make a significant contribution to the planetary atmosphere. For example, all the water in the atmosphere of Mars today could be accounted for by a recent impact of a small comet. Newton noted that the matter in the tails of comets is dissipated in interplanetary space, lost to the comet and little by little attracted gravitationally to nearby planets. He believed that the water on the Earth is gradually being lost, "spent upon vegetation and putrefaction, and converted into dry earth. . . . The fluids, if they are not supplied from without, must be in a continual decrease, and quite fail at last." Newton seems to have believed that the Earth's oceans are of cometary origin, and that life is possible only because cometary matter falls upon our planet. In a mystical reverie, he went still further: "I suspect, moreover, that it is chiefly from the comets that spirit comes, which is indeed the smallest but the most subtle and useful part of our air, and so much required to sustain the life of all things with us."

As early as 1868 the astronomer William Huggins found an identity between some features in the spectrum of a comet and the spectrum of natural or "olefiant" gas. Huggins had found organic matter in the comets; in subsequent years cyanogen, CN, consisting of a carbon and a nitrogen atom, the molecular fragment that makes cyanides, was identified in the tails of comets. When the Earth was about to pass through the tail of Halley's Comet in 1910, many people panicked. They overlooked the fact that the tail of a comet is extravagantly diffuse: the actual danger from the poison in a comet's tail is far less than the danger, even in 1910, from industrial pollution in large cities.

But that reassured almost no one. For example, headlines in the San Francisco *Chronicle* for May 15, 1910, include "Comet Camera as Big as a House," "Comet Comes and Husband Reforms," "Comet Parties Now Fad in New York." The Los Angeles *Examiner* adopted a light mood: "Say! Has That Comet Cyanogened You Yet? . . . Entire Human Race Due for Free Gaseous Bath," "Expect 'High Jinks,'" "Many Feel Cyanogen Tang," "Victim Climbs Trees, Tries to Phone Comet." In 1910 there were parties, making merry before the world ended of cyanogen pollution. Entrepreneurs hawked anti-comet pills and gas masks, the latter an eerie premonition of the battlefields of World War I.

Some confusion about comets continues to our own time. In 1957, I was a graduate student at the University of Chicago's Yerkes Observatory. Alone in the observatory late one night, I heard the telephone ring persistently. When I answered, a voice, betraying a well-advanced state of inebriation, said, "Lemme talk to a shtrominer." "Can I help you?" "Well, see, we're havin' this garden party out here in Wilmette, and there's somethin' in the sky. The funny part is, though, if you look straight at it, it goes away. But if you don't look at it, there it is." The most sensitive part of the retina is not at the center of the field of view. You can see faint stars and other objects by averting your vision slightly. I knew that, barely visible in the sky at this time, was a newly discovered comet called Arend-Roland. So I told him that he was probably looking at a comet. There was a long pause, followed by the query: "Wash'a comet?" "A comet," I replied, "is a snowball one mile across." There was a longer pause, after which the caller requested, "Lemme talk to a *real* shtrominer." When Halley's Comet reappears in 1986, I wonder what political leaders will fear the apparition, what other silliness will then be upon us.

While the planets move in elliptical orbits around the Sun, their orbits are not *very* elliptical. At first glance they are, by and large, indistinguishable from circles. It is the comets—especially the long-period comets—that have dramatically elliptical orbits. The planets are the old-timers in the inner solar system; the comets are the newcomers. Why are the planetary orbits nearly circular and neatly separated one from the other? Because if planets had very elliptical orbits, so that their paths intersected, sooner or later there would be a collision. In the early history of the solar system, there were probably many planets in the process of formation. Those with elliptical crossing orbits tended to collide and destroy themselves. Those with circular orbits tended to grow and survive. The orbits of the present planets are the orbits of the survivors of this collisional natural selection, the stable middle age of a solar system dominated by early catastrophic impacts.

In the outermost solar system, in the gloom far beyond the planets, there is a vast spherical cloud of a trillion cometary nuclei, orbiting the Sun no faster than a racing car at the Indianapolis 500.* A fairly typical comet would look like a giant tumbling snowball about 1 kilometer across. Most never penetrate the border marked by the orbit of Pluto. But occasionally a passing star makes a gravitational flurry and commotion in the cometary cloud, and a group of comets finds itself in highly elliptical orbits, plunging toward the Sun. After its path is further changed by gravitational encounters with Jupiter or Saturn, it tends to find itself, once every century or so, careering toward the inner solar system. Somewhere between the orbits of Jupiter and Mars it

* The Earth is $r = 1$ astronomical unit = 150,000,000 kilometers from the Sun. Its roughly circular orbit then has a circumference of $2\pi r \simeq 10^9$ km. Our planet circulates once along this path every year. One year = 3×10^7 seconds. So the Earth's orbital speed is 10^9 km/3×10^7 sec $\simeq$ 30 km/sec. Now consider the spherical shell of orbiting comets that many astronomers believe surrounds the solar system at a distance $\simeq$ 100,000 astronomical units, almost halfway to the nearest star. From Kepler's third law (p. 62) it immediately follows that the orbital period about the Sun of any one of them is about $(10^5)^{3/2} = 10^{7.5} \simeq 3 \times 10^7$ or 30 million years. Once around the Sun is a long time if you live in the outer reaches of the solar system. The cometary orbit is $2\pi a = 2\pi \times 10^5 \times 1.5 \times 10^8$ km $\simeq 10^{14}$ km around, and its speed is therefore only 10^{14} km/10^{15} sec = 0.1 km/sec $\simeq$ 220 miles per hour.

would begin heating and evaporating. Matter blown outward from the Sun's atmosphere, the solar wind, carries fragments of dust and ice back behind the comet, making an incipient tail. If Jupiter were a meter across, our comet would be smaller than a speck of dust, but when fully developed, its tail would be as great as the distances between the worlds. When within sight of the Earth on each of its orbits, it would stimulate outpourings of superstitious fervor among the Earthlings. But eventually they would understand that it lived not in their atmosphere, but out among the planets. They would calculate its orbit. And perhaps one day soon they would launch a small space vehicle devoted to exploring this visitor from the realm of the stars.

Sooner or later comets will collide with planets. The Earth and its companion the Moon must be bombarded by comets and small asteroids, debris left over from the formation of the solar system. Since there are more small objects than large ones, there should be more impacts by small objects than by large ones. An impact of a small cometary fragment with the Earth, as at Tunguska, should occur about once every thousand years. But an impact with a large comet, such as Halley's Comet, whose nucleus is perhaps twenty kilometers across, should occur only about once every billion years.

When a small, icy object collides with a planet or a moon, it may not produce a very major scar. But if the impacting object is larger or made primarily of rock, there is an explosion on impact that carves out a hemispherical bowl called an impact crater. And if no process rubs out or fills in the crater, it may last for billions of years. Almost no erosion occurs on the Moon and when we examine its surface, we find it covered with impact craters, many more than can be accounted for by the rather sparse population of cometary and asteroidal debris that now fills the inner solar system. The lunar surface offers eloquent testimony of a previous age of the destruction of worlds, now billions of years gone.

Impact craters are not restricted to the Moon. We find them

throughout the inner solar system—from Mercury, closest to the Sun, to cloud-covered Venus to Mars and its tiny moons, Phobos and Deimos. These are the terrestrial planets, our family of worlds, the planets more or less like the Earth. They have solid surfaces, interiors made of rock and iron, and atmospheres ranging from near-vacuum to pressures ninety times higher than the Earth's. They huddle around the Sun, the source of light and heat, like campers around a fire. The planets are all about 4.6 billion years old. Like the Moon, they all bear witness to an age of impact catastrophism in the early history of the solar system.

As we move out past Mars we enter a very different regime—the realm of Jupiter and the other giant or jovian planets. These are great worlds, composed largely of hydrogen and helium, with smaller amounts of hydrogen-rich gases such as methane, ammonia and water. We do not see solid surfaces here, only the atmosphere and the multicolored clouds. These are serious planets, not fragmentary worldlets like the Earth. A thousand Earths could fit inside Jupiter. If a comet or an asteroid dropped into the atmosphere of Jupiter, we would not expect a visible crater, only a momentary break in the clouds. Nevertheless, we know there has been a many-billion-year history of collisions in the outer solar system as well—because Jupiter has a great system of more than a dozen moons, five of which were examined close up by the Voyager spacecraft. Here again we find evidence of past catastrophes. When the solar system is all explored, we will probably have evidence for impact catastrophism on all nine worlds, from Mercury to Pluto, and on all the smaller moons, comets and asteroids.

There are about 10,000 craters on the near side of the Moon, visible to telescopes on Earth. Most of them are in the ancient lunar highlands and date from the time of the final accretion of the Moon from interplanetary debris. There are about a thousand craters larger than a kilometer across in the *maria* (Latin for "seas"), the lowland regions that were flooded, perhaps by lava, shortly after the formation of the Moon, covering over the preexisting craters. Thus, very roughly, craters on the Moon should be formed today at the rate of about 10^9 years/10^4 craters, = 10^5 years/crater, a hundred thousand years between cratering events. Since there may have been more interplanetary debris a few billion years ago than there is today, we might have to wait even longer than a hundred thousand years to see a crater form on the Moon. Because the Earth has a larger area than the Moon, we might have to wait something like ten thousand years between collisions that would make craters as big as a kilometer across on our planet. And since Meteor Crater, Arizona, an impact crater about a kilometer across, has been found to be twenty or thirty thousand years old, the observations on the Earth are in agreement with such crude calculations.

The actual impact of a small comet or asteroid with the Moon might make a momentary explosion sufficiently bright to be visible from the Earth. We can imagine our ancestors gazing idly up on some night a hundred thousand years ago and noting a strange cloud arising from the unilluminated part of the Moon, suddenly struck by the Sun's rays. But we would not expect such an event to have happened in historical times. The odds against it must be something like a hundred to one. Nevertheless, there is an historical account which may in fact describe an impact on the Moon seen from Earth with the naked eye: On the evening of June 25, 1178, five British monks reported something extraordinary, which was later recorded in the chronicle of Gervase of Canterbury, generally considered a reliable reporter on the political and cultural events of his time, after he had interviewed the eyewitnesses who asserted, under oath, the truth of their story. The chronicle reads:

> There was a bright New Moon, and as usual in that phase its horns were tilted towards the east. Suddenly, the upper horn split in two. From the midpoint of the divi-

> sion, a flaming torch sprang up, spewing out fire, hot coals, and sparks.

The astronomers Derral Mulholland and Odile Calame have calculated that a lunar impact would produce a dust cloud rising off the surface of the Moon with an appearance corresponding rather closely to the report of the Canterbury monks.

If such an impact were made only 800 years ago, the crater should still be visible. Erosion on the Moon is so inefficient, because of the absence of air and water, that even small craters a few billion years old are still comparatively well preserved. From the description recorded by Gervase, it is possible to pinpoint the sector of the Moon to which the observations refer. Impacts produce rays, linear trails of fine powder spewed out during the explosion. Such rays are associated with the very youngest craters on the Moon—for example, those named after Aristarchus and Copernicus and Kepler. But while the craters may withstand erosion on the Moon, the rays, being exceptionally thin, do not. As time goes on, even the arrival of micrometeorites—fine dust from space—stirs up and covers over the rays, and they gradually disappear. Thus rays are a signature of a recent impact.

The meteoriticist Jack Hartung has pointed out that a very recent, very fresh-looking small crater with a prominent ray system lies exactly in the region of the Moon referred to by the Canterbury monks. It is called Giordano Bruno after the sixteenth-century Roman Catholic scholar who held that there are an infinity of worlds and that many are inhabited. For this and other crimes he was burned at the stake in the year 1600.

Another line of evidence consistent with this interpretation has been provided by Calame and Mulholland. When an object impacts the Moon at high speed, it sets the Moon slightly wobbling. Eventually the vibrations die down but not in so short a period as eight hundred years. Such a quivering can be studied by laser reflection techniques. The Apollo astronauts emplaced in several locales on the Moon special mirrors called laser retroreflectors. When a laser beam from Earth strikes the mirror and bounces back, the round-trip travel time can be measured with remarkable precision. This time multiplied by the speed of light gives us the distance to the Moon at that moment to equally remarkable precision. Such measurements, performed over a period of years, reveal the Moon to be librating, or quivering with a period (about three years) and amplitude (about three meters), consistent with the idea that the crater Giordano Bruno was gouged out less than a thousand years ago.

All this evidence is inferential and indirect. The odds, as I have said, are against such an event happening in historical times. But the evidence is at least suggestive. As the Tunguska Event and Meteor Crater, Arizona, also remind us, not all impact catastrophes occurred in the early history of the solar system. But the fact that only a few of the lunar craters have extensive ray systems also reminds us that, even on the Moon, some erosion occurs.* By noting which craters overlap which and other signs of lunar stratigraphy, we can reconstruct the sequence of impact and flooding events of which the production of crater Bruno is perhaps the most recent example.

The Earth is very near the Moon. If the Moon is so severely cratered by impacts, how has the Earth avoided them? Why is Meteor Crater so rare? Do the comets and asteroids think it inadvisable to impact an inhabited planet? This is an unlikely forbearance. The only possible explanation is that impact craters are formed at very similar rates on both the Earth and the Moon, but that on the airless, waterless Moon they are preserved for immense periods of time, while on the Earth slow erosion wipes

* On Mars, where erosion is much more efficient, although there are many craters there are virtually no ray craters, as we would expect.

them out or fills them in. Running water, windblown sand and mountain-building are very slow processes. But over millions or billions of years, they are capable of utterly erasing even very large impact scars.

On the surface of any moon or planet, there will be external processes, such as impacts from space, and internal processes, such as earthquakes; there will be fast, catastrophic events, such as volcanic explosions, and processes of excruciating slowness, such as the pitting of a surface by tiny airborne sand grains. There is no general answer to the question of which processes dominate, the outside ones or the inside ones; the rare but violent events, or the common and inconspicuous occurrences. On the Moon, the outside, catastrophic events hold sway; on Earth, the inside, slow processes dominate. Mars is an intermediate case.

Between the orbits of Mars and Jupiter are countless asteroids, tiny terrestrial planets. The largest are a few hundred kilometers across. Many have oblong shapes and are tumbling through space. In some cases there seem to be two or more asteroids in tight mutual orbits. Collisions among the asteroids happen frequently, and occasionally a piece is chipped off and accidentally intercepts the Earth, falling to the ground as a meteorite. In the exhibits, on the shelves of our museums are the fragments of distant worlds. The asteroid belt is a great grinding mill, producing smaller and smaller pieces down to motes of dust. The bigger asteroidal pieces, along with the comets, are mainly responsible for the recent craters on planetary surfaces. The asteroid belt may be a place where a planet was once prevented from forming because of the gravitational tides of the giant nearby planet Jupiter; or it may be the shattered remains of a planet that blew itself up. This seems improbable because no scientist on Earth knows how a planet might blow itself up, which is probably just as well.

The rings of Saturn bear some resemblance to the asteroid belt: trillions of tiny icy moonlets orbiting the planet. They may represent debris prevented by the gravity of Saturn from accreting into a nearby moon, or they may be the remains of a moon that wandered too close and was torn apart by the gravitational tides. Alternatively, they may be the steady state equilibrium between material ejected from a moon of Saturn, such as Titan, and material falling into the atmosphere of the planet. Jupiter and Uranus also have ring systems, discovered only recently, and almost invisible from the Earth. Whether Neptune has a ring is a problem high on the agenda of planetary scientists. Rings may be a typical adornment of Jovian-type planets throughout the cosmos.

Major recent collisions from Saturn to Venus were alleged in a popular book, *Worlds in Collision*, published in 1950 by a psychiatrist named Immanuel Velikovsky. He proposed that an object of planetary mass, which he called a comet, was somehow generated in the Jupiter system. Some 3,500 years ago, it careered in toward the inner solar system and made repeated encounters with the Earth and Mars, having as incidental consequences the parting of the Red Sea, allowing Moses and the Israelites to escape from Pharaoh, and the stopping of the Earth from rotating on Joshua's command. It also caused, he said, extensive vulcanism and floods.* Velikovsky imagined the comet, after a complicated game of interplanetary billiards, to settle down into a stable, nearly circular orbit, becoming the planet Venus—which he claimed never existed before then.

As I have discussed at some length elsewhere, these ideas are almost certainly wrong. Astronomers do not object to the idea of major collisions, only to major *recent* collisions. In any model of the solar system it is impossible to show the sizes of the planets on the same scale as their orbits, because the planets would then be

* As far as I know, the first essentially nonmystical attempt to explain a historical event by cometary intervention was Edmund Halley's proposal that the Noachic flood was "the casual Choc [shock] of a Comet."

almost too small to see. If the planets were really shown to scale, as grains of dust, we would easily note that the chance of collision of a particular comet with the Earth in a few thousand years is extraordinarily low. Moreover, Venus is a rocky and metallic, hydrogen-poor planet, whereas Jupiter—where Velikovsky supposed it comes from—is made almost entirely of hydrogen. There are no energy sources for comets or planets to be ejected by Jupiter. If one passed by the Earth, it could not "stop" the Earth's rotation, much less start it up again at twenty-four hours a day. No geological evidence supports the idea of an unusual frequency of vulcanism or floods 3,500 years ago. There are Mesopotamian inscriptions referring to Venus that predate the time when Velikovsky says Venus changed from a comet into a planet.* It is very unlikely that an object in such a highly elliptical orbit could be rapidly moved into the nearly perfectly circular orbit of present-day Venus. And so on.

Many hypotheses proposed by scientists as well as by nonscientists turn out to be wrong. But science is a self-correcting enterprise. To be accepted, all new ideas must survive rigorous standards of evidence. The worst aspect of the Velikovsky affair is not that his hypotheses were wrong or in contradiction to firmly established facts, but that some who called themselves scientists attempted to suppress Velikovsky's work. Science is generated by and devoted to free inquiry: the idea that any hypothesis, no matter how strange, deserves to be considered on its merits. The suppression of uncomfortable ideas may be common in religion and politics, but it is not the path to knowledge; it has no place in the endeavor of science. We do not know in advance who will discover fundamental new insights.

* The Adda cylinder seal, dating from the middle of the third millennium B.C., prominently displays Inanna, the goddess of Venus, the morning star, and precursor of the Babylonian Ishtar.

Venus has almost the same mass,* size, and density as the Earth. As the nearest planet, it has for centuries been thought of as the Earth's sister. What is our sister planet really like? Might it be a balmy, summer planet, a little warmer than the Earth because it is a little closer to the Sun? Does it have impact craters, or have they all eroded away? Are there volcanoes? Mountains? Oceans? Life?

The first person to look at Venus through the telescope was Galileo in 1609. He saw an absolutely featureless disk. Galileo noted that it went through phases, like the Moon, from a thin crescent to a full disk, and for the same reason: we are sometimes looking mostly at the night side of Venus and sometimes mostly at the day side, a finding that incidentally reinforced the view that the Earth went around the Sun and not vice versa. As optical telescopes became larger and their resolution (or ability to discriminate fine detail) improved, they were systematically turned toward Venus. But they did no better than Galileo's. Venus was evidently covered by a dense layer of obscuring cloud. When we look at the planet in the morning or evening skies, we are seeing sunlight reflected off the clouds of Venus. But for centuries after their discovery, the composition of those clouds remained entirely unknown.

The absence of anything to see on Venus led some scientists to the curious conclusion that the surface was a swamp, like the Earth in the Carboniferous Period. The argument—if we can dignify it by such a word—went something like this:

> "I can't see a thing on Venus."
> "Why not?"
> "Because it's totally covered with clouds."
> "What are clouds made of?"

* It is, incidentally, some 30 million times more massive than the most massive comet known.

> "Water, of course."
>
> "Then why are the clouds of Venus thicker than the clouds on Earth?"
>
> "Because there's more water there."
>
> "But if there is more water in the clouds, there must be more water on the surface. What kind of surfaces are very wet?"
>
> "Swamps."

And if there are swamps, why not cyacads and dragonflies and perhaps even dinosaurs on Venus? Observation: There was absolutely nothing to see on Venus. Conclusion: It must be covered with life. The featureless clouds of Venus reflected our own predispositions. We are alive, and we resonate with the idea of life elsewhere. But only careful accumulation and assessment of the evidence can tell us whether a given world is inhabited. Venus turns out not to oblige our predispositions.

The first real clue to the nature of Venus came from work with a prism made of glass or a flat surface, called a diffraction grating, covered with fine, regularly spaced, ruled lines. When an intense beam of ordinary white light passes through a narrow slit and then through a prism or grating, it is spread into a rainbow of colors called a spectrum. The spectrum runs from high frequencies* of visible light to low ones—violet, blue, green, yellow, orange and red. Since we see these colors, it is called the spectrum of visible light. But there is far more light than the small segment of the spectrum we can see. At higher frequencies, beyond the violet, is a part of the spectrum called the ultraviolet: a perfectly real kind of light, carrying death to the microbes. It is invisible to us, but readily detectable by bumblebees and photoelectric cells.

* Light is a wave motion; its frequency is the number of wave crests, say, entering a detection instrument, such as a retina, in a given unit of time, such as a second. The higher the frequency, the more energetic the radiation.

There is much more to the world than we can see. Beyond the ultraviolet is the X-ray part of the spectrum, and beyond the X-rays are the gamma rays. At lower frequencies, on the other side of red, is the infrared part of the spectrum. It was first discovered by placing a sensitive thermometer in what to our eyes is the dark beyond the red. The temperature rose. There was light falling on the thermometer even though it was invisible to our eyes. Rattlesnakes and doped semiconductors detect infrared radiation perfectly well. Beyond the infrared is the vast spectral region of the radio waves. From gamma rays to radio waves, all are equally respectable bands of light. All are useful in astronomy. But because of the limitations of our eyes, we have a prejudice, a bias, toward that tiny rainbow band we call the spectrum of visible light.

In 1844, the philosopher Auguste Comte was searching for an example of a sort of knowledge that would be always hidden. He chose the composition of distant stars and planets. We would never physically visit them, he thought, and with no sample in hand it seemed we would forever be denied knowledge of their composition. But only three years after Comte's death, it was discovered that a spectrum can be used to determine the chemistry of distant objects. Different molecules and chemical elements absorb different frequencies or colors of light, sometimes in the visible and sometimes elsewhere in the spectrum. In the spectrum of a planetary atmosphere, a single dark line represents an image of the slit in which light is missing, the absorption of sunlight during its brief passage through the air of another world. Each such line is made by a particular kind of molecule or atom. Every substance has its characteristic spectral signature. The gases on Venus can be identified from the Earth, 60 million kilometers away. We can divine the composition of the Sun (in which helium, named after the Greek sun god Helios, was first found); of magnetic A stars rich in europium; of distant galaxies analyzed through the collective light of a hundred billion constituent stars.

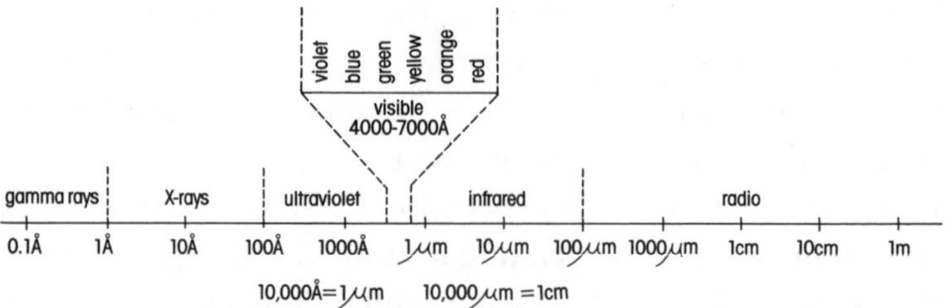

Schematic diagram of the electromagnetic spectrum. The wavelength of light is measured in Ångstroms (Å), micrometers (μm), centimeters (cm) and meters (m).

Astronomical spectroscopy is an almost magical technique. It amazes me still. Auguste Comte picked a particularly unfortunate example.

If Venus were soaking wet, it should be easy to see the water vapor lines in its spectrum. But the first spectroscopic searches, attempted at Mount Wilson Observatory around 1920, found not a hint, not a trace, of water vapor above the clouds of Venus, suggesting an arid, desert-like surface, surmounted by clouds of fine drifting silicate dust. Further study revealed enormous quantities of carbon dioxide in the atmosphere, implying to some scientists that all the water on the planet had combined with hydrocarbons to form carbon dioxide, and that therefore the surface of Venus was a global oil field, a planet-wide sea of petroleum. Others concluded that there was no water vapor above the clouds because the clouds were very cold, that all the water had condensed out into water droplets, which do not have the same pattern of spectral lines as water vapor. They suggested that the planet was totally covered with water—except perhaps for an occasional limestone-encrusted island, like the cliffs of Dover. But because of the vast quantities of carbon dioxide in the atmosphere, the sea could not be ordinary water; physical chemistry required carbonated water. Venus, they proposed, had a vast ocean of seltzer.

The first hint of the true situation came not from spectroscopic studies in the visible or near-infrared parts of the spectrum, but rather from the radio region. A radio telescope works more like a light meter than a camera. You point it toward some fairly broad region of the sky, and it records how much energy, in a particular radio frequency, is coming down to Earth. We are used to radio signals transmitted by some varieties of intelligent life—namely, those who run radio and television stations. But there are many other reasons for natural objects to give off radio waves. One is that they are hot. And when, in 1956, an early radio telescope was turned toward Venus, it was discovered to be emitting radio waves as if it were at an extremely high temperature. But the real demonstration that the surface of Venus is astonishingly hot came when the Soviet spacecraft of the Venera series first penetrated the obscuring clouds and landed on the mysterious and inaccessible surface of the nearest planet. Venus, it turns out, is broiling hot. There are no swamps, no oil fields, no seltzer oceans. With insufficient data, it is easy to go wrong.

When I greet a friend, I am seeing her in reflected visible light, generated by the Sun, say, or by an incandescent lamp. The light rays bounce off my friend and into my eye. But the ancients, including no less a figure than Euclid, believed that we see by virtue of rays somehow emitted by the eye and tangibly, actively contacting the object observed. This is a natural notion and can still be encountered, although it does not account for the invisibility of objects in a darkened room. Today we combine a laser and a photocell, or a radar transmitter and a radio telescope, and in this way make active contact by light with distant objects. In radar astronomy, radio waves are transmitted by a telescope on Earth, strike, say, that hemisphere of Venus that happens to be facing the Earth, and bounce back. At many wavelengths the clouds and atmosphere of Venus are entirely transparent to radio waves. Some places on the surface will absorb them or, if they are very rough, will scatter them sideways and so will appear dark to radio waves. By following the surface features moving with Venus as it rotates, it was possible for the first time to determine reliably the length of its day—how long it takes Venus to spin once on its axis. It turns out that, with respect to the stars, Venus turns once every 243 Earth days, but backward, in the opposite direction from all other planets in the inner solar system. As a result, the Sun rises in the west and sets in the east, taking 118 Earth days from sunrise to sunrise. What is more, it presents almost exactly the same face to the Earth each time it is closest to our planet. However the Earth's gravity has managed to nudge Venus into this Earth-locked rotation rate, it cannot have happened rapidly. Venus could not be a mere few thousand years old but, rather, it must be as old as all the other objects in the inner solar system.

Radar pictures of Venus have been obtained, some from ground-based radar telescopes, some from the Pioneer Venus vehicle in orbit around the planet. They show provocative evidence of impact craters. There are just as many craters that are not too big or too small on Venus as there are in the lunar highlands, so many that Venus is again telling us that it is very old. But the craters of Venus are remarkably shallow, almost as if the high surface temperatures have produced a kind of rock that flows over long periods of time, like taffy or putty, gradually softening the relief. There are great mesas here, twice as high as the Tibetan plateau, an immense rift valley, possibly giant volcanoes and a mountain as high as Everest. We now see before us a world previously hidden entirely by clouds—its features first explored by radar and by space vehicles.

The surface temperatures on Venus, as deduced from radio astronomy and confirmed by direct spacecraft measurements, are around 480°C or 900°F, hotter than the hottest household oven. The corresponding surface pressure is 90 atmospheres, 90 times the pressure we feel from the Earth's atmosphere, the equivalent of the weight of water 1 kilometer below the surface of the oceans. To survive for long on Venus, a space vehicle would have to be refrigerated as well as built like a deep submersible.

Something like a dozen space vehicles from the Soviet Union

and United States have entered the dense Venus atmosphere, and penetrated the clouds; a few of them have actually survived for an hour or so on the surface.* Two spacecraft in the Soviet Venera series have taken pictures down there. Let us follow in the footsteps of these pioneering missions, and visit another world.

In ordinary visible light, the faintly yellowish clouds of Venus can be made out, but they show, as Galileo first noted, virtually no features at all. If the cameras look in the ultraviolet, however, we see a graceful, complex swirling weather system in the high atmosphere, where the winds are around 100 meters per second, some 220 miles per hour. The atmosphere of Venus is composed of 96 percent carbon dioxide. There are small traces of nitrogen, water vapor, argon, carbon monoxide and other gases, but the only hydrocarbons or carbohydrates present are there in less than 0.1 parts per million. The clouds of Venus turn out to be chiefly a concentrated solution of sulfuric acid. Small quantities of hydrochloric acid and hydrofluoric acid are also present. Even at its high, cool clouds, Venus turns out to be a thoroughly nasty place.

High above the visible cloud deck, at about 70 kilometers altitude, there is a continuous haze of small particles. At 60 kilometers, we plunge into the clouds, and find ourselves surrounded by droplets of concentrated sulfuric acid. As we go deeper, the cloud particles tend to get bigger. The pungent gas, sulfur dioxide, SO_2, is present in trace amounts in the lower atmosphere. It is circu-

* *Pioneer Venus* was a successful U.S. mission in 1978–79, combining an orbiter and four atmospheric entry probes, two of which briefly survived the inclemencies of the Venus surface. There are many unexpected developments in mustering spacecraft to explore the planets. This is one of them: Among the instruments aboard one of the Pioneer Venus entry probes was a net flux radiometer, designed to measure simultaneously the amount of infrared energy flowing upward and downward at each position in the Venus atmosphere. The instrument required a sturdy window that was also transparent to infrared radiation. A 13.5-karat diamond was imported and milled into the desired window. However, the contractor was required to pay a $12,000 import duty. Eventually, the U.S. Customs service decided that after the diamond was launched to Venus it was unavailable for trade on Earth and refunded the money to the manufacturer.

lated up above the clouds, broken down by ultraviolet light from the Sun and recombined with water there to form sulfuric acid—which condenses into droplets, settles, and at lower altitudes is broken down by heat into SO_2 and water again, completing the cycle. It is always raining sulfuric acid on Venus, all over the planet, and not a drop ever reaches the surface.

The sulfur-colored mist extends downward to some 45 kilometers above the surface of Venus, where we emerge into a dense but crystal-clear atmosphere. The atmospheric pressure is so high, however, that we cannot see the surface. Sunlight is bounced about by atmospheric molecules until we lose all images from the surface. There is no dust here, no clouds, just an atmosphere getting palpably denser. Plenty of sunlight is transmitted by the overlying clouds, about as much as on an overcast day on the Earth.

With searing heat, crushing pressures, noxious gases and everything suffused in an eerie, reddish glow, Venus seems less the goddess of love than the incarnation of hell. As nearly as we can make out, at least some places on the surface are strewn fields of jumbled, softened irregular rocks, a hostile, barren landscape relieved only here and there by the eroded remnants of a derelict spacecraft from a distant planet, utterly invisible through the thick, cloudy, poisonous atmosphere.*

* In this stifling landscape, there is not likely to be anything alive, even creatures very different from us. Organic and other conceivable biological molecules would simply fall to pieces. But, as an indulgence, let us imagine that intelligent life once evolved on such a planet. Would it then invent science? The development of science on Earth was spurred fundamentally by observations of the regularities of the stars and planets. But Venus is completely cloud-covered. The night is pleasingly long—about 59 Earth days long—but nothing of the astronomical universe would be visible if you looked up into the night sky of Venus. Even the Sun would be invisible in the daytime; its light would be scattered and diffused over the whole sky—just as scuba divers see only a uniform enveloping radiance beneath the sea. If a radio telescope were built on Venus, it could detect the Sun, the Earth and other distant objects. If astrophysics developed, the existence of stars could eventually be deduced from the principles of physics, but they would be theoretical constructs only. I sometimes wonder what their reaction would be if intelligent beings on Venus one day learned to fly, to sail in the dense air, to penetrate the mysterious cloud veil 45 kilometers above them and eventu-

Venus is a kind of planet-wide catastrophe. It now seems reasonably clear that the high surface temperature comes about through a massive greenhouse effect. Sunlight passes through the atmosphere and clouds of Venus, which are semi-transparent to visible light, and reaches the surface. The surface being heated endeavors to radiate back into space. But because Venus is much cooler than the Sun, it emits radiation chiefly in the infrared rather than the visible region of the spectrum. However, the carbon dioxide and water vapor* in the Venus atmosphere are almost perfectly opaque to infrared radiation, the heat of the Sun is efficiently trapped, and the surface temperature rises—until the little amount of infrared radiation that trickles out of this massive atmosphere just balances the sunlight absorbed in the lower atmosphere and surface.

Our neighboring world turns out to be a dismally unpleasant place. But we will go back to Venus. It is fascinating in its own right. Many mythic heroes in Greek and Norse mythology, after all, made celebrated efforts to visit Hell. There is also much to be learned about our planet, a comparative Heaven, by comparing it with Hell.

---

ally to emerge out the top of the clouds, to look up and for the first time witness that glorious universe of Sun and planets and stars.

* At the present time there is still a little uncertainty about the abundance of water vapor on Venus. The gas chromatograph on the Pioneer Venus entry probes gave an abundance of water in the lower atmosphere of a few tenths of a percent. On the other hand, infrared measurements by the Soviet entry vehicles, Veneras 11 and 12, gave an abundance of about a hundredth of a percent. If the former value applies, then carbon dioxide and water vapor alone are adequate to seal in almost all the heat radiation from the surface and keep the Venus ground temperature at about 480°C. If the latter number applies—and my guess is that it is the more reliable estimate—then carbon dioxide and water vapor alone are adequate to keep the surface temperature only at about 380°C, and some other atmospheric constituent is necessary to close the remaining infrared frequency windows in the atmospheric greenhouse. However, the small quantities of SO_2, CO and HCl, all of which have been detected in the Venus atmosphere, seem adequate for this purpose. Thus recent American and Soviet missions to Venus seem to have provided verification that the greenhouse effect is indeed the reason for the high surface temperature.

The Sphinx, half human, half lion, was constructed more than 5,500 years ago. Its face was once crisp and cleanly rendered. It is now softened and blurred by thousands of years of Egyptian desert sandblasting and by occasional rains. In New York City there is an obelisk called Cleopatra's Needle, which came from Egypt. In only about a hundred years in that city's Central Park, its inscriptions have been almost totally obliterated, because of smog and industrial pollution—chemical erosion like that in the atmosphere of Venus. Erosion on Earth slowly wipes out information, but because they are gradual—the patter of a raindrop, the sting of a sand grain—those processes can be missed. Big structures, such as mountain ranges, survive tens of millions of years; smaller impact craters, perhaps a hundred thousand*; and large-scale human artifacts only some thousands. In addition to such slow and uniform erosion, destruction also occurs through catastrophes large and small. The Sphinx is missing a nose. Someone shot it off in a moment of idle desecration—some say it was Mameluke Turks, others, Napoleonic soldiers.

On Venus, on Earth and elsewhere in the solar system, there is evidence for catastrophic destruction, tempered or overwhelmed by slower, more uniform processes: on the Earth, for example, rainfall, coursing into rivulets, streams and rivers of running water, creating huge alluvial basins; on Mars, the remnants of ancient rivers, perhaps arising from beneath the ground; on Io, a moon of Jupiter, what seem to be broad channels made by flowing liquid sulfur. There are mighty weather systems on the Earth—and in the high atmosphere of Venus and on Jupiter. There are sandstorms on the Earth and on Mars; lightning on Jupiter and Venus and Earth. Volcanoes inject debris into the at-

* More precisely, an impact crater 10 kilometers in diameter is produced on the Earth about once every 500,000 years; it would survive erosion for about 300 million years in areas that are geologically stable, such as Europe and North America. Smaller craters are produced more frequently and destroyed more rapidly, especially in geologically active regions.

mospheres of the Earth and Io. Internal geological processes slowly deform the surfaces of Venus, Mars, Ganymede and Europa, as well as Earth. Glaciers, proverbial for their slowness, produce major reworkings of landscapes on the Earth and probably also on Mars. These processes need not be constant in time. Most of Europe was once covered with ice. A few million years ago, the present site of the city of Chicago was buried under three kilometers of frost. On Mars, and elsewhere in the solar system, we see features that could not be produced today, landscapes carved hundreds of millions or billions of years ago when the planetary climate was probably very different.

There is an additional factor that can alter the landscape and the climate of Earth: intelligent life, able to make major environmental changes. Like Venus, the Earth also has a greenhouse effect due to its carbon dioxide and water vapor. The global temperature of the Earth would be below the freezing point of water if not for the greenhouse effect. It keeps the oceans liquid and life possible. A little greenhouse is a good thing. Like Venus, the Earth also has about 90 atmospheres of carbon dioxide; but it resides in the crust as limestone and other carbonates, not in the atmosphere. If the Earth were moved only a little closer to the Sun, the temperature would increase slightly. This would drive some of the CO_2 out of the surface rocks, generating a stronger greenhouse effect, which would in turn incrementally heat the surface further. A hotter surface would vaporize still more carbonates into CO_2, and there would be the possibility of a runaway greenhouse effect to very high temperatures. This is just what we think happened in the early history of Venus, because of Venus' proximity to the Sun. The surface environment of Venus is a warning: something disastrous can happen to a planet rather like our own.

The principal energy sources of our present industrial civilization are the so-called fossil fuels. We burn wood and oil, coal and natural gas, and, in the process, release waste gases, principally CO_2, into the air. Consequently, the carbon dioxide content of the Earth's atmosphere is increasing dramatically. The possibility of a runaway greenhouse effect suggests that we have to be careful: Even a one- or two-degree rise in the global temperature can have catastrophic consequences. In the burning of coal and oil and gasoline, we are also putting sulfuric acid into the atmosphere. Like Venus, our stratosphere even now has a substantial mist of tiny sulfuric acid droplets. Our major cities are polluted with noxious molecules. We do not understand the long-term effects of our course of action.

But we have also been perturbing the climate in the opposite sense. For hundreds of thousands of years human beings have been burning and cutting down forests and encouraging domestic animals to graze on and destroy grasslands. Slash-and-burn agriculture, industrial tropical deforestation and overgrazing are rampant today. But forests are darker than grasslands, and grasslands are darker than deserts. As a consequence, the amount of sunlight that is absorbed by the ground has been declining, and by changes in the land use we are lowering the surface temperature of our planet. Might this cooling increase the size of the polar ice cap, which, because it is bright, will reflect still more sunlight from the Earth, further cooling the planet, driving a runaway albedo* effect?

Our lovely blue planet, the Earth, is the only home we know. Venus is too hot. Mars is too cold. But the Earth is just right, a heaven for humans. After all, we evolved here. But our congenial climate may be unstable. We are perturbing our poor planet in serious and contradictory ways. Is there any danger of driving the environment of the Earth toward the planetary Hell of Venus or the global ice age of Mars? The simple answer is that nobody

* The albedo is the fraction of the sunlight striking a planet that is reflected back to space. The albedo of the Earth is some 30 to 35 percent. The rest of the sunlight is absorbed by the ground and is responsible for the average surface temperature.

knows. The study of the global climate, the comparison of the Earth with other worlds, are subjects in their earliest stages of development. They are fields that are poorly and grudgingly funded. In our ignorance, we continue to push and pull, to pollute the atmosphere and brighten the land, oblivious of the fact that the long-term consequences are largely unknown.

A few million years ago, when human beings first evolved on Earth, it was already a middle-aged world, 4.6 billion years along from the catastrophes and impetuosities of its youth. But we humans now represent a new and perhaps decisive factor. Our intelligence and our technology have given us the power to affect the climate. How will we use this power? Are we willing to tolerate ignorance and complacency in matters that affect the entire human family? Do we value short-term advantages above the welfare of the Earth? Or will we think on longer time scales, with concern for our children and our grandchildren, to understand and protect the complex life-support systems of our planet? The Earth is a tiny and fragile world. It needs to be cherished.

CHAPTER V

BLUES FOR A RED PLANET

In the orchards of the gods, he watches the canals . . .

—*Enuma Elish,* Sumer, c. 2500 B.C.

A man that is of Copernicus' Opinion, that this Earth of ours is a Planet, carry'd round and enlightn'd by the Sun, like the rest of them, cannot but sometimes have a fancy . . . that the rest of the Planets have their Dress and Furniture, nay and their Inhabitants too as well as this Earth of ours. . . . But we were always apt to conclude, that 'twas in vain to enquire after what Nature had been pleased to do there, seeing there was no likelihood of ever coming to an end of the Enquiry . . . but a while ago, thinking somewhat seriously on this matter (not that I count my self quicker sighted than those great Men [of the past], but that I had the happiness to live after most of them) me thoughts the Enquiry was not so impracticable nor the way so stopt up with Difficulties, but that there was very good room left for probable Conjectures.

—Christiaan Huygens, *New Conjectures Concerning the Planetary Worlds, Their Inhabitants and Productions,* c. 1690

Many years ago, so the story goes, a celebrated newspaper publisher sent a telegram to a noted astronomer: WIRE COLLECT IMMEDIATELY FIVE HUNDRED WORDS ON WHETHER

THERE IS LIFE ON MARS. The astronomer dutifully replied: NOBODY KNOWS, NOBODY KNOWS, NOBODY KNOWS . . . 250 times. But despite this confession of ignorance, asserted with dogged persistence by an expert, no one paid any heed, and from that time to this, we hear authoritative pronouncements by those who think they have deduced life on Mars, and by those who think they have excluded it. Some people very much want there to be life on Mars; others very much want there to be no life on Mars. There have been excesses in both camps. These strong passions have somewhat frayed the tolerance for ambiguity that is essential to science. There seem to be many people who simply wish to be told an answer, any answer, and thereby avoid the burden of keeping two mutually exclusive possibilities in their heads at the same time. Some scientists have believed that Mars is inhabited on what has later proved to be the flimsiest evidence. Others have concluded the planet is lifeless because a preliminary search for a particular manifestation of life has been unsuccessful or ambiguous. The blues have been played more than once for the red planet.

Why Martians? Why so many eager speculations and ardent fantasies about Martians, rather than, say, Saturnians or Plutonians? Because Mars seems, at first glance, very Earth-like. It is the nearest planet whose surface we can see. There are polar ice caps, drifting white clouds, raging dust storms, seasonally changing patterns on its red surface, even a twenty-four-hour day. It is tempting to think of it as an inhabited world. Mars has become a kind of mythic arena onto which we have projected our earthly hopes and fears. But our psychological predispositions pro or con must not mislead us. All that matters is the evidence, and the evidence is not yet in. The real Mars is a world of wonders. Its future prospects are far more intriguing than our past apprehensions about it. In our time we have sifted the sands of Mars, we have established a presence there, we have fulfilled a century of dreams!

> No one would have believed in the last years of the nineteenth century that this world was being watched keenly and closely by intelligences greater than man's and yet as mortal as his own; that as men busied themselves about their various concerns, they were scrutinised and studied, perhaps almost as narrowly as a man with a microscope might scrutinise the transient creatures that swarm and multiply in a drop of water. With infinite complacency, men went to and fro over this globe about their little affairs, serene in their assurances of their empire over matter. It is possible that the infusoria under the microscope do the same. No one gave a thought to the older worlds of space as sources of human danger, or thought of them only to dismiss the idea of life upon them as impossible or improbable. It is curious to recall some of the mental habits of those departed days. At most, terrestrial men fancied there might be other men upon Mars, perhaps inferior to themselves and ready to welcome a missionary enterprise. Yet across the gulf of space, minds that are to our minds as ours are to those of the beasts that perish, intellects vast and cool and unsympathetic, regarded this Earth with envious eyes, and slowly and surely drew their plans against us.

These opening lines of H. G. Wells' 1897 science fiction classic *The War of the Worlds* maintain their haunting power to this day.* For all of our history, there has been the fear, or hope, that there might be life beyond the Earth. In the last hundred years, that premonition has focused on a bright red point of light in the night sky. Three years before *The War of the Worlds* was pub-

* In 1938, a radio version, produced by Orson Welles, transposed the Martian invasion from England to the eastern United States, and frightened millions in war-jittery America into believing that the Martians were in fact attacking.

lished, a Bostonian named Percival Lowell founded a major observatory where the most elaborate claims in support of life on Mars were developed. Lowell dabbled in astronomy as a young man, went to Harvard, secured a semi-official diplomatic appointment to Korea, and otherwise engaged in the usual pursuits of the wealthy. Before he died in 1916, he had made major contributions to our knowledge of the nature and evolution of the planets, to the deduction of the expanding universe and, in a decisive way, to the discovery of the planet Pluto, which is named after him. The first two letters of the name Pluto are the initials of Percival Lowell. Its symbol is ♇, a planetary monogram.

But Lowell's lifelong love was the planet Mars. He was electrified by the announcement in 1877 by an Italian astronomer, Giovanni Schiaparelli, of *canali* on Mars. Schiaparelli had reported during a close approach of Mars to Earth an intricate network of single and double straight lines crisscrossing the bright areas of the planet. *Canali* in Italian means channels or grooves, but was promptly translated into English as *canals,* a word that implies intelligent design. A Mars mania coursed through Europe and America, and Lowell found himself swept up with it.

In 1892, his eyesight failing, Schiaparelli announced he was giving up observing Mars. Lowell resolved to continue the work. He wanted a first-rate observing site, undisturbed by clouds or city lights and marked by good "seeing," the astronomer's term for a steady atmosphere through which the shimmering of an astronomical image in the telescope is minimized. Bad seeing is produced by small-scale turbulence in the atmosphere above the telescope and is the reason the stars twinkle. Lowell built his observatory far away from home, on Mars Hill in Flagstaff, Arizona.* He sketched the surface features of Mars, particularly the

* Isaac Newton had written "If the Theory of making Telescopes could at length be fully brought into practice, yet there would be certain Bounds beyond which Telescopes could not perform. For the Air through which we look upon the Stars, is in perpetual tremor. . . . The only remedy is the most serene and quiet Air, such as may

canals, which mesmerized him. Observations of this sort are not easy. You put in long hours at the telescope in the chill of the early morning. Often the seeing is poor and the image of Mars blurs and distorts. Then you must ignore what you have seen. Occasionally the image steadies and the features of the planet flash out momentarily, marvelously. You must then remember what has been vouchsafed to you and accurately commit it to paper. You must put your preconceptions aside and with an open mind set down the wonders of Mars.

Percival Lowell's notebooks are full of what he thought he saw: bright and dark areas, a hint of polar cap, and canals, a planet festooned with canals. Lowell believed he was seeing a globe-girdling network of great irrigation ditches, carrying water from the melting polar caps to the thirsty inhabitants of the equatorial cities. He believed the planet to be inhabited by an older and wiser race, perhaps very different from us. He believed that the seasonal changes in the dark areas were due to the growth and decay of vegetation. He believed that Mars was, very closely, Earth-like. All in all, he believed too much.

Lowell conjured up a Mars that was ancient, arid, withered, a desert world. Still, it was an Earth-like desert. Lowell's Mars had many features in common with the American Southwest, where the Lowell Observatory was located. He imagined the Martian temperatures a little on the chilly side but still as comfortable as "the South of England." The air was thin, but there was enough oxygen to be breathable. Water was rare, but the elegant network of canals carried the life-giving fluid all over the planet.

What was in retrospect the most serious contemporary challenge to Lowell's ideas came from an unlikely source. In 1907, Alfred Russel Wallace, co-discoverer of evolution by natural selection, was asked to review one of Lowell's books. He had been an engineer in his youth and, while somewhat credulous on such

---

perhaps be found on the tops of the highest mountains above the grosser Clouds."

issues as extrasensory perception, was admirably skeptical on the habitability of Mars. Wallace showed that Lowell had erred in his calculation of the average temperatures on Mars; instead of being as temperate as the South of England, they were, with few exceptions, everywhere below the freezing point of water. There should be permafrost, a perpetually frozen subsurface. The air was much thinner than Lowell had calculated. Craters should be as abundant as on the Moon. And as for the water in the canals:

> Any attempt to make that scanty surplus [of water], by means of overflowing canals, travel across the equator into the opposite hemisphere, through such terrible desert regions and exposed to such a cloudless sky as Mr. Lowell describes, would be the work of a body of madmen rather than of intelligent beings. It may be safely asserted that not one drop of water would escape evaporation or insoak at even a hundred miles from its source.

This devastating and largely correct physical analysis was written in Wallace's eighty-fourth year. His conclusion was that life on Mars—by this he meant civil engineers with an interest in hydraulics—was impossible. He offered no opinion on microorganisms.

Despite Wallace's critique, despite the fact that other astronomers with telescopes and observing sites as good as Lowell's could find no sign of the fabled canals, Lowell's vision of Mars gained popular acceptance. It had a mythic quality as old as Genesis. Part of its appeal was the fact that the nineteenth century was an age of engineering marvels, including the construction of enormous canals: the Suez Canal, completed in 1869; the Corinth Canal, in 1893; the Panama Canal, in 1914; and, closer to home, the Great Lake locks, the barge canals of upper New York State, and the irrigation canals of the American Southwest. If Europeans and Americans could perform such feats, why not Martians?

Might there not be an even more elaborate effort by an older and wiser species, courageously battling the advance of desiccation on the red planet?

We have now sent reconnaissance satellites into orbit around Mars. The entire planet has been mapped. We have landed two automated laboratories on its surface. The mysteries of Mars have, if anything, deepened since Lowell's day. However, with pictures far more detailed than any view of Mars that Lowell could have glimpsed, we have found not a tributary of the vaunted canal network, not one lock. Lowell and Schiaparelli and others, doing visual observations under difficult seeing conditions, were misled—in part perhaps because of a predisposition to believe in life on Mars.

The observing notebooks of Percival Lowell reflect a sustained effort at the telescope over many years. They show Lowell to have been well aware of the skepticism expressed by other astronomers about the reality of the canals. They reveal a man convinced that he has made an important discovery and distressed that others have not yet understood its significance. In his notebook for 1905, for example, there is an entry on January 21: "Double canals came out by flashes, convincing of reality." In reading Lowell's notebooks I have the distinct but uncomfortable feeling that he was really seeing something. But what?

When Paul Fox of Cornell and I compared Lowell's maps of Mars with the Mariner 9 orbital imagery—sometimes with a resolution a thousand times superior to that of Lowell's Earthbound twenty-four-inch refracting telescope—we found virtually no correlation at all. It was not that Lowell's eye had strung up disconnected fine detail on the Martian surface into illusory straight lines. There was no dark mottling or crater chains in the position of most of his canals. There were no features there at all. Then how could he have drawn the same canals year after year? How could other astronomers—some of whom said they had not examined Lowell's maps closely until after their own observations—

have drawn the same canals? One of the great findings of the Mariner 9 mission to Mars was that there are time-variable streaks and splotches on the Martian surface—many connected with the ramparts of impact craters—which change with the seasons. They are due to windblown dust, the patterns varying with the seasonal winds. But the streaks do not have the character of the canals, they are not in the position of the canals, and none of them is large enough individually to be seen from the Earth in the first place. It is unlikely that there were real features on Mars even slightly resembling Lowell's canals in the first few decades of this century that have disappeared without a trace as soon as close-up spacecraft investigations became possible.

The canals of Mars seem to be some malfunction, under difficult seeing conditions, of the human hand/eye/brain combination (or at least for some humans; many other astronomers, observing with equally good instruments in Lowell's time and after, claimed there were no canals whatever). But this is hardly a comprehensive explanation, and I have the nagging suspicion that some essential feature of the Martian canal problem still remains undiscovered. Lowell always said that the regularity of the canals was an unmistakable sign that they were of intelligent origin. This is certainly true. The only unresolved question was which side of the telescope the intelligence was on.

Lowell's Martians were benign and hopeful, even a little godlike, very different from the malevolent menace posed by Wells and Welles in *The War of the Worlds*. Both sets of ideas passed into the public imagination through Sunday supplements and science fiction. I can remember as a child reading with breathless fascination the Mars novels of Edgar Rice Burroughs. I journeyed with John Carter, gentleman adventurer from Virginia, to "Barsoom," as Mars was known to its inhabitants. I followed herds of eight-legged beasts of burden, the throats. I won the hand of the lovely Dejah Thoris, Princess of Helium. I befriended a four-meter-high green fighting man named Tars Tarkas. I wandered within the spired cities and domed pumping stations of Barsoom, and along the verdant banks of the Nilosyrtis and Nepenthes canals.

Might it really be possible—in fact and not in fancy—to venture with John Carter to the Kingdom of Helium on the planet Mars? Could we venture out on a summer evening, our way illuminated by the two hurtling moons of Barsoom, for a journey of high scientific adventure? Even if all Lowell's conclusions about Mars, including the existence of the fabled canals, turned out to be bankrupt, his depiction of the planet had at least this virtue: it aroused generations of eight-year-olds, myself among them, to consider the exploration of the planets as a real possibility, to wonder if we ourselves might one day voyage to Mars. John Carter got there by standing in an open field, spreading his hands and wishing. I can remember spending many an hour in my boyhood, arms resolutely outstretched in an empty field, imploring what I believed to be Mars to transport me there. It never worked. There had to be some other way.

Like organisms, machines also have their evolutions. The rocket began, like the gunpowder that first powered it, in China where it was used for ceremonial and aesthetic purposes. Imported to Europe around the fourteenth century, it was applied to warfare, discussed in the late nineteenth century as a means of transportation to the planets by the Russian schoolteacher Konstantin Tsiolkovsky, and first developed seriously for high altitude flight by the American scientist Robert Goddard. The German V-2 military rocket of World War II employed virtually all of Goddard's innovations and culminated in 1948 in the two-stage launching of the V-2/WAC Corporal combination to the then-unprecedented altitude of 400 kilometers. In the 1950's, engineering advances organized by Sergei Korolov in the Soviet Union and Wernher von Braun in the United States, funded as delivery systems for weapons of mass destruction, led to the first artificial satellites. The pace of progress has continued to be brisk:

manned orbital flight; humans orbiting, then landing on the moon; and unmanned spacecraft outward bound throughout the solar system. Many other nations have now launched spacecraft, including Britain, France, Canada, Japan and China, the society that invented the rocket in the first place.

Among the early applications of the space rocket, as Tsiolkovsky and Goddard (who as a young man had read Wells and had been stimulated by the lectures of Percival Lowell) delighted in imagining, were an orbiting scientific station to monitor the Earth from a great height and a probe to search for life on Mars. Both these dreams have now been fulfilled.

Imagine yourself a visitor from some other and quite alien planet, approaching Earth with no preconceptions. Your view of the planet improves as you come closer and more and more fine detail stands out. Is the planet inhabited? At what point can you decide? If there are intelligent beings, perhaps they have created engineering structures that have high-contrast components on a scale of a few kilometers, structures detectable when our optical systems and distance from the Earth provide kilometer resolution. Yet at this level of detail, the Earth seems utterly barren. There is no sign of life, intelligent or otherwise, in places we call Washington, New York, Boston, Moscow, London, Paris, Berlin, Tokyo and Peking. If there are intelligent beings on Earth, they have not much modified the landscape into regular geometrical patterns at kilometer resolution.

But when we improve the resolution tenfold, when we begin to see detail as small as a hundred meters across, the situation changes. Many places on Earth seem suddenly to crystallize out, revealing an intricate pattern of squares and rectangles, straight lines and circles. These are, in fact, the engineering artifacts of intelligent beings: roads, highways, canals, farmland, city streets—a pattern disclosing the twin human passions for Euclidean geometry and territoriality. On this scale, intelligent life can be discerned in Boston and Washington and New York. And at ten-meter resolution, the degree to which the landscape has been reworked first really becomes evident. Humans have been very busy. These photos have been taken in daylight. But at twilight or during the night, other things are visible: oil-well fires in Libya and the Persian Gulf; deepwater illumination by the Japanese squid fishing fleet; the bright lights of large cities. And if, in daylight, we improve our resolution so we can make out things that are a meter across, then we begin to detect for the first time individual organisms—whales, cows, flamingos, people.

Intelligent life on Earth first reveals itself through the geometric regularity of its constructions. If Lowell's canal network really existed, the conclusion that intelligent beings inhabit Mars might be similarly compelling. For life to be detected on Mars photographically, even from Mars orbit, it must likewise have accomplished a major reworking of the surface. Technical civilizations, canal builders, might be easy to detect. But except for one or two enigmatic features, nothing of the sort is apparent in the exquisite profusion of Martian surface detail uncovered by unmanned spacecraft. However, there are many other possibilities, ranging from large plants and animals to microorganisms, to extinct forms, to a planet that is now and was always lifeless. Because Mars is farther from the Sun than is the Earth, its temperatures are considerably lower. Its air is thin, containing mostly carbon dioxide but also some molecular nitrogen and argon and very small quantities of water vapor, oxygen and ozone. Open bodies of liquid water are impossible today because the atmospheric pressure on Mars is too low to keep even cold water from rapidly boiling. There may be minute quantities of liquid water in pores and capillaries in the soil. The amount of oxygen is far too little for a human being to breathe. The ozone abundance is so small that germicidal ultraviolet radiation from the Sun strikes the Martian surface unimpeded. Could any organism survive in such an environment?

To test this question, many years ago my colleagues and I prepared chambers that simulated the Martian environment as it was then known, inoculated them with terrestrial microorganisms and waited to see if anybody survived. Such chambers are called, of course, Mars Jars. The Mars Jars cycled the temperatures within a typical Martian range from a little above the freezing point around noon to about −80°C just before dawn, in an anoxic atmosphere composed chiefly of CO_2 and N_2. Ultraviolet lamps reproduced the fierce solar flux. No liquid water was present except for very thin films wetting individual sand grains. Some microbes froze to death after the first night and were never heard from again. Others gasped and perished from lack of oxygen. Some died of thirst, and some were fried by the ultraviolet light. But there were always a fair number of varieties of terrestrial microbes that did not need oxygen; that temporarily closed up shop when the temperatures dropped too low; that hid from the ultraviolet light under pebbles or thin layers of sand. In other experiments, when small quantities of liquid water were present, the microbes actually grew. If terrestrial microbes can survive the Martian environment, how much better Martian microbes, if they exist, must do on Mars. But first we must get there.

The Soviet Union maintains an active program of unmanned planetary exploration. Every year or two the relative positions of the planets and the physics of Kepler and Newton permit the launch of a spacecraft to Mars or Venus with a minimum expenditure of energy. Since the early 1960's the U.S.S.R. has missed few such opportunities. Soviet persistence and engineering skills have eventually paid off handsomely. Five Soviet spacecraft—Veneras 8 through 12—have landed on Venus and successfully returned data from the surface, no insignificant feat in so hot, dense and corrosive a planetary atmosphere. Yet despite many attempts, the Soviet Union has never landed successfully on Mars—a place that, at least at first sight, seems more hospitable, with chilly temperatures, a much thinner atmosphere and more benign gases; with polar ice caps, clear pink skies, great sand dunes, ancient river beds, a vast rift valley, the largest volcanic construct, so far as we know, in the solar system, and balmy equatorial summer afternoons. It is a far more Earth-like world than Venus.

In 1971, the Soviet Mars 3 spacecraft entered the Martian atmosphere. According to the information automatically radioed back, it successfully deployed its landing systems during entry, correctly oriented its ablation shield downward, properly unfurled its great parachute and fired its retro-rockets near the end of its descent path. According to the data returned by Mars 3, it should have landed successfully on the red planet. But after landing, the spacecraft returned a twenty-second fragment of a featureless television picture to Earth and then mysteriously failed. In 1973, a quite similar sequence of events occurred with the Mars 6 lander, in that case the failure occurring within one second of touchdown. What went wrong?

The first illustration I ever saw of Mars 3 was on a Soviet postage stamp (denomination, 16 kopecks), which depicted the spacecraft descending through a kind of purple muck. The artist was trying, I think, to illustrate dust and high winds: Mars 3 had entered the Martian atmosphere during an enormous global dust storm. We have evidence from the U.S. Mariner 9 mission that near-surface winds of more than 140 meters per second—faster than half the speed of sound on Mars—arose in that storm. Both our Soviet colleagues and we think it likely that these high winds caught the Mars 3 spacecraft with parachute unfurled, so that it landed gently in the vertical direction but with breakneck speed in the horizontal direction. A spacecraft descending on the shrouds of a large parachute is particularly vulnerable to horizontal winds. After landing, Mars 3 may have made a few bounces, hit a boulder or other example of Martian relief, tipped over, lost the radio link with its carrier "bus" and failed.

But why did Mars 3 enter in the midst of a great dust storm? The Mars 3 mission was rigidly organized before launch. Every step it was to perform was loaded into the on-board computer before it left Earth. There was no opportunity to change the computer program, even as the extent of the great 1971 dust storm became clear. In the jargon of space exploration, the Mars 3 mission was preprogrammed, not adaptive. The failure of Mars 6 is more mysterious. There was no planet-wide storm when this spacecraft entered the Martian atmosphere, and no reason to suspect a local storm, as sometimes happens, at the landing site. Perhaps there was an engineering failure just at the moment of touchdown. Or perhaps there is something particularly dangerous about the Martian surface.

The combination of Soviet successes in landing on Venus and Soviet failures in landing on Mars naturally caused us some concern about the U.S. Viking mission, which had been informally scheduled to set one of its two descent craft gently down on the Martian surface on the Bicentennial of the United States, July 4, 1976. Like its Soviet predecessors, the Viking landing maneuver involved an ablation shield, a parachute and retro-rockets. Because the Martian atmosphere is only 1 percent as dense as the Earth's, a very large parachute, eighteen meters in diameter, was deployed to slow the spacecraft as it entered the thin air of Mars. The atmosphere is so thin that if Viking had landed at a high elevation there would not have been enough atmosphere to brake the descent adequately: it would have crashed. One requirement, therefore, was for a landing site in a low-lying region. From Mariner 9 results and ground-based radar studies, we knew many such areas.

To avoid the probable fate of Mars 3, we wanted Viking to land in a place and time at which the winds were low. Winds that would make the lander crash were probably strong enough to lift dust off the surface. If we could check that the candidate landing site was not covered with sifting, drifting dust, we would have at least a fair chance of guaranteeing that the winds were not intolerably high. This was one reason that each Viking lander was carried into Mars orbit with its orbiter, and descent delayed until the orbiter surveyed the landing site. We had discovered with Mariner 9 that characteristic changes in the bright and dark patterns on the Martian surface occur during times of high winds. We certainly would not have certified a Viking landing site as safe if orbital photographs had shown such shifting patterns. But our guarantees could not be 100 percent reliable. For example, we could imagine a landing site at which the winds were so strong that all mobile dust had already been blown away. We would then have had no indication of the high winds that might have been there. Detailed weather predictions for Mars were, of course, much less reliable than for Earth. (Indeed one of the many objectives of the Viking mission was to improve our understanding of the weather on both planets.)

Because of communication and temperature constraints, Viking could not land at high Martian latitudes. Farther poleward than about 45 or 50 degrees in both hemispheres, either the time of useful communication of the spacecraft with the Earth or the period during which the spacecraft would avoid dangerously low temperatures would have been awkwardly short.

We did not wish to land in too rough a place. The spacecraft might have tipped over and crashed, or at the least its mechanical arm, intended to acquire Martian soil samples, might have become wedged or been left waving helplessly a meter too high above the surface. Likewise, we did not want to land in places that were too soft. If the spacecraft's three landing pods had sunk deeply into a loosely packed soil, various undesirable consequences would have followed, including immobilization of the sample arm. But we did not want to land in a place that was too hard either—had we landed in a vitreous lava field, for example, with no powdery surface material, the mechanical arm would have been unable to acquire the samples vital to the projected chemistry and biology experiments.

The best photographs then available of Mars—from the Mariner 9 orbiter—showed features no smaller than 90 meters (100 yards) across. The Viking orbiter pictures improved this figure only slightly. Boulders one meter (three feet) in size were entirely invisible in such photographs, and could have had disastrous consequences for the Viking lander. Likewise, a deep, soft powder might have been indetectable photographically. Fortunately, there was a technique that enabled us to determine the roughness or softness of a candidate landing site: radar. A very rough place would scatter radar from Earth off to the sides of the beam and therefore appear poorly reflective, or radar-dark. A very soft place would also appear poorly reflective because of the many interstices between individual sand grains. While we were unable to distinguish between rough places and soft places, we did not need to make such distinctions for landing-site selection. Both, we knew, were dangerous. Preliminary radar surveys suggested that as much as a quarter to a third of the surface area of Mars might be radar-dark, and therefore dangerous for Viking. But not all of Mars can be viewed by Earth-based radar—only a swath between about 25° N and about 25° S. The Viking orbiter carried no radar system of its own to map the surface.

There were many constraints—perhaps, we feared, too many. Our landing sites had to be not too high, too windy, too hard, too soft, too rough or too close to the pole. It was remarkable that there were any places at all on Mars that simultaneously satisfied all our safety criteria. But it was also clear that our search for safe harbors had led us to landing sites that were, by and large, dull.

When each of the two Viking orbiter-lander combinations was inserted into Martian orbit, it was unalterably committed to landing at a certain *latitude* on Mars. If the low point in the orbit was at 21° Martian north latitude, the lander would touch down at 21° N, although, by waiting for the planet to turn beneath it, it could land at any *longitude* whatever. Thus the Viking science teams selected candidate latitudes for which there was more than one promising site. Viking 1 was targeted for 21° N. The prime site was in a region called Chryse (Greek for "the land of gold"), near the confluence of four sinuous channels thought to have been carved in previous epochs of Martian history by running water. The Chryse site seemed to satisfy all safety criteria. But the radar observations had been made nearby, not in the Chryse landing site itself. Radar observations of Chryse were made for the first time—because of the geometry of Earth and Mars—only a few weeks before the nominal landing date.

The candidate landing latitude for Viking 2 was 44° N; the prime site, a locale called Cydonia, chosen because, according to some theoretical arguments, there was a significant chance of small quantities of liquid water there, at least at some time during the Martian year. Since the Viking biology experiments were strongly oriented toward organisms that are comfortable in liquid water, some scientists held that the chance of Viking finding life would be substantially improved in Cydonia. On the other hand, it was argued that, on so windy a planet as Mars, microorganisms should be everywhere if they are anywhere. There seemed to be merit to both positions, and it was difficult to decide between them. What was quite clear, however, was that 44° N was completely inaccessible to radar site-certification; we had to accept a significant risk of failure with Viking 2 if it was committed to high northern latitudes. It was sometimes argued that if Viking 1 was down and working well we could afford to accept a greater risk with Viking 2. I found myself making very conservative recommendations on the fate of a billion-dollar mission. I could imagine, for example, a key instrument failure in Chryse just after an unfortunate crash landing in Cydonia. To improve the Viking options, additional landing sites, geologically very different from Chryse and Cydonia, were selected in the radar-certified region near 4° S latitude. A decision on whether Viking 2 would set down at high or at low latitude was not made until virtually the last minute, when a place with the hopeful name of Utopia, at the same latitude as Cydonia, was chosen.

For Viking 1, the original landing site seemed, after we examined orbiter photographs and late-breaking Earth-based radar data, unacceptably risky. For a while I worried that Viking 1 had been condemned, like the legendary Flying Dutchman, to wander the skies of Mars forever, never to find safe haven. Eventually we found a suitable spot, still in Chryse but far from the confluence of the four ancient channels. The delay prevented us from setting down on July 4, 1976, but it was generally agreed that a crash landing on that date would have been an unsatisfactory two hundredth birthday present for the United States. We deboosted from orbit and entered the Martian atmosphere sixteen days later.

After an interplanetary voyage of a year and a half, covering a hundred million kilometers the long way round the Sun, each orbiter/lander combination was inserted into its proper orbit about Mars; the orbiters surveyed candidate landing sites; the landers entered the Martian atmosphere on radio command and correctly oriented ablation shields, deployed parachutes, divested coverings, and fired retro-rockets. In Chryse and Utopia, for the first time in human history, spacecraft had touched down, gently and safely, on the red planet. These triumphant landings were due in considerable part to the great skill invested in their design, fabrication and testing, and to the abilities of the spacecraft controllers. But for so dangerous and mysterious a planet as Mars, there was also at least an element of luck.

Immediately after landing, the first pictures were to be returned. We knew we had chosen dull places. But we could hope. The first picture taken by the Viking 1 lander was of one of its own footpads—in case it were to sink into Martian quicksand, we wanted to know about it before the spacecraft disappeared. The picture built up, line by line, until with enormous relief we saw the footpad sitting high and dry above the Martian surface. Soon other pictures came into being, each picture element radioed individually back to Earth.

I remember being transfixed by the first lander image to show the horizon of Mars. This was not an alien world, I thought. I knew places like it in Colorado and Arizona and Nevada. There were rocks and sand drifts and a distant eminence, as natural and unselfconscious as any landscape on Earth. Mars was a *place.* I would, of course, have been surprised to see a grizzled prospector emerge from behind a dune leading his mule, but at the same time the idea seemed appropriate. Nothing remotely like it ever entered my mind in all the hours I spent examining the Venera 9 and 10 images of the Venus surface. One way or another, I knew, this was a world to which we would return.

The landscape is stark and red and lovely: boulders thrown out in the creation of a crater somewhere over the horizon, small sand dunes, rocks that have been repeatedly covered and uncovered by drifting dust, plumes of fine-grained material blown about by the winds. Where did the rocks come from? How much sand had been blown by wind? What must the previous history of the planet have been to create sheared rocks, buried boulders, polygonal gouges in the ground? What are the rocks made of? The same materials as the sand? Is the sand merely pulverized rock or something else? Why is the sky pink? What is the air made of? How fast does the wind blow? Are there marsquakes? How do the atmospheric pressure and the appearance of the landscape change with the seasons?

For every one of these questions Viking has provided definitive or at least plausible answers. The Mars revealed by the Viking mission is of enormous interest—particularly when we remember that the landing sites were chosen for their dullness. But the cameras revealed no sign of canal builders, no Barsoomian aircars or short swords, no princesses or fighting men, no thoats, no footprints, not even a cactus or a kangaroo rat. For as far as we could see, there was not a sign of life.*

* There was a brief flurry when the uppercase letter B, a putative Martian graffito, seemed to be visible on a small boulder in Chryse. But later analysis showed it to be a

Perhaps there are large lifeforms on Mars, but not in our two landing sites. Perhaps there are smaller forms in every rock and sand grain. For most of its history, those regions of the Earth not covered by water looked rather like Mars today—with an atmosphere rich in carbon dioxide, with ultraviolet light shining fiercely down on the surface through an atmosphere devoid of ozone. Large plants and animals did not colonize the land until the last 10 percent of Earth history. And yet for three billion years there were microorganisms everywhere on Earth. To look for life on Mars, we must look for microbes.

The Viking lander extends human capabilities to other and alien landscapes. By some standards, it is about as smart as a grasshopper; by others, only as intelligent as a bacterium. There is nothing demeaning in these comparisons. It took nature hundreds of millions of years to evolve a bacterium, and billions to make a grasshopper. With only a little experience in this sort of business, we are becoming fairly skillful at it. Viking has two eyes as we do, but they also work in the infrared, as ours do not; a sample arm that can push rocks, dig and acquire soil samples; a kind of finger that it puts up to measure wind speed and direction; a nose and taste buds, of a sort, with which it senses, to a much higher precision than we can, the presence of trace molecules; an interior ear with which it can detect the rumbling of marsquakes and the gentler wind-driven jiggling of the spacecraft; and a means of detecting microbes. The spacecraft has its own self-contained radioactive power source. It radios all the scientific information it acquires back to Earth. It receives instructions from Earth, so human beings can ponder the significance of the Viking results and tell the spacecraft to do something new.

---

trick of light and shadow and the human talent for pattern recognition. It also seems remarkable that the Martians should have tumbled independently to the Latin alphabet. But there was just a moment when resounding in my head was the distant echo of a word from my boyhood—Barsoom.

But what is the optimum way, given severe constraints on size, cost and power requirements, to search for microbes on Mars? We cannot—at least as yet—send microbiologists there. I once had a friend, an extraordinary microbiologist named Wolf Vishniac, of the University of Rochester, in New York. In the late 1950's, when we were just beginning to think seriously about looking for life on Mars, he found himself at a scientific meeting where an astronomer expressed amazement that the biologists had no simple, reliable, automated instrument capable of looking for microorganisms. Vishniac decided he would do something about the matter.

He developed a small device to be sent to the planets. His friends called it the Wolf Trap. It would carry a little vial of nutrient organic matter to Mars, arrange for a sample of Martian soil to be mixed with it, and observe the changing turbidity or cloudiness of the liquid as the Martian bugs (if there were any) grew (if they would). The Wolf Trap was selected along with three other microbiology experiments to go aboard the Viking landers. Two of the other three experiments also chose to send food to the Martians. The success of the Wolf Trap required that Martian bugs like liquid water. There were those who thought that Vishniac would only drown the little Martians. But the advantage of the Wolf Trap was that it laid no requirements on what the Martian microbes must do with their food. They had only to grow. All the other experiments made specific assumptions about gases that would be given off or taken in by the microbes, assumptions that were little more than guesses.

The National Aeronautics and Space Administration, which runs the United States planetary space program, is subject to frequent and unpredictable budget cuts. Only rarely are there unanticipated budget increases. NASA scientific activities have very little effective support in the government, and so science is most often the target when money needs to be taken away from NASA. In 1971 it was decided that one of the four microbiology experiments must be removed, and the Wolf Trap was off-loaded. It was a crushing disappointment for Vishniac, who had invested twelve years in its development.

Many others in his place might have stalked off the Viking Biology Team. But Vishniac was a gentle and dedicated man. He decided instead that he could best serve the search for life on Mars by voyaging to the most Mars-like environment on Earth—the dry valleys of Antarctica. Some previous investigators had examined Antarctic soil and decided that the few microbes they were able to find were not really natives of the dry valleys, but had been blown there from other, more clement environments. Recalling the Mars Jars experiments, Vishniac believed that life was tenacious and that Antarctica was perfectly consistent with microbiology. If terrestrial bugs could live on Mars, he thought, why not in Antarctica—which was by and large warmer, wetter, and had more oxygen and much less ultraviolet light. Conversely, finding life in Antarctic dry valleys would correspondingly improve, he thought, the chances of life on Mars. Vishniac believed that the experimental techniques previously used to deduce no indigenous microbes in Antarctica were flawed. The nutrients, while suitable for the comfortable environment of a university microbiology laboratory, were not designed for the arid polar wasteland.

So on November 8, 1973, Vishniac, his new microbiology equipment and a geologist companion were transported by helicopter from McMurdo Station to an area near Mount Balder, a dry valley in the Asgard range. His practice was to implant the little microbiology stations in the Antarctic soil and return about a month later to retrieve them. On December 10, 1973, he left to gather samples on Mount Balder; his departure was photographed from about three kilometers away. It was the last time anyone saw him alive. Eighteen hours later, his body was discovered at the base of a cliff of ice. He had wandered into an area not previously explored, had apparently slipped on the ice and tumbled and bounced for a distance of 150 meters. Perhaps something had caught his eye, a likely habitat for microbes, say, or a patch of green where none should be. We will never know. In the small brown notebook he was carrying that day, the last entry reads, "Station 202 retrieved. 10 December, 1973. 2230 hours. Soil temperature, −10°. Air temperature −16°." It had been a typical summer temperature for Mars.

Many of Vishniac's microbiology stations are still sitting in Antarctica. But the samples that *were* returned were examined, using his methods, by his professional colleagues and friends. A wide variety of microbes, which would have been indetectable with conventional scoring techniques, was found in essentially every site examined. A new species of yeast, apparently unique to Antarctica, was discovered in his samples by his widow, Helen Simpson Vishniac. Large rocks returned from Antarctica in that expedition, examined by Imre Friedmann, turn out to have a fascinating microbiology—one or two millimeters inside the rock, algae have colonized a tiny world in which small quantities of water are trapped and made liquid. On Mars such a place would be even more interesting, because while the visible light necessary for photosynthesis would penetrate to that depth, the germicidal ultraviolet light would be at least partially attenuated.

Because the design of space missions is finalized many years before launch, and because of Vishniac's death, the results of his Antarctic experiments did not influence the Viking design for seeking Martian life. In general, the microbiology experiments were not carried out at the low ambient Martian temperatures, and most did not provide long incubation times. They all made fairly strong assumptions about what Martian metabolism had to be like. There was no way to look for life inside the rocks.

Each Viking lander was equipped with a sample arm to acquire material from the surface and then slowly withdraw it into the innards of the spacecraft, transporting the particles on little hoppers like an electric train to five different experiments: one on the inorganic chemistry of the soil, another to look for organic molecules in the sand and dust, and three to look for microbial life. When we look for life on a planet, we are making certain assumptions. We try, as well as we can, not to assume that life elsewhere will be just like life here. But there are limits to what we can do. We know in detail only about life here. While the Viking biology experiments are a pioneering first effort, they hardly represent a definitive search for life on Mars. The results have been tantalizing, annoying, provocative, stimulating, and, at least until recently, substantially inconclusive.

Each of the three microbiology experiments asked a different kind of question, but in all cases a question about Martian metabolism. If there are microorganisms in the Martian soil, they must take in food and give off waste gases; or they must take in gases from the atmosphere and, perhaps with the aid of sunlight, convert them into useful materials. So we bring food to Mars and hope that the Martians, if there are any, will find it tasty. Then we see if any interesting new gases come out of the soil. Or we provide our own radioactively labeled gases and see if they are converted into organic matter, in which case small Martians are inferred.

By criteria established before launch, two of the three Viking microbiology experiments seem to have yielded positive results. First, when Martian soil was mixed with a sterile organic soup from Earth, something in the soil chemically broke down the soup—almost as if there were respiring microbes metabolizing a food package from Earth. Second, when gases from Earth were introduced into the Martian soil sample, the gases became chemically combined with the soil—almost as if there were photosynthesizing microbes, generating organic matter from atmospheric gases. Positive results in Martian microbiology were achieved in seven different samplings in two locales on Mars separated by 5,000 kilometers.

But the situation is complex, and the criteria of experimental success may have been inadequate. Enormous efforts were made to build the Viking microbiology experiments and test them with a variety of microbes. Very little effort was made to calibrate the experiments with plausible inorganic Martian surface materials. Mars is not the Earth. As the legacy of Percival Lowell reminds us, we can be fooled. Perhaps there is an exotic inorganic chemistry in the Martian soil that is able by itself, in the absence of Martian microbes, to oxidize foodstuffs. Perhaps there is some special inorganic, nonliving catalyst in the soil that is able to fix atmospheric gases and convert them into organic molecules.

Recent experiments suggest that this may indeed be the case. In the great Martian dust storm of 1971, spectral features of the dust were obtained by the Mariner 9 infrared spectrometer. In analyzing these spectra, O. B. Toon, J. B. Pollack and I found that certain features seem best accounted for by montmorillonite and other kinds of clay. Subsequent observations by the Viking lander support the identification of windblown clays on Mars. Now, A. Banin and J. Rishpon have found that they can reproduce some of the key features—those resembling photosynthesis as well as those resembling respiration—of the "successful" Viking microbiology experiments if in laboratory experiments they substitute such clays for the Martian soil. The clays have a complex active surface, given to absorbing and releasing gases and to catalyzing chemical reactions. It is too soon to say that all the Viking microbiology results can be explained by inorganic chemistry, but such a result would no longer be surprising. The clay hypothesis hardly excludes life on Mars, but it certainly carries us far enough to say that there is no compelling evidence for microbiology on Mars.

Even so, the results of Banin and Rishpon are of great biological importance because they show that in the absence of life there can be a kind of soil chemistry that does some of the same things life does. On the Earth before life, there may already have been chemical processes resembling respiration and photosynthesis cycling in the soil, perhaps to be incorporated by life once it arose. In addition, we know that montmorillonite clays are a potent catalyst for combining amino acids into longer chain molecules resembling proteins. The clays of the primitive Earth may have been the forge of life, and the chemistry of contemporary Mars may provide essential clues to the origin and early history of life on our planet.

The Martian surface exhibits many impact craters, each named after a person, usually a scientist. Crater Vishniac lies appropriately in the Antarctic region of Mars. Vishniac did not claim that there had to be life on Mars, merely that it was possible, and that it was extraordinarily important to know if it was there. If life on Mars exists, we will have a unique opportunity to test the generality of our kind of life. And if there is no life on Mars, a planet rather like the Earth, we must understand why—because in that case, as Vishniac stressed, we have the classic scientific confrontation of the experiment and the control.

The finding that the Viking microbiology results can be explained by clays, that they need not imply life, helps to resolve another mystery: the Viking organic chemistry experiment showed not a hint of organic matter in the Martian soil. If there is life on Mars, where are the dead bodies? No organic molecules could be found—no building blocks of proteins and nucleic acids, no simple hydrocarbons, nothing of the stuff of life on Earth. This is not necessarily a contradiction, because the Viking microbiology experiments are a thousand times more sensitive (per equivalent carbon atom) than the Viking chemistry experiments, and seem to detect organic matter synthesized in the Martian soil. But this does not leave much margin. Terrestrial soil is loaded with the organic remains of once-living organisms; Martian soil has less organic matter than the surface of the Moon. If we held to the life hypothesis, we might suppose that the dead bodies have been destroyed by the chemically reactive, oxidizing surface of Mars—like a germ in a bottle of hydrogen peroxide; or that there is life, but of a kind in which organic chemistry plays a less central role than it does in life on Earth.

But this last alternative seems to me to be special pleading: I am, reluctantly, a self-confessed carbon chauvinist. Carbon is abundant in the Cosmos. It makes marvelously complex molecules, good for life. I am also a water chauvinist. Water makes an ideal solvent system for organic chemistry to work in and stays liquid over a wide range of temperatures. But sometimes I wonder. Could my fondness for materials have something to do with the fact that I am made chiefly of them? Are we carbon- and water-based because those materials were abundant on the Earth at the time of the origin of life? Could life elsewhere—on Mars, say—be built of different stuff?

I am a collection of water, calcium and organic molecules called Carl Sagan. You are a collection of almost identical molecules with a different collective label. But is that all? Is there nothing in here but molecules? Some people find this idea somehow demeaning to human dignity. For myself, I find it elevating that our universe permits the evolution of molecular machines as intricate and subtle as we.

But the essence of life is not so much the atoms and simple molecules that make us up as the way in which they are put together. Every now and then we read that the chemicals which constitute the human body cost ninety-seven cents or ten dollars or some such figure; it is a little depressing to find our bodies valued so little. However, these estimates are for human beings reduced to our simplest possible components. We are made mostly of water, which costs almost nothing; the carbon is costed in the form of coal; the calcium in our bones as chalk; the nitrogen in our proteins as air (cheap also); the iron in our blood as rusty nails. If we did not know better, we might be tempted to take all the atoms that make us up, mix them together in a big container and stir. We can do this as much as we want. But in the end all we have is a tedious mixture of atoms. How could we have expected anything else?

Harold Morowitz has calculated what it would cost to put together the correct *molecular* constituents that make up a human being by buying the molecules from chemical supply houses. The answer turns out to be about ten million dollars, which should make us all feel a little better. But even then we could not mix those chemicals together and have a human being emerge from the jar. That is far beyond our capability and will probably be so for a very long period of time. Fortunately, there are other less expensive but still highly reliable methods of making human beings.

I think the lifeforms on many worlds will consist, by and large, of the same atoms we have here, perhaps even many of the same basic molecules, such as proteins and nucleic acids—but put together in unfamiliar ways. Perhaps organisms that float in dense planetary atmospheres will be very much like us in their atomic composition, except they might not have bones and therefore not need much calcium. Perhaps elsewhere some solvent other than water is used. Hydrofluoric acid might serve rather well, although there is not a great deal of fluorine in the Cosmos; hydrofluoric acid would do a great deal of damage to the kind of molecules that make us up, but other organic molecules, paraffin waxes, for example, are perfectly stable in its presence. Liquid ammonia would make an even better solvent system, because ammonia is very abundant in the Cosmos. But it is liquid only on worlds much colder than the Earth or Mars. Ammonia is ordinarily a gas on Earth, as water is on Venus. Or perhaps there are living things that do not have a solvent system at all—solid-state life, where there are electrical signals propagating rather than molecules floating about.

But these ideas do not rescue the notion that the Viking lander experiments indicate life on Mars. On that rather Earth-like world, with abundant carbon and water, life, if it exists, should be based on organic chemistry. The organic chemistry results, like the imaging and microbiology results, are all consistent with no life in the fine particles of Chryse and Utopia in the late 1970's. Perhaps some millimeters beneath the rocks (as in the Antarctic dry valleys), or elsewhere on the planet, or in some earlier, more clement time. But not where and when we looked.

The Viking exploration of Mars is a mission of major historical importance, the first serious search for what other kinds of life may be, the first survival of a functioning spacecraft for more than an hour or so on any other planet (Viking 1 has survived for years), the source of a rich harvest of data on the geology, seismology, mineralogy, meteorology and half a dozen other sciences of another world. How should we follow up on these spectacular advances? Some scientists want to send an automatic device that would land, acquire soil samples, and return them to Earth, where they could be examined in great detail in the large sophisticated laboratories of Earth rather than in the limited microminiaturized laboratories that we are able to send to Mars. In this way most of the ambiguities of the Viking microbiology experiments could be resolved. The chemistry and mineralogy of the soil could be determined; rocks could be broken open to search for subsurface life; hundreds of tests for organic chemistry and life could be performed, including direct microscopic examination, under a wide range of conditions. We could even use Vishniac's scoring techniques. Although it would be fairly expensive, such a mission is probably within our technological capability.

However, it carries with it a novel danger: back-contamination. If we wish on Earth to examine samples of Martian soil for microbes, we must, of course, not sterilize the samples beforehand. The point of the expedition is to bring them back alive. But what then? Might Martian microorganisms returned to Earth pose a public health hazard? The Martians of H. G. Wells and Orson

Welles, preoccupied with the suppression of Bournemouth and Jersey City, never noticed until too late that their immunological defenses were unavailing against the microbes of Earth. Is the converse possible? This is a serious and difficult issue. There may be no micromartians. If they exist, perhaps we can eat a kilogram of them with no ill effects. But we are not sure, and the stakes are high. If we wish to return unsterilized Martian samples to Earth, we must have a containment procedure that is stupefyingly reliable. There are nations that develop and stockpile bacteriological weapons. They seem to have an occasional accident, but they have not yet, so far as I know, produced global pandemics. Perhaps Martian samples *can* be safely returned to Earth. But I would want to be very sure before considering a returned-sample mission.

There is another way to investigate Mars and the full range of delights and discoveries this heterogeneous planet holds for us. My most persistent emotion in working with the Viking lander pictures was frustration at our immobility. I found myself unconsciously urging the spacecraft at least to stand on its tiptoes, as if this laboratory, designed for immobility, were perversely refusing to manage even a little hop. How we longed to poke that dune with the sample arm, look for life beneath that rock, see if that distant ridge was a crater rampart. And not so very far to the southeast, I knew, were the four sinuous channels of Chryse. For all the tantalizing and provocative character of the Viking results, I know a hundred places on Mars which are far more interesting than our landing sites. The ideal tool is a roving vehicle carrying on advanced experiments, particularly in imaging, chemistry and biology. Prototypes of such rovers are under development by NASA. They know on their own how to go over rocks, how not to fall down ravines, how to get out of tight spots. It is within our capability to land a rover on Mars that could scan its surroundings, see the most interesting place in its field of view and, by the same time tomorrow, be there. Every day a new place, a complex, winding traverse over the varied topography of this appealing planet.

Such a mission would reap enormous scientific benefits, even if there is no life on Mars. We could wander down the ancient river valleys, up the slopes of one of the great volcanic mountains, along the strange stepped terrain of the icy polar terraces, or muster a close approach to the beckoning pyramids of Mars.* Public interest in such a mission would be sizable. Every day a new set of vistas would arrive on our home television screens. We could trace the route, ponder the findings, suggest new destinations. The journey would be long, the rover obedient to radio commands from Earth. There would be plenty of time for good new ideas to be incorporated into the mission plan. A billion people could participate in the exploration of another world.

The surface area of Mars is exactly as large as the land area of the Earth. A thorough reconnaissance will clearly occupy us for centuries. But there will be a time when Mars is all explored; a time after robot aircraft have mapped it from aloft, a time after rovers have combed the surface, a time after samples have been returned safely to Earth, a time after human beings have walked the sands of Mars. What then? What shall we do with Mars?

There are so many examples of human misuse of the Earth that even phrasing this question chills me. If there is life on Mars, I believe we should do nothing with Mars. Mars then belongs to the Martians, even if the Martians are only microbes. The existence of an independent biology on a nearby planet is a treasure beyond assessing, and the preservation of that life must, I think, supersede any other possible use of Mars. However, suppose Mars is lifeless. It is not a plausible source of raw materials: the freightage from Mars to Earth would be too expensive for many centu-

* The largest are 3 kilometers across at the base, and 1 kilometer high—much larger than the pyramids of Sumer, Egypt or Mexico on Earth. They seem eroded and ancient, and are, perhaps, only small mountains, sandblasted for ages. But they warrant, I think, a careful look.

ries to come. But might we be able to live on Mars? Could we in some sense make Mars habitable?

A lovely world, surely, but there is—from our parochial point of view—much wrong with Mars, chiefly the low oxygen abundance, the absence of liquid water, and the high ultraviolet flux. (The low temperatures do not pose an insuperable obstacle, as the year-round scientific stations in Antarctica demonstrate.) All of these problems could be solved if we could make more air. With higher atmospheric pressures, liquid water would be possible. With more oxygen we might breathe the atmosphere, and ozone would form to shield the surface from solar ultraviolet radiation. The sinuous channels, stacked polar plates and other evidence suggest that Mars once had such a denser atmosphere. Those gases are unlikely to have escaped from Mars. They are, therefore, on the planet somewhere. Some are chemically combined with the surface rocks. Some are in subsurface ice. But most may be in the present polar ice caps.

To vaporize the caps, we must heat them; perhaps we could dust them with a dark powder, heating them by absorbing more sunlight, the opposite of what we do to the Earth when we destroy forests and grasslands. But the surface area of the caps is very large. The necessary dust would require 1,200 Saturn 5 rocket boosters to be transported from Earth to Mars; even then, the winds might blow the dust off the polar caps. A better way would be to devise some dark material able to make copies of itself, a little dusky machine which we deliver to Mars and which then goes about reproducing itself from indigenous materials all over the polar caps. There is a category of such machines. We call them plants. Some are very hardy and resilient. We know that at least some terrestrial microbes can survive on Mars. What is necessary is a program of artificial selection and genetic engineering of dark plants—perhaps lichens—that could survive the much more severe Martian environment. If such plants could be bred, we might imagine them being seeded on the vast expanse of the

Martian polar ice caps, taking root, spreading, blackening the ice caps, absorbing sunlight, heating the ice, and releasing the ancient Martian atmosphere from its long captivity. We might even imagine a kind of Martian Johnny Appleseed, robot or human, roaming the frozen polar wastes in an endeavor that benefits only the generations of humans to come.

This general concept is called terraforming: the changing of an alien landscape into one more suitable for human beings. In thousands of years humans have managed to perturb the global temperature of the Earth by only about one degree through greenhouse and albedo changes, although at the present rate of burning fossil fuels and destroying forests and grasslands we can now change the global temperature by another degree in only a century or two. These and other considerations suggest that a time scale for a significant terraforming of Mars is probably hundreds to thousands of years. In a future time of greatly advanced technology we might wish not only to increase the total atmospheric pressure and make liquid water possible but also to carry liquid water from the melting polar caps to the warmer equatorial regions. There is, of course, a way to do it. We would build canals.

The melting surface and subsurface ice would be transported by a great canal network. But this is precisely what Percival Lowell, not a hundred years ago, mistakenly proposed was in fact happening on Mars. Lowell and Wallace both understood that the comparative inhospitability of Mars was due to the scarcity of water. If only a network of canals existed, the lack would be remedied, the habitability of Mars would become plausible. Lowell's observations were made under extremely difficult seeing conditions. Others, like Schiaparelli, had already observed something like the canals; they were called *canali* before Lowell began his lifelong love affair with Mars. Human beings have a demonstrated talent for self-deception when their emotions are stirred, and there are few notions more stirring than the idea of a neighboring planet inhabited by intelligent beings.

The power of Lowell's idea may, just possibly, make it a kind of premonition. His canal network was built by Martians. Even this may be an accurate prophecy: If the planet ever is terraformed, it will be done by human beings whose permanent residence and planetary affiliation is Mars. The Martians will be us.

CHAPTER VI
TRAVELERS' TALES

Do there exist many worlds, or is there but a single world? This is one of the most noble and exalted questions in the study of Nature.

—Albertus Magnus, thirteenth century

We may mount from this dull Earth, and viewing it from on high, consider whether Nature has laid out all her cost and finery upon this small speck of Dirt. So, like Travellers into other distant countries, we shall be better able to judge of what's done at home, know how to make a true estimate of, and set its own value upon every thing. We shall be less apt to admire what this World calls great, shall nobly despise those Trifles the generality of Men set their Affections on, when we know that there are a multitude of such Earths inhabited and adorn'd as well as our own.

—Christiaan Huygens, *The Celestial Worlds Discovered*, c. 1690

This is the time when humans have begun to sail the sea of space. The modern ships that ply the Keplerian trajectories to the planets are unmanned. They are beautifully constructed, semi-intelligent robots exploring unknown worlds. Voyages to the outer solar system are controlled from a single place on the planet Earth, the Jet Propulsion Laboratory (JPL) of the National Aeronautics and Space Administration in Pasadena, California.

On July 9, 1979, a spacecraft called Voyager 2 encountered the Jupiter system. It had been almost two years sailing through interplanetary space. The ship is made of millions of separate parts assembled redundantly, so that if some component fails, others will take over its responsibilities. The spacecraft weighs 0.9 tons and would fill a large living room. Its mission takes it so far from the sun that it cannot be powered by solar energy, as other spacecraft are. Instead, Voyager relies on a small nuclear power plant, drawing hundreds of watts from the radioactive decay of a pellet of plutonium. Its three integrated computers and most of its housekeeping functions—for example, its temperature-control system—are localized in its middle. It receives commands from Earth and radios its findings back to Earth through a large antenna, 3.7 meters in diameter. Most of its scientific instruments are on a scan platform, which tracks Jupiter or one of its moons as the spacecraft hurtles past. There are many scientific instruments—ultraviolet and infrared spectrometers, devices to measure charged particles and magnetic fields and the radio emission from Jupiter—but the most productive have been the two television cameras, designed to take tens of thousands of pictures of the planetary islands in the outer solar system.

Jupiter is surrounded by a shell of invisible but extremely dangerous high-energy charged particles. The spacecraft must pass through the outer edge of this radiation belt to examine Jupiter and its moons close up, and to continue its mission to Saturn and beyond. But the charged particles can damage the delicate instruments and fry the electronics. Jupiter is also surrounded by a ring of solid debris, discovered four months earlier by Voyager 1, which Voyager 2 had to traverse. A collision with a small boulder could have sent the spacecraft tumbling wildly out of control, its antenna unable to lock on the Earth, its data lost forever. Just before encounter, the mission controllers were restive. There were some alarms and emergencies, but the combined intelligence of the humans on Earth and the robot in space circumvented disaster.

Launched on August 20, 1977, it moved on an arcing trajectory past the orbit of Mars, through the asteroid belt, to approach the Jupiter system and thread its way past the planet and among its fourteen or so moons. Voyager's passage by Jupiter accelerated it toward a close encounter with Saturn. Saturn's gravity will propel it on to Uranus. After Uranus it will plunge on past Neptune, leaving the solar system, becoming an interstellar spacecraft, fated to roam forever the great ocean between the stars.

These voyages of exploration and discovery are the latest in a long series that have characterized and distinguished human history. In the fifteenth and sixteenth centuries you could travel from Spain to the Azores in a few days, the same time it takes us now to cross the channel from the Earth to the Moon. It took then a few months to traverse the Atlantic Ocean and reach what was called the New World, the Americas. Today it takes a few months to cross the ocean of the inner solar system and make planet-fall on Mars or Venus, which are truly and literally new worlds awaiting us. In the seventeenth and eighteenth centuries you could travel from Holland to China in a year or two, the time it has taken Voyager to travel from Earth to Jupiter.* The annual costs were, relatively, more then than now, but in both cases less than 1 percent of the appropriate Gross National Product. Our present spaceships, with their robot crews, are the harbingers, the vanguards of future human expeditions to the planets. We have traveled this way before.

The fifteenth through seventeenth centuries represent a major

* Or, to make a different comparison, a fertilized egg takes as long to wander from the fallopian tubes and implant itself in the uterus as Apollo 11 took to journey to the Moon; and as long to develop into a full-term infant as Viking took on its trip to Mars. The normal human lifetime is longer than Voyager will take to venture beyond the orbit of Pluto.

turning point in our history. It then became clear that we could venture to all parts of our planet. Plucky sailing vessels from half a dozen European nations dispersed to every ocean. There were many motivations for these journeys: ambition, greed, national pride, religious fanaticism, prison pardons, scientific curiosity, the thirst for adventure and the unavailability of suitable employment in Estremadura. These voyages worked much evil as well as much good. But the net result has been to bind the Earth together, to decrease provincialism, to unify the human species and to advance powerfully our knowledge of our planet and ourselves.

Emblematic of the epoch of sailing-ship exploration and discovery is the revolutionary Dutch Republic of the seventeenth century. Having recently declared its independence from the powerful Spanish Empire, it embraced more fully than any other nation of its time the European Enlightenment. It was a rational, orderly, creative society. But because Spanish ports and vessels were closed to Dutch shipping, the economic survival of the tiny republic depended on its ability to construct, man and deploy a great fleet of commercial sailing vessels.

The Dutch East India Company, a joint governmental and private enterprise, sent ships to the far corners of the world to acquire rare commodities and resell them at a profit in Europe. Such voyages were the life blood of the Republic. Navigational charts and maps were classified as state secrets. Ships often embarked with sealed orders. Suddenly the Dutch were present all over the planet. The Barents Sea in the Arctic Ocean and Tasmania in Australia are named after Dutch sea captains. These expeditions were not merely commercial exploitations, although there was plenty of that. There were powerful elements of scientific adventure and the zest for discovery of new lands, new plants and animals, new people; the pursuit of knowledge for its own sake.

The Amsterdam Town Hall reflects the confident and secular self-image of seventeenth-century Holland. It took shiploads of marble to build. Constantijn Huygens, a poet and diplomat of the time, remarked that the Town Hall dispelled "the Gothic squint and squalor." In the Town Hall to this day, there is a statue of Atlas supporting the heavens, festooned with constellations. Beneath is Justice, brandishing a golden sword and scales, standing between Death and Punishment, and treading underfoot Avarice and Envy, the gods of the merchants. The Dutch, whose economy was based on private profit, nevertheless understood that the unrestrained pursuit of profit posed a threat to the nation's soul.

A less allegorical symbol may be found under Atlas and Justice, on the floor of the Town Hall. It is a great inlaid map, dating from the late seventeenth or early eighteenth centuries, reaching from West Africa to the Pacific Ocean. The whole world was Holland's arena. And on this map, with disarming modesty the Dutch omitted themselves, using only the old Latin name Belgium for their part of Europe.

In a typical year many ships set sail halfway around the world. Down the west coast of Africa, through what they called the Ethiopian Sea, around the south coast of Africa, within the Straits of Madagascar, and on past the southern tip of India they sailed, to one major focus of their interests, the Spice Islands, present-day Indonesia. Some expeditions journeyed from there to a land named New Holland, and today called Australia. A few ventured through the Straits of Malacca, past the Philippines, to China. We know from a mid-seventeenth-century account of an "Embassy from the East India Company of the United Provinces of the Netherlands, to the Grand Tartar, Cham, Emperor of China." The Dutch burgers, ambassadors and sea captains stood wide-eyed in amazement, face to face with another civilization in the Imperial City of Peking.*

Never before or since has Holland been the world power it was

* We even know what gifts they brought the Court. The Empress was presented with "six little chests of divers pictures." And the Emperor received "two fardels of cinnamon."

then. A small country, forced to live by its wits, its foreign policy contained a strong pacifist element. Because of its tolerance for unorthodox opinions, it was a haven for intellectuals who were refugees from censorship and thought control elsewhere in Europe—much as the United States benefited enormously in the 1930's by the exodus of intellectuals from the Nazi-dominated Europe. So seventeenth-century Holland was the home of the great Jewish philosopher Spinoza, whom Einstein admired; of Descartes, a pivotal figure in the history of mathematics and philosophy; and of John Locke, a political scientist who influenced a group of philosophically inclined revolutionaries named Paine, Hamilton, Adams, Franklin and Jefferson. Never before or since has Holland been graced by such a galaxy of artists and scientists, philosophers and mathematicians. This was the time of the master painters Rembrandt and Vermeer and Frans Halls; of Leeuwenhoek, the inventor of the microscope; of Grotius, the founder of international law, of Willebrord Snellius, who discovered the law of the refraction of light.

In the Dutch tradition of encouraging freedom of thought, the University of Leiden offered a professorship to an Italian scientist named Galileo, who had been forced by the Catholic Church under threat of torture to recant his heretical view that the Earth moved about the Sun and not vice versa.* Galileo had close ties with Holland, and his first astronomical telescope was an improvement of a spyglass of Dutch design. With it he discovered sunspots, the phases of Venus, the craters of the Moon, and the four large moons of Jupiter now called, after him, the Galilean satellites. Galileo's own description of his ecclesiastical travails is contained in a letter he wrote in the year 1615 to the Grand Duchess Christina:

* In 1979 Pope John Paul II cautiously proposed reversing the condemnation of Galileo done 346 years earlier by the "Holy Inquisition."

> Some years ago as Your Serene Highness well knows, I discovered in the heavens many things that had not been seen before our own age. The novelty of these things, as well as some consequences which followed from them in contradiction to the physical notions commonly held among academic philosophers, stirred up against me no small number of professors [many of them ecclesiastics]—as if I had placed these things in the sky with my own hands in order to upset Nature and overturn the sciences. They seemed to forget that the increase of known truths stimulates the investigation, establishment, and growth of the arts.*

The connection between Holland as an exploratory power and Holland as an intellectual and cultural center was very strong. The improvement of sailing ships encouraged technology of all kinds. People enjoyed working with their hands. Inventions were prized. Technological advance required the freest possible pursuit of knowledge, so Holland became the leading publisher and bookseller in Europe, translating works written in other languages and permitting the publication of works proscribed elsewhere. Adventures into exotic lands and encounters with strange

---

* The courage of Galileo (and Kepler) in promoting the heliocentric hypothesis was not evident in the actions of others, even those residing in less fanatically doctrinal parts of Europe. For example, in a letter dated April 1634, René Descartes, then living in Holland, wrote:

> Doubtless you know that Galileo was recently censured by the Inquisitors of the Faith, and that his views about the movement of the Earth were condemned as heretical. I must tell you that all the things I explained in my treatise, which included the doctrine of the movement of the Earth, were so interdependent that it is enough to discover that one of them is false to know that all the arguments I was using are unsound. Though I thought they were based on very certain and evident proofs, I would not wish, for anything in the world, to maintain them against the authority of the Church. . . . I desire to live in peace and to continue the life I have begun under the motto *to live well you must live unseen*.

societies shook complacency, challenged thinkers to reconsider the prevailing wisdom and showed that ideas that had been accepted for thousands of years—for example, on geography—were fundamentally in error. In a time when kings and emperors ruled much of the world, the Dutch Republic was governed, more than any other nation, by the people. The openness of the society and its encouragement of the life of the mind, its material well-being and its commitment to the exploration and utilization of new worlds generated a joyful confidence in the human enterprise.*

In Italy, Galileo had announced other worlds, and Giordano Bruno had speculated on other lifeforms. For this they had been made to suffer brutally. But in Holland, the astronomer Christiaan Huygens, who believed in both, was showered with honors. His father was Constantijn Huygens, a master diplomat of the age, a litterateur, poet, composer, musician, close friend and translator of the English poet John Donne, and the head of an archetypical great family. Constantijn admired the painter Rubens, and "discovered" a young artist named Rembrandt van Rijn, in several of whose works he subsequently appears. After their first meeting, Descartes wrote of him: "I could not believe that a single mind could occupy itself with so many things, and equip itself so well in all of them." The Huygens home was filled with goods from all over the world. Distinguished thinkers from other nations were frequent guests. Growing up in this environment, the young Christiaan Huygens became simultaneously adept in languages, drawing, law, science, engineering, mathematics and music. His interests and allegiances were broad. "The world is my country," he said, "science my religion."

* This exploratory tradition may account for the fact that Holland has, to this day, produced far more than its per capita share of distinguished astronomers, among them Gerard Peter Kuiper, who in the 1940's and 1950's was the world's only full-time planetary astrophysicist. The subject was then considered by most professional astronomers to be at least slightly disreputable, tainted with Lowellian excesses. I am grateful to have been Kuiper's student.

Light was a motif of the age: the symbolic enlightenment of freedom of thought and religion, of geographical discovery; the light that permeated the paintings of the time, particularly the exquisite work of Vermeer; and light as an object of scientific inquiry, as in Snell's study of refraction, Leeuwenhoek's invention of the microscope and Huygens' own wave theory of light.* These were all connected activities, and their practitioners mingled freely. Vermeer's interiors are characteristically filled with nautical artifacts and wall maps. Microscopes were drawing-room curiosities. Leeuwenhoek was the executor of Vermeer's estate and a frequent visitor at the Huygens home in Hofwijck.

Leeuwenhoek's microscope evolved from the magnifying glasses employed by drapers to examine the quality of cloth. With it he discovered a universe in a drop of water: the microbes, which he described as "animalcules" and thought "cute." Huygens had contributed to the design of the first microscopes and himself made many discoveries with them. Leeuwenhoek and Huygens were among the first people ever to see human sperm cells, a prerequisite for understanding human reproduction. To explain how microorganisms slowly develop in water previously

* Isaac Newton admired Christiaan Huygens and thought him "the most elegant mathematician" of their time, and the truest follower of the mathematical tradition of the ancient Greeks—then, as now, a great compliment. Newton believed, in part because shadows had sharp edges, that light behaved as if it were a stream of tiny particles. He thought that red light was composed of the largest particles and violet the smallest. Huygens argued that instead light behaved as if it were a wave propagating in a vacuum, as an ocean wave does in the sea—which is why we talk about the wavelength and frequency of light. Many properties of light, including diffraction, are naturally explained by the wave theory, and in subsequent years Huygens' view carried the day. But in 1905, Einstein showed that the particle theory of light could explain the photoelectric effect, the ejection of electrons from a metal upon exposure to a beam of light. Modern quantum mechanics combines both ideas, and it is customary today to think of light as behaving in some circumstances as a beam of particles and in others as a wave. This wave-particle dualism may not correspond readily to our common-sense notions, but it is in excellent accord with what experiments have shown light really does. There is something mysterious and stirring in this marriage of opposites, and it is fitting that Newton and Huygens, bachelors both, were the parents of our modern understanding of the nature of light.

sterilized by boiling, Huygens proposed that they were small enough to float through the air and reproduced on alighting in water. Thus he established an alternative to spontaneous generation—the notion that life could rise, in fermenting grape juice or rotting meat, entirely independent of preexisting life. It was not until the time of Louis Pasteur, two centuries later, that Huygens' speculation was proved correct. The Viking search for life on Mars can be traced in more ways than one back to Leeuwenhoek and Huygens. They are also the grandfathers of the germ theory of disease, and therefore of much of modern medicine. But they had no practical motives in mind. They were merely tinkering in a technological society.

The microscope and telescope, both developed in early seventeenth-century Holland, represent an extension of human vision to the realms of the very small and the very large. Our observations of atoms and galaxies were launched in this time and place. Christiaan Huygens loved to grind and polish lenses for astronomical telescopes and constructed one five meters long. His discoveries with the telescope would by themselves have ensured his place in the history of human accomplishment. In the footsteps of Eratosthenes, he was the first person to measure the size of another planet. He was also the first to speculate that Venus is completely covered with clouds; the first to draw a surface feature on the planet Mars (a vast dark windswept slope called Syrtis Major); and by observing the appearance and disappearance of such features as the planet rotated, the first to determine that the Martian day was, like ours, roughly twenty-four hours long. He was the first to recognize that Saturn was surrounded by a system of rings which nowhere touches the planet.* And he was the discoverer of Titan, the largest moon of Saturn and, as we now know,

* Galileo discovered the rings, but had no idea what to make of them. Through his early astronomical telescope, they seemed to be two projections symmetrically attached to Saturn, resembling, he said in some bafflement, ears.

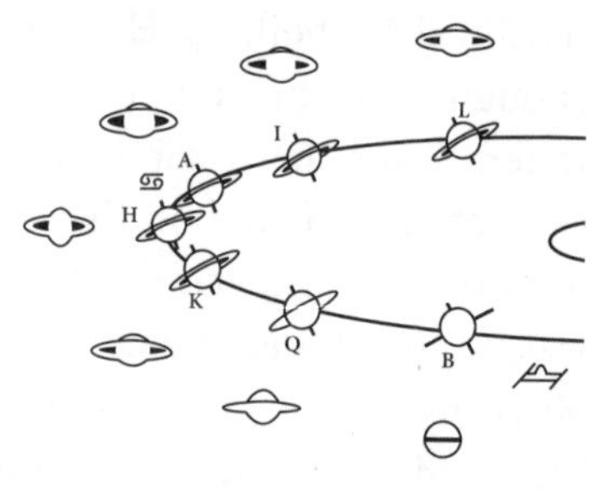

A detail from Christiaan Huygens' *Systema Saturnium*, published in 1659. Shown is his (correct) explanation of the changing appearance of the rings of Saturn over the years as the relative geometry of Earth and Saturn changes. In position B the comparatively paper-thin rings disappear as they are seen edge-on. In position A they display their maximum extent visible from Earth, the configuration that caused Galileo, with a significantly inferior telescope, considerable consternation.

the largest moon in the solar system—a world of extraordinary interest and promise. Most of these discoveries he made in his twenties. He also thought astrology was nonsense.

Huygens did much more. A key problem for marine navigation in this age was the determination of a longitude. Latitude could easily be determined by the stars—the farther south you were, the more southern constellations you could see. But longitude required precise timekeeping. An accurate shipboard clock would tell the time in your home port; the rising and setting of the Sun and stars would specify the local shipboard time; and the difference between the two would yield your longitude. Huygens invented the pendulum clock (its principle had been discovered earlier by Galileo), which was then employed, although not fully successfully, to calculate position in the midst of the great ocean. His efforts introduced an unprecedented accuracy in astronomical and other nautical clocks. He invented the spiral balance spring still used in some watches today; made fundamental contributions to mechanics—e.g., the calculation of centrifugal force—and, from a study of the game of dice, to the theory of probability. He improved the air pump, which was later to revolutionize the mining industry, and the "magic lantern," the ancestor of the slide projector. He also invented something called the "gunpowder engine," which influenced the development of another machine, the steam engine.

Huygens was delighted that the Copernican view of the Earth as a planet in motion around the Sun was widely accepted even by the ordinary people in Holland. Indeed, he said, Copernicus was acknowledged by all astronomers except those who "were a bit slow-witted or under the superstitions imposed by merely human authority." In the Middle Ages, Christian philosophers were fond of arguing that, since the heavens circle the Earth once every day, they can hardly be infinite in extent; and therefore an infinite number of worlds, or even a large number of them (or even one other of them), is impossible. The discovery that the Earth is turning rather than the sky moving had important implications for the uniqueness of the Earth and the possibility of life elsewhere. Copernicus held that not just the solar system but the entire universe was heliocentric, and Kepler denied that the stars have planetary systems. The first person to make explicit the idea of a large—indeed, an infinite—number of other worlds in orbit about other suns seems to have been Giordano Bruno. But others thought that the plurality of worlds followed immediately from the ideas of Copernicus and Kepler and found themselves aghast. In the early seventeenth century, Robert Merton contended that the heliocentric hypothesis implied a multitude of other planetary systems, and that this was an argument of the sort called reductio ad absurdum (Appendix 1), demonstrating the error of the initial assumption. He wrote, in an argument which may once have seemed withering,

> For if the firmament be of such an incomparable bigness, as these Copernical giants will have it . . . , so vast and full of innumerable stars, as being infinite in extent . . . why may we not suppose . . . those infinite stars visible in the firmament to be so many suns, with particular fixed centers; to have likewise their subordinate planets, as the sun hath his dancing still around him? . . . And so, in consequence, there are infinite habitable worlds;

> what hinders? . . . these and suchlike insolent and bold attempts, prodigious paradoxes, inferences must needs follow, if it once be granted which . . . Kepler . . . and others maintain of the Earth's motion.

But the Earth does move. Merton, if he lived today, would be obliged to deduce "infinite, habitable worlds." Huygens did not shrink from this conclusion; he embraced it gladly: Across the sea of space the stars are other suns. By analogy with our solar system, Huygens reasoned that those stars should have their own planetary systems and that many of these planets might be inhabited: "Should we allow the planets nothing but vast deserts . . . and deprive them of all those creatures that more plainly bespeak their divine architect, we should sink them below the Earth in beauty and dignity, a thing very unreasonable."*

These ideas were set forth in an extraordinary book bearing the triumphant title *The Celestial Worlds Discover'd: Conjectures Concerning the Inhabitants, Plants and Productions of the Worlds in the Planets.* Composed shortly before Huygens died in 1690, the work was admired by many, including Czar Peter the Great, who made it the first product of Western science to be published in Russia. The book is in large part about the nature or environments of the planets. Among the figures in the finely rendered first edition is one in which we see, to scale, the Sun and the giant planets Jupiter and Saturn. They are, comparatively, rather small. There is also an etching of Saturn next to the Earth: Our planet is a tiny circle.

By and large Huygens imagined the environments and inhabitants of other planets to be rather like those of seventeenth-century Earth. He conceived of "planetarians" whose "whole

* A few others had held similar opinions. In his *Harmonice Mundi* Kepler remarked "it was Tycho Brahe's opinion concerning that bare wilderness of globes that it does not exist fruitlessly but is filled with inhabitants."

Bodies, and every part of them, may be quite distinct and different from ours . . . 'tis a very ridiculous opinion . . . that it is impossible a rational Soul should dwell in any other shape than ours." You could be smart, he was saying, even if you looked peculiar. But he then went on to argue that they would not look *very* peculiar—that they must have hands and feet and walk upright, that they would have writing and geometry, and that Jupiter has its four Galilean satellites to provide a navigational aid for the sailors in the Jovian oceans. Huygens was, of course, a citizen of his time. Who of us is not? He claimed science as his religion and then argued that the planets must be inhabited because otherwise God had made worlds for nothing. Because he lived before Darwin, his speculations about extraterrestrial life are innocent of the evolutionary perspective. But he was able to develop on observational grounds something akin to the modern cosmic perspective:

> What a wonderful and Amazing scheme have we here of the magnificant vastness of the universe . . . So many Suns, so many Earths . . . and every one of them stock'd with so many Herbs, Trees, and Animals, adorn'd with so many Seas and Mountains! . . . And how must our Wonder and Admiration be increased when we consider the prodigious Distance and Multitude of the Stars.

The Voyager spacecraft are the lineal descendants of those sailing-ship voyages of exploration, and of the scientific and speculative tradition of Christiaan Huygens. The Voyagers are caravels bound for the stars, and on the way exploring those worlds that Huygens knew and loved so well.

One of the main commodities returned on those voyages of centuries ago were travelers' tales,* stories of alien lands and ex-

* Such tales are an ancient human tradition; many of them have had, from the beginning of exploration, a cosmic motif. For example, the fifteenth-century explora-

otic creatures that evoked our sense of wonder and stimulated future exploration. There had been accounts of mountains that reached the sky; of dragons and sea monsters; of everyday eating utensils made of gold; of a beast with an arm for a nose; of people who thought the doctrinal disputes among Protestants, Catholics, Jews and Muslims to be silly; of a black stone that burned; of headless humans with mouths in their chests; of sheep that grew on trees. Some of these stories were true, some were lies. Others had a kernel of truth, misunderstood or exaggerated by the explorers or their informants. In the hands of Voltaire, say, or Jonathan Swift, these accounts stimulated a new perspective on European society, forcing a reconsideration of that insular world.

Modern Voyagers also return travelers' tales, tales of a world shattered like a crystal sphere; a globe where the ground is covered, pole to pole, with what looks like a network of cobwebs; tiny moons shaped like potatoes; a world with an underground ocean; a land that smells of rotten eggs and looks like a pizza pie, with lakes of molten sulfur and volcanic eruptions ejecting smoke directly into space; a planet called Jupiter that dwarfs our own—so large that 1,000 Earths would fit within it.

The Galilean satellites of Jupiter are each almost as big as the planet Mercury. We can measure their sizes and masses and so calculate their density, which tells us something about the composition of their interiors. We find that the inner two, Io and Europa, have a density as high as rock. The outer two, Ganymede and Callisto, have a much lower density, halfway between rock and ice. But the mixture of ice and rocks within these outer moons must contain, as do rocks on Earth, traces of radioactive minerals, which heat their surroundings. There is no effective

---

tions of Indonesia, Sri Lanka, India, Arabia and Africa by the Ming Dynasty Chinese were described by Fei Hsin, one of the participants, in a picture book prepared for the Emperor, as "The Triumphant Visions of the Starry Raft." Unfortunately, the pictures—although not the text—have been lost.

way for this heat, accumulated over billions of years, to reach the surface and be lost to space, and the radioactivity inside Ganymede and Callisto must therefore melt their icy interiors. We anticipate underground oceans of slush and water in these moons, a hint, before we have ever seen the surfaces of the Galilean satellites close up, that they may be very different one from another. When we do look closely, through the eyes of Voyager, this prediction is confirmed. They do not resemble each other. They are different from any worlds we have ever seen before.

The Voyager 2 spacecraft will never return to Earth. But its scientific findings, its epic discoveries, its travelers' tales, do return. Take July 9, 1979, for instance. At 8:04 Pacific Standard Time on this morning, the first pictures of a new world, called Europa after an old one, were received on Earth.

How does a picture from the outer solar system get to us? Sunlight shines on Europa in its orbit around Jupiter and is reflected back to space, where some of it strikes the phosphors of the Voyager television cameras, generating an image. The image is read by the Voyager computers, radioed back across the immense intervening distance of half a billion kilometers to a radio telescope, a ground station on the Earth. There is one in Spain, one in the Mojave Desert of Southern California and one in Australia. (On that July morning in 1979 it was the one in Australia that was pointed toward Jupiter and Europa.) It then passes the information via a communications satellite in Earth orbit to Southern California, where it is transmitted by a set of microwave relay towers to a computer at the Jet Propulsion Laboratory, where it is processed. The picture is fundamentally like a newspaper wirephoto, made of perhaps a million individual dots, each a different shade of gray, so fine and close together that at a distance the constituent dots are invisible. We see only their cumulative effect. The information from the spacecraft specifies how bright or dark each dot is to be. After processing, the dots are then stored on a magnetic disc, something like a phonograph record. There are some eighteen thousand photographs taken in the Jupiter system by Voyager 1 that are stored on such magnetic discs, and an equivalent number for Voyager 1. Finally the end product of this remarkable set of links and relays is a thin piece of glossy paper, in this case showing the wonders of Europa, recorded, processed and examined for the first time in human history on July 9, 1979.

What we saw on such pictures was absolutely astonishing. Voyager 1 obtained excellent imagery of the other three Galilean satellites of Jupiter. But not Europa. It was left for Voyager 2 to acquire the first close-up pictures of Europa, where we see things that are only a few kilometers across. At first glance, the place looks like nothing so much as the canal network that Percival Lowell imagined to adorn Mars, and that, we now know from space vehicle exploration, does not exist at all. We see on Europa an amazing, intricate network of intersecting straight and curved lines. Are they ridges—that is, raised? Are they troughs—that is, depressed? How are they made? Are they part of a global tectonic system, produced perhaps by fracturing of an expanding or contracting planet? Are they connected with plate tectonics on the Earth? What light do they shed on the other satellites of the Jovian system? At the moment of discovery, the vaunted technology has produced something astonishing. But it remains for another device, the human brain, to figure it out. Europa turns out to be as smooth as a billiard ball despite the network of lineations. The absence of impact craters may be due to the heating and flow of surface ice upon impact. The lines are grooves or cracks, their origin still being debated long after the mission.

If the Voyager missions were manned, the captain would keep a ship's log, and the log, a combination of the events of Voyagers 1 and 2, might read something like this:

Day 1 After much concern about provisions and instruments, which seemed to be malfunctioning, we successfully lifted off from Cape Canaveral on our long journey to the planets and the stars.

Day 2 A problem in the deployment of the boom that supports the science scan platform. If the problem is not solved, we will lose most of our pictures and other scientific data.

Day 13 We have looked back and taken the first photograph ever obtained of the Earth and Moon as worlds together in space. A pretty pair.

Day 150 Engines fired nominally for a mid-course trajectory correction.

Day 170 Routine housekeeping functions. An uneventful few months.

Day 185 Successful calibration images taken of Jupiter.

Day 207 Boom problem solved, but failure of main radio transmitter. We have moved to back-up transmitter. If it fails, no one on Earth will ever hear from us again.

Day 215 We cross the orbit of Mars. That planet itself is on the other side of the Sun.

Day 295 We enter the asteroid belt. There are many large, tumbling boulders here, the shoals and reefs of space. Most of them are uncharted. Lookouts posted. We hope to avoid a collision.

Day 475 We safely emerge from the main asteroid belt, happy to have survived.

Day 570 Jupiter is becoming prominent in the sky. We can now make out finer detail on it than the largest telescopes on Earth have ever obtained.

Day 615 The colossal weather systems and changing clouds of Jupiter, spinning in space before us, have us hypnotized. The planet is immense. It is more than twice as massive as all the other planets put together. There are no mountains, valleys, volcanoes, rivers; no boundaries between land and air; just a vast ocean of dense gas and floating clouds—a world without a surface. Everything we can see on Jupiter is floating in its sky.

Day 630 The weather on Jupiter continues to be spectacular. This ponderous world spins on its axis in less than ten hours. Its atmospheric motions are driven by the rapid rotation, by sunlight and by the heat bubbling and welling up from its interior.

Day 640 The cloud patterns are distinctive and gorgeous. They remind us a little of Van Gogh's *Starry Night,* or works by William Blake or Edvard Munch. But only a little. No artist ever painted like this because none of them ever left our planet. No painter trapped on Earth ever imagined a world so strange and lovely.

We observe the multicolored belts and bands of Jupiter close up. The white bands are thought to be high clouds, probably ammonia crystals; the brownish-colored belts, deeper and hotter places where the atmosphere is sinking. The blue places are apparently deep holes in the overlying clouds through which we see clear sky.

We do not know the reason for the reddish-brown color of Jupiter. Perhaps it is due to the chemistry of phosphorus or sulfur. Perhaps it is due to complex brightly colored organic molecules produced when ultraviolet light from the Sun breaks down the methane, ammonia, and water in the Jovian atmosphere and the molecular fragments recombine. In that case, the colors of Jupiter speak to us of chemical events that four billion years ago back on Earth led to the origin of life.

Day 647 The Great Red Spot. A great column of gas

reaching high above the adjacent clouds, so large that it could hold half a dozen Earths. Perhaps it is red because it is carrying up to view the complex molecules produced or concentrated at greater depth. It may be a great storm system a million years old.

Day 650 Encounter. A day of wonders. We successfully negotiate the treacherous radiation belts of Jupiter with only one instrument, the photopolarimeter, damaged. We accomplish the ring plane crossing and suffer no collisions with the particles and boulders of the newly discovered rings of Jupiter. And wonderful images of Amalthea, a tiny, red, oblong world that lives in the heart of the radiation belt; of multicolored Io; of the linear markings on Europa; the cobwebby features of Ganymede; the great multi-ringed basin on Callisto. We round Callisto and pass the orbit of Jupiter 13, the outermost of the planet's known moons. We are outward bound.

Day 662 Our particle and field detectors indicate that we have left the Jovian radiation belts. The planet's gravity has boosted our speed. We are free of Jupiter at last and sail again the sea of space.

Day 874 A loss of the ship's lock on the star Canopus—in the lore of constellations the rudder of a sailing vessel. It is our rudder too, essential for the ship's orientation in the dark of space, to find our way through this unexplored part of the cosmic ocean. Canopus lock reacquired. The optical sensors seem to have mistaken Alpha and Beta Centauri for Canopus. Next port of call, two years hence: the Saturn system.

Of all the travelers' tales returned by Voyager, my favorites concern the discoveries made on the innermost Galilean satellite,

Io.* Before Voyager, we were aware of something strange about Io. We could resolve few features on its surface, but we knew it was red—extremely red, redder than Mars, perhaps the reddest object in the solar system. Over a period of years something seemed to be changing on it, in infrared light and perhaps in its radar reflection properties. We also know that partially surrounding Jupiter in the orbital position of Io was a great doughnut-shaped tube of atoms, sulfur and sodium and potassium, material somehow lost from Io.

When Voyager approached this giant moon we found a strange multicolored surface unlike any other in the solar system. Io is near the asteroid belt. It must have been thoroughly pummeled throughout its history by falling boulders. Impact craters must have been made. Yet there were none to be seen. Accordingly, there had to be some process on Io that was extremely efficient in rubbing craters out or filling them in. The process could not be atmospheric, since Io's atmosphere has mostly escaped to space because of its low gravity. It could not be running water; Io's surface is far too cold. There were a few places that resembled the summits of volcanoes. But it was hard to be sure.

Linda Morabito, a member of the Voyager Navigation Team responsible for keeping Voyager precisely on its trajectory, was routinely ordering a computer to enhance an image of the edge of Io, to bring out the stars behind it. To her astonishment, she saw a bright plume standing off in the darkness from the satellite's surface and soon determined that the plume was in exactly the position of one of the suspected volcanoes. Voyager had discovered the first active volcano beyond the Earth. We know now of nine large volcanoes, spewing out gas and debris, and hundreds—perhaps thousands—of extinct volcanoes on Io. The debris, rolling and flowing down the sides of the volcanic mountains,

* Frequently pronounced "*eye*-oh" by Americans, because this is the preferred enunciation in the *Oxford English Dictionary.* But the British have no special wisdom here. The word is of Eastern Mediterranean origin and is pronounced throughout the rest of Europe, correctly, as "*ee*-oh."

arching in great jets over the polychrome landscape, is more than enough to cover the impact craters. We are looking at a fresh planetary landscape, a surface newly hatched. How Galileo and Huygens would have marveled.

The volcanoes of Io were predicted, before they were discovered, by Stanton Peale and his co-workers, who calculated the tides that would be raised in the solid interior of Io by the combined pulls of the nearby moon Europa and the giant planet Jupiter. They found that the rocks inside Io should have been melted, not by radioactivity but by tides; that much of the interior of Io should be liquid. It now seems likely that the volcanoes of Io are tapping an underground ocean of liquid sulfur, melted and concentrated near the surface. When solid sulfur is heated a little past the normal boiling point of water, to about 115°C, it melts and changes color. The higher the temperature, the deeper the color. If the molten sulfur is quickly cooled, it retains its color. The pattern of colors that we see on Io resembles closely what we would expect if rivers and torrents and sheets of molten sulfur were pouring out of the mouths of the volcanoes: black sulfur the hottest, near the top of the volcano; red and orange, including the rivers, nearby; and great plains covered by yellow sulfur at a greater remove. The surface of Io is changing on a time scale of months. Maps will have to be issued regularly, like weather reports on Earth. Those future explorers on Io will have to keep their wits about them.

The very thin and tenuous atmosphere of Io was found by Voyager to be composed mainly of sulfur dioxide. But this thin atmosphere can serve a useful purpose, because it may be just thick enough to protect the surface from the intense charged particles in the Jupiter radiation belt in which Io is embedded. At night the temperature drops so low that the sulfur dioxide should condense out as a kind of white frost; the charged particles would then immolate the surface, and it would probably be wise to spend the nights just slightly underground.

The great volcanic plumes of Io reach so high that they are close to injecting their atoms directly into the space around Jupiter. The volcanoes are the probable source of the great doughnut-shaped ring of atoms that surrounds Jupiter in the position of Io's orbit. These atoms, gradually spiraling in toward Jupiter, should coat the inner moon Amalthea and may be responsible for its reddish coloration. It is even possible that the material outgassed from Io contributes, after many collisions and condensations, to the ring system of Jupiter.

A substantial human presence on Jupiter itself is much more difficult to imagine—although I suppose great balloon cities permanently floating in its atmosphere are a technological possibility for the remote future. As seen from the near sides of Io or Europa, that immense and variable world fills much of the sky, hanging aloft, never to rise or set, because almost every satellite in the solar system keeps a constant face to its planet, as the Moon does to the Earth. Jupiter will be a source of continuing provocation and excitement for the future human explorers of the Jovian moons.

As the solar system condensed out of instellar gas and dust, Jupiter acquired most of the matter that was not ejected into interstellar space and did not fall inward to form the Sun. Had Jupiter been several dozen times more massive, the matter in its interior would have undergone thermonuclear reactions, and Jupiter would have begun to shine by its own light. The largest planet is a star that failed. Even so, its interior temperatures are sufficiently high that it gives off about twice as much energy as it receives from the Sun. In the infrared part of the spectrum, it might even be correct to consider Jupiter a star. Had it become a star in visible light, we would today inhabit a binary or double-star system, with two suns in our sky, and the nights would come more rarely—a commonplace, I believe, in countless solar systems throughout the Milky Way Galaxy. We would doubtless think the circumstances natural and lovely.

Deep below the clouds of Jupiter the weight of the overlying layers of atmosphere produces pressures much higher than any found on Earth, pressures so great that electrons are squeezed off hydrogen atoms, producing a remarkable substance, liquid metallic hydrogen—a physical state that has never been achieved on Earth. (There is some hope that metallic hydrogen is a superconductor at moderate temperatures. If it could be manufactured on Earth, it would work a revolution in electronics.) In the interior of Jupiter, where the pressures are about three million times the atmospheric pressure at the surface of the Earth, there is almost nothing but a great dark sloshing ocean of metallic hydrogen. But at the very core of Jupiter there may be a lump of rock and iron, an Earth-like world in a pressure vise, hidden forever at the center of the largest planet.

The electrical currents in the liquid metal interior of Jupiter may be the source of the planet's enormous magnetic field, the largest in the solar system, and of its associated belt of trapped electrons and protons. These charged particles are ejected from the Sun in the solar wind and captured and accelerated by Jupiter's magnetic field. Vast numbers of them are trapped far above the clouds and are condemned to bounce from pole to pole until by chance they encounter some high-altitude atmospheric molecule and are removed from the radiation belt. Io moves in an orbit so close to Jupiter that it plows through the midst of this intense radiation, creating cascades of charged particles, which in turn generate violent bursts of radio energy. (They may also influence eruptive processes on the surface of Io.) It is possible to predict radio bursts from Jupiter with better reliability than weather forecasts on Earth, by computing the position of Io.

That Jupiter is a source of radio emission was discovered accidentally in the 1950's, the early days of radio astronomy. Two young Americans, Bernard Burke and Kenneth Franklin, were examining the sky with a newly constructed and for that time very sensitive radio telescope. They were searching the cosmic radio background—that is, radio sources far beyond our solar system. To their surprise, they found an intense and previously unreported source that seemed to correspond to no prominent star, nebula or galaxy. What is more, it gradually moved, with respect to the distant stars, much faster than any remote object could.* After finding no likely explanation of all this in their charts of the distant Cosmos, they one day stepped outside the observatory and looked up at the sky with the naked eye to see if anything interesting happened to be there. Bemusedly they noted an exceptionally bright object in the right place, which they soon identified as the planet Jupiter. This accidental discovery is, incidentally, entirely typical of the history of science.

Every evening before Voyager 1's encounter with Jupiter, I could see that giant planet twinkling in the sky, a sight our ancestors have enjoyed and wondered at for a million years. And on the evening of Encounter, on my way to study the Voyager data arriving at JPL, I thought that Jupiter would never be the same, never again just a point of light in the night sky, but would forever after be a *place* to be explored and known. Jupiter and its moons are a kind of miniature solar system and exquisite worlds with much to teach us.

In composition and in many other respects Saturn is similar to Jupiter, although smaller. Rotating once every ten hours, it exhibits colorful equatorial banding, which is, however, not so prominent as Jupiter's. It has a weaker magnetic field and radiation belt than Jupiter and a more spectacular set of circumplanetary rings. And it also is surrounded by a dozen or more satellites.

The most interesting of the moons of Saturn seems to be Titan, the largest moon in the solar system and the only one with a substantial atmosphere. Prior to the encounter of Voyager 1 with Titan in November 1980, our information about Titan was scanty and tantalizing. The only gas known unambiguously to be

* Because the speed of light is finite (see Chapter 8).

present was methane, CH_4, discovered by G. P. Kuiper. Ultraviolet light from the sun converts methane to more complex hydrocarbon molecules and hydrogen gas. The hydrocarbons should remain on Titan, covering the surface with a brownish tarry organic sludge, something like that produced in experiments on the origin of life on Earth. The lightweight hydrogen gas should, because of Titan's low gravity, rapidly escape to space by a violent process known as "blowoff," which should carry the methane and other atmospheric constituents with it. But Titan has an atmospheric pressure at least as great as that of the planet Mars. Blowoff does not seem to be happening. Perhaps there is some major and as yet undiscovered atmospheric constituent—nitrogen, for example—which keeps the average molecular weight of the atmosphere high and prevents blowoff. Or perhaps blowoff is happening, but the gases lost to space are being replenished by others released from the satellite's interior. The bulk density of Titan is so low that there must be a vast supply of water and other ices, probably including methane, which are at unknown rates being released to the surface by internal heating.

When we examine Titan through the telescope we see a barely perceptible reddish disk. Some observers have reported variable white clouds above that disk—most likely, clouds of methane crystals. But what is responsible for the reddish coloration? Most students of Titan agree that complex organic molecules are the most likely explanation. The surface temperature and atmospheric thickness are still under debate. There have been some hints of an enhanced surface temperature due to an atmospheric greenhouse effect. With abundant organic molecules on its surface and in its atmosphere, Titan is a remarkable and unique denizen of the solar system. The history of our past voyages of discovery suggests that Voyager and other spacecraft reconnaissance missions will revolutionize our knowledge of this place.

Through a break in the clouds of Titan, you might glimpse Saturn and its rings, their pale yellow color diffused by the intervening atmosphere. Because the Saturn system is ten times farther from the sun than is the Earth, the sunshine on Titan is only 1 percent as intense as we are accustomed to, and the temperatures should be far below the freezing point of water even with a sizable atmospheric greenhouse effect. But with abundant organic matter, sunlight and perhaps volcanic hot spots, the possibility of life on Titan* cannot be readily dismissed. In that very different environment, it would, of course, have to be very different from life on Earth. There is no strong evidence either for or against life on Titan. It is merely possible. We are unlikely to determine the answer to this question without landing instrumented space vehicles on the Titanian surface.

To examine the individual particles composing the rings of Saturn we must approach them closely, for the particles are small—snowballs and ice chips and tiny tumbling bonsai glaciers, a meter or so across. We know they are composed of water ice, because the spectral properties of sunlight reflected off the rings match those of ice in the laboratory measurements. To approach the particles in a space vehicle, we must slow down, so that we move along with them as they circle Saturn at some 45,000 miles per hour; that is, we must be in orbit around Saturn ourselves, moving at the same speed as the particles. Only then will we be able to see them individually and not as smears or streaks.

* The view of Huygens, who discovered Titan in 1655, was: "Now can any one look upon, and compare these Systems [of Jupiter and Saturn] together, without being amazed at the vast Magnitude and noble Attendants of these two Planets, in respect of this little pitiful Earth of ours? Or can they force themselves to think, that the wise Creator has disposed of all his Animals and Plants here, has furnished and adorn'd this Spot only, and has left all those Worlds bare and destitute of Inhabitants, who might adore and worship Him; or that all those prodigious Bodies were made only to twinkle to, and be studied by some few perhaps of us poor Fellows?" Since Saturn moves around the sun once every thirty years, the length of the seasons on Saturn and its moons is much longer than on Earth. Of the presumed inhabitants of the moons of Saturn, Huygens therefore wrote: "It is impossible but that their way of living must be very different from ours, having such tedious Winters."

Why is there not a single large satellite instead of a ring system around Saturn? The closer a ring particle is to Saturn, the faster its orbital speed (the faster it is "falling" around the planet—Kepler's third law); the inner particles are streaming past the outer ones (the "passing lane" as we see it is always to the left). Although the whole assemblage is tearing around the planet itself at some 20 kilometers per second, the *relative* speed of two adjacent particles is very low, only some few centimeters per minute. Because of this relative motion, the particles can never stick together by their mutual gravity. As soon as they try, their slightly different orbital speeds pull them apart. If the ring were not so close to Saturn, this effect would not be so strong, and the particles could accrete, making small snowballs and eventually growing into satellites. So it is probably no coincidence that outside the rings of Saturn there is a system of satellites varying in size from a few hundred kilometers across to Titan, a giant moon nearly as large as the planet Mars. The matter in all the satellites and the planets themselves may have been originally distributed in the form of rings, which condensed and accumulated to form the present moons and planets.

For Saturn as for Jupiter, the magnetic field captures and accelerates the charged particles of the solar wind. When a charged particle bounces from one magnetic pole to the other, it must cross the equatorial plane of Saturn. If there is a ring particle in the way, the proton or electron is absorbed by this small snowball. As a result, for both planets, the rings clear out the radiation belts, which exist only interior and exterior to the particle rings. A close moon of Jupiter or Saturn will likewise gobble up radiation belt particles, and in fact one of the new moons of Saturn was discovered in just this way: Pioneer 11 found an unexpected gap in the radiation belts, caused by the sweeping up of charged particles by a previously unknown moon.

The solar wind trickles into the outer solar system far beyond the orbit of Saturn. When Voyager reaches Uranus and the orbits of Neptune and Pluto, if the instruments are still functioning, they will almost certainly sense its presence, the wind between the worlds, the top of the sun's atmosphere blown outward toward the realm of the stars. Some two or three times farther from the Sun than Pluto is, the pressure of the interstellar protons and electrons becomes greater than the minuscule pressure there exerted by the solar wind. That place, called the heliopause, is one definition of the outer boundary of the Empire of the Sun. But the Voyager spacecraft will plunge on, penetrating the heliopause sometime in the middle of the twenty-first century, skimming through the ocean of space, never to enter another solar system, destined to wander through eternity far from the stellar islands and to complete its first circumnavigation of the massive center of the Milky Way a few hundred million years from now. We have embarked on epic voyages.

CHAPTER VII

THE BACKBONE OF NIGHT

I would rather understand one cause than be King of Persia.

—Democritus of Abdera

If a faithful account was rendered of Man's ideas upon Divinity, he would be obliged to acknowledge, that for the most part the word "gods" has been used to express the concealed, remote, unknown causes of the effects he witnessed; that he applies this term when the spring of the natural, the source of known causes, ceases to be visible: as soon as he loses the thread of these causes, or as soon as his mind can no longer follow the chain, he solves the difficulty, terminates his research, by ascribing it to his gods . . . When, therefore, he ascribes to his gods the production of some phenomenon . . . does he, in fact, do any thing more than substitute for the darkness of his own mind, a sound to which he has been accustomed to listen with reverential awe?

—Paul Heinrich Dietrich, Baron von Holbach, *Système de la Nature*, London, 1770

When I was little, I lived in the Bensonhurst section of Brooklyn in the City of New York. I knew my immediate neighborhood intimately, every apartment building, pigeon coop, backyard, front stoop, empty lot, elm tree, ornamental railing, coal chute and wall for playing Chinese handball, among which the brick exterior of a theater called the Loew's Stillwell was of superior quality. I knew where many people lived: Bruno and Dino, Ronald and Harvey, Sandy, Bernie, Danny, Jackie and Myra. But more than a few blocks away, north of the raucous automobile traffic and elevated railway on 86th Street, was a strange unknown territory, off-limits to my wanderings. It could have been Mars for all I knew.

Even with an early bedtime, in winter you could sometimes see the stars. I would look at them, twinkling and remote, and wonder what they were. I would ask older children and adults, who would only reply, "They're lights in the sky, kid." I could *see* they were lights in the sky. But what *were* they? Just small hovering lamps? Whatever for? I felt a kind of sorrow for them: a commonplace whose strangeness remained somehow hidden from my incurious fellows. There had to be some deeper answer.

As soon as I was old enough, my parents gave me my first library card. I think the library was on 85th Street, an alien land. Immediately, I asked the librarian for something on stars. She returned with a picture book displaying portraits of men and women with names like Clark Gable and Jean Harlow. I complained, and for some reason then obscure to me, she smiled and found another book—the right kind of book. I opened it breathlessly and read until I found it. The book said something astonishing, a very big thought. It said that the stars were suns, only very far away. The Sun was a star, but close up.

Imagine that you took the Sun and moved it so far away that it was just a tiny twinkling point of light. How far away would you have to move it? I was innocent of the notion of angular size. I was ignorant of the inverse square law for light propagation. I had not a ghost of a chance of calculating the distance to the stars. But I could tell that if the stars were suns, they had to be very far away—farther away than 85th Street, farther away than

Manhattan, farther away, probably, than New Jersey. The Cosmos was much bigger than I had guessed.

Later I read another astonishing fact. The Earth, which includes Brooklyn, is a planet, and it goes around the Sun. There are other planets. They also go around the Sun; some are closer to it and some are farther away. But the planets do not shine by their own light, as the Sun does. They merely reflect light from the Sun. If you were a great distance away, you would not see the Earth and the other planets at all; they would be only faint luminous points, lost in the glare of the Sun. Well, then, I thought, it stood to reason that the other stars must have planets too, ones we have not yet detected, and some of those other planets should have life (why not?), a kind of life probably different from life as we know it, life in Brooklyn. So I decided I would be an astronomer, learn about the stars and planets and, if I could, go and visit them.

It has been my immense good fortune to have parents and some teachers who encouraged this odd ambition and to live in this time, the first moment in human history when we are, in fact, visiting other worlds and engaging in a deep reconnaissance of the Cosmos. If I had been born in a much earlier age, no matter how great my dedication, I would not have understood what the stars and planets are. I would not have known that there were other suns and other worlds. This is one of the great secrets, wrested from Nature through a million years of patient observation and courageous thinking by our ancestors.

What are the stars? Such questions are as natural as an infant's smile. We have always asked them. What is different about our time is that at last we know some of the answers. Books and libraries provide a ready means for finding out what those answers are. In biology there is a principle of powerful if imperfect applicability called recapitulation: in our individual embryonic development we retrace the evolutionary history of the species. There is, I think, a kind of recapitulation that occurs in our individual intellectual developments as well. We unconsciously retrace the thoughts of our remote ancestors. Imagine a time before science, a time before libraries. Imagine a time hundreds of thousands of years ago. We were then just about as smart, just as curious, just as involved in things social and sexual. But the experiments had not yet been done, the inventions had not yet been made. It was the childhood of genus *Homo.* Imagine the time when fire was first discovered. What were human lives like then? What did our ancestors believe the stars were? Sometimes, in my fantasies, I imagine there was someone who thought like this:

We eat berries and roots. Nuts and leaves. And dead animals. Some animals we find. Some we kill. We know which foods are good and which are dangerous. If we taste some foods we are struck down, in punishment for eating them. We did not mean to do something bad. But foxglove or hemlock can kill you. We love our children and our friends. We warn them of such foods.

When we hunt animals, then also can we be killed. We can be gored. Or trampled. Or eaten. What animals do means life and death for us: how they behave, what tracks they leave, their times for mating and giving birth, their times for wandering. We must know these things. We tell our children. They will tell their children.

We depend on animals. We follow them—especially in winter when there are few plants to eat. We are wandering hunters and gatherers. We call ourselves the hunterfolk.

Most of us fall asleep under the sky or under a tree or in its branches. We use animal skins for clothing: to keep us warm, to cover our nakedness and sometimes as a hammock. When we wear the animal skins we feel the animal's power. We leap with the gazelle. We hunt with the bear. There is a bond between us and the animals. We hunt and eat the animals. They hunt and eat us. We are part of one another.

We make tools and stay alive. Some of us are experts at splitting, flaking, sharpening and polishing, as well as finding, rocks.

Some rocks we tie with animal sinew to a wooden handle and make an ax. With the ax we strike plants and animals. Other rocks are tied to long sticks. If we are quiet and watchful, we can sometimes come close to an animal and stick it with the spear.

Meat spoils. Sometimes we are hungry and try not to notice. Sometimes we mix herbs with the bad meat to hide the taste. We fold foods that will not spoil into pieces of animal skin. Or big leaves. Or the shell of a large nut. It is wise to put food aside and carry it. If we eat this food too early, some of us will starve later. So we must help one another. For this and many other reasons we have rules. Everyone must obey the rules. We have always had rules. Rules are sacred.

One day there was a storm, with much lightning and thunder and rain. The little ones are afraid of storms. And sometimes so am I. The secret of the storm is hidden. The thunder is deep and loud; the lightning is brief and bright. Maybe someone very powerful is very angry. It must be someone in the sky, I think.

After the storm there was a flickering and crackling in the forest nearby. We went to see. There was a bright, hot, leaping thing, yellow and red. We had never seen such a thing before. We now call it "flame." It has a special smell. In a way it is alive. It eats food. It eats plants and tree limbs and even whole trees, if you let it. It is strong. But it is not very smart. If all the food is gone, it dies. It will not walk a spear's throw from one tree to another if there is no food along the way. It cannot walk without eating. But where there is much food, it grows and makes many flame children.

One of us had a brave and fearful thought: to capture the flame, feed it a little, and make it our friend. We found some long branches of hard wood. The flame was eating them, but slowly. We could pick them up by the end that had no flame. If you run fast with a small flame, it dies. Their children are weak. We did not run. We walked, shouting good wishes. "Do not die," we said to the flame. The other hunterfolk looked with wide eyes.

Ever after, we have carried it with us. We have a flame mother *to feed the flame slowly so it does not die of hunger.*[*] *Flame is a wonder, and useful too; surely a gift from powerful beings. Are they the same as the angry beings in the storm?*

The flame keeps us warm on cold nights. It gives us light. It makes holes in the darkness when the Moon is new. We can fix spears at night for tomorrow's hunt. And if we are not tired, even in the darkness we can see each other and talk. Also—a good thing!—fire keeps animals away. We can be hurt at night. Sometimes we have been eaten, even by small animals, hyenas and wolves. Now it is different. Now the flame keeps the animals back. We see them baying softly in the dark, prowling, their eyes glowing in the light of the flame. They are frightened of the flame. But we are not frightened. The flame is ours. We take care of the flame. The flame takes care of us.

The sky is important. It covers us. It speaks to us. Before the time we found the flame, we would lie back in the dark and look up at all the points of light. Some points would come together to make a picture in the sky. One of us could see the pictures better than the rest. She taught us the star pictures and what names to call them. We would sit around late at night and make up stories about the pictures in the sky: lions, dogs, bears, hunterfolk. Other, stranger things. Could they be the pictures of the powerful beings in the sky, the ones who make the storms when angry?

Mostly, the sky does not change. The same star pictures are there year after year. The Moon grows from nothing to a thin sliver

* This sense of fire as a living thing, to be protected and cared for, should not be dismissed as a "primitive" notion. It is to be found near the root of many modern civilizations. Every home in ancient Greece and Rome and among the Brahmans of ancient India had a hearth and a set of prescribed rules for caring for the flame. At night the coals were covered with ashes for insulation; in the morning twigs were added to revive the flame. The death of the flame in the hearth was considered synonymous with the death of the family. In all three cultures, the hearth ritual was connected with the worship of ancestors. This is the origin of the eternal flame, a symbol still widely employed in religious, memorial, political and athletic ceremonials throughout the world.

to a round ball, and then back again to nothing. When the Moon changes, the women bleed. Some tribes have rules against sex at certain times in the growing and shrinking of the Moon. Some tribes scratch the days of the Moon or the days that the women bleed on antler bones. Then they can plan ahead and obey their rules. Rules are sacred.

The stars are very far away. When we climb a hill or a tree they are no closer. And clouds come between us and the stars: the stars must be behind the clouds. The Moon, as it slowly moves, passes in front of stars. Later you can see that the stars are not harmed. The Moon does not eat stars. The stars must be behind the Moon. They flicker. A strange, cold, white faraway light. Many of them. All over the sky. But only at night. I wonder what they are.

After we found the flame, I was sitting near the campfire wondering about the stars. Slowly a thought came: The stars are flame, I thought. Then I had another thought: The stars are campfires that other hunterfolk light at night. The stars give a smaller light than campfires. So the stars must be campfires very far away. "But," they ask me, "how can there be campfires in the sky? Why do the campfires and the hunter people around those flames not fall down at our feet? Why don't strange tribes drop from the sky?"

Those are good questions. They trouble me. Sometimes I think the sky is half of a big eggshell or a big nutshell. I think the people around those faraway campfires look down at us—except for them it seems up—and say that we are in their sky, and wonder why we do not fall up to them, if you see what I mean. But hunterfolk say, "Down is down and up is up." That is a good answer too.

There is another thought that one of us had. His thought is that night is a great black animal skin, thrown up over the sky. There are holes in the skin. We look through the holes. And we see flame. His thought is not just that there is flame in a few places where we see stars. He thinks there is flame everywhere. He thinks flame covers the whole sky. But the skin hides the flame. Except where there are holes.

Some stars wander. Like the animals we hunt. Like us. If you watch with care over many months, you find they move. There are only five of them, like the fingers on a hand. They wander slowly among the stars. If the campfire thought is true, those stars must be tribes of wandering hunterfolk, carrying big fires. But I don't see how wandering stars can be holes in a skin. When you make a hole, there it is. A hole is a hole. Holes do not wander. Also, I don't want to be surrounded by a sky of flame. If the skin fell, the night sky would be bright—too bright—like seeing flame everywhere. I think a sky of flame would eat us all. Maybe there are two kinds of powerful beings in the sky. Bad ones, who wish the flame to eat us. And good ones who put up the skin to keep the flame away. We must find some way to thank the good ones.

I don't know if the stars are campfires in the sky. Or holes in a skin through which the flame of power looks down on us. Sometimes I think one way. Sometimes I think a different way. Once I thought there are no campfires and no holes but something else, too hard for me to understand.

Rest your neck on a log. Your head goes back. Then you can see only the sky. No hills, no trees, no hunterfolk, no campfire. Just sky. Sometimes I feel I may fall up into the sky. If the stars are campfires, I would like to visit those other hunterfolk—the ones who wander. Then I feel good about falling up. But if the stars are holes in a skin, I become afraid. I don't want to fall up through a hole and into the flame of power.

I wish I knew which was true. I don't like not knowing.

I do not imagine that many members of a hunter/gatherer group had thoughts like these about the stars. Perhaps, over the ages, a few did, but never all these thoughts in the same person. Yet, sophisticated ideas are common in such communities. For example, the !Kung* Bushmen of the Kalahari Desert in Botswana

* The exclamation point is a click, made by touching the tongue against the inside of the incisors, and simultaneously pronouncing the K.

have an explanation for the Milky Way, which at their latitude is often overhead. They call it "the backbone of night," as if the sky were some great beast inside which we live. Their explanation makes the Milky Way useful as well as understandable. The !Kung believe the Milky Way holds up the night; that if it were not for the Milky Way, fragments of darkness would come crashing down at our feet. It is an elegant idea.

Metaphors like those about celestial campfires or galactic backbones were eventually replaced in most human cultures by another idea: The powerful beings in the sky were promoted to gods. They were given names and relatives, and special responsibilities for the cosmic services they were expected to perform. There was a god or goddess for every human concern. Gods ran Nature. Nothing could happen without their direct intervention. If they were happy, there was plenty of food, and humans were happy. But if something displeased the gods—and sometimes it took very little—the consequences were awesome: droughts, storms, wars, earthquakes, volcanoes, epidemics. The gods had to be propitiated, and a vast industry of priests and oracles arose to make the gods less angry. But because the gods were capricious, you could not be sure what they would do. Nature was a mystery. It was hard to understand the world.

Little remains of the Heraion on the Aegean isle of Samos, one of the wonders of the ancient world, a great temple dedicated to Hera, who began her career as goddess of the sky. She was the patron deity of Samos, playing the same role there as Athena did in Athens. Much later she married Zeus, the chief of the Olympian gods. They honeymooned on Samos, the old stories tell us. The Greek religion explained that diffuse band of light in the night sky as the milk of Hera, squirted from her breast across the heavens, a legend that is the origin of the phrase Westerners still use—the Milky Way. Perhaps it originally represented the important insight that the sky nurtures the Earth; if so, that meaning seems to have been forgotten millennia ago.

We are, almost all of us, descended from people who responded to the dangers of existence by inventing stories about unpredictable or disgruntled deities. For a long time the human instinct to understand was thwarted by facile religious explanations, as in ancient Greece in the time of Homer, where there were gods of the sky and the Earth, the thunderstorm, the oceans and the underworld, fire and time and love and war; where every tree and meadow had its dryad and maenad.

For thousands of years humans were oppressed—as some of us still are—by the notion that the universe is a marionette whose strings are pulled by a god or gods, unseen and inscrutable. Then, 2,500 years ago, there was a glorious awakening in Ionia: on Samos and the other nearby Greek colonies that grew up among the islands and inlets of the busy eastern Aegean Sea.* Suddenly there were people who believed that everything was made of atoms; that human beings and other animals had sprung from simpler forms; that diseases were not caused by demons or the gods; that the Earth was only a planet going around the Sun. And that the stars were very far away.

This revolution made Cosmos out of Chaos. The early Greeks had believed that the first being was Chaos, corresponding to the phrase in Genesis in the same context, "without form." Chaos created and then mated with a goddess called Night, and their offspring eventually produced all the gods and men. A universe created from Chaos was in perfect keeping with the Greek belief in an unpredictable Nature run by capricious gods. But in the sixth century B.C., in Ionia, a new concept developed, one of the great ideas of the human species. The universe is knowable, the ancient Ionians argued, because it exhibits an internal order: there are regularities in Nature that permit its secrets to be uncovered. Nature is not entirely unpredictable; there are rules even

* As an aid to confusion, Ionia is not in the Ionian Sea; it was named by colonists from the coast of the Ionian Sea.

she must obey. This ordered and admirable character of the universe was called Cosmos.

But why Ionia, why in these unassuming and pastoral landscapes, these remote islands and inlets of the Eastern Mediterranean? Why not in the great cities of India or Egypt, Babylonia, China or Mesoamerica? China had an astronomical tradition millennia old; it invented paper and printing, rockets, clocks, silk, porcelain, and ocean-going navies. Some historians argue it was nevertheless too traditionalist a society, too unwilling to adopt innovations. Why not India, an extremely rich, mathematically gifted culture? Because, some historians maintain, of a rigid fascination with the idea of an infinitely old universe condemned to an endless cycle of deaths and rebirths, of souls and universes, in which nothing fundamentally new could ever happen. Why not Mayan and Aztec societies, which were accomplished in astronomy and captivated, as the Indians were, by large numbers? Because, some historians declare, they lacked the aptitude or impetus for mechanical invention. The Mayans and the Aztecs did not even—except for children's toys—invent the wheel.

The Ionians had several advantages. Ionia is an island realm. Isolation, even if incomplete, breeds diversity. With many different islands, there was a variety of political systems. No single concentration of power could enforce social and intellectual conformity in all the islands. Free inquiry became possible. The promotion of superstition was not considered a political necessity. Unlike many other cultures, the Ionians were at the crossroads of civilizations, not at one of the centers. In Ionia, the Phoenician alphabet was first adapted to Greek usage and widespread literacy became possible. Writing was no longer a monopoly of the priests and scribes. The thoughts of many were available for consideration and debate. Political power was in the hands of the merchants, who actively promoted the technology on which their prosperity depended. It was in the Eastern Mediterranean that

African, Asian, and European civilizations, including the great cultures of Egypt and Mesopotamia, met and cross-fertilized in a vigorous and heady confrontation of prejudices, languages, ideas and gods. What do you do when you are faced with several different gods each claiming the same territory? The Babylonian Marduk and the Greek Zeus was each considered master of the sky and king of the gods. You might decide that Marduk and Zeus were really the same. You might also decide, since they had quite different attributes, that one of them was merely invented by the priests. But if one, why not both?

And so it was that the great idea arose, the realization that there might be a way to know the world without the god hypothesis; that there might be principles, forces, laws of nature, through which the world could be understood without attributing the fall of every sparrow to the direct intervention of Zeus.

China and India and Mesoamerica would, I think, have tumbled to science too, if only they had been given a little more time. Cultures do not develop with identical rhythms or evolve in lockstep. They arise at different times and progress at different rates. The scientific world view works so well, explains so much and resonates so harmoniously with the most advanced parts of our brains that in time, I think, virtually every culture on the Earth, left to its own devices, would have discovered science. Some culture had to be first. As it turned out, Ionia was the place where science was born.

Between 600 and 400 B.C., this great revolution in human thought began. The key to the revolution was the hand. Some of the brilliant Ionian thinkers were the sons of sailors and farmers and weavers. They were accustomed to poking and fixing, unlike the priests and scribes of other nations, who, raised in luxury, were reluctant to dirty their hands. They rejected superstition, and they worked wonders. In many cases we have only fragmentary or secondhand accounts of what happened. The metaphors used then may be obscure to us now. There was almost certainly a conscious effort a few centuries later to suppress the new insights. The leading figures in this revolution were men with Greek names, largely unfamiliar to us today, but the truest pioneers in the development of our civilization and our humanity.

The first Ionian scientist was Thales of Miletus, a city in Asia across a narrow channel of water from the island of Samos. He had traveled in Egypt and was conversant with the knowledge of Babylon. It is said that he predicted a solar eclipse. He learned how to measure the height of a pyramid from the length of its shadow and the angle of the Sun above the horizon, a method employed today to determine the heights of the mountains of the Moon. He was the first to prove geometric theorems of the sort codified by Euclid three centuries later—for example, the proposition that the angles at the base of an isosceles triangle are equal. There is a clear continuity of intellectual effort from Thales to Euclid to Isaac Newton's purchase of the *Elements of Geometry* at Stourbridge Fair in 1663 (p. 70), the event that precipitated modern science and technology.

Thales attempted to understand the world without invoking the intervention of the gods. Like the Babylonians, he believed the world to have once been water. To explain the dry land, the Babylonians added that Marduk had placed a mat on the face of the waters and piled dirt upon it.* Thales held a similar view, but, as Benjamin Farrington said, "left Marduk out." Yes, everything was once water, but the Earth formed out of the oceans by a natu-

* There is some evidence that the antecedent, early Sumerian creation myths were largely naturalistic explanations, later codified around 1000 B.C. in the *Enuma elish* ("When on high," the first words of the poem); but by then the gods had replaced Nature, and the myths offers a theogony, not a cosmogony. The *Enuma elish* is reminiscent of the Japanese and Ainu myths in which an originally muddy cosmos is beaten by the wings of a bird, separating the land from the water. A Fijian creation myth says: "Rokomautu created the land. He scooped it up out of the bottom of the ocean in great handfuls and accumulated it in piles here and there. These are the Fiji Islands." The distillation of land from water is a natural enough idea for island and seafaring peoples.

ral process—similar, he thought, to the silting he had observed at the delta of the Nile. Indeed, he thought that water was a common principle underlying all of matter, just as today we might say the same of electrons, protons and neutrons, or of quarks. Whether Thales' conclusion was correct is not as important as his approach: The world was not made by the gods, but instead was the work of material forces interacting in Nature. Thales brought back from Babylon and Egypt the seeds of the new sciences of astronomy and geometry, sciences that would sprout and grow in the fertile soil of Ionia.

Very little is known about the personal life of Thales, but one revealing anecdote is told by Aristotle in his *Politics:*

> [Thales] was reproached for his poverty, which was supposed to show that philosophy is of no use. According to the story, he knew by his skill [in interpreting the heavens] while it was yet winter that there would be a great harvest of olives in the coming year; so, having a little money, he gave deposits for the use of all the olive-presses in Chios and Miletus, which he hired at a low price because no one bid against him. When the harvest time came, and many were wanted all at once, he let them out at any rate which he pleased and made a quantity of money. Thus he showed the world philosophers can easily be rich if they like, but that their ambition is of another sort.

He was also famous as a political sage, successfully urging the Milesians to resist assimilation by Croesus, King of Lydia, and unsuccessfully urging a federation of all the island states of Ionia to oppose the Lydians.

Anaximander of Miletus was a friend and colleague of Thales, one of the first people we know of to do an experiment. By examining the moving shadow cast by a vertical stick he determined accurately the length of the year and the seasons. For ages men had used sticks to club and spear one another. Anaximander used one to measure time. He was the first person in Greece to make a sundial, a map of the known world and a celestial globe that showed the patterns of the constellations. He believed the Sun, the Moon and the stars to be made of fire seen through moving holes in the dome of the sky, probably a much older idea. He held the remarkable view that the Earth is not suspended or supported from the heavens, but that it remains by itself at the center of the universe; since it was equidistant from all places on the "celestial sphere," there was no force that could move it.

He argued that we are so helpless at birth that, if the first human infants had been put into the world on their own, they would immediately have died. From this Anaximander concluded that human beings arose from other animals with more self-reliant newborns: He proposed the spontaneous origin of life in mud, the first animals being fish covered with spines. Some descendants of these fishes eventually abandoned the water and moved to dry land, where they evolved into other animals by the transmutation of one form into another. He believed in an infinite number of worlds, all inhabited, and all subject to cycles of dissolution and regeneration. "Nor," as Saint Augustine ruefully complained, "did he, any more than Thales, attribute the cause of all this ceaseless activity to a divine mind."

In the year 540 B.C. or thereabouts, on the island of Samos, there came to power a tyrant named Polycrates. He seems to have started as a caterer and then gone on to international piracy. Polycrates was a generous patron of the arts, sciences and engineering. But he oppressed his own people; he made war on his neighbors; he quite rightly feared invasion. So he surrounded his capital city with a massive wall, about six kilometers long, whose remains stand to this day. To carry water from a distant spring through the fortifications, he ordered a great tunnel built. A kilometer long, it pierces a mountain. Two cuttings were dug from either end which met almost perfectly in the middle. The project took about fifteen years to complete, a testament to the civil engineering of the day and an indication of the extraordinary practical capability of the Ionians. But there is another and more ominous side to the enterprise: it was built in part by slaves in chains, many captured by the pirate ships of Polycrates.

This was the time of Theodorus, the master engineer of the age, credited among the Greeks with the invention of the key, the ruler, the carpenter's square, the level, the lathe, bronze casting and central heating. Why are there no monuments to this man? Those who dreamed and speculated about the laws of Nature talked with the technologists and the engineers. They were often the same people. The theoretical and the practical were one.

About the same time, on the nearby island of Cos, Hippocrates was establishing his famous medical tradition, now barely remembered because of the Hippocratic oath. It was a practical and effective school of medicine, which Hippocrates insisted had to be based on the contemporary equivalent of physics and chemistry.* But it also had its theoretical side. In his book *On Ancient Medicine,* Hippocrates wrote: "Men think epilepsy divine, merely because they do not understand it. But if they called everything divine which they do not understand, why, there would be no end of divine things."

In time, the Ionian influence and the experimental method spread to the mainland of Greece, to Italy, to Sicily. There was once a time when hardly anyone believed in air. They knew about breathing, of course, and they thought the wind was the breath of the gods. But the idea of air as a static, material but invisible substance was unimagined. The first recorded experiment on air was

* And astrology, which was then widely regarded as a science. In a typical passage, Hippocrates writes: "One must also guard against the risings of the stars, especially of the Dog Star [Sirius], then of Arcturus, and also of the setting of the Pleiades."

performed by a physician* named Empedocles, who flourished around 450 B.C. Some accounts claim he identified himself as a god. But perhaps it was only that he was so clever that others thought him a god. He believed that light travels very fast, but not infinitely fast. He taught that there was once a much greater variety of living things on the Earth, but that many races of beings "must have been unable to beget and continue their kind. For in the case of every species that exists, either craft or courage or speed has from the beginning of its existence protected and preserved it." In this attempt to explain the lovely adaptation of organisms to their environments, Empedocles, like Anaximander and Democritus (see below), clearly anticipated some aspects of Darwin's great idea of evolution by natural selection.

Empedocles performed his experiment with a household implement people had used for centuries, the so-called *clepsydra* or "water thief," which was used as a kitchen ladle. A brazen sphere with an open neck and small holes in the bottom, it is filled by immersing it in water. If you pull it out with the neck uncovered, the water pours out of the holes, making a little shower. But if you pull it out properly, with your thumb covering the neck, the water is retained within the sphere until you lift your thumb. If you try to fill it with the neck covered, nothing happens. Some material substance must be in the way of the water. We cannot *see* such a substance. What could it be? Empedocles argued that it could only be air. A thing we cannot see can exert pressure, can frustrate my wish to fill a vessel with water if I were dumb enough to leave my finger on the neck. Empedocles had discovered the invisible. Air, he thought, must be matter in a form so finely divided that it could not be seen.

Empedocles is said to have died in an apotheotic fit by leaping

* The experiment was performed in support of a totally erroneous theory of the circulation of the blood, but the idea of performing any experiment to probe Nature is the important innovation.

into the hot lava at the summit caldera of the great volcano of Aetna. But I sometimes imagine that he merely slipped during a courageous and pioneering venture in observational geophysics.

This hint, this whiff, of the existence of atoms was carried much further by a man named Democritus, who came from the Ionian colony of Abdera in northern Greece. Abdera was a kind of joke town. If in 430 B.C. you told a story about someone from Abdera, you were guaranteed a laugh. It was in a way the Brooklyn of its time. For Democritus all of life was to be enjoyed and understood; understanding and enjoyment were the same thing. He said that "a life without festivity is a long road without an inn." Democritus may have come from Abdera, but he was no dummy. He believed that a large number of worlds had formed spontaneously out of diffuse matter in space, evolved and then decayed. At a time when no one knew about impact craters, Democritus thought that worlds on occasion collide; he believed that some worlds wandered alone through the darkness of space, while others were accompanied by several suns and moons; that some worlds were inhabited, while others had no plants or animals or even water; that the simplest forms of life arose from a kind of primeval ooze. He taught that perception—the reason, say, I think there is a pen in my hand—was a purely physical and mechanistic process; that thinking and feeling were attributes of matter put together in a sufficiently fine and complex way and not due to some spirit infused into matter by the gods.

Democritus invented the word *atom,* Greek for "unable to be cut." Atoms were the ultimate particles, forever frustrating our attempts to break them into smaller pieces. Everything, he said, is a collection of atoms, intricately assembled. Even we. "Nothing exists," he said, "but atoms and the void."

When we cut an apple, the knife must pass through empty spaces between the atoms, Democritus argued. If there were no such empty spaces, no void, the knife would encounter the impenetrable atoms, and the apple could not be cut. Having cut a slice from a cone, say, let us compare the cross sections of the two pieces. Are the exposed areas equal? No, said Democritus. The slope of the cone forces one side of the slice to have a slightly smaller cross section than the other. If the two areas were exactly equal, we would have a cylinder, not a cone. No matter how sharp the knife, the two pieces have unequal cross sections. Why? Because, on the scale of the very small, matter exhibits some irreducible roughness. This fine scale of roughness Democritus identified with the world of the atoms. His arguments were not those we use today, but they were subtle and elegant, derived from everyday life. And his conclusions were fundamentally correct.

In a related exercise, Democritus imagined calculating the volume of a cone or a pyramid by a very large number of extremely small stacked plates tapering in size from the base to the apex. He had stated the problem that, in mathematics, is called the theory of limits. He was knocking at the door of the differential and integral calculus, that fundamental tool for understanding the world that was not, so far as we know from written records, in fact discovered until the time of Isaac Newton. Perhaps if Democritus' work had not been almost completely destroyed, there would have been calculus by the time of Christ.*

Thomas Wright marveled in 1750 that Democritus had believed the Milky Way to be composed mainly of unresolved stars: "long before astronomy reaped any benefit from the improved sciences of optics; [he] saw, as we may say, through the eye of reason, full as far into infinity as the most able astronomers in more advantageous times have done since." Beyond the Milk of Hera, past the Backbone of Night, the mind of Democritus soared.

As a person, Democritus seems to have been somewhat unusual. Women, children and sex discomfited him, in part because they took time away from thinking. But he valued friendship,

* The frontiers of the calculus were also later breached by Eudoxus and Archimedes.

held cheerfulness to be the goal of life and devoted a major philosophical inquiry to the origin and nature of enthusiasm. He journeyed to Athens to visit Socrates and then found himself too shy to introduce himself. He was a close friend of Hippocrates. He was awed by the beauty and elegance of the physical world. He felt that poverty in a democracy was preferable to wealth in a tyranny. He believed that the prevailing religions of his time were evil and that neither immortal souls nor immortal gods exist: "Nothing exists, but atoms and the void."

There is no record of Democritus having been persecuted for his opinions—but then, he came from Abdera. However, in his time the brief tradition of tolerance for unconventional views began to erode and then to shatter. People came to be punished for having unusual ideas. A portrait of Democritus is now on the Greek hundred-drachma bill. But his insights were suppressed, his influence on history made minor. The mystics were beginning to win.

Anaxagoras was an Ionian experimentalist who flourished around 450 B.C. and lived in Athens. He was a rich man, indifferent to his wealth but passionate about science. Asked what was the purpose of life, he replied, "the investigation of the Sun, the Moon, and the heavens," the reply of a true astronomer. He performed a clever experiment in which a single drop of white liquid, like cream, was shown not to lighten perceptibly the contents of a great pitcher of dark liquid, like wine. There must, he concluded, be changes deducible by experiment that are too subtle to be perceived directly by the senses.

Anaxagoras was not nearly so radical as Democritus. Both were thoroughgoing materialists, not in prizing possessions but in holding that matter alone provided the underpinnings of the world. Anaxagoras believed in a special mind substance and disbelieved in the existence of atoms. He thought humans were more intelligent than other animals because of our hands, a very Ionian idea.

He was the first person to state clearly that the Moon shines by reflected light, and he accordingly devised a theory of the phases of the Moon. This doctrine was so dangerous that the manuscript describing it had to be circulated in secret, an Athenian *samizdat.* It was not in keeping with the prejudices of the time to explain the phases or eclipses of the Moon by the relative geometry of the Earth, the Moon and the self-luminous Sun. Aristotle, two generations later, was content to argue that those things happened because it was the nature of the Moon to have phases and eclipses—mere verbal juggling, an explanation that explains nothing.

The prevailing belief was that the Sun and Moon were gods. Anaxagoras held that the Sun and stars are fiery stones. We do not feel the heat of the stars because they are too far away. He also thought that the Moon has mountains (right) and inhabitants (wrong). He held that the Sun was so huge that it was probably larger than the Peloponnesus, roughly the southern third of Greece. His critics thought this estimate excessive and absurd.

Anaxagoras was brought to Athens by Pericles, its leader in its time of greatest glory, but also the man whose actions led to the Peloponnesian War, which destroyed Athenian democracy. Pericles delighted in philosophy and science, and Anaxagoras was one of his principal confidants. There are those who think that in this role Anaxagoras contributed significantly to the greatness of Athens. But Pericles had political problems. He was too powerful to be attacked directly, so his enemies attacked those close to him. Anaxagoras was convicted and imprisoned for the religious crime of impiety—because he had taught that the Moon was made of ordinary matter, that it was a place, and that the Sun was a red-hot stone in the sky. Bishop John Wilkins commented in 1638 on these Athenians: "Those zealous idolators [counted] it a great blasphemy to make their God a stone, whereas notwithstanding they were so senseless in their adoration of idols as to make a stone their God." Pericles seems to have engineered Anaxagoras' release from prison, but it was too late. In Greece the tide was turning, although the Ionian tradition continued in Alexandrian Egypt two hundred years later.

The great scientists from Thales to Democritus and Anaxagoras have usually been described in history or philosophy books as "Presocratics," as if their main function was to hold the philosophical fort until the advent of Socrates, Plato and Aristotle and perhaps influence them a little. Instead, the old Ionians represent a different and largely contradictory tradition, one in much better accord with modern science. That their influence was felt powerfully for only two or three centuries is an irreparable loss for all those human beings who lived between the Ionian Awakening and the Italian Renaissance.

Perhaps the most influential person ever associated with Samos was Pythagoras,* a contemporary of Polycrates in the sixth century B.C. According to local tradition, he lived for a time in a cave on the Samian Mount Kerkis, and was the first person in the history of the world to deduce that the Earth is a sphere. Perhaps he argued by analogy with the Moon and the Sun, or noticed the curved shadow of the Earth on the Moon during a lunar eclipse, or recognized that when ships leave Samos and recede over the horizon, their masts disappear last.

He or his disciples discovered the Pythagorean theorem: the sum of the squares of the shorter sides of a right triangle equals the square of the longer side. Pythagoras did not simply enumerate examples of this theorem; he developed a method of mathematical deduction to prove the thing generally. The modern

* The sixth century B.C. was a time of remarkable intellectual and spiritual ferment across the planet. Not only was it the time of Thales, Anaximander, Pythagoras and others in Ionia, but also the time of the Egyptian Pharaoh Necho who caused Africa to be circumnavigated, of Zoroaster in Persia, Confucius and Lao-tse in China, the Jewish prophets in Israel, Egypt and Babylon, and Gautama Buddha in India. It is hard to think these activities altogether unrelated.

tradition of mathematical argument, essential to all of science, owes much to Pythagoras. It was he who first used the word *Cosmos* to denote a well-ordered and harmonious universe, a world amenable to human understanding.

Many Ionians believed the underlying harmony of the universe to be accessible through observation and experiment, the method that dominates science today. However, Pythagoras employed a very different method. He taught that the laws of Nature could be deduced by pure thought. He and his followers were not fundamentally experimentalists.* They were mathematicians. And they were thoroughgoing mystics. According to Bertrand Russell, in a perhaps uncharitable passage, Pythagoras "founded a religion, of which the main tenets were the transmigration of souls and the sinfulness of eating beans. His religion was embodied in a religious order, which, here and there, acquired control of the State and established a rule of the saints. But the unregenerate hankered after beans, and sooner or later rebelled."

The Pythagoreans delighted in the certainty of mathematical demonstration, the sense of a pure and unsullied world accessible to the human intellect, a Cosmos in which the sides of right triangles perfectly obey simple mathematical relationships. It was in striking contrast to the messy reality of the workaday world. They believed that in their mathematics they had glimpsed a perfect reality, a realm of the gods, of which our familiar world is but

* Although there were a few welcome exceptions. The Pythagorean fascination with whole-number ratios in musical harmonies seems clearly to be based on observation, or even experiment on the sounds issued from plucked strings. Empedocles was, at least in part, a Pythagorean. One of Pythagoras' students, Alcmaeon, is the first person known to have dissected a human body; he distinguished between arteries and veins, was the first to discover the optic nerve and the eustachian tubes, and identified the brain as the seat of the intellect (a contention later denied by Aristotle, who placed intelligence in the heart, and then revived by Herophilus of Chalcedon). He also founded the science of embryology. But Alcmaeon's zest for the impure was not shared by most of his Pythagorean colleagues in later times.

an imperfect reflection. In Plato's famous parable of the cave, prisoners were imagined tied in such a way that they saw only the shadows of passersby and believed the shadows to be real—never guessing the complex reality that was accessible if they would but turn their heads. The Pythagoreans would powerfully influence Plato and, later, Christianity.

They did not advocate the free confrontation of conflicting points of view. Instead, like all orthodox religions, they practiced a rigidity that prevented them from correcting their errors. Cicero wrote:

> In discussion it is not so much weight of authority as force of argument that should be demanded. Indeed, the authority of those who profess to teach is often a positive hindrance to those who desire to learn; they cease to employ their own judgment, and take what they perceive to be the verdict of their chosen master as settling the question. In fact I am not disposed to approve the practice traditionally ascribed to the Pythagoreans, who, when questioned as to the grounds of any assertion that they advanced in debate, are said to have been accustomed to reply "The Master said so," "the Master" being Pythagoras. So potent was an opinion already decided, making authority prevail unsupported by reason.

The Pythagoreans were fascinated by the regular solids, symmetrical three-dimensional objects all of whose sides are the same regular polygon. The cube is the simplest example, having six squares as sides. There are an infinite number of regular polygons, but only five regular solids. (The proof of this statement, a famous example of mathematical reasoning, is given in Appendix 2.) For some reason, knowledge of a solid called the dodecahedron having twelve pentagons as sides seemed to them dangerous. It was mystically associated with the Cosmos. The

The Milky Way from slightly above the plane of its spiral arms, which are illuminated by billions of hot, young blue stars. The galactic core, illuminated by older, redder stars, is seen in the distance. Painting by Jon Lomberg.

A globular cluster of stars, orbiting the galactic core. Painting by Anne Norcia.

The Great Hall of the ancient Library of Alexandria in Egypt. A reconstruction based on scholarly evidence.

A Heike crab from the Japanese Inland Sea.

The Moon from the Earth: the view from just outside the atmosphere.

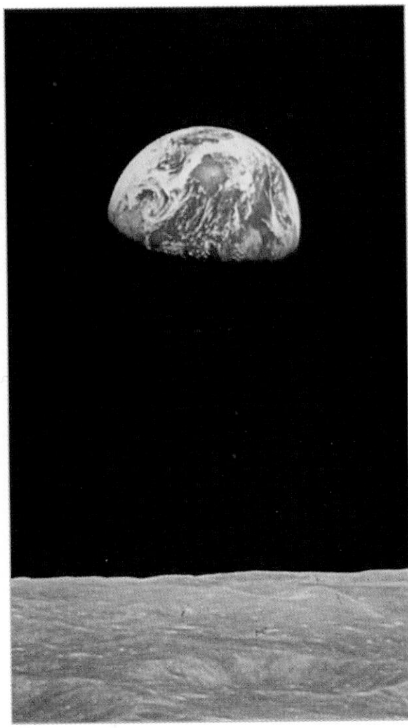

The Earth from the Moon: the view that Kepler dreamed of.

Comet West, photographed from Earth in February 1976 by Martin Grossman of Gromau, West Germany. The great tail is blown away from the icy nucleus of the comet by a wind of protons and electrons from the Sun, which has set below this horizon.

Meteor Crater, Arizona. This crater is 1.2 kilometers in diameter and was probably produced 15,000 to 40,000 years ago when a lump of iron 25 meters across impacted the Earth at a speed of 15 kilometers per second. The energy released was equivalent to that of a 4-megaton nuclear explosion.

Earthrise over rolling hills and complex overlapping craters on the Moon. Apollo Orbiter photo. Courtesy NASA.

Frost in Utopia. A thin layer of water frost covers the ground at 44° North latitude on Mars, in October 1977, at the beginning of northern winter. The vertical structure supports the high-gain antenna for direct communication of Viking 2 with Earth. Colored squares and black strips are calibration targets for the cameras. The black square with white border, bottom left, is a microdot on which are written—very small—the signatures of ten thousand human beings responsible for the design, fabrication, testing, launch and mission operations of the Viking spacecraft. Humans are becoming, almost without noticing it, a multi-planet species. Courtesy NASA.

A portion of Kasei Vallis, an ancient river valley on Mars. Kasei is Japanese for Mars. The impact craters in the channel floor are evidence of its great age. Abundant surface liquid water earlier in Martian history suggests that conditions for life were once more favorable. Viking Orbiter photo, courtesy NASA.

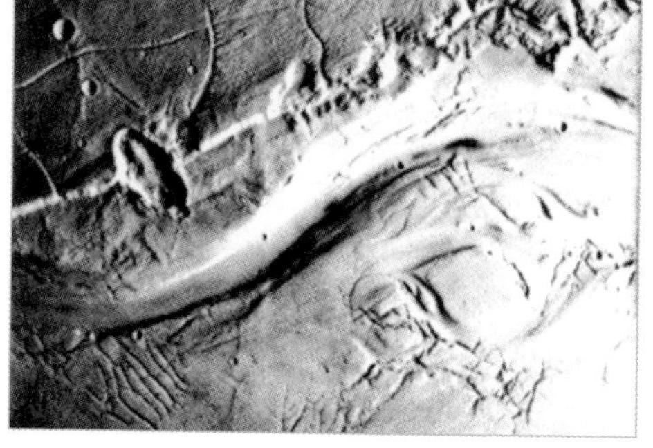

A portrait of another world: strewn boulders and gently rolling sand dunes at the Viking 1 landing site in Chryse. Courtesy NASA.

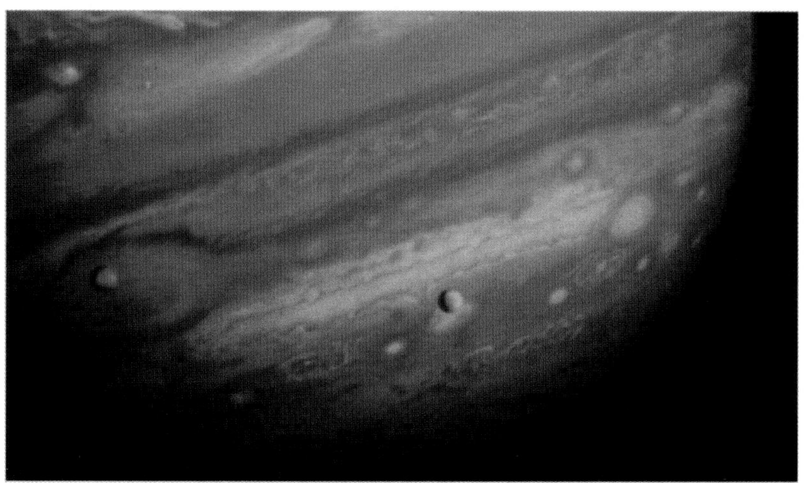

Voyager approaches Jupiter with the moons Io and Callisto in foreground. Courtesy NASA.

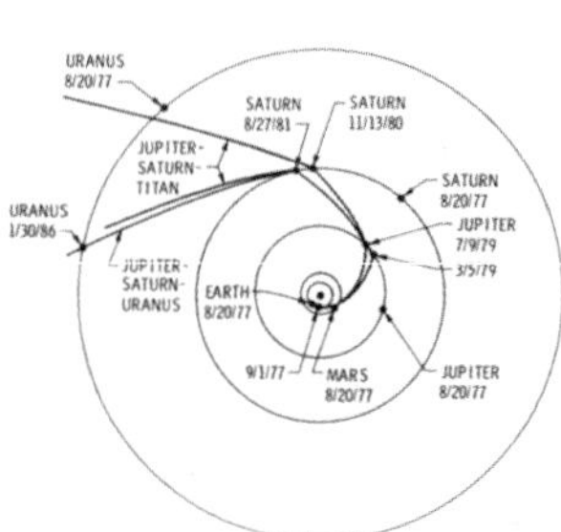

Flight paths of Voyager 1 (crossing the orbit of Uranus, top left) and Voyager 2 (encountering Uranus in January 1986). Also shown is the alternative trajectory were Voyager 2 to have made a close encounter with Titan, as Voyager 1 did.

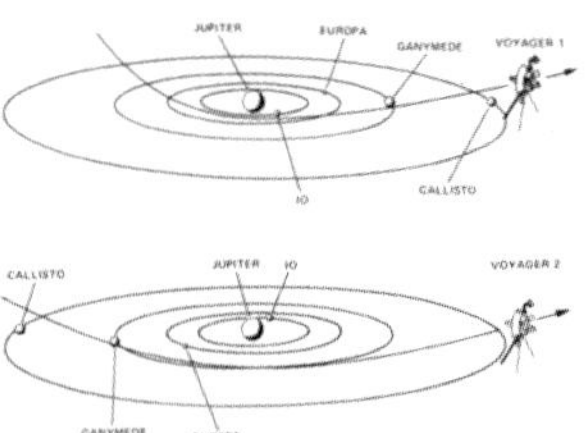

The passage of Voyager 1 (*top*) and Voyager 2 (*bottom*) past the Galilean satellites of Jupiter on March 5 and July 9, 1979.

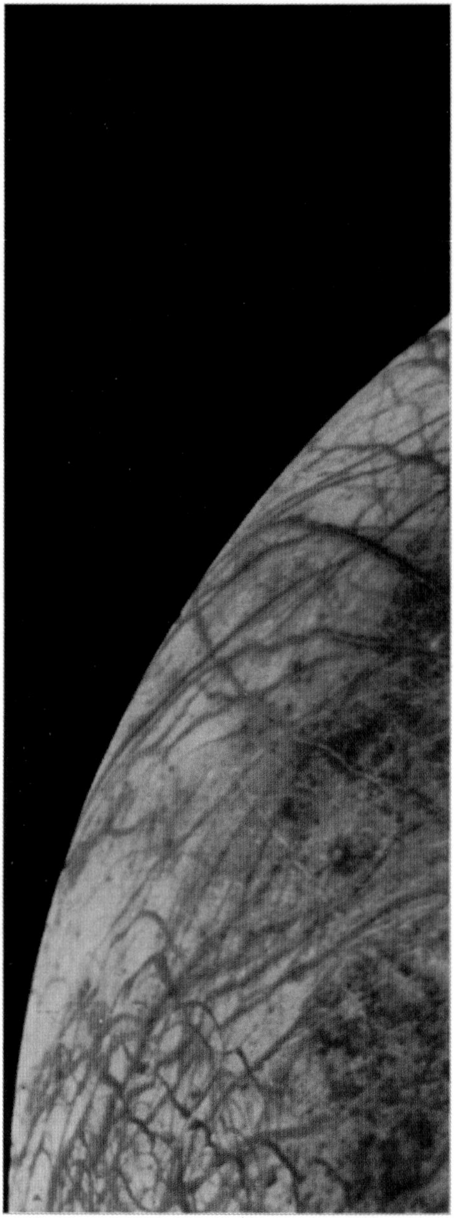

The Jovian moon Europa, as seen by Voyager 2 during close encounter on July 9, 1979. Europa is about the size of our moon but its topography is markedly different. The lack of craters and mountains strongly suggests that a thick ice crust, perhaps 100 kilometers deep, jackets the silicate interior. The complex pattern of dark lines may be ice fractures which have been filled in with material from beneath the crust. The high brightness of Europa is consistent with this hypothesis. Courtesy NASA.

False color image of the Great Red Spot, in which the computer has exaggerated reds and blues at the expense of greens. High clouds temporarily overlie about a third of the GRS. Voyager 1 image. Courtesy NASA.

Voyager 1 image of the surface of Io. Each of the dark, roughly circular features is a recently active volcano. The volcano with a bright halo at the rough center of the disc was observed in eruption just fifteen hours before this image was acquired: it has since been named Prometheus. The black, red, orange and yellow colors are thought to be frozen sulfur, originally spewed from the volcanoes in a molten state with the initial temperatures highest for black deposits and lowest for yellow. White deposits, including those around Prometheus, may be frozen sulfur dioxide. Io is 3,640 kilometers in diameter. Courtesy NASA.

The volcanic plume of the Loki Patera volcano on Io. Ultraviolet light is here transcribed as blue. Surrounding the plume seen in visible light is a vast cloud, bright in reflected ultraviolet sunlight and composed of very small particles. The effect is similar to the blue cast of the light reflected by fine smoke particles. The top of the ultraviolet cloud is more than 200 kilometers above the surface of Io and may eject extremely small particles and atoms directly into space. The ejected matter would still be in orbit about Jupiter, as Io is, and supply the great tube of atoms which surround Jupiter at Io's distance. Voyager 1 image. Courtesy NASA.

A hypothetical ice planet in the system of the Ring Nebula in Lyra. The central star has shed its outer atmosphere, producing a multicolored slowly expanding shell of glowing gas. This system is 1,500 light-years distant, an objective for human exploration in the far future. Painting by David Egge, 1979.

A lifeform and its star. Through a solar telescope equipped with a filter admitting only the red light emitted by hot hydrogen gas, the sunspots appear dark. In foreground, on a mountain, is an exultant human being. Courtesy National Oceanic and Atmospheric Administration. Photograph by Joseph Sutorick.

The Whirlpool Galaxy, M51 (the 51st object in the catalogue of Charles Messier), also known as NGC 5194. In 1845, William Parsons, third Earl of Rosse, discovered the spiral structure of this "nebula," the first galaxy to have such structure observed. Thirteen million light-years distant, it is being gravitationally distorted by its small irregular galactic companion, NGC 5195 (below). Courtesy Hale Observatories.

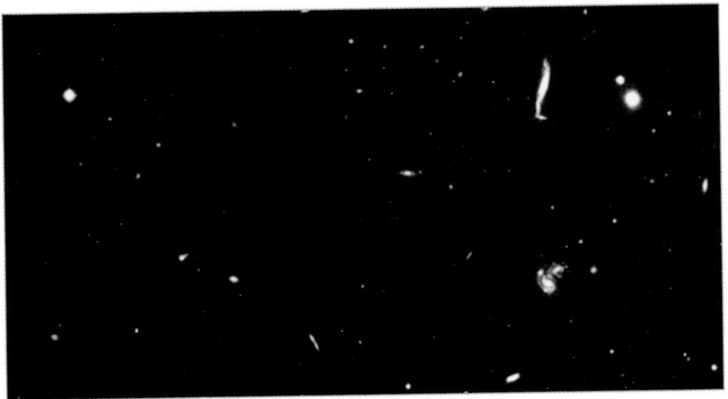

A portion of the Hercules Cluster of galaxies, with about 300 known members, retreating from our region of the Cosmos at some 10,000 kilometers per second. In this photograph there are more galaxies (in excess of 300 million light-years distant) than there are foreground stars in our Milky Way Galaxy. If the Hercules Cluster is not flying apart, there must be five times more mass there, gravitationally gluing the cluster together, than we see in its galaxies. Such "missing mass," if common in intergalactic space, would make a major contribution to closing the universe. Courtesy Hale Observatories.

An intelligent being: A humpback whale breaches the surface of the waters, Frederick Sound, Alaska, summer 1979. Humpbacks are known for their remarkable leaps and their extraordinary communications. An average humpback weighs 50 tons, and is 15 meters long. Their brains are much larger than the brains of humans. Courtesy Dan McSweeney.

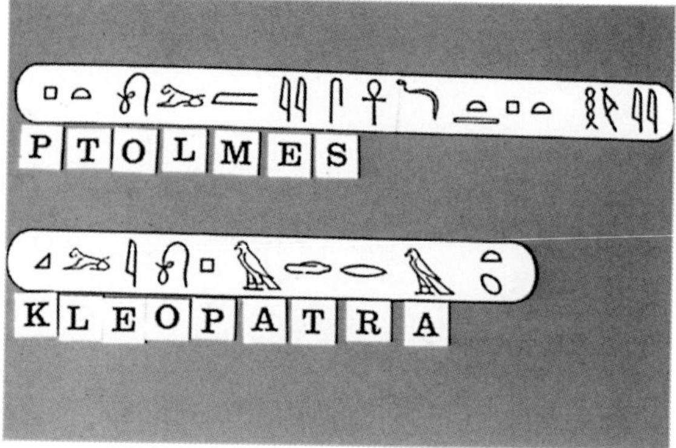

The transliteration of a cartouche of Ptolemy from the Rosetta stone and one of Cleopatra from the Philae obelisk.

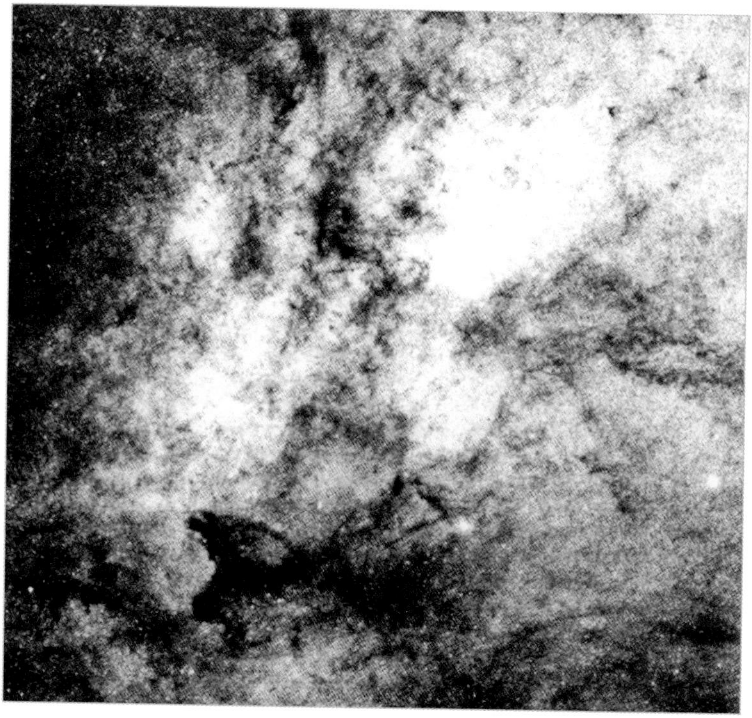

A great star cloud in the constellation Sagittarius, looking towards the center of the Milky Way Galaxy. The obscuring lanes of dust contain organic molecules; some of them contain stars in the earliest stages of formation. In this photograph there are about a million stars. According to the estimates of this chapter, one of them is the sun of a civilization more advanced than ours. Courtesy Hale Observatories.

Two human footprints. Above, from Tanzania, 3.6 million years ago. Below, from Mare Tranquilitatis, 1969. Courtesy Mary Leakey and the National Geographic Society; and NASA.

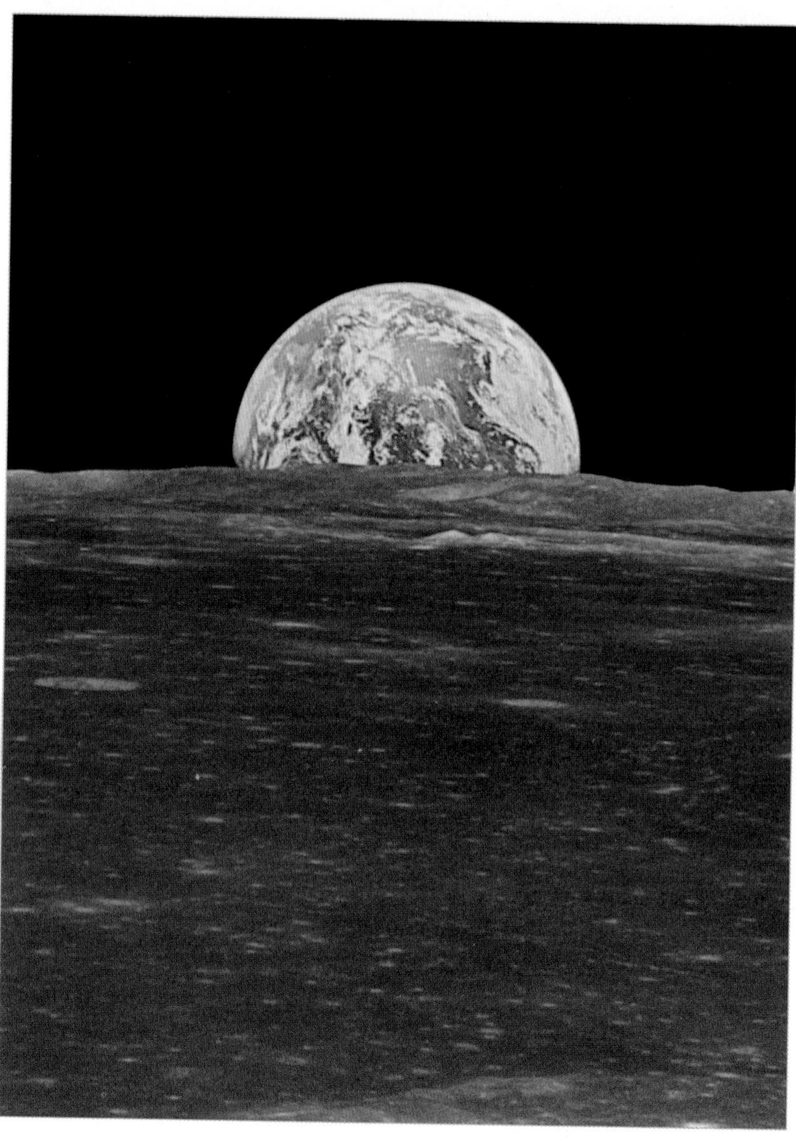

The home planet of an emerging technical civilization, struggling to avoid self-destruction. This world is observed from a temporary outpost near its lone satellite. The Earth travels some 2½ million kilometers every day around the Sun; eight times faster than that around the center of the Milky Way Galaxy; and, perhaps, twice faster still as the Milky Way falls towards the Virgo cluster of galaxies. We have always been space travelers. Courtesy NASA.

other four regular solids were identified, somehow, with the four "elements" then imagined to constitute the world; earth, fire, air and water. The fifth regular solid must then, they thought, correspond to some fifth element that could only be the substance of the heavenly bodies. (This notion of a fifth essence is the origin of our word *quintessence.*) Ordinary people were to be kept ignorant of the dodecahedron.

In love with whole numbers, the Pythagoreans believed all things could be derived from them, certainly all other numbers. A crisis in doctrine arose when they discovered that the square root of two (the ratio of the diagonal to the side of a square) was irrational, that $\sqrt{2}$ cannot be expressed accurately as the ratio of any two whole numbers, no matter how big these numbers are. Ironically this discovery (reproduced in Appendix 1) was made with the Pythagorean theorem as a tool. "Irrational" originally meant only that a number could not be expressed as a ratio. But for the Pythagoreans it came to mean something threatening, a hint that their world view might not make sense, which is today the other meaning of "irrational." Instead of sharing these important mathematical discoveries, the Pythagoreans suppressed the knowledge of $\sqrt{2}$ and the dodecahedron. The outside world was not to know.* Even today there are scientists opposed to the popularization of science: the sacred knowledge is to be kept within the cult, unsullied by public understanding.

The Pythagoreans believed the sphere to be "perfect," all points on its surface being at the same distance from its center. Circles were also perfect. And the Pythagoreans insisted that planets moved in circular paths at constant speeds. They seemed to believe that moving slower or faster at different places in the orbit would be unseemly; noncircular motion was somehow

* A Pythagorean named Hippasus published the secret of the "sphere with twelve pentagons," the dodecahedron. When he later died in a shipwreck, we are told, his fellow Pythagoreans remarked on the justice of the punishment. His book has not survived.

flawed, unsuitable for the planets, which, being free of the Earth, were also deemed "perfect."

The pros and cons of the Pythagorean tradition can be seen clearly in the life's work of Johannes Kepler (Chapter 3). The Pythagorean idea of a perfect and mystical world, unseen by the senses, was readily accepted by the early Christians and was an integral component of Kepler's early training. On the one hand, Kepler was convinced that mathematical harmonies exist in nature (he wrote that "the universe was stamped with the adornment of harmonic proportions"); that simple numerical relationships must determine the motion of the planets. On the other hand, again following the Pythagoreans, he long believed that only uniform circular motion was admissible. He repeatedly found that the observed planetary motions could not be explained in this way, and repeatedly tried again. But unlike many Pythagoreans, he believed in observation and experiment in the real world. Eventually the detailed observations of the apparent motion of the planets forced him to abandon the idea of circular paths and to realize that planets travel in ellipses. Kepler was both inspired in his search for the harmony of planetary motion and delayed for more than a decade by the attractions of Pythagorean doctrine.

A disdain for the practical swept the ancient world. Plato urged astronomers to think about the heavens, but not to waste their time observing them. Aristotle believed that: "The lower sort are by nature slaves, and it is better for them as for all inferiors that they should be under the rule of a master. . . . The slave shares in his master's life; the artisan is less closely connected with him, and only attains excellence in proportion as he becomes a slave. The meaner sort of mechanic has a special and separate slavery." Plutarch wrote: "It does not of necessity follow that, if the work delight you with its grace, the one who wrought it is worthy of esteem." Xenophon's opinion was: "What are called the mechanical arts carry a social stigma and are rightly dishon-

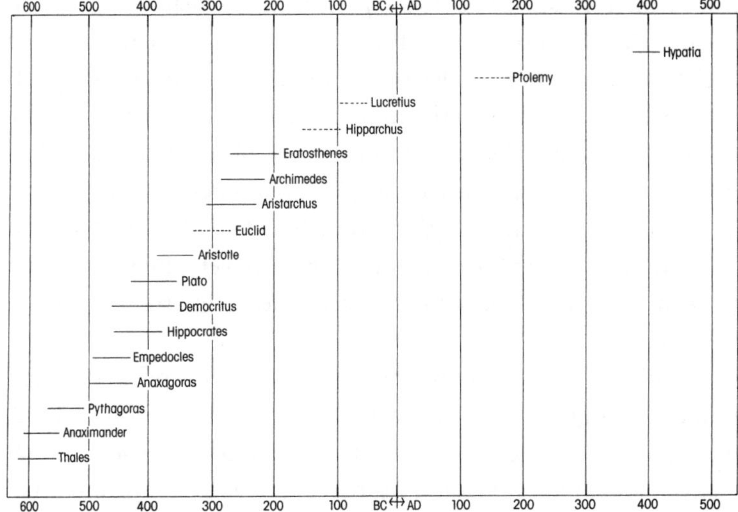

Approximate lifetimes of Ionian and other Greek scientists between the seventh century B.C. and the fifth century. The decline of Greek science is indicated by the relatively few individuals shown after the first century B.C.

oured in our cities." As a result of such attitudes, the brilliant and promising Ionian experimental method was largely abandoned for two thousand years. Without experiment, there is no way to choose among contending hypotheses, no way for science to advance. The antiempirical taint of the Pythagoreans survives to this day. But why? Where did this distaste for experiment come from?

An explanation for the decline of ancient science has been put forward by the historian of science Benjamin Farrington: The mercantile tradition, which led to Ionian science, also led to a slave economy. The owning of slaves was the road to wealth and power. Polycrates' fortifications were built by slaves. Athens in the time of Pericles, Plato and Aristotle had a vast slave population. All the brave Athenian talk about democracy applied only to a privileged few. What slaves characteristically perform is manual labor. But scientific experimentation is manual labor, from which the slaveholders are preferentially distanced; while it is only the slaveholders—politely called "gentle-men" in some societies—who have the leisure to do science. Accordingly, almost no one did science. The Ionians were perfectly able to make machines of some elegance. But the availability of slaves undermined the economic motive for the development of technology. Thus the mercantile tradition contributed to the great Ionian awakening around 600 B.C., and, through slavery, may have been the cause of its decline some two centuries later. There are great ironies here.

Similar trends are apparent throughout the world. The high point in indigenous Chinese astronomy occurred around 1280, with the work of Kuo Shou-ching, who used an observational baseline of 1,500 years and improved both astronomical instruments and mathematical techniques for computation. It is generally thought that Chinese astronomy thereafter underwent a steep decline. Nathan Sivin believes that the reason lies at least partly "in increasing rigidity of elite attitudes, so that the educated were less inclined to be curious about techniques and less willing to value science as an appropriate pursuit for a gentleman." The occupation of astronomer became a hereditary office, a practice inconsistent with the advance of the subject. Additionally, "the responsibility for the evolution of astronomy remained centered in the Imperial Court and was largely abandoned to foreign technicians," chiefly the Jesuits, who had introduced Euclid and Copernicus to the astonished Chinese, but who, after the censorship of the latter's book, had a vested interest in disguising and suppressing heliocentric cosmology. Perhaps science was stillborn in Indian, Mayan and Aztec civilizations for the same reason it declined in Ionia, the pervasiveness of the slave economy. A major problem in the contemporary (political) Third World is that the educated classes tend to be the children of the wealthy, with a vested interest in the status quo, and are unaccustomed either to working with their hands or to challenging conventional wisdom. Science has been very slow to take root.

Plato and Aristotle were comfortable in a slave society. They offered justifications for oppression. They served tyrants. They taught the alienation of the body from the mind (a natural enough ideal in a slave society); they separated matter from thought; they divorced the Earth from the heavens—divisions that were to dominate Western thinking for more than twenty centuries. Plato, who believed that "all things are full of gods," actually used the metaphor of slavery to connect his politics with his cosmology. He is said to have urged the burning of all the books of Democritus (he had a similar recommendation for the books of Homer), perhaps because Democritus did not acknowledge immortal souls or immortal gods or Pythagorean mysticism, or because he believed in an infinite number of worlds. Of the seventy-three books Democritus is said to have written, covering all of human knowledge, not a single work survives. All we know is from fragments, chiefly on ethics, and secondhand accounts. The same is true of almost all the other ancient Ionian scientists.

In the recognition by Pythagoras and Plato that the Cosmos is knowable, that there is a mathematical underpinning to nature, they greatly advanced the cause of science. But in the suppression of disquieting facts, the sense that science should be kept for a small elite, the distaste for experiment, the embrace of mysticism and the easy acceptance of slave societies, they set back the human enterprise. After a long mystical sleep in which the tools of scientific inquiry lay moldering, the Ionian approach, in some cases transmitted through scholars at the Alexandrian Library, was finally rediscovered. The Western world reawakened. Experiment and open inquiry became once more respectable. Forgotten books and fragments were again read. Leonardo and Columbus and Copernicus were inspired by or independently retraced parts of this ancient Greek tradition. There is in our time much Ionian science, although not in politics and religion, and a fair amount of courageous free inquiry. But there are also appalling superstitions and deadly ethical ambiguities. We are flawed by ancient contradictions.

The Platonists and their Christian successors held the peculiar notion that the Earth was tainted and somehow nasty, while the heavens were perfect and divine. The fundamental idea that the Earth is a planet, that we are citizens of the Universe, was rejected and forgotten. This idea was first argued by Aristarchus, born on Samos three centuries after Pythagoras. Aristarchus was one of the last of the Ionian scientists. By this time, the center of intellectual enlightenment had moved to the great Library of Alexandria. Aristarchus was the first person to hold that the Sun rather than the Earth is at the center of the planetary system, that all the planets go around the Sun rather than the Earth. Typically, his writings on this matter are lost. From the size of the Earth's shadow on the Moon during a lunar eclipse, he deduced that the Sun had to be much larger than the Earth, as well as very far away. He may then have reasoned that it is absurd for so large a body as the Sun to revolve around so small a body as the Earth. He put the Sun at the center, made the Earth rotate on its axis once a day and orbit the Sun once a year.

It is the same idea we associate with the name of Copernicus, whom Galileo described as the "restorer and confirmer," not the inventor, of the heliocentric hypothesis.* For most of the 1,800 years between Aristarchus and Copernicus nobody knew the correct disposition of the planets, even though it had been laid

* Copernicus may have gotten the idea from reading about Aristarchus. Recently discovered classical texts were a source of great excitement in Italian universities when Copernicus went to medical school there. In the manuscript of his book, Copernicus mentioned Aristarchus' priority, but he omitted the citation before the book saw print. Copernicus wrote in a letter to Pope Paul III: "According to Cicero, Nicetas had thought the Earth was moved . . . According to Plutarch [who discusses Aristarchus] . . . certain others had held the same opinion. When from this, therefore, I had conceived its possibility, I myself also began to meditate upon the mobility of the Earth."

out perfectly clearly around 280 B.C. The idea outraged some of Aristarchus' contemporaries. There were cries, like those voiced about Anaxagoras and Bruno and Galileo, that he be condemned for impiety. The resistance to Aristarchus and Copernicus, a kind of geocentrism in everyday life, remains with us: we still talk about the Sun "rising" and the Sun "setting." It is 2,200 years since Aristarchus, and our language still pretends that the Earth does not turn.

The separation of the planets from one another—forty million kilometers from Earth to Venus at closest approach, six billion kilometers to Pluto—would have stunned those Greeks who were outraged by the contention that the Sun might be as large as the Peloponnesus. It was natural to think of the solar system as much more compact and local. If I hold my finger before my eyes and examine it first with my left and then with my right eye, it seems to move against the distant background. The closer my finger is, the more it seems to move. I can estimate the distance to my finger from the amount of this apparent motion, or parallax. If my eyes were farther apart, my finger would seem to move substantially more. The longer the baseline from which we make our two observations, the greater the parallax and the better we can measure the distance to remote objects. But we live on a moving platform, the Earth, which every six months has progressed from one end of its orbit to the other, a distance of 300,000,000 kilometers. If we look at the same unmoving celestial object six months apart, we should be able to measure very great distances. Aristarchus suspected the stars to be distant suns. He placed the Sun "among" the fixed stars. The absence of detectable stellar parallax as the Earth moved suggested that the stars were much farther away than the Sun. Before the invention of the telescope, the parallax of even the nearest stars was too small to detect. Not until the nineteenth century was the parallax of a star first measured. It then became clear, from straightforward Greek geometry, that the stars were light-years away.

There is another way to measure the distance to the stars which the Ionians were fully capable of discovering, although, so far as we know, they did not employ it. Everyone knows that the farther away an object is, the smaller it seems. This inverse proportionality between apparent size and distance is the basis of perspective in art and photography. So the farther away we are from the Sun, the smaller and dimmer it appears. How far would we have to be from the Sun for it to appear as small and as dim as a star? Or, equivalently, how small a piece of the Sun would be as bright as a star?

An early experiment to answer this question was performed by Christiaan Huygens, very much in the Ionian tradition. Huygens drilled small holes in a brass plate, held the plate up to the Sun and asked himself which hole seemed as bright as he remembered the bright star Sirius to have been the night before. The hole was effectively* 1/28,000 the apparent size of the Sun. So Sirius, he reasoned, must be 28,000 times farther from us than the Sun, or about half a light-year away. It is hard to remember just how bright a star is many hours after you look at it, but Huygens remembered very well. If he had known that Sirius was intrinsically brighter than the Sun, he would have come up with almost exactly the right answer: Sirius is 8.8 light-years away. The fact that Aristarchus and Huygens used imprecise data and derived imperfect answers hardly matters. They explained their methods so clearly that, when better observations were available, more accurate answers could be derived.

Between the times of Aristarchus and Huygens, humans answered the question that had so excited me as a boy growing up in Brooklyn: What are the stars? The answer is that the stars are mighty suns, light-years away in the vastness of interstellar space.

The great legacy of Aristarchus is this: neither we nor our

* Huygens actually used a glass bead to reduce the amount of light passed by the hole.

planet enjoys a privileged position in Nature. This insight has since been applied upward to the stars, and sideways to many subsets of the human family, with great success and invariable opposition. It has been responsible for major advances in astronomy, physics, biology, anthropology, economics and politics. I wonder if its social extrapolation is a major reason for attempts at its suppression.

The legacy of Aristarchus has been extended far beyond the realm of the stars. At the end of the eighteenth century, William Herschel, musician and astronomer to George III of England, completed a project to map the starry skies and found apparently equal numbers of stars in all directions in the plane or band of the Milky Way; from this, reasonably enough, he deduced that we were at the center of the Galaxy.* Just before World War I, Harlow Shapley of Missouri devised a technique for measuring the distances to the globular clusters, those lovely spherical arrays of stars which resemble a swarm of bees. Shapley had found a stellar standard candle, a star noticeable because of its variability, but which had always the same average intrinsic brightness. By comparing the faintness of such stars when found in globular clusters with their real brightness, as determined from nearby representatives, Shapley could calculate how far away they are—just as, in a field, we can estimate the distance of a lantern of known intrinsic brightness from the feeble light that reaches us—essentially, the method of Huygens. Shapley discovered that the globular clusters were not centered around the solar neighborhood but rather about a distant region of the Milky Way, in the direction of the constellation Sagittarius, the Archer. It seemed to him very likely that the globular clusters used in this investigation, nearly a hundred of them, would be

* This supposed privileged position of the Earth, at the center of what was then considered the known universe, led A. R. Wallace to the anti-Aristarchian position, in his book *Man's Place in the Universe* (1903), that ours may be the only inhabited planet.

orbiting about, paying homage to, the massive center of the Milky Way.

Shapley had in 1915 the courage to propose that the solar system was in the outskirts and not near the core of our galaxy. Herschel had been misled because of the copious amount of obscuring dust in the direction of Sagittarius; he had no way to know of the enormous numbers of stars beyond. It is now very clear that we live some 30,000 light-years from the galactic core, on the fringes of a spiral arm, where the local density of stars is relatively sparse. There may be those who live on a planet that orbits a central star in one of Shapley's globular clusters, or one located in the core. Such beings may pity us for our handful of naked-eye stars, because their skies will be ablaze with them. Near the center of the Milky Way, millions of brilliant stars would be visible to the naked eye, compared to our paltry few thousand. Our Sun or suns might set, but the night would never come.

Well into the twentieth century, astronomers believed that there was only one galaxy in the Cosmos, the Milky Way—although in the eighteenth century Thomas Wright of Durban and Immanuel Kant of Königsberg each had a premonition that the exquisite luminous spiral forms, viewed through the telescope, were other galaxies. Kant suggested explicity that M31 in the constellation Andromeda was another Milky Way, composed of enormous numbers of stars, and proposed calling such objects by the evocative and haunting phrase "island universes." Some scientists toyed with the idea that the spiral nebulae were not distant island universes but rather nearby condensing clouds of interstellar gas, perhaps on their way to make solar systems. To test the distance of the spiral nebulae, a class of intrinsically much brighter variable stars was needed to furnish a new standard candle. Such stars, identified in M31 by Edwin Hubble in 1924, were discovered to be alarmingly dim, and it became apparent that M31 was a prodigious distance away, a number now estimated at a little more than two million light-years. But if M31 were at such a distance, it could not be a cloud of mere interstellar dimensions; it had to be much larger—an immense galaxy in its own right. And the other, fainter galaxies must be more distant still, a hundred billion of them, sprinkled through the dark to the frontiers of the known Cosmos.

As long as there have been humans, we have searched for our place in the Cosmos. In the childhood of our species (when our ancestors gazed a little idly at the stars), among the Ionian scientists of ancient Greece, and in our own age, we have been transfixed by this question: Where are we? Who are we? We find that we live on an insignificant planet of a humdrum star lost between two spiral arms in the outskirts of a galaxy which is a member of a sparse cluster of galaxies, tucked away in some forgotten corner of a universe in which there are far more galaxies than people. This perspective is a courageous continuation of our penchant for constructing and testing mental models of the skies; the Sun as a red-hot stone, the stars as celestial flame, the Galaxy as the backbone of night.

Since Aristarchus, every step in our quest has moved us farther from center stage in the cosmic drama. There has not been much time to assimilate these new findings. The discoveries of Shapley and Hubble were made within the lifetimes of many people still alive today. There are those who secretly deplore these great discoveries, who consider every step a demotion, who in their heart of hearts still pine for a universe whose center, focus and fulcrum is the Earth. But if we are to deal with the Cosmos we must first understand it, even if our hopes for some unearned preferential status are, in the process, contravened. Understanding where we live is an essential precondition for improving the neighborhood. Knowing what other neighborhoods are like also helps. If we long for our planet to be important, there is something we can do about it. We make our world significant by the courage of our questions and by the depth of our answers.

We embarked on our cosmic voyage with a question first framed in the childhood of our species and in each generation asked anew with undiminished wonder: What are the stars? Exploration is in our nature. We began as wanderers, and we are wanderers still. We have lingered long enough on the shores of the cosmic ocean. We are ready at last to set sail for the stars.

CHAPTER VIII

TRAVELS IN SPACE AND TIME

We have loved the stars too fondly to be fearful of the night.

—Tombstone epitaph of two amateur astronomers

The rising and falling of the surf is produced in part by tides. The Moon and the Sun are far away. But their gravitational influence is very real and noticeable back here on Earth. The beach reminds us of space. Fine sand grains, all more or less uniform in size, have been produced from larger rocks through ages of jostling and rubbing, abrasion and erosion, again driven through waves and weather by the distant Moon and Sun. The beach also reminds us of time. The world is much older than the human species.

A handful of sand contains about 10,000 grains, more than the number of stars we can see with the naked eye on a clear night. But the number of stars we can *see* is only the tiniest fraction of the number of stars that *are.* What we see at night is the merest smattering of the nearest stars. Meanwhile the Cosmos is rich beyond measure: the total number of stars in the universe is greater than all the grains of sand on all the beaches of the planet Earth.

Despite the efforts of ancient astronomers and astrologers to put pictures in the skies, a constellation is nothing more than an arbitrary grouping of stars, composed of intrinsically dim stars that seem to us bright because they are nearby, and intrinsically brighter stars that are somewhat more distant. All places on Earth are, to high precision, the same distance from any star. This is why the star patterns in a given constellation do not change as we go from, say, Soviet Central Asia to the American Midwest. Astronomically, the U.S.S.R. and the United States are the same place. The stars in any constellation are all so far away that we cannot recognize them as a three-dimensional configuration as long as we are tied to Earth. The average distance between the stars is a few light-years, a light-year being, we remember, about ten trillion kilometers. For the patterns of the constellations to change, we must travel over distances comparable to those that separate the stars; we must venture across the light-years. Then some nearby stars will seem to move out of the constellation, others will enter it, and its configuration will alter dramatically.

Our technology is, so far, utterly incapable of such grand interstellar voyages, at least in reasonable transit times. But our computers can be taught the three-dimensional positions of all the nearby stars, and we can ask to be taken on a little trip—a circumnavigation of the collection of bright stars that constitute the Big Dipper, say—and watch the constellations change. We connect the stars in typical constellations, in the usual celestial follow-the-dots drawings. As we change our perspective, we see their apparent shapes distort severely. The inhabitants of the planets of distant stars witness quite different constellations in their night skies than we do in ours—other Rorschach tests for other minds. Perhaps sometime in the next few centuries a spaceship from Earth will actually travel such distances at some re-

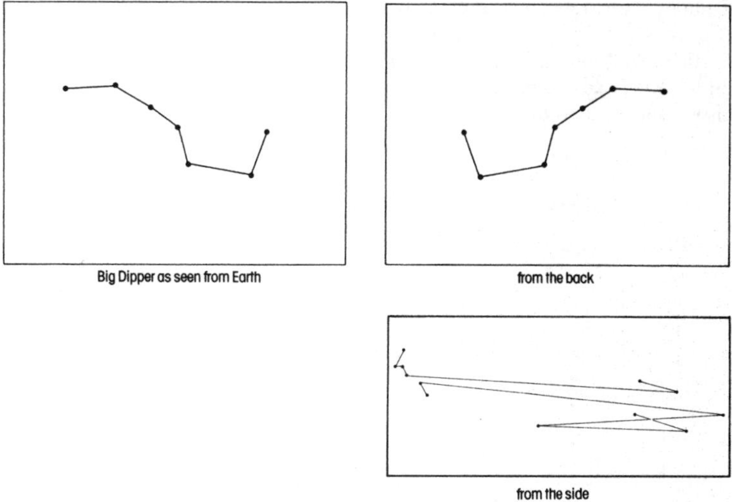

The Big Dipper, as seen from the Earth (*top left*), from the back (*top right*) and from the side (*right*). The last two views would be seen if we were able to travel to the proper vantage points, about 150 light-years away.

markable speed and see new constellations that no human has ever viewed before—except with such a computer.

The appearance of the constellations changes not only in space but also in time; not only if we alter our position but also if we merely wait sufficiently long. Sometimes stars move together in a group or cluster; other times a single star may move very rapidly with respect to its fellows. Eventually such stars leave an old constellation and enter a new one. Occasionally, one member of a double-star system explodes, breaking the gravitational shackles that bound its companion, which then leaps into space at its former orbital velocity, a slingshot in the sky. In addition, stars are born, stars evolve, and stars die. If we wait long enough, new stars appear and old stars vanish. The patterns in the sky slowly melt and alter.

Even over the lifetime of the human species—a few million

Computer-generated images of the Big Dipper as it would have been seen on Earth one million years ago and half a million years ago. Its present appearance is shown at bottom.

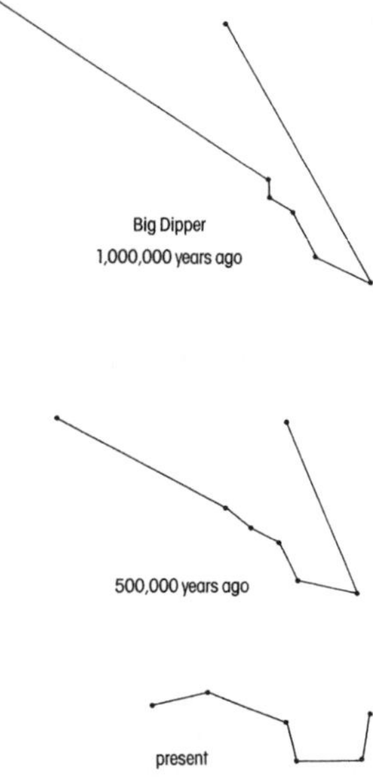

years—constellations have been changing. Consider the present configuration of the Big Dipper, or Great Bear. Our computer can carry us in time as well as in space. As we run the Big Dipper backward into the past, allowing for the motion of its stars, we find quite a different appearance a million years ago. The Big Dipper then looked quite a bit like a spear. If a time machine dropped you precipitously in some unknown age in the distant past, you could in principle determine the epoch by the configuration of the stars: If the Big Dipper is a spear, this must be the Middle Pleistocene.

We can also ask the computer to run a constellation forward into time. Consider Leo the Lion. The zodiac is a band of twelve constellations seemingly wrapped around the sky in the apparent annual path of the Sun through the heavens. The root of the word is that for *zoo,* because the zodiacal constellations, like Leo, are mainly fancied to be animals. A million years from now, Leo will look still less like a lion than it does today. Perhaps our remote descendants will call it the constellation of the radio telescope—although I suspect a million years from now the radio telescope will have become more obsolete than the stone spear is now.

The (nonzodiacal) constellation of Orion, the hunter, is outlined by four bright stars and bisected by a diagonal line of three stars, which represent the belt of the hunter. Three dimmer stars hanging from the belt are, according to the conventional astronomical projective test, Orion's sword. The middle star in the sword is not actually a star but a great cloud of gas called the Orion Nebula, in which stars are being born. Many of the stars in Orion are hot and young, evolving rapidly and ending their lives in colossal cosmic explosions called supernovae. They are born and die in periods of tens of millions of years. If, on our computer, we were to run Orion rapidly into the far future, we would see a startling effect, the births and spectacular deaths of many of its stars, flashing on and winking off like fireflies in the night.

The solar neighborhood, the immediate environs of the Sun in space, includes the nearest star system, Alpha Centauri. It is really a triple system, two stars revolving around each other, and a third, Proxima Centauri, orbiting the pair at a discreet distance. At some positions in its orbit, Proxima is the closest known star to the Sun—hence its name. Most stars in the sky are members of double or multiple star systems. Our solitary Sun is something of an anomaly.

The second brightest star in the constellation Andromeda, called Beta Andromedae, is seventy-five light-years away. The light by which we see it now has spent seventy-five years traversing the dark of interstellar space on its long journey to Earth. In the unlikely event that Beta Andromedae blew itself up last Tuesday, we would not know it for another seventy-five years, as this interesting information, traveling at the speed of light, would require seventy-five years to cross the enormous interstellar distances. When the light by which we now see this star set out on its long voyage, the young Albert Einstein, working as a Swiss patent clerk, had just published his epochal special theory of relativity here on Earth.

Space and time are interwoven. We cannot look out into space without looking back into time. Light travels very fast. But space is very empty, and the stars are far apart. Distances of seventy-five light-years or less are very small compared to other distances in astronomy. From the Sun to the center of the Milky Way Galaxy is 30,000 light-years. From our galaxy to the nearest spiral galaxy, M31, also in the constellation Andromeda, is 2,000,000 light-years. When the light we see today from M31 left for Earth, there were no humans on our planet, although our ancestors were evolving rapidly to our present form. The distance from the Earth to the most remote quasars is eight or ten billion light-years. We see them today as they were before the Earth accumulated, before the Milky Way was formed.

This is not a situation restricted to astronomical objects, but only astronomical objects are so far away that the finite speed of light becomes important. If you are looking at a friend three meters (ten feet) away, at the other end of the room, you are not seeing her as she is "now"; but rather as she "was" a hundred millionth of a second ago. [$(3 \text{ m}) / (3 \times 10^8 \text{ m/sec}) = 1/(10^8 / \text{sec}) = 10^{-8}$ sec, or a hundredth of a microsecond. In this calculation we have merely divided the distance by the speed to get the travel time.] But the difference between your friend "now" and now minus a hundred-millionth of a second is too small to notice. On the other hand, when we look at a quasar eight billion light-years away, the fact that we are seeing it as it was eight billion years ago may be very important. (For example, there are those who think that quasars are explosive events likely to happen only in the early history of galaxies. In that case, the more distant the galaxy, the earlier in its history we are observing it, and the more likely it is that we should see it as a quasar. Indeed, the number of quasars increases as we look to distances of more than about five billion light-years.)

The two Voyager interstellar spacecraft, the fastest machines ever launched from Earth, are now traveling at one ten-thousandth the speed of light. They would need 40,000 years to go the distance to the nearest star. Do we have any hope of leaving Earth and traversing the immense distances even to Proxima Centauri in convenient periods of time? Can we do something to approach the speed of light? What is magic about the speed of light? Might we someday be able to go faster than that?

If you had walked through the pleasant Tuscan countryside in the 1890's, you might have come upon a somewhat long-haired teenage high school dropout on the road to Pavia. His teachers in Germany had told him that he would never amount to anything, that his questions destroyed classroom discipline, that he would be better off out of school. So he left and wandered, delighting in the freedom of Northern Italy, where he could ruminate on matters remote from the subjects he had been force-fed in his highly disciplined Prussian schoolroom. His name was Albert Einstein, and his ruminations changed the world.

Einstein had been fascinated by Bernstein's *People's Book of Natural Science,* a popularization of science that described on its very first page the astonishing speed of electricity through wires and light through space. He wondered what the world would look like if you could travel on a wave of light. To travel at the speed of light? What an engaging and magical thought for a boy on the road in a countryside dappled and rippling in sunlight. You could not tell you were on a light wave if you traveled with it. If you started on a wave crest, you would stay on the crest and lose all notion of it being a wave. Something strange happens at the speed of light. The more Einstein thought about such questions, the more troubling they became. Paradoxes seemed to emerge everywhere if you could travel at the speed of light. Certain ideas had been accepted as true without sufficiently careful thought. Einstein posed simple questions that could have been asked centuries earlier. For example, what do we mean when we say that two events are simultaneous?

Imagine that I am riding a bicycle toward you. As I approach an intersection I nearly collide, so it seems to me, with a horse-drawn cart. I swerve and barely avoid being run over. Now think of the event again, and imagine that the cart and the bicycle are both traveling close to the speed of light. If you are standing down the road, the cart is traveling at right angles to your line of sight. You see me, by reflected sunlight, traveling toward you. Would not my speed be added to the speed of light, so that my image would get to you considerably before the image of the cart? Should you not see me swerve before you see the cart arrive? Can the cart and I approach the intersection simultaneously from my point of view, but not from yours? Could I experience a near collision with the cart while you perhaps see me swerve around nothing and pedal cheerfully on toward the town of Vinci? These are curious and subtle questions. They challenge the obvious. There is a reason that no one thought of them before Einstein. From such elementary questions, Einstein produced a fundamental rethinking of the world, a revolution in physics.

If the world is to be understood, if we are to avoid such logical paradoxes when traveling at high speeds, there are some rules, commandments of Nature, that must be obeyed. Einstein codified these rules in the special theory of relativity. Light (reflected or emitted) from an object travels at the same velocity whether the object is moving or stationary: *Thou shalt not add thy speed to the speed of light.* Also, no material object may move faster than light: *Thou shalt not travel at or beyond the speed of light.* Nothing in physics prevents you from traveling as close to the speed of light as you like; 99.9 percent of the speed of light would be just fine. But no matter how hard you try, you can never gain that last decimal point. For the world to be logically consistent, there must be a cosmic speed limit. Otherwise, you could get to any speed you wanted by adding velocities on a moving platform.

Europeans around the turn of the century generally believed in privileged frames of reference: that German, or French, or British culture and political organization were better than those of other countries; that Europeans were superior to other peoples who were fortunate enough to be colonized. The social and political application of the ideas of Aristarchus and Copernicus was rejected or ignored. The young Einstein rebelled against the notion of privileged frames of reference in physics as much as he did in politics. In a universe filled with stars rushing helter-skelter in all directions, there was no place that was "at rest," no framework from which to view the universe that was superior to any other framework. This is what the word *relativity* means. The idea is very simple, despite its magical trappings: in viewing the universe, every place is as good as every other place. The laws of Nature must be identical no matter who is describing them. If this is to be true—and it would be stunning if there were something special about our insignificant location in the Cosmos—then it follows that no one may travel faster than light.

We hear the crack of a bullwhip because its tip is moving faster than the speed of sound, creating a shock wave, a small sonic boom. A thunderclap has a similar origin. It was once thought that airplanes could not travel faster than sound. Today supersonic flight is commonplace. But the light barrier is different from the sound barrier. It is not merely an engineering problem like the one the supersonic airplane solves. It is a fundamental law of Nature, as basic as gravity. And there are no phenomena in our experience—like the crack of the bullwhip or the clap of thunder for sound—to suggest the possibility of traveling in a vacuum faster than light. On the contrary, there is an extremely wide range of experience—with nuclear accelerators and atomic clocks, for example—in precise quantitative agreement with special relativity.

The problems of simultaneity do not apply to sound as they do to light because sound is propagated through some material medium, usually air. The sound wave that reaches you when a friend is talking is the motion of molecules in the air. Light, however, travels in a vacuum. There are restrictions on how molecules of air can move which do not apply to a vacuum. Light from the Sun reaches us across the intervening empty space, but no matter how carefully we listen, we do not hear the crackle of sunspots or the thunder of the solar flares. It was once thought, in the days before relativity, that light did propagate through a special medium that permeated all of space, called "the luminiferous aether." But the famous Michelson-Morley experiment demonstrated that such an aether does not exist.

We sometimes hear of things that can travel faster than light. Something called "the speed of thought" is occasionally proffered. This is an exceptionally silly notion—especially since the speed of impulses through the neurons in our brains is about the same as the speed of a donkey cart. That human beings have been clever enough to devise relativity shows that we think well, but I do not think we can boast about thinking fast. The electrical impulses in modern computers do, however, travel nearly at the speed of light.

Special relativity, fully worked out by Einstein in his middle twenties, is supported by every experiment performed to check it. Perhaps tomorrow someone will invent a theory consistent with everything else we know that circumvents paradoxes on such matters as simultaneity, avoids privileged reference frames and still permits travel faster than light. But I doubt it very much. Einstein's prohibition against traveling faster than light may clash with our common sense. But on this question, why should we trust common sense? Why should our experience at 10 kilometers an hour constrain the laws of nature at 300,000 kilometers per second? Relativity does set limits on what humans can ultimately do. But the universe is not required to be in perfect harmony with human ambition. Special relativity removes from our grasp one way of reaching the stars, the ship that can go faster than light. Tantalizingly, it suggests another and quite unexpected method.

Following George Gamow, let us imagine a place where the speed of light is not its true value of 300,000 kilometers per second, but something very modest: 40 kilometers per hour, say—and strictly enforced. (There are no penalties for breaking laws of Nature, because there are no crimes: Nature is self-regulating and merely arranges things so that its prohibitions are impossible to transgress.) Imagine that you are approaching the speed of light on a motor scooter. (Relativity is rich in sentences beginning "Imagine . . ." Einstein called such an exercise a *Gedankenexperiment,* a thought experiment.) As your speed increases, you begin to see around the corners of passing objects. While you are rigidly facing forward, things that are behind you appear within your forward field of vision. Close to the speed of light, from your point of view, the world looks very odd—ultimately everything is squeezed into a tiny circular window, which stays just ahead of you. From the standpoint of a stationary observer, light reflected off you is reddened as you depart and blued as you return. If you travel toward the observer at almost the speed of light, you will become enveloped in an eerie chromatic radiance: your usually invisible infrared emission will be shifted to the shorter visible wavelengths. You become compressed in the direction of motion, your mass increases, and time, as you experience it, slows down, a breathtaking consequence of traveling close to the speed of light called time dilation. But from the standpoint of an observer moving with you—perhaps the scooter has a second seat—none of these effects occur.

These peculiar and at first perplexing predictions of special relativity are true in the deepest sense that anything in science is true. They depend on your relative motion. But they are real, not optical illusions. They can be demonstrated by simple mathematics, mainly first-year algebra and therefore understandable to any educated person. They are also consistent with many experiments. Very accurate clocks carried in airplanes slow down a little compared to stationary clocks. Nuclear accelerators are designed to allow for the increase of mass with increasing speed; if they were not designed in this way, accelerated particles would all smash into the walls of the apparatus, and there would be little to do in experimental nuclear physics. A speed is a distance divided by a time. Since near the velocity of light we cannot simply add speeds, as we are used to doing in the workaday world, the familiar notions of absolute space and absolute time—independent of your *relative* motion—must give way. That is why you shrink. That is the reason for time dilation.

Traveling close to the speed of light you would hardly age at all, but your friends and your relatives back home would be aging at the usual rate. When you returned from your relativistic journey, what a difference there would be between your friends and you, they having aged decades, say, and you having aged hardly at all! Traveling close to the speed of light is a kind of elixir of life. Because time slows down close to the speed of light, special relativity provides us with a means of going to the stars. But is it possible, in terms of practical engineering, to travel close to the speed of light? Is a starship feasible?

Tuscany was not only the caldron of some of the thinking of the young Albert Einstein; it was also the home of another great genius who lived 400 years earlier, Leonardo da Vinci, who delighted in climbing the Tuscan hills and viewing the ground from a great height, as if he were soaring like a bird. He drew the first aerial perspectives of landscapes, towns and fortifications. Among Leonardo's many interests and accomplishments—in painting, sculpture, anatomy, geology, natural history, military and civil engineering—he had a great passion: to devise and fabricate a machine that could fly. He drew pictures, constructed models, built full-size prototypes—and not one of them worked.

No sufficiently powerful and lightweight engine then existed. The designs, however, were brilliant and encouraged the engineers of future times. Leonardo himself was depressed by these failures. But it was hardly his fault. He was trapped in the fifteenth century.

A similar case occurred in 1939 when a group of engineers calling themselves the British Interplanetary Society designed a ship to take people to the Moon—using 1939 technology. It was by no means identical to the design of the Apollo spacecraft, which accomplished exactly this mission three decades later, but it suggested that a mission to the Moon might one day be a practical engineering possibility.

Today we have preliminary designs for ships to take people to the stars. None of these spacecraft is imagined to leave the Earth directly. Rather, they are constructed in Earth orbit from where they are launched on their long interstellar journeys. One of them was called Project Orion after the constellation, a reminder that the ship's ultimate objective was the stars. Orion was designed to utilize explosions of hydrogen bombs, nuclear weapons, against an inertial plate, each explosion providing a kind of "putt-putt," a vast nuclear motorboat in space. Orion seems entirely practical from an engineering point of view. By its very nature it would have produced vast quantities of radioactive debris, but for conscientious mission profiles only in the emptiness of interplanetary or interstellar space. Orion was under serious development in the United States until the signing of the international treaty that forbids the detonation of nuclear weapons in space. This seems to me a great pity. The Orion starship is the best use of nuclear weapons I can think of.

Project Daedalus is a recent design of the British Interplanetary Society. It assumes the existence of a nuclear fusion reactor—something much safer as well as more efficient than existing fission power plants. We do not have fusion reactors yet, but they are confidently expected in the new few decades. Orion and Daedalus might travel at 10 percent the speed of light. A trip to Alpha Centauri, 4.3 light-years away, would then take forty-three years, less than a human lifetime. Such ships could not travel close enough to the speed of light for special relativistic time dilation to become important. Even with optimistic projections on the development of our technology, it does not seem likely that Orion, Daedalus or their ilk will be built before the middle of the twenty-first century, although if we wished we could build Orion now.

For voyages beyond the nearest stars, something else must be done. Perhaps Orion and Daedalus could be used as multigeneration ships, so those arriving at a planet of another star would be the remote descendants of those who had set out some centuries before. Or perhaps a safe means of hibernation for humans will be found, so that the space travelers could be frozen and then reawakened centuries later. These nonrelativistic starships, enormously expensive as they would be, look relatively easy to design and build and use compared to starships that travel close to the speed of light. Other star systems are accessible to the human species, but only after great effort.

Fast interstellar spaceflight—with the ship velocity approaching the speed of light—is an objective not for a hundred years but for a thousand or ten thousand. But it is in principle possible. A kind of interstellar ramjet has been proposed by R. W. Bussard which scoops up the diffuse matter, mostly hydrogen atoms, that floats between the stars, accelerates it into a fusion engine and ejects it out the back. The hydrogen would be used both as fuel and as reaction mass. But in deep space there is only about one atom in every ten cubic centimeters, a volume the size of a grape. For the ramjet to work, it needs a frontal scoop hundreds of kilometers across. When the ship reaches relativistic velocities, the hydrogen atoms will be moving with respect to the spaceship at close to the speed of light. If adequate precautions are not taken, the spaceship and its passengers will be fried by these induced cosmic rays. One proposed solution uses a laser to strip the electrons off the interstellar atoms and make them electrically charged while they are still some distance away, and an extremely strong magnetic field to deflect the charged atoms into the scoop and away from the rest of the spacecraft. This is engineering on a scale so far unprecedented on Earth. We are talking of engines the size of small worlds.

But let us spend a moment thinking about such a ship. The Earth gravitationally attracts us with a certain force, which if we are falling we experience as an acceleration. Were we to fall out of a tree—and many of our proto-human ancestors must have done so—we would plummet faster and faster, increasing our fall speed by ten meters (or thirty-two feet) per second, every second. This acceleration, which characterizes the force of gravity holding us to the Earth's surface, is called 1 g, *g* for Earth gravity. We are comfortable with accelerations of 1 g; we have grown up with 1 g. If we lived in an interstellar spacecraft that could accelerate at 1 g, we would find ourselves in a perfectly natural environment. In fact, the equivalence between gravitational forces and the forces we would feel in an accelerating spaceship is a major feature of Einstein's later general theory of relativity. With a continuous 1 g acceleration, after one year in space we would be traveling very close to the speed of light [$(0.01 \text{ km/sec}^2) \times (3 \times 10^7 \text{ sec}) = 3 \times 10^5$ km/sec].

Suppose that such a spacecraft accelerates at 1 g, approaching more and more closely to the speed of light until the midpoint of the journey; and then is turned around and decelerates at 1 g until arriving at its destination. For most of the trip the velocity would be very close to the speed of light and time would slow down enormously. A nearby mission objective, a sun that may have planets, is Barnard's Star, about six light-years away. It could be reached in about eight years as measured by clocks aboard the ship; the center of the Milky Way, in twenty-one years; M31, the Andromeda galaxy, in twenty-eight years. Of course, people left behind on Earth would see things differently. Instead of twenty-one years to the center of the Galaxy, they would measure an elapsed time of 30,000 years. When we got home, few of our friends would be left to greet us. In principle, such a journey, mounting the decimal points ever closer to the speed of light, would even permit us to circumnavigate the known universe in some fifty-six years ship time. We would return tens of billions of years in our future—to find the Earth a charred cinder and the Sun dead. Relativistic spaceflight makes the universe accessible to advanced civilizations, but only to those who go on the journey. There seems to be no way for information to travel back to those left behind any faster than the speed of light.

The designs for Orion, Daedalus and the Bussard Ramjet are probably farther from the actual interstellar spacecraft we will one day build than Leonardo's models are from today's supersonic transports. But if we do not destroy ourselves, I believe that we will one day venture to the stars. When our solar system is all explored, the planets of other stars will beckon.

Space travel and time travel are connected. We can travel fast into space only by traveling fast into the future. But what of the past? Could we return to the past and change it? Could we make events turn out differently from what the history books assert? We travel slowly into the future all the time, at the rate of one day every day. With relativistic spaceflight we could travel fast into the future. But many physicists believe that a voyage into the past is impossible. Even if you had a device that could travel backward in time, they say, you would be unable to do anything that would make any difference. If you journeyed into the past and prevented your parents from meeting, then you would never have been born—which is something of a contradiction, since you clearly exist. Like the proof of the irrationality of $\sqrt{2}$, like the discussion of simultaneity in special relativity, this is an argument in which the premise is challenged because the conclusion seems absurd.

But other physicists propose that two alternative histories, two equally valid realities, could exist side by side—the one you know and the one in which you were never born. Perhaps time itself has many potential dimensions, despite the fact that we are condemned to experience only one of them. Suppose you could go back into the past and change it—by persuading Queen Isabella not to support Christopher Columbus, for example. Then, it is argued, you would have set into motion a different sequence of historical events, which those you left behind in our time line would never know about. If *that* kind of time travel were possible, then every imaginable alternative history might in some sense really exist.

History consists for the most part of a complex bundle of deeply interwoven threads, social, cultural and economic forces that are not easily unraveled. The countless small, unpredictable and random events that flow on continually often have no long-range consequences. But some, those occurring at critical junctures or branch points, may change the pattern of history. There may be cases where profound changes can be made by relatively trivial adjustments. The farther in the past such an event is, the more powerful may be its influence—because the longer the lever arm of time becomes.

A polio virus is a tiny microorganism. We encounter many of them every day. But only rarely, fortunately, does one of them infect one of us and cause this dread disease. Franklin D. Roosevelt, the thirty-second President of the United States, had polio. Because the disease was crippling, it may have provided Roosevelt with a greater compassion for the underdog; or perhaps it improved his striving for success. If Roosevelt's personality had been different, or if he had never had the ambition to be President of the United States, the Great Depression of the 1930's, World War II and the development of nuclear weapons might just possibly have turned out differently. The future of the world might have been altered. But a virus is an insignificant thing, only a millionth of a centimeter across. It is hardly anything at all.

On the other hand, suppose our time traveler had persuaded Queen Isabella that Columbus' geography was faulty, that from Eratosthenes' estimate of the circumference of the Earth, Columbus could never reach Asia. Almost certainly some other European would have come along within a few decades and sailed west to the New World. Improvements in navigation, the lure of the spice trade and competition among rival European powers made the discovery of America around 1500 more or less inevitable. Of course, there would today be no nation of Colombia, or District of Columbia or Columbus, Ohio, or Columbia University in the Americas. But the overall course of history might have turned out more or less the same. In order to affect the future profoundly, a time traveler would probably have to intervene in a number of carefully chosen events, to change the weave of history.

It is a lovely fantasy, to explore those worlds that never were. By visiting them we could truly understand how history works; history could become an experimental science. If an apparently pivotal person had never lived—Plato, say, or Paul, or Peter the Great—how different would the world be? What if the scientific tradition of the ancient Ionian Greeks had survived and flourished? That would have required many of the social forces of the time to have been different—including the prevailing belief that slavery was natural and right. But what if that light that dawned in the eastern Mediterranean 2,500 years ago had not flickered out? What if science and the experimental method and the dignity of crafts and mechanical arts had been vigorously pursued 2,000 years before the Industrial Revolution? What if the power of this new mode of thought had been more generally appreciated? I sometimes think we might then have saved ten or twenty centuries. Perhaps the contributions of Leonardo would have been made a thousand years ago and those of Albert Einstein five hundred years ago. In such an alternate Earth, Leonardo and Einstein would, of course, never have been born. Too many things would have been different. In every ejaculation there are hundreds of millions of sperm cells, only one of which can fertilize an egg and produce a member of the next generation of human beings. But which sperm succeeds in fertilizing an egg must depend on the most minor and insignificant of factors, both internal and external. If even a little thing had gone differently 2,500 years ago, none of us would be here today. There would be billions of others living in our place.

If the Ionian spirit had won, I think we—a different "we," of course—might by now be venturing to the stars. Our first survey ships to Alpha Centauri and Barnard's Star, Sirius and Tau Ceti would have returned long ago. Great fleets of interstellar transports would be under construction in Earth orbit—unmanned survey ships, liners for immigrants, immense trading ships to plow the seas of space. On all these ships there would be symbols and writing. If we looked closely, we might see that the language was Greek. And perhaps the symbol on the bow of one of the first starships would be a dodecahedron, with the inscription "Starship Theodorus of the Planet Earth."

In the time line of our world, things have gone somewhat more slowly. We are not yet ready for the stars. But perhaps in another century or two, when the solar system is all explored, we will also have put our planet in order. We will have the will and the resources and the technical knowledge to go to the stars. We will have examined from great distances the diversity of other planetary systems, some very much like our own and some extremely different. We will know which stars to visit. Our machines and our descendants will then skim the light-years, the children of Thales and Aristarchus, Leonardo and Einstein.

We are not yet certain how many planetary systems there are, but there seem to be a great abundance. In our immediate vicinity, there is not just one, but in a sense four: Jupiter, Saturn and Uranus each has a satellite system that, in the relative sizes and spacings of the moons, resembles closely the planets about the

Sun. Extrapolation of the statistics of double stars which are greatly disparate in mass suggests that almost all single stars like the Sun should have planetary companions.

We cannot yet directly see the planets of other stars, tiny points of light swamped in the brilliance of their local suns. But we are becoming able to detect the gravitational influence of an unseen planet on an observed star. Imagine such a star with a large "proper motion," moving over decades against the backdrop of more distant constellations; and with a large planet, the mass of Jupiter, say, whose orbital plane is by chance aligned at right angles to our line of sight. When the dark planet is, from our perspective, to the right of the star, the star will be pulled a little to the right, and conversely when the planet is to the left. Consequently, the path of the star will be altered, or perturbed, from a straight line to a wavy one. The nearest star for which this gravitational perturbation method can be applied is Barnard's Star, the nearest single star. The complex interactions of the three stars in the Alpha Centauri system would make the search for a low-mass companion there very difficult. Even for Barnard's Star, the investigation must be painstaking, a search for microscopic displacements of position on photographic plates exposed at the telescope over a period of decades. Two such quests have been performed for planets around Barnard's Star, and both have been by some criteria successful, implying the presence of two or three planets of Jovian mass moving in an orbit (calculated by Kepler's third law) somewhat closer to their star than Jupiter and Saturn are to the Sun. But unfortunately the two sets of observations seem mutually incompatible. A planetary system around Barnard's Star may well have been discovered, but an unambiguous demonstration awaits further study.

Other methods of detecting planets around the stars are under development, including one where the obscuring light from the star is artificially occulted—with a disk in front of a space telescope, or by using the dark edge of the Moon as such a disk—and the reflected light from the planet, no longer hidden by the brightness of the nearby star, emerges. In the next few decades we should have definite answers to which of the hundred nearest stars have large planetary companions.

In recent years, infrared observations have revealed a number of likely preplanetary disk-shaped clouds of gas and dust around some of the nearby stars. Meanwhile, some provocative theoretical studies have suggested that planetary systems are a galactic commonplace. A set of computer investigations has examined the evolution of a flat, condensing disk of gas and dust of the sort that is thought to lead to stars and planets. Small lumps of matter—the first condensations in the disk—are injected at random times into the cloud. The lumps accrete dust particles as they move. When they become sizable, they also gravitationally attract gas, mainly hydrogen, in the cloud. When two moving lumps collide, the computer program makes them stick. The process continues until all the gas and dust has been in this way used up. The results depend on the initial conditions, particularly on the distribution of gas and dust density with distance from the center of the cloud. But for a range of plausible initial conditions, planetary systems—about ten planets, terrestrials close to the star, Jovians on the exterior—recognizably like ours are generated. Under other circumstances, there are no planets—just a smattering of asteroids; or there may be Jovian planets near the star; or a Jovian planet may accrete so much gas and dust as to become a star, the origin of a binary star system. It is still too early to be sure, but it seems that a splendid variety of planetary systems is to be found throughout the Galaxy, and with high frequency—all stars must come, we think, from such clouds of gas and dust. There may be a hundred billion planetary systems in the Galaxy awaiting exploration.

Not one of those worlds will be identical to Earth. A few will be hospitable; most will appear hostile. Many will be achingly beautiful. In some worlds there will be many suns in the daytime sky, many moons in the heavens at night, or great particle ring systems soaring from horizon to horizon. Some moons will be so close that their planet will loom high in the heavens, covering half the sky. And some worlds will look out onto a vast gaseous nebula, the remains of an ordinary star that once was and is no longer. In all those skies, rich in distant and exotic constellations, there will be a faint yellow star—perhaps barely seen by the naked eye, perhaps visible only through the telescope—the home star of the fleet of interstellar transports exploring this tiny region of the great Milky Way Galaxy.

The themes of space and time are, as we have seen, intertwined. Worlds and stars, like people, are born, live and die. The lifetime of a human being is measured in decades; the lifetime of the Sun is a hundred million times longer. Compared to a star, we are like mayflies, fleeting ephemeral creatures who live out their whole lives in the course of a single day. From the point of view of a mayfly, human beings are stolid, boring, almost entirely immovable, offering hardly a hint that they ever do anything. From the point of view of a star, a human being is a tiny flash, one of billions of brief lives flickering tenuously on the surface of a strangely cold, anomalously solid, exotically remote sphere of silicate and iron.

In all those other worlds in space there are events in progress, occurrences that will determine their futures. And on our small planet, this moment in history is a historical branch point as profound as the confrontation of the Ionian scientists with the mystics 2,500 years ago. What we do with our world in this time will propagate down through the centuries and powerfully determine the destiny of our descendants and their fate, if any, among the stars.

CHAPTER IX

THE LIVES OF THE STARS

We had the sky, up there, all speckled with stars, and we used to lay on our backs and look up at them, and discuss about whether they was made, or only just happened.

—Mark Twain, *Huckleberry Finn*

I have . . . a terrible need . . . shall I say the word? . . . of religion. Then I go out at night and paint the stars.

—Vincent van Gogh

To make an apple pie, you need wheat, apples, a pinch of this and that, and the heat of the oven. The ingredients are made of molecules—sugar, say, or water. The molecules, in turn, are made of atoms—carbon, oxygen, hydrogen and a few others. Where do these atoms come from? Except for hydrogen, they are all made in stars. A star is a kind of cosmic kitchen inside which atoms of hydrogen are cooked into heavier atoms. Stars condense from interstellar gas and dust, which are composed mostly of hydrogen. But the hydrogen was made in the Big Bang, the explosion that began the Cosmos. If you wish to make an apple pie from scratch, you must first invent the universe.

Suppose you take an apple pie and cut it in half; take one of the two pieces, cut *it* in half; and, in the spirit of Democritus, continue. How many cuts before you are down to a single atom? The answer is about ninety successive cuts. Of course, no knife could be sharp enough, the pie is too crumbly, and the atom would in any case be too small to see unaided. But there is a way to do it.

At Cambridge University in England, in the forty-five years centered on 1910, the nature of the atom was first understood—partly by shooting pieces of atoms at atoms and watching how they bounce off. A typical atom has a kind of cloud of electrons on the outside. Electrons are electrically charged, as their name suggests. The charge is arbitrarily called negative. Electrons determine the chemical properties of the atom—the glitter of gold, the cold feel of iron, the crystal structure of the carbon diamond. Deep inside the atom, hidden far beneath the electron cloud, is the nucleus, generally composed of positively charged protons and electrically neutral neutrons. Atoms are very small—one hundred million of them end to end would be as large as the tip of your little finger. But the nucleus is a hundred thousand times smaller still, which is part of the reason it took so long to be discovered.* Nevertheless, most of the mass of an atom is in its nucleus; the electrons are by comparison just clouds of moving fluff. Atoms are mainly empty space. Matter is composed chiefly of nothing.

* It had previously been thought that the protons were uniformly distributed throughout the electron cloud, rather than being concentrated in a nucleus of positive charge at the center. The nucleus was discovered by Ernest Rutherford at Cambridge when some of the bombarding particles were bounced back in the direction from which they had come. Rutherford commented: "It was quite the most incredible event that has ever happened to me in my life. It was almost as incredible as if you fired a 15-inch [cannon] shell at a piece of tissue paper and it came back and hit you."

I am made of atoms. My elbow, which is resting on the table before me, is made of atoms. The table is made of atoms. But if atoms are so small and empty and the nuclei smaller still, why does the table hold me up? Why, as Arthur Eddington liked to ask, do the nuclei that comprise my elbow not slide effortlessly through the nuclei that comprise the table? Why don't I wind up on the floor? Or fall straight through the Earth?

The answer is the electron cloud. The outside of an atom in my elbow has a negative electrical charge. So does every atom in the table. But negative charges repel each other. My elbow does not slither through the table because atoms have electrons around their nuclei and because electrical forces are strong. Everyday life depends on the structure of the atom. Turn off the electrical charges and everything crumbles to an invisible fine dust. Without electrical forces, there would no longer be *things* in the universe—merely diffuse clouds of electrons, protons and neutrons, and gravitating spheres of elementary particles, the featureless remnants of worlds.

When we consider cutting an apple pie, continuing down beyond a single atom, we confront an infinity of the very small. And when we look up at the night sky, we confront an infinity of the very large. These infinities represent an unending regress that goes on not just very far, but forever. If you stand between two mirrors—in a barber shop, say—you see a large number of images of yourself, each the reflection of another. You cannot see an infinity of images because the mirrors are not perfectly flat and aligned, because light does not travel infinitely fast, and because you are in the way. When we talk about infinity we are talking about a quantity greater than any number, no matter how large.

The American mathematician Edward Kasner once asked his nine-year-old nephew to invent a name for an extremely large number—ten to the power one hundred (10^{100}), a one followed by a hundred zeroes. The boy called it a googol. Here it is: 10,000, 000, 000, 000, 000, 000, 000, 000, 000, 000, 000, 000, 000, 000,

000, 000, 000, 000, 000, 000, 000, 000, 000, 000, 000, 000, 000, 000, 000, 000, 000, 000, 000. You too can make up your own very large numbers and give them strange names. Try it. It has a certain charm, especially if you happen to be nine.

If a googol seems large, consider a googolplex. It is ten to the power of a googol—that is, a one followed by a googol zeros. By comparison, the total number of atoms in your body is about 10^{28}, and the total number of elementary particles—protons and neutrons and electrons—in the observable universe is about 10^{80}. If the universe were packed solid* with neutrons, say, so there was no empty space anywhere, there would still be only about 10^{128} particles in it, quite a bit more than a googol but trivially small compared to a googolplex. And yet these numbers, the googol and the googolplex, do not approach, they come nowhere near, the idea of infinity. A googolplex is *precisely* as far from infinity as is the number one. We could try to write out a googolplex, but it is a forlorn ambition. A piece of paper large enough to have all the zeroes in a googolplex written out explicitly could not be stuffed into the known universe. Happily, there is a simpler and very concise way of writing a googolplex: $10^{10^{100}}$; and even infinity: ∞ (pronounced "infinity").

In a burnt apple pie, the char is mostly carbon. Ninety cuts and you come to a carbon atom, with six protons and six neutrons in its nucleus and six electrons in the exterior cloud. If we were to pull a chunk out of the nucleus—say, one with two pro-

* The spirit of this calculation is very old. The opening sentences of Archimedes' *The Sand Reckoner* are: "There are some, King Gelon, who think that the number of the sand is infinite in multitude: and I mean by the sand not only that which exists about Syracuse and the rest of Sicily, but also that which is found in every region, whether inhabited or uninhabited. And again, there are some who, without regarding it as infinite, yet think that no number has been named which is great enough to exceed its multitude." Archimedes then went on not only to name the number but to calculate it. Later he asked how many grains of sand would fit, side by side, into the universe that he knew. His estimate: 10^{63}, which corresponds, by a curious coincidence, to 10^{83} or so atoms.

tons and two neutrons—it would be not the nucleus of a carbon atom, but the nucleus of a helium atom. Such a cutting or fission of atomic nuclei occurs in nuclear weapons and conventional nuclear power plants, although it is not carbon that is split. If you make the ninety-first cut of the apple pie, if you slice a carbon nucleus, you make not a smaller piece of carbon, but something else—an atom with completely different chemical properties. If you cut an atom, you transmute the elements.

But suppose we go farther. Atoms are made of protons, neutrons and electrons. Can we cut a proton? If we bombard protons at high energies with other elementary particles—other protons, say—we begin to glimpse more fundamental units hiding inside the proton. Physicists now propose that so-called elementary particles such as protons and neutrons are in fact made of still more elementary particles called quarks, which come in a variety of "colors" and "flavors," as their properties have been termed in a poignant attempt to make the subnuclear world a little more like home. Are quarks the ultimate constituents of matter, or are they too composed of still smaller and *more* elementary particles? Will we ever come to an end in our understanding of the nature of matter, or is there an infinite regression into more and more fundamental particles? This is one of the great unsolved problems in science.

The transmutation of the elements was pursued in medieval laboratories in a quest called alchemy. Many alchemists believed that all matter was a mixture of four elementary substances: water, air, earth and fire, an ancient Ionian speculation. By altering the relative proportions of earth and fire, say, you would be able, they thought, to change copper into gold. The field swarmed with charming frauds and con men, such as Cagliostro and the Count of Saint-Germain, who pretended not only to transmute the elements but also to hold the secret of immortality. Sometimes gold was hidden in a wand with a false bottom, to appear miraculously in a crucible at the end of some arduous experimental demonstration. With wealth and immortality the bait, the European nobility found itself transferring large sums to the practitioners of this dubious art. But there were more serious alchemists such as Paracelsus and even Isaac Newton. The money was not altogether wasted—new chemical elements, such as phosphorus, antimony and mercury, were discovered. In fact, the origin of modern chemistry can be traced directly to these experiments.

There are ninety-two chemically distinct kinds of naturally occurring atoms. They are called the chemical elements and until recently constituted everything on our planet, although they are mainly found combined into molecules. Water is a molecule made of hydrogen and oxygen atoms. Air is made mostly of the atoms nitrogen (N), oxygen (O), carbon (C), hydrogen (H) and argon (Ar), in the molecular forms N_2, O_2, CO_2, H_2O and Ar. The Earth itself is a very rich mixture of atoms, mostly silicon,* oxygen, aluminum, magnesium and iron. Fire is not made of chemical elements at all. It is a radiating plasma in which the high temperature has stripped some of the electrons from their nuclei. Not one of the four ancient Ionian and alchemical "elements" is in the modern sense an element at all: one is a molecule, two are mixtures of molecules, and the last is a plasma.

Since the time of the alchemists, more and more elements have been discovered, the latest to be found tending to be the rarest. Many are familiar—those that primarily make up the Earth; or those fundamental to life. Some are solids, some gases, and two (bromine and mercury) are liquids at room temperature. Scientists conventionally arrange them in order of complexity. The simplest, hydrogen, is element 1; the most complex, uranium, is element 92. Other elements are less familiar—hafnium, erbium, dyprosium and praseodymium, say, which we do not much bump

* Silicon is an atom. Silicone is a molecule, one of billions of different varieties containing silicon. Silicon and silicone have different properties and applications.

into in everyday life. By and large, the more familiar an element is, the more abundant it is. The Earth contains a great deal of iron and rather little yttrium. There are, of course, exceptions to this rule, such as gold or uranium, elements prized because of arbitrary economic conventions or aesthetic judgments, or because they have remarkable practical applications.

The fact that atoms are composed of three kinds of elementary particles—protons, neutrons and electrons—is a comparatively recent finding. The neutron was not discovered until 1932. Modern physics and chemistry have reduced the complexity of the sensible world to an astonishing simplicity: three units put together in various patterns make, essentially, everything.

The neutrons, as we have said and as their name suggests, carry no electrical charge. The protons have a positive charge and the electrons an equal negative charge. The attraction between the unlike charges of electrons and protons is what holds the atom together. Since each atom is electrically neutral, the number of protons in the nucleus must exactly equal the number of electrons in the electron cloud. The chemistry of an atom depends only on the number of electrons, which equals the number of protons, and which is called the atomic number. Chemistry is simply numbers, an idea Pythagoras would have liked. If you are an atom with one proton, you are hydrogen; two, helium; three, lithium; four, beryllium; five, boron; six, carbon; seven, nitrogen; eight, oxygen; and so on, up to 92 protons, in which case your name is uranium.

Like charges, charges of the same sign, strongly repel one another. We can think of it as a dedicated mutual aversion to their own kind, a little as if the world were densely populated by anchorites and misanthropes. Electrons repel electrons. Protons repel protons. So how can a nucleus stick together? Why does it not instantly fly apart? Because there is another force of nature: not gravity, not electricity, but the short-range nuclear force, which, like a set of hooks that engage only when protons and neutrons come very close together, thereby overcomes the electrical repulsion among the protons. The neutrons, which contribute nuclear forces of attraction and no electrical forces of repulsion, provide a kind of glue that helps to hold the nucleus together. Longing for solitude, the hermits have been chained to their grumpy fellows and set among others given to indiscriminate and voluble amiability.

Two protons and two neutrons are the nucleus of a helium atom, which turns out to be very stable. Three helium nuclei make a carbon nucleus; four, oxygen; five, neon; six, magnesium; seven, silicon; eight, sulfur; and so on. Every time we add one or more protons and enough neutrons to keep the nucleus together, we make a new chemical element. If we subtract one proton and three neutrons from mercury, we make gold, the dream of the ancient alchemists. Beyond uranium there are other elements that do not naturally occur on Earth. They are synthesized by human beings and in most cases promptly fall to pieces. One of them, Element 94, is called plutonium and is one of the most toxic substances known. Unfortunately, it falls to pieces rather slowly.

Where do the naturally occurring elements come from? We might contemplate a separate creation of each atomic species. But the universe, all of it, almost everywhere, is 99 percent hydrogen and helium,* the two simplest elements. Helium, in fact, was detected on the Sun before it was found on the Earth—hence its name (from Helios, one of the Greek sun gods). Might the other chemical elements have somehow evolved from hydrogen and helium? To balance the electrical repulsion, pieces of nuclear matter would have to be brought very close together so that the short-range nuclear forces are engaged. This can happen only at very

* The Earth is an exception, because our primordial hydrogen, only weakly bound by our planet's comparatively feeble gravitational attraction, has by now largely escaped to space. Jupiter, with its more massive gravity, has retained at least much of its original complement of the lightest element.

high temperatures where the particles are moving so fast that the repulsive force does not have time to act—temperatures of tens of millions of degrees. In nature, such high temperatures and attendant high pressures are common only in the insides of the stars.

We have examined our Sun, the nearest star, in various wavelengths from radio waves to ordinary visible light to X-rays, all of which arise only from its outermost layers. It is not exactly a red-hot stone, as Anaxagoras thought, but rather a great ball of hydrogen and helium gas, glowing because of its high temperatures, in the same way that a poker glows when it is brought to red heat. Anaxagoras was at least partly right. Violent solar storms produce brilliant flares that disrupt radio communications on Earth; and immense arching plumes of hot gas, guided by the Sun's magnetic field, the solar prominences, which dwarf the Earth. The sunspots, sometimes visible to the naked eye at sunset, are cooler regions of enhanced magnetic field strength. All this incessant, roiling, turbulent activity is in the comparatively cool visible surface. We see only to temperatures of about 6,000 degrees. But the hidden interior of the Sun, where sunlight is being generated, is at 40 million degrees.

Stars and their accompanying planets are born in the gravitational collapse of a cloud of interstellar gas and dust. The collision of the gas molecules in the interior of the cloud heats it, eventually to the point where hydrogen begins to fuse into helium: four hydrogen nuclei combine to form a helium nucleus, with an attendant release of a gamma-ray photon. Suffering alternate absorption and emission by the overlying matter, gradually working its way toward the surface of the star, losing energy at every step, the photon's epic journey takes a million years until, as visible light, it reaches the surface and is radiated to space. The star has turned on. The gravitational collapse of the prestellar cloud has been halted. The weight of the outer layers of the star is now supported by the high temperatures and pressures generated in the interior nuclear reactions. The Sun has been in such a stable situation for the past five billion years. Thermonuclear reactions like those in a hydrogen bomb are powering the Sun in a contained and continuous explosion, converting some four hundred million tons (4×10^{14} grams) of hydrogen into helium every second. When we look up at night and view the stars, everything we see is shining because of distant nuclear fusion.

In the direction of the star Deneb, in the constellation of Cygnus the Swan, is an enormous glowing superbubble of extremely hot gas, probably produced by supernova explosions, the deaths of stars, near the center of the bubble. At the periphery, interstellar matter is compressed by the supernova shock wave, triggering new generations of cloud collapse and star formation. In this sense, stars have parents; and, as is sometimes also true for humans, a parent may die in the birth of the child.

Stars like the Sun are born in batches, in great compressed cloud complexes such as the Orion Nebula. Seen from the outside, such clouds seem dark and gloomy. But inside, they are brilliantly illuminated by the hot newborn stars. Later, the stars wander out of their nursery to seek their fortunes in the Milky Way, stellar adolescents still surrounded by tufts of glowing nebulosity, residues still gravitationally attached of their amniotic gas. The Pleiades are a nearby example. As in the families of humans, the maturing stars journey far from home, and the siblings see little of each other. Somewhere in the Galaxy there are stars—perhaps dozens of them—that are the brothers and sisters of the Sun, formed from the same cloud complex, some 5 billion years ago. But we do not know which stars they are. They may, for all we know, be on the other side of the Milky Way.

The conversion of hydrogen into helium in the center of the Sun not only accounts for the Sun's brightness in photons of visible light; it also produces a radiance of a more mysterious and ghostly kind: The Sun glows faintly in neutrinos, which, like photons, weigh nothing and travel at the speed of light. But neutrinos are not photons. They are not a kind of light. Neutrinos, like protons, electrons and neutrons, carry an intrinsic angular momentum, or spin, while photons have no spin at all. Matter is transparent to neutrinos, which pass almost effortlessly through the Earth and through the Sun. Only a tiny fraction of them is stopped by the intervening matter. As I look up at the Sun for a second, a billion neutrinos pass through my eyeball. Of course, they are not stopped at the retina as ordinary photons are but continue unmolested through the back of my head. The curious part is that if at night I look down at the ground, toward the place where the Sun would be (if the Earth were not in the way), almost exactly the same number of solar neutrinos pass through my eyeball, pouring through an interposed Earth which is as transparent to neutrinos as a pane of clear glass is to visible light.

If our knowledge of the solar interior is as complete as we think, and if we also understand the nuclear physics that makes neutrinos, then we should be able to calculate with fair accuracy how many solar neutrinos we should receive in a given area—such as my eyeball—in a given unit of time, such as a second. Experimental confirmation of the calculation is much more difficult. Since neutrinos pass directly through the Earth, we cannot catch a given one. But for a vast number of neutrinos, a small fraction will interact with matter and in the appropriate circumstances might be detected. Neutrinos can on rare occasion convert chlorine atoms into argon atoms, with the same total number of protons and neutrons. To detect the predicted solar neutrino flux, you need an immense amount of chlorine, so American physicists have poured a huge quantity of cleaning fluid into the Homestake Mine in Lead, South Dakota. The chlorine is microchemically swept for the newly produced argon. The more argon found, the more neutrinos inferred. These experiments imply that the Sun is dimmer in neutrinos than the calculations predict.

There is a real and unsolved mystery here. The low solar neutrino flux probably does not put our view of stellar nucleosynthesis in jeopardy, but it surely means something important. Proposed explanations range from the hypothesis that neutrinos fall to pieces during their passage between the Sun and the Earth to the idea that the nuclear fires in the solar interior are temporarily banked, sunlight being generated in our time partly by slow gravitational contraction. But neutrino astronomy is very new. For the moment we stand amazed at having created a tool that can peer directly into the blazing heart of the Sun. As the sensitivity of the neutrino telescope improves, it may become possible to probe nuclear fusion in the deep interiors of the nearby stars.

But hydrogen fusion cannot continue forever: in the Sun or any other star, there is only so much hydrogen fuel in its hot interior. The fate of a star, the end of its life cycle, depends very much on its initial mass. If, after whatever matter it has lost to space, a star retains two or three times the mass of the Sun, it ends its life cycle in a startlingly different mode than the Sun. But the Sun's fate is spectacular enough. When the central hydrogen has all reacted to form helium, five or six billion years from now, the zone of hydrogen fusion will slowly migrate outward, an expanding shell of thermonuclear reactions, until it reaches the place where the temperatures are less than about ten million degrees. Then hydrogen fusion will shut itself off. Meanwhile the self-gravity of the Sun will force a renewed contraction of its helium-rich core and a further increase in its interior temperatures and pressures. The helium nuclei will be jammed together still more tightly, so much so that *they* begin to stick together, the hooks of their short-range nuclear forces becoming engaged despite the mutual electrical repulsion. The ash will become fuel, and the Sun will be triggered into a second round of fusion reactions.

This process will generate the elements carbon and oxygen and provide additional energy for the Sun to continue shining for a limited time. A star is a phoenix, destined to rise for a time from its own ashes.* Under the combined influence of hydrogen fusion in a thin shell far from the solar interior and the high temperature helium fusion in the core, the Sun will undergo a major change: its exterior will expand and cool. The Sun will become a red giant star, its visible surface so far from its interior that the gravity at its surface grows feeble, its atmosphere expanding into space in a kind of stellar gale. When the Sun, ruddy and bloated, becomes a red giant, it will envelop and devour the planets Mercury and Venus—and probably the Earth as well. The inner solar system will then reside within the Sun.

Billions of years from now, there will be a last perfect day on Earth. Thereafter the Sun will slowly become red and distended, presiding over an Earth sweltering even at the poles. The Arctic and Antarctic ice caps will melt, flooding the coasts of the world. The high oceanic temperatures will release more water vapor into the air, increasing cloudiness, shielding the Earth from sunlight and delaying the end a little. But solar evolution is inexorable. Eventually the oceans will boil, the atmosphere will evaporate away to space and a catastrophe of the most immense proportions imaginable will overtake our planet.** In the meantime, human beings will almost certainly have evolved into something quite different. Perhaps our descendants will be able to control or moderate stellar evolution. Or perhaps they will merely pick up and leave for Mars or Europa or Titan or, at last, as Robert Goddard envisioned, seek out an uninhabited planet in some young and promising planetary system.

The Sun's stellar ash can be reused for fuel only up to a point. Eventually the time will come when the solar interior is all car-

* Stars more massive than the Sun achieve higher central temperatures and pressures in their late evolutionary stages. They are able to rise more than once from their ashes, using carbon and oxygen as fuel for synthesizing still heavier elements.

** The Aztecs foretold a time "when the Earth has become tired . . . , when the seed of Earth has ended." On that day, they believed, the Sun will fall from the sky and the stars will be shaken from the heavens.

bon and oxygen, when at the prevailing temperatures and pressures no further nuclear reactions can occur. After the central helium is almost all used up, the interior of the Sun will continue its postponed collapse, the temperatures will rise again, triggering a last round of nuclear reactions and expanding the solar atmosphere a little. In its death throes, the Sun will slowly pulsate, expanding and contracting once every few millennia, eventually spewing its atmosphere into space in one or more concentric shells of gas. The hot exposed solar interior will flood the shell with ultraviolet light, inducing a lovely red and blue fluorescence extending beyond the orbit of Pluto. Perhaps half the mass of the Sun will be lost in this way. The solar system will then be filled with an eerie radiance, the ghost of the Sun, outward bound.

When we look around us in our little corner of the Milky Way, we see many stars surrounded by spherical shells of glowing gas, the planetary nebulae. (They have nothing to do with planets, but some of them seemed reminiscent in inferior telescopes of the blue-green disks of Uranus and Neptune.) They appear as rings, but only because, as with soap bubbles, we see more of them at the periphery than at the center. Every planetary nebula is a token of a star *in extremis.* Near the central star there may be a retinue of dead worlds, the remnants of planets once full of life and now airless and ocean-free, bathed in a wraithlike luminance. The remains of the Sun, the exposed solar core at first enveloped in its planetary nebula, will be a small hot star, cooling to space, collapsed to a density unheard of on Earth, more than a ton per teaspoonful. Billions of years hence, the Sun will become a degenerate white dwarf, cooling like all those points of light we see at the centers of planetary nebulae from high surface temperatures to its ultimate state, a dark and dead black dwarf.

Two stars of roughly the same mass will evolve roughly in parallel. But a more massive star will spend its nuclear fuel faster, become a red giant sooner, and be first to enter the final white dwarf decline. There should therefore be, as there are, many cases of binary stars, one component a red giant, the other a white dwarf. Some such pairs are so close together that they touch, and the glowing stellar atmosphere flows from the distended red giant to the compact white dwarf, tending to fall on a particular province of the surface of the white dwarf. The hydrogen accumulates, compressed to higher and higher pressures and temperatures by the intense gravity of the white dwarf, until the stolen atmosphere of the red giant undergoes thermonuclear reactions, and the white dwarf briefly flares into brilliance. Such a binary is called a nova and has quite a different origin from a supernova. Novae occur only in binary systems and are powered by hydrogen fusion; supernovae occur in single stars and are powered by silicon fusion.

Atoms synthesized in the interiors of stars are commonly returned to the interstellar gas. Red giants find their outer atmospheres blowing away into space; planetary nebulae are the final stages of Sunlike stars blowing their tops. Supernovae violently eject much of their stellar mass into space. The atoms returned are, naturally, those most readily made in the thermonuclear reactions in stellar interiors: Hydrogen fuses into helium, helium into carbon, carbon into oxygen and thereafter, in massive stars, by the successive addition of further helium nuclei, neon, magnesium, silicon, sulfur, and so on are built—additions by stages, two protons and two neutrons per stage, all the way to iron. Direct fusion of silicon also generates iron, a pair of silicon atoms, each with twenty-eight protons and neutrons, joining, at a temperature of billions of degrees, to make an atom of iron with fifty-six protons and neutrons.

These are all familiar chemical elements. We recognize their names. Such stellar nuclear reactions do not readily generate erbium, hafnium, dyprosium, praseodymium or yttrium, but rather the elements we know in everyday life, elements returned to the interstellar gas, where they are swept up in a subsequent generation of cloud collapse and star and planet formation. All the elements of the Earth except hydrogen and some helium have been cooked by a kind of stellar alchemy billions of years ago in stars, some of which are today inconspicuous white dwarfs on the other side of the Milky Way Galaxy. The nitrogen in our DNA, the calcium in our teeth, the iron in our blood, the carbon in our apple pies were made in the interiors of collapsing stars. We are made of starstuff.

Some of the rarer elements are generated in the supernova explosion itself. We have relatively abundant gold and uranium on Earth only because many supernova explosions had occurred just before the solar system formed. Other planetary systems may have somewhat different amounts of our rare elements. Are there planets where the inhabitants proudly display pendants of niobium and bracelets of protactinium, while gold is a laboratory curiosity? Would our lives be improved if gold and uranium were as obscure and unimportant on Earth as praseodymium?

The origin and evolution of life are connected in the most intimate way with the origin and evolution of the stars. First: The very matter of which we are composed, the atoms that make life possible, were generated long ago and far away in giant red stars. The relative abundance of the chemical elements found in the Cosmos matches the relative abundance of atoms generated in stars so well as to leave little doubt that red giants and supernovae are the ovens and crucibles in which matter has been forged. The Sun is a second- or third-generation star. All the matter in it, all the matter you see around you, has been through one or two previous cycles of stellar alchemy. Second: The existence of certain varieties of heavy atoms on the Earth suggests that there was a nearby supernova explosion shortly before the solar system was formed. But this is unlikely to be a mere coincidence; more likely, the shock wave produced by the supernova compressed interstellar gas and dust and triggered the condensation of the solar system. Third: When the Sun turned on, its ultraviolet radiation poured into the atmosphere of the Earth; its warmth generated lightning; and these energy sources sparked the complex organic molecules that led to the origin of life. Fourth: Life on Earth runs almost exclusively on sunlight. Plants gather the photons and convert solar to chemical energy. Animals parasitize the plants. Farming is simply the methodical harvesting of sunlight, using plants as grudging intermediaries. We are, almost all of us, solar-powered. Finally, the hereditary changes called mutations provide the raw material for evolution. Mutations, from which nature selects its new inventory of lifeforms, are produced in part by cosmic rays—high-energy particles ejected almost at the speed of light in supernova explosions. The evolution of life on Earth is driven in part by the spectacular deaths of distant, massive suns.

Imagine carrying a Geiger counter and a piece of uranium ore to some place deep beneath the Earth—a gold mine, say, or a lava tube, a cave carved through the Earth by a river of molten rock. The sensitive counter clicks when exposed to gamma rays or to such high-energy charged particles as protons and helium nuclei. If we bring it close to the uranium ore, which is emitting helium nuclei in a spontaneous nuclear decay, the count rate, the number of clicks per minute, increases dramatically. If we drop the uranium ore into a heavy lead canister, the count rate declines substantially; the lead has absorbed the uranium radiation. But some clicks can still be heard. Of the remaining counts, a fraction come from natural radioactivity in the walls of the cave. But there are more clicks than can be accounted for by radioactivity. Some of them are caused by high-energy charged particles penetrating the roof. We are listening to cosmic rays, produced in another age in the depths of space. Cosmic rays, mainly electrons and protons, have bombarded the Earth for the entire history of life on our planet. A star destroys itself thousands of light-years away and produces cosmic rays that spiral through the Milky Way Galaxy for millions of years until, quite by accident, some of them strike the Earth, and our hereditary material. Perhaps some key steps in the development of the genetic code, or the Cambrian explosion, or bipedal stature among our ancestors were initiated by cosmic rays.

On July 4, in the year 1054, Chinese astronomers recorded what they called a "guest star" in the constellation of Taurus, the Bull. A star never before seen became brighter than any star in the sky. Halfway around the world, in the American Southwest, there was then a high culture, rich in astronomical tradition, that also witnessed this brilliant new star.* From carbon 14 dating of the remains of a charcoal fire, we know that in the middle eleventh century some Anasazi, the antecedents of the Hopi of today, were living under an overhanging ledge in what is today New Mexico. One of them seems to have drawn on the cliff overhang, protected from the weather, a picture of the new star. Its position relative to the crescent moon would have been just as was depicted. There is also a handprint, perhaps the artist's signature.

This remarkable star, 5,000 light-years distant, is now called the Crab Supernova, because an astronomer centuries later was unaccountably reminded of a crab when looking at the explosion remnant through his telescope. The Crab Nebula is the remains of a massive star that blew itself up. The explosion was seen on Earth with the naked eye for three months. Easily visible in broad daylight, you could read by it at night. On the average, a supernova occurs in a given galaxy about once every century. During the lifetime of a typical galaxy, about ten billion years, a hundred million stars will have exploded—a great many, but still only about one star in a thousand. In the Milky Way, after the event of 1054, there was a supernova observed in 1572, and described by Tycho Brahe, and another, just after, in 1604, described by Johannes Kepler.** Unhappily, no supernova explosions have been

* Moslem observers noted it as well. But there is not a word about it in all the chronicles of Europe.

** Kepler published in 1606 a book called *De Stella Nova*, "On the New Star," in which he wonders if a supernova is the result of some random concatenation of atoms in the heavens. He presents what he says is ". . . not my own opinion, but my wife's:

observed in our Galaxy since the invention of the telescope, and astronomers have been chafing at the bit for some centuries.

Supernovae are now routinely observed in other galaxies. Among my candidates for the sentence that would most thoroughly astonish an astronomer of the early 1900's is the following, from a paper by David Helfand and Knox Long in the December 6, 1979, issue of the British journal *Nature:* "On 5 March, 1979, an extremely intense burst of hard x-rays and gamma rays was recorded by the nine interplanetary spacecraft of the burst sensor network, and localized by time-of-flight determinations to a position coincident with the supernova remnant N49 in the Large Magellanic Cloud." (The Large Magellanic Cloud, so-called because the first inhabitant of the Northern Hemisphere to notice it was Magellan, is a small satellite galaxy of the Milky Way, 180,000 light-years distant. There is also, as you might expect, a Small Magellanic Cloud.) However, in the same issue of *Nature,* E. P. Mazets and colleagues of the Ioffe Institute, Leningrad—who observed this source with the gamma ray burst detector aboard the Venera 11 and 12 spacecraft on their way to land on Venus—argue that what is being seen is a flaring pulsar only a few hundred light-years away. But despite the close agreement in position Helfand and Long do not insist that the gamma ray outburst is associated with the supernova remnant. They charitably consider many alternatives, including the surprising possibility that the source lies within the solar system. Perhaps it is the exhaust of an alien starship on its long voyage home. But a rousing of the stellar fires in N49 is a simpler hypothesis: we are sure there are such things as supernovae.

The fate of the inner solar system as the Sun becomes a red

Yesterday, when weary with writing, I was called to supper, and a salad I had asked for was set before me. 'It seems then,' I said, 'if pewter dishes, leaves of lettuce, grains of salt, drops of water, vinegar, oil and slices of eggs had been flying about in the air for all eternity, it might at last happen by chance that there would come a salad.' 'Yes,' responded my lovely, 'but not so nice as this one of mine.'"

giant is grim enough. But at least the planets will never be melted and frizzled by an erupting supernova. That is a fate reserved for planets near stars more massive than the Sun. Since such stars with higher temperatures and pressures run rapidly through their store of nuclear fuel, their lifetimes are much shorter than the Sun's. A star tens of times more massive than the Sun can stably convert hydrogen to helium for only a few million years before moving briefly on to more exotic nuclear reactions. Thus there is almost certainly not enough time for the evolution of advanced forms of life on any accompanying planets; and it will be rare that beings elsewhere can ever know that their star will become a supernova: if they live long enough to understand supernovae, their star is unlikely to become one.

The essential preliminary to a supernova explosion is the generation by silicon fusion of a massive iron core. Under enormous pressure, the free electrons in the stellar interior are forceably melded with the protons of the iron nuclei, the equal and opposite electrical charges canceling each other out; the inside of the star is turned into a single giant atomic nucleus, occupying a much smaller volume than the precursor electrons and iron nuclei. The core implodes violently, the exterior rebounds and a supernova explosion results. A supernova can be brighter than the combined radiance of all the other stars in the galaxy within which it is embedded. All those recently hatched massive blue-white super-giant stars in Orion are destined in the next few million years to become supernovae, a continuing cosmic fireworks in the constellation of the hunter.

The awesome supernova explosion ejects into space most of the matter of the precursor star—a little residual hydrogen and helium and significant amounts of other atoms, carbon and silicon, iron and uranium. Remaining is a core of hot neutrons, bound together by nuclear forces, a single, massive atomic nucleus with an atomic weight about 10^{56}, a sun thirty kilometers across; a tiny, shrunken, dense, withered stellar fragment, a rapidly rotating neutron star. As the core of a massive red giant collapses to form such a neutron star, it spins faster. The neutron star at the center of the Crab Nebula is an immense atomic nucleus, about the size of Manhattan, spinning thirty times a second. Its powerful magnetic field, amplified during the collapse, traps charged particles rather as the much tinier magnetic field of Jupiter does. Electrons in the rotating magnetic field emit beamed radiation not only at radio frequencies but in visible light as well. If the Earth happens to lie in the beam of this cosmic lighthouse, we see it flash once each rotation. This is the reason it is called a pulsar. Blinking and ticking like a cosmic metronome, pulsars keep far better time than the most accurate ordinary clock. Long-term timing of the radio pulse rate of some pulsars, for instance, one called PSR 0329 + 54, suggests that these objects may have one or more small planetary companions. It is perhaps conceivable that a planet could survive the evolution of a star into a pulsar; or a planet could be captured at a later time. I wonder how the sky would look from the surface of such a planet.

Neutron star matter weighs about the same as an ordinary mountain per teaspoonful—so much that if you had a piece of it and let it go (you could hardly do otherwise), it might pass effortlessly through the Earth like a falling stone through air, carving a hole for itself completely through our planet and emerging out the other side—perhaps in China. People there might be out for a stroll, minding their own business, when a tiny lump of neutron star plummets out of the ground, hovers for a moment, and then returns beneath the Earth, providing at least a diversion from the routine of the day. If a piece of neutron star matter were dropped from nearby space, with the Earth rotating beneath it as it fell, it would plunge repeatedly through the rotating Earth, punching hundreds of thousands of holes before friction with the interior of our planet stopped the motion. Before it comes to rest at the center of the Earth, the inside of our planet might look briefly like a Swiss cheese until the subterranean flow of rock and metal healed the wounds. It is just as well that large lumps of neutron star matter are unknown on Earth. But small lumps are everywhere. The awesome power of the neutron star is lurking in the nucleus of every atom, hidden in every teacup and dormouse, every breath of air, every apple pie. The neutron star teaches us respect for the commonplace.

A star like the Sun will end its days, as we have seen, as a red giant and then a white dwarf. A collapsing star twice as massive as the Sun will become a supernova and then a neutron star. But a more massive star, left, after its supernova phase, with, say, five times the Sun's mass, has an even more remarkable fate reserved for it—its gravity will turn it into a black hole. Suppose we had a magic gravity machine—a device with which we could control the Earth's gravity, perhaps by turning a dial. Initially the dial is set at 1 g* and everything behaves as we have grown up to expect. The animals and plants on Earth and the structures of our buildings are all evolved or designed for 1 g. If the gravity were much less, there might be tall, spindly shapes that would not be tumbled or crushed by their own weight. If the gravity were much more, plants and animals and architecture would have to be short

* 1 g is the acceleration experienced by falling objects on the Earth, almost 10 meters per second every second. A falling rock will reach a speed of 10 meters per second after one second of fall, 20 meters per second after two seconds, and so on until it strikes the ground or is slowed by friction with the air. On a world where the gravitational acceleration was much greater, falling bodies would increase their speed by correspondingly greater amounts. On a world with 10 g acceleration, a rock would travel 10 × 10 m/sec or almost 100 m/sec after the first second, 200 m/sec after the next second, and so on. A slight stumble could be fatal. The acceleration due to gravity should always be written with a lowercase g, to distinguish it from the Newtonian gravitational constant, G, which is a measure of the strength of gravity everywhere in the universe, not merely on whatever world or sun we are discussing. (The Newtonian relationship of the two quantities is $F = mg = GMm/r^2$; $g = GM/r^2$, where F is the gravitational force, M is the mass of the planet or star, m is the mass of the falling object, and r is the distance from the falling object to the center of the planet or star.)

and squat and sturdy in order not to collapse. But even in a fairly strong gravity field, light would travel in a straight line, as it does, of course, in everyday life.

Consider a possibly typical group of Earth beings at the tea party from *Alice in Wonderland.* As we lower the gravity, things weigh less. Near 0 g the slightest motion sends our friends floating and tumbling up in the air. Spilled tea—or any other liquid—forms throbbing spherical globs in the air: the surface tension of the liquid overwhelms gravity. Balls of tea are everywhere. If now we dial 1 g again, we make a rain of tea. When we increase the gravity a little—from 1 g to, say, 3 or 4 g's—everyone becomes immobilized: even moving a paw requires enormous effort. As a kindness we remove our friends from the domain of the gravity machine before we dial higher gravities still. The beam from a lantern travels in a perfectly straight line (as nearly as we can see) at a few g's, as it does at 0 g. At 1000 g's, the beam is still straight, but trees have become squashed and flattened; at 100,000 g's, rocks are crushed by their own weight. Eventually, nothing at all survives except, through a special dispensation, the Cheshire cat. When the gravity approaches a billion g's, something still more strange happens. The beam of light, which has until now been heading straight up into the sky, is beginning to bend. Under extremely strong gravitational accelerations, even light is affected. If we increase the gravity still more, the light is pulled back to the ground near us. Now the cosmic Cheshire cat has vanished; only its gravitational grin remains.

When the gravity is sufficiently high, nothing, not even light, can get out. Such a place is called a black hole. Enigmatically indifferent to its surroundings, it is a kind of cosmic Cheshire cat. When the density and gravity become sufficiently high, the black hole winks out and disappears from our universe. That is why it is called black: no light can escape from it. On the inside, because the light is trapped down there, things may be attractively well-lit. Even if a black hole is invisible from the outside, its gravitational presence can be palpable. If, on an interstellar voyage, you are not paying attention, you can find yourself drawn into it irrevocably, your body stretched unpleasantly into a long, thin thread. But the matter accreting into a disk surrounding the black hole would be a sight worth remembering, in the unlikely case that you survived the trip.

Thermonuclear reactions in the solar interior support the outer layers of the Sun and postpone for billions of years a catastrophic gravitational collapse. For white dwarfs, the pressure of the electrons, stripped from their nuclei, holds the star up. For neutron stars, the pressure of the neutrons staves off gravity. But for an elderly star left after supernova explosions and other impetuosities with more than several times the Sun's mass, there are no forces known that can prevent collapse. The star shrinks incredibly, spins, reddens and disappears. A star twenty times the mass of the Sun will shrink until it is the size of greater Los Angeles; the crushing gravity becomes 10^{10} g's, and the star slips through a self-generated crack in the space-time continuum and vanishes from our universe.

Black holes were first thought of by the English astronomer John Mitchell in 1783. But the idea seemed so bizarre that it was generally ignored until quite recently. Then, to the astonishment of many, including many astronomers, evidence was actually found for the existence of black holes in space. The Earth's atmosphere is opaque to X-rays. To determine whether astronomical objects emit such short wavelengths of light, an X-ray telescope must be carried aloft. The first X-ray observatory was an admirably international effort, orbited by the United States from an Italian launch platform in the Indian Ocean off the coast of Kenya and named Uhuru, the Swahili word for "freedom." In 1971, Uhuru discovered a remarkably bright X-ray source in the constellation of Cygnus, the Swan, flickering on and off a thousand times a second. The source, called Cygnus X-1, must therefore be very small. Whatever the reason for the flicker, information on when to turn on and off can cross Cyg X-1 no faster than the speed of light, 300,000 km/sec. Thus Cyg X-1 can be no larger than [300,000 km/sec] × [(1/1000) sec] = 300 kilometers across. Something the size of an asteroid is a brilliant, blinking source of X-rays, visible over interstellar distances. What could it possibly be? Cyg X-1 is in precisely the same place in the sky as a hot blue supergiant star, which reveals itself in visible light to have a massive close but unseen companion that gravitationally tugs it first in one direction and then in another. The companion's mass is about ten times that of the Sun. The supergiant is an unlikely source of X-rays, and it is tempting to identify the companion inferred in visible light with the source detected in X-ray light. But an invisible object weighing ten times more than the Sun and collapsed into a volume the size of an asteroid can only be a black hole. The X-rays are plausibly generated by friction in the disk of gas and dust accreted around Cyg X-1 from its supergiant companion. Other stars called V861 Scorpii, GX339-4, SS433, and Circinus X-2 are also candidate black holes. Cassiopeia A is the remnant of a supernova whose light should have reached the Earth in the seventeenth century, when there were a fair number of astronomers. Yet no one reported the explosion. Perhaps, as I. S. Shklovskii has suggested, there is a black hole hiding there, which ate the exploding stellar core and damped the fires of the supernova. Telescopes in space are the means for checking these shards and fragments of data that may be the spoor, the trail, of the legendary black hole.

A helpful way to understand black holes is to think about the curvature of space. Consider a flat, flexible, lined two-dimensional surface, like a piece of graph paper made of rubber. If we drop a small mass, the surface is deformed or puckered. A marble rolls around the pucker in a orbit like that of a planet around the Sun. In this interpretation, which we owe to Einstein, gravity is a distortion in the fabric of space. In our example, we see two-dimensional space warped by mass into a third physical dimension. Imagine we live in a three-dimensional universe, locally distorted by matter into a fourth physical dimension that we cannot perceive directly. The greater the local mass, the more intense the local gravity, and the more severe the pucker, distortion or warp of space. In this analogy, a black hole is a kind of bottomless pit. What happens if you fall in? As seen from the outside, you would take an infinite amount of time to fall in, because all your clocks—mechanical and biological—would be perceived as having stopped. But from *your* point of view, all your clocks would be ticking away normally. If you could somehow survive the gravitational tides and radiation flux, and (a likely assumption) if the black hole were rotating, it is just possible that you might emerge in another part of space-time—somewhere else in space, somewhen else in time. Such worm holes in space, a little like those in an apple, have been seriously suggested, although they have by no means been proved to exist. Might gravity tunnels provide a kind of interstellar or intergalactic subway, permitting us to travel to inaccessible places much more rapidly than we could in the ordinary way? Can black holes serve as time machines, carrying us to the remote past or the distant future? The fact that such ideas are being discussed even semi-seriously shows how surreal the universe may be.

We are, in the most profound sense, children of the Cosmos. Think of the Sun's heat on your upturned face on a cloudless summer's day; think how dangerous it is to gaze at the Sun directly. From 150 million kilometers away, we recognize its power. What would we feel on its seething self-luminous surface, or immersed in its heart of nuclear fire? The Sun warms us and feeds us and permits us to see. It fecundated the Earth. It is powerful beyond human experience. Birds greet the sunrise with an audible ecstasy. Even some one-celled organisms know to swim to the light. Our ancestors worshiped the Sun,* and they were far from foolish. And yet the Sun is an ordinary, even a mediocre star. If we must worship a power greater than ourselves, does it not make sense to revere the Sun and stars? Hidden within every astronomical investigation, sometimes so deeply buried that the researcher himself is unaware of its presence, lies a kernel of awe.

The Galaxy is an unexplored continent filled with exotic beings of stellar dimensions. We have made a preliminary reconnaissance and have encountered some of the inhabitants. A few of them resemble beings we know. Others are bizarre beyond our most unconstrained fantasies. But we are at the very beginning of our exploration. Past voyages of discovery suggest that many of the most interesting inhabitants of the galactic continent remain as yet unknown and unanticipated. Not far outside the Galaxy there are almost certainly planets, orbiting stars in the Magellanic Clouds and in the globular clusters that surround the Milky Way. Such worlds would offer a breathtaking view of the Galaxy rising—an enormous spiral form comprising 400 billion stellar inhabitants, with collapsing gas clouds, condensing planetary systems, luminous supergiants, stable middle-aged stars, red giants, white dwarfs, planetary nebulae, novae, supernovae, neutron stars and black holes. It would be clear from such a world, as it is beginning to be clear from ours, how our matter, our form and much of our character is determined by the deep connection between life and the Cosmos.

* The early Sumerian pictograph for god was an asterisk, the symbol of the stars. The Aztec word for god was *Teotl*, and its glyph was a representation of the Sun. The heavens were called the Teoatl, the godsea, the cosmic ocean.

CHAPTER X

THE EDGE OF FOREVER

There is a way on high, conspicuous in the clear heavens, called the Milky Way, brilliant with its own brightness. By it the gods go to the dwelling of the great Thunderer and his royal abode . . . Here the famous and mighty inhabitants of heaven have their homes. This is the region which I might make bold to call the Palatine [Way] of the Great Sky.

—Ovid, *Metamorphoses* (Rome, first century)

Some foolish men declare that a Creator made the world. The doctrine that the world was created is ill-advised, and should be rejected.

If God created the world, where was He before creation? . . . How could God have made the world without any raw material? If you say He made this first, and then the world, you are faced with an endless regression . . .

Know that the world is uncreated, as time itself is, without beginning and end.

And it is based on the principles . . .

—The Mahapurana (The Great Legend), Jinasena (India, ninth century)

Ten or twenty billion years ago, something happened—the Big Bang, the event that began our universe. Why it happened is the greatest mystery we know. *That* it happened is reasonably clear. All the matter and energy now in the universe was concentrated at extremely high density—a kind of cosmic egg, reminiscent of the creation myths of many cultures—perhaps into a mathematical point with no dimensions at all. It was not that all the matter and energy were squeezed into a minor corner of the present universe; rather, the entire universe, matter and energy and the space they fill, occupied a very small volume. There was not much room for events to happen in.

In that titanic cosmic explosion, the universe began an expansion which has never ceased. It is misleading to describe the expansion of the universe as a sort of distending bubble viewed from the outside. By definition, nothing we can ever know about *was* outside. It is better to think of it from the inside, perhaps with grid lines—imagined to adhere to the moving fabric of space—expanding uniformly in all directions. As space stretched, the matter and energy in the universe expanded with it and rapidly cooled. The radiation of the cosmic fireball, which, then as now, filled the universe, moved through the spectrum—from gamma rays to X-rays to ultraviolet light; through the rainbow colors of the visible spectrum; into the infrared and radio regions. The remnants of that fireball, the cosmic background radiation, emanating from all parts of the sky can be detected by radio telescopes today. In the early universe, space was brilliantly illuminated. As time passed, the fabric of space continued to expand, the radiation cooled and, in ordinary visible light, for the first time space became dark, as it is today.

The early universe was filled with radiation and a plenum of matter, originally hydrogen and helium, formed from elementary particles in the dense primeval fireball. There was very little to see, if there had been anyone around to do the seeing. Then little pockets of gas, small nonuniformities, began to grow. Tendrils of vast gossamer gas clouds formed, colonies of great lumbering, slowly spinning things, steadily brightening, each a kind of beast eventually to contain a hundred billion shining points. The largest recognizable structures in the universe had formed. We see them today. We ourselves inhabit some lost corner of one. We call them galaxies.

About a billion years after the Big Bang, the distribution of matter in the universe had become a little lumpy, perhaps because the Big Bang itself had not been perfectly uniform. Matter was more densely compacted in these lumps than elsewhere. Their gravity drew to them substantial quantities of nearby gas, growing clouds of hydrogen and helium that were destined to become clusters of galaxies. A very small initial nonuniformity suffices to produce substantial condensations of matter later on.

As the gravitational collapse continued, the primordial galaxies spun increasingly faster, because of the conservation of angular momentum. Some flattened, squashing themselves along the axis of rotation where gravity is not balanced by centrifugal force. These became the first spiral galaxies, great rotating pinwheels of matter in open space. Other protogalaxies with weaker gravity or less initial rotation flattened very little and became the first elliptical galaxies. There are similar galaxies, as if stamped from the same mold, all over the Cosmos because these simple laws of nature—gravity and the conservation of angular momentum—are the same all over the universe. The physics that works for falling bodies and pirouetting ice skaters down here in the microcosm of the Earth makes galaxies up there in the macrocosm of the universe.

Within the nascent galaxies, much smaller clouds were also experiencing gravitational collapse; interior temperatures became very high, thermonuclear reactions were initiated, and the first stars turned on. The hot, massive young stars evolved rapidly, profligates carelessly spending their capital of hydrogen fuel, soon ending their lives in brilliant supernova explosions, returning thermonuclear ash—helium, carbon, oxygen and heavier elements—to the interstellar gas for subsequent generations of star formation. Supernova explosions of massive early stars produced successive overlapping shock waves in the adjacent gas, compressing the intergalactic medium and accelerating the generation of clusters of galaxies. Gravity is opportunistic, amplifying even small condensations of matter. Supernova shock waves may have contributed to accretions of matter at every scale. The epic of cosmic evolution had begun, a hierarchy in the condensation of matter from the gas of the Big Bang—clusters of galaxies, galaxies, stars, planets, and, eventually, life and an intelligence able to understand a little of the elegant process responsible for its origin.

Clusters of galaxies fill the universe today. Some are insignificant, paltry collections of a few dozen galaxies. The affectionately titled "Local Group" contains only two large galaxies of any size, both spirals: the Milky Way and M31. Other clusters run to immense hordes of thousands of galaxies in mutual gravitational embrace. There is some hint that the Virgo cluster contains tens of thousands of galaxies.

On the largest scale, we inhabit a universe of galaxies, perhaps a hundred billion exquisite examples of cosmic architecture and decay, with order and disorder equally evident: normal spirals, turned at various angles to our earthly line of sight (face-on we see the spiral arms, edge-on, the central lanes of gas and dust in which the arms are formed); barred spirals with a river of gas and dust and stars running through the center, connecting the spiral arms on opposite sides; stately giant elliptical galaxies containing more than a trillion stars which have grown so large because they have swallowed and merged with other galaxies; a plethora of dwarf ellipticals, the galactic midges, each containing some paltry millions of suns; an immense variety of mysterious irregulars, indications that in the world of galaxies there are places where something has gone ominously wrong; and galaxies orbiting each other so closely that their edges are bent by the gravity of their companions and in some cases streamers of gas and stars are drawn out gravitationally, a bridge between the galaxies.

Some clusters have their galaxies arranged in an unambiguously spherical geometry; they are composed chiefly of ellipticals, often dominated by one giant elliptical, the presumptive galactic cannibal. Other clusters with a far more disordered geometry have, comparatively, many more spirals and irregulars. Galactic collisions distort the shape of an originally spherical cluster and may also contribute to the genesis of spirals and irregulars from ellipticals. The form and abundance of the galaxies have a story to tell us of ancient events on the largest possible scale, a story we are just beginning to read.

The development of high-speed computers makes possible numerical experiments on the collective motion of thousands or tens of thousands of points, each representing a star, each under the gravitational influence of all the other points. In some cases, spiral arms form all by themselves in a galaxy that has already flattened to a disk. Occasionally a spiral arm may be produced by the close gravitational encounter of two galaxies, each of course composed of billions of stars. The gas and dust diffusely spread through such galaxies will collide and become warmed. But when two galaxies collide, the stars pass effortlessly by one another, like bullets through a swarm of bees, because a galaxy is made mostly of nothing and the spaces between the stars are vast. Nevertheless, the configuration of the galaxies can be distorted severely. A direct impact on one galaxy by another can send the constituent stars pouring and careening through intergalactic space, a galaxy wasted. When a small galaxy runs into a larger one face-on it can produce one of the loveliest of the rare irregulars, a ring galaxy thousands of light-years across, set against the velvet of intergalactic space. It is a splash in the galactic pond, a temporary configuration of disrupted stars, a galaxy with a central piece torn out.

The unstructured blobs of irregular galaxies, the arms of spiral galaxies and the torus of ring galaxies exist for only a few frames in the cosmic motion picture, then dissipate, often to be reformed again. Our sense of galaxies as ponderous rigid bodies is mistaken. They are fluid structures with 100 billion stellar components. Just as a human being, a collection of 100 trillion cells, is typically in a steady state between synthesis and decay and is more than the sum of its parts, so also is a galaxy.

The suicide rate among galaxies is high. Some nearby examples, tens or hundreds of millions of light-years away, are powerful sources of X-rays, infrared radiation and radio waves, have extremely luminous cores and fluctuate in brightness on time scales of weeks. Some display jets of radiation, thousand-light-year-long plumes, and disks of dust in substantial disarray. These galaxies are blowing themselves up. Black holes ranging from millions to billions of times more massive than the Sun are suspected in the cores of giant elliptical galaxies such as NGC 6251 and M87. There is something very massive, very dense, and very small ticking and purring inside M87—from a region smaller than the solar system. A black hole is implicated. Billions of light-years away are still more tumultuous objects, the quasars, which may be the colossal explosions of young galaxies, the mightiest events in the history of the universe since the Big Bang itself.

The word "quasar" is an acronym for "quasi-stellar radio source." After it became clear that not all of them were powerful radio sources, they were called QSO's ("quasi-stellar objects"). Because they are starlike in appearance, they were naturally thought to be stars within our own galaxy. But spectroscopic observations of their red shift (see below) show them likely to be immense distances away. They seem to partake vigorously in the expansion of the universe, some receding from us at more than 90 percent the speed of light. If they are very far, they must be intrinsically extremely bright to be visible over such distances; some are as bright as a thousand supernovae exploding at once. Just as for Cyg X-1, their rapid fluctuations show their enormous brightness to be confined to a very small volume, in this case less then the size of the solar system. Some remarkable process must be responsible for the vast outpouring of energy in a quasar. Among the proposed explanations are: (1) quasars are monster versions of pulsars, with a rapidly rotating supermassive core connected to a strong magnetic field; (2) quasars are due to multiple collisions of millions of stars densely packed into the galactic core, tearing away the outer layers and exposing to full view the billion-degree temperatures of the interiors of massive stars; (3) a related idea, quasars are galaxies in which the stars are so densely packed that a supernova explosion in one will rip away the outer layers of another and make it a supernova, producing a stellar chain reaction; (4) quasars are powered by the violent mutual annihilation of matter and antimatter, somehow preserved in the quasar until now; (5) a quasar is the energy released when gas and dust and stars fall into an immense black hole in the core of such a galaxy, perhaps itself the product of ages of collision and coalescence of smaller black holes; and (6) quasars are "white holes," the other side of black holes, a funneling and eventual emergence into view of matter pouring into a multitude of black holes in other parts of the universe, or even in other universes.

In considering the quasars, we confront profound mysteries. Whatever the cause of a quasar explosion, one thing seems clear: such a violent event must produce untold havoc. In every quasar explosion millions of worlds—some with life and the intelligence to understand what is happening—may be utterly destroyed. The study of the galaxies reveals a universal order and beauty. It also shows us chaotic violence on a scale hitherto undreamed of. That we live in a universe which permits life is remarkable. That we live in one which destroys galaxies and stars and worlds is also remarkable. The universe seems neither benign nor hostile, merely indifferent to the concerns of such puny creatures as we.

Even a galaxy so seemingly well-mannered as the Milky Way has its stirrings and its dances. Radio observations show two enormous clouds of hydrogen gas, enough to make millions of suns, plummeting out from the galactic core, as if a mild explosion happened there every now and then. A high-energy astronomical observatory in Earth orbit has found the galactic core to be a strong source of a particular gamma ray spectral line, consistent with the idea that a massive black hole is hidden there. Galaxies like the Milky Way may represent the staid middle age in a continuous evolutionary sequence, which encompasses, in their violent adolescence, quasars and exploding galaxies: because the quasars are so distant, we see them in their youth, as they were billions of years ago.

The stars of the Milky Way move with systematic grace. Globular clusters plunge through the galactic plane and out the other side, where they slow, reverse and hurtle back again. If we could follow the motion of individual stars bobbing about the galactic plane, they would resemble a froth of popcorn. We have never seen a galaxy change its form significantly only because it takes so long to move. The Milky Way rotates once every quarter billion years. If we were to speed the rotation, we would see that the Galaxy is a dynamic, almost organic entity, in some ways resembling a multi-cellular organism. Any astronomical photograph of a galaxy is merely a snapshot of one stage in its ponderous motion and evolution.* The inner region of a galaxy rotates as a solid body. But, beyond that, like the planets around the Sun following Kepler's third law, the outer provinces rotate progressively more slowly. The arms have a tendency to wind up around the core in an ever-tightening spiral, and gas and dust accumulate in spiral patterns of greater density, which are in turn the locales for the formation of young, hot, bright stars, the stars that outline the spiral arms. These stars shine for ten million years or so, a period corresponding to only 5 percent of a galactic rotation. But as the stars that outline a spiral arm burn out, new stars and their associated nebulae are formed just behind them, and the spiral pat-

* This is not quite true. The near side of a galaxy is tens of thousands of light-years closer to us than the far side; thus we see the front as it was tens of thousands of years before the back. But typical events in galactic dynamics occupy tens of millions of years, so the error in thinking of an image of a galaxy as frozen in one moment of time is small.

tern persists. The stars that outline the arms do not survive even a single galactic rotation; only the spiral pattern remains.

The speed of any given star around the center of the Galaxy is generally not the same as that of the spiral pattern. The Sun has been in and out of spiral arms often in the twenty times it has gone around the Milky Way at 200 kilometers per second (roughly half a million miles per hour). On the average, the Sun and the planets spend forty million years in a spiral arm, eighty million outside, another forty million in, and so on. Spiral arms outline the region where the latest crop of newly hatched stars is being formed, but not necessarily where such middle-aged stars as the Sun happen to be. In this epoch, we live between spiral arms.

The periodic passage of the solar system through spiral arms may conceivably have had important consequences for us. About ten million years ago, the Sun emerged from the Gould Belt complex of the Orion Spiral Arm, which is now a little less than a thousand light-years away. (Interior to the Orion arm is the Sagittarius arm; beyond the Orion arm is the Perseus arm.) When the Sun passes through a spiral arm it is more likely than it is at present to enter into gaseous nebulae and interstellar dust clouds and to encounter objects of substellar mass. It has been suggested that the major ice ages on our planet, which recur every hundred million years or so, may be due to the interposition of interstellar matter between the Sun and the Earth. W. Napier and S. Clube have proposed that a number of the moons, asteroids, comets and circumplanetary rings in the solar system once freely wandered in interstellar space until they were captured as the Sun plunged through the Orion spiral arm. This is an intriguing idea, although perhaps not very likely. But it is testable. All we need do is procure a sample of, say, Phobos or a comet and examine its magnesium isotopes. The relative abundance of magnesium isotopes (all sharing the same number of protons, but having differing numbers of neutrons) depends on the precise sequence of stellar nucleosynthetic events, including the timing of nearby supernova

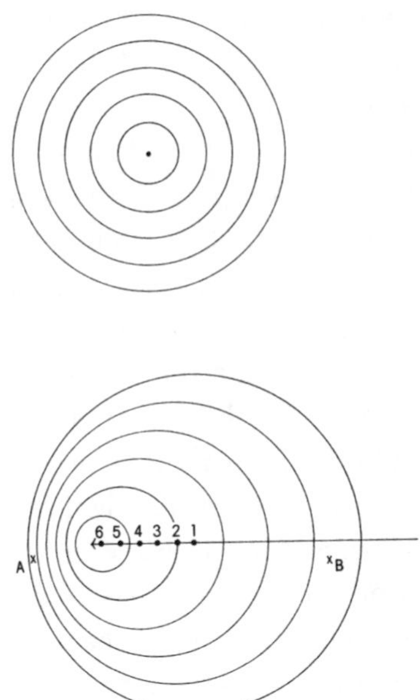

The Doppler effect. A stationary source of sound or light emits a set of spherical waves. If the source is in motion from right to left, it emits spherical waves progressively centered on points 1 through 6, as shown. But an observer at B sees the waves as stretched out, while an observer at A sees them as compressed. A receding source is seen as red-shifted (the wavelengths made longer); an approaching source is seen as blue-shifted (the wavelengths made shorter). The Doppler effect is the key to cosmology.

explosions, that produced any particular sample of magnesium. In a different corner of the Galaxy, a different sequence of events should have occurred and a different ratio of magnesium isotopes should prevail.

The discovery of the Big Bang and the recession of the galaxies came from a commonplace of nature called the Doppler effect. We are used to it in the physics of sound. An automobile driver speeding by us blows his horn. Inside the car, the driver hears a steady blare at a fixed pitch. But outside the car, we hear a characteristic change in pitch. To us, the sound of the horn elides from high frequencies to low. A racing car traveling at 200 kilometers per hour (120 miles per hour) is going almost one-fifth the speed of sound. Sound is a succession of waves in air, a crest and a trough, a crest and a trough. The closer together the waves are, the higher the frequency or pitch; the farther apart the waves are, the lower the pitch. If the car is racing away from us, it stretches out the sound waves, moving them, from our point of view, to a lower pitch and producing the characteristic sound with which we are all familiar. If the car were racing toward us, the sound waves would be squashed together, the frequency would be increased, and we would hear a high-pitched wail. If we knew what the ordinary pitch of the horn was when the car was at rest, we could deduce its speed blindfolded, from the change in pitch.

Light is also a wave. Unlike sound, it travels perfectly well through a vacuum. The Doppler effect works here as well. If instead of sound the automobile were for some reason emitting, front and back, a beam of pure yellow light, the frequency of the light would increase slightly as the car approached and decrease slightly as the car receded. At ordinary speeds the effect would be imperceptible. If, however, the car were somehow traveling at a good fraction of the speed of light, we would be able to observe the color of the light changing toward higher frequency, that is, toward blue, as the car approached us; and toward lower frequencies, that is, toward red, as the car receded from us. An object approaching us at very high velocities is perceived to have the color of its spectral lines blue-shifted. An object receding from us at very high velocities has its spectral lines red-shifted.* This red shift, observed in the spectral lines of distant galaxies and interpreted as a Doppler effect, is the key to cosmology.

During the early years of this century, the world's largest telescope, destined to discover the red shift of remote galaxies, was being built on Mount Wilson, overlooking what were then the clear skies of Los Angeles. Large pieces of the telescope had to be hauled to the top of the mountain, a job for mule teams. A young mule skinner named Milton Humason helped to transport mechanical and optical equipment, scientists, engineers and dignitaries up the mountain. Humason would lead the column of

* The object itself might be any color, even blue. The red shift means only that each spectral line appears at longer wavelengths than when the object is at rest; the amount of the red shift is proportional both to the velocity and to the wavelength of the spectral line when the object is at rest.

mules on horseback, his white terrier standing just behind the saddle, its front paws on Humason's shoulders. He was a tobacco-chewing roustabout, a superb gambler and pool player and what was then called a ladies' man. In his formal education, he had never gone beyond the eighth grade. But he was bright and curious and naturally inquisitive about the equipment he had laboriously carted to the heights. Humason was keeping company with the daughter of one of the observatory engineers, a man who harbored reservations about his daughter seeing a young man who had no higher ambition than to be a mule skinner. So Humason took odd jobs at the observatory—electrician's assistant, janitor, swabbing the floors of the telescope he had helped to build. One evening, so the story goes, the night telescope assistant fell ill and Humason was asked if he might fill in. He displayed such skill and care with the instruments that he soon became a permanent telescope operator and observing aide.

After World War I, there came to Mount Wilson the soon-to-be famous Edwin Hubble—brilliant, polished, gregarious outside the astronomical community, with an English accent acquired during a single year as a Rhodes scholar at Oxford. It was Hubble who provided the final demonstration that the spiral nebulae were in fact "island universes," distant aggregations of enormous numbers of stars, like our own Milky Way Galaxy; he had figured out the stellar standard candle required to measure the distances to the galaxies. Hubble and Humason hit it off splendidly, a perhaps unlikely pair who worked together at the telescope harmoniously. Following a lead by the astronomer V. M. Slipher at Lowell Observatory, they began measuring the spectra of distant galaxies. It soon became clear that Humason was better able to obtain high-quality spectra of distant galaxies than any professional astronomer in the world. He became a full staff member of the Mount Wilson Observatory, learned many of the scientific underpinnings of his work and died rich in the respect of the astronomical community.

The light from a galaxy is the sum of the light emitted by the billions of stars within it. As the light leaves these stars, certain frequencies or colors are absorbed by the atoms in the stars' outermost layers. The resulting lines permit us to tell that stars millions of light-years away contain the same chemical elements as our Sun and the nearby stars. Humason and Hubble found, to their amazement, that the spectra of all the distant galaxies are red-shifted and, still more startling, that the more distant the galaxy was, the more red-shifted were its spectral lines.

The most obvious explanation of the red shift was in terms of the Doppler effect: the galaxies were receding from us; the more distant the galaxy the greater its speed of recession. But why should the galaxies be fleeing *us*? Could there be something special about our location in the universe, as if the Milky Way had performed some inadvertent but offensive act in the social life of galaxies? It seemed much more likely that the universe itself was expanding, carrying the galaxies with it. Humason and Hubble, it gradually became clear, had discovered the Big Bang—if not the origin of the universe then at least its most recent incarnation.

Almost all of modern cosmology—and especially the idea of an expanding universe and a Big Bang—is based on the idea that the red shift of distant galaxies is a Doppler effect and arises from their speed of recession. But there are other kinds of red shifts in nature. There is, for example, the gravitational red shift, in which the light leaving an intense gravitational field has to do so much work to escape that it loses energy during the journey, the process perceived by a distant observer as a shift of the escaping light to longer wavelengths and redder colors. Since we think there may be massive black holes at the centers of some galaxies, this is a conceivable explanation of their red shifts. However, the particular spectral lines observed are often characteristic of very thin, diffuse gas, and not the astonishingly high density that must prevail near black holes. Or the red shift might be a Doppler effect due not to the general expansion of the universe but rather to a more modest and local galactic explosion. But then we should expect as many explosion fragments traveling toward us as away from us, as many blue shifts as red shifts. What we actually see, however, is almost exclusively red shifts no matter what distant objects beyond the Local Group we point our telescopes to.

There is nevertheless a nagging suspicion among some astronomers that all may not be right with the deduction, from the red shifts of galaxies via the Doppler effect, that the universe is expanding. The astronomer Halton Arp has found enigmatic and disturbing cases where a galaxy and a quasar, or a pair of galaxies, that are in apparent physical association have very different red shifts. Occasionally there seems to be a bridge of gas and dust and stars connecting them. If the red shift is due to the expansion of the universe, very different red shifts imply very different distances. But two galaxies that are physically connected can hardly also be greatly separated from each other—in some cases by a billion light-years. Skeptics say that the association is purely statistical: that, for example, a nearby bright galaxy and a much more distant quasar, each having very different red shifts and very different speeds of recession, are merely accidentally aligned along the line of sight; that they have no real physical association. Such statistical alignments must happen by chance every now and then. The debate centers on whether the number of coincidences is more than would be expected by chance. Arp points to other cases in which a galaxy with a small red shift is flanked by two quasars of large and almost identical red shift. He believes the quasars are not at cosmological distances but instead are being ejected, left and right, by the "foreground" galaxy; and that the red shifts are the result of some as-yet-unfathomed mechanism. Skeptics argue coincidental alignment and the conventional Hubble-Humason interpretation of the red shift. If Arp is right, the exotic mechanisms proposed to explain the energy source of distant quasars—supernova chain reactions, supermassive black holes and the like—would prove unnecessary. Quasars need not then be very distant. But some other exotic mechanism will be required to explain the red shift. In either case, something very strange is going on in the depths of space.

The apparent recession of the galaxies, with the red shift interpreted through the Doppler effect, is not the only evidence for the Big Bang. Independent and quite persuasive evidence derives from the cosmic black body background radiation, the faint static of radio waves coming quite uniformly from all directions in the Cosmos at just the intensity expected in our epoch from the now substantially cooled radiation of the Big Bang. But here also there is something puzzling. Observations with a sensitive radio antenna carried near the top of the Earth's atmosphere in a U-2 aircraft have shown that the background radiation is, to first approximation, just as intense in all directions—as if the fireball of the Big Bang expanded quite uniformly, an origin of the universe with a very precise symmetry. But the background radiation, when examined to finer precision, proves to be imperfectly symmetrical. There is a small systematic effect that could be understood if the entire Milky Way Galaxy (and presumably other members of the Local Group) were streaking toward the Virgo cluster of galaxies at more than a million miles an hour (600 kilometers per second). At such a rate, we will reach it in ten billion years, and extragalactic astronomy will then be a great deal easier. The Virgo cluster is already the richest collection of galaxies known, replete with spirals and ellipticals and irregulars, a jewel box in the sky. But why should we be rushing toward it? George Smoot and his colleagues, who made these high-altitude observations, suggest that the Milky Way is being gravitationally dragged toward the center of the Virgo cluster; that the cluster has many more galaxies than have been detected heretofore; and, most startling, that the cluster is of immense proportions, stretching across one or two billion light-years of space.

The observable universe itself is only a few tens of billions of light-years across and, if there is a vast supercluster in the Virgo group, perhaps there are other such superclusters at much greater distances, which are correspondingly more difficult to detect. In the lifetime of the universe there has apparently not been enough time for an initial gravitational nonuniformity to collect the amount of mass that seems to reside in the Virgo supercluster. Thus Smoot is tempted to conclude that the Big Bang was much less uniform than his other observations suggest, that the original distribution of matter in the universe was very lumpy. (Some little lumpiness is to be expected, and indeed even needed to understand the condensation of galaxies; but a lumpiness on this scale is a surprise.) Perhaps the paradox can be resolved by imagining two or more nearly simultaneous Big Bangs.

If the general picture of an expanding universe and a Big Bang is correct, we must then confront still more difficult questions. What were conditions like at the time of the Big Bang? What happened before that? Was there a tiny universe, devoid of all matter, and then the matter suddenly created from nothing? How does *that* happen? In many cultures it is customary to answer that God created the universe out of nothing. But this is mere temporizing. If we wish courageously to pursue the question, we must of course ask next where God comes from. And if we decide this to be unanswerable, why not save a step and decide that the origin of the universe is an unanswerable question. Or, if we say that God has always existed, why not save a step and conclude that the universe has always existed?

Every culture has a myth of the world before creation, and of the creation of the world, often by the mating of the gods or the hatching of a cosmic egg. Commonly, the universe is naively imagined to follow human or animal precedent. Here, for example, are five small extracts from such myths, at different levels of sophistication, from the Pacific Basin:

In the very beginning everything was resting in perpetual darkness: night oppressed everything like an impenetrable thicket.

—The Great Father myth of the
Aranda people of Central Australia

All was in suspense, all calm, all in silence; all motionless and still; and the expanse of the sky was empty.

—The Popol Vuh of the Quiché Maya

Na Arean sat alone in space as a cloud that floats in nothingness. He slept not, for there was no sleep; he hungered not, for as yet there was no hunger. So he remained for a great while, until a thought came to his mind. He said to himself, "I will make a thing."

—A myth from Maiana, Gilbert Islands

First there was the great cosmic egg. Inside the egg was chaos, and floating in chaos was P'an Ku, the Undeveloped, the divine Embryo. And P'an Ku burst out of the egg, four times larger than any man today, with a hammer and chisel in his hand with which he fashioned the world.

—The P'an Ku myths, China
(around third century)

Before heaven and earth had taken form all was vague and amorphous . . . That which was clear and light drifted up to become heaven, while that which was heavy and turbid solidified to become earth. It was very easy for the pure, fine material to come together, but extremely difficult for the heavy, turbid material to solidify. Therefore heaven was completed first and earth assumed shape after. When heaven and earth were joined in emptiness and all was unwrought simplicity, then without having been created

> things came into being. This was the Great Oneness. All things issued from this Oneness but all became different . . .
>
> —Huai-nan Tzu, China (around first century B.C.)

These myths are tributes to human audacity. The chief difference between them and our modern scientific myth of the Big Bang is that science is self-questioning, and that we can perform experiments and observations to test our ideas. But those other creation stories are worthy of our deep respect.

Every human culture rejoices in the fact that there are cycles in nature. But how, it was thought, could such cycles come about unless the gods willed them? And if there are cycles in the years of humans, might there not be cycles in the aeons of the gods? The Hindu religion is the only one of the world's great faiths dedicated to the idea that the Cosmos itself undergoes an immense, indeed an infinite, number of deaths and rebirths. It is the only religion in which the time scales correspond, no doubt by accident, to those of modern scientific cosmology. Its cycles run from our ordinary day and night to a day and night of Brahma, 8.64 billion years long, longer than the age of the Earth or the Sun and about half the time since the Big Bang. And there are much longer time scales still.

There is the deep and appealing notion that the universe is but the dream of the god who, after a hundred Brahma years, dissolves himself into a dreamless sleep. The universe dissolves with him—until, after another Brahma century, he stirs, recomposes himself and begins again to dream the great cosmic dream. Meanwhile, elsewhere, there are an infinite number of other universes, each with its own god dreaming the cosmic dream. These great ideas are tempered by another, perhaps still greater. It is said that men may not be the dreams of the gods, but rather that the gods are the dreams of men.

In India there are many gods, and each god has many manifestations. The Chola bronzes, cast in the eleventh century, include several different incarnations of the god Shiva. The most elegant and sublime of these is a representation of the creation of the universe at the beginning of each cosmic cycle, a motif known as the cosmic dance of Shiva. The god, called in this manifestation Nataraja, the Dance King, has four hands. In the upper right hand is a drum whose sound is the sound of creation. In the upper left hand is a tongue of flame, a reminder that the universe, now newly created, will billions of years from now be utterly destroyed.

These profound and lovely images are, I like to imagine, a kind of premonition of modern astronomical ideas.* Very likely, the universe has been expanding since the Big Bang, but it is by no means clear that it will continue to expand forever. The expansion may gradually slow, stop and reverse itself. If there is less than a certain critical amount of matter in the universe, the gravitation of the receding galaxies will be insufficient to stop the expansion, and the universe will run away forever. But if there is more matter than we can see—hidden away in black holes, say, or in hot but invisible gas between the galaxies—then the universe will hold together gravitationally and partake of a very Indian succession of cycles, expansion followed by contraction, universe upon universe, Cosmos without end. If we live in such an oscillating universe, then the Big Bang is not the creation of the Cosmos but merely the end of the previous cycle, the destruction of the last incarnation of the Cosmos.

Neither of these modern cosmologies may be altogether to

* The dates on Mayan inscriptions also range deep into the past and occasionally far into the future. One inscription refers to a time more than a million years ago and another perhaps refers to events of 400 million years ago, although this is in some dispute among Mayan scholars. The events memorialized may be mythical, but the time scales are prodigious. A millennium before Europeans were willing to divest themselves of the Biblical idea that the world was a few thousand years old, the Mayans were thinking of millions, and the Indians of billions.

our liking. In one, the universe is created, somehow, ten or twenty billion years ago and expands forever, the galaxies mutually receding until the last one disappears over our cosmic horizon. Then the galactic astronomers are out of business, the stars cool and die, matter itself decays and the universe becomes a thin cold haze of elementary particles. In the other, the oscillating universe, the Cosmos has no beginning and no end, and we are in the midst of an infinite cycle of cosmic deaths and rebirths with no information trickling through the cusps of the oscillation. Nothing of the galaxies, stars, planets, lifeforms or civilizations evolved in the previous incarnation of the universe oozes into the cusp, flutters past the Big Bang, to be known in our present universe. The fate of the universe in either cosmology may seem a little depressing, but we may take solace in the time scales involved. These events will occupy tens of billions of years, or more. Human beings and our descendants, whoever they might be, can accomplish a great deal in tens of billions of years, before the Cosmos dies.

If the universe truly oscillates, still stranger questions arise. Some scientists think that when expansion is followed by contraction, when the spectra of distant galaxies are all blue-shifted, causality will be inverted and effects will precede causes. First the ripples spread from a point on the water's surface, then I throw a stone into the pond. First the torch bursts into flame and then I light it. We cannot pretend to understand what such causality inversion means. Will people at such a time be born in the grave and die in the womb? Will time flow backward? Do these questions have any meaning?

Scientists wonder about what happens in an oscillating universe at the cusps, at the transition from contraction to expansion. Some think that the laws of nature are then randomly reshuffled, that the kind of physics and chemistry that orders this universe represent only one of an infinite range of possible natural laws. It is easy to see that only a very restricted range of laws of nature are consistent with galaxies and stars, planets, life and intelligence. If the laws of nature are unpredictably reassorted at the cusps, then it is only by the most extraordinary coincidence that the cosmic slot machine has this time come up with a universe consistent with us.*

Do we live in a universe that expands forever or in one in which there is an infinite set of cycles? There are ways to find out: by making an accurate census of the total amount of matter in the universe, or by seeing to the edge of the Cosmos.

Radio telescopes can detect very faint, very distant objects. As we look deep into space we also look far back into time. The nearest quasar is perhaps half a billion light-years away. The farthest may be ten or twelve or more billions. But if we see an object twelve billion light-years away, we are seeing it as it was twelve billion years ago in time. By looking far out into space we are also looking far back into time, back toward the horizon of the universe, back toward the epoch of the Big Bang.

The Very Large Array (VLA) is a collection of twenty-seven separate radio telescopes in a remote region of New Mexico. It is a phased array, the individual telescopes electronically connected, as if it were a single telescope of the same size as its remotest elements, as if it were a radio telescope tens of kilometers

* The laws of nature cannot be *randomly* reshuffled at the cusps. If the universe has already gone through many oscillations, many possible laws of gravity would have been so weak that, for any given initial expansion, the universe would not have held together. Once the universe stumbles upon such a gravitational law, it flies apart and has no further opportunity to experience another oscillation and another cusp and another set of laws of nature. Thus we can deduce from the fact that the universe exists either a finite age, or a severe restriction on the kinds of laws of nature permitted in each oscillation. If the laws of physics are not randomly reshuffled at the cusps, there must be a regularity, a set of rules, that determines which laws are permissible and which are not. Such a set of rules would comprise a new physics standing over the existing physics. Our language is impoverished; there seems to be no suitable name for such a new physics. Both "paraphysics" and "metaphysics" have been preempted by other rather different and, quite possibly, wholly irrelevant activities. Perhaps "transphysics" would do.

across. The VLA is able to resolve or discriminate fine detail in the radio regions of the spectrum comparable to what the largest ground-based telescopes can do in the optical region of the spectrum.

Sometimes such radio telescopes are connected with telescopes on the other side of the Earth, forming a baseline comparable to the Earth's diameter—in a certain sense, a telescope as large as the planet. In the future we may have telescopes in the Earth's orbit, around toward the other side of the Sun, in effect a radio telescope as large as the inner solar system. Such telescopes may reveal the internal structure and nature of quasars. Perhaps a quasar standard candle will be found, and the distances to the quasars determined independent of their red shifts. By understanding the structure and the red shift of the most distant quasars it may be possible to see whether the expansion of the universe was faster billions of years ago, whether the expansion is slowing down, whether the universe will one day collapse.

Modern radio telescopes are exquisitely sensitive; a distant quasar is so faint that its detected radiation amounts perhaps to a quadrillionth of a watt. The total amount of energy from outside the solar system ever received by all the radio telescopes on the planet Earth is less than the energy of a single snowflake striking the ground. In detecting the cosmic background radiation, in counting quasars, in searching for intelligent signals from space, radio astronomers are dealing with amounts of energy that are barely there at all.

Some matter, particularly the matter in the stars, glows in visible light and is easy to see. Other matter, gas and dust in the outskirts of galaxies, for example, is not so readily detected. It does not give off visible light, although it seems to give off radio waves. This is one reason that the unlocking of the cosmological mysteries requires us to use exotic instruments and frequencies different from the visible light to which our eyes are sensitive. Observatories in Earth orbit have found an intense X-ray glow between the galaxies. It was first thought to be hot intergalactic hydrogen, an immense amount of it never before seen, perhaps enough to close the Cosmos and to guarantee that we are trapped in an oscillating universe. But more recent observations by Ricardo Giacconi may have resolved the X-ray glow into individual points, perhaps an immense horde of distant quasars. They contribute previously unknown mass to the universe as well. When the cosmic inventory is completed, and the mass of all the galaxies, quasars, black holes, intergalactic hydrogen, gravitational waves and still more exotic denizens of space is summed up, we will know what kind of universe we inhabit.

In discussing the large-scale structure of the Cosmos, astronomers are fond of saying that space is curved, or that there is no center to the Cosmos, or that the universe is finite but unbounded. Whatever are they talking about? Let us imagine we inhabit a strange country where everyone is perfectly flat. Following Edwin Abbott, a Shakespearean scholar who lived in Victorian England, we call it Flatland. Some of us are squares; some are triangles; some have more complex shapes. We scurry about, in and out of our flat buildings, occupied with our flat businesses and dalliances. Everyone in Flatland has width and length, but no height whatever. We know about left-right and forward-back, but have no hint, not a trace of comprehension, about up-down—except for flat mathematicians. They say, "Listen, it's really very easy. Imagine left-right. Imagine forward-back. Okay, so far? Now imagine another dimension, at right angles to the other two." And we say, "What are you talking about? 'At right angles to the other two'! There *are* only two dimensions. Point to that third dimension. Where is it?" So the mathematicians, disheartened, amble off. Nobody listens to mathematicians.

Every square creature in Flatland sees another square as merely a short line segment, the side of the square nearest to him. He can see the other side of the square only by taking a short walk. But the *inside* of a square is forever mysterious, unless some terrible accident or autopsy breaches the sides and exposes the interior parts.

One day a three-dimensional creature—shaped like an apple, say—comes upon Flatland, hovering above it. Observing a particularly attractive and congenial-looking square entering its flat house, the apple decides, in a gesture of interdimensional amity, to say hello. "How are you?" asks the visitor from the third dimension. "I am a visitor from the third dimension." The wretched square looks about his closed house and sees no one. What is worse, to him it appears that the greeting, entering from above, is emanating from his own flat body, a voice from within. A little insanity, he perhaps reminds himself gamely, runs in the family.

Exasperated at being judged a psychological aberration, the apple descends into Flatland. Now a three-dimensional creature can exist, in Flatland, only partially; only a cross section can be seen, only the points of contact with the plane surface of Flatland. An apple slithering through Flatland would appear first as a point and then as progressively larger, roughly circular slices. The square sees a point appearing in a closed room in his two-dimensional world and slowly growing into a near circle. A creature of strange and changing shape has appeared from nowhere.

Rebuffed, unhappy at the obtuseness of the very flat, the apple bumps the square and sends him aloft, fluttering and spinning into that mysterious third dimension. At first the square can make no sense of what is happening; it is utterly outside his experience. But eventually he realizes that he is viewing Flatland from a peculiar vantage point: "above." He can see into closed rooms. He can see into his flat fellows. He is viewing his universe from a unique and devastating perspective. Traveling through another dimension provides, as an incidental benefit, a kind of X-ray vision. Eventually, like a falling leaf, our square slowly descends to the surface. From the point of view of his fellow Flatlanders, he has unaccountably disappeared from a closed room and then distressingly materialized from nowhere. "For heaven's sake," they say, "what's happened to you?" "I think," he finds himself replying, "I was 'up.'" They pat him on his sides and comfort him. Delusions always ran in his family.

In such interdimensional contemplations, we need not be restricted to two dimensions. We can, following Abbott, imagine a world of one dimension, where everyone is a line segment, or even the magical world of zero-dimensional beasts, the points. But perhaps more interesting is the question of higher dimensions. Could there be a fourth physical dimension?*

We can imagine generating a cube in the following way: Take a line segment of a certain length and move it an equal length at right angles to itself. That makes a square. Move the square an equal length at right angles to itself, and we have a cube. We understand this cube to cast a shadow, which we usually draw as two squares with their vertices connected. If we examine the shadow of a cube in two dimensions, we notice that not all the lines appear equal, and not all the angles are right angles. The three-dimensional object has not been perfectly represented in its transfiguration into two dimensions. This is the cost of losing a dimension in the geometrical projection. Now let us take our three-dimensional cube and carry it, at right angles to itself, through a fourth physical dimension: not left-right, not forward-back, not up-down, but simultaneously at right angles to all those directions. I cannot show you what direction that is, but I can imagine it to exist. In such a case, we would have generated a four-dimensional hypercube, also called a tesseract. I cannot show you a tesseract, because we are trapped in three dimen-

* If a fourth-dimensional creature existed it could, in our three-dimensional universe, appear and dematerialize at will, change shape remarkably, pluck us out of locked rooms and make us appear from nowhere. It could also turn us inside out. There are several ways in which we can be turned inside out: the least pleasant would result in our viscera and internal organs being on the outside and the entire Cosmos—glowing intergalactic gas, galaxies, planets, everything—on the inside. I am not sure I like the idea.

sions. But what I can show you is the shadow in three dimensions of a tesseract. It resembles two nested cubes, all the vertices connected by lines. But for a real tesseract, in four dimensions, all the lines would be of equal length and all the angles would be right angles.

Imagine a universe just like Flatland, except that unbeknownst to the inhabitants, their two-dimensional universe is curved through a third physical dimension. When the Flatlanders take short excursions, their universe looks flat enough. But if one of them takes a long enough walk along what seems to be a perfectly straight line, he uncovers a great mystery: although he has not reached a barrier and has never turned around, he has somehow come back to the place from which he started. His two-dimensional universe must have been warped, bent or curved through a mysterious third dimension. He cannot imagine that third dimension, but he can deduce it. Increase all dimensions in this story by one, and you have a situation that may apply to us.

Where is the center of the Cosmos? Is there an edge to the universe? What lies beyond that? In a two-dimensional universe, curved through a third dimension, there *is* no center—at least not on the surface of the sphere. The center of such a universe is not *in* that universe; it lies, inaccessible, in the third dimension, *inside* the sphere. While there is only so much area on the surface of the sphere, there is no edge to this universe—it is finite but unbounded. And the question of what lies beyond is meaningless. Flat creatures cannot, on their own, escape their two dimensions.

Increase all dimensions by one, and you have the situation that may apply to us: the universe as a four-dimensional hypersphere with no center and no edge, and nothing beyond. Why do all the galaxies seem to be running away from *us*? The hypersphere is expanding from a point, like a four-dimensional balloon being inflated, creating in every instant more space in the universe. Sometime after the expansion begins, galaxies condense and are carried outward on the surface of the hypersphere. There are astronomers in each galaxy, and the light they see is also trapped on the curved surface of the hypersphere. As the sphere expands, an astronomer in any galaxy will think all the other galaxies are running away from him. There are no privileged reference frames.* The farther away the galaxy, the faster its recession. The galaxies are embedded in, attached to space, and the fabric of space is expanding. And to the question, Where in the present universe did the Big Bang occur? the answer is clearly, everywhere.

If there is insufficient matter to prevent the universe from expanding forever, it must have an open shape, curved like a saddle with a surface extending to infinity in our three-dimensional analogy. If there is enough matter, then it has a closed shape, curved like a sphere in our three-dimensional analogy. If the universe is closed, light is trapped within it. In the 1920's, in a direction opposite to M31, observers found a distant pair of spiral galaxies. Was it possible, they wondered, that they were seeing the Milky Way and M31 from the other direction—like seeing the back of your head with light that has circumnavigated the universe? We now know that the universe is much larger than they imagined in the 1920's. It would take more than the age of the universe for light to circumnavigate it. And the galaxies are younger than the universe. But if the Cosmos is closed and light cannot escape from it, then it may be perfectly correct to describe the universe as a black hole. If you wish to know what it is like inside a black hole, look around you.

We have previously mentioned the possibility of wormholes to get from one place in the universe to another without covering the intervening distance—through a black hole. We can imagine these wormholes as tubes running through a fourth physical di-

* The view that the universe looks by and large the same no matter from where we happen to view it was first proposed, so far as we know, by Giordano Bruno.

mension. We do not know that such wormholes exist. But if they do, must they always hook up with another place in our universe? Or is it just possible that wormholes connect with other universes, places that would otherwise be forever inaccessible to us? For all we know, there may be many other universes. Perhaps they are, in some sense, nested within one another.

There is an idea—strange, haunting, evocative—one of the most exquisite conjectures in science or religion. It is entirely undemonstrated; it may never be proved. But it stirs the blood. There is, we are told, an infinite hierarchy of universes, so that an elementary particle, such as an electron, in our universe would, if penetrated, reveal itself to be an entire closed universe. Within it, organized into the local equivalent of galaxies and smaller structures, are an immense number of other, much tinier elementary particles, which are themselves universes at the next level and so on forever—an infinite downward regression, universes within universes, endlessly. And upward as well. Our familiar universe of galaxies and stars, planets and people, would be a single elementary particle in the next universe up, the first step of another infinite regress.

This is the only religious idea I know that surpasses the endless number of infinitely old cycling universes in Hindu cosmology. What would those other universes be like? Would they be built on different laws of physics? Would they have stars and galaxies and worlds, or something quite different? Might they be compatible with some unimaginably different form of life? To enter them, we would somehow have to penetrate a fourth physical dimension—not an easy undertaking, surely, but perhaps a black hole would provide a way. There may be small black holes in the solar neighborhood. Poised at the edge of forever, we would jump off . . .

CHAPTER XI

THE PERSISTENCE OF MEMORY

Now that the destinies of Heaven and Earth have been fixed;
Trench and canal have been given their proper course;
The banks of the Tigris and the Euphrates
have been established;
What else shall we do?
What else shall we create?
Oh Anunaki, you great gods of the sky,
what else shall we do?

—The Assyrian account of the creation of Man, 800 B.C.

When he, whoever of the gods it was, had thus arranged in order and resolved that chaotic mass, and reduced it, thus resolved, to cosmic parts, he first moulded the Earth into the form of a mighty ball so that it might be of like form on every side ... And, that no region might be without its own forms of animate life, the stars and divine forms occupied the floor of heaven, the sea fell to the shining fishes for their home, Earth received the beasts, and the mobile air the birds ... Then Man was born: ... though all other animals are prone, and fix their gaze upon the earth, he gave to Man an uplifted face and bade him stand erect and turn his eyes to heaven.

—Ovid, *Metamorphoses*, first century

In the great cosmic dark there are countless stars and planets both younger and older than our solar system. Although we cannot yet be certain, the same processes that led on Earth to the evolution of life and intelligence should have been operating throughout the Cosmos. There may be a million worlds in the Milky Way Galaxy alone that at this moment are inhabited by beings who are very different from us, and far more advanced. Knowing a great deal is not the same as being smart; intelligence is not information alone but also judgment, the manner in which information is coordinated and used. Still, the amount of information to which we have access is one index of our intelligence. The measuring rod, the unit of information, is something called a bit (for binary digit). It is an answer—either yes or no—to an unambiguous question. To specify whether a lamp is on or off requires a single bit of information. To designate one letter out of the twenty-six in the Latin alphabet takes five bits ($2^5 = 2 \times 2 \times 2 \times 2 \times 2 = 32$, which is more than 26). The verbal information content of this book is a little less than ten million bits, 10^7. The total number of bits that characterizes an hour-long television program is about 10^{12}. The information in the words and pictures of different books in all the libraries on the Earth is something like 10^{16} or 10^{17} bits.* Of course much of it is redundant. Such a number calibrates crudely what humans know. But elsewhere, on older worlds, where life has evolved billions of years earlier than on Earth, perhaps they know 10^{20} bits or 10^{30}—not just more information but significantly different information.

Of those million worlds inhabited by advanced intelligences, consider a rare planet, the only one in its system with a surface ocean of liquid water. In this rich aquatic environment, many relatively intelligent creatures live—some with eight appendages for grasping; others that communicate among themselves by

* Thus all of the books in the world contain no more information than is broadcast as video in a single large American city in a single year. Not all bits have equal value.

changing an intricate pattern of bright and dark mottling on their bodies; even clever little creatures from the land who make brief forays into the ocean in vessels of wood or metal. But we seek the dominant intelligences, the grandest creatures on the planet, the sentient and graceful masters of the deep ocean, the great whales.

They are the largest animals* ever to evolve on the planet Earth, larger by far than the dinosaurs. An adult blue whale can be thirty meters long and weigh 150 tons. Many, especially the baleen whales, are placid browsers, straining through vast volumes of ocean for the small animals on which they graze; others eat fish and krill. The whales are recent arrivals in the ocean. Only seventy million years ago their ancestors were carnivorous mammals who migrated in slow steps from the land into the ocean. Among the whales, mothers suckle and care tenderly for their offspring. There is a long childhood in which the adults teach the young. Play is a typical pastime. These are all mammalian characteristics, all important for the development of intelligent beings.

The sea is murky. Sight and smell, which work well for mammals on the land, are not of much use in the depths of the ocean. Those ancestors of the whales who relied on these senses to locate a mate or a baby or a predator did not leave many offspring. So another method was perfected by evolution; it works superbly well and is central to any understanding of the whales: the sense of sound. Some whale sounds are called songs, but we are still ignorant of their true nature and meaning. They range over a broad band of frequencies, down to well below the lowest sound the human ear can detect. A typical whale song lasts for perhaps fifteen minutes; the longest, about an hour. Often it is repeated, identically, beat for beat, measure for measure, note for note. Occasionally a group of whales will leave their winter waters in the

* Some sequoia trees are both larger and more massive than any whale.

midst of a song and six months later return to continue at precisely the right note, as if there had been no interruption. Whales are very good at remembering. More often, on their return, the vocalizations have changed. New songs appear on the cetacean hit parade.

Very often the members of the group will sing the same song together. By some mutual consensus, some collaborative songwriting, the piece changes month by month, slowly and predictably. These vocalizations are complex. If the songs of the humpback whale are enunciated as a tonal language, the total information content, the number of bits of information in such songs, is some 10^6 bits, about the same as the information content of the *Illiad* or the *Odyssey*. We do not know what whales or their cousins the dolphins have to talk or sing about. They have no manipulative organs, they make no engineering constructs, but they are social creatures. They hunt, swim, fish, browse, frolic, mate, play, run from predators. There may be a great deal to talk about.

The primary danger to the whales is a newcomer, an upstart animal, only recently, through technology, become competent in the oceans, a creature that calls itself human. For 99.99 percent of the history of the whales, there were no humans in or on the deep oceans. During this period the whales evolved their extraordinary audio communication system. The finbacks, for example, emit extremely loud sounds at a frequency of twenty Hertz, down near the lowest octave on the piano keyboard. (A Hertz is a unit of sound frequency that represents one sound wave, one crest and one trough, entering your ear every second.) Such low-frequency sounds are scarcely absorbed in the ocean. The American biologist Roger Payne has calculated that using the deep ocean sound channel, two whales could communicate with each other at twenty Hertz essentially anywhere in the world. One might be off the Ross Ice Shelf in Antarctica and communicate with another in the Aleutians. For most of their history, the whales may have established a global communications network. Perhaps when separated by 15,000 kilometers, their vocalizations are love songs, cast hopefully into the vastness of the deep.

For tens of millions of years these enormous, intelligent, communicative creatures evolved with essentially no natural enemies. Then the development of the steamship in the nineteenth century introduced an ominous source of noise pollution. As commercial and military vessels became more abundant, the noise background in the oceans, especially at a frequency of twenty Hertz, became noticeable. Whales communicating across the oceans must have experienced increasingly greater difficulties. The distance over which they could communicate must have decreased steadily. Two hundred years ago, a typical distance across which finbacks could communicate was perhaps 10,000 kilometers. Today, the corresponding number is perhaps a few hundred kilometers. Do whales know each other's names? Can they recognize each other as individuals by sounds alone? We have cut the whales off from themselves. Creatures that communicated for tens of millions of years have now effectively been silenced.*

And we have done worse than that, because there persists to this day a traffic in the dead bodies of whales. There are humans who hunt and slaughter whales and market the products for lipstick or industrial lubricant. Many nations understand that the systematic murder of such intelligent creatures is monstrous, but the traffic continues, promoted chiefly by Japan, Norway and the Soviet Union. We humans, as a species, are interested in commu-

* There is a curious counterpoint to this story. The preferred radio channel for interstellar communication with other technical civilizations is near a frequency of 1.42 billion Hertz, marked by a radio spectral line of hydrogen, the most abundant atom in the Universe. We are just beginning to listen here for signals of intelligent origin. But the frequency band is being increasingly encroached upon by civilian and military communications traffic on Earth, and not only by the major powers. We are jamming the interstellar channel. Uncontrolled growth of terrestrial radio technology may prevent us from ready communication with intelligent beings on distant worlds. Their songs may go unanswered because we have not the will to control our radio-frequency pollution and listen.

nication with extraterrestrial intelligence. Would not a good beginning be improved communication with terrestrial intelligence, with other human beings of different cultures and languages, with the great apes, with the dolphins, but particularly with those intelligent masters of the deep, the great whales?

For a whale to live there are many things it must know how to do. This knowledge is stored in its genes and in its brains. The genetic information includes how to convert plankton into blubber; or how to hold your breath on a dive one kilometer below the surface. The information in the brains, the learned information, includes such things as who your mother is, or the meaning of the song you are hearing just now. The whale, like all the other animals on the Earth, has a gene library and a brain library.

The genetic material of the whale, like the genetic material of human beings, is made of nucleic acids, those extraordinary molecules capable of reproducing themselves from the chemical building blocks that surround them, and of turning hereditary information into action. For example, one whale enzyme, identical to one you have in every cell of your body, is called hexokinase, the first of more than two dozen enzyme-mediated steps required to convert a molecule of sugar obtained from the plankton in the whale's diet into a little energy—perhaps a contribution to a single low-frequency note in the music of the whale.

The information stored in the DNA double helix of a whale or a human or any other beast or vegetable on Earth is written in a language of four letters—the four different kinds of nucleotides, the molecular components that make up DNA. How many bits of information are contained in the hereditary material of various lifeforms? How many yes/no answers to the various biological questions are written in the language of life? A virus needs about 10,000 bits—roughly equivalent to the amount of information on this page. But the viral information is simple, exceedingly compact, extraordinarily efficient. Reading it requires very close attention. These are the instructions it needs to infect some other organism and to reproduce itself—the only things that viruses are any good at. A bacterium uses roughly a million bits of information—which is about 100 printed pages. Bacteria have a lot more to do than viruses. Unlike the viruses, they are not thoroughgoing parasites. Bacteria have to make a living. And a free-swimming one-celled amoeba is much more sophisticated; with about four hundred million bits in its DNA, it would require some eighty 500-page volumes to make another amoeba.

A whale or a human being needs something like five billion bits. The 5×10^9 bits of information in our encyclopaedia of life—in the nucleus of each of our cells—if written out in, say, English, would fill a thousand volumes. Every one of your hundred trillion cells contains a complete library of instructions on how to make every part of you. Every cell in your body arises by successive cell divisions from a single cell, a fertilized egg generated by your parents. Every time that cell divided, in the many embryological steps that went into making you, the original set of genetic instructions was duplicated with great fidelity. So your liver cells have some unemployed knowledge about how to make your bone cells, and vice versa. The genetic library contains everything your body knows how to do on its own. The ancient information is written in exhaustive, careful, redundant detail—how to laugh, how to sneeze, how to walk, how to recognize patterns, how to reproduce, how to digest an apple.

Eating an apple is an immensely complicated process. In fact, if I had to synthesize my own enzymes, if I *consciously* had to remember and direct all the chemical steps required to get energy out of food, I would probably starve. But even bacteria do anaerobic glycolysis, which is why apples rot: lunchtime for the microbes. They and we and all creatures in between possess many similar genetic instructions. Our separate gene libraries have many pages in common, another reminder of our common evolutionary heritage. Our technology can duplicate only a tiny fraction of the intricate biochemistry that our bodies effortlessly perform: we have only just begun to study these processes. Evolution, however, has had billions of years of practice. DNA knows.

But suppose what you had to do was so complicated that even several billion bits was insufficient. Suppose the environment was changing so fast that the precoded genetic encyclopaedia, which served perfectly well before, was no longer entirely adequate. Then even a gene library of 1,000 volumes would not be enough. That is why we have brains.

Like all our organs, the brain has evolved, increasing in complexity and information content, over millions of years. Its structure reflects all the stages through which it has passed. The brain evolved from the inside out. Deep inside is the oldest part, the brainstem, which conducts the basic biological functions, including the rhythms of life—heartbeat and respiration. According to a provocative insight by Paul MacLean, the higher functions of the brain evolved in three successive stages. Capping the brainstem is the R-complex, the seat of aggression, ritual, territoriality and social hierarchy, which evolved hundreds of millions of years ago in our reptilian ancestors. Deep inside the skull of every one of us there is something like the brain of a crocodile. Surrounding the R-complex is the limbic system or mammalian brain, which evolved tens of millions of years ago in ancestors who were mammals but not yet primates. It is a major source of our moods and emotions, of our concern and care for the young.

And finally, on the outside, living in uneasy truce with the more primitive brains beneath, is the cerebral cortex, which evolved millions of years ago in our primate ancestors. The cerebral cortex, where matter is transformed into consciousness, is the point of embarkation for all our cosmic voyages. Comprising more than two-thirds of the brain mass, it is the realm of both intuition and critical analysis. It is here that we have ideas and inspirations, here that we read and write, here that we do mathematics and compose music. The cortex regulates our conscious lives. It is the distinction of our species, the seat of our humanity. Civilization is a product of the cerebral cortex.

The language of the brain is not the DNA language of the genes. Rather, what we know is encoded in cells called neurons—microscopic electrochemical switching elements, typically a few hundredths of a millimeter across. Each of us has perhaps a hundred billion neurons, comparable to the number of stars in the Milky Way Galaxy. Many neurons have thousands of connections with their neighbors. There are something like a hundred trillion, 10^{14}, such connections in the human cerebral cortex.

Charles Sherrington imagined the activities in the cerebral cortex upon awakening:

> [The cortex] becomes now a sparkling field of rhythmic flashing points with trains of traveling sparks hurrying hither and thither. The brain is waking and with it the mind is returning. It is as if the Milky Way entered upon some cosmic dance. Swiftly the [cortex] becomes an enchanted loom where millions of flashing shuttles weave a dissolving pattern, always a meaningful pattern though never an abiding one; a shifting harmony of sub-patterns. Now as the waking body rouses, sub-patterns of this great harmony of activity stretch down into the unlit tracks of the [lower brain]. Strings of flashing and traveling sparks engage the links of it. This means that the body is up and rises to meet its waking day.

Even in sleep, the brain is pulsing, throbbing and flashing with the complex business of human life—dreaming, remembering, figuring things out. Our thoughts, visions and fantasies have a physical reality. A thought is made of hundreds of electrochemical impulses. If we were shrunk to the level of the neurons, we might witness elaborate, intricate, evanescent patterns. One might be the spark of a memory of the smell of lilacs on a country road in childhood. Another might be part of an anxious all-points bulletin: "Where did I leave the keys?"

There are many valleys in the mountains of the mind, convolutions that greatly increase the surface area available in the cerebral cortex for information storage in a skull of limited size. The neurochemistry of the brain is astonishingly busy, the circuitry of a machine more wonderful than any devised by humans. But there is no evidence that its functioning is due to anything more than the 10^{14} neural connections that build an elegant architecture of consciousness. The world of thought is divided roughly into two hemispheres. The right hemisphere of the cerebral cortex is mainly responsible for pattern recognition, intuition, sensitivity, creative insights. The left hemisphere presides over rational, analytical and critical thinking. These are the dual strengths, the essential opposites, that characterize human thinking. Together, they provide the means both for generating ideas and for testing their validity. A continuous dialogue is going on between the two hemispheres, channeled through an immense bundle of nerves, the corpus callosum, the bridge between creativity and analysis, both of which are necessary to understand the world.

The information content of the human brain expressed in bits is probably comparable to the total number of connections among the neurons—about a hundred trillion, 10^{14}, bits. If written out in English, say, that information would fill some twenty million volumes, as many as in the world's largest libraries. The equivalent of twenty million books is inside the heads of every one of us. The brain is a very big place in a very small space. Most of the books in the brain are in the cerebral cortex. Down in the basement are the functions our remote ancestors mainly depended on—aggression, child-rearing, fear, sex, the willingness to follow leaders blindly. Of the higher brain functions, some—reading, writing, speaking—seem to be localized in particular places in the cerebral cortex. Memories, on the other hand, are stored redundantly in many locales. If such a thing as telepathy existed, one of its glories would be the opportunity for each of us to read the books in the cerebral cortices of our loved ones. But there is no compelling evidence for telepathy, and the communication of such information remains the task of artists and writers.

The brain does much more than recollect. It compares, synthesizes, analyzes, generates abstractions. We must figure out much more than our genes can know. That is why the brain library is some ten thousand times larger than the gene library. Our passion for learning, evident in the behavior of every toddler, is the tool for our survival. Emotions and ritualized behavior patterns are built deeply into us. They are part of our humanity. But they are not *characteristically* human. Many other animals have feelings. What distinguishes our species is thought. The cerebral cortex is a liberation. We need no longer be trapped in the genetically inherited behavior patterns of lizards and baboons. We are, each of us, largely responsible for what gets put into our brains, for what, as adults, we wind up caring for and knowing about. No longer at the mercy of the reptile brain, we can change ourselves.

Most of the world's great cities have grown haphazardly, little by little, in response to the needs of the moment; very rarely is a city planned for the remote future. The evolution of a city is like the evolution of the brain: it develops from a small center and slowly grows and changes, leaving many old parts still functioning. There is no way for evolution to rip out the ancient interior of the brain because of its imperfections and replace it with something of more modern manufacture. The brain must function during the renovation. That is why our brainstem is surrounded by the R-complex, then the limbic system and finally the cerebral cortex. The old parts are in charge of too many fundamental functions for them to be replaced altogether. So they wheeze along, out-of-date and sometimes counterproductive, but a necessary consequence of our evolution.

In New York City, the arrangement of many of the major streets dates to the seventeenth century, the stock exchange to the eighteenth century, the waterworks to the nineteenth, the electrical power system to the twentieth. The arrangement might be more efficient if all civic systems were constructed in parallel and replaced periodically (which is why disastrous fires—the great conflagrations of London and Chicago, for example—are sometimes an aid in city planning). But the slow accretion of new functions permits the city to work more or less continuously through the centuries. In the seventeenth century you traveled between Brooklyn and Manhattan across the East River by ferry. In the nineteenth century, the technology became available to construct a suspension bridge across the river. It was built precisely at the site of the ferry terminal, both because the city owned the land and because major thoroughfares were already converging on the preexisting ferry service. Later when it was possible to construct a tunnel under the river, it too was built in the same place for the same reasons, and also because small abandoned precursors of tunnels, called caissons, had already been emplaced during the construction of the bridge. This use and restructuring of previous systems for new purposes is very much like the pattern of biological evolution.

When our genes could not store all the information necessary for survival, we slowly invented them. But then the time came, perhaps ten thousand years ago, when we needed to know more than could conveniently be contained in brains. So we learned to stockpile enormous quantities of information outside our bodies. We are the only species on the planet, so far as we know, to have invented a communal memory stored neither in our genes nor in our brains. The warehouse of that memory is called the library.

A book is made from a tree. It is an assemblage of flat, flexible parts (still called "leaves") imprinted with dark pigmented squiggles. One glance at it and you hear the voice of another person—perhaps someone dead for thousands of years. Across the millennia, the author is speaking, clearly and silently, inside your head, directly to you. Writing is perhaps the greatest of human inventions, binding together people, citizens of distant epochs, who never knew one another. Books break the shackles of time, proof that humans can work magic.

Some of the earliest authors wrote on clay. Cuneiform writing, the remote ancestor of the Western alphabet, was invented in the Near East about 5,000 years ago. Its purpose was to keep records: the purchase of grain, the sale of land, the triumphs of the king, the statutes of the priests, the positions of the stars, the prayers to the gods. For thousands of years, writing was chiseled into clay and stone, scratched onto wax or bark or leather; painted on bamboo or papyrus or silk—but always one copy at a time and, except for the inscriptions on monuments, always for a tiny readership. Then in China between the second and sixth centuries, paper, ink and printing with carved wooden blocks were all invented, permitting many copies of a work to be made and distributed. It took a thousand years for the idea to catch on in remote and backward Europe. Then, suddenly, books were being printed all over the world. Just before the invention of movable type, around 1450, there were no more than a few tens of thousands of books in all of Europe, all handwritten; about as many as in China in 100 B.C., and a tenth as many as in the Great Library of Alexandria. Fifty years later, around 1500, there were ten million printed books. Learning had become available to anyone who could read. Magic was everywhere.

More recently, books, especially paperbacks, have been printed in massive and inexpensive editions. For the price of a modest meal you can ponder the decline and fall of the Roman Empire, the origin of species, the interpretation of dreams, the nature of things. Books are like seeds. They can lie dormant for centuries and then flower in the most unpromising soil.

The great libraries of the world contain millions of volumes, the equivalent of about 10^{14} bits of information in words, and perhaps 10^{15} bits in pictures. This is ten thousand times more information than in our genes, and about ten times more than in our brains. If I finish a book a week, I will read only a few thousand books in my lifetime, about a tenth of a percent of the contents of the greatest libraries of our time. The trick is to know which books to read. The information in books is not preprogrammed at birth but constantly changed, amended by events, adapted to the world. It is now twenty-three centuries since the founding of the Alexandrian Library. If there were no books, no written records, think how prodigious a time twenty-three centuries would be. With four generations per century, twenty-three centuries occupies almost a hundred generations of human beings. If information could be passed on merely by word of mouth, how little we should know of our past, how slow would be our progress! Everything would depend on what ancient findings we had accidentally been told about, and how accurate the account was. Past information might be revered, but in successive retellings it would become progressively more muddled and eventually lost. Books permit us to voyage through time, to tap the wisdom of our ancestors. The library connects us with the insights and knowledge, painfully extracted from Nature, of the greatest minds that ever were, with the best teachers, drawn from the entire planet and from all of our history, to instruct us without tiring, and to inspire us to make our own contribution to the collective knowledge of the human species. Public libraries depend on voluntary contributions. I think the health of our civilization, the depth of our awareness about the underpinnings of our culture and our concern for the future can all be tested by how well we support our libraries.

Were the Earth to be started over again with all its physical features identical, it is extremely unlikely that anything closely resembling a human being would ever again emerge. There is a powerful random character to the evolutionary process. A cosmic ray striking a different gene, producing a different mutation, can have small consequences early but profound consequences late. Happenstance may play a powerful role in biology, as it does in history. The farther back the critical events occur, the more powerfully can they influence the present.

For example, consider our hands. We have five fingers, including one opposable thumb. They serve us quite well. But I think we would be served equally well with six fingers including a thumb, or four fingers including a thumb, or maybe five fingers and two thumbs. There is nothing intrinsically best about our particular configuration of fingers, which we ordinarily think of as so natural and inevitable. We have five fingers because we have descended from a Devonian fish that had five phalanges or bones in its fins. Had we descended from a fish with four or six phalanges, we would have four or six fingers on each hand and would think them perfectly natural. We use base ten arithmetic only because we have ten fingers on our hands.* Had the arrangement been otherwise, we would use base eight or base twelve arithmetic and relegate base ten to the New Math. The same point applies, I believe, to many more essential aspects of our being—our hereditary material, our internal biochemistry, our form, stature, organ systems, loves and hates, passions and despairs, tenderness and aggression, even our analytical processes—all of these are, at least in part, the result of apparently minor accidents in our immensely long evolutionary history. Perhaps if one less dragonfly had drowned in the Carboniferous swamps, the intelligent organisms on our planet today would have feathers and teach their young in rookeries. The pattern of evolutionary causality is a web of astonishing complexity; the incompleteness of our understanding humbles us.

Just sixty-five million years ago our ancestors were the most

* The arithmetic based on the number 5 or 10 seems so obvious that the ancient Greek equivalent of "to count" literally means "to five."

unprepossessing of mammals—creatures with the size and intelligence of moles or tree shrews. It would have taken a very audacious biologist to guess that such animals would eventually produce the line that dominates the Earth today. The Earth then was full of awesome, nightmarish lizards—the dinosaurs, immensely successful creatures, which filled virtually every ecological niche. There were swimming reptiles, flying reptiles, and reptiles—some as tall as a six-story building—thundering across the face of the Earth. Some of them had rather large brains, an upright posture and two little front legs very much like hands, which they used to catch small, speedy mammals—probably including our distant ancestors—for dinner. If such dinosaurs had survived, perhaps the dominant intelligent species on our planet today would be four meters tall with green skin and sharp teeth, and the human form would be considered a lurid fantasy of saurian science fiction. But the dinosaurs did not survive. In one catastrophic event all of them and many, perhaps most, of the other species on the Earth, were destroyed.* But not the tree shrews. Not the mammals. They survived.

No one knows what wiped out the dinosaurs. One evocative idea is that it was a cosmic catastrophe, the explosion of a nearby star—a supernova like the one that produced the Crab Nebula. If there were by chance a supernova within ten or twenty light-years of the solar system some sixty-five million years ago, it would have sprayed an intense flux of cosmic rays into space, and some of these, entering the Earth's envelope of air, would have burned the atmospheric nitrogen. The oxides of nitrogen thus generated would have removed the protective layer of ozone from the atmosphere, increasing the flux of solar ultraviolet radiation at the surface and frying and mutating the many organisms imperfectly

* A recent analysis suggests that 96 percent of all the species in the oceans may have died at this time. With such an enormous extinction rate, the organisms of today can have evolved from only a small and unrepresentative sampling of the organisms that lived in late Mesozoic times.

protected against intense ultraviolet light. Some of those organisms may have been staples of the dinosaur diet.

The disaster, whatever it was, that cleared the dinosaurs from the world stage removed the pressure on the mammals. Our ancestors no longer had to live in the shadow of voracious reptiles. We diversified exuberantly and flourished. Twenty million years ago, our immediate ancestors probably still lived in the trees, later descending because the forests receded during a major ice age and were replaced by grassy savannahs. It is not much good to be supremely adapted to life in the trees if there are very few trees. Many arboreal primates must have vanished with the forests. A few eked out a precarious existence on the ground and survived. And one of those lines evolved to become us. No one knows the cause of that climatic change. It may have been a small variation in the intrinsic luminosity of the Sun or in the orbit of the Earth; or massive volcanic eruptions injecting fine dust into the stratosphere, reflecting more sunlight back into space and cooling the Earth. It may have been due to changes in the general circulation of the oceans. Or perhaps the passage of the Sun through a galactic dust cloud. Whatever the cause, we see again how tied our existence is to random astronomical and geological events.

After we came down from the trees, we evolved an upright posture; our hands were free; we possessed excellent binocular vision—we had acquired many of the preconditions for making tools. There was now a real advantage in possessing a large brain and in communicating complex thoughts. Other things being equal, it is better to be smart than to be stupid. Intelligent beings can solve problems better, live longer and leave more offspring; until the invention of nuclear weapons, intelligence powerfully aided survival. In our history it was some horde of furry little mammals who hid from the dinosaurs, colonized the treetops and later scampered down to domesticate fire, invent writing, construct observatories and launch space vehicles. If things had been a little different, it might have been some other creature whose intelligence and manipulative ability would have led to comparable accomplishments. Perhaps the smart bipedal dinosaurs, or the raccoons, or the otters, or the squid. It would be nice to know how different other intelligences can be; so we study the whales and the great apes. To learn a little about what other kinds of civilizations are possible, we can study history and cultural anthropology. But we are all of us—us whales, us apes, us people—too closely related. As long as our inquiries are limited to one or two evolutionary lines on a single planet, we will remain forever ignorant of the possible range and brilliance of other intelligences and other civilizations.

On another planet, with a different sequence of random processes to make hereditary diversity and a different environment to select particular combinations of genes, the chances of finding beings who are physically very similar to us is, I believe, near zero. The chances of finding another form of intelligence is not. Their brains may well have evolved from the inside out. They may have switching elements analogous to our neurons. But the neurons may be very different; perhaps superconductors that work at very low temperatures rather than organic devices that work at room temperature, in which case their speed of thought will be 10^7 times faster than ours. Or perhaps the equivalent of neurons elsewhere would not be in direct physical contact but in radio communication so that a single intelligent being could be distributed among many different organisms, or even many different planets, each with a part of the intelligence of the whole, each contributing by radio to an intelligence much greater than itself.* There may be planets where the intelligent beings have about 10^{14} neural connections, as we do. But there may be places where the number is 10^{24} or 10^{34}. I wonder what they would know. Because

* In some sense such a radio integration of separate individuals is already beginning to happen on the planet Earth.

we inhabit the same universe as they, we and they must share some substantial information in common. If we could make contact, there is much in their brains that would be of great interest to ours. But the opposite is also true. I think extraterrestrial intelligence—even beings substantially further evolved than we—will be interested in us, in what we know, how we think, what our brains are like, the course of our evolution, the prospects for our future.

If there are intelligent beings on the planets of fairly nearby stars, could they know about us? Might they somehow have an inkling of the long evolutionary progression from genes to brains to libraries that has occurred on the obscure planet Earth? If the extraterrestrials stay at home, there are at least two ways in which they might find out about us. One way would be to listen with large radio telescopes. For billions of years they would have heard only weak and intermittent radio static caused by lightning and the trapped electrons and protons whistling within the Earth's magnetic field. Then, less than a century ago, the radio waves leaving the Earth would become stronger, louder, less like noise and more like signals. The inhabitants of Earth had finally stumbled upon radio communication. Today there is a vast international radio, television and radar communications traffic. At some radio frequencies the Earth has become by far the brightest object, the most powerful radio source, in the solar system—brighter than Jupiter, brighter than the Sun. An extraterrestrial civilization monitoring the radio emission from Earth and receiving such signals could not fail to conclude that something interesting had been happening here lately.

As the Earth rotates, our more powerful radio transmitters slowly sweep the sky. A radio astronomer on a planet of another star would be able to calculate the length of the day on Earth from the times of appearance and disappearance of our signals. Some of our most powerful sources are radar transmitters; a few are used for radar astronomy, to probe with radio fingers the surfaces of the nearby planets. The size of the radar beam projected against the sky is much larger than the size of the planets, and much of the signal wafts on, out of the solar system into the depths of interstellar space to any sensitive receivers that may be listening. Most radar transmissions are for military purposes; they scan the skies in constant fear of a massive launch of missiles with nuclear warheads, an augury fifteen minutes early of the end of human civilization. The information content of these pulses is negligible: a succession of simple numerical patterns coded into beeps.

Overall, the most pervasive and noticeable source of radio transmissions from the Earth is our television programming. Because the Earth is turning, some television stations will appear at one horizon of the Earth while others disappear over the other. There will be a confused jumble of programs. Even these might be sorted out and pieced together by an advanced civilization on a planet of a nearby star. The most frequently repeated messages will be station call signals and appeals to purchase detergents, deodorants, headache tablets, and automobile and petroleum products. The most noticeable messages will be those broadcast simultaneously by many transmitters in many time zones—for example, speeches in times of international crisis by the President of the United States or the Premier of the Soviet Union. The mindless contents of commercial television and the integuments of international crisis and internecine warfare within the human family are the principal messages about life on Earth that we choose to broadcast to the Cosmos. What must they think of us?

There is no calling those television programs back. There is no way of sending a faster message to overtake them and revise the previous transmission. Nothing can travel faster than light. Large-scale television transmission on the planet Earth began only in the late 1940's. Thus, there is a spherical wave front centered on the Earth expanding at the speed of light and containing Howdy Doody, the "Checkers" speech of then Vice-President

Richard M. Nixon and the televised inquisitions by Senator Joseph McCarthy. Because these transmissions were broadcast a few decades ago, they are only a few tens of light-years away from Earth. If the nearest civilization is farther away than that, then we can continue to breathe easy for a while. In any case, we can hope that they will find these programs incomprehensible.

The two Voyager spacecraft are bound for the stars. Affixed to each is a gold-plated copper phonograph record with a cartridge and stylus and, on the aluminum record jacket, instructions for use. We sent something about our genes, something about our brains, and something about our libraries to other beings who might sail the sea of interstellar space. But we did not want to send primarily scientific information. Any civilization able to intercept Voyager in the depths of interstellar space, its transmitters long dead, would know far more science than we do. Instead we wanted to tell those other beings something about what seems unique about ourselves. The interests of the cerebral cortex and limbic system are well represented; the R-complex less so. Although the recipients may not know any languages of the Earth, we included greetings in sixty human tongues, as well as the hellos of the humpback whales. We sent photographs of humans from all over the world caring for one another, learning, fabricating tools and art and responding to challenges. There is an hour and a half of exquisite music from many cultures, some of it expressing our sense of cosmic loneliness, our wish to end our isolation, our longing to make contact with other beings in the Cosmos. And we have sent recordings of the sounds that would have been heard on our planet from the earliest days before the origin of life to the evolution of the human species and our most recent burgeoning technology. It is, as much as the sounds of any baleen whale, a love song cast upon the vastness of the deep. Many, perhaps most, of our messages will be indecipherable. But we have sent them because it is important to try.

In this spirit we included on the Voyager spacecraft the

thoughts and feelings of one person, the electrical activity of her brain, heart, eyes and muscles, which were recorded for an hour, transcribed into sound, compressed in time and incorporated into the record. In one sense we have launched into the Cosmos a direct transcription of the thoughts and feelings of a single human being in the month of June in the year 1977 on the planet Earth. Perhaps the recipients will make nothing of it, or think it is a recording of a pulsar, which in some superficial sense it resembles. Or perhaps a civilization unimaginably more advanced than ours will be able to decipher such recorded thoughts and feelings and appreciate our efforts to share ourselves with them.

The information in our genes is very old—most of it more than millions of years old, some of it billions of years old. In contrast, the information in our books is at most thousands of years old, and that in our brains is only decades old. The long-lived information is not the characteristically human information. Because of erosion on the Earth, our monuments and artifacts will not, in the natural course of things, survive to the distant future. But the Voyager record is on its way out of the solar system. The erosion in interstellar space—chiefly cosmic rays and impacting dust grains—is so slow that the information on the record will last a billion years. Genes and brains and books encode information differently and persist through time at different rates. But the persistence of the memory of the human species will be far longer in the impressed metal grooves on the Voyager interstellar record.

The Voyager message is traveling with agonizing slowness. The fastest object ever launched by the human species, it will still take tens of thousands of years to go the distance to the nearest star. Any television program will traverse in hours the distance that Voyager has covered in years. A television transmission that has just finished being aired will, in only a few hours, overtake the Voyager spacecraft in the region of Saturn and beyond and speed outward to the stars. If it is headed that way, the signal will reach Alpha Centauri in a little more than four years. If, some decades or centuries hence, anyone out there in space hears our television broadcasts, I hope they will think well of us, a product of fifteen billion years of cosmic evolution, the local transmogrification of matter into consciousness. Our intelligence has recently provided us with awesome powers. It is not yet clear that we have the wisdom to avoid our own self-destruction. But many of us are trying very hard. We hope that very soon in the perspective of cosmic time we will have unified our planet peacefully into an organization cherishing the life of every living creature on it and will be ready to take that next great step, to become part of a galactic society of communicating civilizations.

CHAPTER XII
ENCYCLOPAEDIA GALACTICA

"What are you? From where did you come? I have never seen anything like you." The Creator Raven looked at Man and was . . . surprised to find that this strange new being was so much like himself.

—An Eskimo creation myth

The author of Nature . . . has made it impossible for us to have any communication from this earth with the other great bodies of the universe, in our present state; and it is highly possible that he has likewise cut off all communication betwixt the other planets, and betwixt the different systems. . . . We observe, in all of them, enough to raise our curiosity, but not to satisfy it . . . It does not appear to be suitable to the wisdom that shines throughout all nature, to suppose that we should see so far, and have our curiosity so much raised . . . only to be disappointed at the end . . . This, therefore, naturally leads us to consider our present state as only the dawn or beginning of our existence, and as a state of preparation or probation for farther advancement. . . .

—Colin Maclaurin, 1748

We have launched four ships to the stars, Pioneers 10 and 11 and Voyagers 1 and 2. They are backward and primitive craft, moving, compared to the immense interstellar distances, with the slowness of a race in a dream. But in the future we will do better. Our ships will travel faster. There will be designated interstellar objectives, and sooner or later our spacecraft will have human crews. In the Milky Way Galaxy there must be many planets millions of years older than Earth, and some that are billions of years older. Should we not have been visited? In all the billions of years since the origin of our planet, has there not been even once a strange craft from a distant civilization surveying our world from above, and slowly settling down to the surface to be observed by iridescent dragonflies, incurious reptiles, screeching primates or wondering humans? The idea is natural enough. It has occurred to everyone who has contemplated, even casually, the question of intelligent life in the universe. But has it happened in fact? The critical issue is the quality of the purported evidence, rigorously and skeptically scrutinized—not what sounds plausible, not the unsubstantiated testimony of one or two self-professed eyewitnesses. By this standard there are no compelling cases of extraterrestrial visitation, despite all the claims about UFOs and ancient astronauts which sometimes make it seem that our planet is awash in uninvited guests. I wish it were otherwise. There is something irresistible about the discovery of even a token, perhaps a complex inscription, but, best by far, a key to the understanding of an alien and exotic civilization. It is an appeal we humans have felt before.

In 1801 a physicist named Joseph Fourier* was the prefect of a *departement* of France called Isère. While inspecting the schools in his province, Fourier discovered an eleven-year-old boy whose remarkable intellect and flair for oriental languages had already earned him the admiring attention of scholars. Fourier invited

* Fourier is now famous for his study of the propagation of heat in solids, used today to understand the surface properties of the planets, and for his investigation of waves and other periodic motion—a branch of mathematics known as Fourier analysis.

him home for a chat. The boy was fascinated by Fourier's collection of Egyptian artifacts, collected during the Napoleonic expedition where he had been responsible for cataloging the astronomical monuments of that ancient civilization. The hieroglyphic inscriptions roused the boy's sense of wonder. "But what do they mean?" he asked. "Nobody knows," was the reply. The boy's name was Jean François Champollion. Fired by the mystery of the language no one could read, he became a superb linguist and passionately immersed himself in ancient Egyptian writing. France at that time was flooded with Egyptian artifacts, stolen by Napoleon and later made available to Western scholars. The description of the expedition was published, and devoured by the young Champollion. As an adult, Champollion succeeded; fulfilling his childhood ambition, he provided a brilliant decipherment of the ancient Egyptian hieroglyphics. But it was not until 1828, twenty-seven years after his meeting with Fourier, that Champollion first set foot in Egypt, the land of his dreams, and sailed upstream from Cairo, following the course of the Nile, paying homage to the culture he had worked so hard to understand. It was an expedition in time, a visit to an alien civilization:

> The evening of the 16th we finally arrived at Dendera. There was magnificent moonlight and we were only an hour away from the Temples: Could we resist the temptation? I ask the coldest of you mortals! To dine and leave immediately were the orders of the moment: alone and without guides, but armed to the teeth we crossed the fields . . . the Temple appeared to us at last . . . One could well measure it but to give an idea of it would be impossible. It is the union of grace and majesty in the highest degree. We stayed there two hours in ecstasy, running through the huge rooms . . . and trying to read the exterior inscriptions in the moonlight. We did not return to the boat until three in the morning, only to return to the Tem-

> ple at seven . . . What had been magnificent in the moonlight was still so when the sunlight revealed to us all the details . . . We in Europe are only dwarfs and no nation, ancient or modern, has conceived the art of architecture on such a sublime, great, and imposing style, as the ancient Egyptians. They ordered everything to be done for people who are a hundred feet high.

On the walls and columns of Karnak, at Dendera, everywhere in Egypt, Champollion delighted to find that he could read the inscriptions almost effortlessly. Many before him had tried and failed to decipher the lovely hieroglyphics, a word that means "sacred carvings." Some scholars had believed them to be a kind of picture code, rich in murky metaphor, mostly about eyeballs and wavy lines, beetles, bumblebees and birds—especially birds. Confusion was rampant. There were those who deduced that the Egyptians were colonists from ancient China. There were those who concluded the opposite. Enormous folio volumes of spurious translations were published. One interpreter glanced at the Rosetta stone, whose hieroglyphic inscription was then still undeciphered, and instantly announced its meaning. He said that the quick decipherment enabled him "to avoid the systematic errors which invariably arise from prolonged reflection." You get better results, he argued, by not thinking too much. As with the search for extraterrestrial life today, the unbridled speculation of amateurs had frightened many professionals out of the field.

Champollion resisted the idea of hieroglyphs as pictorial metaphors. Instead, with the aid of a brilliant insight by the English physicist Thomas Young, he proceeded something like this: The Rosetta stone had been uncovered in 1799 by a French soldier working on the fortifications of the Nile Delta town of Rashid, which the Europeans, largely ignorant of Arabic, called Rosetta. It was a slab from an ancient temple, displaying what seemed clearly to be the same message in three different writings: in hieroglyphics at the top, in a kind of cursive hieroglyphic called demotic in the middle, and, the key to the enterprise, in Greek at the bottom. Champollion, who was fluent in ancient Greek, read that the stone had been inscribed to commemorate the coronation of Ptolemy V Epiphanes, in the spring of the year 196 B.C. On this occasion the king released political prisoners, remitted taxes, endowed temples, forgave rebels, increased military preparedness and, in short, did all the things that modern rulers do when they wish to stay in office.

The Greek text mentions Ptolemy many times. In roughly the same positions in the hieroglyphic text is a set of symbols surrounded by an oval or cartouche. This, Champollion reasoned, very probably also denotes Ptolemy. If so, the writing could not be fundamentally pictographic or metaphorical; rather, most of the symbols must stand for letters or syllables. Champollion also had the presence of mind to count up the number of Greek words and the number of individual hieroglyphs in what were presumably equivalent texts. There were many fewer of the former, again suggesting that the hieroglyphs were mainly letters and syllables. But which hieroglyphs correspond to which letters? Fortunately, Champollion had available to him an obelisk, which had been excavated at Philae, that included the hieroglyphic equivalent of the Greek name Cleopatra. Ptolemy begins with P; the first symbol in the cartouche is a square. Cleopatra has for its fifth letter a P, and in the Cleopatra cartouche in the fifth position is the same square. P it is. The fourth letter in Ptolemy is an L. Is it represented by the lion? The second letter of Cleopatra is an L and, in hieroglyphics, here is a lion again. The eagle is an A, appearing twice in Cleopatra, as it should. A clear pattern is emerging. Egyptian hieroglyphics are, in significant part, a simple substitution cipher. But not every hieroglyph is a letter or syllable. Some *are* pictographs. The end of the Ptolemy cartouche means "Ever-living, beloved of the god Ptah." The semicircle and egg at the end of Cleopatra are a conventional ideogram for "daughter of Isis." This mix of letters and pictographs caused some grief for earlier interpreters.

In retrospect it sounds almost easy. But it had taken many centuries to figure out, and there was a great deal more to do, especially in the decipherment of the hieroglyphs of much earlier times. The cartouches were the key within the key, almost as if the pharaohs of Egypt had circled their own names to make the going easier for the Egyptologists two thousand years in the future. Champollion walked the Great Hypostyle Hall at Karnak and casually read the inscriptions, which had mystified everyone else, answering the question he had posed as a child to Fourier. What a joy it must have been to open this one-way communication channel with another civilization, to permit a culture that had been mute for millennia to speak of its history, magic, medicine, religion, politics and philosophy.

Today we are again seeking messages from an ancient and exotic civilization, this time hidden from us not only in time but also in space. If we should receive a radio message from an extraterrestrial civilization, how could it possibly be understood? Extraterrestrial intelligence will be elegant, complex, internally consistent and utterly alien. Extraterrestrials would, of course, wish to make a message sent to us as comprehensible as possible. But how could they? Is there in any sense an interstellar Rosetta stone? We believe there is. We believe there is a common language that all technical civilizations, no matter how different, must have. That common language is science and mathematics. The laws of Nature are the same everywhere. The patterns in the spectra of distant stars and galaxies are the same as those for the Sun or for appropriate laboratory experiments: not only do the same chemical elements exist everywhere in the universe, but also the same laws of quantum mechanics that govern the absorption and emission of radiation by atoms apply everywhere as well. Distant galaxies revolving about one another follow the same laws of gravitational physics as govern the motion of an apple falling to Earth, or Voyager on its way to the stars. The patterns of Nature are everywhere the same. An interstellar message, intended to be understood by an emerging civilization, should be easy to decode.

We do not expect an advanced technical civilization on any other planet in our solar system. If one were only a little behind us—10,000 years, say—it would have no advanced technology at all. If it were only a little ahead of us—we who are already exploring the solar system—its representatives should by now be here. To communicate with other civilizations, we require a method adequate not merely for interplanetary distances but for interstellar distances. Ideally, the method should be inexpensive, so that a huge amount of information could be sent and received at very little cost; fast, so an interstellar dialogue is rendered possible; and obvious, so any technological civilization, no matter what its evolutionary path, will discover it early. Surprisingly, there is such a method. It is called radio astronomy.

The largest semi-steerable radio/radar observatory on the planet Earth is the Arecibo facility, which Cornell University operates for the National Science Foundation. In the remote hinterland of the island of Puerto Rico, it is 305 meters (a thousand feet) across, its reflecting surface a section of a sphere laid down in a preexisting bowl-shaped valley. It receives radio waves from the depths of space, focusing them onto the feed arm antenna high above the dish, which is in turn electronically connected to the control room, where the signal is analyzed. Alternatively, when the telescope is used as a radar transmitter, the feed arm can broadcast a signal into the dish, which reflects it into space. The Arecibo Observatory has been used both to search for intelligent signals from civilizations in space and, just once, to broadcast a message—to M13, a distant globular cluster of stars, so that our technical capability to engage in both sides of an interstellar dialogue would be clear, at least to us.

In a period of a few weeks, the Arecibo Observatory could transmit to a comparable observatory on a planet of a nearby star all of the *Encyclopaedia Britannica.* Radio waves travel at the speed of light, 10,000 times faster than a message attached to our fastest interstellar spaceship. Radio telescopes generate, in narrow frequency ranges, signals so intense they can be detected over immense interstellar distances. The Arecibo Observatory could communicate with an identical radio telescope on a planet 15,000 light-years away, halfway to the center of the Milky Way Galaxy, if we knew precisely where to point it. And radio astronomy is a natural technology. Virtually any planetary atmosphere, no matter what its composition, should be partially transparent to radio waves. Radio messages are not much absorbed or scattered by the gas between the stars, just as a San Francisco radio station can be heard easily in Los Angeles even when smog there has reduced the visibility at optical wavelengths to a few kilometers. There are many natural cosmic radio sources having nothing to do with intelligent life—pulsars and quasars, the radiation belts of planets and the outer atmospheres of stars; from almost any planet there are bright radio sources to discover early in the local development of radio astronomy. Moreover, radio represents a large fraction of the electromagnetic spectrum. Any technology able to detect radiation of *any* wavelength would fairly soon stumble on the radio part of the spectrum.

There may be other effective methods of communication that have substantial merit: interstellar spacecraft; optical or infrared lasers; pulsed neutrinos; modulated gravity waves; or some other kind of transmission that we will not discover for a thousand years. Advanced civilizations may have graduated far beyond radio for their own communications. But radio is powerful, cheap, fast and simple. They will know that a backward civilization like ours, wishing to receive messages from the skies, is likely to turn first to radio technology. Perhaps they will have to wheel the radio telescopes out of the Museum of Ancient Technology. If we were to receive a radio message we would know that there would be at the very least one thing we could talk about: radio astronomy.

But is there anyone out there to talk to? With a third or half a trillion stars in our Milky Way Galaxy alone, could ours be the only one accompanied by an inhabited planet? How much more likely it is that technical civilizations are a cosmic commonplace, that the Galaxy is pulsing and humming with advanced societies, and, therefore, that the nearest such culture is not so very far away—perhaps transmitting from antennas established on a planet of a naked-eye star just next door. Perhaps when we look up at the sky at night, near one of those faint pinpoints of light is a world on which someone quite different from us is then glancing idly at a star *we* call the Sun and entertaining, for just a moment, an outrageous speculation.

It is very hard to be sure. There may be severe impediments to the evolution of a technical civilization. Planets may be rarer than we think. Perhaps the origin of life is not so easy as our laboratory experiments suggest. Perhaps the evolution of advanced lifeforms is improbable. Or it may be that complex lifeforms evolve readily, but intelligence and technical societies require an unlikely set of coincidences—just as the evolution of the human species depended on the demise of the dinosaurs and the ice-age recession of the forests in whose trees our ancestors screeched and dimly wondered. Or perhaps civilizations arise repeatedly, inexorably, on innumerable planets in the Milky Way, but are generally unstable; so all but a tiny fraction are unable to survive their technology and succumb to greed and ignorance, pollution and nuclear war.

It is possible to explore this great issue further and make a crude estimate of N, the number of advanced technical civilizations in the Galaxy. We define an advanced civilization as one capable of radio astronomy. This is, of course, a parochial if essential definition. There may be countless worlds on which the inhabitants are accomplished linguists or superb poets but indifferent radio astronomers. We will not hear from them. N can be written as the product or multiplication of a number of factors, each a kind of filter, every one of which must be sizable for there to be a large number of civilizations:

> N_*, the number of stars in the Milky Way Galaxy;
> f_p, the fraction of stars that have planetary systems;
> n_e, the number of planets in a given system that are ecologically suitable for life;
> f_l, the fraction of otherwise suitable planets on which life actually arises;
> f_i, the fraction of inhabited planets on which an intelligent form of life evolves;
> f_c, the fraction of planets inhabited by intelligent beings on which a communicative technical civilization develops; and
> f_L, the fraction of a planetary lifetime graced by a technical civilization.

Written out, the equation reads $N = N_* f_p n_e f_l f_i f_c f_L$. All the f's are fractions, having values between 0 and 1; they will pare down the large value of N_*.

To derive N we must estimate each of these quantities. We know a fair amount about the early factors in the equation, the numbers of stars and planetary systems. We know very little about the later factors, concerning the evolution of intelligence or the lifetime of technical societies. In these cases our estimates will be little better than guesses. I invite you, if you disagree with my estimates below, to make your own choices and see what implications your alternative suggestions have for the number of advanced civilizations in the Galaxy. One of the great virtues of this equation, due originally to Frank Drake of Cornell, is that it involves subjects ranging from stellar and planetary astronomy to organic chemistry, evolutionary biology, history, politics and abnormal psychology. Much of the Cosmos is in the span of the Drake equation.

We know N_*, the number of stars in the Milky Way Galaxy, fairly well, by careful counts of stars in small but representative regions of the sky. It is a few hundred billion; some recent estimates place it at 4×10^{11}. Very few of these stars are of the massive short-lived variety that squander their reserves of thermonuclear fuel. The great majority have lifetimes of billions or more years in which they are shining stably, providing a suitable energy source for the origin and evolution of life on nearby planets.

There is evidence that planets are a frequent accompaniment of star formation: in the satellite systems of Jupiter, Saturn and Uranus, which are like miniature solar systems; in theories of the origin of the planets; in studies of double stars; in observations of accretion disks around stars; and in some preliminary investigations of gravitational perturbations of nearby stars. Many, perhaps even most, stars may have planets. We take the fraction of stars that have planets, f_p, as roughly equal to ⅓. Then the total number of planetary systems in the Galaxy would be $N_* f_p \simeq 1.3 \times 10^{11}$ (the symbol $\simeq$ means "approximately equal to"). If each system were to have about ten planets, as ours does, the total number of worlds in the Galaxy would be more than a trillion, a vast arena for the cosmic drama.

In our own solar system there are several bodies that may be suitable for life of some sort: the Earth certainly, and perhaps Mars, Titan and Jupiter. Once life originates, it tends to be very adaptable and tenacious. There must be many different environments suitable for life in a given planetary system. But conservatively we choose $n_e = 2$. Then the number of planets in the Galaxy suitable for life becomes $N_* f_p n_e \simeq 3 \times 10^{11}$.

Experiments show that under the most common cosmic conditions the molecular basis of life is readily made, the building blocks of molecules able to make copies of themselves. We are now on less certain ground; there may, for example, be impediments in the evolution of the genetic code, although I think this unlikely over billions of years of primeval chemistry. We choose $f_l \simeq 1/3$, implying a total number of planets in the Milky Way on which life has arisen at least once as $N_* f_p n_e f_l \simeq 1 \times 10^{11}$, a hundred billion inhabited worlds. That in itself is a remarkable conclusion. But we are not yet finished.

The choices of f_i and f_c are more difficult. On the one hand, many individually unlikely steps had to occur in biological evolution and human history for our present intelligence and technology to develop. On the other hand, there must be many quite different pathways to an advanced civilization of specified capabilities. Considering the apparent difficulty in the evolution of large organisms represented by the Cambrian explosion, let us choose $f_i \times f_c = 1/100$, meaning that only 1 percent of planets on which life arises eventually produce a technical civilization. This estimate represents some middle ground among the varying scientific opinions. Some think that the equivalent of the step from the emergence of trilobites to the domestication of fire goes like a shot in all planetary systems; others think that, even given ten or fifteen billion years, the evolution of technical civilizations is unlikely. This is not a subject on which we can do much experimentation as long as our investigations are limited to a single planet. Multiplying these factors together, we find $N_* f_p n_e f_l f_i f_c \simeq 1 \times 10^9$, a billion planets on which technical civilizations have arisen at least once. But that is very different from saying that there are a billion planets on which technical civilizations now exist. For this, we must also estimate f_L.

What percentage of the lifetime of a planet is marked by a technical civilization? The Earth has harbored a technical civilization characterized by radio astronomy for only a few decades out of a lifetime of a few billion years. So far, then, for our planet f_L is less than $1/10^8$, a millionth of a percent. And it is hardly out of the question that we might destroy ourselves tomorrow. Suppose this were to be a typical case, and the destruction so complete that no other technical civilization—of the human or any other species—were able to emerge in the five or so billion years remaining before the Sun dies. Then $N = N_* f_p f_l f_i f_c f_L \simeq 10$, and at any given time there would be only a tiny smattering, a handful, a pitiful few technical civilizations in the Galaxy, the steady state number maintained as emerging societies replace those recently self-immolated. The number N might even be as small as 1. If civilizations tend to destroy themselves soon after reaching a technological phase, there might be no one for us to talk with but ourselves. And that we do but poorly. Civilizations would take billions of years of tortuous evolution to arise, and then snuff themselves out in an instant of unforgivable neglect.

But consider the alternative, the prospect that at least some civilizations learn to live with high technology; that the contradictions posed by the vagaries of past brain evolution are consciously resolved and do not lead to self-destruction; or that, even if major disturbances do occur, they are reversed in the subsequent billions of years of biological evolution. Such societies might live to a prosperous old age, their lifetimes measured perhaps on geological or stellar evolutionary time scales. If 1 percent of civilizations can survive technological adolescence, take the proper fork at this critical historical branch point and achieve maturity, then $f_L \simeq 1/100$, $N \simeq 10^7$, and the number of extant civilizations in the Galaxy is in the millions. Thus, for all our concern about the possible unreliability of our estimates of the early factors in the Drake equation, which involve astronomy, organic chemistry and evolutionary biology, the principal uncertainty comes down to economics and politics and what, on Earth, we call human nature. It seems fairly clear that if self-destruction is not the overwhelmingly preponderant fate of galactic civilizations, then the sky is softly humming with messages from the stars.

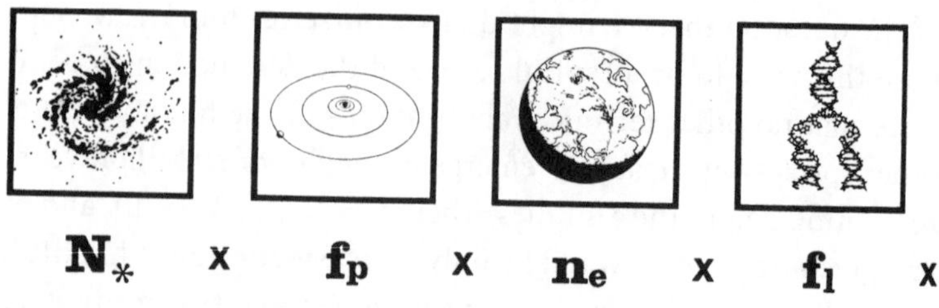

These estimates are stirring. They suggest that the receipt of a message from space is, even before we decode it, a profoundly hopeful sign. It means that someone has learned to live with high technology; that it is possible to survive technological adolescence. This alone, quite apart from the contents of the message, provides a powerful justification for the search for other civilizations.

If there are millions of civilizations distributed more or less randomly through the Galaxy, the distance to the nearest is about two hundred light-years. Even at the speed of light it would take two centuries for a radio message to get from there to here. If we had initiated the dialogue, it would be as if the question had been asked by Johannes Kepler and the answer received by us. Especially because we, new to radio astronomy, must be comparatively backward, and the transmitting civilization advanced, it makes more sense for us to listen than to send. For a more advanced civilization, the positions are, of course, reversed.

We are at the earliest stages of our radio search for other civilizations in space. In an optical photograph of a dense star field, there are hundreds of thousands of stars. By our more optimistic estimates, one of them is the site of an advanced civilization. But which one? Toward which stars should we point our radio telescopes? Of the millions of stars that may mark the location of advanced civilizations, we have so far examined by radio no more than thousands. We have made about one-tenth of one percent of the required effort. But a serious, rigorous, systematic search will come soon. The preparatory steps are now under way, both in the United States and in the Soviet Union. It is comparatively inex-

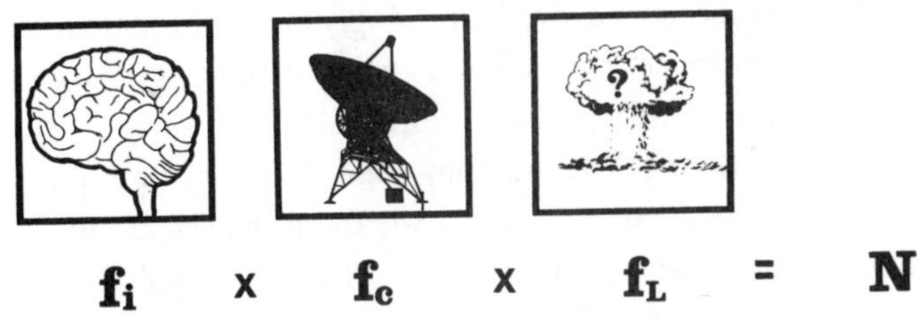

pensive: the cost of a single naval vessel of intermediate size—a modern destroyer, say—would pay for a decade-long program in the search for extraterrestrial intelligence.

Benevolent encounters have not been the rule in human history, where transcultural contacts have been direct and physical, quite different from the receipt of a radio signal, a contact as light as a kiss. Still, it is instructive to examine one or two cases from our past, if only to calibrate our expectations: Between the times of the American and the French Revolutions, Louis XVI of France outfitted an expedition to the Pacific Ocean, a voyage with scientific, geographic, economic and nationalistic objectives. The commander was the Count of La Pérouse, a noted explorer who had fought for the United States in its War of Independence. In July 1786, almost a year after setting sail, he reached the coast of Alaska, a place now called Lituya Bay. He was delighted with the harbor and wrote: "Not a port in the universe could afford more conveniences." In this exemplary location, La Pérouse

> perceived some savages, who made signs of friendship, by displaying and waving white mantles, and different skins. Several of the canoes of these Indians were fishing in the Bay. . . . [We were] continually surrounded by the canoes of the savages, who offered us fish, skins of otters and other animals, and different little articles of their dress in exchange for our iron. To our great surprise, they appeared well accustomed to traffic, and bargained with us with as much skill as any tradesman of Europe.

The Native Americans drove increasingly harder bargains. To La Pérouse's annoyance, they also resorted to pilferage, largely of iron objects, but once of the uniforms of French naval officers hidden under their pillows as they were sleeping one night surrounded by armed guards—a feat worthy of Harry Houdini. La Pérouse followed his royal orders to behave peaceably but complained that the natives "believed our forbearance inexhaustible." He was disdainful of their society. But no serious damage was done by either culture to the other. After reprovisioning his two ships La Pérouse sailed out of Lituya Bay, never to return. The expedition was lost in the South Pacific in 1788; La Pérouse and all but one of the members of his crew perished.*

Exactly a century later Cowee, a chief of the Tlingit, related to the Canadian anthropologist G. T. Emmons a story of the first meeting of his ancestors with the white man, a narrative handed down by word of mouth only. The Tlingit possessed no written records, nor had Cowee ever heard of La Pérouse. This is a paraphrase of Cowee's story:

> Late one spring a large part of Tlingit ventured North to Yakutat to trade for copper. Iron was even more precious, but it was unobtainable. In entering Lituya Bay four canoes were swallowed by the waves. As the survivors made camp and mourned for their lost companions two strange objects entered the Bay. No one knew what they were. They seemed to be great black birds with immense white

* When La Pérouse was mustering the ship's company in France, there were many bright and eager young men who applied but were turned down. One of them was a Corsican artillery officer named Napoleon Bonaparte. It was an interesting branch point in the history of the world. If La Pérouse had accepted Bonaparte, the Rosetta stone might never have been found. Champollion might never have decrypted Egyptian hieroglyphics, and in many more important respects our recent history might have been changed significantly.

wings. The Tlingit believed the world had been created by a great bird which often assumed the form of a raven, a bird which had freed the Sun, the Moon, and the stars from boxes in which they had been imprisoned. To look upon the Raven was to be turned to stone. In their fright, the Tlingit fled into the forest and hid. But after a while, finding that no harm had come to them, a few more enterprising souls crept out and rolled leaves of the skunk cabbage into crude telescopes, believing that this would prevent being turned to stone. Through the skunk cabbage, it seemed that the great birds were folding their wings and that flocks of small black messengers arose from their bodies and crawled upon their feathers.

Now one nearly blind old warrior gathered the people together and announced that his life was far behind him; for the common good he would determine whether the Raven would turn his children into stone. Putting on his robe of sea otter fur, he entered his canoe and was paddled seaward to the Raven. He climbed upon it and heard strange voices. With his impaired vision he could barely make out the many black forms moving before him. Perhaps they were crows. When he returned safely to his people they crowded about him, surprised to see him alive. They touched him and smelled him to see if it was really he. After much thought the old man convinced himself that it was not the god-raven that he had visited, but rather a giant canoe made by men. The black figures were not crows but people of a different sort. He convinced the Tlingit, who then visited the ships and exchanged their furs for many strange articles, chiefly iron.

The Tlingit had preserved in oral tradition an entirely recognizable and accurate account of their first, almost fully peaceable encounter with an alien culture.* If someday we make contact with a more advanced extraterrestrial civilization, will the encounter be largely peaceable, even if lacking a certain rapport, like that of the French among the Tlingit, or will it follow some more ghastly prototype, where the society that was a little more advanced utterly destroyed the society that was technically more backward? In the early sixteenth century a high civilization flourished in central Mexico. The Aztecs had monumental architecture, elaborate record-keeping, exquisite art and an astronomical calendar superior to that of any in Europe. Upon viewing the Aztec artifacts returned by the first Mexican treasure ships, the artist Albrecht Dürer wrote in August 1520: "I have never seen anything heretofore that has so rejoiced my heart. I have seen . . . a sun entirely of gold a whole fathom broad [in fact, the Aztec astronomical calendar]; likewise a moon entirely of silver, equally large . . . also two chambers full of all sorts of weapons, armor, and other wonderous arms, all of which is fairer to see than marvels." Intellectuals were stunned at the Aztec books, "which," one of them said, "almost resemble those of the Egyptians." Hernán Cortés described their capital Tenochtitlán as "one of the most beautiful cities in the world . . . The people's activities and behavior are on almost as high a level as in Spain, and as well-organized and orderly. Considering that these people are barbarous, lacking knowledge of God and communication with other civilized nations, it is remarkable to see all that they have." Two years after writing these words, Cortés utterly destroyed Tenochtitlán along with the rest of the Aztec civilization. Here is an Aztec account:

* The account of Cowee, the Tlingit chief, shows that even in a preliterate culture a recognizable account of contact with an advanced civilization can be preserved for generations. If the Earth had been visited hundreds of thousands of years ago by an advanced extraterrestrial civilization, even if the contacted culture was preliterate, we might well expect to have some recognizable form of the encounter preserved. But there is not a single case in which a legend reliably dated from earlier pretechnological times can be understood only in terms of contact with an extraterrestrial civilization.

> Moctezuma [the Aztec Emperor] was shocked, terrified by what he heard. He was much puzzled by their food, but what made him almost faint away was the telling of how the great Lombard gun, at the Spaniards' command, expelled the shot which thundered as it went off. The noise weakened one, dizzied one. Something like a stone came out of it in a shower of fire and sparks. The smoke was foul; it had a sickening, fetid smell. And the shot, which struck a mountain, knocked it to bits—dissolved it. It reduced a tree to sawdust—the tree disappeared as if they had blown it away . . . When Moctezuma was told all this, he was terror-struck. He felt faint. His heart failed him.

Reports continued to arrive: "We are not as strong as they," Moctezuma was told: "We are nothing compared to them." The Spaniards began to be called "the Gods come from the Heavens." Nevertheless, the Aztecs had no illusions about the Spaniards, whom they described in these words:

> They seized upon the gold as if they were monkeys, their faces gleaming. For clearly their thirst for gold was insatiable; they starved for it; they lusted for it; they wanted to stuff themselves with it as if they were pigs. So they went about fingering, taking up the streamers of gold, moving them back and forth, grabbing them to themselves, babbling, talking gibberish among themselves.

But their insight into the Spanish character did not help them defend themselves. In 1517 a great comet had been seen in Mexico. Moctezuma, captured by the legend of the return of the Aztec god Quetzalcoatl as a white-skinned man arriving across the Eastern sea, promptly executed his astrologers. They had not predicted the comet, and they had not explained it. Certain of forthcoming disaster, Moctezuma became distant and gloomy. Aided by the superstition of the Aztecs and their own superior technology, an armed party of 400 Europeans and their native allies in the year 1521 entirely vanquished and utterly destroyed a high civilization of a million people. The Aztecs had never seen a horse; there were none in the New World. They had not applied iron metallurgy to warfare. They had not invented firearms. Yet the technological gap between them and the Spaniards was not very great, perhaps a few centuries.

We must be the most backward technical society in the Galaxy. Any society still more backward would not have radio astronomy at all. If the doleful experience of cultural conflict on Earth were the galactic standard, it seems we would already have been destroyed, perhaps with some passing admiration expressed for Shakespeare, Bach and Vermeer. But this has not happened. Perhaps alien intentions are uncompromisingly benign, more like La Pérouse than Cortés. Or might it be, despite all the pretensions about UFOs and ancient astronauts, that our civilization has not yet been discovered?

On the one hand, we have argued that if even a small fraction of technical civilizations learn to live with themselves and with weapons of mass destruction, there should now be an enormous number of advanced civilizations in the Galaxy. We already have slow interstellar flight, and think fast interstellar flight a possible goal for the human species. On the other hand, we maintain that there is no credible evidence for the Earth being visited, now or ever. Is this not a contradiction? If the nearest civilization is, say, 200 light-years away, it takes only 200 years to get from there to here at close to the speed of light. Even at 1 percent or a tenth of a percent of the speed of light, beings from nearby civilizations could have come during the tenure of humanity on Earth. Why are they not here? There are many possible answers. Although it runs contrary to the heritage of Aristarchus and Copernicus, perhaps we are the first. Some technical civilization must be the first to emerge in the history of the Galaxy. Perhaps we are mistaken in our belief that at least occasional civilizations avoid self-destruction. Perhaps there is some unforeseen problem to interstellar spaceflight—although, at speeds much less than the velocity of light it is difficult to see what such an impediment might be. Or perhaps they are here, but in hiding because of some *Lex Galactica,* some ethic of noninterference with emerging civilizations. We can imagine them, curious and dispassionate, observing us, as we would watch a bacterial culture in a dish of agar, to determine whether, this year again, we manage to avoid self-destruction.

But there is another explanation that is consistent with everything we know. If a great many years ago an advanced interstellar spacefaring civilization emerged 200 light-years away, it would have no reason to think there was something special about the Earth unless it had been here already. No artifact of human technology, not even our radio transmissions, has had time, even traveling at the speed of light, to go 200 light-years. From their point of view, all nearby star systems are more or less equally attractive for exploration or colonization.*

An emerging technical civilization, after exploring its home planetary system and developing interstellar spaceflight, would slowly and tentatively begin exploring the nearby stars. Some stars would have no suitable planets—perhaps they would all be giant gas worlds, or tiny asteroids. Others would carry an entourage of suitable planets, but some would be already inhabited, or the atmosphere would be poisonous or the climate uncomfortable. In many cases the colonists might have to change—or as we

* There may be many motivations to go to the stars. If our Sun or a nearby star were about to go supernova, a major program of interstellar spaceflight might suddenly become attractive. If we were very advanced, the discovery that the galactic core was imminently to explode might even generate serious interest in transgalactic or intergalactic spaceflight. Such cosmic violence occurs sufficiently often that nomadic spacefaring civilizations may not be uncommon. Even so, their arrival here remains unlikely.

would parochially say, terraform—a world to make it adequately clement. The re-engineering of a planet will take time. Occasionally, an already suitable world would be found and colonized. The utilization of planetary resources so that new interstellar spacecraft could be constructed locally would be a slow process. Eventually a second-generation mission of exploration and colonization would take off toward stars where no one had yet been. And in this way a civilization might slowly wend its way like a vine among the worlds.

It is possible that at some later time with third and higher orders of colonies developing new worlds, another independent expanding civilization would be discovered. Very likely mutual contact would already have been made by radio or other remote means. The new arrivals might be a different sort of colonial society. Conceivably two expanding civilizations with different planetary requirements would ignore each other, their filigree patterns of expansion intertwining, but not conflicting. They might cooperate in the exploration of a province of the Galaxy. Even nearby civilizations could spend millions of years in such separate or joint colonial ventures without ever stumbling upon our obscure solar system.

No civilization can possibly survive to an interstellar spacefaring phase unless it limits its numbers. Any society with a marked population explosion will be forced to devote all its energies and technological skills to feeding and caring for the population on its home planet. This is a very powerful conclusion and is in no way based on the idiosyncrasies of a particular civilization. On any planet, no matter what its biology or social system, an exponential increase in population will swallow every resource. Conversely, any civilization that engages in serious interstellar exploration and colonization must have exercised zero population growth or something very close to it for many generations. But a civilization with a low population growth rate will take a long time to colonize many worlds, even if the strictures on rapid population growth are eased after reaching some lush Eden.

My colleague William Newman and I have calculated that if a million years ago a spacefaring civilization with a low population growth rate emerged two hundred light-years away and spread outward, colonizing suitable worlds along the way, their survey starships would be entering our solar system only about now. But a million years is a very long period of time. If the nearest civilization is younger than this, they would not have reached us yet. A sphere two hundred light-years in radius contains 200,000 suns and perhaps a comparable number of worlds suitable for colonization. It is only after 200,000 other worlds have been colonized that, in the usual course of things, our solar system would be accidentally discovered to harbor an indigenous civilization.

What does it mean for a civilization to be a million years old? We have had radio telescopes and spaceships for a few decades; our technical civilization is a few hundred years old, scientific ideas of a modern cast a few thousand, civilization in general a few tens of thousands of years; human beings evolved on this planet only a few million years ago. At anything like our present rate of technical progress, an advanced civilization millions of years old is as much beyond us as we are beyond a bush baby or a macaque. Would we even recognize its presence? Would a society a million years in advance of us be interested in colonization or interstellar spaceflight? People have a finite lifespan for a reason. Enormous progress in the biological and medical sciences might uncover that reason and lead to suitable remedies. Could it be that we are so interested in spaceflight because it is a way of perpetuating ourselves beyond our own lifetimes? Might a civilization composed of essentially immortal beings consider interstellar exploration fundamentally childish? It may be that we have not been visited because the stars are strewn abundantly in the expanse of space, so that before a nearby civilization arrives, it has altered its exploratory motivations or evolved into forms indetectable to us.

A standard motif in science fiction and UFO literature assumes extraterrestrials roughly as capable as we. Perhaps they have a different sort of spaceship or ray gun, but in battle—and science fiction loves to portray battles between civilizations—they and we are rather evenly matched. In fact, there is almost no chance that two galactic civilizations will interact at the same level. In any confrontation, one will always utterly dominate the other. A million years is a great many. If an advanced civilization were to arrive in our solar system, there would be nothing whatever we could do about it. Their science and technology would be far beyond ours. It is pointless to worry about the possible malevolent intentions of an advanced civilization with whom we might make contact. It is more likely that the mere fact they have survived so long means they have learned to live with themselves and others. Perhaps our fears about extraterrestrial contact are merely a projection of our own backwardness, an expression of our guilty conscience about our past history: the ravages that have been visited on civilizations only slightly more backward than we. We remember Columbus and the Arawaks, Cortés and the Aztecs, even the fate of the Tlingit in the generations after La Pérouse. We remember and we worry. But if an interstellar armada appears in our skies, I predict we will be very accommodating.

A very different kind of contact is much more likely—the case we have already discussed in which we receive a rich, complex message, probably by radio, from another civilization in space, but do not make, at least for a while, physical contact with them. In this case there is no way for the transmitting civilization to know whether we have received the message. If we find the contents offensive or frightening, we are not obliged to reply. But if the message contains valuable information, the consequences for our own civilization will be stunning—insights on alien science and technology, art, music, politics, ethics, philosophy and religion, and most of all, a profound deprovincialization of the human condition. We will know what else is possible.

Because we will share scientific and mathematical insights with any other civilization, I believe that understanding the interstellar message will be the easiest part of the problem. Convincing the U.S. Congress and the Council of Ministers of the U.S.S.R. to fund a search for extraterrestrial intelligence is the hard part.* In fact, it may be that civilizations can be divided into two great categories: one in which the scientists are unable to convince nonscientists to authorize a search for extraplanetary intelligence, in which energies are directed exclusively inward, in which conventional perceptions remain unchallenged and society falters and retreats from the stars; and another category in which the grand vision of contact with other civilizations is shared widely, and a major search is undertaken.

This is one of the few human endeavors where even a failure is a success. If we were to carry out a rigorous search for extraterrestrial radio signals encompassing millions of stars and heard nothing, we would conclude that galactic civilizations were at best extremely rare, a calibration of our place in the universe. It would speak eloquently of how rare are the living things of our planet, and would underscore, as nothing else in human history has, the individual worth of every human being. If we were to succeed, the history of our species and our planet would be changed forever.

It would be easy for extraterrestrials to make an unambiguously artificial interstellar message. For example, the first ten prime numbers—numbers divisible only by themselves and by one—are 1, 2, 3, 5, 7, 11, 13, 17, 19, 23. It is extremely unlikely that any natural physical process could transmit radio messages containing prime numbers only. If we received such a message we would deduce a civilization out there that was at least fond of

* Or other national organs. Consider this pronouncement from a British Defence Department spokesman as reported in the London *Observer* for February 26, 1978: "Any messages transmitted from outer space are the responsibility of the BBC and the Post Office. It is their responsibility to track down illegal broadcasts."

prime numbers. But the most likely case is that interstellar communication will be a kind of palimpsest, like the palimpsests of ancient writers short of papyrus or stone who superimposed their messages on top of preexisting messages. Perhaps at an adjacent frequency or a faster timing, there would be another message, which would turn out to be a primer, an introduction to the language of interstellar discourse. The primer would be repeated again and again because the transmitting civilization would have no way to know when we tuned in on the message. And then, deeper in the palimpsest, underneath the announcement signal and the primer, would be the real message. Radio technology permits that message to be inconceivably rich. Perhaps when we tuned in, we would find ourselves in the midst of Volume 3,267 of the *Encyclopaedia Galactica.*

We would discover the nature of other civilizations. There would be many of them, each composed of organisms astonishingly different from anything on this planet. They would view the universe somewhat differently. They would have different arts and social functions. They would be interested in things we never thought of. By comparing our knowledge with theirs, we would grow immeasurably. And with our newly acquired information sorted into a computer memory, we would be able to see which sort of civilization lived where in the Galaxy. Imagine a huge galactic computer, a repository, more or less up-to-date, of information on the nature and activities of all the civilizations in the Milky Way Galaxy, a great library of life in the Cosmos. Perhaps among the contents of the *Encyclopaedia Galactica* will be a set of summaries of such civilizations, the information enigmatic, tantalizing, evocative—even after we succeed in translating it.

Eventually, taking as much time as we wished, we would decide to reply. We would transmit some information about ourselves—just the basics at first—as the start of a long interstellar dialogue which we would begin but which, because of the vast distances of interstellar space and the finite velocity of light, would be continued by our remote descendants. And someday, on a planet of some far distant star, a being very different from any of us would request a printout from the latest edition of the *Encyclopaedia Galactica* and acquire a little information about the newest society to join the community of galactic civilizations.

Civilization Type: 1.8 L.
Society Code: 2A11, "We Who Survived".
Star: F0V, spectrum variable, r = 9.717 kpc, $\theta = 0°07'51''$, $\phi = 210°20'37''$.
Planet: sixth, $a = 2.4 \times 10^{13}$ cm, $M = 7 \times 10^{18}$ g, $R = 2.1 \times 10^{9}$ cm, $p = 2.7 \times 10^{6}$ s, $P = 4.5 \times 10^{7}$ s.
Extraplanetary colonies: none.
Planet age: 1.14×10^{17} s.
First locally initiated contact: 2.6040×10^{8} s ago.
Receipt first galactic nested code: 2.6040×10^{8} s ago.
Biology: C,N,O,H,S,Se,Cl,Br,H_2O, S_8, polyaromatic sulfonyl halides. Mobile photochemosynthetic autotrophs in weakly reducing atmosphere.
Polytaxic, monochromatic.
$m \approx 3 \times 10^{12}$g, $t \approx 5 \times 10^{10}$ s.
No genetic prosthesis.
Genomes: $\sim 6 \times 10^{7}$ (nonredundant bits/genome: $\sim 2 \times 10^{12}$).
Technology: exponentiating, approaching asymptotic limit.
Culture: global, nongregarious, polyspecific (2 genera, 41 species); arithmetic poetry.
Prepartum/postpartum: 0.52 [30],
Individual/communal: 0.73 [14],
Artistic/technological: 0.81 [18].
Probability of survival (per 100 yr): 80%.

Civilization Type: 2.3 R.
Society Code: 1H1, "We Who Became One".
Interstellar civilization, no planetary communities, utilizes 1504 supergiants, 0V, BV, AV stars and pulsars.
Civilization Age: 6.09×10^{15} s.
First locally initiated contact: 6.09×10^{15} s ago.
Receipt first galactic nested code: 6.09×10^{15} s ago.
Source civilization, neutrino channel.
Local Group polylogue.
Biology: C,H,O,Be,Fe,Ge,He. 4K metal-chelated organic semiconductors, types various.
Cryogenic superconducting electrovores with neutron crystal dense packing and modular starminers; polytaxic.
m various, $t \approx 5 \times 10^{15}$ s.
Genomes: 6×10^{17} (nonredundant bits/mean genome: $\sim 3 \times 10^{17}$).
Probability of survival (per 10^{6} yr): 99%.

Hypothetical computer summaries of two advanced civilizations from the *Encyclopaedia Galactica*. By Jon Lomberg and the author.

Civilization Type: 1.0 J.
Society Code: 4G4, "Humanity".
Star: G2V, r = 9.844 kpc, θ = 00°05′24″,θ = 206°28′49″.
Planet: third, $a = 1.5 \times 10^{13}$ cm, $M = 6 \times 10^{27}$ g, $R = 6.4 \times 10^{8}$ cm, $p = 8.6 \times 10^{4}$ s, $P = 3.2 \times 10^{7}$ s.
Extraplanetary colonies: none.
Planet age: 1.45×10^{17} s.
First locally initiated contact: 1.21×10^{9} s ago.
Receipt first galactic nested code: application pending.
Biology: C,N,O,S,H_2O,PO_4. Deoxyribonucleic acid.
No genetic prosthesis.
Mobile heterotrophs, symbionts with photosynthetic autotrophs. Surface dwellers, monospecific, polychromatic O_2 breathers. Fe-chelated tetrapyroles in circulatory fluid. Sexual mammals. $m \approx 7 \times 10^{4}$ g, $t \approx 2 \times 10^{9}$ s. Genomes: 4×10^{9}.
Technology: exponentiating/fossil fuels/nuclear weapons/ organized warfare/ environmental pollution.
Culture: ~200 nation states, ~6 global powers; cultural and technological homogeneity under way.
Prepartum/postpartum: 0.21 [18],
Individual/communal: 0.31 [17],
Artistic/technological: 0.14 [11].
Probability of survival (per 100 yr): 40%.

Hypothetical summary of a newly emerged technical civilization from the *Encyclopaedia Galactica*. By Jon Lomberg and the author.

CHAPTER XIII
WHO SPEAKS FOR EARTH?

To what purpose should I trouble myself in searching out the secrets of the stars, having death or slavery continually before my eyes?

—A question put to Pythagoras by Anaximenes (c. 600 B.C.), according to Montaigne

How vast those Orbs must be, and how inconsiderable this Earth, the Theatre upon which all our mighty Designs, all our Navigations, and all our Wars are transacted, is when compared to them. A very fit consideration, and matter of Reflection, for those Kings and Princes who sacrifice the Lives of so many People, only to flatter their Ambition in being Masters of some pitiful corner of this small Spot.

—Christiaan Huygens, *New Conjectures Concerning the Planetary Worlds, Their Inhabitants and Productions,* c. 1690

We look back through countless millions of years and see the great will to live struggling out of the intertidal slime, struggling from shape to shape and from power to power, crawling and then walking confidently upon the land, struggling generation after generation to master the air, creeping down into the darkness of the deep; we see it turn upon itself in rage and hunger and reshape itself anew, we watch it draw nearer and more akin to us, expanding, elaborating itself, pursuing its relentless inconceivable purpose, until at last it reaches us and its being beats through our brains and arteries . . . It is possible to believe that all the past is but

> the beginning of a beginning, and that all that is and has been is but the twilight of the dawn. It is possible to believe that all that the human mind has ever accomplished is but the dream before the awakening . . . Out of our . . . lineage, minds will spring, that will reach back to us in our littleness to know us better than we know ourselves. A day will come, one day in the unending succession of days, when beings, beings who are now latent in our thoughts and hidden in our loins, shall stand upon this earth as one stands upon a footstool, and shall laugh and reach out their hands amidst the stars.
>
> —H. G. Wells, "The Discovery of the Future," *Nature 65*, 326 (1902)

The Cosmos was discovered only yesterday. For a million years it was clear to everyone that there were no other places than the Earth. Then in the last tenth of a percent of the lifetime of our species, in the instant between Aristarchus and ourselves, we reluctantly noticed that we were not the center and purpose of the Universe, but rather lived on a tiny and fragile world lost in immensity and eternity, drifting in a great cosmic ocean dotted here and there with a hundred billion galaxies and a billion trillion stars. We have bravely tested the waters and have found the ocean to our liking, resonant with our nature. Something in us recognizes the Cosmos as home. We are made of stellar ash. Our origin and evolution have been tied to distant cosmic events. The exploration of the Cosmos is a voyage of self-discovery.

As the ancient mythmakers knew, we are the children equally of the sky and the Earth. In our tenure on this planet we have accumulated dangerous evolutionary baggage, hereditary propensities for aggression and ritual, submission to leaders and hostility to outsiders, which place our survival in some question. But we have also acquired compassion for others, love for our children and our children's children, a desire to learn from history, and a great soaring passionate intelligence—the clear tools for our continued survival and prosperity. Which aspects of our nature will prevail is uncertain, particularly when our vision and understanding and prospects are bound exclusively to the Earth—or, worse, to one small part of it. But up there in the immensity of the Cosmos, an inescapable perspective awaits us. There are not yet any obvious signs of extraterrestrial intelligence and this makes us wonder whether civilizations like ours always rush implacably, headlong, toward self-destruction. National boundaries are not evident when we view the Earth from space. Fanatical ethnic or religious or national chauvinisms are a little difficult to maintain when we see our planet as a fragile blue crescent fading to become an inconspicuous point of light against the bastion and citadel of the stars. Travel is broadening.

There are worlds on which life has never arisen. There are worlds that have been charred and ruined by cosmic catastrophes. We are fortunate: we are alive; we are powerful; the welfare of our civilization and our species is in our hands. If we do not speak for Earth, who will? If we are not committed to our own survival, who will be?

The human species is now undertaking a great venture that if successful will be as important as the colonization of the land or the descent from the trees. We are haltingly, tentatively breaking the shackles of Earth—metaphorically, in confronting and taming the admonitions of those more primitive brains within us; physically, in voyaging to the planets and listening for the messages from the stars. These two enterprises are linked indissolubly. Each, I believe, is a necessary condition for the other. But our energies are directed far more toward war. Hypnotized by mutual mistrust, almost never concerned for the species or the planet, the nations prepare for death. And because what we are doing is so horrifying, we tend not to think of it much. But what we do not consider we are unlikely to put right.

Every thinking person fears nuclear war, and every technological state plans for it. Everyone knows it is madness, and every nation has an excuse. There is a dreary chain of causality: The Germans were working on the bomb at the beginning of World War II; so the Americans had to make one first. If the Americans had one, the Soviets had to have one, and then the British, the French, the Chinese, the Indians, the Pakistanis . . . By the end of the twentieth century many nations had collected nuclear weapons. They were easy to devise. Fissionable material could be stolen from nuclear reactors. Nuclear weapons became almost a home handicraft industry.

The conventional bombs of World War II were called blockbusters. Filled with twenty tons of TNT, they could destroy a city block. All the bombs dropped on all the cities in World War II amounted to some two million tons, two megatons, of TNT—Coventry and Rotterdam, Dresden and Tokyo, all the death that rained from the skies between 1939 and 1945: a hundred thousand blockbusters, two megatons. By the late twentieth century, two megatons was the energy released in the explosion of a single more or less humdrum thermonuclear bomb: one bomb with the destructive force of the Second World War. But there are tens of thousands of nuclear weapons. By the ninth decade of the twentieth century the strategic missile and bomber forces of the Soviet Union and the United States were aiming warheads at over 15,000 designated targets. No place on the planet was safe. The energy contained in these weapons, genies of death patiently awaiting the rubbing of the lamps, was far more than 10,000 megatons—but with the destruction concentrated efficiently, not over six years but over a few hours, a blockbuster for every family on the planet, a World War II every second for the length of a lazy afternoon.

The immediate causes of death from nuclear attack are the blast wave, which can flatten heavily reinforced buildings many kilometers away, the firestorm, the gamma rays and the neutrons, which effectively fry the insides of passersby. A school girl who survived the American nuclear attack on Hiroshima, the event that ended the Second World War, wrote this first-hand account:

> Through a darkness like the bottom of hell, I could hear the voices of the other students calling for their

> mothers. And at the base of the bridge, inside a big cistern that had been dug out there, was a mother weeping, holding above her head a naked baby that was burned bright red all over its body. And another mother was crying and sobbing as she gave her burned breast to her baby. In the cistern the students stood with only their heads above the water, and their two hands, which they clasped as they imploringly cried and screamed, calling for their parents. But every single person who passed was wounded, all of them, and there was no one, there was no one to turn to for help. And the singed hair on the heads of the people was frizzled and whitish and covered with dust. They did not appear to be human, not creatures of this world.

The Hiroshima explosion, unlike the subsequent Nagasaki explosion, was an air burst high above the surface, so the fallout was insignificant. But on March 1, 1954, a thermonuclear weapons test at Bikini in the Marshall Islands detonated at higher yield than expected. A great radioactive cloud was deposited on the tiny atoll of Rongalap, 150 kilometers away, where the inhabitants likened the explosion to the Sun rising in the West. A few hours later, radioactive ash fell on Rongalap like snow. The average dose received was only about 175 rads, a little less than half the dose needed to kill an average person. Being far from the explosion, not many people died. Of course, the radioactive strontium they ate was concentrated in their bones, and the radioactive iodine was concentrated in their thyroids. Two-thirds of the children and one-third of the adults later developed thyroid abnormalities, growth retardation or malignant tumors. In compensation, the Marshall Islanders received expert medical care.

The yield of the Hiroshima bomb was only thirteen kilotons, the equivalent of thirteen thousand tons of TNT. The Bikini test yield was fifteen megatons. In a full nuclear exchange, in the paroxysm of thermonuclear war, the equivalent of a million Hiroshima bombs would be dropped all over the world. At the Hiroshima death rate of some hundred thousand people killed per equivalent thirteen-kiloton weapon, this would be enough to kill a hundred billion people. But there were less than five billion people on the planet in the late twentieth century. Of course, in such an exchange, not everyone would be killed by the blast and the firestorm, the radiation and the fallout—although fallout does last for a longish time: 90 percent of the strontium 90 will decay in 96 years; 90 percent of the cesium 137, in 100 years; 90 percent of the iodine 131 in only a month.

The survivors would witness more subtle consequences of the war. A full nuclear exchange would burn the nitrogen in the upper air, converting it to oxides of nitrogen, which would in turn destroy a significant amount of the ozone in the high atmosphere, admitting an intense dose of solar ultraviolet radiation.* The increased ultraviolet flux would last for years. It would produce skin cancer preferentially in light-skinned people. Much more important, it would affect the ecology of our planet in an unknown way. Ultraviolet light destroys crops. Many microorganisms would be killed; we do not know which ones or how many, or what the consequences might be. The organisms killed might, for all we know, be at the base of a vast ecological pyramid at the top of which totter we.

The dust put into the air in a full nuclear exchange would reflect sunlight and cool the Earth a little. Even a little cooling can have disastrous agricultural consequences. Birds are more easily killed by radiation than insects. Plagues of insects and consequent further agricultural disorders are a likely consequence of nuclear war. There is also another kind of plague to worry about:

* The process is similar to, but much more dangerous than, the destruction of the ozone layer by the fluorocarbon propellants in aerosol spray cans, which have accordingly been banned by a number of nations; and to that invoked in the explanation of the extinction of the dinosaurs by a supernova explosion a few dozen light-years away.

the plague bacillus is endemic all over the Earth. In the late twentieth century humans did not much die of plague—not because it was absent, but because resistance was high. However, the radiation produced in a nuclear war, among its many other effects, debilitates the body's immunological system, causing a deterioration of our ability to resist disease. In the longer term, there are mutations, new varieties of microbes and insects, that might cause still further problems for any human survivors of a nuclear holocaust; and perhaps after a while, when there has been enough time for the recessive mutations to recombine and be expressed, new and horrifying varieties of humans. Most of these mutations, when expressed, would be lethal. A few would not. And then there would be other agonies: the loss of loved ones; the legions of the burned, the blind and the mutilated; disease, plague, long-lived radioactive poisons in the air and water; the threat of tumors and stillbirths and malformed children; the absence of medical care; the hopeless sense of a civilization destroyed for nothing; the knowledge that we could have prevented it and did not.

L. F. Richardson was a British meteorologist interested in war. He wished to understand its causes. There are intellectual parallels between war and weather. Both are complex. Both exhibit regularities, implying that they are not implacable forces but natural systems that can be understood and controlled. To understand the global weather you must first collect a great body of meteorological data; you must discover how the weather actually behaves. Our approach must be the same, Richardson decided, if we are to understand warfare. So, for the years between 1820 and 1945, he collected data on the hundreds of wars that had been fought on our poor planet.

Richardson's results were published posthumously in a book called *The Statistics of Deadly Quarrels.* Because he was interested in how long you had to wait for a war that would claim a specified number of victims, he defined an index, M, the magnitude of a war, a measure of the number of immediate deaths it causes. A war of magnitude M = 3 might be merely a skirmish, killing only a thousand people (10^3). M = 5 or M = 6 denote more serious wars, where a hundred thousand (10^5) or a million (10^6) people are killed. World Wars I and II had larger magnitudes. He found that the more people killed in a war, the less likely it was to occur, and the longer before you could witness it, just as violent storms occur less frequently than cloudbursts.

Richardson proposed that if you continue the curve to very small values of M, all the way to M = 0, it roughly predicts the worldwide incidence of murder; somewhere in the world someone is murdered every five minutes. Individual killings and wars on the largest scale are, he said, two ends of a continuum, an unbroken curve. It follows, not only in a trivial sense but also I believe in a very deep psychological sense, that war is murder writ large. When our well-being is threatened, when our illusions about ourselves are challenged, we tend—some of us at least—to fly into murderous rages. And when the same provocations are applied to nation states, they too sometimes fly into murderous rages, egged on often enough by those seeking personal power or profit. But as the technology of murder improves and the penalties of war increase, a great many people must be made to fly into murderous rages simultaneously for a major war to be mustered. Because the organs of mass communication are often in the hands of the state, this can commonly be arranged. (Nuclear war is the exception. It can be triggered by a very small number of people.)

We see here a conflict between our passions and what is sometimes called our better natures; between the deep, ancient reptilian part of the brain, the R-complex, in charge of murderous rages, and the more recently evolved mammalian and human parts of the brain, the limbic system and the cerebral cortex. When humans lived in small groups, when our weapons were comparatively paltry, even an enraged warrior could kill only a few. As our technology improved, the means of war also improved. In the same brief interval, *we* also have improved. We have tempered our anger, frustration and despair with reason. We have ameliorated on a planetary scale injustices that only recently were global and endemic. But our weapons can now kill billions. Have we improved fast enough? Are we teaching reason as effectively as we can? Have we courageously studied the causes of war?

What is often called the strategy of nuclear deterrence is remarkable for its reliance on the behavior of our nonhuman ancestors. Henry Kissinger, a contemporary politician, wrote: "Deterrence depends, above all, on psychological criteria. For purposes of deterrence, a bluff taken seriously is more useful than a serious threat interpreted as a bluff." Truly effective nuclear bluffing, however, includes occasional postures of irrationality, a distancing from the horrors of nuclear war. Then the potential enemy is tempted to submit on points of dispute rather than unleash a global confrontation, which the aura of irrationality has made plausible. The chief danger of adopting a credible pose of irrationality is that to succeed in the pretense you have to be very good. After a while, you get used to it. It becomes pretense no longer.

The global balance of terror, pioneered by the United States and the Soviet Union, holds hostage the citizens of the Earth. Each side draws limits on the permissible behavior of the other. The potential enemy is assured that if the limit is transgressed, nuclear war will follow. However, the definition of the limit changes from time to time. Each side must be quite confident that the other understands the new limits. Each side is tempted to increase its military advantage, but not in so striking a way as seriously to alarm the other. Each side continually explores the limits of the other's tolerance, as in flights of nuclear bombers over the Arctic wastes; the Vietnam and Afghanistan wars—a few entries from a long and dolorous list. The global balance of terror is a very delicate balance. It depends on things not going wrong, on mistakes not being made, on the reptilian passions not being seriously aroused.

And so we return to Richardson. In the diagram the solid line is the waiting time for a war of magnitude M—that is, the average time we would have to wait to witness a war that kills 10^m people (where M represents the number of zeroes after the one in our usual exponential arithmetic). Also shown, as a vertical bar at the right of the diagram, is the world population in recent years, which reached one billion people (M = 9) around 1835 and is now about 4.5 billion people (M = 9.7). When the Richardson curve crosses the vertical bar we have specified the waiting time to Doomsday: how many years until the population of the Earth is destroyed in some great war. With Richardson's curve and the simplest extrapolation for the future growth of the human population, the two curves do not intersect until the thirtieth century or so, and Doomsday is deferred.

But World War II was of magnitude 7.7: some fifty million military personnel and noncombatants were killed. The technology of death advanced ominously. Nuclear weapons were used for the first time. There is little indication that the motivations and propensities for warfare have diminished since, and both conventional and nuclear weaponry has become far more deadly. Thus, the top of the Richardson curve is shifting downward by an unknown amount. If its new position is somewhere in the shaded region of the figure, we may have only another few decades until Doomsday. A more detailed comparison of the incidence of wars before and after 1945 might help to clarify this question. It is of more than passing concern.

This is merely another way of saying what we have known for decades: the development of nuclear weapons and their delivery systems will, sooner or later, lead to global disaster. Many of the American and European émigré scientists who developed the first nuclear weapons were profoundly distressed about the demon they had let loose on the world. They pleaded for the global abolition of nuclear weapons. But their pleas went unheeded; the prospect of a national strategic advantage galvanized both the U.S.S.R. and the United States, and the nuclear arms race began.

In the same period, there was a burgeoning international trade in the devastating non-nuclear weapons coyly called "conventional." In the past twenty-five years, in dollars corrected for inflation, the annual international arms trade has gone from $300 million to much more than $20 billion. In the years between 1950 and 1968, for which good statistics seem to be available, there were, on the average, worldwide several accidents involving nuclear weapons per year, although perhaps no more than one or two accidental nuclear explosions. The weapons establishments in the Soviet Union, the United States and other nations are large and powerful. In the United States they include major corporations famous for their homey domestic manufactures. According to one estimate, the corporate profits in military weapons procurement are 30 to 50 percent higher than in an equally technological but competitive civilian market. Cost overruns in military weapons systems are permitted on a scale that would be considered unacceptable in the civilian sphere. In the Soviet Union the resources, quality, attention and care given to military production is in striking contrast to the little left for consumer goods. According to some estimates, almost half the scientists and high technologists on Earth are employed full- or part-time on military matters. Those engaged in the development and manufacture of weapons of mass destruction are given salaries, perquisites of power and, where possible, public honors at the highest levels available in their respective societies. The secrecy of weapons development, carried to especially extravagant lengths in the Soviet Union, implies that individuals so employed need almost never accept responsibility for their actions. They are protected and anonymous. Military secrecy makes the military the most difficult sector of any society for the citizens to monitor. If we do not know what they do, it is very hard for us to stop them. And with the rewards so substantial, with the hostile military establishments beholden to each other in some ghastly mutual embrace, the world discovers itself drifting toward the ultimate undoing of the human enterprise.

Every major power has some widely publicized justification for its procurement and stockpiling of weapons of mass destruction, often including a reptilian reminder of the presumed character and cultural defects of potential enemies (as opposed to us stout fellows), or of the intentions of others, but never ourselves, to conquer the world. Every nation seems to have its set of forbidden possibilities, which its citizenry and adherents must not at any cost be permitted to think seriously about. In the Soviet Union these include capitalism, God, and the surrender of national sovereignty; in the United States, socialism, atheism, and the surrender of national sovereignty. It is the same all over the world.

How would we explain the global arms race to a dispassionate extraterrestrial observer? How would we justify the most recent destabilizing developments of killer-satellites, particle beam weapons, lasers, neutron bombs, cruise missiles, and the proposed conversion of areas the size of modest countries to the enterprise of hiding each intercontinental ballistic missile among hundreds of decoys? Would we argue that ten thousand targeted nuclear warheads are likely to enhance the prospects for our survival? What account would we give of our stewardship of the planet Earth? We have heard the rationales offered by the nuclear superpowers. We know who speaks for the nations. But who speaks for the human species? Who speaks for Earth?

About two-thirds of the mass of the human brain is in the cerebral cortex, devoted to intuition and reason. Humans have evolved gregariously. We delight in each other's company; we care for one another. We cooperate. Altruism is built into us. We have brilliantly deciphered some of the patterns of Nature. We have sufficient motivation to work together and the ability to figure out how to do it. If we are willing to contemplate nuclear war and the wholesale destruction of our emerging global society, should we not also be willing to contemplate a wholesale restructuring of our societies? From an extraterrestrial perspective, our global civilization is clearly on the edge of failure in the most important task it faces: to preserve the lives and well-being of the citizens of the planet. Should we not then be willing to explore vigorously, in every nation, major changes in the traditional ways of doing things, a fundamental redesign of economic, political, social and religious institutions?

Faced with so disquieting an alternative, we are always tempted to minimize the seriousness of the problem, to argue that those who worry about doomsdays are alarmists; to hold that fundamental changes in our institutions are impractical or contrary to "human nature," as if nuclear war were practical, or as if there were only one human nature. Full-scale nuclear war has never happened. Somehow this is taken to imply that it never will. But we can experience it only once. By then it will be too late to reformulate the statistics.

The United States is one of the few governments that actually supports an agency devoted to reversing the arms race. But the comparative budgets of the Department of Defense (153 billion dollars per year in 1980) and of the Arms Control and Disarmament Agency (0.018 billion dollars per year) remind us of the relative importance we have assigned to the two activities. Would not a rational society spend more on understanding and preventing, than on preparing for, the next war? It is possible to study the causes of war. At present our understanding is meager—probably because disarmament budgets have, since the time of Sargon of Akkad, been somewhere between ineffective and nonexistent. Microbiologists and physicians study diseases mainly to cure people. Rarely are they rooting for the pathogen. Let us study war as if it were, as Einstein aptly called it, an illness of childhood. We have reached the point where proliferation of nuclear arms and resistance to nuclear disarmament threaten every person on the planet. There are no more special interests or special cases. Our survival depends on committing our intelligence and resources on a massive scale to take charge of our own destiny, to guarantee that Richardson's curve does not veer to the right.

We, the nuclear hostages—all the peoples of the Earth—must educate ourselves about conventional and nuclear warfare. Then we must educate our governments. We must learn the science and technology that provide the only conceivable tools for our survival. We must be willing to challenge courageously the conventional social, political, economic and religious wisdom. We must make every effort to understand that our fellow humans, all over the world, *are* human. Of course, such steps are difficult. But as Einstein many times replied when his suggestions were rejected as impractical or as inconsistent with "human nature": What is the alternative?

Mammals characteristically nuzzle, fondle, hug, caress, pet, groom and love their young, behavior essentially unknown among the reptiles. If it is really true that the R-complex and limbic systems live in an uneasy truce within our skulls and still partake of their ancient predelictions, we might expect affectionate parental indulgence to encourage our mammalian natures, and the absence of physical affection to prod reptilian behavior. There is some evidence that this is the case. In laboratory experiments, Harry and Margaret Harlow found that monkeys raised in cages and physically isolated—even though they could see, hear and smell their simian fellows—developed a range of morose, withdrawn, self-destructive and otherwise abnormal characteristics. In humans the same is observed for children raised without physical affection—usually in institutions—where they are clearly in great pain.

The neuropsychologist James W. Prescott has performed a startling cross-cultural statistical analysis of 400 preindustrial societies and found that cultures that lavish physical affection on infants tend to be disinclined to violence. Even societies without notable fondling of infants develop nonviolent adults, provided sexual activity in adolescents is not repressed. Prescott believes that cultures with a predisposition for violence are composed of individuals who have been deprived—during at least one of two critical stages in life, infancy and adolescence—of the pleasures of the body. Where physical affection is encouraged, theft, organized religion and invidious displays of wealth are inconspicuous; where infants are physically punished, there tends to be slavery, frequent killing, torturing and mutilation of enemies, a devotion to the inferiority of women, and a belief in one or more supernatural beings who intervene in daily life.

We do not understand human behavior well enough to be sure of the mechanisms underlying these relationships, although we can conjecture. But the correlations are significant. Prescott writes: "The percent likelihood of a society becoming physically violent if it is physically affectionate toward its infants *and* tolerant of premarital sexual behavior is 2 percent. The probability of this relationship occurring by chance is 125,000 to one. I am not aware of any other developmental variable that has such a high degree of predictive validity." Infants hunger for physical affection; adolescents are strongly driven to sexual activity. If youngsters had their way, societies might develop in which adults have little tolerance for aggression, territoriality, ritual and social hierarchy (although in the course of growing up the children might well experience these reptilian behaviors). If Prescott is right, in an age of nuclear weapons and effective contraceptives, child abuse and severe sexual repression are crimes against humanity. More work on this provocative thesis is clearly needed. Meanwhile, we can each make a personal and noncontroversial contribution to the future of the world by hugging our infants tenderly.

If the inclinations toward slavery and racism, misogyny and violence are connected—as individual character and human history, as well as cross-cultural studies, suggest—then there is room for some optimism. We are surrounded by recent fundamental changes in society. In the last two centuries, abject slavery, with us for thousands of years or more, has been almost eliminated in a stirring planet-wide revolution. Women, patronized for millennia, traditionally denied real political and economic power, are gradually becoming, even in the most backward societies, equal partners with men. For the first time in modern history, major wars of aggression were stopped partly because of the revulsion felt by the citizens of the aggressor nations. The old exhortations to nationalist fervor and jingoist pride have begun to lose their appeal. Perhaps because of rising standards of living, children are being treated better worldwide. In only a few decades, sweeping global changes have begun to move in precisely the directions needed for human survival. A new consciousness is developing which recognizes that we are one species.

"Superstition [is] cowardice in the face of the Divine," wrote Theophrastus, who lived during the founding of the Library of Alexandria. We inhabit a universe where atoms are made in the centers of stars; where each second a thousand suns are born; where life is sparked by sunlight and lightning in the airs and waters of youthful planets; where the raw material for biological evolution is sometimes made by the explosion of a star halfway across the Milky Way; where a thing as beautiful as a galaxy is formed a hundred billion times—a Cosmos of quasars and quarks, snowflakes and fireflies, where there may be black holes and other universes and extraterrestrial civilizations whose radio messages are at this moment reaching the Earth. How pallid by comparison are the pretensions of superstition and pseudoscience; how important it is for us to pursue and understand science, that characteristically human endeavor.

Every aspect of Nature reveals a deep mystery and touches our sense of wonder and awe. Theophrastus was right. Those afraid of the universe as it really is, those who pretend to nonexistent knowledge and envision a Cosmos centered on human beings will prefer the fleeting comforts of superstition. They avoid rather than confront the world. But those with the courage to explore the weave and structure of the Cosmos, even where it differs profoundly from their wishes and prejudices, will penetrate its deepest mysteries.

There is no other species on Earth that does science. It is, so far, entirely a human invention, evolved by natural selection in the cerebral cortex for one simple reason: it works. It is not perfect. It can be misused. It is only a tool. But it is by far the best tool we have, self-correcting, ongoing, applicable to everything. It has two rules. First: there are no sacred truths; all assumptions must be critically examined; arguments from authority are worthless. Second: whatever is inconsistent with the facts must be discarded or revised. We must understand the Cosmos as it is and not confuse how it is with how we wish it to be. The obvious is sometimes false; the unexpected is sometimes true. Humans everywhere share the same goals when the context is large enough. And the study of the Cosmos provides the largest possible context. Present global culture is a kind of arrogant newcomer. It arrives on the planetary stage following four and a half billion years of other acts, and after looking about for a few thousand years declares itself in possession of eternal truths. But in a world that is changing as fast as ours, this is a prescription for disaster. No nation, no religion, no economic system, no body of knowledge, is likely to have all the answers for our survival. There must be many social systems that would work far better than any now in existence. In the scientific tradition, our task is to find them.

Only once before in our history was there the promise of a brilliant scientific civilization. Beneficiary of the Ionian Awakening, it had its citadel at the Library of Alexandria, where 2,000 years ago the best minds of antiquity established the foundations for the systematic study of mathematics, physics, biology, astronomy, literature, geography and medicine. We build on those foundations still. The Library was constructed and supported by the Ptolemys, the Greek kings who inherited the Egyptian portion of the empire of Alexander the Great. From the time of its creation in the third century B.C. until its destruction seven centuries later, it was the brain and heart of the ancient world.

Alexandria was the publishing capital of the planet. Of course, there were no printing presses then. Books were expensive; every one of them was copied by hand. The Library was the repository of the most accurate copies in the world. The art of critical editing was invented there. The Old Testament comes down to us mainly from the Greek translations made in the Alexandrian Library. The Ptolemys devoted much of their enormous wealth to the acquisition of every Greek book, as well as works from Africa, Persia, India, Israel and other parts of the world. Ptolemy III Euergetes wished to borrow from Athens the original manuscripts or official state copies of the great ancient tragedies of Sophocles, Aeschylus and Euripides. To the Athenians, these were a kind of cultural patrimony—something like the original handwritten copies and first folios of Shakespeare might be in England. They were reluctant to let the manuscripts out of their hands even for a moment. Only after Ptolemy guaranteed their return with an enormous cash deposit did they agree to lend the plays. But Ptolemy valued those scrolls more than gold or silver. He forfeited the deposit gladly and enshrined, as well he might, the originals in the Library. The outraged Athenians had to content themselves with the copies that Ptolemy, only a little shamefacedly, presented to them. Rarely has a state so avidly supported the pursuit of knowledge.

The Ptolemys did not merely collect established knowledge; they encouraged and financed scientific research and so generated new knowledge. The results were amazing: Eratosthenes accurately calculated the size of the Earth, mapped it, and argued that India could be reached by sailing westward from Spain. Hipparchus anticipated that stars come into being, slowly move during the course of centuries and eventually perish; it was he who first catalogued the positions and magnitudes of the stars to detect such changes. Euclid produced a textbook on geometry from which humans learned for twenty-three centuries, a work that was to help awaken the scientific interest of Kepler, Newton and Einstein. Galen wrote basic works on healing and anatomy which dominated medicine until the Renaissance. There were, as we have noted, many others.

Alexandria was the greatest city the Western world had ever seen. People of all nations came there to live, to trade, to learn. On any given day, its harbors were thronged with merchants, scholars and tourists. This was a city where Greeks, Egyptians, Arabs, Syrians, Hebrews, Persians, Nubians, Phoenicians, Italians, Gauls and Iberians exchanged merchandise and ideas. It is probably here that the word *cosmopolitan* realized its true meaning—citizen, not just of a nation, but of the Cosmos.* To be a citizen of the Cosmos . . .

Here clearly were the seeds of the modern world. What prevented them from taking root and flourishing? Why instead did the West slumber through a thousand years of darkness until Columbus and Copernicus and their contemporaries rediscovered the work done in Alexandria? I cannot give you a simple answer. But I do know this: there is no record, in the entire history of the Library, that any of its illustrious scientists and scholars ever seriously challenged the political, economic and religious assumptions of their society. The permanence of the stars was questioned; the justice of slavery was not. Science and learning in general

* The word *cosmopolitan* was first invented by Diogenes, the rationalist philosopher and critic of Plato.

were the preserve of a privileged few. The vast population of the city had not the vaguest notion of the great discoveries taking place within the Library. New findings were not explained or popularized. The research benefited them little. Discoveries in mechanics and steam technology were applied mainly to the perfection of weapons, the encouragement of superstition, the amusement of kings. The scientists never grasped the potential of machines to free people.* The great intellectual achievements of antiquity had few immediate practical applications. Science never captured the imagination of the multitude. There was no counterbalance to stagnation, to pessimism, to the most abject surrenders to mysticism. When, at long last, the mob came to burn the Library down, there was nobody to stop them.

The last scientist who worked in the Library was a mathematician, astronomer, physicist and the head of the Neoplatonic school of philosophy—an extraordinary range of accomplishments for any individual in any age. Her name was Hypatia. She was born in Alexandria in 370. At a time when women had few options and were treated as property, Hypatia moved freely and unselfconsciously through traditional male domains. By all accounts she was a great beauty. She had many suitors but rejected all offers of marriage. The Alexandria of Hypatia's time—by then long under Roman rule—was a city under grave strain. Slavery had sapped classical civilization of its vitality. The growing Christian Church was consolidating its power and attempting to eradicate pagan influence and culture. Hypatia stood at the epicenter of these mighty social forces. Cyril, the Archbishop of Alexandria, despised her because of her close friendship with the Roman governor, and because she was a symbol of learning and science, which were largely identified by the early Church with

* With the single exception of Archimedes, who during his stay at the Alexandrian Library invented the water screw, which is used in Egypt to this day for the irrigation of cultivated fields. But even he considered such mechanical contrivances far beneath the dignity of science.

paganism. In great personal danger, she continued to teach and publish, until, in the year 415, on her way to work she was set upon by a fanatical mob of Cyril's parishioners. They dragged her from her chariot, tore off her clothes, and, armed with abalone shells, flayed her flesh from her bones. Her remains were burned, her works obliterated, her name forgotten. Cyril was made a saint.

The glory of the Alexandrian Library is a dim memory. Its last remnants were destroyed soon after Hypatia's death. It was as if the entire civilization had undergone some self-inflicted brain surgery, and most of its memories, discoveries, ideas and passions were extinguished irrevocably. The loss was incalculable. In some cases, we know only the tantalizing titles of the works that were destroyed. In most cases, we know neither the titles nor the authors. We do know that of the 123 plays of Sophocles in the Library, only seven survived. One of those seven is *Oedipus Rex.* Similar numbers apply to the works of Aeschylus and Euripides. It is a little as if the only surviving works of a man named William Shakespeare were *Coriolanus* and *A Winter's Tale,* but we had heard that he had written certain other plays, unknown to us but apparently prized in his time, works entitled *Hamlet, Macbeth, Julius Caesar, King Lear, Romeo and Juliet.*

Of the physical contents of that glorious Library not a single scroll remains. In modern Alexandria few people have a keen appreciation, much less a detailed knowledge, of the Alexandrian Library or of the great Egyptian civilization that preceded it for thousands of years. More recent events, other cultural imperatives have taken precedence. The same is true all over the world. We have only the most tenuous contact with our past. And yet just a stone's throw from the remains of the Serapaeum are reminders of many civilizations: enigmatic sphinxes from pharaonic Egypt; a great column erected to the Roman Emperor Diocletian by a provincial flunky for not altogether permitting the citizens of Alexandria to starve to death; a Christian

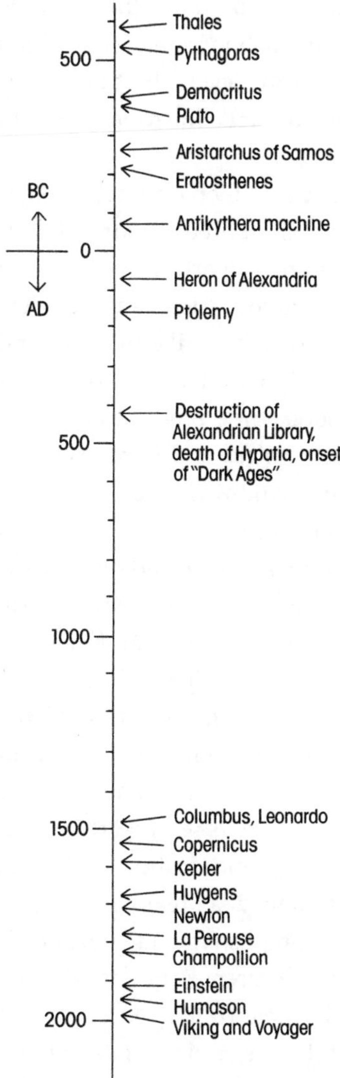

A time line of some of the people, machines and events described in this book. The Antikythera machine was an astronomical computer developed in ancient Greece. Heron of Alexandria experimented with steam engines. The millennium gap in the middle of the diagram represents a poignant lost opportunity for the human species.

church; many minarets; and the hallmarks of modern industrial civilization—apartment houses, automobiles, streetcars, urban slums, a microwave relay tower. There are a million threads from the past intertwined to make the ropes and cables of the modern world.

Our achievements rest on the accomplishments of 40,000 generations of our human predecessors, all but a tiny fraction of whom are nameless and forgotten. Every now and then we stumble on a major civilization, such as the ancient culture of Ebla, which flourished only a few millennia ago and about which we knew nothing. How ignorant we are of our own past! Inscriptions, papyruses, books time-bind the human species and permit us to hear those few voices and faint cries of our brothers and sisters, our ancestors. And what a joy of recognition when we realize how like us they were!

We have in this book devoted attention to some of our ancestors whose names have not been lost: Eratosthenes, Democritus, Aristarchus, Hypatia, Leonardo, Kepler, Newton, Huygens, Champollion, Humason, Goddard, Einstein—all from Western culture because the emerging scientific civilization on our planet is mainly a Western civilization; but every culture—China, India, West Africa, Mesoamerica—has made its major contributions to our global society and had its seminal thinkers. Through technological advances in communication our planet is in the final stages of being bound up at a breakneck pace into a single global society. If we can accomplish the integration of the Earth without obliterating cultural differences or destroying ourselves, we will have accomplished a great thing.

Near the site of the Alexandrian Library there is today a headless sphinx sculpted in the time of the pharaoh Horemheb, in the Eighteenth Dynasty, a millennium before Alexander. Within easy view of that leonine body is a modern microwave relay tower. Between them runs an unbroken thread in the history of the human species. From sphinx to tower is an instant of cosmic time—a moment in the fifteen or so billion years that have elapsed since the Big Bang. Almost all record of the passage of the universe from then to now has been scattered by the winds of time. The evidence of cosmic evolution has been more thoroughly ravaged than all the papyrus scrolls in the Alexandrian Library. And yet through daring and intelligence we have stolen a few glimpses of that winding path along which our ancestors and we have traveled.

For unknown ages after the explosive outpouring of matter and energy of the Big Bang, the Cosmos was without form. There were no galaxies, no planets, no life. Deep, impenetrable darkness was everywhere, hydrogen atoms in the void. Here and there denser accumulations of gas were imperceptibly growing, globes of matter were condensing—hydrogen raindrops more massive than suns. Within these globes of gas was first kindled the nuclear fire latent in matter. A first generation of stars was born, flooding the Cosmos with light. There were in those times not yet any planets to receive the light, no living creatures to admire the radiance of the heavens. Deep in the stellar furnaces the alchemy of nuclear fusion created heavy elements, the ashes of hydrogen burning, the atomic building materials of future planets and lifeforms. Massive stars soon exhausted their stores of nuclear fuel. Rocked by colossal explosions, they returned most of their substance back into the thin gas from which they had once condensed. Here in the dark lush clouds between the stars, new raindrops made of many elements were forming, later generations of stars being born. Nearby, smaller raindrops grew, bodies far too little to ignite the nuclear fire, droplets in the interstellar mist on their way to form the planets. Among them was a small world of stone and iron, the early Earth.

Congealing and warming, the Earth released the methane, ammonia, water and hydrogen gases that had been trapped within, forming the primitive atmosphere and the first oceans. Starlight from the Sun bathed and warmed the primeval Earth, drove storms, generated lightning and thunder. Volcanoes overflowed with lava. These processes disrupted molecules of the primitive atmosphere; the fragments fell back together again into more and more complex forms, which dissolved in the early oceans. After a time the seas achieved the consistency of a warm, dilute soup. Molecules were organized, and complex chemical reactions driven, on the surface of clays. And one day a molecule arose that quite by accident was able to make crude copies of itself out of the other molecules in the broth. As time passed, more elaborate and more accurate self-replicating molecules arose. Those combinations best suited to further replication were favored by the sieve of natural selection. Those that copied better produced more copies. And the primitive oceanic broth gradually grew thin as it was consumed by and transformed into complex condensations of self-replicating organic molecules. Gradually, imperceptibly, life had begun.

Single-celled plants evolved, and life began to generate its own food. Photosynthesis transformed the atmosphere. Sex was invented. Once free-living forms banded together to make a complex cell with specialized functions. Chemical receptors evolved, and the Cosmos could taste and smell. One-celled organisms evolved into multicellular colonies, elaborating their various parts into specialized organ systems. Eyes and ears evolved, and now the Cosmos could see and hear. Plants and animals discovered that the land could support life. Organisms buzzed, crawled, scuttled, lumbered, glided, flapped, shimmied, climbed and soared. Colossal beasts thundered through the steaming jungles. Small creatures emerged, born live instead of in hard-shelled containers, with a fluid like the early oceans coursing through their veins. They survived by swiftness and cunning. And then, only a moment ago, some small arboreal animals scampered down from the trees. They became upright and taught themselves the use of tools, domesticated other animals, plants and fire, and devised language. The ash of stellar alchemy was now emerging into consciousness. At an ever-accelerating pace, it invented writing, cities, art and science, and sent spaceships to the planets and the stars. These are some of the things that hydrogen atoms do, given fifteen billion years of cosmic evolution.

It has the sound of epic myth, and rightly. But it is simply a description of cosmic evolution as revealed by the science of our time. We are difficult to come by and a danger to ourselves. But any account of cosmic evolution makes it clear that all the creatures of the Earth, the latest manufactures of the galactic hydrogen industry, are beings to be cherished. Elsewhere there may be other equally astonishing transmutations of matter, so wistfully we listen for a humming in the sky.

We have held the peculiar notion that a person or society that is a little different from us, whoever we are, is somehow strange or bizarre, to be distrusted or loathed. Think of the negative connotations of words like *alien* or *outlandish.* And yet the monuments and cultures of each of our civilizations merely represent different ways of being human. An extraterrestrial visitor, looking at the differences among human beings and their societies, would find those differences trivial compared to the similarities. The Cosmos may be densely populated with intelligent beings. But the Darwinian lesson is clear: There will be no humans elsewhere. Only here. Only on this small planet. We are a rare as well as an endangered species. Every one of us is, in the cosmic perspective, precious. If a human disagrees with you, let him live. In a hundred billion galaxies, you will not find another.

Human history can be viewed as a slowly dawning awareness that we are members of a larger group. Initially our loyalties were to ourselves and our immediate family, next, to bands of wandering hunter-gatherers, then to tribes, small settlements, city-states, nations. We have broadened the circle of those we love. We have now organized what are modestly described as superpowers, which include groups of people from divergent ethnic and cultural backgrounds working in some sense together—surely a humanizing and character-building experience. If we are to survive, our loyalties must be broadened further, to include the whole human community, the entire planet Earth. Many of those who run the nations will find this idea unpleasant. They will fear the loss of power. We will hear much about treason and disloyalty. Rich nation-states will have to share their wealth with poor ones. But the choice, as H. G. Wells once said in a different context, is clearly the universe or nothing.

A few million years ago there were no humans. Who will be here a few million years hence? In all the 4.6-billion-year history of our planet, nothing much ever left it. But now, tiny unmanned exploratory spacecraft from Earth are moving, glistening and elegant, through the solar system. We have made a preliminary reconnaissance of twenty worlds, among them all the planets visible to the naked eye, all those wandering nocturnal lights that stirred our ancestors toward understanding and ecstasy. If we survive, our time will be famous for two reasons: that at this dangerous moment of technological adolescence we managed to avoid self-destruction; and because this is the epoch in which we began our journey to the stars.

The choice is stark and ironic. The same rocket boosters used to launch probes to the planets are poised to send nuclear warheads to the nations. The radioactive power sources on Viking and Voyager derive from the same technology that makes nuclear weapons. The radio and radar techniques employed to track and guide ballistic missiles and defend against attack are also used to monitor and command the spacecraft on the planets and to listen for signals from civilizations near other stars. If we use these technologies to destroy ourselves, we surely will venture no more to the planets and the stars. But the converse is also true. If we continue to the planets and the stars, our chauvinisms will be shaken further. We will gain a cosmic perspective. We will recognize that our explorations can be carried out only on behalf of all the people of the planet Earth. We will invest our energies in an enterprise devoted not to death but to life: the expansion of our understanding of the Earth and its inhabitants and the search for life elsewhere. Space exploration—unmanned and manned—uses many of the same technological and organizational skills and demands the same commitment to valor and daring as does the enterprise of war. Should a time of real disarmament arrive before nuclear war, such exploration would enable the military-industrial establishments of the major powers to engage at long last in an untainted enterprise. Interests vested in preparations for war can relatively easily be reinvested in the exploration of the Cosmos.

A reasonable—even an ambitious—program of unmanned exploration of the planets is inexpensive. The budget for space sciences in the United States and the Soviet Union together represents the equivalent of two or three nuclear submarines per decade, or the cost overruns on one of the many weapon systems in a single year. In the last quarter of 1979, the program cost of the U.S. F/A-18 aircraft increased by $5.1 billion, and the F-16 by $3.4 billion. Since their inceptions, significantly less has been spent on the unmanned planetary programs of both the United States and the Soviet Union than has been wasted shamefully—for example, between 1970 and 1975, in the U.S. bombing of Cambodia, an application of national policy that cost $7 billion. The total cost of a mission such as Viking to Mars, or Voyager to the outer solar system, is less than that of the 1979–80 Soviet invasion of Afghanistan. Through technical employment and the stimulation of high technology, money spent on space exploration has an economic multiplier effect. One study suggests that for every dollar spent on the planets, seven dollars are returned to the national economy. And yet there are many important and entirely feasible missions that have not been attempted because of lack of funds—including roving vehicles to wander across the surface of Mars, a comet rendezvous, Titan entry probes and a full-scale search for radio signals from other civilizations in space.

The cost of major ventures into space—permanent bases on the Moon or human exploration of Mars, say—is so large that they will not, I think, be mustered in the very near future unless we make dramatic progress in nuclear and "conventional" disarmament. Even then there are probably more pressing needs here on Earth. But I have no doubt that, if we avoid self-destruction, we will sooner or later perform such missions. It is almost impossible to maintain a static society. There is a kind of psychological compound interest: even a small tendency toward retrenchment, a turning away from the Cosmos, adds up over many generations to a significant decline. And conversely, even a slight commitment to ventures beyond the Earth—to what we might call, after Columbus, "the enterprise of the stars"—builds over many generations to a significant human presence on other worlds, a rejoicing in our participation in the Cosmos.

Some 3.6 million years ago, in what is now northern Tanzania, a volcano erupted, the resulting cloud of ash covering the surrounding savannahs. In 1979, the paleoanthropologist Mary Leakey found in that ash footprints—the footprints, she believes, of an early hominid, perhaps an ancestor of all the people on the Earth today. And 380,000 kilometers away, in a flat dry plain that humans have in a moment of optimism called the Sea of Tranquility, there is another footprint, left by the first human to walk another world. We have come far in 3.6 million years, and in 4.6 billion and in 15 billion.

For we are the local embodiment of a Cosmos grown to self-awareness. We have begun to contemplate our origins: starstuff pondering the stars; organized assemblages of ten billion billion

billion atoms considering the evolution of atoms; tracing the long journey by which, here at least, consciousness arose. Our loyalties are to the species and the planet. *We* speak for Earth. Our obligation to survive is owed not just to ourselves but also to that Cosmos, ancient and vast, from which we spring.

ACKNOWLEDGMENTS

Besides those thanked in the introduction, I am very grateful to the many people who generously contributed their time and expertise to this book, including Carol Lane, Myrna Talman, and Jenny Arden; David Oyster, Richard Wells, Tom Weidlinger, Dennis Gutierrez, Rob McCain, Nancy Kinney, Janelle Balnicke, Judy Flannery, and Susan Racho of the *Cosmos* television staff; Nancy Inglis, Peter Mollman, Marylea O'Reilly, and Jennifer Peters of Random House; Paul West for generously lending me the title of Chapter 5; and George Abell, James Allen, Barbara Amago, Lawrence Anderson, Jonathon Arons, Halton Arp, Asma El Bakri, James Blinn, Bart Bok, Zeddie Bowen, John C. Brandt, Kenneth Brecher, Frank Bristow, John Callendar, Donald B. Campbell, Judith Campbell, Elof Axel Carlson, Michael Carra, John Cassani, Judith Castagno, Catherine Cesarsky, Martin Cohen, Judy-Lynn del Rey, Nicholas Devereux, Michael Devirian, Stephen Dole, Frank D. Drake, Frederick C. Durant III, Richard Epstein, Von R. Eshleman, Ahmed Fahmy, Herbert Friedman, Robert Frosch, Jon Fukuda, Richard Gammon, Ricardo Giacconi, Thomas Gold, Paul Goldenberg, Peter Goldreich,

Paul Goldsmith, J. Richard Gott III, Stephen Jay Gould, Bruce Hayes, Raymond Heacock, Wulff Heintz, Arthur Hoag, Paul Hodge, Dorrit Hoffleit, William Hoyt, Icko Iben, Mikhail Jaroszynski, Paul Jepsen, Tom Karp, Bishun N. Khare, Charles Kohlhase, Edwin Krupp, Arthur Lane, Paul MacLean, Bruce Margon, Harold Masursky, Edmond Momjian, Linda Morabito, Edward Moreno, William Murnane, Bruce Murray, Thomas A. Mutch, Kenneth Norris, Tobias Owen, Linda Paul, Roger Payne, Vahe Petrosian, James B. Pollack, George Preston, Nancy Priest, Boris Ragent, Dianne Rennell, Michael Rowton, Allan Sandage, Fred Scarf, Arnold Scheibel, Maarten Schmidt, Eugene Shoemaker, Frank Shu, Nathan Sivin, Bradford Smith, Laurence A. Soderblom, Hyron Spinrad, Edward Stone, Jeremy Stone, Ed Taylor, Kip S. Thorne, Norman Thrower, O. Brian Toon, Barbara Tuchman, Roger Ulrich, Richard Underwood, Peter van de Kamp, Jurrie J. Van der Woude, Arthur Vaughn, Joseph Veverka, Helen Simpson Vishniac, Dorothy Vitaliano, Robert Wagoner, Pete Waller, Josephine Walsh, Kent Weeks, Donald Yeomans, Stephen Yerazunis, Louise Gray Young, Harold Zirin, and the National Aeronautics and Space Administration. I am also grateful for special photographic help by Edwardo Castañeda and Bill Ray.

APPENDIX 1

Reductio ad Absurdum and the Square Root of Two

The original Pythagorean argument on the irrationality of the square root of 2 depended on a kind of argument called *reductio ad absurdum*, a reduction to absurdity: we assume the truth of a statement, follow its consequences and come upon a contradiction, thereby establishing its falsity. To take a modern example, consider the aphorism by the great twentieth-century physicist, Niels Bohr: "The opposite of every great idea is another great idea." If the statement were true, its consequences might be at least a little perilous. For example, consider the opposite of the Golden Rule, or proscriptions against lying or "Thou shalt not kill." So let us consider whether Bohr's aphorism is itself a great idea. If so, then the converse statement, "The opposite of every great idea is not a great idea," must also be true. Then we have reached a *reductio ad absurdum*. If the converse statement is false, the aphorism need not detain us long, since it stands self-confessed as not a great idea.

We present a modern version of the proof of the irrationality of the square root of 2 using a *reductio ad absurdum*, and simple algebra rather than the exclusively geometrical proof discovered by the Pythagoreans. The style of argument, the mode of thinking, is at least as interesting as the conclusion:

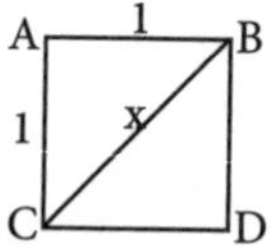

Consider a square in which the sides are 1 unit long (1 centimeter, 1 inch, 1 light-year, it does not matter). The diagonal line BC divides the square into two triangles, each containing a right angle. In such right triangles, the Pythagorean theorem holds: $1^2 + 1^2 = x^2$. But $1^2 + 1^2 = 1 + 1 = 2$, so $x^2 = 2$ and we write $x = \sqrt{2}$, the square root of two. We *assume* $\sqrt{2}$ is a rational number: $\sqrt{2} = p/q$, where p and q are integers, whole numbers. They can be as big as we like and can stand for any integers we like. We can certainly require that they have no common factors. If we were to claim $\sqrt{2} = 14/10$, for example, we would of course cancel out the factor 2 and write $p = 7$ and $q = 5$, not $p = 14$, $q = 10$. Any common factor in numerator or denominator would be canceled out before we start. There are an infinite number of p's and q's we can choose. From $\sqrt{2} = p/q$, by squaring both sides of the equation, we find that $2 = p^2/q^2$, or, by multiplying both sides of the equation by q^2, we find

$$p^2 = 2q^2 \qquad \text{(Equation 1)}$$

p^2 is then some number multiplied by 2. Therefore p^2 is an even number. But the square of any odd number is odd ($1^2 = 1$, $3^2 = 9$, $5^2 = 25$, $7^2 = 49$, etc.). So p itself must be even, and we can write $p = 2s$, where s is some other integer. Substituting for p in Equation (1), we find

$$p^2 = (2s)^2 = 4s^2 = 2q^2$$

Dividing both sides of the last equality by 2, we find

$$q^2 = 2s^2$$

Therefore q^2 is also an even number, and, by the same argument as we just used for p, it follows that q is even too. But if p and q are both even, both divisible by 2, then they have not been reduced to their lowest common factor, contradicting one of our assumptions. *Reductio ad absurdum.* But which assumption? The argument cannot be telling us that reduction to common factors is forbidden, that 14/10 is permitted and 7/5 is not. So the initial assumption must be wrong; p and q cannot be whole numbers; and $\sqrt{2}$ is irrational. In fact, $\sqrt{2} = 1.4142135\ldots$

What a stunning and unexpected conclusion! How elegant the proof! But the Pythagoreans felt compelled to suppress this great discovery.

APPENDIX 2

The Five Pythagorean Solids

A regular polygon (Greek for "many-angled") is a two-dimensional figure with some number, n, of equal sides. So n = 3 is an equilateral triangle, n = 4 is a square, n = 5 is a pentagon, and so on. A polyhedron (Greek for "many-sided") is a three-dimensional figure, all of whose faces are polygons: a cube, for example, with 6 squares for faces. A simple polyhedron, or regular solid, is one with no holes in it. Fundamental to the work of the Pythagoreans and of Johannes Kepler was the fact that there can be 5 and only 5 regular solids. The easiest proof comes from a relationship discovered much later by Descartes and by Leonhard Euler which relates the number of faces, F, the number of edges, E, and the number of corners or vertices, V, of a regular solid:

$$V - E + F = 2 \qquad \text{(Equation 2)}$$

So for a cube, there are 6 faces (F = 6) and 8 vertices (V = 8), and 8 – E + 6 = 2, 14 – E = 2, and E = 12; Equation (2) predicts that the cube has 12 edges, as it does. A simple geometric proof of Equation (2) can be found in the book by Courant and Robbins in the Bibliography. From Equation (2) we can prove that there are only five regular solids:

Every edge of a regular solid is shared by the sides of two adjacent polygons. Think again of the cube, where every edge is a boundary between two squares. If we count up all the sides of all the faces of a polyhedron, n F, we will have counted every edge twice. So

$$n\,F = 2\,E \qquad \text{(Equation 3)}$$

Let r represent how many edges meet at each vertex. For a cube, r = 3. Also, every edge connects two vertices. If we count up all the vertices, r V, we will similarly have counted every edge twice. So

$$r\,V = 2\,E \qquad \text{(Equation 4)}$$

Substituting for V and F in Equation (2) from Equations (3) and (4), we find

$$2\,E/r - E + 2\,E/n = 2$$

If we divide both sides of this equation by 2 E, we have

$$1/n + 1/r = 1/2 + 1/E \qquad \text{(Equation 5)}$$

We know that n is 3 or more, since the simplest polygon is the triangle, with three sides. We also know that r is 3 or more, since at least 3 faces meet at a given vertex in a polyhedron. If both n and r were *simultaneously* more than 3, the left-hand side of Equation (5) would be less than ⅔ and the equation could not be satisfied for any positive value of E. Thus, by another *reductio ad absurdum* argument, either n = 3 and r is 3 or more, or r = 3 and n is 3 or more.

If $n = 3$, Equation (5) becomes $(1/3) + (1/r) = (1/2) + (1/E)$, or

$$1/r = 1/E + 1/6 \qquad \text{(Equation 6)}$$

So in this case r can equal 3, 4, or 5 only. (If E were 6 or more, the equation would be violated.) Now $n = 3$, $r = 3$ designates a solid in which 3 triangles meet at each vertex. By Equation (6) it has 6 edges; by Equation (3) it has 4 faces; by Equation (4) it has 4 vertices. Clearly it is the pyramid or tetrahedron; $n = 3$, $r = 4$ is a solid with 8 faces in which 4 triangles meet at each vertex, the octahedron; and $n = 3$, $r = 5$ represents a solid with 20 faces in which 5 triangles meet at each vertex, the icosahedron (see figures on p. 55).

If $r = 3$, Equation (5) becomes

$$1/n = 1/E + 1/6$$

and by similar arguments n can equal 3, 4, or 5 only. $n = 3$ is the tetrahedron again; $n = 4$ is a solid whose faces are 6 squares, the cube; and $n = 5$ corresponds to a solid whose faces are 12 pentagons, the dodecahedron.

There are no other integer values of n and r possible, and therefore there are only 5 regular solids, a conclusion from abstract and beautiful mathematics that has had, as we have seen, the most profound impact on practical human affairs.

FOR FURTHER READING

(The more technical scientific works are asterisked.)

Chapter 1

Boeke, Kees. *Cosmic View: The Universe in Forty Jumps.* New York: John Day, 1957.

Fraser, Peter Marshall. *Ptolemaic Alexandria.* Three volumes. Oxford: Clarendon Press, 1972.

Morison, Samuel Eliot. *Admiral of the Ocean Sea: A Life of Christopher Columbus.* Boston: Little, Brown, 1942.

Sagan, Carl. *Broca's Brain: Reflections on the Romance of Science.* New York: Random House, 1979.

Chapter 2

Attenborough, David. *Life on Earth: A Natural History.* London: British Broadcasting Corporation, 1979.

*Dobzhansky, Theodosius, Ayala, Francisco J., Stebbins, G. Ledyard and Valentine, James. *Evolution.* San Francisco: W.H. Freeman, 1978.

Evolution. A Scientific American Book. San Francisco: W.H. Freeman, 1978.

Gould, Stephen Jay. *Ever Since Darwin: Reflections on Natural History.* New York: W.W. Norton, 1977.

Handler, Philip (ed.). *Biology and the Future of Man.* Committee on Science and Public Policy, National Academy of Sciences. New York: Oxford University Press, 1970.

Huxley, Julian. *New Bottles for New Wine: Essays.* London: Chatto and Windus, 1957.

Kennedy, D. (ed.). *Cellular and Organismal Biology.* A Scientific American Book. San Francisco: W.H. Freeman, 1974.

*Kornberg, A. *DNA Replication.* San Francisco: W.H. Freeman, 1980.
*Miller, S.L. and Orgel, L. *The Origins of Life on Earth.* Englewood Cliffs, N.J.: Prentice-Hall, 1974.
Orgel, L. *Origins of Life.* New York: Wiley, 1973.
*Roemer, A.S. "Major Steps in Vertebrate Evolution." *Science,* Vol. 158, p. 1629, 1967.
*Roland, Jean Claude. *Atlas of Cell Biology.* Boston: Little, Brown, 1977.
Sagan, Carl. "Life." *Encyclopaedia Britannica,* 1970 and later printings.
*Sagan, Carl and Salpeter, E.E. "Particles, Environments and Hypothetical Ecologies in the Jovian Atmosphere." *Astrophysical Journal Supplement,* Vol. 32, p. 737, 1976.
Simpson, G.G. *The Meaning of Evolution.* New Haven: Yale University Press, 1960.
Thomas, Lewis. *Lives of a Cell: Notes of a Biology Watcher.* New York: Bantam Books, 1974.
*Watson, J.D. *Molecular Biology of the Gene.* New York: W.A. Benjamin, 1965.
Wilson, E.O., Eisner, T., Briggs, W.R., Dickerson, R.E., Metzenberg, R.L., O'Brien, R.D., Susman, M., and Boggs, W.E. *Life on Earth.* Stamford: Sinauer Associates, 1973.

Chapter 3

Abell, George and Singer, B. (eds.) *Science and the Paranormal.* New York: Scribner's, 1980.
*Beer, A. (ed.). *Vistas in Astronomy: Kepler,* Vol. 18. London: Pergamon Press, 1975.
Caspar, Max. *Kepler.* London: Abelard-Schuman, 1959.
Cumont, Franz. *Astrology and Religion Among the Greeks and Romans.* New York: Dover, 1960.
Koestler, Arthur. *The Sleepwalkers.* New York: Grosset and Dunlap, 1963.
Krupp, E.C. (ed.). *In Search of Ancient Astronomies.* New York: Doubleday, 1978.
Pannekoek, Anton. *A History of Astronomy.* London: George Allen, 1961.
Rey, H.A. *The Stars: A New Way to See Them,* third edition. Boston: Houghton Mifflin, 1970.
Rosen, Edward. *Kepler's Somnium.* Madison, Wis.: University of Wisconsin Press, 1967.
Standen, A. *Forget Your Sun Sign.* Baton Rouge: Legacy, 1977.
Vivian, Gordon and Raiter, Paul. *The Great Kivas of Chaco Canyon.* Albuquerque: University of New Mexico Press, 1965.

Chapter 4

Chapman, C. *The Inner Planets.* New York: Scribner's, 1977.
Charney, J.G. (ed.). *Carbon Dioxide and Climate: A Scientific Assessment.* Washington, D.C.: National Academy of Sciences, 1979.
Cross, Charles A. and Moore, Patrick. *The Atlas of Mercury.* New York: Crown Publishers, 1977.
*Delsemme, A.H. (ed.). *Comets, Asteroids, Meteorites.* Toledo: University of Ohio Press, 1977.
*Dunne, James A. and Burgess, Eric. *The Voyage of Mariner 10.* NASA SP-424. Washington, D.C.: U.S. Government Printing Office, 1978.

Ehrlich, Paul R., Ehrlich, Anne H. and Holden, John P. *Ecoscience: Population, Resources, Environment.* San Francisco: W.H. Freeman, 1977.

*El-Baz, Farouk. "The Moon After Apollo." *Icarus,* Vol. 25, p. 495, 1975.

Goldsmith, Donald (ed.). *Scientists Confront Velikovsky.* Ithaca: Cornell University Press, 1977.

Kaufmann, William J. *Planets and Moons.* San Francisco: W.H. Freeman, 1979.

*Keldysh, M.V. "Venus Exploration with the Venera 9 and Venera 10 Spacecraft." *Icarus,* Vol. 30, p. 605, 1977.

*Kresak, L. "The Tunguska Object: A Fragment of Comet Encke?" *Bulletin of the Astronomical Institute of Czechoslovakia,* Vol. 29, p. 129, 1978.

Krinov, E.L. *Giant Meteorites.* New York: Pergamon Press, 1966.

Lovelock, L. *Gaia.* Oxford: Oxford University Press, 1979.

*Marov, M. Ya. "Venus: A Perspective at the Beginning of Planetary Exploration." *Icarus,* Vol. 16, p. 115, 1972.

Masursky, Harold, Colton, C.W. and El-Baz, Farouk (eds.). *Apollo Over the Moon: A View from Orbit.* NASA SP-362. Washington, D.C.: U.S. Government Printing Office, 1978.

*Mulholland, J.D. and Calame, O. "Lunar Crater Giordano Bruno: AD 1178 Impact Observations Consistent with Laser Ranging Results." *Science,* Vol. 199, p. 875, 1978.

*Murray, Bruce and Burgess, Eric. *Flight to Mercury.* New York: Columbia University Press, 1977.

*Murray, Bruce, Greeley, R. and Malin, M. *Earthlike Planets.* San Francisco: W.H. Freeman, 1980.

Nicks, Oran W. (ed.). *This Island Earth.* NASA SP-250. Washington, D.C.: U.S. Government Printing Office, 1970.

Oberg, James. "Tunguska: Collision with a Comet." *Astronomy,* Vol. 5, No. 12, p. 18, December 1977.

*Pioneer Venus Results. *Science,* Vol. 203, No. 4382, p. 743, February 23, 1979.

*Pioneer Venus Results. *Science,* Vol. 205, No. 4401, p. 41, July 6, 1979.

Press, Frank and Siever, Raymond. *Earth,* second edition. San Francisco: W.H. Freeman, 1978.

Ryan, Peter and Pesek, L. *Solar System.* New York: Viking, 1979.

*Sagan, Carl, Toon, O.B. and Pollack, J.B. "Anthropogenic Albedo Changes and the Earth's Climate." *Science,* Vol. 206, p. 1363, 1979.

Short, Nicholas M., Lowman, Paul D., Freden, Stanley C. and Finsh, William A. *Mission to Earth: LANDSAT Views the World.* NASA SP-360. Washington, D.C.: U.S. Government Printing Office, 1976.

Skylab Explores the Earth. NASA SP-380. Washington, D.C.: U.S. Government Printing Office, 1977.

The Solar System. A Scientific American Book. San Francisco: W.H. Freeman, 1975.

Urey, H.C. "Cometary Collisions in Geological Periods." *Nature,* Vol. 242, p. 32, March 2, 1973.

Vitaliano, Dorothy B. *Legends of the Earth.* Bloomington: Indiana University Press, 1973.

*Whipple, F.L. *Comets.* New York: John Wiley, 1980.

Chapter 5

*American Geophysical Union. *Scientific Results of the Viking Project.* Reprinted from the *Journal of Geophysical Research,* Vol. 82, p. 3959, 1977.

Batson, R.M., Bridges, T.M. and Inge, J.L. *Atlas of Mars: The 1:5,000,000 Map Series.* NASA SP-438. Washington, D.C.: U.S. Government Printing Office, 1979.

Bradbury, Ray, Clarke, Arthur C., Murray, Bruce, Sagan, Carl, and Sullivan, Walter. *Mars and the Mind of Man.* New York: Harper and Row, 1973.

Burgess, Eric. *To the Red Planet.* New York: Columbia University Press, 1978.

Gerster, Georg. *Grand Design: The Earth from Above.* New York: Paddington Press, 1976.

Glasstone, Samuel. *Book of Mars.* Washington, D.C.: U.S. Government Printing Office, 1968.

Goddard, Robert H. *Autobiography.* Worcester, Mass.: A.J. St. Onge, 1966.

*Goddard, Robert H. *Papers.* Three volumes. New York: McGraw-Hill, 1970.

Hartmann, W.H. and Raper, O. *The New Mars: The Discoveries of Mariner 9.* NASA SP-337. Washington, D.C.: U.S. Government Printing Office, 1974.

Hoyt, William G. *Lowell and Mars.* Tucson: University of Arizona Press, 1976.

Lowell, Percival. *Mars.* Boston: Houghton Mifflin, 1896.

Lowell, Percival. *Mars and Its Canals.* New York: Macmillan, 1906.

Lowell, Percival. *Mars as an Abode of Life.* New York: Macmillan, 1908.

Mars as Viewed by Mariner 9. NASA SP-329. Washington, D.C.: U.S. Government Printing Office, 1974.

Morowitz, Harold. *The Wine of Life.* New York: St. Martin's, 1979.

*Mutch, Thomas A., Arvidson, Raymond E., Head, James W., Jones, Kenneth L. and Saunders, R. Stephen. *The Geology of Mars.* Princeton: Princeton University Press, 1976.

*Pittendrigh, Colin S., Vishniac, Wolf and Pearman, J.P.T. (eds.). *Biology and the Exploration of Mars.* Washington, D.C.: National Academy of Sciences, National Research Council, 1966.

The Martian Landscape. Viking Lander Imaging Team, NASA SP-425. Washington, D.C.: U.S. Government Printing Office, 1978.

*Viking 1 Mission Results. *Science,* Vol. 193, No. 4255, August 1976.

*Viking 1 Mission Results. *Science,* Vol. 194, No. 4260, October 1976.

*Viking 2 Mission Results. *Science,* Vol. 194, No. 4271, December 1976.

*"The Viking Mission and the Question of Life on Mars." *Journal of Molecular Evolution,* Vol. 14, Nos. 1–3. Berlin: Springer-Verlag, December 1979.

Wallace, Alfred Russel. *Is Mars Habitable?* London: Macmillan, 1907.

Washburn, Mark. *Mars At Last!* New York: G.P. Putnam, 1977.

Chapter 6

*Alexander, A.F.O. *The Planet Saturn.* New York: Dover, 1980.

Bell, Arthur E. *Christiaan Huygens and the Development of Science in the Seventeenth Century.* New York: Longman's Green, 1947.

Dobell, Clifford. *Anton Van Leeuwenhoek and His "Little Animals."* New York: Russell and Russell, 1958.

Duyvendak, J.J.L. *China's Discovery of Africa*. London: Probsthain, 1949.
*"First Scientific Results from Voyager 1." *Science,* Vol. 204, No. 4396, June 1, 1979.
*"First Scientific Results from Voyager 2." *Science,* Vol. 206, No. 4421, p. 927, November 23, 1979.
*Gehrels, T. (ed.). *Jupiter: Studies of the Interior, Atmosphere, Magnetosphere and Satellites.* Tucson: University of Arizona Press, 1976.
Haley, K.H. *The Dutch in the Seventeenth Century.* New York: Harcourt Brace, 1972.
Huizinga, Johan. *Dutch Civilization in the Seventeenth Century.* New York: F. Ungar, 1968.
*Hunten, Donald (ed.). *The Atmosphere of Titan.* NASA SP-340. Washington, D.C.: U.S. Government Printing Office, 1973.
*Hunten, Donald and Morrison, David (eds.). *The Saturn System.* NASA Conference Publication 2068. Washington, D.C.: U.S. Government Printing Office, 1978.
Huygens, Christiaan. *The Celestial Worlds Discover'd: Conjectures Concerning the Inhabitants, Planets and Productions of the Worlds in the Planets.* London: Timothy Childs, 1798.
Manuel, Frank E. *A Portrait of Isaac Newton.* Washington: New Republic Books, 1968.
Morrison, David and Samz, Jane. *Voyager to Jupiter.* NASA SP-439. Washington, D.C.: U.S. Government Printing Office, 1980.
Needham, Joseph. *Science and Civilization in China,* Vol. 4, Part 3, pp. 468–553. New York Cambridge University Press, 1970.
*Palluconi, F.D. and Pettengill, G.H. (eds.). *The Rings of Saturn.* NASA SP-343. Washington, D.C.: U.S. Government Printing Office, 1974.
Rimmel, Richard O., Swindell, William and Burgess, Eric. *Pioneer Odyssey.* NASA SP-349. Washington, D.C.: U.S. Government Printing Office, 1977.
*"Voyager 1 Encounter with Jupiter and Io." *Nature,* Vol. 280, p. 727, 1979.
Wilson, Charles H. *The Dutch Republic and the Civilization of the Seventeenth Century.* London: Weidenfeld and Nicolson, 1968.
Zumthor, Paul. *Daily Life in Rembrandt's Holland.* London: Weidenfeld and Nicolson, 1962.

Chapter 7

Baker, Howard. *Persephone's Cave.* Athens: University of Georgia Press, 1979.
Berendzen, Richard, Hart, Richard and Seeley, Daniel. *Man Discovers the Galaxies.* New York: Science History Publications, 1977.
Farrington, Benjamin. *Greek Science.* London: Penguin, 1953.
Finley, M.I. *Ancient Slavery and Modern Ideology.* London: Chatto, 1980.
Frankfort, H., Frankfort, H.A., Wilson, J.A. and Jacobsen, T. *Before Philosophy: The Intellectual Adventure of Ancient Man.* Chicago: University of Chicago Press, 1946.
Heath, T. *Aristarchus of Samos.* Cambridge: Cambridge University Press, 1913.
Heidel, Alexander. *The Babylonian Genesis.* Chicago: University of Chicago Press, 1942.
Hodges, Henry. *Technology in the Ancient World.* London: Allan Lane, 1970.
Jeans, James. *The Growth of Physical Science,* second edition. Cambridge: Cambridge University Press, 1951.
Lucretius. *The Nature of the Universe.* New York: Penguin, 1951.

Murray, Gilbert. *Five Stages of Greek Religion.* New York: Anchor Books, 1952.
Russell, Bertrand. *A History of Western Philosophy.* New York: Simon and Schuster, 1945.
Sarton, George. *A History of Science,* Vols. 1 and 2. Cambridge: Harvard University Press, 1952, 1959.
Schrödinger, Erwin. *Nature and the Greeks.* Cambridge: Cambridge University Press, 1954.
Vlastos, Gregory. *Plato's Universe.* Seattle: University of Washington Press, 1975.

Chapter 8

Barnett, Lincoln. *The Universe and Dr. Einstein.* New York: Sloane, 1956.
Bernstein, Jeremy. *Einstein.* New York: Viking, 1973.
Borden, M. and Graham, O.L. *Speculations on American History.* Lexington, Mass.: D.C. Heath, 1977.
*Bussard, R.W. "Galactic Matter and Interstellar Flight." *Astronautica Acta,* Vol. 6, p. 179, 1960.
Cooper, Margaret. *The Inventions of Leonardo Da Vinci.* New York: Macmillan, 1965.
*Dole, S.H. "Formation of Planetary Systems by Aggregation: A Computer Simulation." *Icarus,* Vol. 13, p. 494, 1970.
Dyson, F.J. "Death of a Project." [Orion.] *Science,* Vol. 149, p. 141, 1965.
Gamow, George. *Mr. Tompkins in Paperback.* Cambridge: Cambridge University Press, 1965.
Hart, Ivor B. *Mechanical Investigations of Leonardo Da Vinci.* Berkeley: University of California Press, 1963.
Hoffman, Banesh. *Albert Einstein: Creator and Rebel.* New York: New American Library, 1972.
*Isaacman, R. and Sagan, Carl. "Computer Simulation of Planetary Accretion Dynamics: Sensitivity to Initial Conditions." *Icarus,* Vol. 31, p. 510, 1977.
Lieber, Lillian R. and Lieber, Hugh Gray. *The Einstein Theory of Relativity.* New York: Holt, Rinehart and Winston, 1961.
MacCurdy, Edward (ed.). *Notebooks of Leonardo.* Two volumes. New York: Reynal and Hitchcock, 1938.
*Martin, A.R. (ed.). "Project Daedalus: Final Report of the British Interplanetary Society Starship Study." *Journal of the British Interplanetary Society,* Supplement, 1978.
McPhee, John A. *The Curve of Binding Energy.* New York: Farrar, Straus and Giroux, 1974.
*Mermin, David. *Space and Time and Special Relativity.* New York: McGraw-Hill, 1968.
Richter, Jean-Paul. *Notebooks of Leonardo Da Vinci.* New York: Dover, 1970.
Schlipp, Paul A. (ed.). *Albert Einstein: Philosopher-Scientist,* third edition. Two volumes. La Salle, Ill: Open Court, 1970.

Chapter 9

Eddy, John A. *The New Sun: The Solar Results from Skylab.* NASA SP-402. Washington, D.C.: U.S. Government Printing Office, 1979.

*Feynman, R.P., Leighton, R.B. and Sands, M. *The Feynman Lectures on Physics*. Reading, Mass.: Addison-Wesley, 1963.

Gamow, George. *One, Two, Three . . . Infinity*. New York: Bantam Books, 1971.

Kasner, Edward and Newman, James R. *Mathematics and the Imagination*. New York: Simon and Schuster, 1953.

Kaufmann, William J. *Stars and Nebulas*. San Francisco: W.H. Freeman, 1978.

Maffei, Paolo. *Monsters in the Sky*. Cambridge: M.I.T. Press, 1980.

Murdin, P. and Allen, D. *Catalogue of the Universe*. New York: Crown Publishers, 1979.

*Shklovskii, I.S. *Stars: Their Birth, Life and Death*. San Francisco: W.H. Freeman, 1978.

Sullivan, Walter. *Black Holes: The Edge of Space, The End of Time*. New York: Doubleday, 1979.

Weisskopf, Victor. *Knowledge and Wonder*, second edition. Cambridge: M.I.T. Press, 1979.

Excellent introductory college textbooks on astronomy include:

Abell, George. *The Realm of the Universe*. Philadelphia: Saunders College, 1980.

Berman, Louis and Evans, J.C. *Exploring the Cosmos*. Boston: Little, Brown, 1980.

Hartmann, William K. *Astronomy: The Cosmic Journey*. Belmont, Cal.: Wadsworth, 1978.

Jastrow, Robert and Thompson, Malcolm H. *Astronomy: Fundamentals and Frontiers*, third edition. New York: Wiley, 1977.

Pasachoff, Jay M. and Kutner, M.L. *University Astronomy*. Philadelphia: Saunders, 1978.

Zeilik, Michael. *Astronomy: The Evolving Universe*. New York: Harper and Row, 1979.

Chapter 10

Abbott, E. *Flatland*. New York: Barnes and Noble, 1963.

*Arp, Halton. "Peculiar Galaxies and Radio Sources." *Science*, Vol. 151, p. 1214, 1966.

Bok, Bart and Bok, Priscilla. *The Milky Way*, fourth edition. Cambridge: Harvard University Press, 1974.

Campbell, Joseph. *The Mythic Image*. Princeton: Princeton University Press, 1974.

Ferris, Timothy. *Galaxies*. San Francisco: Sierra Club Books, 1980.

Ferris, Timothy. *The Red Limit: The Search by Astronomers for the Edge of the Universe*. New York: William Morrow, 1977.

Gingerich, Owen (ed.). *Cosmology* + 1. A Scientific American Book. San Francisco: W.H. Freeman, 1977.

*Jones, B. "The Origin of Galaxies: A Review of Recent Theoretical Developments and Their Confrontation with Observation." *Reviews of Modern Physics*, Vol. 48, p. 107, 1976.

Kaufmann, William J. *Black Holes and Warped Space-Time*. San Francisco: W.H. Freeman, 1979.

Kaufmann, William J. *Galaxies and Quasars*. San Francisco: W.H. Freeman, 1979.

Rothenberg, Jerome (ed.). *Technicians of the Sacred*. New York: Doubleday, 1968.

Silk, Joseph, *The Big Bang: The Creation and Evolution of the Universe*. San Francisco: W.H. Freeman, 1980.

Sproul, Barbara C. *Primal Myths: Creating the World.* New York: Harper and Row, 1979.

*Stockton, A.N. "The Nature of QSO Red Shifts." *Astrophysical Journal,* Vol. 223, p. 747, 1978.

Weinberg, Steven. *The First Three Minutes: A Modern View of the Origin of the Universe.* New York: Basic Books, 1977.

*White, S.D.M. and Rees, M.J. "Core Condensation in Heavy Halos: A Two-Stage Series for Galaxy Formation and Clustering." *Monthly Notices of the Royal Astronomical Society,* Vol. 183, p. 341, 1978.

Chapter 11

Human Ancestors. Readings from Scientific American. San Francisco: W.H. Freeman, 1979.

Koestler, Arthur. *The Act of Creation.* New York: Macmillan, 1964.

Leakey, Richard E. and Lewin, Roger. *Origins.* New York: Dutton, 1977.

*Lehninger, Albert L. *Biochemistry.* New York: Worth Publishers, 1975.

*Norris, Kenneth S. (ed.). *Whales, Dolphins and Porpoises.* Berkeley: University of California Press, 1978.

*Payne, Roger and McVay, Scott. "Songs of Humpback Whales." *Science,* Vol. 173, p. 585, August 1971.

Restam, Richard M. *The Brain.* New York: Doubleday, 1979.

Sagan, Carl. *The Dragons of Eden: Speculations on the Evolution of Human Intelligence.* New York: Random House, 1977.

Sagan, Carl, Drake, F.D., Druyan, A., Ferris, T., Lomberg, J., and Sagan, L.S. *Murmurs of Earth: The Voyager Interstellar Record.* New York: Random House, 1978.

*Stryer, Lubert. *Biochemistry.* San Francisco: W.H. Freeman, 1975.

The Brain. A Scientific American Book. San Francisco: W.H. Freeman, 1979.

*Winn, Howard E. and Olla, Bori L. (eds.). *Behavior of Marine Animals,* Vol. 3: *Cetaceans.* New York: Plenum, 1979.

Chapter 12

Asimov, Isaac. *Extraterrestrial Civilizations.* New York: Fawcett, 1979.

Budge, E.A. Wallis. *Egyptian Language: Easy Lessons in Egyptian Hieroglyphics.* New York: Dover Publications, 1976.

de Laguna, Frederica. *Under Mount St. Elias: History and Culture of Yacutat Tlingit.* Washington, D.C.: U.S. Government Printing Office, 1972.

Emmons, G.T. *The Chilkat Blanket.* New York: Memoirs of the American Museum of Natural History, 1907.

Goldsmith, D. and Owen, T. *The Search for Life in the Universe.* Menlo Park: Benjamin/Cummings, 1980.

Klass, Philip. *UFOs Explained.* New York: Vintage, 1976.

Krause, Aurel. *The Tlingit Indians.* Seattle: University of Washington Press, 1956.

La Pérouse, Jean F. de G., comte de. *Voyage de la Pérouse Autour du Monde* (four volumes). Paris: Imprimerie de la Republique, 1797.

Mallove, E., Forward, R.L., Paprotny, Z., and Lehmann, J. "Interstellar Travel and

Communication: A Bibliography." *Journal of the British Interplanetary Society,* Vol. 33, No. 6, 1980.

*Morrison, P., Billingham, J. and Wolfe, J. (eds.). *The Search for Extraterrestrial Intelligence.* New York: Dover, 1979.

*Sagan, Carl (ed.). *Communication with Extraterrestrial Intelligence (CETI).* Cambridge: M.I.T. Press, 1973.

Sagan, Carl and Page, Thornton (eds.). *UFO's: A Scientific Debate.* New York: W.W. Norton, 1974.

Shklovskii, I.S. and Sagan, Carl. *Intelligent Life in the Universe.* New York: Dell, 1967.

Story, Ron. *The Space-Gods Revealed: A Close Look at the Theories of Erich von Daniken.* New York: Harper and Row, 1976.

Vaillant, George C. *Aztecs of Mexico.* New York: Pelican Books, 1965.

Chapter 13

Drell, Sidney D. and Von Hippel, Frank. "Limited Nuclear War." *Scientific American,* Vol. 235, p. 2737, 1976.

Dyson, F. *Disturbing the Universe.* New York: Harper and Row, 1979.

Glasstone, Samuel (ed.). *The Effects of Nuclear Weapons.* Washington, D.C.: U.S. Atomic Energy Commission, 1964.

Humboldt, Alexander von. *Cosmos.* Five volumes. London: Bell, 1871.

Murchee, G. *The Seven Mysteries of Life.* Boston: Houghton Mifflin, 1978.

Nathan, Otto and Norden, Heinz (eds.). *Einstein on Peace.* New York: Simon and Schuster, 1960.

Perrin, Noel. *Giving Up the Gun: Japan's Reversion to the Sword 1543–1879.* Boston: David Godine, 1979.

Prescott, James W. "Body Pleasure and the Origins of Violence." *Bulletin of the Atomic Scientists,* p. 10, November 1975.

*Richardson, Lewis F. *The Statistics of Deadly Quarrels.* Pittsburgh: Boxwood Press, 1960.

Sagan, Carl. *The Cosmic Connection. An Extraterrestrial Perspective.* New York: Doubleday, 1973.

World Armaments and Disarmament. SIPRI Yearbook, 1980 and previous years, Stockholm International Peace Research Institute. New York: Crane Russak and Company, 1980 and previous years.

Appendices

Courant, Richard and Robbins, Herbert. *What Is Mathematics? An Elementary Approach to Ideas and Methods.* New York: Oxford University Press, 1969.

INDEX

ABOUT THE AUTHOR

Carl Sagan served as the David Duncan Professor of Astronomy and Space Sciences and director of the Laboratory for Planetary Studies at Cornell University. He played a leading role in the Mariner, Viking, Voyager, and Galileo spacecraft expeditions, for which he received the NASA Medals for Exceptional Scientific Achievement and (twice) for Distinguished Public Service.

His Emmy and Peabody–winning television series, *Cosmos,* became the most widely watched series in the history of American public television. The accompanying book, also called *Cosmos,* is one of the bestselling science books ever published in the English language. Dr. Sagan received the Pulitzer Prize, the Oersted Medal, and many other awards—including twenty honorary degrees from American colleges and universities—for his contributions to science, literature, education, and the preservation of the environment. In their posthumous award of their highest honor to Dr. Sagan, the National Science Foundation declared that his "research transformed planetary science . . . his gifts to mankind were infinite."

Dr. Sagan died on December 20, 1996.